ASSASSIN

ASSASSIN

Doug Casey
and
John Hunt

Book 3 of the High Ground Novels

Assassin
Book 3 of the High Ground Series

© 2020 Doug Casey and John Hunt

Published by High Ground Books, LLC

ISBN-13: 978-1-947449-09-1

Cover design by Jim Ross

Acknowledgments

WE are grateful to Ancha Casey and Kimberly Johnson, who have formidable editorial skills among many other virtues; John Slovensky and Jeffrey James Higgins for their intellectual insights; Marco Wutzer, Paul Rosenberg and Rob Viglione for their crypto brilliance; Jim Ross for his artistic consistency and our many readers who eagerly dove into the manuscript.

Contents

"He who fights with monsters should be careful lest he thereby become a monster. And if thou gaze long into an abyss, the abyss will also gaze into thee."

— Nietzsche

Prologue

SOME people just need killing.

With his rifle's scope focused, Charles Knight could see the condensing breath of the man three hundred yards away. He watched his target walk up a slight incline onto the mostly brown third tee. A caddy handed the man his driver. The club, with a head the size of a small melon, compensated for the man's soft muscles and scrawny frame. This manicured golf course catered to three hundred elite members eager to hit the links as soon as the winter mud cleared. It hadn't yet. Paul Samuels therefore played his early-morning round alone. The caddy would be the only witness.

Concealed among the trees, Charles studied Samuels's balding head and wrinkled countenance; he appeared as harmless as any elderly golfer. He didn't look like a criminal responsible for putting the world's economy on the edge of a precipice and transforming millions into modern-day serfs. But Charles wasn't here to contemplate the man. In fact, he hardly saw him as a man, but as a creature whose essential nature was ... alien.

Samuels pointed to some dirt on the club's face and, cleaning it himself, petulantly berated the caddy. He bent down to place his ball, gripped his club, waggled his hips, bent his knees slightly, drew back on the club, and swung. He stood totally still at the end of his follow-through, staring down the fairway as if waiting for Charles to act.

The choice was binary: kill or don't kill. Charles had debated the issue at length in his mind. It was a question of right and wrong, but not a simple one. If Samuels were threatening him with a weapon, there was

1

no question—of course he'd kill him. He'd kill him if he were threatening a friend. But what if he were threatening some stranger? What if he were threatening a whole society? And what if there were no alternative ways of solving the problem? College sophomores tried to seem clever in philosophy class by asking whether it would be right to kill Hitler as a baby. Charles's mind had played out many arguments for and against similar conundrums.

Once he cut away arbitrary legal and religious norms, the rational arguments were of equal weight. Perhaps a better question was not whether he had the right to kill this man, but rather, did he have the right to let him live? His intellect had yet to provide a definitive answer, but his instinct—the practical combination of wisdom and experience—told him to take the shot.

The forestock of the .300 Winchester Magnum rested on a small mound of dirt that Charles had formed just before he'd settled into a prone position that, while entirely relaxed, provided his desired natural point of aim as he lay protected from view in the brush. He pressed his cheek against the stock and exhaled.

No breeze stirred. The air was crisp. The Winchester was zeroed in for this specifically confirmed distance and so he needed to make no adjustments to his scope. There were no other important variables. The birds stopped chirping then, or so it seemed. He gently contracted his index finger, drawing back on a finely tuned trigger. The final release of the firing pin had to be smooth. For a three-hundred-yard shot, no anticipatory reflex, no muzzle movement could be allowed. His finger drew back farther, enticing the weapon as if caressing the ivory of a piano key. Even through his ear-plugs, the sound of the powder exploding in the cartridge assaulted Charles's ears as the powerful recoil impacted his shoulder. The smell of burned sulfur arrived next, acrid yet refreshing in the small dose. Smoke touched his eyes.

He stayed for a moment to watch the man fall to the ground. There was no blood. Crawling back ten yards into the woods, he arose, stuffed the rifle and its rest into his golf bag, then hiked to the car. He accelerated the rental down a narrow service road, swerving to avoid a wayward squirrel.

No clouds marred the pure-blue sky.

But the clouds of an impending economic and political hurricane marred Charles's mind. The storm would soon overwhelm not just the US, but the whole world. There was real risk in this morning's outing. Its consequences weren't clear.

2

He inhaled deeply in a futile pursuit of calm.

Charles had proved long ago that he had the ability to kill an enemy, with forethought and intent. And that ability had been honed by eighteen months in the system.

But he contemplated a better way to neutralize this golf-playing criminal.

And it would be far more effective than his death.

1

Serving Time

EIGHTEEN months before, Charles had been remanded to incarceration, as the system's insiders liked to phrase it.

Then began a period of incessant boredom, punctuated by moments of fear and pain. The high-decibel noise of men shouting and metal clanging, the stench of overflowing toilets and industrial cleaning fluid, and lighting intense enough for an interrogation chamber all relentlessly assaulted his senses. The environment engendered anger and inchoate criminality in the guards. Still, they could leave after an eight-hour shift. Not so the prisoners.

Bad karma permeated the place. Anger could serve a useful purpose at times, but it's a base emotion, a relative of fear, hatred, antagonism, and hostility. As he sat, lay down, or walked in small circles, Charles felt all of these on a scale. He disliked the person that prison life was turning him into.

He had never before suffered from boredom. Except for his childhood internment in public schools, he stayed free and active. Schools were about being constrained and passive. They tried to direct what he thought, limit what he could say, and make him do pointless things. Prison seemed like an extreme version of school. Involuntary, rule focused, and punishment driven. But more regimented and boring.

Unlike school, it was very, very dangerous.

Confined by institutional concrete, gray steel, and unyielding restrictions, frustration shared a berth with resentment in the minds of most prisoners. The key was to separate the outer situation from his inner being, which took effort. Charles knew it would take iron self-discipline to keep

4

his mind and muscles active and fit. An inactive mind became weak, as did inactive muscles.

He was kept in solitary confinement "for his own safety" in the federal penitentiary at Lee, Virginia, for the first three months after being sentenced to twenty years by a federal court in DC. All but six months of that sentence were supposed to be suspended. Then he'd be free again.

Charles mechanically ate three unappetizing meals a day: variations on cornflakes in the morning, a dry baloney sandwich for lunch, and some mystery meat with overcooked veggies and instant mashed potatoes for dinner. With no connection to the outside world, he gradually lost awareness of current events. It was the worst variety of solitary, an effective sensory-deprivation chamber. No pen, no paper, no books. His home consisted of four rough walls, a high ceiling and a hard floor, all made of cold steel and concrete. No windows: light entered through rectangles near the ceiling designed too narrow for a man to squeeze through, but big enough for rats and roaches.

The absence of things you want, the presence of things you don't want.

Solitary meant different things in different times and places. A genuine nightmare in the days of Henri Charrière's Papillon in French Guiana, where heat and dark ruled. A different flavor of nightmare in the Alcatraz Hole where cold and dark ruled. In modern US pens it meant you were alone in a psychologically dank six- by nine-foot cell. Most prisoners despise it regardless of the century or location; it's a form of torture, one step up from being buried alive, even when granted books, writing materials, or a TV.

But in those first three months, perhaps as punishment for the judge suspending 98 percent of his sentence, Charles was granted nothing.

Enforced isolation and monotony leave little to occupy a prisoner's mind except the scents and sounds of other inmates—and memories of the past, most of them bad. A convict recognizes that his life no longer belongs to him. It drives some psychotic: not a long trip for those who were already writhing balls of neuroses.

In solitary, there's no choice but to mind one's own business. So Charles made it his business to become stronger, and to not let the place destroy him. He decided that just because his surroundings were suboptimal didn't mean he had an excuse to veer from his code: *Mens sana in corpore sano.* A sound mind in a sound body.

He exercised his hands on an imaginary piano keyboard, playing the music that he'd most enjoyed throughout his life. His fingers recalled the motions, his eyes envisioned the keyboard, and his mind synthesized the sounds. He repeated the mechanical actions of the one-hundred-year-old piano he'd first played as a child in Montana. To the limited extent he could, he went through Bach's fugues and Mozart's concertos. After a few weeks, the notes would play in his mind as he fell asleep and as he awoke. Fine music had morphed into auditory hallucination.

Like most prisoners, he performed a routine of pushups, jumping jacks, squat thrusts, and sit ups. But Charles went further. He planned out something more challenging and beneficial.

He'd spend an hour practicing Tae Kwan Do kicks and punches. It was better to have several basic moves down perfectly than have a hundred shaky ones. Then a few katas his muscles had memorized years before. He'd modified them to squeeze onto the deck of his sailboat during long crossings, which proved convenient now, given the space in his cell. Although they amounted to dance moves, the formulaic but powerful strikes and blocks were useful for close combat.

He'd rest for an hour, then practice the tai chi forms he'd learned in the Orient. If karate was a hard martial art—relying on speed and power—tai chi was a soft one, relying on precision and mindfulness: a moving meditation; a different path up the mountain to mental, spiritual, and physical mastery.

Sometimes, he shadowboxed. Western boxing had become unjustifiably underrated by comparison to Oriental self-defense arts. A good boxer was the equal of any karateka. In street fights, many karate students wound up on the ground after trying to impress opponents with high jumping or spinning kicks. The boxer's use of the uppercut, the cross, and the hook—which hardly exist in the Oriental repertoire—could be more useful than exotic kicks.

He worked on the Krav Maga moves he'd learned in a series of courses in Tel Aviv. Unlike karate, tai chi, or boxing, no element of art or sport applied. It combined moves and methods from all the martial arts, based only on their simplicity and deadliness. Highly practical, they were the tools of a fighter intent on severely damaging his opponent.

He dedicated an hour each day for yoga, doing the postures he favored, but also his least favorite, which challenged his body most. Breathing and meditating in a lotus posture was both more enjoyable and harder than any-thing else he did. His other practices, meant to prepare for violence, seemed more logical in a prison. But in solitary the main enemy was the engrams buried in one's own psyche. Repeating a mantra to quiet the monkey mind took time, as the monkey bounced around his consciousness, grasping at distractions. When he sat in zazen, he transported his being out of the prison to a Japanese cherry orchard with a burbling stream.

Other than the barest amenities, a thin Dacron mattress and a worn and stained pillow, time was all he had in this place. Most prisoners thought of time as another enemy, but Charles wouldn't waste his most valuable posses-sion. Of the twenty-four hours, eight went for sleeping, three to catnapping and idle rest, another to eating, washing, and necessities. Of the remaining twelve, six went to his physical and spiritual routines. That left six for the disciplined exercise of his intellect.

Organizing his physical routine was relatively simple and repetitive. Organizing his mental routine was potentially as complex as a giant library. Everything related to everything else, so he could start anywhere. Divide knowledge into the sciences and the arts, starting with A. He accessed and organized what he knew of astronomy—the sizes of the planets, the dis-tances to other galaxies, the characteristics of the stars, how geniuses from Galileo to Hubble had figured it all out. He surprised himself with how much he could access from his memory now that he had the time and moti-vation to do so. But it saddened him to recognize how much he either didn't know or could no longer recall.

Biology, chemistry, geology, physics, and zoology followed, along with topics that blurred boundaries of the fields.

Same with the arts: architecture, history, literature, music, painting, sculpture. Mnemonics and his memory palace reminded him of where he'd been and where he was going. He sifted through his knowledge of ancient Greece and Rome as closely as he could. Everything happening to him now had happened to others before. Was he filling in the historical holes with his imagination? No doubt. That's what the academic historians did these days. Was what he remembered of The Iliad actually from the book or just some reconstruction from a movie? Was there more value to knowing real ancient history than knowing all seventy-three episodes of Game of Thrones? Perhaps it didn't matter. In a thousand years people might think Cato and Pompey were the fiction and Tyrion and Daenerys real. History and literature combined to create myth, and myths are what people actually live by.

He lingered on his knowledge of chemistry. Charles's attempts to visualize the periodic table of the elements proved a struggle. But he remembered that Francium, number 87, was probably the rarest element, with only an ounce present in the earth's crust at any one time because even its most long-lived isotope has only a twenty-two-minute half-life. It was possibly more relevant for his future to know more about Thallium, number 81. Its tasteless salts were a slow-acting poison, easily absorbed, even through the skin. Perhaps he'd later employ his knowledge that Sodium, Potassium, and Cesium were among the metals that were instantly explosive when dropped into water.

His understanding of the way the world worked and the history of technology grew as he integrated everything he knew into a mental encyclopedia.

On the rare nights when he couldn't sleep, he recalled the details of his past friends and foes, contemplating questions many don't adequately consider. What was the essence of a true friend? How can you recognize a foe? He examined what had caused his most negative experiences. To what degree did they occur because of a flaw in himself? How would he remedy that flaw? He considered who had wrongly attacked him, exactly why, and when and how he may have treated others unjustly. He relived the details of his interactions.

Those first three months in solitary allowed him to inventory what he was made of. His incarceration was intended as torture, but he tried to make it as valuable physically as a professional sports training camp, as valuable mentally as a transfusion from a library, and as valuable spiritually and psychologically as time spent in a Taoist monastery.

*　　*　　*

Everybody has flaws. Those flaws caused them to harm themselves and other people. For most, their flaws are not their essence. Some people, however, possessed such bad characters that their flaws overwhelmed their better elements. In prison, inmates and guards alike wore their vices on their faces like badges of honor. The overt criminals needed to be isolated from society.

Less obvious, and vastly more dangerous, were the covert criminals. They destroyed lives as a default setting, sometimes simply for their amusement, as Iago destroyed Othello. They preferred to strike without warning, like a viper hidden behind a log. Charles had a particular aversion to those who tended to erode, rather than add, value. Difficult to identify, they thrived outside of prison as well as inside. He'd suffered sorely from run-ins with them. They derailed peace and progress wherever they went, and they could be anywhere. Charles had learned they concentrated in certain cities and certain occupations, most notably politics.

Washington's politicians and bureaucrats were contemptible. They were self-identified, visible, and in the open but beholden to their backers. The true rot came from the cronies who profited by controlling the whole apparatus from behind the scenes, just out of sight. They'd coalesced like the body's immune system against a foreign bacteria when Charles's drug, Sybillene, first threatened to rationalize society. United in wanting Charles Knight and Sybillene eliminated, they emerged like cockroaches from every sector—drug companies of course, but also finance, major corporations, the media, academia, the military, churches, all collectors of rent from the status quo. The Establishment: some called it The Deep State.

They were the enemy, and they'd attacked him. He had a natural right to defend himself. There were very few good things about a prolonged time in federal prison, but it did allow him to formulate a plan to fight back.

The ideal scenario would be to overthrow the whole corrupt structure, but that was completely unrealistic… an unfocused daydream. It didn't make much sense to attack the government itself; people might whine about it, but they were partial to it because they thought they lived in a democracy. Being "antigovernment" would be counterproductive, likely putting him in an unsavory stewpot with camouflage-wearing rednecks at one extreme and communists at the other. Besides, the government was just a tool. The problem was the failed ethics of the type of people who chose to use the tool.

Politicians? Elected officials? It was pointless to attack them. If one of them joined the ranks of the departed, there were ten more dangerous replacements in the wings.

The real problem was the puppeteers, the cronies, using successive governments to enrich and protect themselves while keeping the proles ignorant and confused. They were most responsible for not only sticking him in this prison, but for the degradation of society itself. Most important, they were discrete individuals who could be identified and held accountable.

He would target the cronies.

Charles crystallized his plan, to be implemented upon his release. Reality, however, intruded on his timing.

One day at 3:00 p.m., he was marched to the administration offices, where the warden informed him that because of his poor behavior, his suspended sentence had been partially revoked. He'd be transferred to a different FCI—federal correctional institute—and his time extended, perhaps indefinitely. Charles started to ask the warden: what poor behavior? But he knew better.

Judge Warren Thomason—the man who'd suspended most of his sentence and thereby thrown some sand in the gears of the Deep State—had retired immediately after doing so. His forced retirement had left Charles without what the Russians called a krysha—a roof—and at the mercy of the powers that be.

He could end up in the slammer for two decades.

And that changed everything.

Hard Time

WHY were they transferring him? Perhaps it was as prosaic as a report from one of the screws who monitored prisoners constantly by remote TV. Perhaps word had filtered up that he was not suffering enough in solitary.

His thoughts changed from temporary tolerance of his loss of freedom to a desperate need to escape. An impossible dream. Escape from any maximum-security prison was the stuff of movies, not the real world. His frustration fused with a righteous anger, and those emotions transmuted. Hatred gained a foothold in his mind. Not as an untamed emotion, but as a cool and logical intention. Charles recognized that his plans of vengeance, with all reasonable certainty, would never materialize. They were now a fantasy. Much of reality had started out as fantasy; over time, fantasies had a way of transforming reality.

Before anyone on the outside knew that he'd been released from solitary in Virginia, faster than the online federal inmate locator could track him, he was whisked off to the New York Metropolitan Correctional Center. That particular federal pen supposedly had some spare space within its Brutalist walls, although Charles couldn't imagine where. It was a pressure cooker filled to capacity and boiling over. Five days into his time in the MCC's General Population, a pock-faced lifer with nothing to lose thrust a five-inch shiv toward Charles's neck. A gasp and a surprised expression on the face of an inmate watching the action provided the heads-up Charles needed to deflect the shiv with his left hand while simultaneously turning and smashing the heel of his right hand into the assailant's nose.

Before the screws arrived, the lifer said, "Next time, you won't get so lucky" through bloody teeth.

Charles didn't feel so lucky this time, with a deep gash in the heel of his hand. They repaired it with fifteen stitches in his left palm, and rewarded him with another thirty days in solitary. He used it to restart his routine. He'd let everything but the calisthenics lapse in genpop. Visibly practicing martial arts was an invitation to fight. So was doing yoga and meditation, just for different reasons.

His reflections on the morality of killing shifted to its practical and immediate implications. Surrounded by criminals, the notion—indeed the occasional necessity—of killing became easier to justify.

A few days after Charles was released from the hole and returned to genpop, the lifer who had tried to knife him was found with a crushed larynx and severe hypoxic brain injury. No one saw anything. In prison, only a fool sees anything; there's zero upside and lots of downside to it. Very unlike the world of the sheep outside, where they were programmed to "See something—say something." Doing so here would be signing your own death warrant. Here there was a slightly different golden rule as well. When you knew someone was out to kill you, the golden rule in a tough prison became: Do unto others—but do it first.

So he did.

The next two months in MCC New York were trouble free. Rainbow managed to extract Uncle Maurice from his apartment for a weekly visit. The direct contact made Charles feel less like he was living in the sewers of an alien planet.

His street cred as the creator of Naked Emperor and his time in MCC's nasty 10 South put him next to a certain notorious Mexican drug lord. The two spent hours comparing notes and swapping anecdotes on running very different kinds of drug empires. Eavesdroppers got a practical street version of an MBA degree. The two men formed a tenuous friendship, based mostly on shared competence and a recognition that neither was a threat to the other. The Mexican had high intelligence, extreme focus, a certain organizational genius, and an iron will—the essentials for success in any business. His main flaws were complete amorality and a predilection for extreme violence.

Charles had two key takeaways from the hours they spent talking. First, he garnered several introductions to the man's confederates on the outside.

12

These were potentially valuable but very dangerous. Association with volatile criminals should be avoided. Calling on them for a favor would require the favor to be returned. Second and more important was an appreciation of the value of a private army, which the Mexican had. That, Charles noted, could be extremely useful. But it was like a machine gun, or dynamite, or a nuclear weapon. Best be very careful even owning it; using it was something else again.

The system decided to move him to yet another FCI, and later another, and then again, for reasons a Kafka or a Solzhenitsyn would recognize.

The prisons were mostly filled with psychopaths, gangsters, lowlifes, and perennial losers. While the justice system was hardly a model of probity, efficiency, or actual justice, it nonetheless skimmed some of the worst scum from the stew of society. But it was also a dragnet, trapping people who were just in the wrong place at the wrong time, or had the wrong views and an ambitious prosecutor. As he moved through the various lockups, now and again in the general population, Charles met some worthwhile humans and memorable characters. It was the one small fringe benefit of being in the slammer.

He spent time with the imprisoned leader of a world-famous motorcycle club, as the man styled it. Most called it an outlaw motorcycle gang. He was pleasant, well read, rather cultured, and highly intelligent. He also had the skills necessary to keep five thousand aggressive thugs under control. Charles looked forward to joining him someday at the club's annual Thanksgiving dinner—the only official event to which outsiders were invited.

They transferred him from state to state, dressed in peels, ankles shackled, hands cuffed, chained at the waist, hop-marching through tunnels, onto a bus and then an airplane to reach a new set of grated metal corridors in a new pen. The inmates called it diesel therapy. The process no doubt served several purposes, but mainly harassment and demoralization. All familiarity was destroyed, any connection he'd made to others terminated. And his prison cash account invariably failed to follow him.

That was more than a nuisance. Items from the canteen provided an important supplement to a horrible diet, and also could be traded to other prisoners. His frustrations grew as rapidly as his funds were lost. A phone call to Uncle Maurice would replenish them—although with delays that could take a month to work through. A prisoner was lucky to overcome even a fraction of the bureaucratic hurdles impeding the simplest of processes.

On the outside, Sybillene, better known by its street name of Naked Emperor, had painted a target on his back. But the wildly popular mind-enhancing pharmaceutical made him a celebrity among criminals, and even some of the screws. That was a plus.

On the minus side, each time they moved him, one predictable event occurred: soon after his arrival to a new prison, someone would try to kill him.

Things like that happen in prison. But not so predictably. So consistently.

Colorado's Fremont ADMAX was built to incarcerate the hardest and most violent career criminals. There, soon after another failed attempt on his life, Charles encountered a pacifist, a few years younger than himself, whom the feds had locked up for two times life plus forty years for building a darknet site for anonymous commerce. Despite its extensive use for illicit drug sales, not a single violent act occurred in its years of operation. Not until the feds violently jammed up the young computer geek into their supermax prison. This required a couple of crooked federal agents to conjure up some crimes. That the agents were themselves subsequently imprisoned for lies and misconduct in their investigation proved insufficient to free the internet merchant. His lifetime imprisonment served as a warning to anyone who defied State controls. His only hope, short of a revolution, was a presidential pardon. With President Cooligan in office, whose only real accomplishment had been the creation of yet another domestic secret police force—the Sybillene Eradication Administration—there wasn't much hope.

Charles didn't have any confidence in politics, but that didn't keep him from imagining himself as the president of the United States. His first act in office would be to pardon everyone locked up for a victimless crime. That alone would reduce the prison population by half.

The prison system had plenty of inmates who, if not always innocent, at least offered something of interest, but it was a mistake to seek them out. The wisest policy was to keep to yourself for the simple reason that so many of the inmates were active sociopaths. General population was dangerous, but at least it allowed him to visit the library, use writing materials, see sunlight, and have some semihuman contact.

14

A week after he was shipped to Lompoc, in California, another lifer he'd never seen before wrapped a cord around his neck in an effort to garrote him.

His attacker had said simply, "Don't blame me" as he cranked down to squeeze Charles's carotids off.

Just before he would have passed out and then died, Charles reflexively stomped on his attacker's foot with his heel, swiveled his hips to the right, and used the edge of his hand to hit the man hard in the groin. As the garrote loosened, he was able to reach around and jam his fingers up the man's nostrils, practically tearing his nose off. The wire burn on his neck faded during the two months that they stuck him, for the bad behavior of defending himself, in the Special Housing Unit. Solitary again. Living his life in a cube made him feel a little like Steve McQueen's character in The Great Escape.

He resumed his solitary routine. The growing realization that this was what the next twenty years would look like—assuming nobody succeeded in assassinating him—reinforced his anger and every other low-grade emotion. It seemed almost metaphysically impossible to feel things that could make life in this place worthwhile. He recognized what was happening in his mind and fought against it.

He forced himself to smile; the exercise of those muscles resulted in a notable improvement in his mental state. At the risk of a guard reporting him as a candidate for the dreaded psych ward with its drugs and injections, he forced himself to laugh. That simple act made him feel better, partly because it recognized the cosmic absurdity of his condition.

Making himself laugh didn't ease his righteous hatred for the system. He continued planning revenge. Even if he couldn't execute, it helped keep him sane.

Revenge. Like so many other things in a morally askew world, it had an undeserved reputation. Far from being wrong, revenge was a morally correct response to aggression. It served, in many cases, as the practical application of justice. Was there anything more important than justice? And what was justice other than a matter of people getting what they deserved?

Their just deserts.

Some said that only God has the right to dispense justice, but that made no sense. Charles saw no evidence that Yahweh existed anywhere in these prisons outside the pages of the Bible. There was even less evidence that he actively dispensed justice.

Some said that justice should be left to the State. His personal experience, in fact all of history, convinced him that the State dispensed vastly more injustice than justice. That was its nature, simply because of the type of people who wanted to work in it and for it. The very worst criminals were dug into the State like ticks.

If justice was to be served, it made no sense to look to either the Church or the State. Acting like a whipped dog while hoping some innately corrupt institution would kiss the situation and make it better only made a sane person feel vulnerable and insecure. It made much more sense for the market to dispense justice.

Upon his next release into general population, Charles approached the man with the garotte, nostrils now healing, and made an agreement that would help keep them both alive. The inmate wasn't about to rat out who had put him up to it; that would have been signing his own death warrant. But he recognized that since Charles was alive and could be a deadly enemy, it was wise to defuse the situation. He allowed that "T'weren't nutin' personal, dawg. D' order come fum outside."

Generally speaking—unless they were both members of the same race-based prison gang—one prisoner will never help another who's being assaulted. The reason is simple: you can't expect return help, but you could definitely expect retribution from the attackers. The guy figured Charles didn't fit the usual prison mold. Charles was what some called a gamma rat. The alphas staked out territories and beat up the betas, who did what they were told. The gammas—a small minority—neither kowtowed to the alphas nor beat up the betas.

Charles formed a dozen hypotheses for why he was so often a target.

He figured he was being both dieseled and cycled between solitary and genpop for a reason. The attempted homicides continued, especially when he was at a new FCI before he could show he was a hard target. In order to better his odds, Charles parlayed his fame outside to put together an informal crew to keep an eye out. But every altercation harshened the conditions of his incarceration. He survived, but with scars, bloody knuckles, and broken teeth.

Increasingly, his innate good nature failed to protect him from dark thoughts.

16

It wasn't just the physical damage; Charles changed in other ways. Like a dog forced to live in the wild, he remained on red alert, trusting no one. Adrenaline coursed through his veins while in genpop. When he got kicked back to solitary, it took days for him to come down from the sudden withdrawal of the fight-or-flight physiology. Only his routine in solitary saved him from both physical and mental collapse.

And they transferred him yet again. Which among the lifers would try to kill him this time? The federal pen at Marion had an especially unsavory reputation.

The warden, a large man with graying close-cropped hair, minced no words after an incident the day he arrived.

"Someone out there despises you, son."

"What do you mean, sir?" Charles replied, suppressing a gag reflex on the word sir. "I never met that man before. I just got here." He feigned surprise as he dug for more information.

The warden studied Charles's bloodied scalp where a hired hit man had tried to bust the new arrival's skull open. The warden shook his head. "I feel for you son. I do. Heck, your drug, Sybillene, saved my marriage and made my wife happy. I'm well aware of the word around the cellblocks; you're a hunted man. My own view is that you shouldn't be in prison. But since you have to be, you're best off in solitary. I'll do what I can for you."

Charles stepped back, flummoxed. He'd judged the man based only on the fact that he was the warden. Now he looked at him in a new light, considering that he might have prejudged incorrectly. He cared neither for prejudice nor for being incorrect.

"I truly appreciate your intentions, Warden. But I'd prefer to stay in genpop for the time being. I may do better in solitary than some others, but it's still miserable. I'd prefer to stay a bit more free."

"Free, here? Even a taste of it, huh? Well, as you wish."

But after four weeks and three attempts on his life, solitary provided a needed reprieve. He decided to take advantage of the warden's offer, and sacrificed minimal liberty for temporary safety. Ben Franklin would roll in his grave.

As the door clanked closed on the gray cell, Charles knew that he'd fallen further than he'd ever imagined.

Dumas's Count of Monte Cristo had found a way through it, a way out of it. Maybe so could he.

Three months in the Control Unit should have meant twenty-three hours a day in a windowless cell with only the disciplined routine he'd developed to keep him grounded. Fortunately, this time was different. Books arrived for him to read. A guard told him they'd been selected by the warden himself.

Rainbow sent him a book on blockchain and cryptocurrency. She'd taken an interest in it, and Charles could see why: it had potential to expand individual sovereignty by taking money out of the hands of the central banks and therefore bringing both competition and privacy back to money. He inhaled its contents and asked her to send everything she thought worthwhile on it. If only he had a computer, he could have learned by doing. He replaced parts of his routine with reading and became perhaps the only person in solitary, anywhere, who didn't have enough hours in the day. He suspected—no, he knew—that cryptocurrencies were changing far faster than he could assess by reading books. Reading at least gave him a grip on the fundamentals.

A couple of history books from Maurice made it through the prison censor. One with a suspicious emphasis on revolutions, terrorism, and assassinations, and another about Lincoln and the Civil War. Something of a surprise, as the litany of banned or disapproved books in prison was a mile long and included anything that verged on sex, escape, or crime.

Reading the last book brought him back to when he was a teenager, to a conversation with Uncle Maurice about the assassination of Abraham Lincoln. It was completely uncontroversial in the eyes of almost all Americans. To them Lincoln was a saint.

Maurice had adjusted his position, closing his eyes for a few moments to gather his thoughts. "After a leading politician like Lincoln is killed, the tendency is to make him into a hero, even a demigod. People like to emphasize that he brought himself up from nowhere, studied by firelight, and worked as a log splitter. Fair enough. He had virtues. But so what? The real issue should revolve around what he did. Why? And who benefitted at whose expense. What was the essence of the man? The fact is that politics were as corrupt in his day as they are in ours; he made his money and got his power as a corporate lawyer, selling patronage, representing major railroads. He lobbied for a new central bank to more easily fund his clients. His whole career, and one hundred percent of his personal fortune, was about directing political favors to the fat cats of his day."

18

Charles had replied, "Okay. But that was legal. And I don't think they called him 'Honest Abe' for nothing. And he freed the slaves … and won the Civil War."

"That's all true. Let's not talk about whether 'Honest Abe' was just a marketing slogan, and whether or not Lincoln was in office mainly to self-aggrandize and pad his and his supporters' bank accounts. I don't like to be an iconoclast of national heroes these days—even if I don't believe they were really heroes. In today's world, the way things are going, Americans soon won't have anything left to believe in. Yes, he won the Civil War—although it's a mistake to call it that. It's more accurate to call it the War Between the States. Although the War of Northern Aggression might be even more correct. A civil war is one where two or more groups are fighting for the control of a government. The unpleasantness of 1861 to 1865 was actually a failed secession, which is very different. The Confederacy didn't want control of Washington, DC and the northern states. The secession didn't have to be violent.

"Lincoln won it, but he also started it. And the war wasn't about slavery, per se. This is a perfect example of Will Rogers's comment, that the problem isn't what people don't know—it's what people think they know that just ain't so. Although slavery was a hot button issue, it wasn't what the war was about. Lincoln had no intention of abolishing the 'peculiar institution,' as they called it, in the South. He said so emphatically, and there's no doubt he was sincere.

"There were two big issues: new states, and import duties. Would new states, like Kansas, be slave or free? If a new state became 'slave,' that would decide whether the agricultural South, or the industrial North, controlled the DC government.

"Why was that worth a war? It boiled down to money, as is usually the case. The group that controlled Congress would decide the level of import duties. High duties benefitted Northern industrialists but devastated Southern planters.

"Of course Lincoln was against slavery on moral grounds. Most people were, in both the North and the South. Especially after Uncle Tom's Cabin was published, the whole country argued about whether it was right or wrong. The average Northerner was certainly against slavery, but that didn't mean he wanted blacks for neighbors. Most important, he wasn't interested in labor competition from them.

"People today just quote Lincoln when what he said suits the mythos that's grown up around him. It suits our national self-image to represent the war as a moral crusade, even though it was actually about the control of Congress—and who paid the taxes. Nobody wants to admit seven hundred thousand men died, brother against brother, over filthy lucre.

"In his first inaugural address Lincoln defended the South's right to slavery on constitutional grounds. He promised, numerous times, that he wouldn't interfere with the institution of slavery, directly or indirectly, in the states where it already existed. That was a key part of the Republican Party platform of 1860. Lincoln supported the Fugitive Slave Act, which compelled Northerners to hunt down runaway slaves. He supported a proposed amendment to the Constitution to prohibit the US government from ever interfering with Southern slavery.

"Freeing the slaves? Lincoln didn't do that until January 1863, almost two years after the war began. And even then only in the states that seceded. Why? Perhaps it was to incite a slave rebellion to help the Union war effort. At a minimum it would encourage runaways and hurt the South's labor-short economy. He purposefully didn't free the slaves in the border states—Delaware, Maryland, Kentucky, and Missouri—that stuck with the Union. In fact, Lincoln actively wanted to transplant ex-slaves back to Africa. It was all very cynical and had zero to do with morality.

"Anyway, slavery was already a dying institution because of the ongoing Industrial Revolution. Unwilling slaves couldn't compete with machines. Brazil, in 1888, was the last country in the West to abolish slavery—it would have fallen by the wayside in the South way before that.

"So why, if Lincoln didn't threaten slavery, did the South want out? They were going to be devastated by import duties that basically only they would pay. It would have forced them to import goods from the North rather than Europe. You've got to remember that, at the time, about 90 percent of federal tax revenue came from import duties. The South was already paying most of that because they imported most of their machinery—most of everything—from Europe. It was higher quality and lower in cost than what the North had to offer.

"But in 1860, even though they were already paying a disproportionate share of federal taxes, it was about to get worse. Just before Lincoln's inauguration, President Buchanan signed the Morrill Tariff into law, which more than doubled the average tariff rate from fifteen percent to over thirty percent, and promised to take it to nearly fifty percent. Not only that, but it greatly increased the number of items covered by the tariff.

"The North and South were at loggerheads. They had totally different economic interests, and their cultures had diverged as well. The North was about big cities, industry, shopkeepers, traders, and small farms. The South was mostly rural, with large single-crop plantations, worked mostly by slave labor. It no longer made any sense for them to remain in the same political unit—any more than it made sense for the original colonies to stay subservient to England.

"A parting of the ways was inevitable, and it should have and could have been peaceful. But Lincoln's first priority wasn't peace, and had nothing to do with freeing slaves. It was keeping the Union together.

"Why? Perhaps he might just have thought it was his duty as president. No doubt it was also an ego issue; he certainly didn't want to suffer the embarrassment of the Union—dysfunctional or not—dissolving on his watch. But, most important, he didn't want Washington to lose most of its tax revenue. At the same time, his cronies, relatively inefficient Northern manufacturers, would lose their Southern markets to Europe. Southerners already exported at least three-fourths of all their agricultural products to Europe.

"The Confederate government already existed before Lincoln took office. Their secession didn't necessitate war, but Lincoln promised war over collection of tariffs in his first inaugural address. After the South foolishly bombarded Fort Sumter in April 1861, Lincoln used that as a casus belli to mobilize and invade. I'd say the South had every right to take him out after he invaded.

"The strange thing about Lincoln's assassination is that it happened after the war was over—when it no longer served any useful purpose. In fact, Reconstruction would likely have been much less destructive under him. His assassination can only be explained as an act of revenge for the immense destruction the unnecessary war caused. If Booth had shot Lincoln just after he was elected, however, or at least before he declared war on the South, the whole unpleasantness would almost certainly have been avoided."

As Charles sat in his prison cell, surrounded by cold concrete and foul stenches, he remembered in vivid detail the next words that Maurice spoke.

"If you ask me, Lincoln's assassination in 1865 was a disaster, and a mistake. But in good part because it didn't happen four years earlier."

*   *   *

In the early-morning cold before the guards changed shift, Charles was released from Marion without a warning. The warden himself walked him out of the walls, toward the gate.

Charles looked through the parallel chain-link fences enclosing a sea of barbed wire. Then across Prison Drive to the woods and fields surrounding the penitentiary. He'd made no preparations, and there'd be no one to pick him up. He packed his underwear, toiletries, and a couple of books in a small prison-issued sack along with a bottle of water and a box of crackers. They gave him back his wallet, his watch, and the clothes he'd worn eighteen months earlier—plus a cheap Carhartt coat, the type favored by Midwestern farmers to take the edge off an early-April Illinois chill. The warden handed him $500 in cash from his own pocket.

Outside the gate, flat terrain extended in all directions. He could see a decrepit trailer park in the distance, off to the right, probably where many of the guards and menial helpers lived. Somewhere to the left, far past a long-unused security gatehouse, there'd have to be a road to freedom. There was no traffic at this hour of the morning on Prison Drive—no cars at all, but for a mud-stained sedan parked fifty yards up. A decrepit-looking man, with unkempt gray hair draggling out of his wool cap, leaned his kyphotic back against the vehicle. Perhaps the old geezer, probably an ex-con, was awaiting the release of his son or an elderly brother.

The outside was almost as depressing as the prison itself.

A dog barked in the distance. Charles glanced at the overcast sky. He breathed in the damp, chill air and closed his eyes. He assessed his resources. His body was strong, healthy, ready, but he was more concerned about his mind and emotions. Prison changes everybody. Although gratitude for his unexpected freedom helped keep negative thoughts at bay, Charles knew his future was headed in a new and uncharted direction. His well-incubated quest for vengeance would serve as a navigational beacon on the path forward.

"Thank you, Warden, for the books. Your empathy helped make these last months tolerable. Maybe that kept me alive as much as keeping me out of the reach of men who wanted to kill me."

"They didn't want to kill you. They just wanted privileges."

Charles treasured standing in the first truly unguarded space for the first time in eighteen months. "I figured as much. Do you know who has it in for me?"

"No. But I'm aware of your history in the system. No question that powerful people want you either dead or locked up for the full twenty years. Preferably the former. They barely even tried to disguise their efforts."

"Then how come you're able to walk me out of here today?"

"Just threading a needle through some paperwork that got lost somewhere." He winked and smiled dourly. "I'm confident your twenty-year suspended sentence would have continued being unsuspended, year after year, forever. Or until someone killed you. Unsuspending a sentence is an active process requiring a judge to keep you in prison. Regular paperwork has been required to keep you incarcerated. You fell through the bureaucratic cracks somehow after you came to my prison. We just now walked out these gates through one of those cracks."

"Did you have anything to do with opening that crack?"

The warden shrugged. "I don't like paperwork. And I figure I owed you."

Charles nodded and looked into the man's eyes. "Thank you. Aren't you putting yourself at risk?"

"Probably. But the system's about as efficient as a DMV; there's lots of plausible deniability. I can blame it on a virus. Plus, it's hard to hold me accountable for not doing the wrong thing. But do me a favor. If you end up on the FBI's Most Wanted list, just make sure to be at the very top. If I'm to go down, it might as well be in flames."

"I'll try to stay out of the FBI's sights."

The warden grinned, fleetingly. "I should warn you. I'm releasing you back into a restless country. It feels to me like a low-security pen just before a riot breaks out. The economy's verging on collapse. Fear spreads on the internet faster than the most aggressive pandemic. The presidential election cycle is heating up, and that's not calming things down any."

Charles chuckled. "I don't care about the election, but I've heard a little about the trouble in the cities and the economic problems. Thanks for the warning. I'll make sure not to turn on the news. I doubt it's more reliable than the rumors you hear in genpop anyway."

The warden snorted agreement. "You know you aren't actually a free man? They can stick you back in the pen if you wriggle in a way they don't like. They say that people commit on average three felonies a day. If they want you back inside, they'll find a way. That's what they just might do if you stay alive out there too long."

"Then I best live life to the fullest in the short amount of time that I have."

"If they happen to send you back here, I'll do my best to keep you comfortable. But there're over a hundred federal pens and most wardens not only won't give a damn, they'll be glad to see you dead and gone."

"That I've learned."

"You've a right to be angry. For many reasons and at many people. You've got a lot of enemies, but I know for a fact that you also have a lot of friends out there in the world. They'll find you. Or you'll find them where and when you don't expect to. Some of the friends will be in plain sight; some hidden right next to you. Similarly, not all of the enemies will be easy to spot. Check in with your probation officer in New York City right away. You have a few days. Stay off the streets at night and don't get swept up in the riots."

They shook hands. The warden pointed down the road to the left. "That's your way home. It's closer than you think. Good luck, Mr. Knight."

Charles wondered if this was the way most prisoners felt when released: geographically and psychologically disoriented, uncertain of bearings or distances, walking alone in the cold gray of an extended winter. He didn't care how far he might need to walk, nor did he know where a bus station might be found. Nobody would pick up a hitchhiker near a prison. He stepped into freedom and away from this anteroom to hell. He closed his eyes for several steps and felt the pebbles under his feet. It was cold and gray, but at least it wasn't snowing.

Loss of freedom was one step removed from death itself. Even this partial recovery of his freedom was like rebirth or like opening the lid on a casket wherein he'd been buried. It didn't matter if the world was falling apart; he had his own prospects, his own agenda. His body shivered, and not from the cold. He couldn't label his emotions at this point. He'd been stoic for eighteen months. Now, finally free, he had nothing left to draw on. He'd used it all up. He knew deep in his bones that he'd depleted his reserves. He was like a soldier just out of the front lines, trying to decompress. He wondered whether a shrink would diagnose him with post-traumatic stress syndrome.

Then he opened his eyes, threw the small bag of prison belongings over his shoulder, and set out with the stride of an experienced walker who, late in the day, found he had further to go than he previously thought. He didn't look back at the fenced walls, the warden walking back through the gate, or up at the sky. He gave a perfunctory nod to the withered man leaning against the muddy car and walked on past. His vision focused on a future that, as it always did, began right now. This future was about vengeance and justice.

"Hey, kid." The voice came from behind, from the old man leaning on the car.

Charles stopped.

The sound of that voice made a decade fall away in an instant. It loosed a flood of emotion that he'd bottled up, concealed and denied, and now suddenly refused to stay imprisoned by Charles's practiced rationality. The neurochemicals he'd strained to keep in balance chaotically flooded into his body: his heart sped, his breathing tightened, his throat clamped tight. He sobbed.

He felt a hand upon his shoulder.

"It's okay, kid."

He recognized the hand. He knew the faintly accented voice.

He turned and his tear-blurred eyes saw through the stranger's camouflage. It wasn't a stranger, but his comrade from a life-changing adventure, long ago and far away.

It took Charles more than a minute to regain composure. During this time, the old cripple straightened his crooked back. He removed the wool cap with its attached greasy gray locks, revealing a well-groomed silver-highlighted head of brown hair. He stood a foot taller than when he rested against the car. Those eyes and that smile could belong to no one other than Xander Winn.

Xander reached around Charles with both arms and hugged him with strength that his appearance belied.

"It's good to see you, Charles. Welcome back to the land of the living. I trust you didn't mind the disguise. I wasn't sure if the media had gotten wind of this somehow, and I like to stay private."

Three weeks later, Charles found himself at an exclusive golf course on another cool morning, where his instincts told him at the last moment to not yet assassinate the man who had played a central role in the hell of his imprisonment.

If nothing else, prison had taught him patience.

3

Erinyes

THE assassination attempt on one of the world's most quietly powerful men fed the national news. The masses had been taught that the Federal Reserve kept the economy alive during this time of unprecedented uncertainty by pumping out dollars and controlling interest rates. Indeed, just a few months earlier, Time magazine had named Paul Samuels their Man of the Year. The FBI had no leads, but that didn't prevent the reporters and anchors from speculating as to what had happened and why. News was, after all, infotainment.

The emerging consensus—a notion that, for the media, had become the new definition of the archaic concept of fact—held that the attempt was related to the waves of demonstrations and riots. Mobs rampaged through New York and most other large cities. Spontaneous violence and wanton destruction erupted uptown, downtown, in Brooklyn, the Bronx, Queens, and across the river in Jersey.

Apparently, the assassin had missed Paul Samuels's head by inches. The high velocity bullet had instead burrowed through the titanium and composite head of his customized 460 cc TaylorMade driver.

The unexpected impact of the bullet had transferred along the shaft and through the golfer's overly tight grip, throwing the president of the New York Federal Reserve off balance, spinning him around as he tumbled awkwardly. With his shoulder like a fulcrum, the twisted remains of the titanium-nickel/carbon fiber shaft of his club crushed into his neck leaving a bruise that would shine red, then purple, then brown and yellow-green for a fortnight. A disabling pain would hinder his golf swing for much longer.

The shot did far more than throw Paul Samuels off balance on the golf course. The man would now fear for his security. Not only could he be reached, but someone cared enough to target him.

Was it narcissistic overconfidence that prevented Charles from dispatching Paul Samuels? How confident, or arrogant, was he to think that, instead of killing Samuels, he could devise a more satisfactory way to neutralize a man who, for all practical purposes, lived above the law? At least above conventional law.

After so many months of confinement, his objective was to exact revenge—however risky that might be. But instead all he'd done was to harshly remind the man of his own mortality, an awareness that sociopaths generally lacked. It was at least a good first step to replace, with fear, the man's complacent arrogance.

Charles was rueful, but only for destroying the man's golf club. It was the product of talented craftsmen who'd created a veritable piece of art. His time in prison may have suppressed the aesthetic side of his nature, but the months he'd spent in solitary contemplation had sharpened his moral sentiments. Taking the shot was completely illegal. But was it within the bounds of Natural Law?

Treatises have been written about Natural Law throughout history, but for Charles it boiled down to the dictum "Don't do to others what you don't want them to do to you." It didn't invoke action; it advised inaction. Basically, live and let live. Like most people, at least decent ones, Charles intuitively lived by Natural Law.

He reasoned that his action against Samuels wasn't the initiation of force, just a necessarily delayed reaction to Samuels's direct aggression. After all, Samuels sought to destroy him. He may have failed to murder him, so far, but he had succeeded in stealing a major part of Charles's life.

But was it moral to react with lethal force after the passage of time, as opposed to just in the moment of immediate danger, if there were no other reasonable alternative? Or was it just and moral to act preemptively only if there appeared to be what the Supreme Court called a clear and present danger? These were questions that philosophers, lawyers, and priests had written libraries about. He realized he was teetering on a slippery moral slope. He had to be cautious, but his care was strictly intellectual. Eighteen months in prison had reshaped his attitude.

Law. Most of it was argumentative and arbitrary. Arcane and convoluted. Should one approach it as a Kantian, a utilitarian, a positivist, a rationalist? Should one see it from a Christian, a Mohammedan, or a Talmudic point of view? Buddhists might see things differently.

All of these traditions were interesting, but none provided the entire answer—if any of them were even right. The fact was that people basically did what they wanted to do and found justifications after the fact.

Charles settled on his own philosophy, a direct and personal ethics even more concise than Natural Law. The only moral code that made practical sense was a very simple one: Do what thou wilt … but be prepared to accept the consequences.

The critical part was the second clause. If someone thought through the indirect and delayed as well as the direct and immediate results and was prepared to accept them, then at least he'd act more rationally than he would otherwise. More importantly, he'd have to take personal responsibility for what he did. The purpose of morality was to make for a sane world, but that was only possible when people acted as adults as opposed to toddlers intent on immediate gratification.

He assumed that most people would never initiate violence or fraud. That was certainly true in his case, whether for purely aesthetic reasons or the chance that karma would punish him. Even if the concept of cosmic blowback proved to be hogwash and there were no karmic penalties, the essence of character was standing by your actions.

Disregarding media speculation about the supposed assassination attempt, Charles looked instead for red herrings and false clues the police might release. Most reports praised Paul Samuels lavishly, saying he was critical to the Federal Reserve interventions that were necessary to keep the economy on an even keel during the many recent shocks to the system. They all offered an obligatory dollop of pompous gratitude for how incompetent the assassin had been. Which was just annoying. In fact, it had been a superb shot.

He was pleased when Xander told him he'd been invited to play a piece at a small recital. Maybe he'd been invited because of his notoriety, but perhaps it was because he still had many fans. Maybe it was just because he was recognized as an excellent stylist. He accepted the invitation. An evening playing to a refined audience under the bright lights of a small concert hall would help him regain his aesthetic balance.

Charles had spent much of his first week of freedom practicing on the Steinway in Xander's apartment, creating real sound. It was an antidote to the negativity encroaching on him. Xander had urged him to take a month to transition before visiting with Maurice and Rainbow.

"You need to become human again, kid. You don't want to inflict your current self on those you most love, do you? Take a few weeks with me to reacclimate. Then a small performance on stage, to help you remember what it feels like to be constructive. You've spent a year and half deep underwater. You can't resurface all of a sudden. You need to decompress gradually."

In part, Charles agreed with Xander, but he had no desire to decompress entirely. He planned to retain some of that pressure for righteous, but patient, vengeance. The result of that vengeance, Charles knew, could be the most productive thing he'd ever do.

The reigning powers at the Philharmonic lacked the courage to invite back a convicted felon just out of prison, even though—before he'd become known as a notorious drug lord— the Sunday edition of the New York Times had celebrated him with a review on the front page of the arts section. So Xander had pulled a different string—that of a friend with connections in New York society.

A few music-loving socialites who'd heard him play before showed up. Some of tonight's audience were curiosity seekers, hoping to see the notorious drug lord make a fool of himself. But it turned out that most of the audience were fans, for reasons that had nothing to do with music. They came to reassure themselves that a semblance of normalcy existed in a city that moved from one arbitrary lockdown to another, a city that might soon be on fire in a world on the precipice of economic calamity. They came because he had become their hero in the days when Naked Emperor was available. They would have come even if he banged on the piano keys like a chimpanzee.

The orchestra finished shifting, their instruments at temporary rest. The only audible sound was the air passing through the center of his chest. He positioned his hands on the keys he loved and centered his emotions to supercharge his performance. He shut his eyes, preparing himself.

In his left pocket, his cell phone vibrated. No one but Xander had the number, but the phone still managed to ring several times a day. After eighteen months of technological disconnection, he'd forgotten how important it was to turn the blasted device off. He took his fingers off the keyboard and reached into his pocket. He glanced at the screen, shook his head, and replaced the now deactivated phone. Then he looked out at the audience and cast a sheepish grin while turning his palms up. "Telemarketers!" Ripples of light laughter told him he'd smoothed over a potentially major faux pas.

He sat still, and the concert hall hushed into silence.

He then took thirty seconds to center himself—a long time in front of a silent audience. Then, finally, his index finger gently moved, as on the trigger of a gun. But this time its motion was from the F, to the D-flat, and then to the C.

Although he was born after Glenn Gould died, he seemed to channel the famous pianist, exceeding the audience's expectations. The pace was far faster than most expected to ever hear Clair de Lune performed. He played as if he had a dozen independent fingers on each hand. The piano's keys were an extension not of his hands, but of his heart and mind.

After the concert, a cocktail party had been arranged in the mezzanine for VIPs to meet the performers. His hands ached, but more from greeting scores of admirers than massaging the keyboard. He lost count of the people who had come just to say thank you, not just for the music, but for Sybillene—Naked Emperor. The drug had started a revolution to overthrow the reign of lies and self-delusion: a stillborn revolution, quashed by Paul Samuels, Sabina Heidel, their minions, and their sympathizers.

They'd declared war against Naked Emperor. As in all wars, truth was the first casualty.

During the meet and greet, there were a few uncomfortable moments.

A woman behind him spoke loudly, to be sure he'd hear her clearly through the muffling of her surgical mask. "How can such beauty come from such a monster? It's a contradiction."

He could feel her hatred—and disliked that more than the silly biddy herself. She was an indication that perhaps the whole planet was just a milder version of the prisons he'd just left. Was there any point in trying to communicate with such a person? He knew the likely answer but decided to indulge himself.

"When you find yourself in a contradiction, question your assumptions." He smiled again and turned his back on her.

Another woman, with a light fur draped on her shoulders and a more pleasant countenance, approached but stayed a polite distance away. "Mr. Knight," she said in a quivering voice that reflected her age, "I always appreciated Debussy. But you've added a degree of passion and energy. I cried."

Then she added, while conspiratorially tilting her head toward a silver-haired man, "He won't likely admit it, but he shivered at the start of the second movement."

Her husband smiled diffidently.

"I'm honored, and happy, in equal measures, madam. It sounds like he had what some call a musical moment. It's happened to me too. They're rare and should be treasured and remembered. To quote Glenn Gould, 'The purpose of art is not the release of a momentary ejection of adrenaline but is, rather, the gradual, lifelong construction of a state of wonder and serenity.' I hope you both have many more such moments."

"A musical moment. Yes... I like that." She smiled at him, turned away, and then turned back. "Thank you," she whispered.

He had created value here, tonight, as he had earlier by sending Samuels a message that even the purest evil could not ignore. Both actions invigorated him.

His thoughts returned to Samuels. He'd killed before—and not purely in self-defense. Eliminating Seth Fowler, the head of the Sybillene Eradication Administration, had, in part, been about preventing more destruction, but Charles admitted to himself that it was mostly about vengeance. Paul Samuels? The whole world would have benefitted from his death.

It would have been a "greater good."

What a perverse concept. Perhaps that manipulative phrase would someday disappear back into the Eye of Sauron, or back down the throats of the fascists and socialists who loved to use it to justify their quest for power. In fact, the "greater good" was always whatever best served the kind of people who liked to use the phrase.

Had they known of his actions at the golf course, there were some who would criticize his restraint. Charles wondered who would kill the one who would inevitably replace Samuels? And whoever followed next? And next?

It would never end.

Sharks' teeth. They fall out, but there are always others to take their place.

He knew that he could kill such people; he had the ability and the will. But removing rotten teeth just to make room for the next one wasn't practical.

The object was to destroy not just the man, but his destructive power, his work. It was a battle of ideals, not biology. A criminal's death didn't kill what he stood for. In fact, it might amplify it, if the media made him into a martyr. That's what happened with Che Guevara. He would have been

31

forgotten as just another psycho, a Latin version of Charles Manson, if the Bolivian army—instead of killing him—had held an open trial to expose all his misdeeds. Then the romantic photo of him wearing a beret would never have been put on millions of t-shirts.

Just then an odd little man, with a potbelly and a scrunched-up face, intruded on his ruminations by tugging on his elbow. "Charles," he said, "that was a wonderful performance."

Charles drew his mind back to the mezzanine in which dozens of patrons still lingered. He struggled to place the man but couldn't, so he said, "Thank you, sir."

"I'm Thomas Jackson." Jackson stared up into his face for too long before saying, "I need your advice." He then guided Charles away from the throng, into a corner, behind a table.

"You know what they say about free advice, Mr. Jackson."

Jackson had a degree of fetid breath that can only persist in people who have no idea how bad it is. Involuntarily stepping back, Charles lifted his glass of Macallan's to his mouth, and inhaled deeply through his nose—a mild anesthetic against the insult.

"Charles, I know you've been through the wringer. But you… you bounce back like a rubber ball." Jackson let his eyes fall to the floor. "I need your help."

"What kind of help?" After the performance, Charles had no emotional energy to spare, but he didn't want to disappoint a fan.

Jackson said, "You've known some of the toughest characters in the world. You've been in prison, right? You got some friends from there, right? You learned a lot, right?"

Charles didn't like the man's style, nor where this seemed to be going. Prison has an effect on everybody, mostly bad. Character isn't formed so much by the things that happen to you as how you react to them—including your reaction to intrusive questions.

"It's no secret I've done time, but only a short stretch. Most of the people in prison are actual criminals, and most criminals are basically stupid. What I learned is that I don't want to associate with stupid people, Mr. Jackson."

The man nodded his head, impatient and paying no attention. "But you know some people who can do things that people like you and I can't do, don't you?"

Charles braced himself. Jackson was in trouble. He was about to learn what sort of trouble, although he didn't want to know.

Jackson moved odoriferously closer, exhaling as he spoke sotto voce. "Look. There's this shithead having an affair with my wife. All winter, and still going on. I've got proof. Real proof. Pictures!" Jackson's eyes were angry, not sad. "I need this fixed."

"And you want me to introduce you to someone who has the skills to fix it?"

"Yes."

"Fix it how?" Charles didn't whisper.

The man spat back, "Dead. Or beat to shit. That's how."

"Your wife or the man or both?"

Jackson shook his head. "I suppose just the man. Yeah, just the man."

"What's his crime?"

"What? What do you mean? He's having an affair with my wife!"

"Has he threatened you?"

"No. He's probably too frightened to come near me."

Charles doubted that. "Has he committed rape?"

Jackson grimaced. "She seemed willing enough."

"It sounds to me like seduction and consensual fornication."

"Well, you say tomato, I say potato."

"I'm sorry for your plight. But you don't own her. And I can't help you, Mr. Jackson, other than to advise you not to do anything stupid."

Charles walked away leaving Jackson standing in a perturbed silence.

He kept walking, past admirers and whisperers, out the door and into a taxicab.

At Xander's building, he opened the door to the spacious top-floor apartment with stunning views of Manhattan and beyond. Its market value had probably risen twentyfold since its purchase. Xander didn't treat it as an investment, but he mentioned that it was probably time to sell. "When the ducks are quacking, it's time to feed them. Besides, this city has seen its best days for years to come." He came to New York for business, but also art collection. Like his other apartments in Washington, Buenos Aires, and Bangkok, the place was as much a gallery as a home. For Charles, for the time being, it was home.

"Well played, Charles!" Xander said, handing him a glass of Ardbeg.

Charles asked, "You stick around for the whole thing, or did you duck out part way through?"

"I stayed for your part, but I didn't stay for the cocktails because I don't like hanging out with the public. The chances are that few are worth meeting. The older I get the less time I have to waste finding out which they are."

"I empathize, Xander."

Charles kicked his shoes off and positioned himself on an overstuffed, but very comfortable, leather sofa. To his right was a Vermeer self-portrait. In the art world, there were only thirty-four Vermeer paintings believed to remain in existence, yet this was a thirty-fifth, out of the public eye and presumed destroyed or lost centuries earlier. Xander had not acquired it through conventional channels.

Charles gazed over the city savoring the smoky, peaty single malt. It mandated small sips. Xander sat near him, looking more at the art than the city. His sun-worn face softened as he gazed at a large modern painting dealing with Greek myths, done by a living Bulgarian artist. It was probably only worth thousands, but he liked it more than the Vermeer worth millions.

"Now that the concert's over, what's on your mind, kid?"

"I'm thinking there's a market for a set of skills I've come to possess. People who need problems solved. If I stay away from stupid people, I could occupy myself filling that need."

During his confinement, he'd had the time to assess not just himself, but the others locked away with him. His forced association with people who'd lowered their masks of sanity had given him valuable insights. He mentioned the stupidity of criminals to Jackson earlier at the concert hall. Stupid didn't mean bad scores on an IQ test. It meant an inability to predict consequences. Not just the delayed and indirect consequences of their actions, but even the immediate and direct ones. Stupidity was an unwitting tendency to self-destruction. It made many people in prison irrational and unpredictable.

He knew what he would allow himself to do and what he would never do. He knew what made him different from the criminals—whether the criminals were in prison or in power.

True, his mind, his psyche, had been bent. But in some ways it was stronger than ever for the experience. As a consolation prize, he was probably in the best physical shape of his life.

He thought back to the first time he'd set foot in New York, at just thirteen. He'd come to stay with Maurice just after his mother had died. He'd carried a book with him in his backpack from Montana.

He spoke to Xander somberly, musing out loud. "When I was a kid, my favorite book was The Count of Monte Cristo. I liked who he made himself become. And the way that he—because he was seeking revenge for himself—created justice in the world at large. My favorite TV show when I was a kid was Have Gun—Will Travel. I liked who Paladin was and the way he solved problems. He didn't need the money people paid him to solve their problems. What he needed was the challenge of doing so. Paladin preferred peaceful, nonviolent solutions to problems, but he was willing and able to right wrongs in whatever way necessary. With you, I've dipped more than just a toe into the profession, solving the John-John problem in Gondwana. You pulled that trigger. And then again when I pulled the trigger to punch Seth Fowler's ticket in DC. Those were last resorts, but necessary and correct.

"Edmund Dantes and Paladin are modern versions of the Greek Erinyes, the Roman Furies. Personifications of justice. Paul Samuels and his cronies want me dead. Am I going to walk on eggshells for the rest of my life, trying to hide from them? Should I try to look for some way to placate them? No. That's not the way I'm wired. It wouldn't work anyway. They're determined to hang me out to dry. All I know is that I'd rather be hanged as a wolf than a lamb. They want a war? Okay. I can do war."

Xander had watched Charles closely all month. "There are people who need to shed their mortal coil. There are people who need killing. The high-risk, high-reward aspect of that work fits your character. You've been way up and way down a couple of times already. Maybe that's modified the way your brain responds to the dopamine it produces. Becoming a ... problem solver ... is a reasonable next step. It's certainly a valuable skillset to have anytime, but especially as the world gets more chaotic. Sure, you could live a life of reasonable leisure with just the assets you set aside from our little adventure in Gondwana. But your enemies are unlikely to leave you alone no matter what you do or where you go."

To destroy destroyers. Charles considered that it could be quite productive. There was no point in being a sitting duck. It made sense to go on the offensive.

But he had zero interest in being a hired killer. In fact he didn't like the

35

idea of killing; he didn't even have an interest in hunting animals, unusual for a kid from Montana. And he had chosen not to kill Samuels.

Killing Samuels wouldn't have been murder. Murder is defined as an unjustifiable killing. The laws of most cultures prohibited murder, but not killing. How many Christian martyrs had gone to their violent deaths without even defending themselves, failing to recognize that the commandment might have been better translated as "Thou shalt not murder," not "Thou shalt not kill." But there was no point in parsing what was going on in the mind of some prophet or budding theologian thousands of years ago—and similarly little value in playing Talmudic scholar, trying to determine the correct translation of an ancient word.

More to the point, common law tradition guarantees everyone the right to defend himself or hire others to defend him. Only police states put that power exclusively in the hands of the police. The Soviet Union, Nazi Germany, and Communist China all denied their subjects the right to self-defense. In essence they were just criminal fantasies acted out on a grand scale. They were the stand-outs in the twentieth century, but now the twenty-first century was chockablock with coercive governments.

It wasn't a question of becoming a one-man Star Chamber. Although, in a way, he had done just that earlier when he, alone, had chosen to let Paul Samuels live, not die. What right did he have to make that decision? Did twelve men, or a thousand, or a million, have any more right than an individual?

Perhaps the opinion of a large group wasn't worth more, but less than that of one man, in a matter of life or death. A lone man has a conscience; he has to live with the consequences of his actions and take responsibility for them. A million people, even if they set themselves up as The Law or The State, can evade any hint of individual responsibility. They're essentially a mob. Prison had provided him with practice acting as judge and jury, for there was no other justice there. When necessary, he'd also served as executioner.

The United Nations had murdered everyone at Charles's manufacturing operation in Gondwana, at the direct request of Paul Samuels. Sure, French naval aircraft were the specific tools; Aristotle would have termed them the material cause. But blaming the French navy's planes was like blaming a gun for shooting up a school. Although the philosopher would term them the efficient cause, the pilots weren't moral actors: the information they'd been given was neither sufficient nor accurate enough for them to know that following those orders was wrong. So, following orders, they had turned the hilltop in Africa—and all the good people who stood on it—into dust. Paul Samuels was the ultimate cause, the one that counted. He had pulled the trigger releasing the jets and their air to ground missiles, bombs, and cannons on Charles's friends on that faraway African hill.

"I agree that evil should be extinguished. The problem is that someone has to do it," Xander continued. "Surely Charles Manson, Jeffrey Dahmer, and other serial murderers would have continued if they hadn't been caught. It was their nature. Evil exists. Do you know the story of the frog and the scorpion?"

Charles did, but he didn't mind hearing it again from someone who might add another dash of flavor.

"So a frog and a scorpion were caught on an island about to be washed away in a flood. The scorpion asked the frog to give him a ride to dry land. The frog said, 'But if I do, you'll sting me, and I'll die.' The scorpion replied, 'That makes no sense. If I sting you, we'd both drown.' The frog thought about it and said 'Okay, hop on.' In the middle of the river the scorpion stung him. With his dying breath, the frog asked the scorpion, 'Why did you do that? Now we're both going to die.' The scorpion answered, 'Why? Because I'm a scorpion.'"

Samuels was a scorpion who routinely committed offenses that were subtler than Dahmer's, but vastly more destructive. He was in a class with Stalin or Mao—wholesale criminals who, even long after their deaths, were worshipped by vast numbers of people around the world. Samuels held the second-most-powerful position in the Federal Reserve. But because of his immense personal wealth, influence, and connections, he was more important than the Fed's chairman.

Charles looked into the eyes of his friend and mentor—a man who had made fortunes, fought in bush wars, traveled everywhere, and protected and shaped him. They'd risked their lives together, enriching themselves while doing the right thing. Charles cared immensely for Xander, and he was sorry they didn't spend much more time together.

"Should I have killed him, Xander?"

"Probably. Stop second-guessing yourself, Charles. You've made your choice. Act on it."

Paul Samuels still lived. For that reason among many, Charles slept poorly.

37

4

Render unto Caesar

LATE the next morning, Charles phoned his uncle.

"Hi, Charles. What the hell do you need me for now?" The sounds gurgled out his uncle's throat. Maurice's harsh tone in no way reflected how the great man felt about his nephew, and Charles smiled at hearing his voice.

Until the last couple of years, the obese man had rarely left his apartment but for annual trips to the doctor and the dentist. According to his uncle's self-serving reports of the visits, the doctor spoke only of his perfect health. Recently things had begun to change, however. He was still terribly overweight, but Rainbow said that he'd lost fifty pounds. More important, his muscles had regained some of the tone they once had.

"Maurice. Mission accomplished. At least as far as I'm concerned."

His uncle replied in words chosen carefully in recognition of the ever-present potential of listening ears on any phone line, anywhere. "I hear you. But if I were you, it would have ended differently ... with more of a crescendo, as you musicians might say."

Charles also chose his words carefully. Artificial intelligence audited millions of conversations everywhere in the world, sorting them by interest level before relaying them to live agents, and likely doing a far better job than the agents themselves. "I know. I've got a lot to learn. There's no better way to learn than by doing. Let's get together tonight."

He contemplated his prospective new avocation. Unresolved, inadequately compartmentalized feelings battled within him.

He heard a loud snore. Was there a cure for his uncle's narcolepsy?

"Uncle Maurice... Maurice!"

"Yeah, what the hell are you waking me for?" The words came slurred with sleep.

"Stay awake, Maurice."

"Yeah. All right. I will." There was no chance he would.

Charles said firmly, "I'm coming over."

"About time," Maurice replied gruffly.

*   *   *

Charles seated himself next to his uncle in the apartment at the Royal Major General in Chelsea. Maurice had a box of Cohiba Esplendidos and a half-consumed glass of Chateau Margaux on the table to his right. Crumpled papers that had not reached their target lay scattered around the wastebasket. In contrast to Maurice's somewhat Hefneresque appearance in Egyptian cotton pajamas and a silk robe, the apartment was untidy—neither the maid nor Rainbow had been there that day. Empty fast food containers lay open on counters while trash containers stood unused. But the coffee table was organized by a conscientious mind with specific intent. Two hard-wired telephones—one of which was red—three cellular phones, and two laptop computers were situated in arm's reach. Another laptop computer lay open on the end table to his left. Each had split-screen views on which ran streaming quotes from the highly volatile global stock and commodity exchanges; C-SPAN; weather data; and international news feeds pouring forth bad earnings reports, new quarantine measures, travel restrictions, and capital controls. Behind the screens lay stacks of reports and magazines. The area around Maurice's couch was like a Combat Information Center in a nuclear-powered dumpster.

Charles waited patiently for his uncle's next alert period. A disturbed sleeping pattern occurred when Maurice's tongue fell back in his throat and obstructed his breathing enough that he'd have to wake up and reposition himself to catch his breath. His snores sounded like a subway failing to stop as it raced through a station. It was an endearing trait, but it seriously compromised his health and needed a medical solution.

On the bright side, there was no question his uncle had lost weight—a reversal of a very long-term trend. It was probably Rainbow's regular influence.

"What? What is it?" His uncle roused himself.

"Maurice, it's me, Charles."

39

"Oh. Thanks for coming." Maurice Templeton pried his body out of the chair's leather cushions sufficiently to sit up. "Or should I ask what you want from me this time?"

"Synergy, Maurice. Mutual benefit."

"The idea is most appealing. Let's celebrate it, and your freedom, with a small repast." He stretched out his oak trunk of an arm, pressed a button on one of the telephones, and picked up the receiver. "Jerry, send up some Chinese. Yeah the usual. Plus..." He looked at Charles with raised eyebrows.

"Dumplings. Steamed," Charles replied without thinking.

"Plus an order of steamed dumplings. Make that two orders."

After hanging up, Maurice spoke pidgin, mimicking the Peking Palace's order taker. "It take ten minute onry. It oways be taking ten minute onry." He then took that ten minutes to work his way to the bathroom. By the time he returned, the posh building's bowtie-wearing concierge knocked at the door, carrying two large paper bags.

When they ate together, usually Maurice talked and Charles listened. That suited Charles; his uncle was a veritable encyclopedia of knowledge, curated by wisdom and experience. He knew he couldn't learn much by talking, but a lot by listening. This, however, turned into more of a two-way conversation.

"Where's Rainbow?" Charles asked.

"You can tell she's not been here, you mean?" Maurice's hand held his chopsticks as he waved his arm over the disarray of the apartment. "The maid will be in tomorrow. Rainbow's been in Washington for a couple of weeks, touching base with her crew. She's coming home today."

Charles smiled, pleased that Maurice considered his apartment to be the girl's home.

"She's working for you, huh?"

"It's good to have the kid around."

"She's a good combination of smart and street smart. With lots of energy."

"Yeah, I miss her. I backslide without her riding herd on me. Anyway, when she's here, she's busy learning the trade."

Charles raised his eyebrows. "Really? You trust her that much?"

"She earned your trust, didn't she? Besides, she's already saved my life—or at least extended it a few years. I don't want everything I know to get buried six feet under with me. You gotta trust a few people in the world. Sometimes even the most trusted will let you down, but that's usually a misunderstanding rather than the emergence of evil. Talk it through and the misunderstandings go away. I've chosen to trust Rainbow, you, and a few others. Not many. The more people you trust, the greater the chances you're gonna be disappointed."

Charles nodded. "Well, I trust you. Enough to ask you to abet me in another high-risk venture that you'll find intellectually stimulating. I know you don't need the money, but it should be financially rewarding. Maybe it can keep me off the road back to prison as a bonus."

"More like a highway to hell. Death is more likely than a prison sentence for either one of us at this point."

"I didn't enjoy prison."

"You're not supposed to. But if there's a next time, it'll probably be a super-max in the middle of nowhere, not a white-collar establishment with gourmet grub and conjugal visits every Tuesday, Thursday, and twice on weekends."

"Yeah, that's exactly how I remember my last eighteen months. By the way, I don't intend to go back."

Maurice snorted and shook his head.

Charles insisted. "Not just that. I think we might be able to change the course of history."

"What's that aphorism, something about pride goeth before a fall?"

"I like 'Go big, or go home.' But, also, 'I am too enamored of my freedom, too fond of my own ideas!'"

"Yeah, I taught you that line. But Claude Debussy isn't going to keep you out of prison. And quoting him won't impress anyone back in prison. That's if they don't kill you out here first. You still like to play piano?"

"You know I do—even though you skipped my performance last night."

"Can't play piano much in prison, can you?"

This line of conversation was pointless, so Charles concluded it with a simple statement. "Okay, you've convinced me to stay out of prison."

Maurice closed his eyes momentarily but didn't fall asleep. "Why this career path all of a sudden?"

"I'm a felon. It's hard to get a job."

"But you don't want a job. You don't need one."

"I spent the last year and a half engaged in trench warfare against boredom. I can tell you there's a lot of truth to the old saying about 'Busy hands are happy hands,' or something like that . . . I need a business that allows me to do well by doing good, taking the fight to the enemy. Part of my plan is to take The Count of Monte Cristo and Have Gun—Will Travel and turn them into reality. The more criminal the opponents, the more appealing the target.

Maurice, I'd like to believe I can do good that others are afraid to do. Or aren't capable of doing. It should be possible to earn a living taking out truly evil people."

"Are you sure? Samuels is a truly evil person. You didn't kill him."

Charles shook his head. "I'm not necessarily talking about killing; I want to avoid it for all kinds of reasons. Samuels's type of evil would live on after his death anyway. I'm looking for a more permanent solution."

Maurice pushed a large hand against his belly, as if trying to make room for the next dumpling. He chewed as he thought, the wheels of his brain grinding, calculating.

Charles could read his uncle well, and he could tell that the proposition thrilled Uncle Maurice. In his professional circles, Maurice had the occasional need for a competent problem solver, a knight without armor, a modern Paladin. Who would be more trustworthy than his own nephew?

Maurice swallowed with a twanging reverberation. "Beware of your inner being, m'boy. This sort of work requires taking some on the chin. Emotionally, I mean. And perhaps spiritually. You're going to suffer some tough hits. Your targets are going to be mostly political. Which means both ultrarisky and ultrahigh profile."

Maurice sat back in his couch. Charles recognized the contemplative expression on his uncle's face. It was the look of a professor about to impart wisdom.

"You know, Charles," Maurice began, "the most famous assassination in history was that of Julius Caesar. Caesar was a dictator, but the Republic was by then already a fiction. After Rome destroyed Carthage a hundred years before, it was well on its way to being an empire, with possessions around the Mediterranean. It was no longer a city-state run by sturdy yeoman farmers. During the wars, those farmers picked up a lot of bad habits killing people professionally overseas. When they returned, they found their farms had gone back to bush. Rich men who'd made a fortune on the wars bought their farms for sesterces on the denarius and then imported slaves—captured Carthaginians—to work them. So, many of the penniless unemployed former farmer-soldiers moved into the capital to live on the dole. Rome gave the displaced farmers free food and kept them busy with free entertainment. But not busy enough. Romans were easy to recruit into political gangs.

"The famous Gracchi brothers tried to reform the situation and met with violent deaths. Theirs were the first important political murders in hundreds of years. Was Rome destabilized by the murders—or was an unstable Rome the cause of the murders? My guess is both—a feedback loop. In any event, the society became even more unstable. These things take on a life of their own. It's as hard to turn around a country that's headed downhill as it is to stop an avalanche once it's started.

"Then came the dictatorships, civil wars, and proscriptions under Marius and Sulla. Thousands of upper-class Romans were murdered and their properties were confiscated. Slave rebellions. The Catiline conspiracy with more murders. Armed political mobs roaming the streets.

"Caesar fabricated an excuse to invade Gaul. By conquering it, he covered himself in military glory while looting the country, which made him Rome's richest man. It gave him control of enough money and men to cross the Rubicon and try to take over Rome. He was popular; the mob loves a conquering hero. After a successful civil war with his ex–fellow triumvir and rival Pompey the Great, Caesar was now a king in everything but the title itself, although he never would have used that word because the Romans saw themselves as citizens, not subjects.

"In 44 BC Caesar was just three days away from leaving on a long war against the Persians. The Persians had recently killed the ex-triumvir Crassus and wiped out several legions. Brutus, Cassius, and a couple dozen other senators decided to kill him because Caesar was treating the Republic like his personal property.

"I've always had respect for Brutus. You know, Brutus was a direct descendant of the Brutus who centuries earlier vanquished the last king of Rome and instituted the Republic. No doubt this young Brutus felt it his duty to protect the family legacy. I've also asked myself why Brutus misread things so badly. In the context of the times, Caesar was better than most. He was famously generous and forgiving with his enemies. He didn't engage in proscriptions or try to set up a police state. He was extremely popular with the common people. Most important, he was about to leave town for at least several years—maybe forever. The war against Persia might not have cost anything. In those days, if you won a war, you stole all the loser's gold, cattle, and artwork and shipped them home accompanied by a large assortment of slaves. Unlike today, war was a potentially profitable business.

"The conspirators had an impossible dream about restoring the Republic. It wasn't as if the people really cared whether Caesar was a dictator. Sulla had been one before him, and Augustus was one after him. All they really cared about was free food, free entertainment, and an orderly society—just like today once you strip away the propaganda about democracy.

"Killing the guy in charge, in any time or place, is usually a formula for chaos. Until he's starved, with his back up against the wall, the average guy doesn't typically like political change—as Brutus discovered. Caesar was transformed into an even bigger hero—one for the ages—and all the conspirators were dead within three years.

"It didn't much matter what they said they were trying to do. Dante put Brutus and Cassius in the lowest rung of his Inferno, alongside Judas. The betrayers of Julius and the betrayer of Jesus, to be ground by Satan's teeth for eternity. The assassination of Caesar not only didn't resurrect the republic, it ushered in the formal Empire—after more civil war. It was morally correct, but a strategic mistake. So it accomplished nothing… Hell, it made things worse—and gave assassination a bad name that it still has.

"The general rule is that things get worse after a head of state is killed. There are exceptions, of course. Take Caligula, Rome's third emperor and a despicable criminal—and the first emperor we know, for sure, that was assassinated. Certainly one who needed killing. He was walking in his garden and stopped to praise a group of young men who were performing. Probably picking one out for an evening of pleasure; he had violent inclinations. One of his praetorians, a former centurion named Cassius Chaerea, slashed his throat, shouting, 'Take that.' A praetorian tribune named Cornelius Sabinus—basically one of the commanders—then stabbed Caligula in the chest, breaking the emperor's jaw as he pulled his sword out.

"Very few people know their names. I think they should be remembered—as should Brutus—as good Romans, and memorialized for ridding the world of Caligula. He was replaced by Claudius, a much better emperor. But no good deed goes unpunished in the world of politics. Chaerea was executed by Claudius. Sabinus, perhaps figuring he was next, suicided."

Charles's cell phone rang in his pocket. He nodded apologetically to his uncle. "Excuse me." He answered the phone, listened for ten seconds, and hung up. "Believe it or not, Maurice, the guy was trying to sell me Viagra."

Maurice laughed. "Poor sod had no idea who he was calling." The irony was that a knockoff of Viagra, marketed by the inner-city Alpha Crew, had been a major part of Charles's rise to the position of a drug lord.

"It doesn't appear you can get away from the bastards, unless you go incommunicado." He recalled the near-disaster at the concert.

"Get used to it. It'll only get worse when they develop artificial intelligence to reach out and touch you."

Charles shook his head. "Looking at the bright side, there were no robocallers in prison. So what were you saying?"

"What I've been saying is that political assassination has gotten a bad name—starting with Caesar's. Some of that bad name is deserved because it rarely accomplishes much, but it can be useful. Is there a way to restore the good name of people like Brutus and make Cassius Chaerea and Cornelius Sabinus into heroes? If you think you can, sign me up."

"That's the idea," Charles nodded. "Like Brutus, I'll need a co-conspirator or two."

"I'll keep my eye out, but for the most part, you're gonna to have to do your own marketing. It's not like you can advertise in the New York Times. Don't jump into the deep end. Take this on a gradient, and start off with small fry. Taking out a world leader isn't an amateur-hour event."

Charles agreed with his uncle, as he usually did. "I do need to gain some experience. Avenging angels don't hatch full blown from the egg." He needed to gain some time, some recovery, some moderation of this sensation that persisted inside his chest.

"While you're plotting a life of death, Charles, how do you intend to move the money? Like in the drug trade, the feds always follow the money."

"I understand. It's harder than ever to move dollars with all the new restrictions. More every day. They illegalized Naked Emperor because they said it was a health risk. They're making everything about health; it's a perfect excuse for the Sybillene Eradication Administration to expand their reach. It was bad enough before, when every foreign account had to be reported. But, Maurice, cryptocurrencies can change everything."

"Sure, Charles. Even taxi drivers and shoeshine boys have touted it. Blockchain, Bitcoin. Interesting stuff. Rainbow's all gawgaw over it. She put most of what she made from Sybillene in it—and then took a ninety percent hit at one point. She's tech savvy, but has a lot to learn about market timing. Crypto was beyond my ken initially. The old-dog syndrome. Took me a while to grasp the utility of blockchain. But she thinks some of the cryptos are the best thing since butter on bread, and she nagged me into buying some. I considered it tuition money and let her do the technical work and make day-to-day trading decisions. Tiny fraction of my portfolio, but it's the fraction that's paid off the best, despite its huge ups and downs. It's a crazy roller coaster. A speculator's wet dream.

"I treated Bitcoin like a trading sardine, not an eating sardine, and suggested she sell out when it was obviously frothy. But no, she always wants to HODL, as they say—hold on for dear life. Maybe she's learned a lesson. Maybe not. She's gotten very involved with the tech." Maurice inhaled a portion of General Tso's chicken. "But you think the boys at Goldman Sachs are really going to let some upstart newfangled money like crypto castrate their ability to control the universe? Samuels—who, by the way, isn't dead—isn't about to hang around playing golf while some cryptocurrency makes the Federal Reserve's Monopoly money look like… well… Monopoly money."

Charles had heard all this before, and he had gained his own expertise in the area since Rainbow had introduced it to him in the joint. "That's the thing, Maurice. Stopping cryptocurrency would require the concerted efforts of most of the governments and central banks on the planet. That's not going to happen. It's nearly impossible to get two—forget about two hundred—heads of state to even agree the sky is blue. It's far harder than banning marijuana or alcohol. What's important is that the nations who buck Samuels and Goldman and the central banks—the ones that encourage crypto economies—are gonna flourish. A few countries have figured that out already. I'm thinking about buying property in those."

"Too bad you lost your passport to the criminal-justice system, Charles."

"Just my US passport, Maurice. I have others."

"I expected no less. You never impressed me as a fool, m'boy."

"The progressives have been pushing compulsory wealth redistribution for decades. Well, they'll get it—but not the way they want. What's going to happen is voluntary wealth redistribution. Crypto will move money away from Wall Street, out of high-tax, high-regulation countries, and toward the individual—and do it in complete privacy."

"That's a nice hope. But if the money flow is enough, Wall Street will find a way to control it and profit from it. Or, if they can't, then they'll suppress it. I know those guys. Many of them have lower ethics than the average gangster. Willy Sutton was asked why he robbed banks. You know what he said? 'Because that's where the money is.' Smart bad guys figured out that owning banks is way easier and safer than robbing them. That's the way the world is. But I understand the argument for the things. In a way, cryptocurrencies are commoditizing—monetizing—your ideology, aren't they?"

"Yes. Commoditized freedom. I like that," reflected Charles. "In a way, it lets people put a financial value on freedom, and speculate in it. The cryptocurrency universe was built by anarchists to put their theories about a free and peaceful world into practice. And boom! Look what's happened! A lot of penniless libertarians became overnight centimillionaires or billionaires. There's a global pent-up demand for freedom, Maurice! And it's not just the kids in Rainbow's generation that see these things as digital freedom. When Bitcoin went from a few pennies to five figures, a bunch of libertarians all over the planet got rich. Rich libertarians, Maurice. It's unheard of, but it's just gotta be good for the world. They don't give a damn for political borders, and they're immune to nationalist propaganda. They're not about to fight pointless wars to keep politicians in power, and now they have money that governments can't touch."

Maurice nodded.

"We need to make another fortune. A really big one. The business I'm going to create will be built around a new cryptocurrency, Maurice."

"You and whose uncle? What do you know about blockchain coding, Charles?"

"I know some basics. More important, I know that for the right price, I can find a blockchain coder or two. Most important, I have a way to put the theory of what we've been talking about into practice."

"Coders are in demand. There aren't enough to go around."

"So I'll have to pay a lot of money."

Maurice jerked upright. Charles thought perhaps he was choking on some moo goo gai pan, but that wasn't it. Which was fortunate because, despite his recent weight loss, Maurice remained far too large for Charles to be able to reach around his torso to perform a Heimlich maneuver.

Maurice held up his index finger. "Maybe not a lot of money, Charles. Maybe this can start out as more of a barter deal." He struggled forward in his chair, grabbed a pen and paper from the coffee table, scribbled a number, and gave it to Charles. "Call this number from an untraceable phone. Don't use your name; don't give any identification. Sure as hell don't mention me."

Charles nodded. "Whose number is this?"

"Someone who needs a serious problem solved."

Charles raised his eyebrows impatiently and asked, "Is this someone who needs assistance for reasons that would appeal to Brutus?"

"Not a political target. Not a noble desire to return to a republic. More practical. Smaller. But otherwise, yes. And it's someone who may be able to return a favor. That number will connect you."

"You know him pretty well?"

"Who are you talking to? You can fill in the blanks after you call him. Play private eye, collect whatever evidence you need to assuage your moral qualms. Personally, I suspect somebody needs to transcend to the next spiritual plane. Or, more likely, descend to a lower one. But you figure it out for yourself. I have no doubt that you'll do the right thing. Whatever right is."

Charles nodded. "Okay, Maurice. What's the crypto connection here?"

Maurice investigated the order of Hunan beef. "The man who needs help is named Chiang. He owns an electronics store in Manhattan."

Charles's eyebrows raised.

After a frustrating delay, Maurice swallowed audibly.

"And?" Charles prompted.

"And his daughter is a hacker, and she knows her way around crypto. From what I hear, she's a natural. Supposedly she's a genius. Maybe true, maybe not. Genius is an overused word. But at least a very smart kid who speaks computer fluently."

"So Mr. Chiang needs a problem solved, and his daughter knows blockchain. Maybe a deal?"

"Maybe, m'boy. I don't know. I can't hand you everything on a platter."

The two men loved and respected each other, and they had made money together since Charles's youth, speculating in stocks using his uncle's trading accounts. He'd taken his first overseas trip to investigate what turned out to be a hyped-up gold-mining fraud in Africa, where he'd met Xander Winn. While the world thought the company was sitting on the biggest deposit ever discovered, he and Xander made an even bigger discovery: there was no gold at all. Aggressively shorting that stock was a gigantic win—although the IRS and SEC confiscated all of Charles's money they could get their hands on. But for that government theft, Charles would have had $200 million, not just $10 million, sequestered in the Caymans.

In part to steer clear of the sociopathic agents that had targeted him, Charles subsequently spent seven years traveling most of the world, including the mountainous tropical forests of Colombia. Colombia yielded no immediate profit, just adventure with a people who still lived very close to nature. He had collected something there so rare, so unusual, that perhaps he alone in the whole of North America possessed so much of it. He kept it to this day, very secure, untouchable. Now, after all these years, he just might have a use for it.

5

A Rainbow Tornado

THE DOOR to the apartment burst open and a tornado of energy entered in the form of a teenage ghetto girl dressed as if she'd just emerged from a rave or some other place with limited appeal to either Charles or Maurice. Before Charles could get up from his chair, she ran toward him and jumped on him. "Paladin! You're here!"

"Better late than never!" Charles replied, hugging her.

"What took you so long to visit? You been off the farm for like … months!"

"Three weeks. An adjustment period, Rainbow. I've been at the bottom of the ocean; I needed a decompression stop. Copious apologies."

"Ah damn, Paladin. What … you needing time to yo'self? You did less than two bullets in the joint. You gettin' weak?" She pushed her fist into his jaw playfully and climbed off his lap. "Hell, anybody can do a year or two in Club Fed standing on their head and get right back into action on day one."

Maurice held his hand up in a pointless effort to restrain her words. Rainbow came over with a smile and slapped it in greeting on her way to the kitchen. She stepped around the corner. Charles could hear her open the refrigerator and shift things around inside.

Both men called to her simultaneously, "Don't drink out of the carton!"

Rainbow stepped back into the living room and stood in profile so the men could see her defy them as she drank half the remaining contents directly from a quart container of orange juice. She returned it to the refrigerator and walked back to the living room.

"What did you two gentlemen just say? I missed it."

Maurice shook his head. "You see what you put me through, Charles? A teenager. I had my fill of teenagers back when you lived with me."

Rainbow moved a stack of papers and plunked herself down on the other soft chair near the couch.

"So, how was the rest of your time in the slammer, Paladin?"

"Standard fare, I suspect. Get up in the morning, go jogging on the beach, a massage, check email, play some golf."

"Really, man. What was it like?"

"Well, when I wasn't in solitary, I found some compatriots—homied up with a few OGs. Otherwise, it was a giant suck. Get up in the AM, do nothing most of the day, an hour rec in the yard with my road dogs, eat crappy food, feed the warden, dash a coupla screws, back to the cell."

Maurice said, "I don't know what half of that means."

Rainbow sneered, "Cuz you never been up the river, Maurice. OG: original gangsta—long-time inmate."

Charles cut in, "And feeding the warden means using the bathroom. Dashing is... umm... a related concept."

"Hey, Paladin, you ever keister?" Rainbow chuckled.

"Nah, kid. I don't ever take it to the hoop. I keep it outa the safe. No packing the rabbit. Maybe a little choking the chicken or spanking the monkey."

Rainbow laughed loudly and Maurice shook his head.

Charles said, "You don't want to know what the rest means, Maurice."

"I get the picture," he replied. "Sounds like a waste of valuable life to me."

Charles said, "No time is wasted if you try to make the most of it. Think of Bakunin and Solzhenitsyn. Doing time in Siberia makes my trip up river look like a vacation."

"Maybe," Maurice replied. "I used to have a friend, Karl Hess. This is an interesting story, Rainbow, so listen up. He started out as a corporate suit, then got involved in Goldwater's presidential campaign in '64. The only thing people remember out of that campaign was a line Karl wrote: 'Extremism in the defense of liberty is no vice; moderation in the pursuit of justice is no virtue.' It was perfectly logical thinking, but of course it scandalized the usual suspects, even then. Today they'd crucify anybody who said that. Unless they were social justice warriors. Among other things, Karl went on to become the only white member of the Black Panthers. He was a philosopher, but learned to be a welder. Rather in the mold of Eric Hoffer. They were both great writers. He was the interviewee for Playboy one month. We were talking about how civilization was on a slippery slope and, as I recall, he told me, 'Maurice, they could put either one of us in a fifty-five-gallon drum and seal it. We'd just use it as an opportunity for some self-discipline, to dig into the recesses of our minds and come up with something worth thinking about.' It sounds like that's what you did during your imprisonment, Charles."

Rainbow chuckled. "We've got more work to do, Maurice, before you'll ever fit in a fifty-five-gallon drum."

Charles winked at Rainbow. "Pretty much, Maurice. But it wasn't easy. When I was running around the Third World after my time in Gondwana, I spent a lot of time with people of all colors and creeds. Never a problem. We were just individuals relating to each other as individuals. But, in the joint, you better not be seen consorting with people outside your racial group. If you associate with members of an enemy tribe, you're viewed as a traitor. Your chances of something bad happening go way up. This is lowest-common-denominator stuff. It's stupid. But fighting that tide in any pen would have been like waving a Japanese or German flag in Times Square during World War II."

Rainbow asked, "So you had to be a racist?"

Rainbow knew full well how it worked; she'd grown up among blacks in the DC ghettos.

Charles spelled it out. "Prison is tribal. Break that big rule, you'll get sideways in the joint. The rest of the rules? Mind your own business. Don't ask questions. Be respectful. If you're challenged, don't back down or try to worm out of a situation. It's better to take the ass-kicking than show fear—a weakness that will haunt you the rest of your stay. If you have a problem, the last thing you do is report it. They hate rats more than they hate child molesters. Be calm and polite, but don't get friendly with the guards. The guards—they like to be called corrections officers—come from the bottom of the barrel. After all, what kind of person would put himself in a place where everybody hates him, the noise is constant, and you're surrounded by locked steel doors? Answer: the type who wants to boss around and brutalize the people under him."

51

Rainbow shifted from hip-hop ghetto-speak to proper English. "I'm sorry you had to go through all that, Charles."

"Well, you know what Nietzsche said…" In this case, she probably did, having spent many hours under the guidance of Maurice's massive brain and massive library.

"Yeah. 'That which doesn't kill us, makes us stronger.' But life on the street is a better teacher than any German philosopher. And that line is bullshit anyway." She changed the subject. "Hey, Uncle Maurice, did you leave any dumplings for me?"

Charles glanced at Maurice and mouthed the word "Uncle?"

Maurice shrugged and whispered back, "I'm a courtesy uncle. It works for us both."

Charles nodded. His uncle was a great mentor for the girl, just as he had been for Charles. He trusted no one more than Maurice to do right by Rainbow. Rainbow, now all of eighteen years old, had no biological family that she knew of. She'd grown up in Southeast DC and spent years under the informal guardianship of a middle-aged gang leader, Alpha, who'd supplied the drugs that killed her mother. She'd rescued Charles from getting his ass kicked on his first trip down to her 'hood over three years ago now. She'd then worked with Charles for a full year before he'd been sent up the river, assisting the CEO of Visioryme Pharmaceuticals on the one hand and running bootlegged drugs and Naked Emperor for Charles and Alpha on the other. Her street smarts matched her intellect and natural good looks.

Charles didn't want to talk of prison anymore, for the same reason soldiers don't like to talk of their war experiences. He turned to Rainbow. "I know you know quite a bit about crypto. PS, thanks for the stuff you sent me on it."

Rainbow's eyes lit up in a way common to cryptocurrency geeks. She fell back into talking jive, tending toward Ebonics. "Yo, Paladin, crypto be changin' everything. Ol' dudes don' know what's hittin' 'em, an' don' got no clue dey bein' hit. Goin' change da way it works. The man's goin' down! Crypto gon' scoop his place."

Maurice shrugged. "I told you she's into the stuff."

"I need to start my own cryptocurrency, Rainbow. You in?"

"If, and only if, you do it smartly. If you do it smartly, hell yeah!" Rainbow again transitioned out of one culture and into another with the ease of a chameleon. Charles watched her morph back into her professional persona, her language and tone changing to a version a retired couple from Toledo would be comfortable with. "When it comes to new cryptocurrencies, Paladin, things have changed. The third wave of cryptos were mostly frauds. People are alert now, cautious about climbing aboard scams looking for a greater fool. Can't get away with the big con anymore. Maurice says the market's beginning to mature. That's probably right. If you want to put out a new crypto token, it needs to have real utility. Hype is out. Diligence is in. You'll have to do something that serves an actual purpose. And scarcity too. There needs to be a reason why people will want to accumulate and trade your token."

"I believe I've got that covered."

"And there needs to be a marketing program, so that people will have a clue it exists."

"That may be the hard part. Or not. I've got some ideas on that, but this crypto will be unique and outrageous. Word of mouth might spread like news of a gold strike."

"Don't count on that. You need to have a competent and experienced blockchain dev team if you're going to offer any functionality beyond what the current chains provide. The team needs blockchain street cred, some respect, to get attention."

"Doesn't sound like anybody I've met in the last couple of years. As far as respect—I think they're gonna want to stay unknown and anonymous."

"That's going to be a tough sell to early investors."

"I'm willing to finance the startup expenses myself. This token has to be constructed for a maximum of secrecy and untraceability. Its utility is to be ideal for illegal activities while still being in demand for legal ones."

Maurice said, "Investors will come in if it works. But early on it'll be tough to get people to send money into the ether to whomever for who-knows-what. These things have become the next iteration of Nigerian-prince scams."

"I said I'd be the early investor; other investors can join the party at higher prices after they can see it works. We shouldn't stress that this is a cryptocurrency. It's better as a community that happens to use lots of cryptography."

That cued Rainbow to jump in again. "The ecosystem has to be real. A new crypto may hype to the sky, but it isn't going to stay there if it doesn't do something special, or if it isn't easy to use. Forget about the price in government money. That won't matter for much longer." She shifted back to urban culture. "So what's yo' shit gon' buy a man, Paladin? Jus' what you sellin' that people gon' need ya token to buy?"

Charles replied, "They'll need it to buy information that they can't get elsewhere."

Maurice interjected, "So you're creating a market to compete with me."

Charles said, "Just moving your work into what PC types like to call the sharing economy. I prefer gig economy. I'm most interested in a particular set of products. Let's call them extrajudicial solutions."

Maurice nodded. "Perhaps to engage the services of a Ronin warrior... or maybe an entire A-Team?"

"Eventually a bunch of A-Teams, competing on price and their reputation as problem solvers. Special-ops forces dedicated to neutralizing the black-hat hackers, the Nigerian princes, cronies, sociopaths, and other parasites beyond the reach of the law. Doing what the governments have failed to do because the criminals write the laws. Anonymous teams, of course, with identities secured by anonymous transactions on blockchain. I expect a competent programming team could install layers of protection for the mercs, for the victims, and for those being accused, of course."

"A mercenary marketplace?" Maurice asked.

"Yes, but it can be more than that. We know that politics attracts sociopaths. It's a perfect job for them. Lie to get the job, and then control people with the power of the job. We need to even out the playing field to make the sociopaths suffer if they get the job. The cryptocurrency can be an integral part of that. A real money needs to be convertible. You need to be able to trade it for work, or property, or energy, or something of definite value. Cryptocurrencies like Bitcoin are backed by proof of work; that's what crypto mining is, rather like digging gold out of the ground. Other cryptos require proof of stake, which is like equity, meaning that ownership of the tokens is needed to participate in the ecosystem."

"So... what are you proposing, Charles?" Maurice prompted.

Rainbow chimed in and said what Charles had considered but not put into words. "I've got an idea. People can mine the tokens in a couple of ways. One, by operating the nodes on the network, like most crypto. But mostly by actual work, as a member in a network of checks and balances to keep the government rulers accountable. Any A-Team will need specialized intelligence to get a job done right."

54

Charles smiled. Rainbow was coming into her own. "Exactly! Tokens can be earned by individuals participating in the constant, ubiquitous monitoring and tracking of politicians, their puppet masters, ordinary criminals, and sociopaths in general. Boots on the ground and boots in cyberspace. Gig workers. Uber drivers part time, token miners part time. Politicians are always going on about how they want transparency in everything—but especially into other people's lives. We'll offer a little transparency into the Deep State.

"I'm talking teams of paparazzi that have no interest in annoying movie stars. Instead they'll track down liars, cheats, thugs, and cronies who swim in the political swamp. Imagine people paid, anonymously, in tokens, to inform the network what a specified sociopathic bureaucrat is up to. Imagine that there's a way to pay those who track down and document political corruption? What the DC swamp rats are doing, who they're with, who's influencing them, who's trying to hire them, what revolving private-public doors they're going through, and what backroom deals they're making. Open wide the daily lives of the cronies who hide while using government force to enrich themselves. Get the skeletons out of their closets. Dig into corporate-government collusion. Expose union coercion and scams. What I'm talking about is a decentralized, citizen-run version of the NSA, but with ethical controls, dedicated to exposing the crimes of government and its minions! If every action of government employees was observed, it would act as a real disincentive to be a bureaucrat in order to abuse the public trust."

The enthusiasm was infectious, but in need of tempering. Maurice observed, "So you want to make the Deep State suffer. That's a double-edged sword. The Chinese have installed their social-credit system. You get a parking ticket, you're late on a mortgage payment, you say things considered unpatriotic, you have friends with low social-credit scores—and a thousand other things—and your score gets dinged and that affects everything in your future."

Charles shook his head. "Yes, that's the government spying on citizens. I'm saying we balance it by having the citizens keep the government honest. Journalists are supposed to be doing that, but they've abrogated their duty. Very few are ethical or professional anymore; H.L. Mencken's ghost has got to be angry. Journalists today are just part of the entertainment industry. Those that still care can barely investigate officials because, at a minimum, they won't get access. If they get too close to the bone, well, then it's top secret for national security. All the important mainstream media is owned by just five corporations, and those companies are completely intertwined with the State. It's time to replace the media as the watchers; they've been co-opted and corrupted.

"And yes, protection of the innocent has to be an integral part of the system. Rainbow, I've got some ideas on that already. Bearing false witness has always been considered one of the worst crimes throughout history. But in this country, false witnessing has become a standard tool for social engineering and political positioning. Our network has to make sure that unsubstantiated character assassination and bearing false witness is punished, hard."

The three chatted at length about the new cryptocurrency and how the network would operate to protect the innocent and expose, humiliate, and destroy antisocial actors. If successful, the cryptotokens could become immensely valuable over time. That took them out of the realm of theory, down to a practical level. They talked about what the A-Teams might look like. They changed the designation to Alpha Team after a phone call to one of Charles's favorite people, Alpha. The morally reformed drug dealer, whose product had inadvertently killed Rainbow's mom, jumped on board the moment he was asked if he'd like to become a modern-day Paladin.

They also talked more somberly about the risks of such a network of paparazzi and Paladins. The fact that the State had granted itself a monopoly on legalized violence in no way made such violence moral, but an attack focused on the State's immorality was not in itself an argument to expand righteous violence to non-state enterprises. What if nefarious actors managed to dominate the network and turned it to unethical purposes? Could they avoid this?

They accepted the reality that they would be struggling with these issues for a long time to come.

*   *   *

After taking leave from his uncle and Rainbow, Charles strolled six blocks and turned south on Fifth. He felt a need to both reinvigorate his mind and get some light exercise. As he moved through the city in the late afternoon, he saw evidence of economic decline everywhere. Poverty, decay, and pollution. Trash decorated the streets, and bums wandered like zombies. Graffiti covered walls like an unintelligible alien language.

His mind jumped from thought to thought. Cool it. Settle your mind. Rely on logic. Rationality. Clear thinking.

Anticipation of the impending venture caused a flood of emotions and made that hard to do.

The friendly, amused smile of his younger years appeared less often now, partly because of accumulated anger, partly because of loss, and partly because of a growing cynicism about the nature of mankind—an attitude based not just on reading history, but on personal experience. His trademark smile had once been a constant. Happiness makes one smile; what's less obvious is that smiling also makes one happy, an exercise he practiced in prison. Indeed, the mind isn't as in charge as many presume; the body feeds back to the brain in unexpected ways. Charles's natural optimism and curiosity went with him everywhere, even to prison, but hate, stupidity, and injustice can displace a good nature, measure for measure.

His good nature was a survival tool in prison, when surrounded by people full of negative emotions. A sincere smile could move a potential aggressor from a feeling of incipient fear, up to a state of simple anxiety—a big improvement. It might enable someone with a covert unexpressed resentment to say what's on his mind. That might nudge him from active hostility on the edge of violence, to simple antagonism—also an improvement. It defused situations and made people feel better in spite of themselves. His smile helped him to make friends easily.

Hatred had never before been part of his emotional makeup, but it now allowed him to stay focused. It wasn't a good thing, but it could serve a useful purpose.

Emotions had to be kept in their place. It was one thing if they arose from reason, but if they were only a reaction to some past pain or damage, that was something else entirely. Charles thought emotions should complement rationality, not supersede it. Except—of course—while playing the piano.

There were still a few payphones scattered around the city. When he was a little kid, there used to be banks of the things everywhere, and even lots of phone booths where—as the old comic books illustrated—Superman could slip into uniform. They were now uneconomic for the phone company. As the dollar declined, dimes and quarters made of base metals became worth so little that few people even bothered to keep them, let alone carry them. During his walk, he found one of the remaining anachronistic devices and used a few silver-colored twenty-five-cent disks to call the number his uncle had provided.

"Wei?" a man's voice answered.

Charles hesitated for a moment, analyzing. It was the word the Chinese commonly used when picking up the phone. This was a man who expected calls from Chinese people, not from an English-speaking mei guo ren. Then he said, slowly, "Is this Mr. Chiang?"

"Yes. Who you?"

Charles considered the alias he used as a drug lord: Paladin. The TV character he'd modeled himself on as a boy would be his template for what was to come. "No name needed now. I was told you have a problem that might benefit from my services."

After a moment, the heavily accented voice said, "Who tell you call me?"

"Nobody I can name."

"Call me back. Three minute. Okay?"

Charles hung up and used the time to observe others on the street. He scrutinized the shadows and scanned for anyone who looked too guilty—or too innocent. When he called back, the voice said, "Okay. We meet face to face. Yes?"

"Not my preferred next step."

"What to do, then?"

"Are you a Catholic?" Charles asked the voice.

He imagined Chiang looking at his phone, confused.

"Fah flom it," Chiang replied.

"Close enough."

6

Evil, and Some Sins Confessed

"DO IT. Do it now!" Blaize Forestal ordered, sounding like a cop with a dangerous suspect.

"Get away from me, psycho!" The nearly naked girl wrenched her wrist free of his grasp and twisted on the carpet, crying.

Her satin shirt remained secured only by the buttons at each wrist. He exploited the shirt to jerk her back toward himself and squeezed her arms tight against her nude hips. Her soft hair, nearly as light as her white shirt, hung over breasts compressed against his lower chest.

"Do it," he whispered downward, into her ear. "Or else. I don't mean to imply that you have a choice." Tall, pale, with slick black hair, Forestal had black eyes that conveyed the same certainty and control as his words.

She strained to get away. That was out of the question. She squirmed futilely, but the teenager's slight build was no match for his wiry muscles. She couldn't escape unless he decided to show mercy. Today, as always, he felt no mercy. He planned on taking out on her the frustration of his meetings on Capitol Hill. His pet congressmen weren't behaving like trained lapdogs. The day's failure ripened his anger. She started to scream, so he thrust her back, smashing his elbow into her head to shut her up.

The blow landed on her temple, and far too hard. She stood straight up with eyes wide open. He watched as her pupils dilated beyond the bounds of simple fear. Then the eyes went dull, expressionless, like a doll's. Her legs crumpled under her, and she fell in a pile on the floor, motionless. He watched her long enough to know that she'd stopped breathing.

Crap. He was hardly even aroused yet. Forestal looked down at the small mass of now-useless flesh at his feet in disgust. He thought a moment, picked up his cell phone, and dialed the person who would clean up the mess.

A short, thick, bald fireplug of a man with big hands arrived within an hour, carting two large suitcases that contained quiet electric saws, knives, chemicals, protective surgical garb, small freezer boxes, and the other trappings of the Cleaner. His high-pitched voice did not fit with his muscular physique. His name was Lichen, and he said, "Let me take your current attire for disposal. Better safe than sorry."

Forestal stripped to his underwear and handed the man his silk shirt (minus its ostentatious cufflinks), tie, suit and shoes. The Cleaner stuffed them into a trash bag.

"Fresh clothes, sir."

Forestal donned the proffered jogging attire.

The human fireplug moved with the smoothness of a practiced professional. After dissecting the corpse into small pieces, the Cleaner would save the valuable portions while flushing the unusable biological detritus down the hotel toilet and then wash and bleach every surface in the bathroom. No blood, no DNA, no trace of the girl would remain. This wasn't the first time.

People disappeared fairly often in DC.

Forestal wouldn't leave the hotel room until he'd inspected the Cleaner's work, accomplished for the most part with a minimum of noise. Even the toilet, overworked for the next two hours, operated in reasonable silence. The luxurious Park Hyatt in DC's posh Foggy Bottom area was not far from the Eccles Building, where new dollars were created. That building's spigots of currency were very important to him, as he, like many well-connected denizens of the Deep State, received those dollars before their purchasing power got diluted. It was a major reason Forestal had become so rich. The high cost of the Cleaner was less than a rounding error.

After his mind adjusted to the activity behind the bathroom's closed door and the change in his evening's plans, Forestal returned to his work. It was just as well. An evening with that girl would have been substandard at best, entirely apart from the fact that he needed to prepare for what lay ahead.

He hoped that Sabina wouldn't call. She did so sporadically, demanding attention on the spur of the moment. He found it difficult to refuse her.

Few men could. She was always a sensual delight, but he resented being used as her sex toy; she made him feel ... disposable.

In any event, tonight was out of the question, but not because of the activity in the bathroom. Sabina wouldn't bat an eye at that, even as she made a note for future use. Rather, he couldn't chance Sabina Heidel twisting his mind in circles. She tended to do just that.

He had to be in top form, for he was running in a race against Sabina among others, up the hill of power.

He opened his laptop and began searching and scanning websites, digging in deeper when it seemed worthwhile. His work at the Justice Department was useful on a personal level as well as being reasonably interesting from an academic viewpoint.

He scratched at his chest. The old scar itched, in some kind of psychosomatic reaction, on nights like these. He was glad the exit wound, inconveniently located on his back, didn't bother him. The bitch who shot him a decade ago was herself an itch he was desperate to scratch. Her time would come.

A mechanical whine screeched from the bathroom, and the room's lights flickered. The Cleaner quickly turned off his jammed saw and said sorry in his high-pitched voice just loud enough to be heard in the living room. It only distracted Forestal for a fleeting instant.

Not long thereafter, mission accomplished.

"We good, Lichen?"

"Yes, Mr. Forestal. Clean as the driven snow. Show me where she touched anything out here. Anything." The smell of bleach lingered in the air.

"We'd just arrived. She touched nothing other than the floor where she landed."

The Cleaner went to work on the hard floor with a spray bottle and a sponge.

"No oversights?" Forestal asked.

"Triple-checked."

Forestal nodded. "You'll find the usual on the table by the door."

The fireplug stepped back into the bathroom and changed back into his wrinkled blue business suit with a nondescript clip-on tie held by a simple clasp. He glanced over and saw a brick of $100 bills. The original Bureau of Engraving and Printing band around them was so tight that none could be removed without breaking it. Increasingly people left the band on for convenience. A standalone C-note wasn't worth what it once was.

"I'll be stopping by The Store in the next little while," Forestal said.

"Thank you, Mr. Forestal. I look forward to seeing you at The Store again. It's been a while."

"Yes, I've been busy."

Forestal watched the man leave before turning back to his work. He would stay in the hotel for the night. He had important matters to consider.

* * *

"Ten Hail Marys, five Our Fathers, and you promise to return twice weekly to confess your sins."

"Why so often, Father?"

Spiritual guidance and comedy seemed natural companions, so Charles replied with a grin that the penitent couldn't see. "Because from what I'm hearing, if you wait longer than a week you might not remember some of the best ones."

The man on the other side of the screen coughed to stifle laughter and then said, "Thank you, Father."

"No problem, my son. May the next supplicant live with as much temptation as you do. Dominus vobiscum."

Charles, camouflaged by a black robe and a white dog collar, had commandeered the confessional outside of appointed hours. The devotee had seen him enter the booth and taken the opportunity of unburdening his conscience. His costume had convinced at least one guy. In this age of omnipresent surveillance, Charles would need to perfect the art of masquerade.

Charles now knew how a charlatan felt, at least one possessed of an otherwise-normal psyche. He'd make an effort to avoid these accidental true confessions in the future. Amusing perhaps, but distracting. And perhaps not quite right. Were the penitent's sins truly forgiven because he hadn't confessed to a real priest? Was it possible the poor fellow would have to spend eternity in a lake of fire because of him? Had he himself committed a mortal sin in the process? Perhaps only the Bishop of Rome, who was infallible in matters of faith and morals, knew for sure.

Not many people visited churches anymore, at least when Mass wasn't scheduled. Those who did were often bums looking for a safe place out of the weather or away from the violent thugs that roamed the streets most nights. The buildings were increasingly locked overnight, and there were other constraints on his ability to use them. But could there be a safer place to meet in person without being seen?

His cell phone vibrated. Charles checked it. Unknown number. Almost certainly a telemarketer, but he answered, listened for a few seconds, and hung up.

A heavily accented voice came through the confessional screen, a parody of devoutness, sounding like it was reading a written formula. "Fo'give me, Father, fo' I have sin. It been nine hundred nineteen days since my rast confession."

Charles recognized the voice from the phone without needing to hear the agreed-upon code number. He rubbed at his Maori tattoo, which bore a rough resemblance to the number 919. An impressively obese Polynesian artist, himself an illustrated man covered head to toe in multicolored ink, had emblazoned it on his shoulder years before in the back of a bar in Pape'ete. The artist was mildly annoyed needling the simple tattoo; it was like asking Rembrandt to draw a stick figure. To his haole client, however, it was a permanent reminder of a temporary feeling, although the temporary feeling was long forgotten.

"Okay, Mr. Chiang. I'm here. Tell me about your problem."

The kneeling man spoke quietly through the screen. "I own store on East Side. TVs, radio, and camera. I run honest business. Four month ago, two guy come my store. Tear it up. Break thumb of employee. Come each week. Thousand dollars each time. Not easy. Especially now. No people buying anything."

"Police?" Charles interrupted.

"They no help anyone in neighborhood."

"Have you been paying the bastards?"

"The police?"

"No, the other bastards."

"No, but they threaten me. Two week ago, the big guy, Jacques, stuck gun my head. Cocksukka. Make me take off clothes. Tell me next time he come, if I no have his money, he make me his bitch. That what he say."

"You don't want that."

"No. Bettah be dead."

63

"Why don't you kill him? Defend yourself." Charles's tone was frosty cold. In part, he was testing the man. He was also testing himself.

Chiang replied slowly. His dialect improved a bit as he took time to structure his thoughts. "If shoot someone New York City, no matter why, I go jail. My family depend on me. Have gun here? Cannot! Velly irregal to defend self or famry in this city."

"Have you tried to hire anyone before? To solve this Jacques problem?"

"No. Such person just do same thing like Jacques. Kirrers not good people."

"Yet you're talking to me."

"You supposed to be okay."

"So, maybe killers can sometimes be good people?"

Chiang hesitated before replying. "Yeah, maybe."

"When do you expect Jacques and his pal will come back?" Charles asked.

"Maybe next day. Come when they want."

Charles said, "There's a piece of paper and a pen under the step that you're kneeling on. Write the address of your business there." He added with little pause, "If I solve your problem with Jacques, permanently, it will cost you twenty thousand dollars."

The response from Chiang came slowly. He said, "That is much money."

"Not as much as it'll cost for the emergency room bill, or worse." Charles gave the man time to consider. It was a huge expense for him—and only small money in Charles's former world, before prison. It was still small money to him, but principle was involved. People undervalue things they got for free. Good business always involved a two-way exchange.

Chiang's voice quivered. "Jacques... he... say he... do same to my daughter."

Before prison, Charles rarely succumbed to anger, but he was different now and found that not only anger but hate was justifiable—and useful. Such a threat filled him with disgust.

"What age is your daughter?"

"Sixteen. She smart girl."

Charles sat silently.

After a minute, Chiang said, "Pay you... when?"

"After I've solved your problem."

"What if I not pay you?"

"Then we'll have a problem. I don't look kindly upon anybody who commits fraud."

"I will pay you."

"I know you will. Now go home. Don't stick around this cathedral, Mr. Chiang. You'll see me when I'm needed, but not until."

Charles sat in his side of the confessional for ten minutes, hoping no more penitent sinners would seek his or God's forgiveness. He replayed the conversation with Chiang in his mind. Charles tested it against his sixth sense, his gut instincts: the sum of all his knowledge and experiences filtered by judgment. It told him that Chiang was shooting straight. If this Jacques character proved to be as Chiang described, then the situation demanded action. Action for which Chiang didn't have the skills.

7

An Unexpected Encounter

UPON leaving the church and Mr. Chiang, Charles headed toward Battery Park. He'd doffed the robe and Roman collar, because priests stand out and Charles wanted to blend in. Now he wished he hadn't, for the night had grown cooler. The city's lights reflecting off low clouds made for an eerie, almost post-apocalyptic effect on the deserted streets.

The rioters' evening rampage brewed in the north of Manhattan, giving this part of the city a rest, although plenty of trash and broken windows provided evidence of the previous night's destruction. Cryptic symbols tagged the walls of buildings. It was increasingly hard to say when, or even if, they'd be washed off, as people had lost heart. Tension crackled like the air before an electrical storm; if you were smart, you stayed inside because it was hard to know where lightning would strike.

Relatively few were involved in the nightly riots, but it only took a small percentage of the population to provoke civil unrest or even start a revolution. From what Charles could glean, community organizers fomented discontent about pretty much anything. Individuality was submerged under race and gender identity. Individual responsibility was very un-PC. The country was splitting into irreconcilable groups that not only didn't understand, but genuinely hated each other. New York, like most other cities, was a pressure cooker filled with inflammable volatiles just awaiting a match.

He turned the corner past the World Trade Center site and headed toward the water through Battery Park's winding paths. Even though the long winter had finally yielded to spring, the place attracted far fewer visitors in the evening than during the day. The old-style light poles scattering sepia shadows over the paved walkways once looked quaint and charming; they now seemed derelict and threatening. Vendor booths lay shuttered, some closed for the night, some closed for good. Charles counted less than a dozen people.

He looked farther south and saw the object of his walk.

She stood tall and majestic over a tiny island in the harbor, alight from her base to the torch she held high with her right arm. He wondered how long the statue would continue to exist. Surely the ancient Greeks thought the Colossus of Rhodes, which was about the same size, would last forever too.

The inscription on a plaque in the base of the American icon included the famous line "Give me your tired, your poor, your huddled masses yearning to breathe free, the wretched refuse of your teeming shore." Unbeknownst to most who read it, the phrase had nothing to do with the Statue of Liberty's original intent. Neither the statue's designer nor its donors had given any consideration to immigrants or what they might be like. If they'd even thought about it, they would have asked the world—from whatever parts—to send them more people like the original Americans. Self-reliant risk takers who demanded only freedom from oppression. No one in his right mind would solicit and subsidize wretched refuse from teeming shores, encouraging them to become parasites. Yet, somehow, the United States now competed with Europe in creating a welfare state to do just that.

No, those words had been grafted onto the statue during the early years of the Progressive Era, twenty years after the statue was erected. France had gifted the Statue of Liberty in celebration of America's success in creating a republic where liberty seemed secure, but now, with its original meaning forgotten, the statue mainly reflected Americans' amnesia about their own history.

He leaned on a thick wooden railing, rough with splinters. His cotton oxford shirt did little to protect him from the evening chill. Wryly, he imagined her waking up and smashing that torch down on the top floors of the financial district. It could equally well be King Kong or the giant Stay Puft Marshmallow Man as long as the job got done.

Many of the most important financial buildings were just a few blocks away, on Wall Street, West Street and Maiden Lane. Paul Samuels worked there, running the Federal Reserve Bank of New York, disturbingly and perversely housed at 33 Liberty Street.

How did men like that come into being? What evolutionary pressures created such people? Was it just a matter of Darwinian selection? After all, fungi evolved to live on the carcasses of other life forms. Leopards evolved to take advantage of weak or unsuspecting herbivores. Maybe it was the same with creatures like Samuels.

But those weren't good analogies: concepts like right and wrong and good and evil probably didn't exist in nature. Elephants seemed to mourn their dead, and dogs displayed loyalty. Thinking that was due to philosophy on their part is likely just anthropomorphizing on our part.

That said, the contemplation of good and evil differentiated psychologically healthy humans from the rest of the animals. Understanding the nature of good and evil was the essence of philosophy and the key to Adam—man—escaping the allegorical walls of the Garden of Eden, a story with analogs in most religions. Risking their lives by eating from the tree of the knowledge of good and evil provided evidence that at least some humans prioritized becoming moral agents over living forever as protected pets. Charles considered that the exodus from the garden opened the door to mankind someday joining the divine.

But the struggle to survive ensured that somebody—something—filled every niche. Sociopaths probably just viewed themselves as the equivalent of farmers, using the rest of the world as milk cows—or, if necessary, beef cows. Al Capone, after all, saw himself as just a businessman. That might have been true if it weren't for the fact that his empire was built on violence. Sociopaths came in many shapes, sizes, flavors, and degrees.

What made them all alike, however, was their lack of compunction or regret for what they did. It's what defined their character. The more power they obtained, the more damage they could do. If only they all sported swastikas on their sleeves or wore Che Guevara t-shirts, they'd be easy to spot. But they weren't easy to spot. They disguised themselves in suits and ties and pretended to be normal. Liars, cheats, thieves... dead souls all, but they seemed to rule the world. These people were arguably insane on a very basic level. If they ever dropped their mask of sanity, not only would they not rule. They'd be outcast. Or dead.

The old term for a sociopath was morally insane. Charles considered that a far more fitting term for such people. Recently, the label sociopath had even been softened further as progressive academics renamed it antisocial personality disorder. As if it were a medical condition, which the patient had no control over. Charles wondered how soon the progressives would start labeling the moral people—those who obeyed natural law instead of the rule of the mob—as the antisocial personalities. That would complete the 180-degree reversal. Such blatant perversion of the language played a critical role in the destruction of a culture.

Unfortunately for millions—billions—of people worldwide, the political system naturally moved sociopaths into positions of power. How could it not, when the key to getting elected was promising the masses something for nothing and inciting envy? Sociopaths controlled the system, and the system was self-reinforcing and self-perpetuating.

It couldn't realistically be changed from within. An outside force was needed. A new player in the game.

Charles looked at himself from the outside. A vigilante? Yes. Was his judgment better than that of the system? If so, what made his judgment better? As he pursued the profession of problem solver, could he avoid becoming a narcissist, like the people he'd be neutralizing? It was a risk. Everything and everybody is influenced by their surroundings and what they do. Predators survived by trying to rule over everyone as if they were a flock of sheep, always preaching that it was for their own good. He had no desire to do that. If they were predators, like wolves, he would be a sheepdog. Sheepdogs, even very fierce ones like Komondors, German shepherds, and Tibetan mastiffs, weren't predators. They were force equalizers.

It would be hard to avoid moral pitfalls along the path he had begun to tread. He could act as an arm of truth, justice, and whatever was left of the American way only where the wrong was clear. Unfortunately, there was enough criminality in the world that he could afford to be selective—and be absolutely sure. He smiled as he thought of one of Davy Crockett's aphorisms: "Be sure you're right. Then go ahead."

Heady thoughts. He wondered if there were others out there thinking the same things and with the same will to act. There had to be a few.

He sensed a presence behind him. A breath, a shuffle of cloth against cloth. Charles turned, preparing his 190 pounds on a 6 '1" frame to confront the potential threat.

"Take it easy, friend." The man possessed a confident but gentle voice. The right side of his dark sportscoat was tucked conspicuously behind what was otherwise a well-concealed small holster. Charles recognized the gun it contained because he owned the exact same weapon—a Ruger LCP. The pistol weighed only nine ounces empty but could fire seven .380 ACP hollow-point bullets with reasonable effect at close range. The average New York mugger wouldn't choose such a weapon—because it appeared relatively unthreatening, but it made for a perfect carry gun, thin and light. It could disappear into a tuxedo's pocket; even a pair of running shorts could conceal it. A possible downside: all seven bullets might be required to stop an adrenaline-pumped attacker, depending on the skill of the user. Few knew that Ian Fleming's James Bond used a puny .25 auto before he was convinced to upgrade to .380 in a Walther PPK.

Charles, foolishly, did not have his Ruger with him. Why not? Fear of getting caught by the authorities? In New York, unlicensed carry could land a citizen in jail for ten years. A felon on probation, like Charles, might well get a life sentence. Still, the penalty for getting caught without a gun could be even worse. He wouldn't make the mistake again.

Charles's heartbeat quickened, but he caught himself, remembered to take a breath, and assessed the situation.

"Why are you showing me the gun, friend?" Charles maintained his composure.

"The city is on edge. I figured you would be too. I didn't want to take a chance you'd beat me to a pulp," the man replied. "You've been in prison for a year and a half. You've picked up some bad habits, and your responses are honed. But your instincts about me would be wrong, Mr. Knight."

The man knew him. So, not a mugging. Maybe something worse. Just like in prison, soon after arrival at a new place, someone always tried to kill him. Charles said, "Are you planning a long friendship?"

"Yes. Exactly that."

"Who are you?"

"I am, in fact, a friend."

"A friend showing me his weapon?" Charles said, raising his eyebrows.

"It's holstered. If you were in your normal state of mind, you wouldn't consider a holstered weapon to be threatening. Would you?"

"You seem to know me. I don't know you."

"Can I call you Charles? You can call me Jeffrey."

"Is that really your name?"

"It is."

"Nice to meet you, Jeffrey," Charles said as he turned away from him to lean his arms on the rail again and gaze out over the water toward Lady Liberty. "At least I hope it turns out to be nice to meet you."

Jeffrey moved next to Charles and likewise leaned on the railing. After a time, he said, "What a beautiful night."

Charles nodded and turned his head to further study the man, trying to make out his features in the dim light of the park's lampposts. Olive-colored skin, black hair—a bit long—and a chiseled face that suggested a fit body. Charles guessed he was in his late forties.

The man exhaled audibly. Charles waited and wondered what was next. His heart began to slow further toward normal when Jeffrey asked a disarming question.

"What makes for a good life, Charles?"

Charles took immediate note. It was a question to which he'd devoted a lot of thought.

"We live in an increasingly strange world," the man continued. "A world where laws contradict themselves, where criminality is acceptable. Where politicians are respected while entrepreneurs are suspect. Incentives are twisted, morality is punished, and dishonor rewarded. Hypocrisy and confusion rule. It's easier to become wealthy by gaming the system than producing something of value."

Charles agreed with the short dissertation. He himself had given up trying to change others' beliefs, although he would go through the motions when he wanted some amusement or wanted to relearn the lesson not to bother. "What you said describes the situation on this planet since about day one. It's stating the obvious … except it doesn't seem so obvious to most people."

Jeffrey continued. "You're right. But it's getting worse. Most people go to college for four years today but only learn things antithetical to Western civilization. The classics have been made irrelevant. Not many even study subjects that acquaint them with physical reality—science, technology, engineering, math, physics, or medicine. Most of the professors are leftists. The students are rewarded for accepting their prof's views as doctrine. Subjects like English, sociology, economics, political science, history, anthropology— all the soft subjects—have become platforms for indoctrination into cultural Marxism. Some kids even major in gender studies. Their core values are unsound.

"No matter how strong your logic, you can't win an argument with someone whose core values are radically different than your own. Even if they're able to think logically, if their basic assumptions are different, trying to convince them is pointless. Most have a vested interest in defending what they spent lots of time and money to learn. Their reasoning proceeds from a false starting point and therefore must arrive at a false conclusion. Debating such people is futile. They have to change their own minds."

Charles replied, "One of many reasons why I don't argue. It only serves to cement people in their positions. So, Jeffrey, what do you want? I doubt it has much to do with fighting global warming, giving everybody a kitten, or, for that matter, my living a good life."

Jeffrey didn't answer at first. But after a minute during which both men gazed out across the water toward the Statue of Liberty, he spoke.

"It's said that you can't fix stupid. But, Charles, your drug actually could and did. Neither you nor I can convince people to identify their own failed and contradictory thinking. Ten puffs of Sybillene can."

Charles knew this. He replied, "If the person is basically of good will, yes, you're right. So, you want to me to supply you with Naked Emperor, is that it? Some kind of entrapment? Bust my parole so I'm down for life. Make my probation officer happy?"

Jeffrey chuckled. He started to walk away, along the rail parallel to the water's edge. He turned and called back, "We'll talk about that someday." He strode on, but, before vanishing into the dark shadows around the side of a building, continued, "I'm one of those people the warden in Illinois said would be a friend looking out for you."

While Charles watched, bemused and concerned, he disappeared into the night's shadows.

Charles was inclined to think he had a new friend.

Or he could be an enemy trying to deceive him for some unknown purpose. A devil in disguise.

Then again, perhaps the devil had an unjustly besmirched reputation.

8

Asasiyun

"BOSS, where were you yesterday?" The middle-aged man's flaccid muscles matched his paunchy gut. His skin, the color of a fish's belly, said he spent all his time indoors. He looked up at Tony.

Tony Scibbera regarded the desks filling the room. Coffee cups rested on top of stacked papers. A half-hearted attempt at putting up cubicle walls resulted in only a dozen or so scattered among the thirty desks. The facility had given up on the pretense of either privacy or efficiency. The coated windows on the far wall made even a sunny sky appear gray and dull. The result was to further numb the spirits of the time servers shuffling paper at their desks.

"Working, Phil. Taking care of business," Tony replied after Phil had given up on getting a response and started to walk away, shaking his head.

Phil turned back. "How can you have been working? You weren't here all day. I know, because I was here." Phil was second-in-command of the grungy office, and visibly resented having been passed over in favor of Tony, an outsider.

"It's the twenty-first century, Phil. They say viruses are running rampant. I was working from home."

Tony looked at his recently acquired underling with barely concealed distaste. He was a bold little fellow, insolent even, daring to question his superior. The anemic little pedant wouldn't hesitate to enforce any and every rule in the book; it gave his life a sort of meaning. Phil seemed to worship the authorities that made the rules; to him, they were his gods and and his Ten Commandments.

Tony imagined mounting a plastic model of Phil—just a little one, because he was a little guy—at the entrance to the building as a warning of what the office workers were trained to become. But he quashed the thought—it would certainly be workplace intimidation or, these days, maybe even sexual harassment. Anyway, the very fact that these people worked here meant they probably weren't worth saving. Phil was a reminder of what Tony fought against every day.

Phil petulantly tried a different tactic. "You know, questions come up. I was confused about some of what you said the other day, when you took control of this office."

"Sorry, Phil. I'll try to supervise you more closely to make sure you have a safe space."

Phil flared his nostrils in a vain attempt to seem like an alpha male, aided by the knowledge that his seniority as a civil servant made him nearly immune to being fired for anything short of an axe murder. "What did you mean when you said that we're going to redirect our efforts? For as long as I've been here, this office has followed department protocols to deal with perps. We know these assholes. We know how they lie and weasel out from under their obligations. We know their tactics, and we're really good at what we do."

Tony caught himself before laughing out loud as Phil, the prototypical weasel, described the actions of others as weaseling.

"Yes, Phil. I know a … professional … when I see one," he said honestly. "Your skills are part of what attracted me to this office." No lie, but Phil would never know the more complete truth. "I'm here mainly to observe. I may pick up a few cases myself to get a hands-on feeling for the way you manage these felons."

Phil looked confused—a sign that he'd be easy to handle.

Tony walked toward his new office; his predecessor's nameplate was still displayed on the left of the door. A clerk in Requisitions had ordered a replacement, to be delivered eventually. Cheap vinyl louvered blinds, their stained drawstrings hanging like confused spaghetti, kept eyes from peering through the glass walls. A dozen boxes bursting with papers were stacked on the floor.

I can do this, he thought. I can pretend until after the elections. That's all Jeffrey has asked.

He took his annual one-month vacation on the island, and that would help him do the time, feeling only slightly more at liberty than the parolees cycling through the office. The work was depressing, but it was necessary to keep Albert Peale and many others in circulation. As the editor and publisher of his small newspaper, Peale exposed the criminality of those in power, but those in power don't take lightly to being outed. So Albert ended up being thrown in prison and then restricted for an extended probation. Tony worked the probation system as a double agent to help Albert and others gain their wrongly stolen freedom. He had to elude discovery for a bit longer.

It was a dangerous time. The world walked on a high wire, and Tony was one of the few people walking it in the opposite direction.

The high purpose of his work barely overcame his distaste for dealing with people like Phil.

He closed his door and sighed. Tony reminded himself how important it would be to watch over Charles Knight so people like Phil wouldn't get in his way.

*   *   *

Seeing Jeffrey's pistol the night before prompted Charles to pull his own identical weapon out of the lockbox sequestered under the seat of Xander's car, parked in an underground garage. He tucked his LCP into an unusual holster that, when in a pocket, looked like a wallet. Its design left the trigger accessible so that the gun—with its internal hammer—could remain in the holster when fired, the bullet unimpeded. He hadn't yet had a chance to fire it that way, and he wondered whether the action would jam. There was a good chance it would. Best to take the extra time to withdraw the pistol if he needed more than one shot.

The holster had an innovative design for concealment but shoddy workmanship. Among other flaws, its leather hadn't been tanned appropriately, so the thing smelled like sour socks. Made in China. If China didn't collapse from the inside first, they were going to take over the world in twenty years like the Borg took over the galaxy in Star Trek. But, for the moment, they had a lot to learn about quality control on holsters.

The risk of getting caught with the little Ruger was a minor concern, given that he had another Ruger in a shoulder holster under his blue sports coat: a suppressed .22 MK II. The gun was illegal to own anywhere in the US without extensive permitting. Obtaining one legally required copious paperwork and a six-month wait. The Bureau of Alcohol, Tobacco, Firearms and Explosives knew neither the location nor the ownership of this gun, however. Strange agency, the ATF. It regulated three of the things needed for a standard hunting trip as if they were nuclear weapons. Many of its employees were FBI wannabes who couldn't make the cut at Quantico.

The suppressed MK II served as the classic choice of the close-in assassin, almost completely silent. Its subsonic .22 Long Rifle round was far quieter than a suppressed 9 mm. Then the muffling along the length of its long barrel effectively eliminated the sound of gunpowder exploding. The only noise the gun made when fired was the cycling of the action back and forth.

In Hollywood movies, people fall instantly dead when shot, as if the bullet has magical sedating properties. Other than a shot to the head, this almost never happens. And the "pop" sound of a Hollywood silencer? Fabricated out of whole cloth. Gunsmiths called them suppressors because they only reduced, not eliminated, the sound of a gunshot. Hollywood pandered to the expectations of a viewing public trained to accept fibs as fact. They thought the truth was unrealistic. That's why most movies are projected at a slow twenty-four frames per second, which is what viewers are used to. The more realistic modern technology at forty-eight to sixty frames per second looks so smooth and lifelike that people interpret it as fake.

Fake had become most everyone's reality.

Charles had dyed his hair a dark reddish brown. His sideburns looked real but sometimes itched, as did a large latex nose, enhanced by an expert imitation of rosacea and underlined by a thin synthetic mustache, just above his lips, that spread out past the corners of his mouth. Some concealer altered his complexion, simultaneously hiding the lines from the nose prosthesis. Although he disliked putting anything in his eyes, he'd inserted brown contacts to obscure his blue irises. A high arch insert placed in only one of his shoes caused him to walk askew. It was inconvenient but necessary to fool gait-analysis surveillance software. He wore a hoodie over his baseball cap to further confuse the omnipresent cameras. He left Xander's apartment using the back stairs, looking nothing like himself and quite a bit like Paladin. The city's noises already filled the early-morning streets of Manhattan.

Jacques. He knew nothing about Jacques.

But Maurice had told him quite a bit about his new client, Chiang, who needed a solution to his Jacques problem. Maurice had been referred to Chiang by a client he'd known since the days when he'd traveled extensively. He needed secure communications technology more than most, because nowadays he rarely went out. Maurice had been skeptical about using Chinese tech or Chinese advice, but as they spent time together he gained confidence that Chiang was on the right side of the philosophical barricades.

It was a challenge for a Shanghai émigré with marginal English to run a shop outside the confines of Chinatown. Some blacks and Hispanics felt threatened by newcomers they believed should be below them on the totem pole. They were especially threatened by someone of another race who was obviously climbing higher. Identity politics poisoned the minds of many in Chiang's neighborhood.

Not much different from prison culture.

Chiang's business struggled against a lot of obstacles in New York, but it was nothing compared to what his family had endured in China during the Great Leap Forward, which featured tens of millions of deaths from starvation—or, even worse, the Great Cultural Revolution, when Mao tried to purge the country of ideological impurity using his Red Guards. Millions of traditionalists, suspected right-wing deviationists, and capitalist roaders met untimely ends.

Chiang was used to dealing with thugs; in China's socialist utopia, they were as ubiquitous as air and water. After a while, even living in hell becomes background noise when you have nothing to lose. Conditions in America were vastly better; that made Jacques's protection racket more than just background noise. Chiang wasn't about to lose everything a second time without a fight.

Jacques claimed to provide some value by assuring Chiang that no competing store would open up nearby. It was another sign of Jacques's stupidity. What Chiang needed was more electronic stores nearby so the area would become known as the go-to for those products. It was an academic observation. What Chiang needed most was for Jacques to ... go away.

The long walk to the Lower East Side allowed Charles time to reflect, despite the city's noise and distractions. He mulled over his personal rules of engagement. Obeying the law was obviously out of the question, but he was determined to abide by his own rules. He'd need to catch Jacques in the act of violence or a credible threat of violence. It made no sense to rely on Chiang's word alone for proof of culpability. People lied. In prison, you didn't assume someone was telling the truth until a lie was proven; you assumed a lie until the truth was proven. At least Maurice trusted the storeowner, and he didn't give his trust lightly.

From what he'd gleaned so far, this Jacques seemed beyond redemption. It was necessary to be prepared for an ugly confrontation, including bloodshed. There might be no way around it. He was confronting a series of risks, known and unknown. Risk required compensation.

Maurice knew Charles's objectives. He saw the big picture: Charles was positioning himself to solve much bigger problems than the one facing Chiang. It seemed clear he'd soon be facing the government itself.

Jacques offered his services for $4,000 per month, and failure to pay would be dangerous. The IRS charged more, and their penalties were different but likewise painful. Chiang had to pay off both of these protection rackets, plus another overseen by the mayor of New York, and a fourth run by the governor. Today Charles might end one of those rackets. In some future tomorrow, he planned to confront the others.

When trying to solve a homicide, the police bracket suspects by figuring who had three things: the motive, the means, and the opportunity. They naturally look first, and most closely, at people with some contact, some relationship, with the victim. But an outside assassin could be absolutely anybody. If money was the presumed motive, the pool of potential perpetrators becomes unlimited. In Charles's case, should he have to act with extreme prejudice, the money was incidental. Symbolic, really. The motive was justice. Not justice determined by some arbitrary law administered by some appointed judge, but justice defined as someone getting what he deserved, and Charles was willing to take responsibility for that.

People wanted to believe somebody could set things right, even if that somebody was imaginary. It explained the rise of superheroes in pop culture. Batman, the X-Men, Deadpool, the Watchmen ... they were all vigilantes, defying the police and ignoring the courts. Millions of comic book readers and movie watchers intuited the difference between justice and legality. They cheered their heroes on, dressed their children up in their costumes, and quietly hoped that such people might exist.

Why charge a fee for his services when the superheroes never did? In real life, there should always be an exchange of value. Charity was a bottomless pit, often corrupting both the giver and the recipient. Charles wasn't Batman, but an entrepreneur helping to balance the supply of justice with the demands for it.

He sat down on a bench in the small park across the street from Chiang's store. Pigeons wandered through the park while its human residents, vagrants and bums, lay scattered about with their dirty sleeping bags. The enthusiasm and confidence that used to hallmark the city had morphed into apprehension. Charles struggled to discern whether this sense of foreboding came from his own mind—a residue of his incarceration—or from the vibrations coming from everyone else.

To pass the time productively, he listened to a book on his smartphone, using a single earbud, allowing him to also monitor street noises and the conversations of passersby. The phone was rigged to tune in to bugs he'd planted in the store as well as the miniature video cameras hidden on shelves. He'd told Chiang to disconnect the store's backdoor alarm.

He pulled down the bill of the ball cap under his hoodie. To anyone who might look at him—though nobody did—he appeared to be sleeping. Sunglasses would have offered even more concealment, but without them he offered a less threatening appearance, one more likely to be ignored. The city's people seemed afraid of almost everything. The hoodie was threatening enough. Charles wondered for a moment if most cases of "white cop shoots black man" could also be described as "cop shoots man in hoodie." Probably. But that wouldn't fit the preferred racist narrative.

He found himself paying little attention to the audiobook. His thoughts took him in a different direction. After missing several pages of narration, twice, he turned it off and let his mind go where it wanted. He recalled what he had read about assassination, considering what it would mean to be an assassin.

Most lawyers would say it's about the premeditated murder, usually of a high government official. There's no question that it's against the law unless, of course, it was State sponsored. Legislative laws are arbitrary; common law crimes aren't. Charles questioned whether an assassination is necessarily a crime if one defines crime properly. A crime was an unprovoked aggression against another person or his property, a breach of Natural Law. From that point of view, most crimes were actually committed by the State and were "legal" only because it was the State that committed them. If anyone else did the same, they'd be arrested. Max Stirner was right when he said that the State calls its own violence law, but that of the individual they call crime.

Perhaps, then, in many instances, assassination isn't even immoral. Many assassinations are either for vengeance or perceived self-defense.

Sometimes—perhaps always—vengeance is righteous. Simple people, with gut-level common sense ideas of what's right and wrong, often use the term righteous. Outlaw bikers, who have a code of conduct but operate outside the law, use the word routinely.

Vengeance is complex. You have to be correct on all the facts and motives. Entirely apart from that, a better vengeance involves obtaining recompense from the perpetrator. The legal system wasn't set up to make the victim whole, only to punish the perpetrator. There's always a danger of getting into a feud—a Hatfields-and-McCoys type of thing that takes on a life of its own.

Self-defense is always righteous. But how to defend oneself against the violent State, the powers that be? Assassination is perhaps the oldest answer.

The morality of assassination remained uncertain to Charles, but, then, the origin of the word itself was rooted in confusion. People assumed it derived from hashish, the drug. Assumptions are often false when dealing with ancient history.

In the early twelfth century, about the time of the First Crusade, Hassan bin Sabbah—who later came to be called the Old Man of the Mountain—established himself as a warlord. He was an intellectual, a businessman, a traveler, a mystic, a military genius, and an original thinker. He occupied Alamut Castle, close to the current Syrian-Iranian border, and trained a cadre of warriors to do his bidding. Selected for intelligence and psychological strength, these young men trained in weapons and martial arts. They were experts at stealth and disguise. They could move among beggars and merchants, monks and aristocrats and fit in with any of them. They spoke several languages. They understood the value of psychological warfare as well as asymmetrical warfare.

Rather than building an army to confront his enemies, he used his assassins to murder the opposing ruler or general, not soldiers in the army. It was logical. Armies do what they're told; they're basically just tools. It's their leader that poses a threat. Why engage in expensive wholesale bloodshed when you really only want to kill the guy in command? Hassan bin Sabbah understood the value of Special Forces. He knew that in a game of chess, you won when you took out the king—not when you knocked over a bunch of pawns.

The common belief is that bin Sabbah drugged these men with hashish, making them crazy so they'd go out and commit mayhem. This was just poorly thought-out antidrug propaganda. Pot or hashish makes a man spacey and oblivious—the opposite of what you want in a stealth assassin. Who'd want to send Cheech and Chong or South Park's Towelie out on a mission?

Another meme was that he would expose them to a Garden of Earthly Delights in his castle: get a kid stoned out of his mind and let him wake up surrounded by beautiful promiscuous houris, and tell him that it was a taste of heaven and if he completed his mission, this would be his eternal reward. That version probably makes more sense, but not much. The chances that a sophisticated, well-educated, psychologically sound warrior could be taken in by a charade like that are slim, although no doubt those delights were made available to competent warriors, without the effort at subterfuge.

A reasonable speculation is that they were called assassins because Hassan bin Sabbah termed them asasiyun, an Arabic word meaning "those who are faithful" or "those who are principled." The origin of the word is a far cry from describing a stoned junkie or a naïve kid or some low-life hit man. Hassan was an Ismaili. Just as the Aga Khan's followers are intensely loyal to him today, Hassan's would have been at least as loyal. He gave them everything, plus a faith to believe in and something to live for.

Perhaps Marco Polo, writing about it a couple of generations later, got the story confused. Then other writers got the word hashishin confused with asasiyun because the words sound alike to someone who doesn't speak Arabic.

Charles recalled what happened to the Old Man of the Mountain. He lived to a ripe old age. He stayed in Alamut, sent out his minions, pursued his interests, and likely made use of his personal Garden of Earthly Delights.

Charles ticked off a few of the boxes that seemed fitting for an asasiyun. He was faithful . . . to his friends. He was principled. And he was happy to immerse himself in the Garden of Earthly Delights. Why wait for heaven?

However, his work today wouldn't include any honorable assassination. No tyrannical political target was in his sights at this moment. Today was just about individual justice.

He felt like a cop, watching. He might need to wait here outside of Chiang's store for days.

It took an hour. Two men stood outside Chiang's Electronics, scoping the area. They looked like the kind of people who demanded respect but didn't deserve it.

Charles put on a pair of thin, black leather gloves.

9

One Store

ONE man stood almost six and a half feet tall, must have weighed at least 270 pounds, and looked like he spent a lot of time in the gym. He could have just been the muscle, but he carried himself like the leader. The second man—small and wiry with an acne-marred face—hung back, his eyes darting. He oozed the persona of a weak-minded sidekick, little more than a frightened jungle rodent. The prisons were full of creatures much like either of them.

"Freak, what did I say I was going to do to this shit if he didn't have our money today?"

The little man called Freak replied with his scratchy voice. "I think you was gonna fuck him up."

"How much money do he owe us?"

"A grand a week, Jock."

"And when he s'posed to pay us?" asked Jock.

Freak looked at a palm-sized notepad. "Two weeks ago. We been taking care of his place all this time for free."

"I don't work for free. Not in this economy. He gotta learn that. Lez go."

Freak held the door open for his bulky boss to squeeze his broad shoulders through. Across the street, Charles switched his signal reception to one of the inside cameras.

Charles's client stood up the moment the two men walked in. The only customer in the store figured it was a good time to leave. The big man stood close to Chiang.

"You have what you owe us, right?"

Chiang backed away. "Jacques. Have not!" he said with a tone at once defiant and fearful, and a pronunciation of Jacques suggesting that Chiang spoke better French than English.

"My name is Jock, you chink piece a crap. J-O-C-K. I ain't no fuckin' frog!"

Chiang shrank farther away, trying to blend with the wall behind him. His eyes flickered toward the door. "So solly, umm, Jock. This money... not possible."

The man now more correctly identified as Jock followed Chiang's eyes to the door of the store. No observers. "I don't care, little man. What I know is that we have a contract, and you ain't holdin' up your end."

"Look... Jock." It still somehow came out sounding something like Jacques with his thick accent. "Have some money. Heah." Chiang proffered a handful of assorted bills.

"Some ain't all, Chinaman. I don't do my job half-assed. I don't expect half-assed pay." He reached over the counter and grabbed as Chiang tried to slide sideways, hindered by a glass display case filled with binoculars and camera lenses. Jock pulled Chiang forward, dragged him around the corner of the counter, and then pressed him down backward on the glass surface.

"What did I say would happen if you don't pay?"

Chiang couldn't speak. He was shaking.

Freak took the moment to smash the glass of another cabinet, pulling out some Wi-Fi devices that drew his attention.

"Man, see what happens when you don't pay your insurance?" Jock sneered. "If you don't pay your insurance, how d' ya expect to keep your store functioning? If you don't have insurance, bad things like this happen. Everybody gotta have insurance. It's a fuckin' mandate!" Jock's voice increased in pitch when excited.

Jock slapped Chiang's ear and pressed him on the counter in front of him.

A small girl—somewhere in her teens—emerged from the backroom, carrying an expression of bitter hatred and a black metal baseball bat. She yelled out and swung at Jock with real ferocity. Had she been able to reach his head, and had he been entirely off guard, she could have done some damage.

But Jock heard her, turned his head toward the back entrance, and saw her in time to deflect the blow with his forearm. It had little more effect than to raise some fury in him, which he then focused on the girl.

"Bitch!" he groaned as he jerked the bat out of her hands. He pulled it back, as if to strike her with it, but then he sneered as he saw the bitterness in the girl's eyes. His face twisted into a grimace. He eyed the girl up and down and turned away from Chiang.

"Your daddy owes me a lot of money he can't pay…" He looked at her appraisingly.

The girl spat back, "He owes you nothing!"

Jock ignored it. "You can cover the debt for him, huh?" He turned back to Chiang. "What do you think, Chiang? How about you tell your daughter here to pay some debt for her daddy?"

Freak smashed a glass cabinet containing camera lenses and laughed.

Chiang glared at Jock with a face full of hate, moving to intercede. Jock picked him up as if he were a feather and threw him to the floor near his daughter. "Sit yo'self down, chink, and watch. Come here, girly. I'll introduce you to a real man."

Jock loosened his belt. He pulled his pants down, and started to drop his laundry, overconfident about what would happen next. When he looked up, his eyes met those of Paladin, who was standing by the back entry.

A second later he howled in agony.

A suppressed pistol held in a black-gloved hand sent a .22-caliber hollow-point round silently exploding out of the weapon at a thousand feet per second to bury itself in Jock's groin.

Charles didn't pause for a response from Jock. He fired again, hitting Jock in his hand as he reached for something at his side. He targeted the weapon at Freak next but kept his eyes on Jock. Freak stepped back and put his hands out, pleading. Charles felt no compunction, none of the uncertainty that preoccupied him earlier. The criminal Jock stood in front of him in shock, disbelief, and pain. There was copious evidence the bullet had affected his genitals as well as his bladder. He tried to cover the source of the fluids with his bleeding hand.

"Jock, or Jacques, or whatever," said Charles. "I don't care how you got to be the person that you are now. I don't care if your old man beat you or you have mommy problems, or if you're just having a bad day. I'm here to be sure you pay the consequences of your actions." He held the gun at his waist and turned the muzzle slowly back toward Jock.

Jock's expression changed from horror to vicious anger. He screamed and, although hobbled by the pants at his knees, tried to charge at Charles as if the blood pouring from his groin injury was from a minor scratch.

A .22-caliber round is small, relatively slow, and doesn't have the force to penetrate through both sides of a skull, as would a larger bullet. So when it enters a skull, it spins wildly, slicing through gelatinous brain tissue like a blender. In transferring its kinetic energy to the nasty work of cutting and burrowing through bone and brain, the bullet loses so much speed that it can only bounce off the far side of the skull, ricocheting back through the brain. There is no exit wound through which a larger bullet might carry away some of its energy. The force of the .22 is limited, but it's all used on the destruction of brain tissue. It's an advantage for close-range commerce.

Jock collapsed limply to the floor. Brain and blood oozed through a single hole in his forehead like pahoehoe lava. Jock's legs shuddered violently, and his right arm spasmed. His brain was dead, but his body had yet to receive the message.

Charles had no time to contemplate the consequences of Jock getting what he deserved.

Off to the side, humiliation and relief competed to control Chiang's face as he moved toward his daughter and took her in his arms. He looked with gratitude to the man with the bulbous nose, his confessor of the night before.

Charles was not proficient in such an extreme version of problem solving. Out of shock and concern for himself, Chiang, and the girl, he had compromised his broader situational awareness. He got the reminder he needed a moment later as a knife hurled by Freak careened toward his head. The near miss had nothing to do with Charles's skills or reflexes. It was sheer luck—luck that he turned his head at that moment to look empathetically at Chiang's daughter as she grasped her father tightly. In a way, she saved his life.

As Charles turned his head again, he moved just enough that the knife flew just in front of his eyes, disfiguring the tip of his latex nose before clattering against the wall beyond. The fake nose hung off his face as if he were in a cheap horror movie.

As more adrenaline pumped into his bloodstream, Charles's survival instincts took over. Instinctively, far faster than his cognitive mind could calculate, his arm thrust toward Freak, and he pulled the Ruger's trigger twice. Two near-silent bullets entered Freak's torso, one in the chest, one in the belly.

It's generally stupid to bring a knife to a gunfight.

Freak groaned, whimpered, and then pleaded with Charles. "Look, man. Jock, he's no friend of mine. I ain't workin' for him no more. Now, now I work for you. Man, don't let me die. Call an ambulance!" Tears of pain and fear welled up and streamed down the man's rough cheeks.

Charles commanded, "Freak, you wriggle wrong and you'll be right alongside your pal Jock there for the rest of eternity." But Charles knew that the disgusting creature was already on his way to non-existence, hell, or reincarnation as a cockroach, depending on one's cosmic preferences.

Charles spoke to his client. "Please search this man for any more weapons. Don't miss his ankles, his groin, and the small of his back."

The shop owner, regaining some composure, let go of his daughter and moved toward Freak. Freak, knowing his life was oozing away, offered no resistance. Chiang found no more weapons.

Charles felt the dangling latex nose on his face and discovered a small amount of blood. Nothing more than an abrasion. He shook his head, angry at himself, but grateful the Fates had kept him alive. "Mr. Chiang, please lock the doors and turn off most of the lights; business is closed for the day. Give Mr. Freak here a paper and pen." Charles kept his gun trained at Freak.

After Chiang secured the store, Charles leaned in close to Freak. "So, you work for me now, right?"

"Right. Tha's right." Freak breathed hard; his eyes frequently flashed to his left, looking first at Jock's corpse on the floor and then at the blood on his belly. He coughed.

Charles said, "Look at me. I want you to write down the names, addresses, and dollar figures for all the businesses you've been extorting. I want to know how much money each week you've been taking from them."

"If you da police, I want my lawyer." Freak said, coughing again.

"Do I look like police?" Charles held his weapon sideways briefly so that Freak could see the suppressor more completely.

Freak shook his head and started writing. "Man, I need the hospital, bad."

"First things first. Start writing—and I want a complete list."

86

Charles turned toward the door leading to the backroom. "Mr. Chiang, may I ask your daughter's name?"

The girl emerged from the backroom and dropped a box of trash bags next to Jock's corpse. She spoke for herself. "My name is Mei-li."

Charles glanced at the still-conscious and desperately scribbling Freak, then turned to the girl—the first chance he had to study her. His overwhelming impression was that she was young. Young enough that Charles's psyche reflexively adopted the protective attitude of mentor or uncle, as it had when he'd met Rainbow—just as Maurice had done when he'd met Rainbow.

At about 5'2" and a hundred pounds, she was small in both stature and weight. But standing with her arms akimbo, she seemed formidable as well as pretty, with shoulder-length straight black hair, an unblemished complexion, a symmetric face with an unexpectedly sharp nose, and eyes so dark that he could not distinguish the iris from the pupil.

"Mei-li, hello. I hope to provide you with an opportunity."

Mei-li replied in a sardonic tone. "Does this opportunity involve my dressing in a gold bikini with a chain around my ankle?"

Charles looked at her squarely. "Not in the least."

And then he said to Chiang, "You go to the bank. Meet me back here."

Chiang nodded slowly, looked at Jock's body, muttered something in Chinese that sounded like "BUN tyen-shung duh ee-DWAY-RO," and stole out the back door.

Charles looked questioningly at Mei-li.

She said, "It's... impolite. Dad called him a stupid inbred sack of meat."

He smiled and then turned back to the pitiful Freak. "Keep writing your list."

Searching Jock's clothes, he extracted what looked like about $10,000 from the big dead man's pockets. All hundreds, but still a stack about an inch high. Smart, keeping his money out of the banks; he likely had more stashed away someplace.

While Freak completed his inventory of Jock's victims, Charles studied the electronic devices as he put some back on shelves. Freak reached out a weak hand with the paper. Charles read it through; it seemed genuine. There was no need to say, "Thank you," for when he next looked up, it was to see Freak's head fall to the side. The man would have no more conscious thoughts.

The store's bathroom had a mirror. He went to work on his face, repairing his latex nose with a small kit he carried with him. He'd need a larger supply of noses.

"When's trash day, Mei-li?"

"Today. I don't think they've come yet though."

"That's good. Lucky."

Charles had been prepared to kill Jock. He'd determined in advance how and when killing Jock would be moral or immoral. He'd contemplated the potential effect on his own psyche, but he had failed to consider the most direct consequence of the action. Among other things, he hadn't considered what to do with a body.

He'd been stupid and forgotten the Six P's: proper planning prevents piss-poor performance. A score of things could have gone wrong, and the day had barely started.

Wouldn't it be nice, even a bit poetic, to just flush this sack of meat, as Chiang colorfully termed him, down a giant toilet.

He wrapped Freak in multiple layers of black plastic trash bags, the modern solution to a wide range of disposal problems. The classic, but now outmoded, option of rolling the body up in a rug allowed for easy traceability through the accumulated DNA of the carpet owner. Government databanks, combined with data available from companies people paid to analyze their genetic makeup, allowed the authorities to zero in on much of the population. Few realized that their desire to prove they were part Native American or African to gain some affirmative action benefit, virtue signal, or simply identify a hidden risk of disease, could one day draw themselves or their relatives into a police dragnet.

Wrapped in plastic, Freak's light body easily slid along the floor. Charles peered through the alley door, looking for cameras. Seeing neither windows nor cameras, he carried the diminutive Freak to the dumpster a half block down in the shadows of the back alley, hoisted him over its edge, and dropped him where he belonged, onto a soft pile of stinking garbage.

Mei-li scrubbed the floor while Charles moved on to confront the more challenging corpse. Jock was both big and heavy, and hefting a dead weight was much harder than pumping the same weight of iron in a gym. All the exercise Charles had undertaken in prison would now pay a dividend. He packaged the dead man in several layers of plastic and turned his mind to how to get Jock's bulk into the dumpster.

He couldn't toss him over the top as he had Freak; that was impossible without a forklift or another strong man. However the bin had a sliding metal door on its side, about four feet off the ground, providing easier access. It offered some hope, but the bin was already loaded with garbage above that level.

He needed to make some space. He was about to gain some appreciation for what garbagemen had to deal with every day. Not only what he was doing, but the reason why he had to do it, was unsavory, unaesthetic, and degrading.

Charles climbed into the dumpster and started moving the garbage and boxes away from the side access door. He rolled Freak's impromptu body bag toward the far side, and then kept digging away at the miasmatic refuse to clear enough space for Jock's body to go through the side door and be covered.

Charles emerged from the top and looked around for curious observers; if there were any, they'd likely just think he was another dumpster-diving bum. Seeing none, he went into the store's backroom to start hauling Jock.

After Mei-li emptied inventory from a rolling cart constructed of heavy-duty resin, she moved it beside Jock's wrapped body and stood by, ready to assist. Small as she was, she provided just enough extra strength to hoist the heavy plastic-covered mass onto the cart. He rolled it out the door into the alleyway, and then struggled to move the awkward dead weight up and through the sliding door into the dumpster. One final shove and the corpse flopped over into the container. Charles jumped back in to cover it up with refuse. The rest was up to a trash truck.

Most likely Jock and Freak would end up in either a local incinerator or a landfill in North Carolina as part of the twenty-five thousand tons of mixed trash that New York City created each day. Although it was best that the police never discover the bodies, if they were discovered, the chances of being traced were low once they left the premises. It's not like they put ID trackers on trash bags—yet.

It was unlikely the police would have the capacity or the interest to sift through stinking garbage, hoping for hints of the locations where the killing may have occurred—if it were even discovered. What self-respecting cop would waste energy looking for the killer of known lowlifes, particularly in the midst of the worst period of violent discontent in decades? The police were already strained way beyond their capacity.

But still, there was risk. And risk should beget reward.

Chiang returned from the bank with $5,000 in cash. "This all I have in bank. Can please give me time for other $15,000?"

"Chiang, I tell you what. The way things worked out, you only owe me five thousand dollars more." Charles looked quickly around the electronics store, taking a rapid inventory. "I'll be back for it someday. Perhaps you can pay me from your inventory. Don't forget."

"I not forget."

"Good."

10

Another Store

BLAIZE Forestal stared out his office window into Washington, DC's afternoon sun. He felt acutely frustrated but had no one to complain to. He might once have told his wife about it, but he had divorced her years ago, soon after he got shot.

He could never tell Sabina anything; she would unquestionably use any weakness she might discover against him. There were no other women he could vent to. He now just played the field with superficially attractive twenty-somethings. Washington was full of young women who made themselves available to rich and powerful men. Only a fool would ever tell them anything of import—but Washington was full of fools. Forestal mulled over the available women. He attracted gold-diggers easily.

Stepping back and forth through the revolving doors that barely separated investment banks from the government had made him wealthy. Round and round he'd go, so many times that it was a wonder he avoided vertigo. Each trip through the door took him to a bigger office with more rewards. He started with Goldman. Even that entry-level job paid well and, more important, allowed him to meet the Masters of the Universe. After a five-year stint, he took a position as a deputy assistant under secretary at the US Treasury. It was a huge cut in pay, but the position wired him to people with whom he could trade favors. Then, armed with his new connections, he slid into a VP slot at JPMorgan Chase, then a short stint at the New York Fed, then to Citigroup as an executive VP, from which Goldman lured him back with a seven-figure signing bonus.

His current position at Justice had been arranged by Paul Samuels with the enthusiastic approval of the Goldman board, just before the most recent bubble popped. It was always better to be in government during crises. In addition to positioning himself to benefit Paul Samuels, it let him control the purse strings of several increasingly powerful agencies: the ATF, the FBI, the DEA, and, most importantly, the SEA, which was the newest and by far the most aggressive of the praetorian agencies. Almost a law unto itself, the SEA was built to address an existential threat to the Deep State.

The SEA proved uniquely useful, far beyond its original mandate, the eradication of Sybillene. Insofar as they could be controlled—and it was getting harder all the time—the Department of Justice directed the various arms of the police state. The more powerful they grew, the more some citizens resented and feared them. Other citizens thought they needed even more power to keep the country from flying apart.

The media painted whistleblowers and town criers as unpatriotic crazies. Paul Samuels had catalyzed that too, in what he termed pushes. The danger of entities on both sides of Forestal's revolving door getting blamed for economic collapse grew as the financial system walked further out on its tightrope. Controlling important divisions of the Justice Department would help keep the country under control when the impending depression broke that tightrope. It was important that the legal system send the right victims to the guillotine when it came time to mollify the population.

Forestal's time in government always paid off. Most of his friends, if you could call them friends, also rotated through the revolving door. When he "served" in the government (he appreciated the irony of the word), he would take care of his friends. When he stepped out of government and they rolled in, favors would be returned. No one spoke of this arrangement publicly. Sometimes, over whisky and cigars, stories would be told and laughter would echo through the wood-paneled backroom of a luxurious DC restaurant or the plush millionaires' suite of a New York nightclub. But, most of the time, his subculture remained hidden in plain view. Immensely powerful, but discreet. Even though the system was increasingly unstable, the longer it persisted, the more confident everyone was that it would last forever.

The system worked well for the Masters of the Universe who pulled its levers. Like college boys telling tales of their female conquests, they crowed about transferring the downsides of risky deals to either the retail public— the "little people" trying to save for retirement—or the taxpayer. Often one and the same. When the deal went well, they celebrated their new riches. When the deal went poorly, they laughed at the stupidity of the mooches and marks who bore all the pain. The little people were oblivious to their status as indentured servants.

The credit card system channeled 3 percent of every purchase made to the banking system; the convenience amounted to an unseen sales tax on everything. Then most purchases on credit brought in at least 18 percent while the banks borrowed at near zero from the Fed. The banks made money coming and going. The fractional-reserve system itself allowed banks to lend 90–100 percent of every dollar taken in as a deposit. Then when the proceeds were redeposited by the recipient, 90–100 percent of that amount could be lent again. Ad infinitum. Creating money out of thin air had to be the most profitable, highest-margin business in the world.

An evening with faux-friends was better than being by himself; laughter, camaraderie, alcohol, and a snort or two of first-rate cocaine quelled the fear that often rose up from the depths of his psyche. He knew the well-met associates with whom he shared financial interests would as soon cut his throat as look at him, if they thought it would advance their interests. There were long-term risks in associating with people like himself, but they were outweighed by the short-term rewards. Including the fact that sometimes a beautiful and eager girl awaited his arrival. A college student, maybe a graduate student, keen to meet a multimillionaire... or a billionaire, as he sometimes claimed to be. Some he used like the money-grubbing little sluts they were, but a public policy groupie from a well-connected family might more deliberatively be nurtured because she could be useful one day.

Word got around, however. Some ungrateful bitch might post his name—or occasionally even his face—on a website such as DontDate-Him.com or AbusiveBoyfriend.com. He had people on the lookout for unflattering listings, so they wouldn't stay posted for long. His lawyers would threaten the website or its host to remove the listing. If lawyers met resistance, a visit to the victim from a tough-looking thug ensured the item was deleted.

Each time Forestal came up for a government post, the Senate confirmed him by rote. Unless there was a sex scandal, or a top dog was involved, the American public didn't care or even know who worked at the Fed, Treasury, Justice, Homeland Security and the dozens of powerful agencies under them.

So he would attend his confirmation hearing, read his prepared statement, let the senators ask their boilerplate questions, and smile agreeably as they predictably praised his extensive credentials and service in both the public and private sectors. The Kabuki theater showed the system was working. Even if they first came to Capitol Hill as idealists—imagining themselves as real-life models for the Jimmy Stewart character in Mr. Smith Goes to Washington—senators soon learned they weren't in Kansas anymore.

It didn't take long before new-to-Washington types figured out where their personal interests lay. Then they gradually merged into the amorphous club the Ottoman Turks called the Deep State. Democrat or Republican, liberal or conservative, welfare or warfare, business or labor, in the big picture these were nothing more than labels for opinions, psychological quirks, or costumes at a party. Once they wormed their way inside the Beltway, they basked in the respect and social approbation the naïve and deluded plebs lavished upon them. Being at the epicenter of the country's tax revenue, political power, and media attention was addicting. Better than being a movie star in some ways.

Because the Deep State was a completely informal and unacknowledged hierarchy, its very existence was denied or scoffed at. It comprised perhaps a thousand people at its highest level—half of them top senators and representatives, heads of powerful agencies, influential generals, and miscellaneous string pullers within the government. These were complemented by an equal number of academics, media types, money managers, business moguls, and NGO heads. These might be termed the Top Dogs of the Deep State.

The next level down, the Running Dogs, were secondary players and supporting actors in the power centers—a smart researcher, an ambitious minion, an energetic colonel, a properly connected lobbyist. These people enabled the Top Dogs and got some fat table scraps in reward. Perhaps there were twenty thousand spread across the country.

Everybody else, taxpayers and rule obeyers, law-abiding workers and peasants, doctors and lawyers, soldiers and sailors, butchers, bakers, and candlestick makers, were nothing but Whipped Dogs and Underdogs. The servile class, the drones.

Few of the senators had much interest in the details of exactly how the financial system worked, how it entwined itself with the Justice Department, or how Forestal and his ilk knew what buttons to push and when to push them. When asked, "How does it work?" a sincere offhand answer might be: "It works good… it works real good!" The rare congressman who didn't care to join would be marginalized as a rogue or a tinfoil-hat wearer. Even smart people, sophisticated and well read, were prone to swallow anything the Deep State touted as being in the national interest hook, line, and sinker.

It had all almost ended with Naked Emperor. They had stood on the very precipice. Like all wars, the drug war's main result, if not its purpose, was to empower the State. The war against Naked Emperor had been far more important than the war against conventional drugs. It was a war to stop people from seeing through the façade and peeking behind the curtain. Setting up the SEA—the Sybillene Eradication Administration— proved to be an act of genius, although Paul Samuels himself called it an act of desperation.

It had been quite a coup. The only successful battle in all the drug wars had been the war against Sybillene. The continual presence of other illegal drugs served a useful purpose in a number of ways. But Sybillene was dangerous on an existential level. They pulled out all the stops to eradicate it.

It required subtle but complete control of the media, which largely determined what people thought about and how they thought about it, along with the practical elimination of rights that had gradually eroded for decades anyway. And the more or less formal—but "temporary"—abandonment of the Constitution. It was almost academic, since the irritating document had long been a dead letter anyway, essentially interpreted out of existence. Paul Samuels had nurtured growing support for the concept of a new, "living" constitution, more in keeping with the times. All the changes were undertaken in the interests of National Security, which was of unquestioned paramount importance.

Samuels had conducted the process from the shadows, like a magician crossed with an air traffic controller. Forestal had watched the master at work. He didn't like Samuels—maybe nobody did—but his pseudoscientific mumbo jumbo had proven right about that drug.

Notwithstanding his orchestration of massive interdictions and interventions, the residual effects of Naked Emperor continued to percolate. It was likely contributing to the current urban riots, albeit only as a delayed effect of prior use. The penalty for simple possession was so draconian that few now wanted to chance it.

Forestal chuckled to himself as he replayed a scene from a popular movie in his mind. A sociopath is in bed with his girlfriend, and his wife walks in. She says, "What… what is that girl doing in bed with you?" The response is pretty much what Samuels had engineered on a national level: "What girl? What are you talking about? Are you seeing things? There's no girl in bed here! Who are you going to believe? Me, or your lying eyes?"

There was a word for this tactic: gaslighting. Forestal appreciated that most people were unaware how much they suffered from it.

Gaslighting served a key role in the sociopaths' and Deep State armamentaria.

Limits applied to little people, not to Forestal. He considered it a great strength: to be capable of absolutely anything. Normal people were constrained, limited by bounds of what they thought was decent or moral. He suffered no such limitations and took pride in that.

Goebbels had been right. Tell a big-enough lie enough times and with enough conviction, and it becomes the truth. Once people have an idea, whether it's true or false, they'll most likely carry it with them to their grave.

The propaganda machine constructed by Samuels operated night and day, through academia, the media, entertainment, and the government. It helped to redefine inflation, turning it from a verb into a noun and from an intentional process to an unpredictable effect. A liberal was no longer an individualist who believed in free minds and free markets, but instead a statist who believed everything could be and should be controlled by means of sufficient political force. It took time to garner support for concepts such as the social contract, which nobody had ever signed. Or public-private partnerships, which were more like an accommodation between a wolf and a sheep. It had taken substantial resources and a concerted effort, but now almost everyone thought they had a right to health care at someone else's expense. Forestal learned from Samuels that in order to control a culture, it is important to control how people think. To do that, it is helpful to confuse their language in order to confuse their thinking. Burning books, one word at a time.

As long as groupthinkers outnumbered free thinkers, Forestal could enthusiastically support the concept of democracy. The problem with Sybillene was that it cleared the mind—the very opposite of most drugs, which clouded the mind. If minds were clear, the current phony democracy would fall apart. Democracy might work in a city-state, where all the citizens shared a common culture, race, and traditions, but it was necessarily a sham in a domestic multicultural empire like the US. Democracy worked for a while in the case of ancient Greece and the Roman Republic, but it inevitably devolved into oligarchy or dictatorship. Forestal was confident that this time, the transition would continue to oligarchy. It had mostly been achieved already, under the cover of shadows and propaganda. There were still stumbling blocks to be overcome, such as guns in the hands of the population. The guns themselves were a relatively trivial threat; the real problem was psychological. The guns allowed individuals to feel unacceptably empowered, secure on their own.

It had become extraordinarily difficult, expensive, and dangerous to obtain Naked Emperor—far more so than garden-variety substances like heroin and cocaine, but, like anything illegal, it was available with enough money and connections. Forestal kept a supply on hand, using it when it was especially important to see through the manipulations, backbiting, and conspiracies that were the routine modus operandi of his peers. They probably used Sybillene too, although no one would dare admit to it; use carried a potential federal death penalty. National Security trumped everything; Naked Emperor was on a par with traitorous activity during wartime. There was no question that his friends would use that against him if they needed him out of the picture and found out he had a stash.

Or they'd dispense with legal procedures and just have him cleaned. If you live in a snake pit, expect to be bitten.

Naked Emperor would remain illegal as long as Paul Samuels was alive. It made Forestal thankful for small favors, like the lousy aim of whoever had tried to assassinate Samuels on his golf course. These so-called Freedom Fighters were so dysfunctional they couldn't even find a competent assassin. No triggerman he hired would muff such an easy shot.

Forestal had a far more important reason to be pleased that Samuels had survived: he needed Samuels to help him climb the ladder. Forestal could be patient that way. Any young Roman from the Senatorial class had to progress through the cursus honorum: questor; aedile; praetor; and the ultimate prize, consul. In so many ways, the US modeled itself on Rome. Just visit the House of Representatives to see two giant Roman fasces carved into the wall behind the Speaker's podium.

He'd put up with this job at the Justice Department for a year or two before moving further up the ladder. Samuels was still the master. Forestal was proud to be the Sith lord's apprentice.

Except Sabina might stand even closer. Samuels seemed to view her as a replacement for his estranged daughter. No doubt she used her nuanced charms to position herself. Or maybe she just offered him sex. How prosaic.

He should activate some plans to undermine her relationship with Samuels. His position at Justice might prove helpful to that end.

Taking a turn in government made sense. He relished the power unique to government—the legal authority to imprison or kill anyone who did anything they labeled a crime. And everyone could be found guilty of committing some crime or another. A library of laws made sure of that. There's always a way to take someone down. Want someone to squeal on a powerful associate? Threaten him with prison and fines if he doesn't. It's Tactic #1 of the special prosecutor. Kafka's nineteenth-century Europe had nothing on twenty-first-century America. Forestal was in a good position at Justice to get the dirt on anyone. Government was useful for committing crimes legally.

He only had a few days left to pull off his current caper, which would be worth millions once he went back through the revolving door to the private sector. Getting a bill through Congress without alerting watchdogs to its hidden beneficiaries was complicated as well as competitive, with so many others attempting to divert some of the cash tsunami flooding from the Fed into their own pockets. The key was to enrich himself and his friends while appearing to promote the welfare of the downtrodden. Ideally, the legislation's victims built grassroots support for it and lobbied aggressively at their own expense. Virtue signaling provided near perfect cover. The equality of minorities, a living wage, and global warming all worked well.

The legislative business-as-usual grind was slow but low risk. A highly visible crisis-response program was always welcome, though; one should never let a good crisis go to waste. In his previous sabbatical from private banking, at the Federal Reserve, Samuels had personally tutored him in fabricating crises to "move forward," "do something," and "get things done"—all reliable DC mantras. It appealed to the little people, assuring them someone was at the helm of the ship of state. The sheer size of the current financial crisis, however, led to unwanted attention. It wasn't good to have people aware of the Fed. Some fringe types criticized the Fed's interventions as essentially bailouts of the mismanaged megacorporations that paid megamillions to their friends on Wall Street so they could afford their megayachts. Fortunately, Samuels and his colleagues in academia and the media were successful in painting the bailouts as necessary to preserve the jobs, savings, and houses of the little guy. They'd done it for decades.

But where did the dollars come from, and where did they go? The government spent far more than it collected in taxes—far more than the Chinese were willing to lend. Even some people not on the fringe noticed it. Everybody acknowledged a gigantic financial crisis was a bad thing; but somehow it turned into a good thing for the Deep State, with trillions of new dollars flowing into the right places. Some said it was criminal, but no one was ever indicted, because they all had friends—like Forestal—in the Justice Department.

The Federal Reserve System had been justified as a response to a brief banking panic in 1907. It was a brilliant scheme. The old families who built the Fed used it to cement their wealth in place. Forestal knew his fortune was made possible a century ago through the foresight of Aldrich, Warburg, Rothschild, and Morgan, among others. As Nathan Rothschild had commented, "I care not what puppet is placed upon the throne of England to rule the empire on which the sun never sets. The man who controls the British money supply controls the British Empire, and I control the British money supply."

The crisis-response approach worked because when nobody had time to think, any panic button could be pressed. Something had to be done, or it would be 1929 all over again. Those who pointed out that the Great Depression had been caused—directly, entirely, and exclusively—by the Fed and other actors in the government were mocked by the Top Dogs and their numerous Running Dogs. The media assured the masses that the end of the world was imminent if the government didn't do something to save them all. So trillions of new dollars were created to bail out failing companies, so long as those who got bailed out behaved themselves. Proof that an ill wind can blow some good to some people.

If his gambit worked, the good in question would benefit Forestal and his friends handsomely. Most of their wealth and power was a result of the something that got done. Some outsiders, who knew how the game worked, had also made fortunes by speculating when the crisis would occur and how the insiders would respond when it materialized.

But, to the plebs, each crisis was the avoidable fault of the other political party. They hoped their retirement-account mutual funds would bounce back and protect them from poverty. They might get lucky, but the only real certainty was that their fund would pay 1 or 2 percent of their capital every year to its Wall Street managers.

Forestal laughed to himself. The poor fools—the ancient Romans called them the capite censi, the "head count"—thought their votes actually mattered. The voters really seemed to believe that Party A would solve the problems caused by Party B. Their superficial notions of economics and finance just got them into trouble. When the Fed created an inflationary boom and sent the market screaming to manic highs, they figured stocks were the place to be—right at the market top. By the time the panic bottom came, they were desperate to sell just before a new bull market began. As they approached their underfunded retirement, with inflation eroding their savings, they were easy marks for get-rich-quick schemes run by con men.

Then they looked for a political solution to their financial problems, wasting their hard-earned money by donating to candidates from Party A or Party B. Unaware that party labels were meaningless to the Top Dogs in the Deep State, they voted for their party's crony candidate, especially if he, or she, appeared empathetic to their situation. They failed to comprehend that their party's guy was interchangeable with the other party's guy. Instead of taking advantage of the business cycles the Fed created, the capite censi only saw crises as justifications to vote out one set of bums and replace them with the other set every four years. Their expensive universities and dumbed-down televisions—both just Deep State mouthpieces—taught them that this was what democracy meant. Didn't they know that almost all the politicians were on the side of the State? Voting them out of office was like trying to win a coin toss with your opponent's two-headed coin.

At Justice, Forestal helped promote, sponsor, and pass new laws filled with minutiae to benefit very specific people. The party leadership whipped the dogs, and the bills passed unread on a voice vote, with no debate, to be signed by the president on a holiday weekend, without fanfare. Forestal only had to make a few legislators care enough, with the help of threats and bribes, to sponsor his legislation.

His job proved tougher while the news cycle focused on what the press had dubbed the CityFire uprisings in New York, San Francisco, Atlanta, Chicago, Seattle and now here in Washington. The politicians wanted to be in front of that limelight, and so they weren't giving the attention needed to help make Forestal and his friends happy. They had poverty to solve, and fairness and equality to spread around to help assuage the demands of the disenfranchised and dispossessed. The CityFire crisis would provide a useful distraction for some larger moves soon, but for now it only interfered with what Forestal needed to accomplish.

He had much work to do. After his next rotation through the private sector he'd come back into government as treasury secretary. That would bring perks, but also more visibility. The spotlight meant he would have to be more cautious and circumspect about his after-hours pursuits—or fly out of the country for serious dissipated pleasures, taking advantage of the fact that what happens in a Third World shithole usually stayed in a Third World shithole. Their cops were generally incompetent, risk averse, and easy to bribe. As a bonus, the taxpayer should and would, of course, pay for the travel expenses of a public servant, serving at great personal sacrifice.

It had been a trying day, dealing with the self-important worms inhabiting the Rayburn Building. Although well supplied with financial and political power, he felt oddly drained. What might revitalize him? That was a question with an easy answer. He didn't really have time for it, but he needed the biological boost that The Store provided. He would come out feeling like an alpha male victorious after a challenge, testosterone energizing his sense of power. Sky-high cortisol, and dopamine pulsing through his hypothalamus, would reward a return visit. A visit to The Store would augment his self-confidence. The only downside? Obsession. Obsession could slow down any man. He shouldn't risk it.

A brisk spring wind whipped his face as he emerged from the DoJ Building. He drew the collar of his long cashmere overcoat to cover his chin.

As he walked the six blocks to his condo, he noted the girls he passed. They ignored him, presuming he was just another of the depressed, bored, and boring bureaucrats that filled the city. In fact, he felt the way he looked.

He stopped in his tracks. So why go home to the apartment? No. He would go to The Store after all.

As the Cleaner had observed a few days ago, he hadn't been there in a while. When he'd previously been based in DC, the obsession forced him there almost every night for weeks on end. It was an addiction. He accomplished far less at work during those binges. Now again based in DC, the call of The Store proved hard to avoid. This time, he was sure it wouldn't control him.

His hands would come alive with the force of his temper.

The Store had existed for a century in its well-appointed townhouse not far from Union Station, unmolested by the law and unexposed by the media. Those who knew what lay inside—the members and a few highly trusted employees—rightfully feared saying a word. Police protected this area of DC from the growing crime and discontent. Power and influence ensured that the cops kept unwelcome elements at bay and the proclivities of The Store's members under cover.

"Open up," Forestal said, banging on the door of the unmarked townhouse. The Cleaner, dressed in black tie, whose primary job was at The Store, replied in his high-pitched voice, "Of course, Mr. Forestal. I'm sorry. So much unrest and brutality in the city these days. Come in, sir. It's nice and warm inside." He held the door open for Forestal.

The hallway was dominated by a wide staircase with Oriental runners. A life-size marble statue of a naked boy stood off to the side. The sculptor who had carved the boy's face was clearly catering to a certain type of client. It was innocent yet demanding; weak, but petulant. It could have been a Michelangelo but for a blatant and visually intrusive lewdness, a quality particularly attractive to perverts in general and pedophiles in particular. The National Endowment for the Arts considered it a masterpiece and awarded its well-connected sculptor a substantial prize.

Forestal figured the artist deserved it, if only because the statue always stimulated him. It probably excited most of the men who shopped at The Store. Society's mores and rules were irrelevant to him, but clearly moving in his direction.

"And your passcode, please, sir. Type it here." The Cleaner held a tablet computer in his hands, the same hands that had performed such bloody work in his apartment.

"Nice new system, Lichen. Same passcode, right?"

"Yes, Mr. Forestal. If you would like to see your balance, just press the green button. Yes… there."

Forestal tapped the button. The balance came up as less than $1,400. The man in tails raised his eyebrows as he said, "Oh my. I think we will have to do something about that, sir, don't you think?"

Forestal reached into his coat pocket as the greeter secured the door behind him. He handed the man two $10,000 bricks. "Fifteen on account. The rest is for you."

"Certainly, sir. Thank you. You have returned at an excellent time. The selection available this week is superior."

"Good, good. Was that Terrence Kirby that just entered?"

"Yes, sir."

Forestal knew the young and very irritating up-and-comer who worked at the Department of Agriculture. When they'd first met, Forestal thought the man might be an investigative reporter who had somehow—against all odds—surmounted the screening process. He seemed to skulk about and liked to ask oily personal questions. He was smarmy and covert, but what Kirby had done to that girl that first night had entertained and impressed Forestal. Kirby was clearly a connoisseur of violence routinely in need of higher doses. No way that was cover for a journalist or cop. This guy was the real deal.

He'd run into Kirby many other times at The Store during Forestal's last period of outright addiction. He'd learned that Kirby came from wealthy stock and that his father had been a member before him. Kirby didn't work for government because he needed a job, but because he liked being around kindred spirits. He'd wanted to be FBI but couldn't pass either their physical or—more importantly—their psychological evaluations. Kirby discovered that the much less demanding Department of Agriculture was a sufficient launchpad for a career within the Washington Beltway.

Last he'd heard, Kirby was still at Agriculture, worming his way up the ranks with enough finesse to perhaps merit the attention of Paul Samuels.

He'd catch up with the man tonight.

* * *

Three hours later, Forestal emerged from The Store and grabbed a taxi in front of Union Station for the trip home. His knuckles hurt as he brushed them against the rough strap while buckling his seatbelt. Safety first. His knuckles must pale in comparison to Kirby's, who was even more enthusiastic about inflicting pain on the small and defenseless.

The taxi driver glanced back via the mirror. "Why the scowl, mister?"

Forestal hadn't realized he was scowling, but now he could feel that his mouth was turned down and stiff, his eyes narrow, his muscles taut.

"Shut up and drive."

He remembered now. As often happened when he was done at The Store, he felt like he'd been cheated by God. Taunted. He had absolutely everything—money and power—but it wasn't enough. He could never get enough.

*   *   *

Charles spent some days in reflection, meditation, and contemplation.

He'd killed two men a few days ago. They were willfully destructive and actively evil. Even though he was protecting the lives and property of others, killing did not sit well with him.

He could have done it differently. He could have held them until the police arrived, and pressed charges. That might have stopped them for a time, but it would fail as a strategy. The police weren't very effective in the best of times, and now they were exhausted from the nightly CityFire riots. The judicial system was unreliable. Properly lawyered up, the pair could be back on the street in a few days, and the Chiangs might well be the ones that wound up in a dumpster.

In a degraded and degenerating society, there was plenty of room for vigilantes in the mold of Batman or Paladin. It was an unjustly besmirched calling.

Pacifists would decry his solution. But then pacifists ended up slaves to the violent, turning the other cheek so fast that their yokes slid easily over their spinning heads and around their necks. Hoping for nonviolence was fine, but hope was not a plan.

Charles considered the evening in Battery Park. Who was this Jeffrey character? What was his real purpose in contacting him? Even a casual mention of Sybillene could arouse suspicions. Something in his chain of thoughts prompted him to make a call to an old friend, five thousand miles away.

After the usual pleasantries and some time catching up, Charles posed a question to TJ Wandeah. "You think you might be interested in a potentially lucrative, but somewhat speculative, business venture?" Like Charles, TJ used an encrypted voice line.

"Have you forgotten who you are talking to, Charles? Or where I am? This whole country is a giant speculation, my friend." He laughed like Santa.

His thick West African accent brought back powerful memories. Charles envisioned him sitting behind a cheap desk in an office with white walls, bright sunlight shining through a window behind him, the scent of smoldering charcoal pervading the air. Maybe the air conditioning worked, maybe not. Half the time the power grid was offline in the capital city of Gondwana.

"What're your worries now, TJ?"

"Same as usual. No capital. No work ethic. Chinese buying up all the value in exchange for loans to pay them to build the roads and ports that they use to ship out the resources they extract. We get some dog-work jobs for a few years, then the projects go bust and the Chinese take them over and put in their own people. Politicians and bureaucrats get fat with bribes."

"Pretty much like here."

"But, in Gondwana, everyone wants some cold water."

Charles grinned as the old phrases returned to mind. Cold Water. The term was part of the soft language of West African extortion. Anyone who wore a uniform would spend their day jockeying for a position to pull over a car with white passengers. If they sat in a government office, the idea was to get in front of an NGO or foreign businessman and figure a way to be greased with some weekend money.

"TJ, what would you think of opening up shop again?"

The phone stayed silent.

"TJ?"

"I'm thinking," came the delayed response. "Why would you want to do this?"

"I don't know that I do. But it's possible the reward is worth the risk."

"You are just out of prison. There is a target on your back as large as a house."

"That's right. That's why I can't be involved in any way beyond a few phone calls."

"And in supplying the capital, right?"

"And the capital, TJ. But with no trail from me to you. You'd need to do this in the bush. Where no one will know. Entirely locals."

"Locals work only four hours a day—maybe. You know that."

"Remember how you did this before? How you selected the best and incentivized them? It worked. This would be a repeat effort."

"As long as there was money, it worked, Charles. But when the cash flow stopped, so did they."

"Cash flow can start again. Could you round up the same crew?"

"The ones who aren't dead, yes. And what about those airplanes and their missiles?"

"I told you this would be a speculative venture."

"How serious are you?"

"At this point? Just sounding it out. I won't be selling product. I'm out of the drug-lord business."

"You won't be selling it? Then who will? How will you develop distribution channels?"

"I won't."

"Sounds like a bad idea, Charles. Manufacture the drug, and then what, store it in barrels? For how long?"

"I'm not sure yet. But can you give it some thought? Think how you would do it. Consider it a mental exercise, will you?"

"Of course, Charles. I will think about it."

"Do you need travel and expense money?" TJ had made out well when they were in business together, but it was hard to stay rich with legions of relatives always begging for nonrepayable loans. In Gondwana, it was hard to make money and even harder to hold on to it.

TJ grunted. "Of course, Charles. Travel money is always good. It helps me think. You best send it soon, before they have you back in prison... or shot."

The two friends disconnected, and Charles sat back on Xander's couch and considered. The mysterious man from Battery Park wanted Naked Emperor. Not for himself, but for some other purpose. Charles didn't know what that purpose might be, but he knew that to have success, especially outside of the law, you needed a certain amount of luck. Luck always favored those who were both bold and prepared. Something about Jeffrey felt lucky. A few bucks to TJ to fertilize the soil of his mind just might pay off.

11

The Accidental Billionaire

GRAYSON W. Chase won the lottery.

Literally.

It had happened ten years before, when Grayson had glanced down at the dashboard of his fifteen-year-old Ford F250 Superduty to see the fuel gauge redlining. He usually filled up from the five-hundred-gallon tank of off-road diesel that fed the tractors on his hobby farm. It both saved money on fuel taxes and allowed him to deny some revenue to the State—a double win. However, he'd rushed off early that AM to a jobsite. After twelve hours training and supervising the work crew in marginal Spanish, laying shingles with them and dealing with a hundred ad hoc problems, he realized on the way home that both his truck and his body were running on fumes.

His old truck was sad, and so was Grayson. Very sad. It had been eight months… since… He couldn't bear to think about it.

He pulled into the Kwik-E-Mart, stuck the diesel nozzle in the fuel pipe, and headed inside for a Big Gulp and a cheese dog. In line, he noticed that the MegaMillions lottery stood at $1.8 billion. The second highest in history. He couldn't help but buy a lottery ticket about once a year, when the potential reward shot past the moon. Mostly, lotteries were taxes on people who can't do math. You actually got better odds playing the mob's numbers racket, but it was worth a couple of bucks just for the fun of thinking about what he would do if he won. He bought a ticket and stuck it in his wallet.

The freshly fueled truck struggled to start, then limped out of the gas station on perhaps five of its eight cylinders. If it were a horse, he'd put it out to pasture. The Ford had been reliable until recently and didn't quite deserve the glue factory. He could afford a new one but, like any sensible person, dreaded a visit to a car dealership. He was indifferent to the depreciating asset, as long as it ran.

He parked, opened the engine compartment, and systematically appraised the problem. Probably neither electrical or mechanical, more likely the fuel system. The air filter was clear, and no kinks in the turbo ducts. Unlikely it was bad fuel, more likely the injectors. Three hundred forty thousand miles wasn't bad, but they'd be about due for replacement. Even if he did the work himself, it would still cost $1,200 to buy the parts. How, he wondered, did the average American get by?

Distracted, he forgot about the lottery ticket in his wallet and didn't even get his money's worth of fantasy out of it. Days later, he just assumed he'd lost and went about his daily life.

He had succeeded reasonably well in life, at least until last year.

In high school, he'd worked as a carpenter's apprentice. Old Tom was much more than a carpenter though. He knew everything. He could plumb, do complicated electrical wiring, roofing, concrete, and roadbuilding. He knew the county building codes, but he ignored them because what he built was always, on principle, better than code. Old Tom had learned his trades almost fifty years earlier as a shipwright on old wooden vessels. It was a small niche few people could fill or wanted to. There was little future in wooden boats, but it taught him the value of quality in details. Sailors who bought wooden boats were far more particular and demanding than the buyers of tract houses. Tom then served for years as both chief engineer and head carpenter on a decrepit World War II–era wooden minesweeper. It was an antique but served well enough as an oceanographic-research vessel.

The young Grayson learned more than just a set of skills from Tom. Tom practically adopted him since Tom didn't have a family of his own. The man was in the mold of Eric Hoffer, the libertarian intellectual who worked as a longshoreman because he felt being an intellectual without actually working would corrupt anybody's character. Tom's love of reading and suspicion of academia rubbed off on Grayson—as did his attitudes toward business.

Tom knew how to run a business but was more interested in the project itself. As a result, his operation never lacked demand. Old Tom died the day before Grayson finished high school, leaving Grayson to finish two ongoing multiyear projects. He was well equipped for the challenge.

In fact, at age eighteen, he held two jobs—the first completing Tom's projects and the second turning his hobby as a hotrodder into a trade. He took a job in a small shop doing simple mechanical work on average cars. When opportunities arose, he preferred transforming bodywork, building high-performance engines and fitting exotic suspensions. That work was intellectually stimulating, artistically satisfying, and remunerative. Five years later, when the owner wanted to retire to Florida, Grayson bought the place with seller's financing. The other mechanics liked him both as a person and as the boss.

He had a simple formula that it didn't take an MBA to figure out. In fact, it was a formula very few MBAs seemed to understand: make the shop the kind of place he'd want to patronize and tell his friends about. The shop thrived, and in three years he paid off the loan and started banking profits. Perhaps because he didn't chase girls every night and wasn't much of a drinker, he was able to put considerable money aside, buying local rental properties, adding value with his contractor's skills. He compounded the steady cash by reinvesting in new properties.

After considerable reading about economics, finance, and the various markets, he stepped into stocks, following the advice of some financial-newsletter writers whose philosophies he shared. He trusted Wall Street about as much as he trusted used-car salesmen.

Stacks of books filled Grayson's bedroom, living room, and the shelves he built in the hallways. He'd never gone to college, nor did he want to, in part because he hated how slowly school moved. It was clearly a misallocation of time and money. He learned far more efficiently on his own. One of the many things he'd learned from Tom was to be suspicious of people who taught without doing.

Finding the right woman, with not just a pretty face and a shapely body but character and virtues as well, took time. When he did at age forty-two, he fell for her hard, and they were married in six months. She was soon pregnant, and for the next seven months, he learned to be a husband and prepared to be a father. Grayson was happy.

He never fully understood why she had refused to go to the doctor when her first symptoms appeared. "Frankly, Gray, I hate waiting an hour for an expensive five-minute exam. I can take my own temperature, pulse, and blood pressure. They'll say to take two aspirins and get some rest. Anyway, these things come and go. I'll feel better in the morning." A reasonable response; she was a thoughtful woman.

But she didn't feel better.

She'd died from eclampsia. The baby didn't make it either. That was about eight months before he bought the lottery ticket.

He'd always love her and the baby he'd never met.

He worked hard to figure out why it had happened. He did it the old-fashioned way: by studying everything he could. It took him a while to figure out all the pieces to the puzzle. The real problem was a compounding series of laws that, though each seemed like a good idea at the time, wound up destroying all sanity and function in the medical system. Do-gooder lawmakers were the ultimate cause of his wife's and baby's deaths.

He sometimes found himself just sitting and staring at the TV or a wall. Sometimes he'd aimlessly wander around the house during the evening, tinkering here and there. Bored, sad, and wondering what the point of it all was, one evening he killed time thinning out the mess of receipts and paper scraps in his wallet. And so, on the first anniversary of his wife's death, he came upon the now-dog-eared lottery ticket bought at the Kwik-E-Mart. He'd heard on the news a few months back that the winning ticket for the huge jackpot had been bought in state, but he'd forgotten that he was in the running. Among the dozen or so tickets he'd bought in his life, he'd never matched even a single number. Not one. So as he opened his computer to check his ticket against the winning number, he was confident that his ticket wouldn't be a winner. It was hard to imagine the thrill of victory; he didn't allow himself the fantasy of thinking: What if?

He looked at the screen and then the ticket, number by number.

That couldn't be right.

He put on reading glasses and checked the date on the ticket. He checked the numbers again. Then he held up the ticket next to the screen.

He went to another lottery website hosted by the State of Georgia, just to his south, in case South Carolina's website had a typo.

Yup, he'd won it. There, in his hand, was the only winning ticket.

He nodded in acceptance.

He kept some gold coins in a safe in his basement hidden behind a large plastic storage bin and several bags of junk silver in five-gallon paint cans.

He placed the ticket in an envelope, stuck it on top of a small pile of gold eagles, and locked the safe.

Then, after visiting the kitchen to make a cup of hot chocolate, he went to bed and read a book about the collapse of the Roman Republic. The subject echoed the current news yet was much more interesting. Although it was well written and relevant, he couldn't keep his mind on it. You might expect that anyone holding a ticket worth about one billion after-tax dollars would fantasize about being ridiculously wealthy. Except it wouldn't be fantasy. Grayson was ridiculously wealthy. Still, he found he really didn't care. As he fell asleep, he thought about his wife and what it would have been like to watch their baby's first steps together, to have her here to share in this incredible turn of events.

In the morning, he awoke in good spirits. He reconfirmed the numbers on his lottery ticket, stuck it back in the safe, and called his lawyer. They did some quick math, and Grayson nodded his head.

Then he drove to work.

He told nobody else about it and acted the same as always—except for an extra bounce in his step and a lot more thoughts in his mind. The piece of paper in his safe made him feel younger and banished thoughts of a looming midlife crisis. His mind played with a new purpose, with a whole new set of goals.

Grayson continued his work but thought less about the present and more about possible futures. At night, alone in his empty house that once held such love and hope, he planned, networked, and read. Once a week, he'd meet with his attorney, who introduced him to other attorneys who specialized in helping high-wealth clients.

His lawyers met with the South Carolina Lottery Commission and arranged for Grayson to claim his winnings anonymously. The media furor over the huge jackpot had long since faded when no one emerged to claim it. These many months later, few noticed when the lottery commission announced that an anonymous winner had finally come forward. As he had not come far enough forward to be identified, the media had no story. They moved on.

No paparazzi or investment salesmen would bother Grayson Chase. Few people outside of his hometown in South Carolina knew he existed.

No one suspected any change in his status. No orange Lamborghini appeared in front of a megamansion. He lived life as a billionaire with few people having a clue. He read. He learned. He made new connections.

To his colleagues and friends in his little town near Georgetown, South Carolina, he was the same old Grayson Chase, although now he seemed to travel more often.

During those brief trips out of town, Grayson had quietly met the movers and shakers of a certain subsegment of the world. He got to know them, obtained their tentative support, and maintained regular communications with them. They'd be most helpful when the time was right.

And so a decade passed in mostly quiet solitude. He lived like a Taoist monk—in the world, but not of it.

Until Grayson Chase was ready to act.

12

Three Meetings of Minds

RAINBOW kicked some trash from the entranceway and slid, unnoticed, into Chiang's electronic store. She'd stopped by a couple of times before, lingering, getting the feel of the place, keeping an eye out for Mei-li, who had yet to appear. Her father was usually able to keep up with the modest stream of customers, but it was more hectic today during the lunch hour. A half a dozen shoppers fiddled with gadgets and peered into display cases. Chiang looked anxious and chattered in Chinese toward the backroom. A girl emerged and moved toward a customer, who seemed to be losing patience with the slow service.

Upon Mei-li's entrance, Rainbow started paying attention, instinctively employing the survival tactics that had allowed her to thrive in the ghetto. Every movement of a facial muscle had some meaning. Years of observation enabled her to make the right choices under stress. A wrong choice could have fatal consequences when dealing with a hopped-up gangsta. Rainbow could read people, a rare and valuable skill that went beyond simple street smarts.

She studied Mei-li's face and movement, but mostly her eyes. It is said that the eyes are the windows to the soul. More exactly, eyes provided insights into intelligence, intentions, attitude, and a score of other characteristics. It was why many poker players liked to wear dark glasses.

Mei-li's eyes gave Rainbow the impression that if the girl had fear, she kept it under control—which was better than being fearless—and that her brain processed information fast. She possessed self-esteem but wasn't arrogant. Rainbow noted a sense of humor, or at least a bit of tempered amusement at her current customer, who proclaimed extensive knowledge about high-tech audio products. He was the type of person who'd lie about his golf scores.

Rainbow wondered about the survival value of overconfidence, which impressed her as a failing. Bluffing, bragging, baring teeth, and chest thumping seemed to help make men dominant in society. As a gross generality, they seemed genetically programmed to "fake it 'til they make it." The ghetto was full of men with exaggerated egos trying to disguise weak self-esteem. In contrast, women tended to bend in the other direction, underplaying their worth, acting passive and submissive. She wondered if Naked Emperor could have been the Great Equalizer, as people of both sexes learned to stop lying to themselves, pretending to be something they weren't.

Rainbow moved next to Mei-li's annoying customer, who was engrossed in comparing two sets of headphones, nodding to let her know she was just as amused. Mei-li's mouth twitched in an almost-imperceptible equivalent of a wink. Their first connection.

Rainbow pointed to a set of night vision goggles. "Third generation?"

Mei-li replied, "Second gen." She pointed to an adjacent model. "That's third."

Rainbow nodded and said, "K."

She examined them, comparing specs in their manuals, while Mei-li's pretended headphone expert left without buying. Rainbow met her eyes, and Mei-li smiled.

"The gen threes are expensive, but they're far better than gen twos. No comparison. And they last. Gen fours? They're neat, but they sap battery life and they wear out. Gen three is the winner, price for value. I'm not sure about the SWIR yet."

"SWIR?"

"Short-wave infrared. That's some cool tech, but new. It's coming along, but doesn't make sense for most buyers now. It needs time. The quality will improve, and the price will drop."

Rainbow held up the third-generation device. "How much?"

"I'll check. It's around four thousand dollars."

"Is that a good price?"

"Pretty good. Cheaper than Amazon." She put another device on the counter. "But this is the one I would choose if I needed good night vision.

Monocular, so you don't sacrifice your natural night vision in both eyes. That's why the military prefers monocular. And they mostly use gen three too. In fact, gen four isn't really a military term—it's mostly a marketing handle for civilians."

Rainbow figured that Mei-li had no expectation of making a sale. In a recession, what were the odds of a teenage girl walking in, playing with some of the most expensive gadgets in the store, and buying one? Mei-li had to have pegged her as a browser with time to kill, just eyeballing cool but unaffordable stuff. Yet she accommodated her. Decent and wise.

Rainbow asked, "I don't suppose you'll take cryptocurrency for it?"

Mei-li gazed back at Rainbow more closely.

"Sure. Personally I'd prefer it."

"Which crypto would you prefer?"

"Most anything other than some shitcoin will work." Mei-li said it with a wry smile.

"Let's keep it simple. How about just Bitcoin then?"

"K by me, if you're willing to stick around for a bit," Mei-li replied. "I may set up a Lightning node soon, to speed things up."

"I don't mind sticking around and chatting." Rainbow smiled, took out her phone, and the two girls worked together to complete the transaction. In short order, Rainbow owned a night vision scope she didn't have much use for. It would be another five hours and a trip for fast food together before the two girls parted for the evening.

Rainbow had accomplished her major objective in visiting the shop.

Mei-li was fluent in not only blockchain and cryptography, but the marketing and business side of cryptocurrencies as well. Indeed, she was not just adequate, but close to perfect for what Charles was seeking. Was she genius level? Possibly. The girl knew what she was talking about. Rainbow had a sense that Mei-li had the cojones as well as the right attitude and skills to fit in.

All it cost Charles to make this connection was a night vision scope, a couple of homicides, and, potentially, life in prison if they were caught.

* * *

The ulcer returned about this time of year, every year. He could see a doctor, who would stick tubes down his throat to look around, take biopsies, make a guess, call it a diagnosis, and likely start him on antibiotics that would mess up his digestion for months or years. Or he could wait a week or two for the nuisance to go away on its own. Jeffrey trusted only two doctors on the planet, one of whom practiced on the far side of the globe. He drank a glass of Alka-Seltzer and luxuriated as the pain disappeared over the next few minutes. Good enough for now. He made a mental note to address the issue properly someday soon, knowing he wouldn't find the time.

Diana sat perfectly poised, yet perfectly relaxed, in a long white silk dress supported by shapely tanned breasts as much as by two almost microscopically thin shoulder straps. Her blue eyes shimmered as she studied the menu.

Jeffrey appreciated all the effort she had taken for tonight's date. Her daily attire was nothing like this. Overalls, lab coats and jeans were more her style. Few people other than Jeffrey would think of her as beautiful; she was fit and shapely, but also a bit angular and gawky. A little like a flamingo or an ostrich, when he let his imagination roll. He gave her the pet name of Birdy. He couldn't keep his eyes off of her and thought she was the most marvelous creature in the universe.

She was usually too preoccupied with her career to spend much time on makeup, but because they didn't intersect nearly often enough, she had taken some time to deck herself out tonight. Jeffrey wondered if he had done anything to merit it. Apparently she thought so, and that was the important thing.

Her blond hair had the same texture as the white silk of her evening gown. Usually held up in a bun, tonight it fell most of the way down her back, almost as far down as the cut of her dress, low enough to excite the imagination of any reasonable man. Jeffrey was, perhaps above all else, a reasonable man.

"Birdy, you laugh at my pain?"

Diana covered her mouth, but the laughter in her eyes remained. "Oh, I'm sorry, Jeffrey. Are you really in pain?"

"Just looking at you takes it away."

"I've missed you. You need to relax more."

Jeffrey agreed, but his agreement couldn't change the reality. "The boss keeps me busy. And you have your work. There's a lot for us all to do."

"Are you making progress?"

"I don't know. It's an uphill battle."

116

"Are you safe?"

"Safe… I don't really like that word. There are some risks with anything. But I get your point. I'm trying to recruit some more help."

"Help that might keep you safer?"

"I'm getting older. Only an idiot thinks he can overcome the second law of thermodynamics. Everything winds down and falls apart over time. No, the help is for things that I can change."

"I don't like to sound like a negative Nelly, but you're looking pretty beat up. How's your breathing?"

"Good enough. I can't run so well anymore."

"Well, you are missing a bunch of lung."

"Yeah. There's that."

Most knew the restaurant as Chez Pierre, but its actual name was much longer. It received three stars, five diamonds, and unremitting acclaim from both the food critics and run-of-the-mill gourmands. Was that because the chef and most of the staff were gay? Maybe; there was certainly a correlation. Men with a certain sexual orientation tend to be fit, well groomed, fashionably dressed, and blessed with good taste generally. A good rule of thumb for making money in real estate was simply to buy in whatever rundown area they were moving into. Their appreciation for the better things in life definitely extended to food.

But even within that context, Chez Pierre was a couple of standard deviations above simply good. The ambiance, the service, and the cuisine itself never disappointed. Heaven itself would have its food prepared in Pierre's kitchen, if the gods called far enough in advance to get a reservation.

The vice president of the European Central Bank sat at the next table with Paul Samuels, who now was watched over by two readily identifiable bodyguards. Jeffrey, having provided the maître d' with a $100 bill, was positioned where he could hear almost every word the two central bankers said. He couldn't listen as closely as he would have liked, because Diana both expected, and deserved, attention. Fortunately, the restaurant's excellent acoustics and low ambient noise allowed his discreetly placed phone to record anything said at the adjacent table that he might miss. He'd review it for details later.

Diana enjoyed a serving of escargots, and he listened as the executive spoke quietly to another well-dressed man sitting next to him.

"Mr. Samuels. We know it's obvious to you. We believe that with your help we can continue for at best two more years, assuming no further loss of confidence in the euro."

"And that's what we're here to discuss, Mr. Domici," replied the balding man who shared the table. He spoke quietly, barely audible to Jeffrey. "It is why we do what we do and have what we have. We're positioned to help our friends at the ECB. Let's talk specific needs and terms, shall we?"

Diana tapped him on his sleeve. "Mr. Otter," she said, using his pet name, "How do you like the mushrooms?" She asked it between bites of her exquisitely well-prepared aiguillettes de canard.

Jeffrey picked at his duxelles, the finely chopped mushrooms mixed with shallots and heavy cream, placed in delicate crêpes accented by a madeira truffle sauce. It should have been an inspiring sensation, but his mind lingered elsewhere. Instead of living for this moment, he was planning for the next. On a parallel track in his mind, he recognized it was foolish to try to do two things at once, neither very well.

His iPhone's voice recorder would catch what he needed, so he reaffirmed his decision to let it do its work. This enchanting woman and the elegant meal truly deserved all his attention. So Jeffrey pulled himself back to the moment, picked up a forkful of les duxelles, and willed himself to ignore the European crony and his problems. Now was a time to savor life. He let the flavor of the exquisite dish flow through him, triggering those brain hormones that would demand a repeat of the experience. Every healthy human being was addicted to food.

But then his cell phone buzzed. That would override his recording. He glanced at it in frustration, rejected the telemarketer's call, and reset the recording feature.

Diana looked at the device disapprovingly.

"Sorry. I've just gotta find a way to shut down all these irritating telemarketers. The electronic equivalents of mosquitoes. I am enjoying both my meal and the company—two of life's great pleasures." He looked at her hungrily, but with a smile in his eyes and added, "Although there are others."

Diana conveyed mock reproach and said, "That's what I like about you, Jeffrey. You wish you could find a way to make telemarketers disappear. Most everybody else only hopes that someone could find a way to make it so. You, my love, are that someone: a man of solutions." She then added in a whisper, "Very sexy."

Later that evening, she held his arm as he walked her up the stairs to their apartment. He took her hand and led her to the bedroom. After an extended time in which he delighted as much as she did, she fell asleep on his shoulder. He listened to her breathe; she was content. After a bit, he gently moved her aside and tucked a sheet around her before walking down the hall to his library, where he stretched out on a plush chair, feet on an ottoman, and listened intently to the recording of two influential men discussing their mutual needs—or, more exactly, one detailing his fears and the other his requirements.

Jeffrey's face stayed expressionless as he listened, but then a faint smile appeared, just for a moment.

Several hours later, he took in the serenity of Diana's sleeping face. She'd indulged him at the restaurant. She'd sensed his divided attention and accepted it instead of feeling threatened. She never seemed jealous of other demands on his time. If anything, she admired his preoccupation with his business; his life had purpose. Too many men were drones, concerned with trivialities.

He, in turn, respected her dedication to her own work—work that had, so far at least, proven even more valuable than his own.

13

Solving Problems, Creating Networks

MEI-LI and Rainbow sat in the basement of Chiang's store. In a world where many teenage girls only cared about boyfriends and fashion, they found themselves kindred spirits. By early June they'd met a dozen times; their discussions had become serious early on.

Mei-li spoke with confidence. "It's no problem to create and airdrop a new token. The hard part is getting people to use it. That's the payoff. Even with a good product, marketing is crucial. Marketing is mostly your gig. So, what's gonna make a Paladin Token valuable?"

A good name was just a start. Something both memorable and descriptive of its function.

Rainbow replied, "People will earn a Paladin Token by creating value. They'll also create value with the kinds of things they'll spend it on. People can earn it by performing services, which I'll tell you about. The tokens need to be tradable privately either on a peer-to-peer exchange or on centralized exchanges in jurisdictions that protect privacy. Some people will want to pool their resources for especially big… projects."

"Spend it on what?"

"Collecting information and fixing problems—problems you can't fix with blockchain and computers alone. Problems that need hands-on action. Problems that only go away when the person who causes the problem is neutralized. Problems caused by bad people, because the bad people are the problem." Rainbow assumed that Mei-li couldn't help but be reminded of Jock and Freak.

The girl's eyes widened. "You mean a market for problem solvers that don't work within the system? Unlicensed detectives and spies?"

Rainbow nodded. "Spies and detectives certainly. And, yeah, there are other ways to manage a problem. Vigilantes. Muscle. Mercenaries. We need to create a marketplace for problem solving, including methods we can't imagine. Let the market invent new solutions. And, well, extreme measures, when appropriate, can be part of that market."

"An assassination market?"

Rainbow smiled. "We aren't the first to think of it. Some guys once set up kind of a Guessing Game lottery. You bought a ticket and predicted a time by which a bad guy—usually a politician—would be killed. If enough people hated him, the pot could get huge. There was real incentive for people to ensure their ticket became a winner. People would try to kill the guy on their chosen day. The government shut it down easily. But with blockchain and cryptocurrencies, it can happen—privately, and on a much, much bigger scale."

"Yeah, I get the picture. Doesn't killing seem evil to you?"

Rainbow smiled again and planted a few more seeds for her new friend to chew on. "I've talked this over with my family. It's important we define words accurately. Murder is the premeditated killing of someone who hasn't first used fraud or violence against you or yours. It's evil. But homicide? That depends! Was it evil for Princess Leia to choke Jabba the Hut to death using the chain he had her bound up with? Would it have been evil to assassinate Stalin or Hitler or Mao as soon as they started out on mass murder? In fact, even before. Stalin would have been an easy decision. Before he got into the government, he was a thief, bank robber, counterfeiter, and murderer. Mei-li, there are some people who just need to die. It's like they're screaming, Stop me before I kill again!"

"Isn't that the government's job, to decide who lives and dies?"

Rainbow shook her head. "That's a scary thought! Look, I got some mentors with real cred." She slid back into ghetto rap. "They make me read their shit. And they expect me to know what's gone down and pass on the bits that make sense to me. Here's what I got. Governments done killed a hundred sixty million of their own people just in the last century. Did you know that? I'm not talking in war. That number don't include none of the wars that government starts. The people? We're all just government's bitches and tools.

"You basically got two kinds of people in the world. Ones that like to do things, and ones that like to do other people. Good people don't become politicians. Politicians have to promise pie in the sky to stupid-ass voters. They're all liars and thieves. They have to be, to steal shit from some people and give it to other people after taking a big cut. If they get enough power, they're all murderers. Enough power they be mass murderers—and I'm talkin' the hundred sixty million. That's all politics is. They've set things up so that government works for them. That crap about of the people, by the people, and for the people—is just hustle.

"When we hate on the man, it's government that we be hating on! What do you do with those dudes, Mei-li? People who get their kicks from causing destruction all around them? People who control the government, an' make the laws, an' never get what's coming to them? Ain' no justice system! It's an injustice system, girl! Has the government ever provided you with any justice? The IRS would be bustin' your dad's store all up if he didn't pay them their protection money. They call it taxes. And they're supposed to be the ones protecting us? Nah. They're the criminals. Girl got to seek her own justice! Believe me, I been on the front lines. I been in the belly of the beast." It wasn't just talk.

Rainbow's torture at the hands of the SEA before Charles rescued her was burned in her psyche. Even though she was street smart from almost day one, she didn't understand how she could have been so stupid about the way things really worked—until they worked on her.

She wondered if telling her about that experience would help Mei-li put the Paladin operation in context. Even though people didn't like being abused, most accepted it as if they were cattle. Even those with genius-level IQs, like Mei-li, were entirely capable of acting like domestic farmyard animals, idling their way toward execution.

Rainbow said, "We have the right to kick the ass of anyone who threatens us or steals our stuff. I bet you can think of some situation where killing is just the thing to do."

Mei-li didn't hesitate. "I can."

"There you go. There aren't many people out there who can defend themselves. They're not able to because they're weak, or they're scared, or they're sick, or they're ignorant. Or they're afraid of five-oh, and they don' wanna get into the system, cuz they know it's dangerous and expensive and doesn't work. Those people gotta be able to hire a pro who can handle the situation for 'em."

Mei-li slowly replied, "And that can be through us. You're right." She nodded, again slowly. "But this will be illegal."

"Of course it will. Because the bad guys make the laws. They're a lot more dangerous than street thugs, and there's no protection from them. That's where most of our action will be."

Mei-li said, "Quis custodiet ipsos custodes?"

Rainbow smiled and replied, "Who watches the watchmen."

"We can be the ones to try."

Rainbow nodded. "Think of Yoda from Star Wars. He said, There is only 'Do or do not.' There is no try."

"Yeah," Mei-li replied. "If we're gonna be a real-life Justice League, then we can't screw it up."

Apolitical Man Bites Political Dog

"GRAYSON ... Grayson!" Steve Elias shouted to him from across the meeting room they'd rented in Georgetown. They had managed to gather teams from six national news outlets plus a couple of the local South Carolina television crews. Grayson Chase was the 714th person to file his papers as a candidate for president of the United States in the November election. All but a handful were essentially non-entities—tinfoil-hat wearers, deluded political activists, and publicity seekers.

It was June, and the major primaries and caucuses had already determined the Democratic and Republican candidates while entertaining the voters with Kabuki theater. Of course, President Cooligan—who, at 38 percent approval, had been one of the more popular presidents of recent years—represented the Demopublican Party. The Republicrats picked a well-heeled Washington swamp rat named Heather Lear, who surrounded herself with cronies from the same companies and lobby groups as did President Cooligan. The president's re-election prospects had declined to about fifty-fifty, in view of rising inflation, rising unemployment, weakening stock and real estate markets, unending foreign conflicts, a mismanaged viral epidemic, and the rapidly growing CityFire riots. And, of course, the ongoing impeachment hearings—the third of his term.

Impeachment was now thrown around like confetti. Because the Republicrats controlled only the House, it never led to conviction. The House used impeachment like the Senate used the filibuster. Every six months, the congressmen impeached the president and sent over new charges to tie up the

Senate. President Cooligan was probably guilty of some charges, but that wasn't the point. This wasn't an effort to seek truth, but a newly recognized parliamentary weapon, where everyone voted strictly according to party lines. All except the most naïve or stupid congressmen knew they were pots calling the kettle black.

Cooligan put on a bold front but was losing enthusiasm for the game. He was smart enough to see the trend, and it was pretty clear it was only going to accelerate during the next four years. Losing wasn't a bad option. It would allow him to capture his $100 million in the form of delayed paybacks for favors granted. Suitcases or steamer trunks full of $100 bills were only for Third World politicians; America was still a high-trust society. His corporate directorships, consulting contracts, sweetheart deals, six-figure speeches, and eight-figure book contracts awaited. He could look forward to the company of available young political groupies, especially while away from his wife.

Other than Cooligan's unspoken lack of enthusiasm, it was supposed to be the same as every prior presidential election: each side just hating the other's candidate slightly more than their own, with only the two candidates from which to choose.

Grayson had decided to throw a monkey wrench in the machinery of this business-as-usual cycle. So he now faced thirty or so media types. They came in hopes of reporting on something interesting, or at least embarrassing. Their chatter died down as Grayson raised his hand.

"Thank you for coming here tonight," he said. "My name is Grayson Chase. And I do not want to be the president of the United States. Questions?"

It took fifteen seconds before anyone could adequately process the statement. The local media had come tonight because they wondered what the quiet bachelor businessman, who was said to be wealthy, had on his mind. It would certainly be more interesting than reporting on a local traffic accident, or a meeting of the county commissioners. They sat, confused, after Grayson's statement.

The national media however had been prepped with selectively planted tips, to make them feel like insiders. They thought they knew more of what this was about. The CNN guy from Atlanta raised his hand first.

"Yes, Tom." Grayson had made a point of knowing the names of all the people in the room. He'd always been good with names.

"We understand that ten years ago you won the second-largest lottery jackpot in history. Is that true?"

"It is."

The local-news folk started jabbering. Everyone believed, mostly correctly, that only the desperate and destitute ever won the lottery. And they were usually back in their double-wides in a couple of years. Grayson, however, was known as a businessman with a reputation for doing what he said he was going to do. No one had suspected he was anything more than a well-off self-made man.

A bold local reporter didn't bother to raise her hand. She simply spoke out. "Are you the anonymous donor that gave the money to the Boys and Girls Club a few years ago?"

Grayson smiled. "Jennifer, whoever anonymously gave that money obviously wants to be anonymous. Who's got the next question?"

The CNN man followed with "So you won almost two billion and managed to keep it?"

Grayson replied, "Yes. It was only one billion after taxes, of course. I've succeeded in increasing that many times over. Ten years can do a lot of good for a portfolio."

"Even now, with the recession?"

"I got lucky winning the money in the first place, but I'd like to think there was at least some skill involved in growing it, and then not losing it in these past six months."

"And you said you don't want to be president."

"That's entirely true, Tom. I don't. Why would any sane person want to be president? To surround oneself with power-hungry sharks and piranhas? To socialize with socialists and sociopaths? The people who congregate in Washington are the kind of people a sensible person avoids at all costs. Sociopaths are drawn to Washington the same way gamblers are drawn to Las Vegas, surfers to Hawaii, or wannabe actors to Hollywood."

Fox News came next. "So what exactly are you announcing?"

"Kevin. Although I don't want to be president, I'm nonetheless announcing my candidacy for president of the United States. You've heard of a new party, the Jeffersonian Democratic-Republicans, that was formed last year and registered in all fifty states and DC. That, by the way, was the name of Thomas Jefferson's party. Call it the Jeffersonian Party for short, but the ballot will say Jeffersonian Democratic-Republican. Ten minutes ago, I sent text messages to all the field offices to begin open operations. We plan on a large media campaign to explain what we stand for and what we're going to do. The campaign website will be online after this conference. It's straightforward, simple, and clear on every position that I support. I believe you'll find the platform quite different from that of the other parties." Grayson pointed behind him. "The young folks in the back will provide you literature, links, contacts, and such."

A woman from ABC held up her hand.

Grayson nodded to her and said, "Jodi?"

"Why the timing of the announcement, so late in the game? Is it because of today's civil unrest?"

"No. Those people taking part in the riots are upset, just like I am. They're showing their displeasure with the state of affairs by being violent. I don't respect that. I'd like to show my displeasure by changing the conditions that are causing the riots. By the way, I'd ask that we all beware of hyperbole. Myself included. The cities haven't been burning, any more than the oceans have risen to submerge them. Some cars and some stores have burned. That's bad, but it isn't cities burning. Now, because the name City-Fire has been given to what's happening, or adopted by participants, it may prove a self-fulfilling prophecy. Let's hope not.

"To answer your question, I'd prefer to have announced my candidacy even later, after the other candidates have torn each other to pieces with ad hominem attacks. But it takes time to get a party on all the ballots, ramp up a campaign, and get name recognition. My team and I sat around a table many months back and decided today would be our launch day. It gives us just shy of five months to pull this off."

Kevin from Fox then asked, "What on earth makes you think you can win?"

"Four billion dollars is what makes me think I might win. That's much of my accumulated wealth. I'm putting it all on black and spinning the wheel, Kevin. It's twice what all the candidates together wasted in the last election, spewing nonsense and lying through their teeth when they swore to preserve, protect, and defend the Constitution of the United States. I ask you, when was the last time that a president abided by that oath? Maybe Coolidge, a century ago. But sure as hell not Cooligan or any other politician in this century. The other thing that makes me think there's a moderate chance of winning is that the two major parties have selected the standard hacks and swamp monsters to be their nominees. I mean, most people already dislike them both."

"Do you?"

"Dislike them? I dislike telemarketers or Nigerian princes who say they'll make you wealthy for a small fee. As for the candidates that the two-faces-of-the-same-coin party system has chosen for you? I don't know them and I don't want to know them. What I can say is that I don't want either of 'em as a ruler. They each want to be elected. In my view, wanting to be president should disqualify you from running. The more ardently someone wants to rule over others, the better the odds they're an idiot, a sociopath, or both."

"Which is why you said you don't want to be president."

"Partly. I wasn't kidding when I said I don't want to be president."

"Then why are you announcing your candidacy?"

"Because I'm a patriot. I love what America stands for—or at least used to stand for. I'm disappointed in the government and what it has done to America. The government has become a separate entity. Its interests are at odds with those of America; the interests of its employees are different from those of the American people."

"So you won the lottery and want to take the country back?"

"Let's say I'm investing my wealth to create more wealth. Freedom is worth a ton of money to me and almost every other American. I speak to those people who care about their freedom. I'm investing my wealth in you! If part of my wealth has a chance of digging us out of the hole that a century of craven politicians have put us in, then that's money well spent. That's what money's for. Nobody lives forever."

"But you'll still be just one man."

"Yeah. And the swamp is filled with snakes. I can be one man with a sharp veto pen. One man with a soapbox, a bully pulpit, as they say. I'm one man who can be counted on to do what he says he's going to do. One man who can't be bought by anyone because I've paid my own way, and I've got more money than they do. People now fear the government, every day, much, much more than they fear terrorists. It's time to change that, don't you think? And I don't mean we need to fear terrorists more. I mean we should never have to fear our own government. Look, government, and therefore politics, has stuck its nose into every aspect of American life. My job is to break that nose. One man can break a nose."

"But how are you different than other outside candidates before you?"

"Because of the money, of course. Billions of dollars can't buy an election if you're a jerk, but it can get attention if you're not. I have a ton of money, and I live cheap. I live on the same farm that I had before I won the lottery ten years ago. I don't need other people's money to get elected. All I need to do is convince the good people in America—regardless of their color, creed, or national origin—to kick off the shackles of their government. The Jeffersonian Democratic-Republican Party is our chance to fix it. If we don't fix it, those CityFire riots might merge with a whole lot of rational and irrational discontent and become a shooting war.

"My friends, our adversary is the government, with its tentacles wrapped around the country like a vampire squid. We're on the cusp of not just what I call the Greater Depression, but a lockdown police state. As the economy gets worse, the way the red counties and the blue counties hate each other now, we could be looking at something like a civil war. We need to take serious action to get back to our roots if we want to avoid these things. Here are seven key points.

"Point one. We need to allow the collapse of all zombie corporations—banks, brokers, insurers, and government contractors. The real wealth they supposedly own will still exist. It will just change ownership. The American people should no longer be forced to indulge politically connected fat cats.

"Point two. Abolish all regulatory agencies. I know you've been told they exist to protect you, and that may even have been an intention when they were created. But they now exist mainly to serve the industries they regulate. The FDA, for instance, kills more Americans every year than does the Department of Defense in a typical decade. The SEC, the Swindlers Encouragement Consortium, lulls the average investor into thinking he's protected. They and other agencies extract scores of billions out of the economy to feed useless mouths in return for throwing sand in the gears of the economy.

"Point three. Abolish the Federal Reserve. I know most people hardly know it even exists. It benefits the one percent that gets the money it creates first, before it loses value. You need a strong currency to encourage saving, so that your savings keep their value. Actually, you don't need an official currency at all. We used to use gold itself as everyday money. We should again.

"Point four. Cut the size of the military by eighty percent. And while we're at it, abolish the praetorian agencies like the CIA, the NSA, the FBI, the DEA, the SEA, and a bunch of others. In addition to bankrupting the

US, the military is now a huge domestic danger to us all and an instrument for creating enemies abroad.

"Point five. Sell essentially all US government assets. Some have real value, but they're all a drain on the economy and taxpayers. For instance, the Post Office loses five billion dollars a year, and Amtrak loses over a billion dollars. The interstate highway system, airports and the air traffic control system, the six hundred fifty million acres of USG land, and many thousands of other assets should all be distributed in shares to the citizens and operated privately for profit—or sold. This would liberate an immense amount of dead capital. The proceeds could be used to partially satisfy some government obligations.

"Point six. Eliminate the income tax, as a start, which will be possible if the other six things are done. The economy would boom and your lives would be a lot simpler.

"Point seven. Here's one that will shock you. Default on the national debt and contingent liabilities. That's somewhere between thirty and two hundred trillion dollars. The main reason is to avoid turning our younger generations into serfs, given that they are going to have to repay it. Nobody says this, but it's never going to be paid anyway. It's like a giant building that's about to collapse; it's better to bring it down in a controlled demolition than wait for it to collapse unexpectedly.

"Now I'm aware these things seem almost impossible. It's my intention to go as far and as fast toward all of them as we can. Thanks for your attention. I'll have a lot more to say in the months and years to come."

The next day, the campaign began in earnest. As Grayson had expected, there was hardly a mention from any of the national news outlets. It was the biggest man-bites-dog story of the decade. The journalists in attendance were anxious to air it, for that reason, but their editors generally spiked it.

In the past, that might have been the end of the story, but the internet was far more important than the mainstream media. Most people only watched the MSM in an idle moment; they bought the paper because they had a puppy or a parrot that needed a cage liner. But everyone was on the internet. News—true, false, and usually bad—spread like a firestorm through thousands of blogs, newsletters, podcasts, radio shows, video channels, and chat rooms. Three days later, the whole country was talking about Grayson Chase; twenty million had already subscribed to his online updates. His website registered thousands of new visitors per hour. Despite, or perhaps because of, the radical agenda that fit on neither the so-called Left or Right, the Jeffersonian Democratic-Republican Party was overnight being taken more seriously than any previous party that had tried to intrude on the Demopublicans and Republicrats. There was hope among many that this time there might actually be a choice.

It was a simple message. Peace and non-intervention abroad, economic and social liberty at home. Not everybody liked it, but it set him apart—that, and the fact that Grayson had never sought a public office and didn't align with either major party.

The media lapdogs would soon bark in fierce and incessant opposition, and charges of lunacy and psychosis would be hurled at him.

Grayson didn't want to do this, on so many levels.

Like flushing out a sewer, it was dirty work. But somebody had to do it.

*   *   *

The nighttime CityFire riots hadn't yet reached Chiang's neighborhood, so the store escaped looting—at least by mobs. Rainbow and Mei-li established their initial core of operations in its basement. The two girls raided Mei-li's father's inventory for many of the computer and telecom parts they needed, using the expense account of their new company, largely financed by Charles and Maurice—as well as Rainbow herself, who'd become surprisingly wealthy from distributing Sybillene when she was a kid and then getting involved in Bitcoin early on. Mei-li earned sweat equity. Orders for equipment bought by Chiang's Electronics garnered no particular attention from the authorities.

The girls shared a teenager's confidence that they'd conquer the world, which carried over to their view of cryptos. Even if the sector collapsed 99 percent along the way, they were confident it would re-emerge, leaner, meaner, and more ready for the future. There were thousands of cryptocurrencies, most of them rubbish. The victors in the unregulated race would be those with the most use value. The girls planned to be among the winners.

Mei-li lay on her back with a screwdriver gripped in her teeth, under a table, stuffing wires through slots she'd drilled in it. "Rainbow, grab them, will ya?" She didn't even know Charles existed. Nor did she need to know that Rainbow's mentor was the man who had taken out Jock and Freak. All the funding flowed through Rainbow. She was the firewall.

Five servers would soon be at work, the first of the sandbox nodes on the protocol that Mei-li had developed with input, editing, and proofing from her numerous coding friends on GitHub, none of whom knew who she was.

"Never, ever do we provide any hints as to who we are. We agreed?" Mei-li said to Rainbow, in the exact same words she'd used before.

"Never," Rainbow replied, without a hint of frustration upon hearing this for the umpteenth time. They would repeat this to each other every day, to engrain the thought. They were the anonymous heirs of the anonymous creator of Bitcoin: Satoshi Nakamoto.

Rainbow watched with admiration as her new friend and her virtual colleagues sorted through lines of code, combining features from the codebases of several systems—including Horizen's Zendoo and Decred—into two new Paladin blockchains running side by side. Decred provided a good model for how a network could evolve by users directing its growth. Monero's mixing provided anonymity. Horizen's Zendoo taught them how to add a third, and a hundredth, and a millionth parallel blockchain, increasing the number as demand required. The family of Paladin blockchains would communicate with each other in a system more akin to a matrix than the standard block-by-block linearity of a single chain. Bitcoin's slow transaction speeds would not be issues for Paladin.

They would confound metadata analysis by using mixnets and keep secrets using zero-knowledge proofs. They would have security and distributed governance. These models, as Mei-li knew, were good models for phyles in the blockchain universe.

Phyles were a concept coined by Neal Stephenson in his groundbreaking sci-fi novel The Diamond Age, contemplating a world where phyles largely replaced the nation-state and conventional political government. Using the internet, people from anywhere in the world could unite into voluntary organizations based on whatever is important to them—philosophy, religion, occupation, ethnicity, or any of a thousand things. The phyles, virtual and physical communities, would provide justice and security, replacing the most important functions of traditional political government.

Charles hadn't asked for all this new blockchain functionality. All he'd asked for was a unique combination of conditional anonymity and secure accountability. Accomplishing that proved challenging, not because parts hadn't been done before, but because it was hard to decide which systems for

accomplishing those things were best and how to put them together seam-
lessly. How could a balance be struck between ensuring anonymous transactions so that people could comfortably defy unjust government laws, while
holding individuals accountable for infracting natural law?

Various solutions were proposed and experimented with.

Mei-li asked Rainbow, "Only a couple more weeks of school for me this
year, then I can work on this twenty-four/seven. Don't you go to school?"

Rainbow replied with her usual toss-off line. "For sure. The school of
life. twenty-four/seven."

"Your family let you skip?"

"You know I don't have parents anymore," she replied. "My uncles not
only let me skip, but they pretty much insist on it. They aren't fans of school,
but they're big on study and learning. So am I."

"How many uncles you got?"

"Umm. At least three. I got people."

Mei-li probed, looking at Rainbow quizzically.

"A couple of 'em here in New York; others in DC."

"Right. That's where you're from."

"It was. Home now is wherever I am. I've been mostly in New York for
going on two years. How about you? Heading off to college?"

Mei-li replied, "If my father has his way, yeah. He thinks it's how
you climb the ladder, get a good job. But I don't want to be somebody's
employee. And if I take out student loans, I'll just be in debt. I suppose I
could get a scholarship, but what's the point? I grew up programming. I
don't need to spend four years distracting myself from what I want to do. I
don't need to pay a fortune to drink and party."

The thoughts seemed to get her rather worked up. Was it a psychological or a physical reaction? When Mei-li got hungry, she became testy. Rainbow learned when to drag her out of the basement tech room to hit the
Peruvian fusion place they favored. During the better part of a month, the
two spent much of their time together.

Rainbow made her first real friend of her own age.

Mei-li built the protocol and the apps. Rainbow, with the still-anon-
ymous help of Charles and Maurice, prepared for the launch of the Paladin Token, which meant marketing. Rainbow built the token launch
website, PaladinNetwork.io, and drafted instructions for how to mine the
cryptocurrency. The various efforts she undertook morphed into a white

paper—the standard format by which information is disseminated prior to a crypto token launch. She made connections within crypto exchanges and added up the money required to get Paladin listed on some of the better ones so that Paladin Token holders could trade them for other currencies as well as fiat US dollars.

The Paladin Network, a self-improving ecosystem, was born. It would act as a platform, a marketplace, to neutralize all sorts of destructive influences in the world. The next problem would be defining exactly what those might be.

15

The 4th Floor

THE north elevator in the expansive Upper East Side townhouse had no buttons for its first three floors. The 4th Floor, as it was known, required a key that Forestal kept in his pocket. The floor held several sitting rooms of various sizes, two private conference rooms, and a central hall with a café-style eating area supported by a chef and two waiters. Forestal sat alone at a table in the café, sipping a glass of wine. He wasn't alone because he was a naïve schoolboy, afraid to ask a girl to dance. It was because he knew the value of quiet observation.

He should have felt privileged to be among a group of men and women who influenced the course of world events. Forestal considered it his right. Sabina Heidel—his nemesis as well as a most enjoyable sexual partner—was absent. She was by far the youngest member, which was testimony to her talents and her connections.

The usual visitors here weren't circumscribed by any ethos that limited normal people. They were highly intelligent, well informed and well traveled, and capable of being quite charming. If their social veneer was washed away, however, a keen observer would discern their vicious natures through layers of petulance, arrogance, and snark. Keen observers were rare, as Forestal could well attest.

He looked around at the scattered tables of people in the room. They were capable of forming friendships of a sort, although entirely based on utility—or pleasure, like his with Sabina. Here, friendship without an agenda was as rare as a wolf loving a fox or a lion loving a hyena. They inquired as to each other's health, but only to pick up some hint of weakness: secrets were a reserve of ammunition to be used at a vulnerable moment. They postured, manipulated, and positioned. Forestal suspected that they behaved more civilly here with each other than they did with their spouses, children, or employees, whom they could bully and dominate. In this place, with their peers, they wore a cordial veneer with only the occasional outburst. The psychological menu in the café area consisted of a plateful of covert hostility with a dash of jealousy, a heaping pile of ego, and a dusting of fear.

A few people had filtration masks to keep the viruses at bay, even if it amounted to using a chain-link fence to protect from mosquitoes. The paranoia had settled now to a low-grade caution and perhaps a fashion statement. Progressives tended to wear masks more often than conservatives, the same way they drove Volvos. Maybe it was to keep the fear in the forefront. Fear allowed for easier control. Or maybe they just read the most inflammatory headlines, which for many months would report every sneeze as the herald of Armageddon.

The 4th Floor was no Bilderberg Group or secret society; there was no agenda for discussion. Rather, this was just the fourth floor of a particularly influential man's private home, to which he routinely invited people to meet each other and see what might result. Some came to maintain the status quo. Others came to change it radically. In both cases, it was to maximize their profits, make deals where they could, and find alliances where needed. The deals, mergers, and other relationships that originated here often involved billions of dollars.

Many considered New York City the center of the world, with its financial organs pumping dollars into the US economy, and indeed the world economy. The 4th Floor was its heart. Only the rich, the powerful—and those who soon would be—ever received an invitation to the 4th Floor. The phrase "4th Floor" implied a deal in the making.

These people attended Council on Foreign Relations conferences, showed up at special meetings of the United Nations, and gave opening statements at the World Economic Forum in Davos. That sort of thing was good PR, but it was on the 4th Floor that they had potential for real impact.

The owner called the shots. His father and grandfather had lived here before him and hosted similar gatherings over the decades, although much more sporadically. Conspiracy theorists might overestimate the intrigue, collusion, and scheming in such gatherings, while underestimating the effects of simple and often spontaneous conversations. The owner was a catalyst, and the 4th Floor a beaker to bring molecules together. With the chemical-activation energy lowered by liquor and cordial conversation, the molecules reacted to create new compounds. Although most commonly nothing consequential occurred, sometimes a reaction would release substantial energy.

Their host was always the first to know where that energy would flow. It helped the man—now in his seventies—control and grow his truly immense wealth in securities and real estate. He controlled even more wealth in the form of power and influence.

Even so, he was not the wealthiest man here this evening. Forestal believed that honor belonged to a second elderly man who alone was worth more than some medium-sized countries. He had a stubbly gray beard; his remaining silver hair lay unkempt. He wore cheap plastic glasses, with smudged lenses. His perfectly pressed suit, at odds with the rest of his appearance, was evidence that he had an attentive valet, but it couldn't disguise the fact that he hadn't bathed today, or perhaps for several days.

He too was seated alone in the café.

Forestal's phone buzzed. He pulled it out, didn't recognize the number for the twelfth time today, and dismissed it. Telemarketers. Some bureaucrats imagined themselves coming to the rescue by banning and regulating these spam callers. Not Forestal. Instead, he envisioned buying one of their sweatshops in India or Manila and profiting from whatever fraud they were peddling.

Several well-known politicians had deployed themselves about the 4th Floor. There once was a time when the politicians had been lead actors on center stage that held direct control of the government, and therefore a legal right to compel anyone to do almost anything. Corporate executives competed for their favor. Now the unofficial fourth branch of government—the bureaucracy run by appointed functionaries such as Forestal—enjoyed most of the direct power. Politicians mostly busied themselves raising funds, seeking re-election, and heating the air in committee meetings. Becoming a powerful member of the fourth branch was a good stepping stone to the 4th Floor.

Forestal wondered if the man currently reputed to be the wealthiest in the world stopped by here from time to time. He'd never met, or even seen, him. The multibillionaire had two headquarters: one in Manhattan, the locus of financial power; the other just outside Washington, DC, the locus of political power. Money and power had worked together not just since the days of Rome, but likely the dawn of civilization. Anyone who'd created an empire would want to protect it by embedding himself in these two cities. He'd also want an early-warning system as to which way the winds might blow. The 4th Floor was like a political weather satellite for the world's oligarchs.

"Blaize Forestal. It's been too long since I've seen you in person. It's good to again have you here as my guest." His host took a seat before Forestal could rise to greet him.

Forestal smiled faintly and reached out a hand to the demigod. "As always, it is my honor to be here in your home, Mr. Samuels."

16

Situational Awareness

CHARLES walked past the townhome without glancing up at the windows. He knew Paul Samuels lived there and that—as evidenced by the contingent of burly security guards—Samuels now feared for his life even in his own home. But he knew nothing of its 4th Floor.

The morning air refreshed Charles, helping him overcome a lack of sleep. The northern hemisphere floated through its summer solstice today. Soon heat would rise in waves off the streets and sidewalks.

Constant situational awareness had kept Charles alive despite multiple attempts to kill him during his prison stint. It might be even more important here, where there was a natural tendency to relax. An attack from a tattooed and hoodied hoodlum wasn't the most likely risk on this fabulously wealthy Upper East Side street. The danger would come from someone who fit in and looked harmless.

For practice, he kept an eye on the cars with windows rolled down and nearby buildings with open windows. He watched out for police and how others reacted to them. People who seemed to fear or avoid the police might be dangerous—or, potentially, future colleagues. Many people wore breathing masks or scarfs when they were out and about. What would in the past have raised suspicion had become an accepted norm, and even politically correct. On the one hand, it made it difficult for Charles to identify subtle hints of impending aggression in a passerby. On the other hand, combined with large dark sunglasses and a brimmed hat, the now-accepted face scarf provided excellent protection from the prying eyes of security cameras. That could come in handy, turning a nuisance into a convenience.

Observation was a learned competence like any other; it required thoughtfulness and practice. It was a survival skill from the dawn of history. If you lacked situational awareness and didn't see a predator, you were easy prey and likely to die quickly. Or, if you were the predator and didn't find prey, you died slowly. Civilization had dulled the skill in humans. Charles watched the people on the street and noted how most eyes of all ages focused on smartphones while earbuds filled the ears of the younger ones. Each lived in a bubble of his own creation. Perhaps they'd increase their engagement with their surroundings if a CityFire mob started rolling up the street.

Staying constantly on alert exhausts anyone who tries it. It drains energy and takes intense focus. It made Charles feel like he was back in the pen. He worked on structuring his reactions in advance, so as to not always be on a hair trigger.

As someone who might be the object of unwanted attention or aggression at any minute, he tried to keep the color codes of the famous shootist Jeff Cooper in his mind—white, yellow, orange, and red. Most relevant in an actively hostile environment such as a prison, they also applied in the streets of New York.

He could only be in white—relaxed—when things were as safe as they could get.

Outside, on the street or in a shop, he should automatically enter yellow: relaxed but aware of others around and where the exits might be.

If he saw something that got his attention, something that might or might not be a threat but was worth focusing on, he went to orange.

From there things had to clarify. Either move back to yellow or escalate to red: what a security maven might term a clear and present danger. He'd then decide whether fight or flight was the correct—or needed—response and how to play out either scenario. When things went bad, a second or two of advance planning could prove critical.

In prison, flight was a non-option. In the first place, there was nowhere to run to. In the second place, a runner was a chicken and permanently marked as prey. Trying to talk an opponent down was suspect and usually futile. Fighting was necessary.

Back in the real world, however, fighting was always the last alternative. If you lost the fight, it might mean a permanent injury. If you won, the other guy might be severely injured or killed, while the damage to yourself from subsequent police involvement, the criminal courts, and maybe a civil suit could be just as nasty.

For even an expert fighter, flight was by far the preferred choice on the street. Given Charles's compromised legal status, compounded by the fact that he committed a felony every day now simply by carrying a concealed weapon in New York, flight was the only rational choice.

He couldn't afford to be just another city dweller, mind preoccupied with work and play, only a fraction left over for threat awareness. Even though it was barely summer now... winter is coming. Charles knew this was more than the ominous catch phrase of a popular TV drama.

He walked miles each day because he had been unable to for so long. Despite himself, he regularly slipped into distracted contemplation as he traversed the city's streets. In prison, he had no obligations and few ambitions, apart from staying alive and sane. Out here a thousand things intruded on his mind and broke his concentration. The color code system usually lingered in the back of his mind instead of at the front where it belonged.

He'd started frequenting one particularly comfortable coffee shop where cameras didn't peer from the ceiling, the furniture was overstuffed, and the baristas were pleasant. Its ambiance attracted at least superficially likable types. Nothing like the jailbirds he'd come to know.

He practiced his observation skills as he stood in line with the other customers. A young woman who entered just after him caught his eye. She was good looking and projected a certain confidence. He recalled seeing her on the street several minutes earlier, and he was pleased she'd come into the place. She stood in line behind him, caught him looking at her, and glanced away. Then she looked up and held his gaze.

Pumpkin-spiced lattes, frappuccinos, decaf espressos with a twist. Old-timers were nostalgic about the days when ten cents got you a bottomless cup in any diner.

Charles studied the menu above the bar more intently. Coffee house terminology: the only foreign language most Americans ever learned. His situational awareness and observation practice faltered as his mind wandered to languages. Soon all tongues would be translated real-time into an earpiece— the embodiment of the galactic hitchhiker's babelfish—making the onerous study of foreign languages unnecessary. Of course true fluency—allowing a speaker to grasp all the idioms and subtleties—would retain value in the same way an ability to read body language would always provide an edge in negotiations, but for the great majority, language education in high school would soon be just another academic exercise. Few students retained more than a smattering of phrases after scores of hours sitting at a desk while a teacher droned on incomprehensibly in foreign words until the bell rang, so they could be herded off to the next class like a flock of sheep to be pulled, wooled, and culled.

That train of thought was leading him to a gloomy state of mind when the girl behind him in line met his gaze again with a smile. She seemed to smile a lot, rather like he used to do.

He paid, settled down on an old brown leather sofa, and started reading one of the newspapers on the appropriately named coffee table in front of him. He'd been advised by the warden in Illinois to avoid reading newspapers. Yet here he was, little more than two months later, stultifying his brain with one.

Scanning through it, he saw that the new presidential candidate, Grayson Chase, had made unexpected waves during the ten days since his announcement, as had his Jeffersonian Democratic-Republican Party. On election day, the Jeffersonian part of its name might attract some traditionalists. Plus it confused people who thought it might be a happy compromise. Did today's American have a clue what Jefferson stood for? If they really believed in anything—which was unlikely—it was more likely to be Lincolnian, Wilsonian, Rooseveltian, or even Johnsonian ideals. All of which were antithetical to Jefferson's.

The Democratic-Republican part of the moniker caught his attention. Could that possibly stand for anything? If Grayson Chase was a typical politician, he'd just take the worst—but predictably the most popular—tenets of both parties and meld them together: the welfare-state programs of the one, and the warfare-state programs of the other. Charles could hardly remember which party most supported which statist program. They both advanced it all, just with different rhetoric.

True, most overt socialists, progressives, and globalists were Democrats, and most conservatives and nationalists were Republicans. They were all just cattle as far as the leadership was concerned. The Democrats were feed-lot cattle, and the Republicans free-range cattle. They were all headed to the same packing plant.

Maybe this new party would mimic the Progressive Conservative Party of Canada, named after two opposites in a vain hope to please everyone. What had Lincoln said? You can fool most of the people most of the time, but we won't be fooled again? Or was that the Baby Bush? No matter. Charles's signature smile lit up.

But then maybe Grayson Chase was not the typical politician.

The Times seemed unsure what to make of Grayson Chase. Its usual political bias seemed absent from the story. The writers and editors presented him neutrally. Was that because Chase was neutral, like beige cloth? Charles didn't care for politics and politicians. However, the man's picture caught his eye. He was strikingly handsome, which usually helped in elections as in every other aspect of life. But he was probably just another megalomaniac.

He flipped through the pages and found that the attempted assassination of Samuels, now six weeks ago, had made the news again, albeit on an interior page. The FBI apparently concluded that the shot fired at Samuels had been a hunting accident and the perpetrator probably wasn't even aware of the furor he'd caused. After all, the slug found embedded in the base of a tree twenty-five yards beyond the tee box belonged to a typical hunting rifle. The conclusion was logical, although based on nothing solid. It went on to say Samuels was a pillar of the community who gave generously to charities and was well respected by his colleagues in the economics profession. Who would intentionally try to kill him?

Of course the story was transparently bogus. Charles chuckled. An assassin would use exactly the same ammunition as a hunter. The shooting episode had occurred months after the deer season had ended, so hunters would only have been shooting at varmints. And for varmints, a .300 Magnum would be egregious overkill for even the largest coyote, but then Paul Samuels was a very big varmint. The news story was either an intentional misdirection by the FBI or an example of journalistic incompetence. Maybe both.

Another headline stood out. Despite the government's huge ethanol subsidies, a small farmer in North Dakota had switched from corn to a crop that didn't meet with Department of Agriculture approval: hemp. Even after the broad popular acceptance of hemp and cannabis and the federal legalization of hemp, there were still bureaucratic restrictions that attracted the attention of agents interested in taking a scalp. This farm's hemp apparently contained 0.4 percent THC—a tiny fraction above the legal limit of

0.3 percent. So armed federal agents raided the farm, burned the offending crops, and threatened the owner with jail and fines. More disturbing, Social Services, noting the farmer was involved in a major drug enterprise, took his grandchildren "for their protection." Their parents had been killed years earlier in a car accident.

Who would imagine that the Department of Agriculture had the power to burn crops and kidnap children? Weren't they supposed to help farmers? It sounded more like Ukraine in the '30s than Little House on the Prairie or The Waltons.

The unfortunate event might, however, prove synergistic. The farmer clearly needed help. Some well-publicized righteous vigilante justice could be just the ticket to kick off the Paladin Crypto Network's marketing campaign. He smiled at the irony of finding himself in a updated episode of Have Gun—Will Travel. The show usually started with Paladin reading the paper in the lobby of San Francisco's Hotel Carlton, alerted to a citizen somewhere with a problem in need of a solution. Paladin then mailed the article to the beleaguered victim in an envelope with his card. And so the adventure began.

Charles fiddled with one of the one-ounce silver coins that Rainbow had commissioned and had minted for him using some Etsy craftsman. She'd paid for it with Bitcoin through a Samurai wallet with two mixing runs, and she'd had them delivered to a fake-name mailbox at a shipping store. As a long-time street kid who knew how investigators worked, Rainbow covered all the security bases. The coins were very expensive calling cards that ensured the recipient would pay attention. What was a few thousand dollars when many millions were in play?

The Paladin symbol stood out in deep relief on one side—the knight from a chess set with the name PALADIN curving along the top. On the other side were emblazoned the words Have Gun—Will Travel. He had several with him, each individually wrapped in plastic.

Charles opened his computer, connected via VPN and Tor Browser, found the Times article online, and sent the link to his uncle via the Cryptohippie darknet. Twenty minutes later, he had an address for the farmer in question; Maurice must have gotten a good night's sleep to have responded so quickly. Charles put on a pair of thin leather gloves, removed a stamped envelope from a plastic sleeve in his pocket, and borrowed a pen from a barista. He carefully addressed the envelope and prepared a Have Gun—Will

Travel business card with an encrypted email-service address that would only be used once and that would be forwarded through multiple free email services to its final email address. Charles would check it in a week, again using an untraceable Tor Browser through a VPN from a free Wi-Fi connection at some random hotel lobby. He placed the card and the coin—no longer in its plastic in the envelope—sealed it, and put it in his pocket.

Rainbow had become adept in anonymous communication during her time as a Naked Emperor distributor. She kept improving her skills while Charles lingered in prison, and she now advised him how to keep his communications reasonably untraceable. Reasonably was the operative word, and the best he could expect in a world where privacy really no longer existed.

He placed the borrowed pen on the counter and returned to his seat. The pretty girl had settled into a corner against the front window, and she glanced at him again. He smiled at her, and she smiled back. Attractive, certainly, but not exotic. A wholesome-apple-pie sort of American girl who'd probably played soccer in school.

She walked over to the sofa and sat next to him.

Raising his eyebrows, he said, "Hello, I'm Charles."

"I'm Emily."

Charles nodded, folded his newspaper, and directed his attention to Emily. Not all, but most of it. During the next hour that they sat together and talked, he had trouble maintaining proper situational awareness.

* * *

Most people came into coffee shops as zombies and seemed to stay that way even after dosing themselves with some expensive concoction. People seemed to like sugar, milk, and flavorings more than coffee itself. There remained only a hint that a coffee bean, probably decaffeinated, once might have bounced into and back out of the cup. Emily ventured that Americans patronized coffee shops because they amounted to informal clubs, relatively quiet places where you could sit in a comfortable chair for as long as you liked and read a paper. Instead of paying an annual membership in a private club, they paid ten dollars for a warm brew, a soft perch, and a low table.

Few read books here; they seemed concerned only with the news and popular trivia. Perhaps that contributed to Emily Renner's continuous low-grade sense that things were going wrong with the world, a sense that had appeared long before this CityFire movement had started turning recession and frustration over perceived injustices into destructive riots. Maybe the world had always been this way. Even though she wasn't a reader of classical history, she easily recognized the similarities between America and Rome in the days of the Gracchi brothers, Marius, and Sulla, when the constitution was adjudicated by mobs in the street.

Emily once had a boyfriend, years before, who was anything but a zombie. He was fit, alert, and embodied competence. He had plenty of virtues and only a few vices; otherwise he could never have worked with her father. They hadn't been together long enough for the relationship to tolerate an enforced separation of six years, which is what the criminal-justice system had sentenced her to. She'd heard from her father that her once boyfriend dropped off the map after that. But now he was back, mostly here in New York City. He had his own life, a new significant other, and was doing exactly what he and her father had so often dreamed about. She was happy for him. Losing him was bad, but not the worst thing that had happened to her.

Her mistakes were legion during the subsequent years, but she'd survived her sentence at Singer Jail on Rikers Island—a place notorious for prison abuse. Like most convicts, she preferred not talking about it. Protesting her innocence was not only pointless, but counterproductive. It was safer to be known as an attempted murderess, which is what they'd sentenced her for.

In the criminal-justice system, there was precious little justice.

She did her full bit. No early release for good behavior, despite the squalid conditions and judicial injunctions for the state to clean up and clean out Rikers. She should have expected nothing less since the blind eye of justice was wide open for her case. Justice saw that the district attorney was a buddy of the asshole that she'd shot. And the asshole that she'd shot was pretty damn powerful in his own right. Lady Justice—if she knew what was good for her—stayed on the side of the rich and well connected.

If a bright side could be found, it was that serving the full term left her with no probation after release. She was a free woman, although she couldn't vote. Not that it mattered; her vote, like anybody's, counted about as much as a single grain of sand on a beach. Although, from what she'd learned, Grayson Chase seemed worth voting for.

For the last few years, as a fully free woman, she'd worked with her father as they traveled the world, always maintaining some vain hope of finding his long-missing daughter... Emily's younger sister. Somewhere during those years, she'd finally abandoned her dream of medical school, which had long motivated her. Well, at least before that animal had tried to rape her for a second time and she'd put a hole in him. She should have emptied the chamber.

She'd recently come back to New York while her father took some time off in paradise. She'd once found the city life exciting. With no job to go to and a lingering empty space in her heart, she'd contacted her old boyfriend. They'd met and talked about life, and, the next day, he called with a proposition that offered some excitement, even some meaning.

He'd given her this work, which was kind. She preferred being active.

It wasn't like she was new to the world of discreetly spying on people, but she wasn't particularly fond of it, and she told him as much. As questionable as the morality of spying might be, hopefully the worst downside was an end to her usefulness if she was spotted.

The target was Charles Knight. The mission was to follow him around, see what he did, where he hung out. News of his testimony in front of Congress and his sentencing and imprisonment hadn't made it to Southeast Asia or New Zealand where she and her dad had spent much of the last few years. So she knew of him mostly from what she'd learned researching him in the last few days.

Perhaps the fact that Knight had only recently been released from prison explained why he noticed her.

She'd hoped he would just stare at the menu above the counter with a coffee-and-sugar addict's zombie eyes. That would allow her to move inconspicuously to an unobtrusive place to observe him. But once they'd locked eyes, she figured she'd be useless for any further spying. She'd stick out if they walked past each other again. He'd know her face. So she might as well go back to the apartment she'd been bunking down at. Excitement over.

But maybe there was a way to rescue the situation. So she'd smiled at him in line soon sat next to him on the sofa. There was nothing to lose.

There are moments in life when you connect with another person and know that person is important to you. Some call it synchronicity: a melding of personal energies. Some believe they see an aura. Some can pick up on subtle facial expressions, body language, and voice tones. Maybe it was just pheromones—nothing mystical about it, just a biological invention to ensure propagation of the species.

Emily studied Charles, associating the intensity in his eyes and his flashes of good humor with trustworthiness. Perhaps it was his similarity to her father too. He bore a passing resemblance to him physically, but it was more his attitude that made them appear alike. She inhaled deeply through her nose, no doubt filling her lungs with his pheromones, which, after an extended period in prison, flowed out of him in high concentrations. Emily felt a strong animal, biological, attraction to him.

Knowing full well that these things were just evolution successfully manipulating her physiology, she pushed the sensations aside as best as she could. There was work to do.

After their initial and brief exchange of names, neither had said anything for several moments, but it didn't feel awkward. She spoke next.

"Sorry to intrude. You looked like you might consider some company." Then she wondered if that sounded like a hooker's pickup line.

"Kind of you to notice that. Yes, I could use some company, Emily." He pushed the newspaper across the table with his hand and turned so he could see her comfortably, without straining his neck.

Emily got up and moved to the chair adjacent to him to make it easier to talk.

"That's better, isn't it?"

"Better on the neck, yes. Thanks again."

"You don't object to not social distancing?"

"I've had more than enough social distancing lately," he replied. "Where do we start? With our favorite signs and colors?"

"How about our favorite countries?" She told him about her travels over the past few years. He told her about his own. They'd visited the same islands, although his visits were some years earlier than hers. They recalled some of the same bars, hotels, and marinas. Not a lot changed in the islands over half a decade, but much changed in Singapore, Hong Kong, Shanghai, and Bangkok; those cities seemed to reinvent themselves continually. They talked for an hour that flew by.

"This has been great, Emily. Want to get together again?"

She nodded and smiled. "Here's my number." She took a pen from her purse and wrote it on a napkin.

"Do you like to walk?"

"Very much," she said, smiling at him.

She guessed that he couldn't help but smile back at her again.

And she was right.

She liked his smile.

They agreed to meet at 6:00 p.m.

What was supposed to be discreet and distant observation had become, by accident, a first step into Charles Knight's world. It had been a great deal easier than she'd planned. Except that she hadn't planned it at all.

She hoped Jeffrey wouldn't mind how things were developing.

*　　*　　*

Charles left the coffee shop on a high that had nothing to do with caffeine. He knew many women. One whom he had met in his year before prison was stunning—statuesque, gilded, well spoken, and intelligent—but lacking both judgment and a real moral compass. Unlike Emily, Tristana hadn't glowed with a kind of internal light. Emily exuded something Charles craved, beyond sexual attraction and the mating instinct. He couldn't put his finger exactly on the way he felt, but it felt very good.

He felt almost human again.

17

Bad Luck and Lies

EMILY'S green eyes turned blue when she was sad.

Charles first noticed this when she looked up at him as they strolled along the High Line—the park-like elevated walkway along old train tracks that meanders through the buildings of Manhattan between the Meatpacking District and 34th Street.

They took a small table at a neighborhood café. A homey place that had managed to survive the virus hysteria, it was not part of a giant national franchise with plastic furniture and food shipped in from a processing facility in Kansas. Emily leaned on the checkered tablecloth as she told him about her grandfather's death when she was six. Those eyes turned blue again when she talked about her mother, who had died when she was fifteen. Then, green again, her eyes smiled as she spoke of her eighty-four-year-old grandmother, who was still full of life and rebellion, and of her father.

"Yeah, Dad and I were always a team. Still are, really. But he likes the islands. I wanted to see New York in a new light."

"Why a new light?" asked Charles.

She paused and frowned. Then she said, "Damn."

Charles looked at her quizzically.

"I don't like talking about it. But you might understand."

"Okay." Charles's sensors lit up with the prospect of hearing something that was not just amusing or interesting, but meaningful—and perhaps unwelcome.

She said, "For six years, the only lights from New York that I saw were over or through the walls around Rikers Island. I got out four years ago, then I went off traveling the world with my dad. I didn't want to come back to the US for a very long time, if ever."

A hundred thoughts flashed through Charles's mind. Maybe she was a hooker after all? But what kind of a hooker gets a six-year stretch? Or has a loving relationship with her father? His heart sped up; warning lights flashed in his mind. Was she setting him up with an elaborate lie? But he'd need to stay cool. After all, his own experience with the so-called criminal-justice system would hardly reassure most women.

He wouldn't draw any conclusions just yet.

"It's hard to talk about, but you might as well hear it."

He looked at her sympathetically. "There are eight million stories in the Naked City. What were you in for?"

She shrugged and pursed her lips, then smiled, but not nervously. "Attempted murder."

"Oh. One of the real offenses," Charles said, still reserving judgment. He wasn't yet sure if her mistake was getting railroaded, attempting the murder, or failing to accomplish it. Her reasons for it, and the circumstances, were likely more important than the act itself. "Did you do it?"

"No. It was a bum rap. I mean, yes, I did try to kill the guy. One hundred percent self-defense. It wasn't premeditated, so, despite what they called it, it wasn't attempted murder... even though planning to kill that bastard would have been the right thing to do. I mean, why is it wrong to plan something out, if the same thing would be excusable on the spur of the moment? Only thing I feel guilty about is just wounding him. If he'd died on the spot, I would have gotten off and he wouldn't still be out there hurting people. Because he survived, he was able to turn the whole thing on its head."

She scored points for being thoughtful. Charles certainly couldn't find fault with anything she'd said so far, but knowing what prison could do, caution was advisable. It was hard to avoid picking up bad habits in the joint. Men often assumed that a woman with a sweet-looking face also had a sweet disposition. But that same woman could be a very attractive homicidal maniac.

She went on. "About ten years ago, right out of college, I was working on Wall Street. I'd studied biology and ended up analyzing biotech stocks. I was trying to earn some serious money on the way to medical school."

"Are you a doctor?"

"That dream got sidelined, Charles. By what I'm about to tell you. The big boss was a lecher. There were rumors. He noticed me one day and got this leer in his eye. I figured that meant trouble. What it meant was two weeks of hell until I quit."

"That was wise," Charles replied. "The best way to avoid trouble is to avoid bad people like poison, because they are poison. That goes double for bad bosses."

"For sure. He dug up my address from HR and showed up on my doorstep before midnight one night with flowers and asked to come in. Wanted to apologize, he said. I didn't go for that; I told him to go home, closed the door. The next evening, he must have been waiting. He grabbed me, threw me up against the wall in the alley, and tried to rape me. I slammed my knee in his groin, got away, and went straight to the police. Spent all night there. They collected evidence from my clothing and took pictures. They checked out my building. They reached out to the asshole and interviewed him. He denied being anywhere near me, and there was no real proof. They told me to go home and lock the doors. I asked for a restraining order, but they're hard to get and pretty much pointless, or so the cops said."

"Probably right about that. So what did you do?"

"I didn't trust the cops to protect me, so I borrowed a gun from my dad and kept it with me. The jerk must have been stalking me. He tried exactly the same trick in the same alley a week later. I pushed him away and pulled my gun out. He had this grotesque laugh, mocking me, like he didn't take me seriously. He lunged at me. I put a bullet in his chest."

"Sounds like self-defense."

"Except that the district attorney for Manhattan was the creep's good buddy. And he was rich and connected far deeper than that. My lawyer said no one would take the guy on; they all close ranks around each other. The assistant DAs would be risking their jobs, and there's nothing in it for the police when they know the DA isn't going to prosecute. The newspapers reported him as the victim! They said I was a disgruntled employee with a history of mental instability who'd been stalking him."

"True?"

"No! Not in the least. I've always been sane. Mostly—although things like this should drive anybody crazy. So it turns out he'd reported me to the police and filed for a restraining order against me. He was smart, thought ahead; I was just a kid."

"Where was your dad while this is going on? I thought you were tight with him?"

"I'll get to that … The DA's office offered me a deal, which I turned down flat, to the dismay of my attorney. He warned me. But I wasn't going to be one of the ninety-five percent of cases that get plea-bargained. I'd saved some money, I was innocent, and I didn't want a felony on my record. Seemed right, seemed smart. But it was stupid. Innocence had nothing to do with it. I got five years for attempted murder and another year for the handgun violation. It's illegal to defend yourself in this city."

Understanding that she'd spent time in jail helped him connect to her, as much as the conversation itself. Charles knew firsthand that stories like hers happened every day, but how could he know it was all true? As bad as the justice system might be, most of the people in jail belonged there.

There was no way he would get involved with this woman without more information. Her story might only intersect loosely with reality, a fiction concocted during years in jail to help her cope with guilt or keep her ego intact. Perhaps the scales of justice had gotten this one right, and she was living in a dream world of deceit and delusion, two d-words that would obviate any interest he might have in her. How could he know the truth? Anyone could lie. Some people were skilled and enthusiastic liars.

"What's the jerk's name?" Charles asked.

She sighed. "I don't like even thinking of it. His name is Blaize Forestal. There's no way I can touch him. The guy's now some bigwig at the Justice Department, of all places."

Charles studied her face. What enticed him about this girl? She was thoughtful, intelligent, affable, and independent, but were those attributes just a good overlay on an otherwise-vile character? He required good character in his male friends; that was what the Romans termed a sine qua non—without which there is nothing. A bad character was like a rotten foundation in a beautiful building. It didn't matter how elegant the lines, how large, how expensive, or how well finished it might be. If the foundation was rotten, the whole thing would collapse, disastrously.

That was the problem. Beauty was a great disguise—especially effective against a guy fresh out of prison who was just beginning to feel human again. Although nice while it lasted, beauty wasn't necessary. Everyone's youthful good looks disappear in time. If a person had a good character, though, her wisdom and kindness would endure.

He knew the long-term enforced celibacy might be clouding his thinking. She was female, attractive, and here. He'd spent quite enough time alone in a cell and too much time in the company of people he actively disliked.

She said, "And my sentence? It wasn't the worst part."

"What was worse?"

Emily looked down at her lap, looking as if she was choking off a tear. She said in a muted voice, "My mother died when I was young, so it was just Dad, my little sister, and me. When my defense attorney started going after Forestal—investigating him—next thing that happens is my dad's getting investigated for made-up crimes. That prick DA friend of Forestal's sticks him in jail with no bail. Anna—that's my sister—gets taken by Child Protective Services. She was only fourteen. So I'm stuck at Rikers. Dad's in a holding cell. Then my sister disappeared from CPS. Gone. No one knew where. CPS said she ran away. Maybe. Maybe kidnapped, killed, we've never found out. Dad, he was devastated. Furious. But he was stuck in jail until the DA dropped the fake charges on him after a few months. They threatened to raise the charges again if he went after CPS. He was obsessed with finding her, of course. Spent years traveling, following hunches looking for Anna. No leads. Nothing. The police were useless. Written off as a runaway. Just another of thousands of kids who are lucky if they even get their picture on a milk carton. All his fears as a parent, a father, came to life as he was unable to protect either of his daughters. He had this overwhelming feeling of powerlessness."

"I'm so sorry, Emily."

"He's recovered some. So have I. Mostly."

Charles nodded slowly. "What do you want now, Emily?"

She scrutinized his face. Her own face became firm, committed, certain.

"I want to live the way I want to live. Away from nasty, evil people. Is that too much to ask?"

"Alone?" Charles probed.

"I'm fine alone. We're born alone and die alone. There's not much we can do about that." Her eyes shone intently. "But we don't necessarily have to live alone. If there were someone I could be with, who had his own life, that would be better. But he's got to be an intellectual equal. And share my values. We could live, you know, parallel lives, doing our things and traveling along the road of life." She looked straight into his eyes. "I came close once, briefly. He raised my expectations of what's possible."

"Well, that's intimidating," replied Charles.

He thought back on Caroline. They'd been too young, and her life simply could not stay parallel to his unless he lived in Denmark and spent his days posing for the paparazzi. Who would ever want to marry into a royal family? He would have been criticized if he had failed to play his official role as the quiet, respectful, dutiful consort. It would have been living a lie. He would have been ostracized if he'd been himself and spoken his mind while attending the constant functions with political types. Either way, he'd have been a liability to Caroline.

He thought of Tristana. Something kept her in and around the Washington Beltway, where she'd be gradually poisoned by osmosis. He found people of that particular bent not just uninteresting, but actively irksome. He hadn't reached out to her since leaving prison.

He looked at the girl before him. A coffee shop was as good a place as any to meet someone. Maybe not as good as a bookstore, but a lot better than a bar. Likely better than Gondwana, and certainly better than Washington, DC. She might turn out to be a psychotic predator, but his gut told him that she was on the right side of the moral barricades, even if, perhaps, not entirely forthright. Still, he thought ruefully, they'd only just met, and she had revealed a lot about herself, while he hadn't.

He would look into her story and check out this guy Blaize Forestal. And maybe get together with her again when he returned to New York in a few days.

What kind of name was Blaize, anyway? It seemed pompous, pretentious. Was it possible a man's name could influence his character?

"My last name is Renner. I never mentioned it."

"Mine is Knight."

"Charles Knight. A nice name."

"My father gave it to me."

"*The* Charles Knight." She stated it without a question, and with no hint of surprise.

"Indeed. The very one." Charles wished he wasn't so recognizable, but wishing did little to change reality. "So you see how I can empathize with your unjust incarceration."

She took a few moments before saying, "I'm grateful for that. I suppose most people who go to prison belong there; that makes it harder on the ones who don't. It's hard to figure who's who. Not many empathize. I'm glad that you can."

His phone rang. He glanced at it and dismissed the robocall.

155

18

A Quiet, Mostly Nonviolent Revolution

"HOW'S it coming, Rainbow?"

"Mei-li's kickin' it, Paladin. Your Paladin Network is gonna be ten times better than you expected. You know that, right? She's got all her crew working on it. And they're going to town. Soon they'll start having hackathons—to make it solid."

Charles's concern rose. "How are we paying them?"

"They'll get paid in Paladins after we launch."

That seemed reasonable. A form of sweat equity. Paying contractors who had no direct skin in the game was the least desirable alternative. He asked, "They do know those tokens may have little value?"

Rainbow chuckled. "They know that far better than you do. They gonna make sure they're valuable."

"The airdrop?"

"That's just an awareness campaign. Marketing via free tokens."

Charles wondered how much those free tokens would cost him by diluting out potential gains, but it was impossible to calculate. Anyway, profit was far from his primary motive. He asked, "Do you have the conditional-anonymity and accountability aspects set up?"

"That conditional-anonymity shit has been the hardest part. It's a new concept. No good models to work from. You said you wanted everybody to be anonymous unless they defy the rules within the community. For minor infractions of our very simple rules, they can lose some or all of the staked

Paladins each person has to post for collateral, but they can retain their anonymity. But for infractions of natural law, they lose anonymity so that they can be outcast or even outlawed. That's what you wanted, and that's what you'll be getting. But we've had to be very inventive. Should be gettin' a patent on this shit. If it works. Not sure yet."

Charles chuckled. "Unfortunately, a patent on this would just incriminate us. No need to waste our money on that!"

Like most open-source projects built on a sound foundation, the Paladin Network was evolving beyond Charles's initial ideas. Mei-li and Rainbow had gotten way ahead of him. No problem. Ten years ago, he hadn't wanted to get involved in an African bush war. Three years ago, he hadn't been looking to formulate a game-changing drug. He certainly hadn't intended to build a righteous version of Meyer Lansky's and Bugsy Siegel's Murder, Inc. with a cryptocurrency platform to support it. He didn't have to do it himself, any more than Alexander of Macedon had to personally conquer the Persians—his phalanxes did the hands-on work. Specialization and the division of labor made progress possible. Charles just wanted to be sure that the operation stayed ethically sound; there could be no collateral damage to innocent parties. It needed to be ideologically sound as well; the objective of the business had to stay on track. Making a huge amount of money was just a natural fringe benefit of providing a wanted and needed service.

But was the objective of the Paladin Network ethically sound? Was it moral to take the law into your own hands? To be judge, jury, and executioner? It was a decision that Charles had made a decade before. First when he'd shot a man in self-defense. Then when he'd violated the law by failing to involve the police. This brought up the distinction between what was moral and what was legal; they were two totally different things, often with only an accidental overlap. It had been an easy decision then. He'd disliked having to kill the mercenary sent to murder him, but it was urgent, defensible, and necessary. There was no moral imperative to involve the police; that was simply a cost-benefit calculation. Strictly a matter of risk and reward. It would have made no sense to do so.

His involvement in the assassination of John-John in Gondwana was more complex. The crazed warlord hadn't posed an immediate threat to him, but not killing him would have resulted in a civil war with perhaps hundreds of thousands of deaths, peppered with world-class suffering. There was no alternative solution to the problem. In fact, it would have been a moral failure not to kill him, even though killing him violated numerous African laws, for what they were worth.

The situation became even more complex with Seth Fowler, the new head of the SEA who'd been torturing and killing teenagers. Charles took him out as the man was walking from the White House to the Willard Hotel. The act was akin to someone taking out Heinrich Himmler—head of the SS—in 1938. The SS was then completely legal in Germany, just as the SEA was in the US now.

It was a slippery slope and a personal question that each individual had to answer for himself. Religion provided little help. The Bible overflowed with righteous killings, often wholesale and on the orders of Yahweh. The Koran seemed to aggressively advocate them.

The issue, and the problems it presented on many levels, lingered in the back of Charles's mind and came to the fore with increasing frequency as he considered new information and newly learned history. If everybody took the law into their own hands, would society be much better behaved, or would it break down into chaos? Or was society more likely to permanently enshrine evil if some people didn't take the law into their own hands? There were essentially two kinds of people: those who believed in voluntarism, and those who believed in coercion. Those who believed in coercion inevitably gravitated toward the State—which operated on coercion. They ineluctably shaped its laws to their advantage and in line with their character as they entrenched themselves in power.

After a certain point, it was impossible to change a corrupt system from within. What were the chances a reformer could have altered the nature of the Soviet Union, until it collapsed totally in 1990? It could have saved the world oceans of blood if someone had simply removed Lenin or Stalin early on.

Perhaps, ultimately, the only lasting solution was to purge the human race of evil people on a wholesale level. It sounded like a cliché plot for a James Bond movie in which a wealthy genius prepares to drop poisonous orchids on the planet from low orbit. Entirely apart from the obvious ethical problems the concept presented, how was it even possible? How could you determine who was evil … or would be in the future?

"Hey, Paladin. Where'd you go? You off daydreaming?"

Charles shook his head. "Rainbow, tell me how this KYC, know-your-customer, stuff will work if we have anonymity." He was irked to find himself using that lingo. Its main practical effect, besides truckloads of red tape, was to deny certain people the ability to open a financial account and make it clear that everyone's financial life was an open book to the government.

"You said, 'conditional anonymity.' Here's what we're doing. People who want to either mine Paladin tokens or purchase services need to submit their KYC digitally. But we've got some cool new twists that you'll see when you go through the process yourself. Once your identity is confirmed, the data are encrypted on a blockchain and the unencrypted files get deleted. There's no way that any government can then decrypt the data or force any-one to decrypt it, or even know which data to examine to re-identify any-body. No one can decrypt the data. Even the person involved can't be forced to decrypt it."

"So what's the point? Permanently encrypted sounds like a black hole. Nothing's getting out."

"It's not necessarily permanent. The network itself can decide to re-iden-tify a person—but only if numerous conditions are met. Conditional ano-nymity, right? It'll all be in the white paper we're writing. You and Maurice will be contributing to it. We designed the conditions to allow re-identifi-cation only in the setting of fraud or unprovoked violence. Let's say that an anonymous member pays to use network resources to commit an offense against an innocent person."

Charles asked, "By network resources, you mean miners?"

"In part. And by miners, we mean something much more than Bit-coin miners. Paladin Token miners—Mei-li calls them spyminers—are peo-ple on the street, in offices, and on the internet. We expect many of them will be actively working within, for, and around various bureaucracies and crony enterprises. Some of them will work in the anonymous gig economy to track and monitor the activities and deals of those politicians and bureau-crats and their cronies."

Charles smiled. "That's mining the motherlode of problems."

Rainbow nodded. "And of course they can target miscellaneous socio-paths and criminals wherever they find them. Targets of opportunity. Just like we talked about. It's gonna be an independent distributed network that's always on the lookout for criminals. Much better than the centralized net-works of informers set up by police and intelligence agencies."

Charles and Rainbow chatted through the evening, punctuated with numerous calls to Mei-li, who was irritated to be distracted from her work.

The way conditional anonymity would work became clearer in Charles's mind. The network would guarantee anonymity only as long as the individual did not commit fraud. Reporting a provably false location for a target or inventing condemning evidence would amount to being a false witness. The perpetrators would be held to account by losing their anonymity.

If the Paladin Network was successful, the amount of data coming into it—potentially from millions of miners on millions of subjects—would be immense. Far beyond the ability of even an army of full-time analysts to sort. It was a problem only artificial intelligence could solve. AI was developing at least as fast as blockchain, as the world moved toward the Singularity.

Predictably, Mei-li had connections with an artificial intelligence crypto group. They saw the financial upside of involvement with the Paladin Network. It was one thing to play around with a science project but something else again to find an application on a specific project that could immediately spin out profit.

Their AI network would analyze the data pouring in from the Paladin Network's spyminers. If any spyminer data proved inconsistent with the bulk of the facts, the AI system would recognize the conflict and determine whether it was differing opinions, error, or fraud. Fraud was always a potential problem when dealing with the public. In the gold-mining business, fraud often took the form of salting, making it look like the gold was there when there wasn't any. The Paladin Token miners would be submitting data about politicians, bureaucrats, and their cronies. If they salted their data to pretend that their spymining was digging up gold when it really wasn't, the AI network should be able to figure it out based on the inconsistencies. The possibly phony data would then be presented to all interested parties, and the network members would vote on the matter. A majority could agree to put the offending member on probation or remove the offending miner from the network. He could be outcast, no longer able to deal with, use, or earn money from the Paladin Network.

The network needed strong disincentives against lying and bearing false witness. In biblical times, perjury was codified into the Eighth Commandment. It was just as important now. The #MeToo movement had a hard time differentiating between who had a righteous case and who was a female sociopath seeking attention or just trying to make a man's life miserable. Either led to the targeted male being tarred and feathered—whether guilty or innocent. The Court of Instagram was always in session and always prejudicial.

The Paladin Network had to be a tool of justice, not a pervertible weapon. A network member who bore false witness that caused harm risked being labeled an outlaw, which was far worse than being an outcast. It meant they could be targeted by both the network and his victim. Historically, being outlawed was far worse than being on the FBI's Most Wanted list. Unjustly outlawed individuals were the grist for romantic fables and heroic tales, but common outlaws weren't romantic figures; they were criminals, not just unprotected by the law but fair game. On the Paladin Network, any member could collect a bounty. Imagine having your home hacked, your Wi-Fi monitored, your computer's keystrokes logged, and your business and private lives exposed publicly every day. That's what they had designed the Paladin Network to do to cronies in and out of politics. But it also applied to the outlawed.

There were no boundaries to the network's mandates and sanctions. They could range from the relatively trivial shame of having one's criminal acts exposed to, as certain government agencies liked to phrase it, termination with extreme prejudice.

While assassination was always an alternative, and sometimes necessary, it was only a final option. There was rarely any direct upside in killing a miscreant. The world's criminal-justice systems failed to figure this out. They only punished the defendants—which did the victims no good whatsoever. The Paladin Network, as a decentralized profit-making organization, was only sustainable by—rather obviously—making a profit and seeing justice done. The Paladin Network radically departed from the world's existing police, court, and prison systems in that one of its objectives was to make the victim whole—as near as possible. The costs of doing so, including compensation for the Paladin operatives, had to come out of the criminal's hide. Restitution and rehabilitation had to be built in. Charles didn't know how this would be accomplished, but he didn't need to. The developers and miners—in accomplishing their distributive justice—would find a way, if a way existed.

Vigilante hackers and vigilante mercs would be incentivized to track down the Nigerian princes looking to ambush the unwary on the internet. Perhaps they'd just recover the stolen money and punch holes through their digital lives. Perhaps, if the crime warranted it and compensation was adequate, they might punch holes through their biological lives.

Wiki meets blockchain meets Jack Reacher.

* * *

"Have you decided about Charles Knight?" The voice came through the cell phone just a bit rough and slightly delayed because the caller used an app, called Signal, that provided high-end voice encryption but without collecting metadata. It was available for free. The speaker was a billionaire who would spare no expense to communicate safely. Doing so for free? That was even better.

He hadn't needed such technology until he'd declared his candidacy. Now, however, the American Deep State, a dozen foreign intelligence agencies, and, of course, both the DNC and RNC were pinging his network for weaknesses. They bugged everywhere he went, flew drones above him, tried to bribe anyone he knew, and aimed sound-amplifying parabolas and lasers at his windows. Any semblance of his privacy had disappeared.

Jeffrey said, "I've got more to learn about him, Grayson. We only met for a few minutes. So far, I'm optimistic. He's not your typical drug lord; he appears to have a lot of your Boy Scout virtues. On the other hand, the man's done hard time. That can warp anybody's personality. Plus, he's on probation for the better part of the next twenty years, which is inconvenient. On the bright side, he doesn't appear to be the least bit rehabilitated. Not according to the way they define the word. That's typical of the prison system, isn't it? Even if we believed that everybody in prison belonged there, putting men in cages has little chance of improving them."

Grayson Chase replied, "Yes. If he were rehabilitated—started doing what he's told—then he wouldn't be the right guy for us."

"Exactly. He's had run-ins with unsavory types and still wants to fight the good fight. His actions were justified in the B-F Explorations scam; you can't respect someone who just rolls over. He came out with a huge win before the government confiscated almost all his money. He traveled the world for seven years and stayed below the radar. Then, out of the blue, he appeared back in the US and turned Sybillene into Naked Emperor."

"The drug that almost changed the world ... and maybe still will."

"Yes. Like you, I want that drug flooding the streets again. When Paul

162

Samuels and his pals in the Deep State created the Sybillene Eradication Agency, Knight took it personally and considered it a direct attack."

"It was a direct attack."

Jeffrey acknowledged that with a slight nod, inaudible over the phone. "When the government attacked him, Knight defied them. Which is dangerous enough. Then he counterattacked—which is extremely dangerous. You're supposed to roll over on your back like a whipped dog, wet yourself, and apologize. Of course, the best defense is often a good offense, especially when an opponent thinks he's immune from attack. Samuels likes to think he's invulnerable. And not without reason. Nobody in the system would dare try anything against him; he's the man behind the curtain. He's got stuff on everyone. Probably set with dead man's switches. But Charles isn't part of the system."

"I can think of no better person to shed his mortal coil than Paul Samuels. Let all his dead man's switches activate—that would be a bonus for the world, since all his associates are criminals too. Are you still sure it was Knight who took the shot at him?"

"Pretty sure. I believe he intended to miss."

Grayson replied, "Possible. Maybe Knight just wanted to send a message, not kill him. Or maybe it wasn't Knight shooting at him. We may never know. It's amazing how rare political assassinations are. I find the questionable cases most interesting. Particularly the counterintuitive ones. For instance, it's said there was a British plot to kill George Washington in 1776, right at the start of the war, using a chap named Hickey, who was a member of his personal bodyguard. If Washington had been killed, it probably would have aborted the revolution."

Jeffrey said, "That assassination would certainly have changed things."

"Yes. Nobody knows the exact numbers, but something like fifty thousand Americans and the same number of Brits died because of the war. Plus huge destruction of property. Without Washington, there'd likely have been just the thirteen original colonies, each an independent country. And then a bunch of others once the pioneers went west. Today's Americans would probably feel—not think, mind you, but feel—that that would have been a terrible outcome. I'm not so sure. America is an idea, not a place or a government. The things that made the US great—the rule of law, freedom of thought and speech, capitalism, individualism, and the rest—would have gone west with the pioneers, but the taxes and regulations and wars that came out of Washington might not have. We certainly would not have had the so-called Civil War.

"Maybe some state would have provoked the Spanish at the end of the nineteenth century, but it wouldn't likely have ended with imperialism in the Pacific. The Army killed about two hundred thousand natives when they conquered the Philippines. Probably no individual states would've gotten involved in World War I, so it would've ended earlier in a draw... and then there wouldn't have been a Treaty of Versailles, Hitler's rise, or World War II. America's culture and values, which are what made her great, would likely have remained intact—as opposed to being degraded by those wars. It's all speculative, of course. Even though Washington was a decent human being and one of the best presidents, when you consider what the US has mutated into, the world might have been a better place if Hickey had succeeded."

Jeffrey said, "Might have been. I'm more confident that the world would be a better place if Knight had succeeded in assassinating Paul Samuels. What I do know for a fact is that Knight could have killed Samuels. He's competent, motivated, and seems to have a soft spot for the weak. I wouldn't be surprised if he's the one who shot Seth Fowler."

Grayson would know who Seth Fowler had been—the head of the SEA, the man who would be king, who aspired to be the next J. Edgar Hoover. His imperial aspirations had been cut short by a well-placed bullet just before Charles Knight turned himself in to be incarcerated for Sybillene possession.

Jeffrey added, "I'll wager Knight makes his services available to us... but not because he needs money. It's my impression that he's much more likely to do something because he thinks it's right."

"A mercenary who thinks like a vigilante."

Jeffrey replied, "Mercenary? I suppose. I've got no problem with mercenaries. There are many people who simply can't fight successfully for themselves. They need to hire a champion, a knight errant. As for vigilantes, they only arise when the State is either ineffectual or corrupt. They've been given an undeservedly bad reputation. I think Knight may be moving into that space to fill the need for justice."

"There's a lot to be said for vigilante justice. When you've gained more confidence in Knight, let me know before you try to bring him into the fold."

"That goes without saying. I know how important this is, and how dangerous. It would derail your candidacy if it got out that you'd work to put

Naked Emperor back on the street if you won. It's perverse. If it were legal, it would guarantee you'd win by a landslide."

"Hey, if it were legal, I wouldn't need to run. Anyway, if it's late in the campaign, and it looks like I'm not gonna win the election, I plan to announce that I'll work to decriminalize Naked Emperor and end the SEA. Maybe that would turn the tide."

"Hold off on that Hail Mary pass for now, will you?"

"Of course. I'm hoping Knight proves to be a friend, either way. Think of it. If he killed Seth Fowler, we could be socializing with an assassin."

"You already are socializing with an assassin, Grayson."

Grayson chuckled. "Jeffrey, you don't count. You're not a hired gun."

"Ah, but that's not my definition. My definition of a righteous assassination is the justifiable homicide of someone above the law. And Knight won't be a hired gun either. If he's hunting big game, it would hardly be for hire. The Greeks' Erinyes, the Romans' Furies couldn't be hired. The great heroes of mythology—Theseus, Perseus, Hercules—were all self-appointed vigilantes. They weren't on anybody's payroll. They weren't following the orders of some king."

"Yet, one should be paid for value supplied."

"Certainly, Grayson, but he'd probably think of it as a reward, not a wage. I don't think he's the type to take orders from anybody just because they're paying him. He's an unusual character—a lone wolf."

"A rare find."

"Especially for a pretty normal guy. Most people would think only some secret agent with exotic government training could play in this sandbox."

Their conversation paused as the man who would be president deliberated.

Jeffrey intruded on his thoughts. "I'll stay positioned and keep an eye on him. And I'll get to know him better directly."

"Where is he now?"

"I don't know. He's been off the grid for a couple of days."

"You worried?"

"No."

"Who do you have on him?"

"A few people. But one stumbled and fell in too far. She thought he noticed she was tailing him. She had to either back off or go all in. She went all in."

"Who?"

"Emily."

"That's funny. Who could be more prepared than Emily?"

"Yeah, I think it might work out. Knight should like her. If they get close, that could be for the best. Wouldn't be surprised if Emily falls for him. She has good reason to."

"That okay by you?"

"Not entirely. We'll have to apologize to him later. I hate to do something that looks like a honey trap."

"I mean, is it okay with you that Emily might fall for Knight?"

"Of course, Grayson. Hell, they'd probably have good-looking kids."

"Speaking of kids, how is my sister?"

Jeffrey moved the phone away from his cheek and looked over at the kitchen table where Diana sat reading a newspaper. A silk bathrobe fell enticingly loose on her shoulders and she wore nothing else. "She's absolutely stunning," he said.

"Keeping your hands off of her?"

"As always," Jeffrey offered assurance in a tone of voice that would in no way reassure Diana's much older brother.

Grayson laughed, as expected. "I'm friends with an assassin who's sleeping with my little sister. What the hell's wrong with me?"

Jeffrey grinned. "And I'm friends with my girl's jackass brother who's running for president. What the hell's wrong with me?"

He hung up the phone and went over to Diana, where he entirely failed to keep his hands off of her.

19

The Hinterland

"PISS in the cup."

Charles took the cup, pushed past Phil, and moved toward the small malodorous bathroom.

Phil, Charles's probation officer, was cut from the same cloth as the screws and bulls in the prison system. Not very bright, a congealed streak of hostility in lieu of a backbone, and a deep-seated desire to control people. Under the bravado, he was weak and fearful. He wouldn't last more than a day or two in the slammer.

"You know I need to watch," Phil added in a tone that transformed Charles's stoicism to disgust.

"I bet you need to. Is this a fringe benefit for you? Don't worry. I'll make sure you get a good view, Phil."

"That's Mr. Dillwyn to you, Knight. Your attitude is part of your file. Fail the test and you're back in the can."

"And that's Mr. Knight to you. I never asked before, but they're going to test me for what? Meth? Coke? H?"

"They run the standard screen. We know you're not into the usual junk. Naked Emperor is all I expect to see."

"Well, thank god for that. You won't see it. Don't you know that no one sells Naked Emperor anymore?"

"The law's the law. Particularly for you. If anyone has any Naked Emperor lying around, you would."

"Naked Emperor never worked on me," Charles reminded his intensely annoying probation officer.

"Yeah, as if you or anybody else in this shithole would tell the truth. We're checking. You're not so special. Pee in the damn cup, Knight."

Phil's cell phone rang and kept ringing.

"You gonna answer that, Phil?"

"It's spam." He glanced at the phone and dismissed it.

Charles said, "Those constant calls out here almost make me miss prison. Like I'm about to miss this cup." He started to pull the bathroom door closed behind him, but Phil didn't allow that. So he turned to face Phil, who watched intently as Charles filled the cup to near overflowing and capped it carelessly. He shook out some drops in the direction of Phil's shoes as he handed him the cup. Phil took it reflexively, some of the liquid spilling on his hand.

"Get back to my desk. I have to deal with your piss."

Charles walked back to Phil's desk. It was Charles's fifth visit to the building, but the new man in charge of the probation office remained a mystery. Not even a name plaque on the door across from Phil's cubicle. Venetian blinds across the glass wall blocked the view into his office, but his door stood open.

Charles looked over at the paperwork on Phil's desk, making no effort to conceal his interest.

"Get away from that."

"From what, Mr. Dillwad?"

An amused snicker came through the open door of the new office boss.

"Dillwyn. Dillwyn. You know my name!" Charles's probation officer almost screamed as he sat down at his small metal desk.

"All right. Let's get this over with," Charles said, smiling. "What litany of denials do you need me to recite today, Phil?"

Dillwyn pulled some paper from under a file and asked, "Have you left the state of New York?"

"Why do you ask?"

"You know why. You cannot leave the state without my permission."

"What I think you mean is I shouldn't leave, although I can. But, to answer your question: we've got beautiful summer weather. And riots every night. Supply shortages. Why would I want to leave? And since I haven't received your permission, and only you could allow me to leave, then I must not have left." In his pocket, Charles crinkled a recently used Amtrak round-trip ticket stub for Washington, DC—a trip he'd taken over the past few days to perform essential due diligence related to his current avocation. He smiled innocently.

Dillwyn sneered as he checked a box on a computer form.

Charles had snuck in the illicit trip to Washington, DC, both to visit with his friend Alpha and to liberate the laptop of a Department of Agriculture agent named Terrence Kirby. This was Paladin work. Charles and Alpha had followed Kirby from his home looking for the right opportunity. That opportunity came on the first day when Kirby stopped by the publicly accessible Department of Agriculture Library in Beltsville, Maryland.

Charles had morphed into Paladin for the trip, with the latex nose, makeup, wig, mustache, and sideburns, and the added protection against surveillance provided by a breathing mask. Easily replicated TSA ID badges, combined with a dominant attitude, gave Charles and Alpha the proper air of authority. The drones working in the building were loath to question authority. Dressed in cheap wrinkled suits, they fit right into the environment. Charles viewed it as a game. For authenticity, he had feigned low self-esteem, overlain with a sense of superiority and entitlement. His camouflage had let him swim like a native species of fish in the Washington bureaucracy's turgid waters. Alpha might have stuck out a bit more, but, even apart from the fact he was large and tough-looking, no one dared question a black man in DC.

When Kirby had set his laptop bag down on a table, Charles had distracted him for the thirty seconds it took Alpha to snatch the computer and disappear through a side door. While Kirby panicked, Charles slipped away himself, got the computer from Alpha, and hightailed it back to New York City. Perhaps the higher-ups would sentence Kirby to two hours of cybersecurity training for losing his government laptop.

Dillwyn repeated a question that Charles had ignored. "Do you have on your person or in your place of abode any firearms?"

"Am I allowed to?"

"No." Phil rolled his eyes like a teenager. "You're a convicted felon and have no right to bear arms."

"In this city, I'd have no right even if I weren't a convicted felon."

Phil Dillwyn's face twisted to match his petulant voice. "Answer the question, Knight!"

"I feel like I'm on a quiz show. I can't remember the question."

Charles heard another chuckle coming from the boss's office.

Exasperation failed to make Dillwyn's face look any more intelligent. "Yes or no. Do you have possession of a firearm."

"I wish. I mean this city is dangerous!"

"Yes or no, Knight!"

"You have your answer."

"I need you to say yes or no." Dillwyn closed his eyes in frustration.

"Yes or no." Charles said, predictably. Charles detected a snort from within the nearby office of the supervisor.

Dillwyn looked at Knight with a hostile stare in an effort to control and intimidate. Charles was immune to such tactics. Dillwyn must have figured that out, for he gave up with a sigh and scowl, checked a box, and moved on. "Are you gainfully employed?"

"That impresses me as a deeply philosophical question."

"Are you seeking work?"

"Yes."

"How?"

"I'm letting people know that I am available to do work for them."

"Doing what?"

"Cleaning up messes. Why don't you jot down handyman."

A loud guffaw echoed out through Scibbera's open door. Everything in the office was background noise to the people who worked there; it was a little like prison that way. Phil seemed oblivious to the laughter emanating from his boss's office. Charles paid attention though. Either the man was hosting a party in there, or the boss, whoever he was, was listening in on his conversation with this PO and enjoying it.

Phil didn't enjoy it. "Fuck you, Knight."

"That's very professional of you, Phil."

"Look, Knight. You served less than two years of a twenty-year sentence. If I can stick you back in, I will. All you have to do is sneeze in a way that displeases me."

"That's good to know."

"Mr. Knight, how many deaths of school kids are you responsible for?"

"You mean if I add them all up?"

"Yes."

"If I add them all up, the number is precisely zero, Phil." Charles could take a lot of trash talk and stay in control, but an outright lie from the mouth of a petty creature like Dillwyn tested his reserves of patience.

"The SEA under Seth Fowler poisoned the Naked Emperor and set up school shootings."

Dillwyn was oblivious to the discipline Charles required to keep from throttling him. The PO's idea of a clever comeback was "Bullshit conspiracy theory."

Charles looked at Dillwyn. "Phil, you irk me. I find you irksome."

"You're an ass. You are a drug-dealing, child-killing, evil human being."

"But, unlike you, I only have to be with you in this office," Charles slowly scanned the dismal room, "for about a half hour every week or two. You, on the other hand, have to be in this office eight hours a day. And then go home to an apartment where you have to live with yourself. I pity you."

"I will take you down, Knight. I know your type. Wise guy. No respect. Think you're better than the rest of us. I absolutely know you'll break your probation. Then I'll pounce." He made a cat-like motion with his hand as he bared his teeth.

"Well, I suppose you have to inject some kind of meaning to your life." Charles stood up and started to leave.

"Knight. Don't you dare leave New York. Don't even leave Manhattan."

"I'll make a note, Phil," Charles replied without looking at the man. He wanted to get out of the oppressive place. He looked around again, gripped by melancholy. The people and atmosphere here could be mistaken for any of ten thousand rooms in Stalin's USSR, Honecker's East Germany, or Ceausescu's Romania. In fact, the world was full of rooms like this with people like Phil. It was evidence the Earth was some kind of prison planet. But this was today, in what was left of America. At least he was going to walk out, which wouldn't have happened in countless different times and places.

He couldn't resist sneaking a quick peek through the open office door of Dillwyn's new boss. He looked directly into the very amused eyes of Anthony Scibbera.

And he immediately recognized the mustachioed face.

He'd been the probation officer for Albert Peale—the newspaper editor who'd first reported on the amazing effects of high-dose Sybillene. According to Peale, Scibbera had been instrumental in creating Sybillene's street name, Naked Emperor. So Charles owed him, for it was a perfect name. He'd never met him, but Scibbera had been at his sentencing hearing, sitting in the very back row, between Peale and Xander Winn, all boldly applauding in support of him as Charles was perp-walked off in shackles.

171

Tony Scibbera winked at Charles and waved him away with a toss of his hand. Charles took the hint and skedaddled.

The warden who had helped him gain his freedom had mentioned that friends would appear, hidden unless needed.

He had no doubt that Anthony Scibbera was one of them.

*   *   *

Charles left the dingy probation office, inhaled a breath of the city's semi-fresh air, and walked to Penn Station, where he retrieved the bag he'd left in one of the keyed lockers. It was surprising that the lockers still existed since they could serve as completely anonymous low-cost safe-deposit boxes. Undoubtedly, they were but one real, fabricated, or imagined terrorist incident away from disappearing altogether.

He checked the monitor to board the Lake Shore Limited, connecting to the Empire Builder. Together, the trains would take him far outside his legal confines of the state of New York for the second time this week. Fuck you, Dillwyn.

The train ran late. Amtrak's multibillion-dollar annual subsidies were apparently inadequate to secure competent management.

Charles sat down and reviewed the email from the farmer in North Dakota, whose grandchildren had been kidnapped by Child Protective Services because he had dared grow some hemp. It revealed a man who was at once confused, desperate, and hopeful: could Paladin possibly help an old farmer?

He used a prepaid cell phone bought with cash. For an alibi, he'd left his usual cell phone back in Xander's Manhattan apartment, where he'd been living since Xander had flown to Bali for a couple of months with one of his girlfriends. Automatically controlled by an app, the cell would make an occasional call: a trick Rainbow learned from Mei-li. To further document compliance to his probation officer's demands to stay local, he had Rainbow order up at least one meal per day on his credit card. It was a win-win deal.

On this trip, or any trip, he used only cash. One of the advantages of the US falling behind in applied technology was that cash remained practical. In some countries, like Sweden, cash was already an anachronism. Citizens in China could only purchase tickets electronically, and then only if one's social credit rating was sufficiently high. Authorities in the US tracked people via electronic payments, cell phone records, and ubiquitous cameras. Privacy, long threatened, now neared extinction in the developed world. The key to roaming free was to look nothing like a person the authorities might want to track.

Never-ending trench warfare raged between the type of people who worked for the State and those who intuitively worked against it. Those on the defensive weren't necessarily fighting because of any ideology or philosophy—although there were plenty who did—but because they didn't like being bossed around. In recent years, in some measure of desperation, they'd circled their wagons and worked hard to build new defensive weapons. Thanks to them, some cryptocurrencies created channels for private money movement, and internet traffic could be encrypted so that even the NSA couldn't listen in. But travel without being tracked and monitored was more challenging.

He wore his makeup, baseball cap, big nose, mustache, and glasses whenever there might be a camera around, as was the case now, and, for practical purposes, everywhere, at all times. He placed an insert into one shoe to foil gait-recognition software. Practice in applying the makeup and latex meant they no longer itched, but he always kept his touchup kit handy to compensate for sweat resulting from the antiviral mask that concealed even more of his face. He thought of Gondwana. Sweat naturally brought that hellhole to mind.

He'd mailed a few more of his Have Gun—Will Travel coins to various parties who appeared as if they might be in need of his services, each coin accompanied by a card with a carefully written email address, always different, always untraceable, connecting via VPN and Tor Browser. The relative lack of complications, despite his poorly planned effort on behalf of Chiang, could not be relied on to persist. Beginner's luck. The best way to pursue a new line of work was to learn by doing. It was unwise to go after lion and elephant until he'd taken down enough rats.

The train took two days to reach his destination, including a change in Chicago—another city where the CityFire riots had taken hold. Guns were banned, but bullets flew every night and the rioters carried their weapons openly. Would the situation degenerate into open warfare in the streets as the depression deepened?

Renting a car with cash isn't hard, as long as it's from a local business purveying twenty-year-old clunkers. Modern cars run forever with little more than an occasional oil change; the difference between a new car and one with 150,000 miles was mostly cosmetic. The benefit of the old ones was that they didn't come with GPS and couldn't be tracked. The proprietor of the low-rent Hertz knockoff met him at the railroad station, driving a boxy thirty-five-year-old Chrysler with scratched and faded paint. Five hundred dollars, but no license or names, changed hands. The car wasn't worth even that, but it ran and handled well enough. If he returned it within the week, without much additional damage, he'd get four hundred of those dollars back. Who needed corporate offices full of overpaid suits, franchise payments, and long contracts written in expensive legalese that nobody read? Who needed fleets of depreciating new vehicles, financed with debt and rented with credit cards? Who needed layers of intermediaries all taking a piece? All that was a recipe for bankruptcy.

Instead, this was a win-win deal and left the government out of the loop—a practical cash business.

There had been no rain for some time, and the gravel road's dust rose in clouds rendering the rearview mirror mostly useless. A lazy breeze wafted the dust away now and again so that Charles could see that no one followed him, even at a distance. It may be unnecessary here, but it was a good habit to reinforce, and so he kept checking.

He pulled the sun-damaged, paint-peeling maroon Chrysler up to a well-tended house with white clapboards. Tame boxwoods lined the front. A bench swing moved gently on the brick patio leading to the front door. An American flag flew high on a pole, its base surrounded with flowers, their petals sad and wilted.

He tapped on the heavy wooden front door. Some would say the door would benefit from new paint, but to Charles, the faded and rough surface gave it character.

The man who opened the door wore a blue work shirt, the sleeves rolled up over substantial arm muscles that were losing their fight against entropy. He looked twenty years older than the fifty-year-old Marine Corps tattoo on his arm. He had a firm jaw but exhausted eyes, which met Charles warily.

"You didn't used to be suspicious of people who came to your door, did you, Mr. Jannsen?"

The man's eyes settled some as he took in Charles, and the door opened a bit wider as he relaxed.

"You asked for help. I came."

174

"Are you … ?"

"Call me Paladin."

The door opened the rest of the way. "I used to watch that show when I was a youngster." Jannsen said. "My friend Tommy, he's gone now, his father was the first person I knew with a TV. We all loved that show. You know, you sorta look like him, like the actual Paladin."

That was the point of the latex nose: to look like the character Paladin. As a child, Charles had believed Paladin was real. Perhaps now he was.

Mr. Jannsen guided Charles to a bright and warmly decorated living room.

"Maggie, we have a guest." His wife emerged from around a corner, wearing an apron. "This is," he paused ever so slightly, "… Mr. Paladin."

"Hello, Mrs. Jannsen. It's my pleasure."

She was a teacher. He could tell just by looking at her. She slowly nodded to him with a faint smile born of habit, not deference.

She spoke with the brisk voice of a teacher too. "I'll bring you two something to drink. I already have a teapot ready."

"Tea, no milk or sugar, would be welcome. Thank you."

Mr. Jannsen sat on the couch.

Charles said, "To clean up a mess, sometimes a mess needs to be made. Are you able to tolerate that?"

Jannsen took a breath, sighed, and then shook his head. "Look, I'm stuck, Mr. Paladin. I'm furious too. Our grandies have been taken away. They're young and they… they don't understand. Eight and ten years old. That's all they are. I have no money left to pay our attorneys, who I bet are working with the same people who took the kids away, damn them. No one is winning here. Everyone suffers."

"Especially the children!" Mrs. Jannsen emerged from the kitchen. If Charles had heard that phrase back east, he would have connected it to some PC busybody, using it to justify some new law about guns, drugs, climate change, or a half dozen other fashionable causes. Not here.

Mrs. Jannsen would not stay quiet when angry. Righteous fury affected both her voice and appearance; her husband was more phlegmatic. Charles expected that lasers could shoot from her eyes at anyone who opposed her, including any misbehaving child in her classroom. Her hands shook slightly as she passed Charles a cup of tea. It spilled onto the china saucer to be absorbed by two shortbread cookies.

175

"Maggie, do you mind if Mr. Paladin and I go for a walk? We can take your tea with us."

"Yes, why don't you men go out and see what's left of the farm. Go do men things. I'm off to my bridge group anyway. Mr. Paladin, a pleasure to meet you for even a short moment."

The breeze carried some cooler air down from the high hills to the west. Mr. Jannsen kicked at the charred remains of his hemp crop as they walked across a gently sloped terrain.

"Would you believe it was already over ten foot high when they burned it? A hundred eighty acres. A huge investment. Makes good cloth, and it's much better than grinding up trees to make paper. The Declaration of Independence was written on hemp paper. George Washington grew a lot of it himself. I would have made enough on this one crop to pay for the grandkids' college expenses. Now it's all gone."

"I'm sorry."

"Department of Agriculture. Damn that government punk from back east."

"Terrence Kirby. I looked into him before I came. He's what would be called a true believer." Charles referred to Eric Hoffer's classic book by that name.

"If by that, Mr. Paladin, you mean a flaming fascist, then yes, Kirby is a true believer. He didn't care one whit that there was essentially no THC in my hemp, although it's true they found a few plants slightly over their limit. Hell, I wish there had been a bunch so that we coulda got the whole town high when the government bastards burned it. But you'd have to smoke a bushel of it to get the slightest bit wide."

"Hardly what you'd call killer weed."

"Never touched the stuff in my life. Doesn't bother me if other people do, but I don't indulge."

"So, this Kirby guy came in and burned your crop." Charles kicked at a mound of blackened vegetation. The hemp had been converted into charcoal.

"That's just part of the problem. At first it was just a threat. But when I tried to fight it, the county came in and took the children. Said we were endangering them, growing illegal drugs."

Charles's stomach knotted. "I'm so sorry about the kids. Nothing more horrible."

176

"I ain't ashamed to tell you. I'm capable of killing over this. They kidnapped the children. They burned my property. If you don't react to that, then you're hardly a man. Problem is, I just don't have the capabilities I once did. A man's got to know his limitations."

"I saw your tattoo. Have you put someone in your sights and pulled the trigger before?"

"Yes." Jannsen stopped, turned, and looked at Charles. "I assume, based on your card, you've done that too."

"I try to avoid it. Sometimes it's necessary."

"I want three things, Mr. Paladin. I want the children back. I want my property back. I want no one to have to go through this sort of hell ever again."

Charles smiled slightly. "Let's get the children back. We'll try for your property. As for protecting others from going through such hell … that's a tall order. Different chapter. Even a different book."

Jannsen nodded his understanding. "I have no way to pay you."

"Of course you do. The price will be twenty thousand dollars, paid at whatever pace you can, and derived solely from the sale of your future hemp."

Jannsen bent over and picked up some charcoal. "This is my future hemp."

"No, that's your past hemp. Next year you'll have a better crop."

"Are you certain?"

Charles replied as he took the charcoal from the man's hand. "Well, I'm reasonably certain things can't get much worse than this, can they?"

20

Imminent Opportunity

"TROUBLE Brewing in Africa." That was nothing new or unusual. As a break from news of recession, the virus, and the ever-increasing violence in the cities, some producer had decided to do a sixty-second report on the subject.

Tribal warfare with automatic weapons, RPGs, and, of course, machetes. It might be best to let them all kill each other. Had any human rights activists from another continent ever tried to intervene in the era of Europe's constant wars? Would it have helped if they had? The answer was obvious.

Unemployed, testosterone-driven young Africans would rise up with equal fervor to follow a Bible-thumping, Jim Jones–style Christian preacher, a Koran-quoting mullah, or a charismatic self-proclaimed general. The currently popular rebel leader was of the Mohammedan persuasion, like about half of the population. There was always a simmering tension between the Christians and Muslims; to set it ablaze only took an aggressive leader promising one group that he'd eliminate the other group and divvy up their property. It was clever marketing. If you weren't rewarded with wealth and fame in this life, you'd certainly get eternal bliss in either the Prophet's paradise or Jesus's heaven.

Yet another rebel force led by an egomaniacal sociopath had taken up arms against an autocratic government whose sole purpose was to enrich the new president-for-life and his hangers-on. The usual drill. One man, one vote—one time. But for the blood running in the streets, the election cycle of the United States every four years was only a kinder and gentler version of African politics. And this cycle, there was even blood in the streets here.

What could be done? thought Charles.

He revised the question. What—if anything—should be done? Religious wars offering temporal and otherworldly rewards generally had to burn themselves out. So the realistic answer to the question was that nothing should be or could be done. Charles didn't belong to those tribes or their chosen religions. He was an outsider, so their conflict was beyond his ken and none of his business unless it threatened him. He was disinclined, however, to sit idly by if this civil war burned its way through two more national boundaries and into Gondwana, where Charles owned a mountaintop property near a glorious beach, where his friends lived and where his future plans lay. Natural law dictated that when someone threatened his property, he had a right to defend it.

These wars spread across African borders like the tropical diseases endemic to the continent.

Neither diseases nor tribes cared about the borders drawn by cartographers in Europe. There were fifty-four countries on the continent. With perhaps one or two exceptions, none of them were either stable or prosperous. Even if this conflagration was extinguished or ran its course, some neighbor would light up a year or two later.

When he was twenty-three years old, Charles had helped save Gondwana from a civil war. But, for now, he would do nothing. He turned the television news off, something he probably should have done sooner. It was distracting and annoying. It might be worth a few minutes every day or so, but only to find out what the public was expected to believe.

He put Africa out of his mind; first things first. He would focus on solvable problems: smaller problems affecting a small number of people.

Like the Jannsens and their grandchildren.

Charles stepped out of the dingy motel to stand in its cracked and potholed parking lot. The sun approached the horizon at a shallow angle. The daylight would slowly recede over the next few hours, ending in a crimson glow in the sky to the west that would persist until almost 10:00 p.m. Desiccated leaves stirred in a dry, hot breeze as the shadows cast by their trees lengthened. The motel's sign hung from a post by the road, a rusting and broken chain leaving it angled and creaking as it swung. It felt like a post-apocalyptic scene in a movie. The only evidence of another

179

living person lay in the far distance, as a tractor trailer headed downhill with its Jake brake activated.

It was as surreal as what he needed to do tonight. Charles assumed the psychological mantle of Paladin—both a mercenary and a vigilante—pursuing justice. This time it felt natural. He'd tried to mold himself—physically, intellectually, psychologically, and ethically—into a certain form. He was constantly rubbing off the rough edges. He might yet become Paladin—a fictional character, but one that embodied virtue the way few actual humans did.

The concept Thou shalt not kill had been so aggressively propagandized into the American mind and into Charles's own neuronal pathways that he could only overcome it with active rational effort. He revisited his position. Murder differed from simple homicide. In the Judeo-Christian ethic, it meant unjustifiable killing. Even Islam, an intrinsically warlike creed, defined it as the killing of an innocent who has done no wrong. These were reasonable universal principles, and all societies had proscriptions of some type against murder. To the Abrahamic traditions, it was wrong mainly because Yahweh, Jesus, or Allah said it was wrong. In most of the world now, certainly including the US, one could be sentenced as a murderer even if the killing was entirely justified—if that's what the law said. The State reserved for itself, via its own inept agents, the meting out of redress or punishment.

Classical societies had generally followed the reasoning of philosophers, not theologians or legal pedants. Those societies relied on their elders to judge each instance on a case-by-case basis to determine whether it was a justified killing or an unjustified murder. Today, publicity-addicted district attorneys running for re-election decided whether to prosecute based on polls, political correctness, and the softness of the target.

Charles would rely on the rules of neither state nor church for justice. Instead, he would rely on not getting caught. The government agents who had kidnapped the Jannsens' grandchildren and burned down their crop under the cover of an arbitrary regulation were, if anything, less innocent than the engineers who said they were "only driving the train" on the way to Auschwitz. Kidnapping belonged on almost any list of capital offenses. Capital offenses, by definition, could be answered with justified killing.

He drove the stolid Chrysler onto a dirt road leading to the home of the county's chief social service worker. He pulled over and cut the engine. From what he could learn during his study of the woman who owned the place, he expected a person of concrete-bound habits. The type who'd likely be certain that what her parents taught her was right. Certain what she learned in school was right. That everything that anybody in authority told her was right. And that it was her moral obligation—no, duty—as a God-fearing American to do what they said was the right thing.

To all appearances, a salt-of-the-earth, law-abiding, flag-waving, apple-pie-eating American, but only superficially. There was a standard distribution of people just like her in every time and place. Perfectly normal in normal times. They were always there, and you might not notice them until the tenor of the times changed. When certain ideas took hold, these same people became commissars and goose-stepping brownshirts. Things had been changing in that direction for some time.

Jannsen had given Charles the case records from his attorney, including those presented by the Department of Agriculture. Far more useful information was stored on Kirby's laptop, the one Alpha had snatched. Its contents had made for disconcerting reading on the train ride to North Dakota. The documents detailed plans to use the Jannsen farm as an example. Kirby clearly wanted to become known as a man of action who severely nipped transgressions in the bud.

Some states had started legalizing hemp, and now the feds had legalized it too, but with different concentrations of THC as the defining criteria. This presented the national bureaucracy with a conundrum: how could something be both legal and illegal at the same time in the same place? It was a contradiction that would have amused Franz Kafka. To Charles it suggested that the construct of federalism had been kicked to the curb.

Kirby had noted that the situation was entirely out of control in places like California and Colorado, but in conservative rural North Dakota, the Department of Agriculture had a chance to launch a successful counterattack. The best strategy was to act on several fronts at once. It was important to inflict more than economic pain. Marijuana was a notoriously high-profit crop, and money could be replaced. The pain needed to be personal.

The phrase *Take the children* was at the very top of a list titled "Ensuring Effective Interdiction" in Kirby's documents. Take the children. It might be the name of a nonprofit organization dedicated to establishing a progressive utopia by systematic indoctrination of the citizenry's offspring.

Despite his personal experiences with the SEC, IRS, FDA, and DEA, Charles was surprised that anyone employed by something as benign-sounding as the Department of Agriculture would bother with an old farmer in the middle of nowhere. However, with over one hundred thousand employees and a budget of over $150 billion, there was plenty of power and money that might be controlled by an aggressive operator aspiring to burrow into the Deep State. Kirby, clearly interested in climbing the department's institutional ladder, had emerged as a little Napoleon.

A resume of the man's life, supplied by Maurice, painted a picture of a power-hungry narcissist armed with a law degree, a nobody making himself into a somebody at others' expense. His emails showed he fancied himself a ladies' man. He sold himself as a kind of James Bond who used his Ag Department position as a cover for far more exotic and dangerous work. With the sociopath's signature impulsivity and lack of concern for consequences, he'd foolishly maintained a ledger of his female conquests on his work computer and hyperlinked the list to photos. Indeed, he'd successfully seduced a certain married social worker in North Dakota. Such activities weren't crimes, but they could provide useful material for blackmail—not of Kirby, who wouldn't care, but of the social worker.

Charles had no compunction about the use of blackmail. There was nothing intrinsically immoral about it. Blackmail was simply a matter of giving a miscreant the option of doing what he was told or facing up to his past transgressions. There was no force involved, and it could certainly serve a moral purpose. Blackmail had a bad reputation mainly because most people had done things in their life that they shouldn't have done. Charles wondered how much more detailed, and sordid, this deep dive into Kirby could have been, had the Paladin Network already been up and running. How much incriminating dirt could a hundred or a thousand well-motivated Paladin spyminers dig up on power-hungry thieves in Washington? How much in the way of concealed gifts, promises of future rewards, and outright bribes might be discovered as the hacker minds focused their energy on examining the intricate webs connecting the swamp's denizens?

He'd found the strands of one web as he scanned Kirby's emails: the name of Emily Renner's nemesis, Blaize Forestal. The email messages between Kirby and Forestal appeared innocuous enough. Washington's denizens must bump into each other from time to time. By combining this connection with a hundred thousand others, perhaps AI could determine where exactly Charles would need to cut, piece by piece, to destroy the entirety of the Beltway web.

Clearly ambitious and politically adept, Kirby had drafted and submitted dozens of position papers detailing new rules and policies that would expand and empower his department. His efforts, in turn, had put him in charge of moving around the money for ethanol subsidies to agribusiness; he was effectively the ethanol czar. His email inbox was filled with friendly greetings from agribusiness executives reaching out to build relationships and ensure the success of various private-public partnerships. Kirby was automatically positioned to benefit from the favors he could dispense. He'd soon begin his own odyssey through the revolving door to the private sector and then back into public "service."

Ethanol in gasoline made no economic sense for anyone besides the corn lobby, the distillers, and the congressmen who funded them. And perhaps small engine-repair shops that took in a tidy sum replacing the carburetors that the ethanol invariably gunked up. It didn't even make theoretical environmental sense, as corn ethanol's carbon footprint was size 12 compared to a size 10 for oil. Ethanol mandates were essentially bribes to a few farm-state politicians, sometimes to support tricky-to-pass legislation like Obamacare or some other destructive power grab. The benefits to the local congressmen and senators were substantial, immediate, and direct. The harm to drivers and taxpayers, however, was diffuse and delayed. The farmers all knew it was a scam, but it made no sense to turn down easy, free money, even though it grated on some of them, knowing it amounted to burning food as fuel while hurting the environment. Thoughtful economists and environmentalists all knew it was destructive malinvestment, but stupidity and waste were the engines of the political world, and no one got off that train.

It wasn't hard to parse Kirby's grandiose dreams for his future, building on his new position as ethanol czar. Perhaps the operation could be spun off into a new agency, merging it with the Alcohol and Tobacco parts of the Bureau of Alcohol, Tobacco, Firearms and Explosives. Thus the communications between Kirby and Forestal. Kirby's dreams showed unusual ambition for a midlevel bureaucrat. Perhaps he'd studied the career of the late Seth Fowler, who'd been on his way to becoming one of the country's most powerful and dangerous officials until Charles disrupted his plans with a well-placed bullet. Kirby was, thus far, just an ambitious peon.

Kirby's laptop contained hundreds of child-porn photos. It wasn't just a matter of looking at pictures. In many, Kirby was an active participant. Charles couldn't look at the images without visceral disgust. It was an indicator of the man's incurable personality disorder. It spoke of a thirst for power and control over the weak. As a child, he undoubtedly liked to torture small animals. His active participation in the abuse, and the fact that he'd recorded it for future viewing, argued that Kirby could not be reformed and would continue using the cover of his growing government power to wreak destruction.

Like most decent humans, Charles could consider no excuses for such a man. Like most normal human beings, he thought the man should be removed from the ranks of the living. Unlike most, Charles would see that it happened.

As Charles absorbed the data from the computer, Kirby was in North Dakota meeting with the local district attorney and the circuit court judge and undoubtedly looking forward to schmoozing that evening with some new friends on the industry side of the government-agribusiness revolving door. Kirby would probably try to fit into his busy schedule a tryst with a certain county social service worker.

And so Charles started with that social worker.

The door of his high-mileage sedan creaked as he pushed it open. Complementing his nose, mustache, glasses, and wig were a black shirt, black pants and a long black coat—the full Paladin outfit. But no mask this evening. He walked the last three hundred yards to a house illuminated by the dying pink light of the receding sun. He knocked twice, and a minute later he looked into a face that might belong to one of Ian Fleming's female villains—a more attractive and mellower version of Rosa Klebb or Irma Bunt. Charles recognized the cynical counterpoint to Kirby's pretense of being a James Bond.

"My name is Paladin. I'm here to correct a wrong."

The woman stepped back, frightened by the man in black with long sideburns, mustache, and bulging nose who stood before her.

"Don't move too far, Ms. Penure. I want to show you something."

She kept her frizzy hair pulled back severely in a bun. Her voice shook, as did her hands. "Show me what?" She moved another step back, her hand squeezing the edge of the door.

"Your husband is a long-haul truck driver. He's away for some time, I presume."

She did nothing for a moment other than dart her eyes back and forth between the man in front of her and various random places in the shadows outside.

Apprehension. Good.

She nodded faintly in response to his question. "He'll be back very soon."

That was a lie.

She regained a modicum of strength and demanded, "Who are you? What do you want? Why are you here?"

"I'm standing here because you haven't invited me inside. I would like to come inside." Charles's voice was soft but insistent.

"I think not."

"I think so." Charles pulled his suppressed .22 from inside his coat and aimed it from his hip at the center of her chest. Out here—a mile from the nearest neighbor—he didn't need a suppressed weapon, but the long barrel of the assassin's weapon would be psychologically motivating. She stepped back, and the door swung open. From her vantage point, he was a sinister figure, tall and severe, standing against a dusky background. He said, "Again, my name is Paladin. As to who I am, consider me an arm of justice. I'm here because you, who are supposed to protect rights, have instead violated them."

She moved toward the sofa in the living room. "What do … do … do … you mean?"

Charles's stern expression fit the occasion. "You've recently taken children away from a family. Children who lost their parents not long ago. You've extracted them from the loving home of their grandparents. You kidnapped them."

"I've done nothing of the sort. What do you want from me?"

"First, a question. Do you have the power to return the Jannsens' children tonight? Or do you need permissions and approvals to do so?"

She hesitated and shivered.

Charles firmly repeated, "Do you need permission from anyone else, Mrs. Penure, or do you—working for Child Protective Services—have the power to return the children tonight?"

She found a whiff of courage as she remembered her position. "I am CPS in this town. So I could. If I thought it was the right thing to do. Which I don't."

"Good. I'll convince you. I want you to get Mr. Jannsen's family back together. Immediately. The children need to be home with their grandparents."

"The Jannsens are criminals," she replied.

Charles exhaled in disgust. "Why do you think they're criminals?

185

Because a government official told you so? Because they grew hemp on their own farm?"

"Hemp is a source of illegal drugs. We are in the middle of a war on drugs, Mr. Paladin. They're on the wrong side of that war and committed a federal felony. Nobody who breaks the law is fit to raise a child."

"I have neither the time nor the interest to discuss botany or legalities with you. Tell me, did you think the Jannsens were unfit caregivers before all this? I'm sure you've met them. It's a small town."

"I have met them before. But I was naïve. Now I know."

"Do you think the Jannsens are criminals in any other way?"

She replied, "Drugs are enough. More than enough."

"Did you find evidence that the Jannsens were abusing the children?"

She shrugged. "Physically. No. But the drugs... They were growing drugs."

Charles nodded. "So you first learned of their evil from Mr. Kirby, perhaps."

During their conversation, she'd slumped against the side of a couch, and then into it. She raised her chin defiantly. "Yes, that's right. I learned the details from an Agriculture agent, straight from Washington."

"I want you to see what your friend Terrence Kirby is."

"What do you mean?" she asked with a suddenly weaker voice.

"This is his laptop. Take a look at some material on it."

He positioned the laptop in front of her and opened the screen to the summary page of Kirby's sexual conquests. He let her read it until she saw her name located not far from the end of the list.

"Why should I believe this is his laptop?" she murmured with her eyes squeezed tightly closed.

"Click on your name."

She opened her eyes, hesitated, but then clicked on her name. A folder opened. With pictures. Of her, and him, in flagrante delicto.

"Oh no."

"Would you like to see the emails between the two of you? They're all here in this laptop. He cares nothing about your privacy or modesty. Or would you prefer to start with the emails between him and his wife?"

"His wife?"

"Yes. Kirby's married. But then so are you."

The woman shrank into a smaller form, crumpled into the couch. "No. I don't need to see them."

186

"How about the child pornography? He has thousands of images. He himself is a child rapist. You should be protecting children from him, not allowing him to manipulate you."

Charles took a step back. "I generally don't pay heed to people's infidelities. It's none of my business. But at the moment I do care about your infidelity, Ms. Penure. Do you love your husband?"

She replied quietly, "Yes."

"Do you need your husband?"

She looked straight at Charles. "Yes."

Charles nodded. "Good. Your infidelity may save your life, then. We'll see. What worries me is that you're instinctively obedient to authority without regard to justice. You took the children for a weak reason and against their will. You've been so obedient that you've committed what's generally regarded as a capital offense: kidnapping. The sentence for kidnapping is death. The fact you did so as an apparatchik of your employer doesn't excuse you. In fact, the way you revel in your power further compounds your offense. The question is whether I should allow you to live. To allow you and your diseased mindset to continue harming decent people."

The woman somehow sank back even further into the couch, sniveling and whining softly.

"Notwithstanding your brownshirt mentality, I'm inclined to let you live. Mainly because I find it convenient, for the moment. However, you will return the Jannsen children this evening—meaning right now—to their farm. If you do not, I will send copies of these computer files to your husband, to your employer, to the local newspaper, to your church, and to your friends and family. If you ever harm another person again while claiming the power of the law is behind you, I will hear of it and return to kill you without another thought. If you tell anyone that your return of the children to the Jannsens was performed under duress, I will kill you. If you reach out to Kirby for help or to let him know of our understanding, I will kill you. Do you understand everything I've just said?"

She nodded slowly. There was nothing but fear there now. Fear of death, certainly. But with this kind of person, especially in a small traditional town, fear of exposure and humiliation was even more terrifying.

"I see you're stressed. Please repeat back to me, in your own words, everything I just said to you."

She did so.

"Ironically, your infidelity has given you a probation, Mrs. Penure. Your fear of exposure allows me to take a chance on you. Instead of killing you while I rescue the children, I can save myself some trouble. I'll be watching you." He turned away from the despicable woman and walked back to his car.

Charles next drove for an hour to Bismarck, the state capital, parked on the road across from the Hilton Garden Inn, and waited for Terrence Kirby to return from meeting with his crony buddies from big agribusiness.

Charles made a quick call to the Jannsens to learn that the county sheriff had already brought the grandchildren home. The sheriff even stuck around for dinner with the reunited family.

After that good news, sitting in the car for four hours outside a hotel was taxing. Dog work interrupted only by spammers who managed even to call burner phones. After the extended dusk finally turned to darkness, the night vision scope Rainbow had acquired from Mei-li proved moderately useful. He studied each vehicle to make sure he didn't miss anyone entering the hotel.

Kirby arrived just before midnight. Charles traded his coat for a hooded gray sweatshirt, locked his car, and entered the building moments after him. Kirby had his phone to his ear, talking loudly, the way people do who want others to think they must be important. He stood about five and half feet tall, his eyes small and dark, with a narrow mouth and prominent proboscis that reminded Charles of a possum. Had his unfortunate looks formed his character, or had his unfortunate character shaped his looks?

Together, the two men awaited the arrival of the elevator.

Kirby, barely aware of Charles, focused on his phone. "Great, Todd. You know I'm in. I had a great time with you gentlemen tonight... Well, of course. You rub my back. I rub yours. You know how we roll. You've got the grease; I pull the levers."

Charles rode the painfully slow elevator with him to the third floor.

"May lose your signal. I'll get back to you next week, and I'll make sure you get what you need... Yup... Bye."

The man looked self-satisfied but with a twinge of anxiety. Perhaps because he was alone in an elevator with a man in a hoodie. Then, perhaps to allay his hoodie fears, or maybe just because he was both drunk and feeling like a little master of the universe because of whatever deal he'd just done, the cocky bastard started to gloat.

He held up his phone and said, "The CEO himself. The moneybags. The man with the gold. I'm getting the gold!"

"I only get spam calls," Charles replied. "CEO of what?"

"CEO of my new corporate sugar daddy."

Charles let the man walk out of the elevator first. "Strange choice of terms. But I get what you're saying."

Kirby took a quick look over his shoulder toward the hooded man as he fumbled for his plastic key card in front of his motel-room door, but he didn't act on his instinctual fear fast enough. He didn't rush to move inside and close the door.

Charles shoved Kirby into the room and held the suppressed .22 to his head, used his other hand to frisk him, and then pushed him backward. "Sit down, Kirby. On the bed."

"Who are you?" Kirby's panic rose further as he stumbled backward onto the bed. He knew that the elongated suppressed .22 was no typical mugger's weapon.

Charles stood over him. He lowered the gun to his hip, aiming it at the center of Kirby's torso. Kirby shrank against the bed's headboard and pulled a pillow across his chest, as if it were either a comforting stuffed animal or an effective shield against lead.

"The name I use is irrelevant. But who I am matters to you greatly. Because of the failure of the system, I am by default your judge, jury, and quite likely your executioner. Now, defend yourself."

"What?"

"I have your computer. Your actions are unconscionable. What's your defense?"

"You . . . you have my computer?"

"Yes. Do you recognize me now?" Charles asked.

The man looked closely and shook his head.

Charles, pleased, prompted, "Your department library. We talked for a moment. Just as your computer went missing."

Kirby scowled. He seemed to think that revelation gave him some leverage. "My computer's government property. It's a serious crime, and I'll prosecute to the full extent of the law! You have no right to access it."

"Is that what you're worried about right now?"

Kirby eyes widened, and he shivered slightly. "What do you want?"

"Surprisingly little."

"What do you want, you fuck!" The whimpering Kirby added that last bit of pointless defiance with effort.

"I want you to defend yourself. You're corrupt, you're perverted, and you use your position to pointlessly destroy other people's lives. Prove to me otherwise."

"Look, I have money with me."

The man's response was automatic, reflexive. After living in the swamp, he seemed to assume that cash provided all the moral defense one might need.

Charles allowed him to reach into his pocket for his wallet. Six hundred dollars. He told Kirby, "I'll consider this a down payment on what the Jannsens owe me."

"The Jannsens? Is this about the Jannsens?"

Charles nodded. "And the Smythes, and the Friedmanns, and the Cochrans."

It took only a few seconds for Kirby to process the names of farmers on a list in his laptop: hemp growers who'd suffered because their plants had a fraction too much THC.

"So this is about hemp. You're just a stinking drug dealer, aren't you?"

Charles had to smile at that. "Actually, I was more of a drug lord. But I'm not anymore. You're really about the only man at DOA who seems to have a particular vendetta against hemp. I mean, it's legal. Why are you doing this?"

"Some is legal. Not all. Those farmers were growing illegal hemp. It's my job to enforce the law. I didn't write the law."

"Is that law constitutional?"

"What?"

"I spoke clearly."

"Constitutional? What are you talking about?"

Charles knew the type, but he wanted to probe. So he asked, "Is the law actually defensible? Is it even a moral law?" Asking the question made him feel anachronistic. It was a little like asking a gangsta at a rap concert if he liked thirteenth-century Gregorian chants.

Kirby's eyes darted back and forth. "It's the law. What do you mean?"

"Quite simply, does the federal government have the right to make a law banning hemp production that has more than point-four percent THC?"

"Of course we do! We have the right to make any law we want. What the hell is wrong with you?"

Kirby used the first-person plural. In that man's mind, the government and himself were inseparably intertwined.

190

Charles said, "Do you have the right to favor the CEO of that company too? Make sure he gets first dibs on the ethanol subsidy, perhaps?"

"Yeah. Yeah. In my position I do. The money is solid. I can cut you in."

"How much?"

Kirby brightened at the prospect of a solution. "Every month. It's every month. I don't know exactly how much yet, but it'll be a lot."

"Sounds like a good offer." Charles shook his head, unable to control his disgust. He reached into the satchel he carried and removed Kirby's laptop. He opened the screen to reveal the man's extensive folder of images of child sexual abuse as he placed it on the bed next to Kirby. "But I don't want to go into business with you. I don't like you. I not only have your computer, but I saw the pictures you keep on it—before I got nauseated, that is. You're a stupid man, keeping this sort of thing on your work computer. Perhaps your bosses have similar predilections. I don't know. But they'd be pretty pissed off if they knew you were using their computer for this. You might get caught, and that would make them look bad."

"Those files are all password protected!"

"You're a fool, then, as well as a pederast."

"A what?"

"Never mind, you don't need to know what it means. You're a waste of food." Charles lifted the muzzle of the gun to the man's head. He considered for a moment. He acknowledged that Kirby posed no immediate threat to him. Indeed he posed no immediate threat to anyone. Was he justified in pulling the trigger? What does one do when face to face with somebody who just can't help destroying other people's lives and property? What should a farmer do if he catches a weasel in his henhouse? The weasel won't just take one hen for dinner. It will kill every single one, simply because that's the way it's wired. So you've got to kill the weasel. What does one do with a real criminal? Not just a thoughtless thug who commits a spur-of-the-moment crime because he's too stupid to look down the road and see what the consequences are, but a real sociopath, a criminal personality. The easiest solution is to simply take him out. That may, or may not, present a moral problem.

The immediacy of a threat provided one justification for killing, but the severity of a threat might combine with a series of other circumstances to justify killing when the opportunity presented itself. The fact that a man enjoyed looking at pictures of children having all manner of violent and perverted things done to them might, in the minds of many, warrant pulling the trigger. The morality of that would be questionable. That Kirby participated in such violence himself, however, made pulling the trigger mandatory.

Charles fell back onto the steeliness he had learned in prison. Even the worst experiences in life can add to one's capabilities. It helped him now as he pulled the trigger. The gun's action sounded no louder than the noise of the television remote control as it fell from the bed, pushed by Kirby's spasming hand.

He reached into his pocket for two plastic-wrapped Paladin coins, with the Have Gun—Will Travel and the chess-knight logo. He tore open the plastic envelopes. His gloved hand placed one coin on each of the man's eyes. One heads up, one tails. Why take this risk? Because, after a while, word would spread that someone served justice upon this man.

Of course, it was unlikely the FBI agents who came to investigate would release the information about the coins. Instead, it would have to leak out. Charles had a brand to build, so he would see to it. He took a picture of the coins on Kirby's dead face, securing the image with a cryptographic app, in case the phone ever fell into the wrong hands.

As Charles started the Chrysler and drove away, he felt the discomfort in his chest. Not as tight as when he killed Jock, but certainly present. He noted also, with dour satisfaction, that he felt no adrenaline rush, no high, no sensation of excitement, no thrill. Thank god or nature for that, for such responses could lead to pleasure and addiction. There should be nothing addicting about this avocation. It was comparable to being an exterminator eliminating an infestation of rats or cockroaches—not pleasant, but necessary.

He didn't like exposing himself to unpleasant people, but many things that are necessary, or even voluntarily undertaken, may not be pleasant. On the bright side, there was now one less man with a malicious ideology and a malevolent character eager to damage humanity.

It was a dirty job, but perhaps the Paladin Network would create a market for getting it done.

Dirty jobs are performed to make things cleaner.

Tonight, Charles resolved a kidnapping and made the world a slightly safer place for everyone … except himself.

21

Lunch with Frenemies

"SO you believe the hunting-accident story."

"It's been two months and nothing suspicious. No other attempts on my life. Accidents happen."

"Not to us."

"We're not immune to accidents." Samuels's tone reflected many decades of experience.

The pair sat at a quiet corner table on the 4th Floor.

About a dozen others lunched there today; Forestal appraised them. Most were made out of money. The cost of any house, any piece of land, or almost any person for that matter, was an ignorable fraction of their net worth. They were far above a plebeian task like managing their money. They owned wealth.

Forestal ranked comfortably within the top hundredth of the top 1 percent, but he was still way out of their league. He was here because he was useful to them and had shown competence. They recognized the importance of bringing new members, young blood, into the club. Without young blood, even with all their wealth, they'd eventually become ineffectual, doddering old men. That would happen anyway, but younger talent could act as very effective minions—much more so than their own often-worthless sons and daughters or their employees.

Forestal didn't mind that they used him—as he used them. A symbiosis like rhinos and tick birds, or sharks and remoras.

They were people persons, but not in the usual sense of the phrase. They manipulated people the way normal people manipulated things. They were cronies. The word had negative connotations to most; it implied backroom deals and conspiracies against the public. Cronies didn't have real friendships so much as convenient or opportunistic associations. Usually with good access to public funding. Forestal had thought about it and decided cronyism was an apt descriptor for their way of life. If the capite censi didn't like the good-ol'-boy system, it was because they weren't important enough to join the club.

The 4th Floor was the nexus of cronyism in New York City. DC and other large cities had their own counterparts. It was important to have a place to size up associates, trade rumors, and do deals.

Forestal was proud to be a part of it. He might have felt fortunate, but it was simply his due.

Sabina joined them and sat a bit too close to the far-older man. An ever-increasing number of women frequented the 4th Floor. Inevitable, perhaps, but a major error, he thought with some resentment. It would change dynamics here that had been stable for over a hundred years. Sexual tension invariably accompanied the mingling of the sexes, and now they were mingling at levels approaching equality. Women first made inroads in medicine, then literature, science, and academia. They'd gone from about 0 to over 60 percent of college students. They'd gained tremendous influence in politics and the media—and now in business and finance. He wondered if they weren't on the way to becoming the dominant human life form, relegating men to the role of sperm donors. Was that possible? Perhaps. Young males seemed to be turning into gender-fluid metrosexuals. Even fifty years earlier, a woman in this room—other than a paid escort—would have been unthinkable. There were three women evident in the café this afternoon.

Forestal had made his money as he rose through positions in banking and government over the last twenty years. Sabina, substantially younger, was wealthy by the standards of most people—obviously excepting those in this room. She had, so far, focused on gaining power, building a network of connections, and amassing IOUs and extortion tokens she could cash in upon leaving the public sector. The next step in the cursus honorum, as the Romans called it, might be a position in industry with a seven-figure salary plus bonuses and stock options, but Sabina's long-term focus was a key position in central banking. It was an attainable goal. She'd gone to the effort of getting a PhD and writing academic papers with well-known economists

Samuels had introduced her to. She had the necessary ambition, intelligence, and credentials—as did hundreds of other young women moving in these circles. She combined those things with the beauty of a Medici princess and the mind and morals of a Machiavelli. Forestal liked to keep her physically close when he felt the urge but safely distant in every important way. He knew lots of women. Of them all she was most like him and therefore particularly dangerous.

Forestal and Sabina thought alike, but he recognized she was far more proficient at controlling others. Each considered other humans as pawns, toys, or stepping-stones. Where he turned to violence, she chose emotional manipulation. Could a woman with such a captivating smile and engaging manner actually be a female Dorian Grey? How much more successful would a velociraptor have been if it mimicked the looks, manners, and family status of its prey when it went hunting? People served as tools in her survival kit; she was even more of a people person than the others in the room. That made her a successful Deep State denizen and very useful to Paul Samuels.

Sabina nodded provocatively toward Forestal. He nodded back.

Eterio Conti sat nearby. The Eterio Conti—the most recognized member of the group. A glutton for publicity, he demanded attention like a spoiled two-year-old. Getting it made him almost as happy as obtaining more money and power. In fact, he'd routinely risk money, but not power, to gain a bit more attention. He played on the ignorance and apathy of the capite censi. It amused him to watch his dupes fawn and grovel. Conti was like a sophisticated carnival sideshow hustler but on a global scale. He enjoyed putting one over on the rubes even as they applauded him. Had he been born an American, he would have run for president, but, born in Austria of an Italian father and a Lebanese mother, he couldn't pass constitutional muster. He held passports from all four countries.

Across from Conti sat James Wainwright, Forestal's freshman-year roommate. Wainwright had climbed faster up the ladder after graduation than he had. Forestal blamed that on a few unfortunate episodes that had slowed his own climb. He rubbed at the itchy scar on his chest in response to the memory.

Princeton University had been a great launching pad for both of their careers. It wasn't that the average student learned any more than he might at some no-name school in the hinterlands. Its advantage lay in its reputation and the fact that it was notoriously hard to gain admission. That winnowed out the dullards and the lumpenproletariat. If you were a Princeton man, people assumed that either your IQ was at least two standard deviations above the norm or you were a scion of a wealthy and well-connected family. Once you were in, it was fairly easy to stay in and benefit from the aura, despite increasing numbers of outsiders there to provide diversity and PC bona fides. Princeton alumni looked out for each other, passing around opportunities, board memberships, and favors.

After grad school, Wainwright became a faculty member at Harvard and went on to do a stint on the board of the New York Fed. Now he was the secretary of the treasury, clearly on track for moving up the ladder from high government official to Master of the Universe. The prospect was a psychological steroid, allowing him to dominate almost everyone in his personal sphere. In public life, he loved to flex his intellectual muscles before the rubes in Congress, dazzling them with abstruse and recondite mathematical formulae, confidently explaining the economy. His audience had all seen the plus, minus, multiplication, and division signs—and even knew how to use them. Those who'd been in a fraternity at least recognized the Greek letters used in the math, but none of them had a clue what the strange figures— the factorials, asymptotic equivalents, converse implications, ket vectors, functional derivatives, and many others—could possibly mean. Wainwright knew there'd be no questions from the congressional peanut gallery.

The economically naïve and intellectually weak legislators cooperated for fear of embarrassment, even thanking him as a way to hide their confusion. A high-functioning sociopath, Wainwright enjoyed convincing his victims—whether congressmen or his unlucky interns—to join willingly, even enthusiastically, in their own abuse. He indulged his proclivities and used his high IQ and connections to avoid the exposure of compromising situations.

Connections were everything. Wainwright's Senate confirmation process revealed that he owed more back taxes than the average American earned in a decade. While a regular Joe would have been looking at jail time, Wainwright just apologized, blamed it on his accountant's poor computer skills, and wrote a check on the day of his confirmation. One would think that tax evasion might preclude confirmation as treasury secretary. One would be incorrect.

Theodore Solomon, tapped as Goldman Sachs's next CEO, sat across from Wainwright. Yet another Princeton alum, he envied Wainwright's blueblood breeding, Aryan looks, and bravado, but he was just as powerful and even wealthier. They'd had the same professors, albeit a few years apart. Jews and bluebloods came from different tribes that were suspicious and resentful of each other. Solomon resented his people's being excluded by the WASPs for generations; Wainwright resented the Jews now pushing his own people aside. For the potential upside, however, they now held their noses, feigned friendship, and joined the same clubs.

Old-money families were well represented on the 4th Floor. Two distinguished-looking patriarchs sat with each other, politely disdaining the parvenus while discussing the grandchildren of their respective clans. Both subtly boasted of the kids' qualities and success. "Yes," said the first. "Tad is very socially aware—thinking of a major in gender studies." The second countered with his own brood's involvement in impact investing. Each knew the other's little bastard was a spoiled alcoholic, druggie, party animal, and spendthrift. Hopefully the outsiders managing the wealth in their family offices wouldn't steal too much, so there'd be something left for the great grandchildren, if any were birthed. The upper classes weren't reproducing the way they once did.

The two patriarchs were Ivy League, of course, but it didn't matter what college they attended: inherited wealth and connections guaranteed their status. Eschewing publicity, like Samuels, they kept a low profile. Unlike Conti, who sought ego enhancement, these two men sought quiet wealth and power. They looked alike, sharing mannerisms, pale skin, and dead eyes—something like the ex–CIA chief who whelped his baby Bushes, hoping to start a dynasty. Forestal recognized he shared similar physical features and wondered if he might be a lost descendant or a bastard child of one of them.

Sabina sat quietly, perfectly formed legs crossed. Samuels interrupted Forestal's contemplation and returned to the conversation. "Look, the FBI says that it was likely accidental. Isn't that enough?"

"Accidental it is," Forestal replied, as if agreement between two powerful men determined fact.

Samuels nodded. "Europe is on the brink. What do you hear?"

Forestal replied, "One might have thought the Moslem invasion would have angered the hoi polloi. You'd think there'd be some kind of reaction at seeing their culture swept away. Every Nigerian that's made it to Europe is on his cell phone to his pals back home telling them to get on board, come over, and help conquer the Eurotrash. I'm hearing more concern about what's happening right here, with this CityFire movement on top of the recession. But even the Europeans will start waving pitchforks and torches at some point." He hesitated a moment before adding, "The people running Europe aren't nearly as subtle or astute as you, Paul." It was the first time Forestal had ever referred to the president of the New York Fed by his first name, at least to his face.

Samuels didn't seem affronted by the familiarity, and Forestal took that as permission.

"They haven't needed to be as astute, Blaize. The Europeans have had a more advanced welfare state, and for much longer, than the Americans. They're saturated with Marxist thought. Sovietized, for practical purposes. The upper classes are unisex faggots sitting around cafes talking about Sartre, Foucault, Derrida, and feeling sorry for themselves. The lower classes are thoughtless peasants. They control themselves quite well on their own. In the US, we have a more difficult population."

Forestal followed up with another compliment. "Your success with the Charles Knight affair and destroying Naked Emperor before it got too far out of hand… it's the stuff of legend, or at least textbooks."

"I appreciate your kind words. The American media has become easy to manipulate. The days of effective, or at least irritating, investigative reporters are gone, Blaize. They used to be hard-bitten types dredging the street for dirt, acting like characters in a Mickey Spillane novel. Fortunately, there are very few left now. They're all English or journalism majors now. Their idea of original research is Googling some subject and rewriting something somebody else wrote—who probably did the same thing. It's like they're still in high school. No street smarts. When they were in college, all they learned was how to parrot what their professors said, to get an A. They're useful idiots, but distasteful. I understand why Mao sent them all to work in the fields."

He paused, in thought, then continued. "So, Blaize, it's only necessary to take the place of their professor. These new journalists have all got a bundle of college debt, which makes them buyable. A promise of loan forgiveness could be part of a quid pro quo. The few who are independent-minded know they'd better toe the line; nobody can afford to lose their job these days."

Blaize nodded. "At some point soon, journalists and journalism can be replaced with artificial intelligence algorithms. They're going to be better, a lot cheaper, and guaranteed to see things from the right angle."

"We're making progress on that front. For now, it's easy enough to puppeteer, I suppose. But we don't want to become too arrogant. The media has lost the public's respect. The same things that make the media easy to play have destroyed their credibility. The hoi polloi aren't bright, but they can sense a lack of integrity. Kind of on the same gut level an animal can tell when you're afraid. Influence on the media won't matter much if the people don't pay attention to them anymore. As far as the destruction of Naked Emperor, that credit goes in part to Sabina."

Forestal couldn't help but wince at the mention of her name. He wondered if either Sabina or Samuels noticed. Most likely they did; predators were always searching for weakness and could read the tiniest muscle twitch. Forestal scolded himself.

Samuels continued. "As the economy gets worse—and it will—there will be violent uprisings in Europe. Our counterparts there are rightly concerned. As charismatic leaders coalesce from the CityFire protests, uprisings will get worse here in the US as well. The situation can get out of hand. It's like when Mrs. O'Leary's cow kicked over a lantern in Chicago in 1871. Who knew that a little fire in a barn would wind up burning down the whole city? These things can take on lives of their own. In fact, at this point it seems likely to spread. Riots about the economy and politics can cause fractures in society itself.

"With all the monetization of government and corporate debt we're undertaking, at some point the Fed will lose control of the money supply. Retail prices will get out of control, and we'll lose our ability to fix interest rates. The whole economy is a daisy chain of debt, a house of cards built on quicksand. It's true what our critics have said: there aren't any free lunches. Our worker bees at the Fed and Treasury have PhDs but mostly don't have a clue. They're paid to convince everyone that the economy is under control, and they convince themselves in the process. But between us, we're headed for serious trouble. Just not as fast as Europe. For the first time, I've realized I'm old enough to care about my legacy. I don't know why. It shouldn't make any difference after you're dead, but I don't want to be thought of in the history books as stupid."

Forestal looked at him, poker-faced.

Samuels continued. "Many Americans still believe in their heritage.

They see traditional America as a culture that's worth defending. They'll respond violently if they feel threatened. And I don't mean these CityFire rioters either. They're just spoiled brats demanding more handouts. In my mind, they're only useful for cannon fodder. No, I'm talking about the few people who are sincere thinkers who believe in what America was supposed to be but no longer is. Remember, only five percent of the population was truly in favor of rebelling against England in 1774; the rest of the country was about evenly divided between loyalists and those who really didn't care. My guess is that—assuming it wasn't a freak accident—whoever shot at me was politically motivated. Someone who'd feel everyone here on the 4th deserves the same fate—if he knew you existed."

So Samuels was indeed feeling his mortality. It was undoubtedly the near miss. Although he needed to talk to somebody, he had nobody close. The people in this room, this snake pit, were as close to family as he had. Forestal said, "So you don't really accept it was an accident."

"Of course not. It was a botched assassination."

Forestal watched as Samuels rubbed at his neck, still faintly sore from that event. He looked into the man's eyes, noticed the increasing gauntness of his face, and sensed a certain fear. The bodyguards weren't the only evidence that Paul Samuels now lived on edge.

"I'm afraid the natives are getting restless," Samuels said. "Very few Americans have any idea what the Federal Reserve is, but a certain number of them have bought into the idea that it's a threat to their liberty. They're the same types that tend to own assault weapons."

Forestal recalled that the phrase "assault weapons" had been invented and promulgated by a predecessor of Samuels, a few decades earlier.

Samuels turned to Sabina. "This country's on the ragged edge financially, economically, politically, and socially. It all brings me to an issue that Blaize and I have been contemplating between us for some time. I'd like your opinion, Sabina, on the matter of guns in the United States."

Forestal knew this matter hadn't come to Samuels's mind just because he'd been shot at. He also knew that Samuels had positioned him in his current government post for a very specific reason, planned long before the attempted assassination. He glanced around the room again with a new frame of reference. What might the people here on the 4th Floor, today, bring to the table in regard to Samuels's vision for gun control?

Sabina spoke for the first time. "What about guns? Three hundred ninety million guns mostly owned by people who I certainly don't consider my allies. How do you deal with people who like to say, 'Sure, you can have my gun—when you pry it from my cold dead hands'? A lot of it's just big talk, but the masses can sometimes be unpredictable and violent. What do you expect from trailer park trash, right-wing ideologues, and paranoid nationalists? Much worse situation than in Europe. What happened to you is a good reason why guns should be banned."

Forestal had taken his position at Justice in part to flex some muscles, and Samuels had been instrumental in setting that up. He was but a pawn in the great game that Samuels had been designing for years, but at least he was on the board, playing the game. He thought it best to let Sabina carry the conversation. All he said was "True enough, but gun aficionados exist at all economic levels."

Samuels nodded. "The people who visit me here on the 4th Floor generally have substantial means to protect themselves and their assets. Bodyguards and more. Like I've recently been forced to employ. But those people ... out there"—he waved his hand dismissively toward the outside world—"maintain they have the same right, and they tend not to be dissuaded of that notion. The CityFire mobs are just one piece of evidence that the overall situation is ... unstable."

"So you agree it's finally time to disarm the gun nuts?" Sabina asked. Both her voice and posture indicated it was a rhetorical question. Her use of the word nuts stood in obvious counterpoint to Forestal's use of aficionados a moment before. Sabina sneered slightly when she said it.

Samuels didn't answer directly. Instead, he said, "The masses are frustrated, and they don't know who to blame. There's unrest in the world concentrated among the middle classes in developed nations. Third Worlders are too poor and ignorant to make a difference. They only count when millions of them migrate, like locusts. Their rulers know that if we cut off the flow of capital, bribes, technology, and food, they'd revert to bush in no time. They're but a nuisance.

"The United States will survive. But here there will be armed militias and gangs to deal with. Blacks in the ghettos, Latinos in the barrios, whites in the hinterland. Chaotic conditions always sort people out by the lowest common denominators: force and violence. It's been that way for the last two hundred thousand years since the human species emerged. Perhaps for five hundred million years, since multicellular animals evolved. Force and violence are programmed into our genetic makeup. Modern humans may seem civilized, but it's just a social veneer that all these"—he again waved his hand expansively—"naked apes affect. Most are just overfed, drug-addled doughballs; they'll just sit on their couches and watch TV no matter what happens. They hardly count. But there's a certain percentage that will rise up in rebellion."

Sabina interrupted. "It's not possible for the civilians to win."

Forestal smiled as Samuels corrected her.

"But they don't know that, Sabina," Samuels replied. "And that makes things... unpredictable. We might get caught in the crossfire. Of course they'll be crushed if they take on the State; that's not the problem. The problem is that any one of them, as an individual, can take out any of us as individuals. A gun gives them a practical way to reach out and touch us—as individuals. How else can they hurt us? With their bare hands? With a knife? If I could snap my fingers and eliminate all guns in this country—except yours and mine—I'd do so."

Forestal smiled more broadly as Sabina tried again by saying, "It's been done in almost every other country."

"Sabina, we think it has," Samuels replied. "But how many guns are buried in plastic bags in people's backyards? America is different than most all countries. Gun control efforts here suffer from a national history that we've—quite unwisely—not yet corrected in the schools. One reason people in America have guns is so they can defend those guns against people who want to take them. Like I said, they're wrong about that—but what counts is what these people believe.

"Anyway, it triggered the Revolutionary War, which, you'll recall, started when British troops marched to Lexington to seize a cache of weapons." He once again waved his arm to encompass the room and perhaps the whole country. "An outright ban will more likely trigger unrest than contain it."

Sabina tried another tactic to gain favor with Samuels. "So how about ammunition? Put a substantial tax on it. Gradually ban some types, starting with things like hollow-point bullets. And then tax the ingredients. The gunpowder and the lead used for ammunition. At a minimum it will decrease demand."

"Taxing ammunition and its components is on the table. It's a wedge; harder for the Second Amendment to get in the way. But these people, especially the hard core, have billions of rounds stockpiled."

Sabina added, "I understand. The best way to make progress is to wear them down with trench warfare—and psychological warfare."

"But the trenches have moved backwards lately." Forestal took the opportunity to clarify. "The judiciary biases have shifted."

Samuels nodded. "Over the decades, as you well know, the most successful way to push forward an agenda is to have opinion leaders say and write the right things during times of crisis. It's most important to control words; controlling words is as close as you can come to controlling thought. Most people don't actually think, with their reason. All they really do is feel, with their emotions. They conflate the justification of their feelings with reason. This makes it easier to control the high ground on the battlefield. In this battle, control includes defining the terms of the debate. Laying out the meaning of terms the way I need them defined has always been my strength since my academic days. It's the key to sowing confusion in the ranks of the enemy.

"The best example might be how the definition of the word liberal has morphed. Today it means the exact opposite of its original meaning. It comes from the Latin liber, which means free. Liberal used to mean free thought, free minds, free actions, free markets, and the like. So liberal was a good word to capture. Changing language is easier than changing minds. Orwell exposed this in 1984. War is Peace, Freedom is Slavery, etc. Confused language makes for confused thought. Confused thought heightens emotions and makes it easy to control people. Humans are dangerous animals if they're not kept under control.

"Just like Global Warming became Climate Change and then Climate Crisis and then Climate Catastrophe. Violence becomes Gun Violence. Crime becomes Gun Crime. Changing what words mean, and the language itself, are important tools. The gun lobby is aware of the importance of language, but fortunately, they aren't the brightest Crayons in the box."

Sabina said, "Still, any awareness is unfortunate."

"Awareness in your adversary is always unfortunate, of course. Even those with the brains of an oyster know when the tide is going out. They don't say it. They try to keep up a bold front, but they know resistance is futile over the longer term."

Sabina said, "Clearly, you have a notion you're considering?"

Samuels nodded. "Sure, I'm in favor of taxing ammunition and its components. Claim the tax revenues will be used to enhance the safety of students at schools. Who can argue they want unsafe schools? And provide mental health counseling or some such. We know it's ninety percent drivel, but the shrinks are on our side. I'm working on it from a fiscal angle; Forestal is navigating legislation and administration."

Forestal watched Sabina nod cautiously. She looked miffed at having been left out of the loop.

She said, pensively, "But as you mentioned, existing ammunition will be around for decades. These people will hoard it until they need it."

"You're right, Sabina," Samuels responded. "Forestal and I have discussed this at some length over the past two years. We've got bigger initiatives too. What's the path forward when control of language is insufficient? Tell you what. Before we go into details, let's first enlarge this conversation. Using rhetoric to sway the mob is always helpful, and sometimes critical. But, in point of fact, most progress is made with small deals between important people."

Forestal was proud of himself for anticipating that Samuels had arranged today's conversation. He watched as Samuels went into action.

Samuels stood up. As the host, he had certain privileges; when he stood, the guests moved together, like a school of fish or a flock of birds. No one needed to rap on a drinking glass. He spoke formally. "Gentlemen and ladies, I propose a conversation on the issue of gun control in the US, including the methods by which it can be accomplished. I invite anyone interested to the conference room."

It wasn't unusual for a conversation at one table to expand. Within ten minutes, the intended invitees had gathered in the conference room.

Before they entered, Samuels pulled Forestal aside and spoke sotto voce.

"I want you to take a lead role in this discussion and what, if anything, evolves from it. Stick your neck out. Take some risks. It's fine to discuss ammunition tariffs, but you must not raise the matter of the real prize. You understand me?"

Forestal did.

It was a huge vote of confidence on the one hand. On the other hand, Samuels could be setting him up.

Using the conference room was a sensual delight. A spectacular silk Oriental on the buffed wood floors, impressive art on the walls, sumptuous leather chairs around the centerpiece, and a massive redwood table with its layered varnish polished to a mirror finish. It might have come from Muir

Woods. Maybe Samuels had a three-hundred-foot-tall tree, in one of the most famous forests in the world, felled just to make a table. He wouldn't put it past the man. And he certainly didn't object. Forestal glanced out the window, disdaining the mere mortals on the street below.

Samuels addressed the seven people seated around the table. "We've been discussing the possibility of advancing the gun control agenda."

The wealthiest, oldest, and least kempt man at the table grunted. "City-Fires scaring you, are they, Samuels? Or is it that you've been shot at, and that's got your attention? Don't think I didn't notice the guards surrounding you and your house all the time now. It's come too close to home, hasn't it?"

Forestal hoped Samuels would disregard the impertinence, and he did. Forestal cleared his voice and asserted himself. "We have an opportunity."

"How so?" one of the pale men from an old family asked, clearly irritated while managing to sound both bored and pompous with only two words.

Forestal replied, "The gun lobby uses hunting as justification for keeping civilian ownership of guns legal."

"One of many justifications," interrupted Eterio Conti.

"Yes," Forestal agreed. "It's an increasingly weak approach on their part. Relatively few Americans hunt anymore. It's seen as brutal and politically incorrect. Progress has been made on that front. Hunters' rights are a dead duck these days." He smiled at his own bon mot. "It's nowhere on the list of voting priorities. Animals might prefer to roam free and then die suddenly, rather than be factory farmed. But they don't get a vote." He nodded to Samuels.

A woman—the superstar CEO of a Silicon Valley social media powerhouse—said, "These Neanderthals worship the Second Amendment as if it's a god. These people don't understand that the Constitution is a living document. It needs to move with the times." If she'd been referring to blacks, migrants, or Muslims as Neanderthals, it would have been terminally non-PC. But to call gun owners Neanderthals was quite acceptable.

The wealthiest, oldest man took a long view of everything. Perhaps that was just a function of being on the far side of ninety. He said he'd always thought that way, and he attributed his investment success to it. He funded paleontology expeditions and tended to the terminology of those academics. "Assault-rifle bans, handgun permits, and local restrictions come and go. It's a case of punctuated equilibrium. Things move very slowly for a long time.

Then there's a major event that accelerates or entirely reverses a trend. Look how things changed with the Kennedy assassination. Guns were regulated practically overnight."

Forestal imagined that Samuels might have brought this man into the conversation to add precisely that thought. Little that Samuels did should be considered spontaneous. "An excellent point, Mr. Claussen," replied Forestal, extending himself further than he thought safe, doing so because Samuels had prodded him into it. "That's one reason why I'm at this table—and why I'm at the Justice Department. I've found a needle and a way to thread it."

"What is this needle? What color is your thread?"

Forestal wished he could tell these people the whole plan and take credit for it, but Samuels had been clear in his admonition to do no such thing. So Forestal replied, "In the past, the focus was on banning guns. Regulating, criminalizing, and then finally confiscating them. This process advanced the ball but hasn't taken it into the end zone. We need a change in focus. We're now addressing the supply and costs of ammunition, including restrictions on volume purchases and serious taxes. We'll get the president to add sizable tariffs on foreign ammunition—for national-security reasons, or to level the playing field, or some other palatable reason. We're confident that US ammunition manufacturers will support tariffs and bans on imported ammunition because it eliminates their competition and gives them higher margins. Businessmen always support free trade until they find a reason not to. Anyway, prices will shoot up. It's a winning combination. I'm now positioned at Justice to develop and enforce regulations to control ammunition and its various components. The SEA will be in my purview, and that agency has immense powers."

The wealthiest man chuckled. He wasn't quite old enough to remember Prohibition firsthand, but his family would have told him stories; they'd made a good part of their fortune from Prohibition. Every law and any war, including the recent war on drugs, was a godsend to the well connected. Talk of how these things worked was passed down during family dinner conversations much the way tradition was passed from one generation of Gypsies to another over the campfire.

Forestal watched as the man's mind zeroed in on how to take advantage of the trade restrictions.

Esther Diamond, the grande dame of progressive politics, stated what

206

was obvious to everyone in the room but she'd never say in public. "It's simply unconscionable to have... these rednecks... running around with guns in their pickup trucks. They're a danger to themselves and our great nation." Her voice rose at the end as she reflexively fell into campaign mode, then realized where she was. She said more quietly, "Frankly, we should do something about pickup trucks too. They ruin the environment."

"Good luck with that," Wainwright spat out. His lack of respect for the woman's easy demagoguery was evident, despite their shared goal of centralized control.

Diamond was sincere in her desire to have an omnipotent government do what she thought best for the masses. Probably the only thing sincere about her. Wainwright, Forestal knew, had no problem with an omnipotent government as long as it worked on his behalf. Feigning concern for the masses was... degrading. It was only a subtle distinction, but one that made those two dislike each other. Forestal mentally shrugged his shoulders. It was like listening to bickering among the Leninists, Trotskyites, and Stalinists. They ostensibly shared the same socialist ideals, but they hated each other.

Samuels eyed Forestal knowingly, resignedly.

Forestal knew a smile and sincere-sounding flattery were the best way to respond. So he said, "Of course. The rednecks should be controlled for their own sake, but we'll need you to moderate how your followers do it. Look, I'm on your side, but your desire to confiscate their guns has become a major justification for their holding on to them so tightly. When we're too overt in this regard, Ms. Diamond, it supports their fanaticism. Their molon labe posturing. We need to work together to accomplish the goal you want. Just more subtly. With finesse—I know you understand." He was pretty sure she didn't. Nor could he understand how someone so dim and thoughtless had managed to rise so high in the world of politics.

Clark Sassen raised his voice. "Before this bubble burst, before this downturn, weren't guns supposed to be under control already? It seems not, for the downturn is at hand. Samuels, how likely do you think a civil war is?"

Samuels looked at him seriously. "The unrest is just beginning. People forget that there were thousands—not hundreds, but thousands—of bombings in the US starting in 1969. About four thousand in '69 and '70 alone. Most were Molotov cocktails or pipe bombs. Some used dynamite or ammonium nitrate fertilizers mixed with diesel."

Sassen looked back at Samuels. He probably remembered the era fondly, if only because it was also the height of the sexual revolution. "Of course. There were several a day. People took them in stride. If it happened now, there'd be panic."

Samuels interrupted quickly, "And demands for martial law."

Forestal and Samuels both thought of martial law as a goal, not a danger.

The old man nodded. "That is so. Will we have open civil war? Or rather a Revolution?" He pointed at Samuels with a shaking hand and a sneering mouth before continuing. "As Paul so well knows," he chuckled slightly, "what you label something determines how the mob views it." He nodded to his tablemates as if they were but a slight improvement over the mob.

One thing all the people on the 4th Floor had in common was complete disrespect for the average person. To Forestal's mind, it was a disrespect well deserved.

Samuels took over now. In keeping with his academic persona, he spoke to his strength—his specialty of accurately projecting future events based on history. Paul Samuels did not usually provide passive predictions. It would be more accurate to call his predictions active plans. But it seemed different this time. His words had an undertone of fear, or at least uncertainty, and the people at the table noticed.

"The US has already undergone a gradual revolution in economic thinking. Most Americans are now at least sympathetic to, if not active supporters of, socialist ideas and the welfare state. We've also had a slow, quiet political revolution. There's been an irreversible growth in the size of the State and concentration of power in the hands of government at all levels. The next step seems inevitable. Cultural revolution.

"As evidence for that assertion, let me point to China's Great Cultural Revolution from about 1966 to 1976. The Red Guards, mostly teenagers and people in their twenties, took over the country. The idea was to destroy the four olds—old customs, old culture, old habits, and old ideas. China had already undergone economic and political revolutions since Mao took over after World War II. So it came time to destroy what remained of traditional Chinese civilization.

"What we need to remember, my friends, is how violent and out of control it became. Book burnings of pre-Mao literature. Red Guards—and everybody else if they were smart—waved Mao's Little Red Book in the virtue signaling of the times. There was wholesale destruction of artwork, furniture, and clothing. Everyone, everywhere, wore Mao suits—your choice of gray, brown, or blue. Public shaming and beatings were the rage. Millions were sent to the countryside and forced to endure sessions of self- and mutual criticism each day, after twelve hours in the fields.

"Is the US Cultural Revolution going to be like the one in China? Not in its particulars, of course. This is over a half century later. Technology has accelerated the pace of change, and the US isn't full of starving workers and peasants. But something like it is underway. Social movements like Antifa, #MeToo, Black Lives Matter, and many others want major changes. They all want to be rid of old customs, old culture, old ideas, and old habits. Everything associated with the old America is being discredited. Traditional ideas like free speech, the free market, individualism, and limited government are being swept away and replaced with intellectual fluff. They laugh at the work ethic and want to replace it with a guaranteed annual income. Little things—from the car culture, to fast food, to houses in the suburbs—are derided as toxic. Public shamings are rampant and function like a crazed mob; but the public square today is Twitter and Facebook. Millions of online chimpanzees get together to throw virtual rotten fruit at the shamed.

"A wholesale overturning of the culture is dangerous. It's vastly more serious than changes in economics and politics. I believe we're indeed looking at a cultural revolution. We need to recognize the severity of the situation and its ability to get out of our control. I fear this will be much more serious and violent than what we saw in the US in the '60s. Why? In those days, college students were a small minority and not all their professors were hardcore leftists. Now almost everybody goes to college, and the indoctrination and peer pressure is all toward the Left, which teaches, in a nutshell, the acceptability of using force to accomplish aims. Most of the younger generations don't realize they've been taught that it's okay to be violent to accomplish their goals. But that's exactly what's happened. It's more evident every day. Mao didn't have to contend with such dangers. Indeed, he sent the few college educated to be coolies in the fields, or he killed them."

"So we have to contend with a monster of our own creation?" The old man asked, again with a sneer.

Samuels nodded. "That's precisely, and perversely, correct. We are hoist by our own petard. I'm quite aware that we cannot control all outcomes.

We've nurtured the education system to promote progressive centralization of power and ignorance of economics. That's been a huge advantage, but along with that came a collectivist mindset and the broad acceptance of violence that underpins it, which can be problematical. Granted, the progressives don't acknowledge, or even recognize, their violent proclivities. They're mostly, shall we say, violent by proxy. They think if government exerts violence on their behalf, it becomes legitimate and keeps their hands from being bloody. Violence is at their core, and they're increasingly itching to get their hands dirty.

"We ourselves did not adequately understand this. As long as we were the ones who defined what the greater good was, such thinking benefitted us. But someone else, leading a mob, may soon redefine what the greater good is and use it to justify burning our homes, stealing our wealth. And chopping off our heads; it's happened plenty of times in history.

"And the progressives aren't the only ones. The traditionalists are circling their wagons around their own thought leaders, flying their own banners. They'll be violent too . . . defending what they hold dear. The country is divided into traditionalists and antitraditionalists, like two heavyweights on the ends of a barbell, both sides adamant they're correct. The cultural battleground is here and now. I see no indication that current trends are slowing down—rather the contrary. Mutual hate is growing even among family members. We can expect increasing violence.

"My friends, what we want is control. What we're getting is chaos. I fear the direction we've wanted the country to go over the last few generations has gone too far. I fear we might wind up looking like the sorcerer's apprentice. The CityFire movement is mob action with no defined purpose. It's like the violence in Rome at the end of the Republic. Today is more serious. It's about a radical difference in worldviews, cutting across every area of the culture. Because of the way the country is divided into patchwork red areas and blue areas, secession is not a viable option. Perhaps the country will divide into a number of smaller ones—but that's a discussion for another day."

Forestal admired Samuels's ability to salt his speech with classical references, but the man's professorial tendencies risked losing the attention of those at the table. He needed to keep the conversation focused on guns. So, with approval from Samuels, he took the virtual conch to say, "The central issue is crystallizing around gun rights. Even more than abortion—where people also form pretty much along the same lines. The pro-gun and antigun people are irreconcilable, and they're all potentially violent. They're diametrically opposed, two sides of a battle front, each aiming everything they've got at the other. It's a perfect setup for war. Either a civil war," Forestal nodded to the old man, "or perhaps a revolution, depending on how we want to define that word. Either would be an unpredictable change in the status quo that has served us all well. What we've built could get overthrown."

The socialist woman said, "Then we must do something." She'd been elected to the Senate on a platform of doing something. She spent her time jockeying for new positions of power before her planned presidential run, which had to wait until President Cooligan left office.

Forestal viewed her as a dimwitted hysteric but nodded affably. "And, indeed, we must do something. Our host's near demise at the hands of an irresponsible hunter—or somebody—received extensive media coverage."

Conti scoffed. "The talking heads? Whether someone is pro-gun or anti-gun is genetically determined. Nobody's going to be influenced by what some blow-dried TV robot reads off his script. Thousands of blacks killing each other in Chicago only helps the NRA. Frankly, the near death of a banker on a golf course was part of the news cycle for about five minutes."

Forestal responded, "With all due respect to Professor Samuels, I agree with you, Mr. Conti. Although we here would have recognized his death as a horrific tragedy, its terrible consequences would be delayed and therefore unrecognized by the hoi polloi." Forestal at once paid respect to Samuels while gaining points from the room by proclaiming his disdain for the masses, the rabble... the capite censi.

"So let's get to the point. What do you have in mind?" the old man asked.

What he had in mind was something that had proven highly effective in the past. A great deal more of it was now required. He could say something grandiloquent, such as "In great causes, sacrifices are needed. We must do more!" But everybody except the dingbat lady senator would just roll their eyes. He needed to hear what ideas emerged from this table and what they each could bring to the table. So he only said, "What do each of you suggest we do to control the impending dangers to us that can result from mass violence?" And then he listened.

Few of the simple ideas they presented would fly or would accomplish anything significant. Most aimed to simply ban all guns, except for those of the police. That was a nonstarter. So the conversation danced nowhere near what Forestal knew was really needed. During this dance, Forestal identified what help each of them might bring to the cause, although they would avoid getting blood on their hands. He'd have to do the dirty work.

He got the attention of the media-conglomerate owner and said to him, "The fools who claim that school shootings are part of an anti-gun conspiracy get shamed in the public sphere—as they should be. We appreciate your efforts and those of your people in that regard. No one should ever get away with disrespecting the victims by advancing the notion that a school shooting is part of a conspiracy."

The media mogul nodded slowly and skeptically.

Senator Diamond looked at him, nodding with enthusiasm as she said, "Thank you for helping to keep our children safe."

Samuels thanked the group for their input into the theoretical conversation, and the gathering dispersed. He pulled Forestal aside, and they agreed on the next course of action.

Then Samuels said, "It was wise not going too far in presenting what needs to happen. We should keep that between us for now. I'm impressed with how you played it. You held them together. But had you asked anything of them? In my experience, that usually fails. These people have their own priorities; they'll mostly just pay lip service. You won't get what they promise. It's not their way. They'll welch on you. Conspiracies don't last long. In fact, they're mostly the imaginings of the tinfoil-hat crowd. Whenever men of a similar trade get together, the conversation always turns to benefitting themselves at some cost to the public."

"Adam Smith."

"Correct. I would add that after their conversation ends, they all go their separate ways and do whatever they want. It's the same here on the 4th Floor, Blaize."

Forestal nodded. "I hear you, Paul. Count on no one. With what we're planning, I don't need to make any new Best Friends Forever."

"However, with what we're planning, you'll need to work with Sabina. I'm sure you have mixed feelings about her. She's got abilities, skills, and contacts. You share certain character traits. And, like you, she won't hesitate to do what's necessary. In this venture, you will need help."

Samuels was right. Forestal sighed. He knew Sabina's skill sets. One of them was an ability to throw anyone, at any time, under a bus.

Samuels then planted a seed. "And I need you and Sabina to start paying attention to this Grayson Chase."

"Yes, he's rising in the polls and clearly won't be an ally."

"The polls are just evidence of something far more dangerous. Chase has charisma."

"All successful politicians have charisma. It's how they get successful."

"Yes, Blaize. Of course. But Grayson Chase has something the other wannabes lack."

"You mean the money?"

"Well, that too. What I really mean is that Chase has both charisma and integrity. Look at the other two buffoons running for president. They're useful enough, and frankly I don't much care which one wins, as long as he or she stays under control. They're both narcissists who want to be worshipped like movie stars; Washington is Hollywood for ugly people. They want to live in mansions with servants and bodyguards. They want to be worth a hundred million, and that's no problem once they're out of office. They're both just little people with giant egos. Empty suits—pantsuits in her case. Shells with fatuous smiles and glib words. They advocate radical agendas, but they'll fall apart like a wet cardboard box when the going gets rough. They're professional nobodies.

"There have been fewer and fewer people with actual character who've run for president over time. Why? Because anyone with half a brain knows that every peccadillo they've ever even thought about is going to be put in front of the whole world. So you get ciphers running. Anyone who has a life figures it can't be worth the trouble.

"Chase is different. Salt-of-the-earth type, no real vices. Simple and soft spoken. I don't have much respect for the voters; they're stupid enough to believe anything they're told, so they get what they deserve. Things are turbulent in this country, and they can feel it. People are like dogs: they can tell if somebody's the real deal. Chase is the real deal."

Forestal frowned. "So he's a threat?"

Samuels replied, "His type can get followers. With real money behind him, he could be a danger. Idealists aren't easy to manipulate. They don't respond to threats readily, at least not the way we'd want them to. They could market him as a Gandhi, dressed in a loincloth, or a Pepe Mujica, living in a ramshackle farmhouse while he was president of Uruguay. They were both frauds, of course, but that's beside the point."

Forestal considered this. Chase might be the type of person who wouldn't sacrifice his honor or integrity for his own gain—or even to prevent his own harm. Forestal neither understood nor respected those who thought that way. Jesus, Gandhi, maybe Martin Luther King Jr. If Chase were successful in his bid for the presidency, perhaps he'd need to suffer their same fate. "So what do you propose?"

Samuels rubbed his chin. "We wait, we watch, we study. Just as always."

"And then?"

Samuels replied, "And then, as always, we do whatever is necessary."

22

Down Home

"I'M SORRY if any of you fellas feel bad that I didn't tell you," Grayson Chase spoke to his people at the auto-repair shop as one of them, not as a multibillionaire. The men sat in plastic chairs in the small waiting room, vinyl floor under their feet, drop-down ceiling over their heads. The muted TV on the wall was tuned to a financial show, where a rolling tickertape revealed mostly declining stock prices. Nobody cared what the moving mouths of the blow-dried anchors were saying.

"I didn't tell anyone except my lawyer and folks that absolutely needed to know. I didn't see why a sensible man would want to advertise it. It tends to infect relationships and attract the wrong kind of people. I didn't want things to be different—just wanted life to go on smoothly."

Jimmy Vincent said, "Gray, I knew you were doin' okay, sure. But a billionaire?"

Grayson shrugged.

Jimmy asked, "So the money that came outa nowhere to help with my wife's medical expenses? That came from you?"

Grayson sighed. He'd realized early on that it was a ticklish situation. If he'd helped the guys out by giving them money directly, they'd have thought they were causing him a hardship. Nobody wants to see a friend make a painful sacrifice. Then someday—like today—after they had learned the extent of his wealth, they might feel misled and foolish for being overly grateful. If he hadn't helped, it would likely have been even worse. No good deed goes unpunished. It was one reason why the rich tended to separate themselves from the poor.

"Yes, Jimmy. And yes, yours too, Adam. And Jay—your son's. Y'all knew it came from a fund designed to help with medical expenses. I kinda hoped y'all would have your mind on your work and family… and so not give it much thought beyond that."

The men sat silently for a minute as they now, for the first time, actually did give it thought.

Jay said, "The town has done well in the past decade, Grayson. How much of that was you?"

"You guys know I don't believe in conventional charity. A lot of givers do it in order to be big shots, and most of the money gets pissed away. My main focus has been on building this giant war chest."

"Not already big enough, that money bin?" Adam, the youngest, blurted out as he handed Grayson a beer from the Styrofoam icebox on the floor.

"It's pretty big, Adam. I'd like an even bigger one, like the one Scrooge McDuck used to have. I ain't gonna suggest otherwise."

The younger men were puzzled by the reference, though the older workers smiled; they'd read those comics when they were kids. The noble, tough old duck was at once miserly and benevolent, but Scrooge McDuck had been purged from illustrated literature in politically correct times.

"And yes, I've been able to multiply my initial winnings many times over. In part, that's because I didn't blow it on high living and trying to impress people."

Jay, one of the youngest as well as smartest of the bunch, said, "You hold on to your trucks longer than I do. You could have bought a spankin' new one every year!"

"I didn't need a spankin' new one every year, Jay. I just need a truck that works. For me, the purpose of a truck is to move stuff around, not to impress my neighbors."

"When you gone off on all them trips you've been making over the years, it ain't all been fishin', now, was it?"

"Some was. So happens I love fishin'. But yeah, I've been meeting people too—influential people—setting up and getting ready for this."

"I can't believe it, Grayson. Damn. You gonna be president of these United States!"

"Not likely, but it's possible." He nodded and looked out through the big garage windows over the parking lot full of cars in need of repair, over the high grass, to the road where a dozen media vans sat parked. The media had, at first, portrayed him as just another narcissist with fantasies of the White House. Now he was seen as a reasonable, down-to-earth person that anyone would be happy to invite over for a backyard barbecue. Grayson was sure some lingering effects of Naked Emperor had contributed to that.

Few voters actually supported either the Tweedledee from the one party or the Tweedledum representing the other. There wasn't all that much difference between them. The Dems were "progressive," with promises of free education, free medical care, a guaranteed annual income, guaranteed housing, racial diversity, and gender equality. The Republicans would agree with all those things, if their leaders thought it would help them keep power. Just not quite so much, or quite so fast, and supplemented with a heavy helping of nationalism.

The very nature of politics was picking who decides who gets what at whose expense. Democracy was a usually nonviolent way to determine who that was: mob rule dressed in a coat and tie with campaign buttons.

"What do the polls say now, Grayson?"

"They say I'm at ten percent, but it's early still. Things are happening. Seems like everyone running for president has to have a book. My book comes out next week."

"What's it called?"

"The President Doesn't Run the Country. I know hardly anyone's gonna read the book, but lots will see the title. The president should only be running the executive branch of government—which is already way too big—certainly not the whole country."

"Yeah," said Adam, "I heard you say that on TV."

"You're gonna be the president!" Greg jumped up. "You're really gonna be the president."

Grayson didn't much like the thought. "Ten percent. That's all so far. And that's a poll. Polls are just a few people's gut feelings, at the moment." Grayson smiled. "Elections aren't much better. It's all feeling, not much thinking. I'm on the radar screen now. So they're going to start attacking me. They'll make up stories that aren't true, and exaggerate any stories that are true, and take anything I say or do out of context. I'm here to apologize to you in advance." He pointed out toward the collected media outside.

"Because those piranhas out there in the vans are gonna try to tear into you and rip off pieces of flesh. Have fun with 'em if you want, but don't think they're your friends. They're cannibals looking for a story, and they'll eat your liver in the process. My candidacy is a story now."

Jay looked at Adam and the other guys. "Look, if you don't want us to talk to those jerks, we won't talk to them."

"You know what?" Grayson replied. "I don't know what you should do. Just don't be suckered by them. Don't risk your family, your relationships, your friendships. They're manipulative weasels. Just be yourselves and do the right thing as you see fit. I trust y'all. But don't trust them out there, okay? I'm real sorry about putting y'all through this."

Adam said, "Hey, it'll be fun. I'm gonna be your secretary of defense, right?"

"And I want to be ambassador to Tahiti."

"And can you send Chris off as consul to Antarctica? Bastard borrowed my torque wrench yesterday and didn't put it back. Still missing."

Grayson shook his head. "You know that's sin number one around here. Chris, you get that wrench back, you hear? Or you'll end up in the ring with Adam. And he's faster."

"Nah, I'll take the Antarctica gig. I hear the women are gorgeous."

"That's Iceland, moron." Adam punched Chris in the shoulder.

Grayson looked around at the men. They took it pretty well. But everything was in flux. His relationships with friends and colleagues were changing for the worse. It was unavoidable and as predictable as human nature. Even though some of the boys had joked about becoming ambassadors, he knew a little hope flitted through their minds. Everyone would be happy to pick a political plum if it was offered. Innocent desire easily morphed into corruption.

He wondered what his lady friends would think. A few had come into and out of his life over the past several years. Although none had been serious, he expected to get a few calls. Why did he imagine some would be angry that he hadn't told them about his wealth and even shared some of it?

Jay asked him a hard question. "Aren't you worried somebody's gonna take a potshot at you, Grayson? I mean, you're playin' in the big leagues here."

Grayson nodded. "Look guys, there's a risk. Before the election, maybe I'm safe. Though Robert Kennedy wasn't. If I'm elected, I may have to count on the Secret Service." He chuckled to himself about that possibility, for he knew exactly who would lead his detail. "But you're right. I'll be a target for sure because I aim to break a whole bunch of rice bowls and doggy dishes. Anyone in politics is at risk of being taken out—and probably should be. It's been that way since day one. On the other hand, maybe the presidency is the safest place on the totem pole.

"Relatively few leaders who really deserved it have been assassinated, though. I'm surprised more guys who run countries don't die violent deaths. Take Stalin, for instance. He was a paranoid sociopath; most of his close associates were disappeared as time went by—not to mention most of the senior army officers during the late 1930s. All the people around him probably thought about killing Stalin. Why didn't they take him out? My guess is that they knew that when Beria's secret police arrested them, they'd be tortured for weeks. Partly for sport but mainly to get the names of co-conspirators.

"Other than the good karma of taking out Stalin, nothing would change. To make it stick, you have to kill the leader and overthrow his government at the same time. For that, you need a conspiracy, a replacement shadow government with confederates pulling strings, commanding police and military units, distributing propaganda and taking out counter-revolutionaries. That's what von Stauffenberg did in Germany when he tried to kill Hitler with the bomb in 1944. Very dangerous; a leak would amount to a death warrant. It almost worked because the German officers were from the same class, shared professional ideals, and had close bonds of trust. It wouldn't have worked against Stalin because the USSR was a vastly more intrusive police state than Nazi Germany, and Stalin had already purged the officer corps of 'politically unreliable elements'—you've gotta love that Soviet turn of phrase—in the late '30s."

Greg, a good ol' boy older than the rest, was inclined toward conspiracy theories. Some he promulgated made more sense than others. As he was skeptical of authority, he often stumbled into truth. "That's not just in places like Russia, Grayson. There's been dozens of deaths around the Clintons, includin' a bunch of their ex-bodyguards. Bodyguards see everything, who's comin' an' goin'. They're like members of the family, but don' get ta share in the spoils. They go missin' if they know too much. Then there's Ron Brown, Clinton's secretary of commerce, I think. His plane crashed just as he began cooperating with prosecutors. Very suspicious. The air-traffic controller committed suicide a few days later. The big one was Vince Foster. They found his body in Fort Marcy Park, dead of what they said was a suicide. Made no sense at all."

Grayson knew that Greg could go on with extensive details about Vince Foster and the Clintons. He'd heard that tale before. Some or all of it might be true. It was impossible to know because all the sources—official and informal—were unreliable. The information was further filtered and distilled through the press, hearsay, and blogs. Nonetheless, Grayson didn't put it past the Clintons. Hillary seemed capable of anything. There were roughly 140 so-called Arkancides. It was dangerous to be a president, but perhaps even more dangerous to be near a president.

He was loath to cut Greg off, but he was due to appear on a national comedy/news show that evening. He'd prepared by watching a few episodes and needed to organize his thoughts. The host was equipped with a sharp wit. To the younger voters, his opinion mattered far more than those of the talking heads. Grayson knew all he could do was be himself. On live TV with a comedian, authenticity mattered more than policy.

He companionably excused himself while Greg continued providing details about all that the Clintons had gotten away with. Grayson smiled. The vultures out in the media vans wouldn't know what to do with Greg. What do you do with someone who shouts that the king has no clothes?

23

Plan of Action

"WHAT is it?"

"Thirty-ought six. Hollow point. Jacketed." The bald man's whiny, high-pitched voice didn't fit his wide, stubby body, its muscles straining the seams of his clothing.

"What does that mean, Lichen?" asked Forestal.

Sabina Heidel stood next to him and chuckled. "Don't you know anything about ammunition?"

Forestal replied without hesitation, looking offended. "I've barely even held a gun."

The bald man on the other side of his desk frowned and, not quite imperceptibly enough, shook his head.

"Hold this gun, then." He pulled a revolver from his belt and slid it across the desk to Forestal.

Forestal picked up the surprisingly lightweight weapon. He turned the muzzle toward his face and looked down the blackness of the barrel, a thumb on the trigger. He could see the tips of the bullets in the chambers of the cylinder. The man opposite winced, stood up, and reached over for his gun.

"Don't ever do that," the man chastised Forestal without any deference, without the respect that Forestal was used to hearing from him.

Forestal asked, stunned, "Do what?"

Sabina interjected, "Don't aim a gun at your face. Unless you plan on pulling the trigger."

"Don't be stupid," Lichen said, annoyed, with an edge of contempt.

The fellow obviously knew something about weapons; maybe he was just trying to impart some valuable information. Forestal decided to let the deprecating tone slide for now, and, equally annoyed, he simply said, "Okay."

"So you really don't know anything about guns and ammunition."

"I told you I don't. So you shouldn't have handed that one to me."

Lichen seemed to ignore the critique, partly because he knew the fool was right. "Yet your work includes managing the finances of the ATF. The irony amuses me."

Forestal didn't reply to the sarcasm, but he made a note to punish the man's insolence someday.

"So why would I want to help you promote the anti-gun agenda?"

Forestal had a ready answer. "Money. Lots of it."

"I like guns, Forestal. I own lots of guns. I don't want the government inconveniencing me."

More of that disrespectful tone. Lichen had just called him by his last name without title. In front of Sabina, no less. Forestal looked coldly at Lichen and said between clenched teeth, "We won't take your guns away."

"Damn right about that. But whenever a politician says that, he's lying."

"Your guns are safe. Because you'll be on the right team."

"Hmm. For now. What if the G decides later I ain't?"

"That's a risk you'll be taking, Lichen. You'll be paid well for it."

"I suspect I'll need an appointment as an ATF special agent."

"I'll think about it. We can't have a direct link between us if you get caught, can we?"

Forestal disliked the change in the dynamics of their relationship. Lichen was taking a measure of him. Could this be the same subservient cleaner who took care of the gelatinous mess on his hotel room floor? The same obsequious greeter who guarded the entrance of The Store? It seemed impossible. Maybe Lichen had always considered him no more than just another arrogant banker. Lichen was establishing himself as the alpha male at this table. Perhaps it was just Sabina's presence. Ten seconds of exposure to her could and did change the very nature of some men. Like a buck during the rut. But this man seemed different.

"So, what do you propose?" Chemnitz Lichen was a solid man top to bottom. Totally bald, his large head sat on a thick neck over a broad chest.

His full abdomen required his suit to stretch to cover it. His habitually turned-down mouth attested to years of accumulated disgust with human-kind—especially the kind of humans he worked for.

"I've always thought of you," replied Forestal, "as fully reliable in any circumstance."

"Always?" Lichen raised an eyebrow. "Well, glad you do. I don't object to things others are afraid to do, so you're correct."

"Well, you were certainly accommodating when we last met."

The man smiled darkly—a sinister smile, more like a half sneer. "You and I have never before met, Forestal. You must be referring to my brother, Dresden. My identical twin brother. From The Store, right? Hah! I figured you for someone who would use The Store. I was right! Me and him, we're in related fields."

Forestal smiled as it suddenly became clear. He had not actually met this man before. He took a moment to process its implications. "Interesting. I had no idea. I've met your brother many times. I simply assumed."

"Assume is the mother of most fuck-ups. Sometimes my brother and me … we count on that."

Then Forestal realized that the strangeness of Lichen's Hulk-like appearance—the severity of the baldness, the thickness of the neck, the roundness of the abdomen and the gut—had kept him from noticing subtleties of the man's face that differentiated him from his brother. He said, "Your brother shows greater deference."

"Maybe he fakes it. I don't. You have to earn respect from me. It won't come easy."

Forestal resigned himself to that bit of wisdom. He didn't always require deference, but his money and position usually ensured it. He hated losing face with Sabina. After all, he too was a rutting buck. "So have you ever rejected an assignment?"

"They aren't assignments, and I don't take orders. I'm not your employee. They're jobs. I'm a contractor."

"Right. Sorry. Do you ever turn down a contract?"

"Not usually from people who come with good references. And I don't even meet with people who don't have good references."

Apparently, Chemnitz Lichen was a distant cousin of Sabina's. She'd described Chemnitz as having a god complex. He considered himself untouchable, and that made him willing to take extreme risks. If he were ever caught, he'd fight to the death. Two years earlier, he'd performed the same sort of work they needed him for now. Sabina had needed his help manipulating Congress into banning Naked Emperor. They would use the same tool this time, on a much larger scale, to manipulate both the people and their political representatives. Everyone would soon be begging the government to do something to solve gun violence.

It wasn't rocket science. They simply needed to point the herd in the right direction and then scare them. The sheep would all follow the first one as it ran right off the cliff.

Sabina chimed in. "It's not just a matter of shooting up a few schools this time," she said with no hesitation or concern. Perfectly cold.

Forestal respected that. He shared her attitude toward the public.

"Although," she added reasonably, "starting with a school would be fine."

"Schools start up again in, what, six weeks?"

"Plenty of time for you to prepare," Sabina replied.

"But not just schools. What else?" Lichen prompted.

Forestal expanded on Sabina's direction. "For broadest possible impact, we want to affect every demographic. Churches. Playgrounds. Little league baseball games. Elks Club meetings. Bingo groups. Hospitals, clinics. A Planned Parenthood somewhere. Zoos. Orphanages. Families at home. Asians, blacks, latinos, but mostly whites. District attorneys, mayors, school principals. American Legion and VFW halls to throw suspicion around. You get the idea. It's open season. Make sure you always use standard, legal guns. Nothing automatic that's already controlled. That's important."

Lichen took a moment, considering.

Forestal sensed that the sheer scale of the operation intrigued the man.

His first question was simply "Where?"

Forestal stretched his arms apart and pointed his fingers in opposite directions. "Scattered all over the country as fast as you can safely make them happen. Concentrated into several weeks. Mostly in states with loose gun control laws, but some in the tight states too. That will encourage people to complain about the laxity of the neighboring state's laws."

"How many incidents are you hoping for?"

"Unlimited. We want this to be constant. Unending. An incessant, overwhelming series of events. We want this to be so big that the population demands guns be banned nationwide by executive decree."

Sabina said, "It only took a few school shootings to kill Naked Emperor dead. Just a few changed the whole Naked Emperor subculture. Hysteria spreads faster than a viral pandemic."

Forestal replied, "How true. I don't need to know anything about guns to know gun culture is deeply engrained in this country. Changing a culture is like turning a supertanker; it takes a lot of push for a lot of time." He turned to Lichen. "I understand that you're experienced at what we need and excellent at avoiding being seen doing it. Of course, there were people who suspected that those shootings you did were staged, to make it look like the shooters were under the influence of Naked Emperor."

"That's because they were staged." Lichen looked at Forestal with a condescending air.

"But these can't look like the influence of Naked Emperor—nor look staged. They need to look like it was the guns that caused the shooting. So it's essential that you not be caught, and essential that no one considers that it could be one person carrying these out. The obvious enemy needs to be guns and bullets."

"Well, first, it's not going to be one person. I'm going to have a colleague or two. Second, I don't get caught. All the blame will fall on the guns. Unless you want to hang the blame on some group? Maybe disgruntled white males; anybody will believe anything about them now. Maybe followers of the Prophet; they'd be quite credible."

Forestal replied, "No. We want it to be a mystery so everyone can be suspicious and scared of everyone else."

"I understand what you want. I just don't understand why. You people are already at the top of the heap. If you create chaos on this scale, well, it could touch off a revolution. Those usually don't end well for people in your position. Guillotines and heads rolling. The average dummy doesn't know shit about the Constitution, but he still takes the Second Amendment seriously, Forestal."

Forestal replied, "Look. I agree. But this country's heading toward a revolution or a civil war as it is. The financial system and the economy are off the rails, sooner than we planned for. The last thing we want is a bunch of heavily armed yahoos who feel they have nothing to lose running around. We're trying to be proactive before these CityFires get totally out of control or the next cause célèbre catches the attention of the bitchers and moaners and sends them into the streets. This is about damage control, before the real damage is done.

"And, sure, they'll fight gun control in the courts, but after you do your work, they'll be too embarrassed, too demoralized to fight very hard. While you're doing your part, we're going to make sure that the media starts referring to a Nation in Crisis. It'll be the daily banner across CNN's screen. No old piece of parchment is going to stand in the way of the desperate needs of a Nation in Crisis."

Sabina said, "In fact, it's time for a new constitutional convention. In times of chaos, people want change. Half the population can't lay their hands on a thousand dollars for an emergency. If they miss two paychecks they're looking at an eviction notice. They know the rich control all the assets and are getting richer. They want another New Deal. A serious one this time. The best way to get that is a new constitution. And let me assure you, we'll know how to write it."

Forestal nodded faintly, considering. Was a constitutional convention really in Paul Samuels's plans? Or had Sabina made this up on the fly? Most likely the latter. But it was a good idea.

She continued, "Which leads to another target. These things have blown over before. A couple of well-chosen Supreme Court justices can save the Second Amendment. We'd rather not take that risk."

Forestal said, "You're guessing my whole plan, Sabina. The current White House needs an opportunity to make a new appointment or two to the Supreme Court."

Lichen asked, "So you want a supreme to join the ranks of the dearly departed, too?"

"I'm sure you can figure out a way to make one of the conservative ones too sick to work. They're not closely guarded. Terminal sickness by means of an act of senseless gun violence."

Lichen asked, "Interesting. There's bound to be opposition. How about the NRA? They aren't going to stand quietly by."

Forestal said, "The NRA has maybe four or five million members. Less than two percent of the adult population. Duck hunters. They can keep their shotguns for the time being. The NRA will be lucky to keep their building warm with what income they'll have after this is over."

"Perhaps you underestimate them," Lichen replied.

Forestal raised his voice to win the point. "First, I think you underestimate us. We can completely co-opt the NRA. My bet is that they'll wind up endorsing the new laws. In fact, I'm rather counting on them to help write the laws that I want enacted."

"Are you serious?"

"Entirely. They'll be as scared as the little bunnies they hunt. They'll see a compromise as getting in front of the situation."

Lichen shook his head. "Okay, but I'm telling you: do something serious at this point in terms of getting guns banned, and it's a match to a powder keg."

Forestal and Samuels had long ago decided that gun and ammunition bans would not be the real path forward, but rather a distraction. "I'm not talking about bans. Give us some credit. We want the public demanding bans, yes. But we won't give them bans. Look, open violence and civil conflict is a given. It's going to happen. There's a thousand matches that can light this up. We're looking to diminish the explosion when any one of those matches is lit, but we aren't planning on lighting the match ourselves.

"Look at it this way. If the US is now like a giant forest full of dry tinder, what we're doing is like a back burn, causing a fire break when the wind is right so the thing can be controlled."

"So no gun bans?" Lichen shook his head but then held it steady as he considered.

"No gun bans, as such."

"Ammunition?"

"That's an area where we see some possibilities."

"Anything else?"

Forestal smiled. "Yes. There will be a new law that has nothing to do with control of guns and ammunition, yet it will accomplish far more."

Chemnitz Lichen smiled. "What's my budget?"

"What do you need?"

"The scale of what you're proposing is… unprecedented."

Forestal wondered what coursed through Lichen's mind then. Was he recalibrating his own sense of scale? A hundred thousand dollars an event? No. A million?

The image of Dr. Evil in the Austin Powers movies came to mind. Resuscitated from a fifty-year sleep, he named $1 million as a sufficient ransom for not destroying the world. It was funny because he actually thought it was a lot of money. It was likely the only time that much of the millennial generation had been exposed to the reality of compounding inflation.

Forestal knew that the money would be a big number, because after all this, Lichen would have to disappear without a trace, forever. That was hard in today's wired, watched, and obsessively monitored world. He must suspect that these people, giving him this job now, would likely try to clean him when it was all over, notwithstanding that he was Sabina's distant cousin. There was going to be a lot more to this than arranging a few events. Any step Lichen took might lead to quicksand. So Forestal was prepared for a big number.

Sabina responded before Forestal could. "Our funding source has unlimited money. And never gets audited. They could buy the moon from Russia and no one would see any evidence of it. Your budget will be met." She smiled at Lichen and stared at him for too long.

Forestal wondered if Sabina's wiles would have any effect on someone as completely devoid of human empathy as Lichen. It would be interesting to watch them negotiate. Cousin or not.

"Oh, and Lichen," Forestal said, "there're some people you must be careful to not injure during this process. I'm going to provide you with names and locations. Make sure you or your buds don't go near them. Screw that up, we're all dead."

"I understand," Lichen replied.

"And don't get caught."

Lichen frowned. "We won't."

24

Philosophy and Pheromones

EMILY approached the coffee shop with anxiety and anticipation. After more than a week off the radar, Charles Knight had reappeared, calling her the night before to say that he planned to work in the coffee shop this morning and was wondering if she might be coming by.

She let Jeffrey know of the meeting, and he seemed pleased. Emily was pleased for her own reasons.

Walking through the door, she looked around for Charles. There he sat, on the far back right of the shop, looking at her with a welcoming smile. She smiled, waved, and moved to join him.

He stood up at her approach. He cut a good form, no question about that. It was clear he'd just shaved. She controlled an urge to reach her hand to his cheek. His hair was trimmed and natural with no goop—or product as it was strangely called—to distort his appearance or call attention to himself. He'd get enough attention as it was because he was handsome, fit, and exuded an air of calm self-confidence combined with an attractive warmth. It was his eyes, of course, that drew her most. The eyes provided far more useful information than posture or attire.

"I've dropped in a few times," he said, as he placed his hand on the back of her chair while she sat. "I considered camping out here... to catch up with you."

"I'm glad you tried calling. It's more effective."

"But think how cool it would be if we'd just kept bumping into each other."

"What have you been up to for the last couple of weeks?"

"Just working. I'd like to take you out to dinner tonight. Are you free?"

She'd hoped he would ask. "Sounds like a date… got to say I'm a little out of practice."

"That makes two of us. I'll pick you up at seven. I'm looking forward to spending time outside of work hours with you."

She felt a flash of guilt at hearing that. Jeffrey would be paying her to go out with him. She suppressed it quickly.

"Can I get you something?" He glanced at the short line.

"No, you're here to work. I'll get my coffee and then I'll work too. Refill for you?"

Charles smiled as he replied, "Please. Large, black." He lifted a folded newspaper off the table to reveal a pen and paper with a few scrawled diagrams.

He'd really meant it when he said he'd be working this morning. She respected that and found it attractive. Business before pleasure, of course. Her own morning combined the two.

When she returned to the table, he nodded at her as she set his cup down, but he said nothing. She read a few articles and occasionally glanced up. He flipped through several newspapers while making infrequent notes on paper. She wondered what his project related to. Likely Jeffrey would want to know. She refilled her coffee; they might have been the only customers who weren't drinking things with Italian names that no righteous Italian would dream of drinking. An ordinary cup of coffee made little sense from a business point of view, of course; the money was in frou-frou concoctions. Each with about a quarter of a day's calories, costing about twice the daily income of most people in Third World coffee-producing countries.

He sipped at his coffee as he took a break from his reading. Perhaps it was a door to conversation, so she went through it.

"Been having fun?"

"I haven't had much fun lately, Emily. I'm buried under weighty things."

"Weighty. Don't hear that word much. Perhaps I'm running with a lightweight crowd. What kind of things?"

"The world, I guess."

"The world can definitely weigh you down, Atlas."

"Funny." He tossed the Wall Street Journal onto the chair next to him and then lifted his hips to more easily place his few sheets of folded paper into his pants pocket. She couldn't help but imagine him doing the same motion in another, far more intimate setting.

She prodded, "You aren't planning on stopping the motor of the world, are you?"

Charles lifted his eyebrow slightly and then flashed the briefest smile. She knew what that meant. Her father communicated in the same way when he was up to something that might get him in trouble.

"Beware, or you'll end up like my dad." Her mind flickered back to her father's frustration in the days he raged against the machine. She was grateful he no longer wasted his energies that way. "The world has a life of its own, Charles."

He looked into her eyes and said, "How true. World improvers tend to be dangerous busybodies. I'm more focused on pulling one weed at a time, mostly in my own backyard."

"Sounds like hard work. What are you up to?"

Charles smiled at her. "Besides pulling weeds? Well, I'm always looking to learn the meaning of life. If any. "

"That might take some time. And time's a luxury."

"Luxury. An interesting concept. As is time itself. Time unquestionably dilates; nothing like forced confinement or inactivity to bring home how time can drag or flash by in a frame-by-frame instant once adrenaline kicks in. In the long run, time renders us all, and all our efforts, completely irrelevant."

"You underestimate your impact, Charles, and the impact of Naked Emperor."

"Did you ever try it?"

She frowned slightly and closed her eyes for a second. "Do you know what SEA does if you admit to having used Naked Emperor. It's like confessing to a murder."

Charles shook his head. "Of course I know. Who are you talking to? But it shows how far off the rails government's gone... sign of the times."

"I haven't used it, no. I'd like to, though. Do you have some?" Even though the conversation flowed naturally, this went to the core of the question that Jeffrey had asked her to examine.

Charles chuckled. "Did they give you a deal to get you out of Rikers in exchange for dropping a dime on drug dealers like me?"

"I wouldn't have taken it."

"Good. Still, it's best if I don't respond. It's getting so that the only safe answer to any question is name, rank, and serial number."

"I used to watch a television show at Rikers called The Mentalist. Good show, but the perps were generally narcissists who were too clever by half and proud of their crimes. Maybe they let us watch it because the perps always confessed at the end of each episode. We'd all hoot and holler at that. 'Don't confess! Don't do it!' we'd shout at the screen. They didn't need to confess. Always needing to explain themselves. Stupid, really."

Charles said, "Against stupidity, the gods themselves contend in vain."

Emily sat back in surprise. It was that very quote from Schiller that had triggered her father to stop cluttering his mind with worry and prompted him to stop trying to solve the world's problems. He realized it made more sense to improve the state of his own psyche, health, and wealth. That was easier to do isolated in the islands.

Charles continued. "Well. Einstein did say that after hydrogen, the most common thing in the universe is stupidity. Just observe it, don't let it upset you, and capitalize on it when possible. I surely don't want to compete with the gods. I don't try to fight it anymore."

"So what are you fighting, Charles?"

"A topic for another time."

She sized him up. Prison had undoubtedly affected him. He was not just physically hard, but psychologically as well. So many of the men in places like this coffee shop were effeminate or corporate drones. The thought came to her spontaneously, as a surprise. She knew that she was attracted to masculinity; that part didn't surprise her. An involuntary quickening coursed through her as his pheromones had an effect.

"Are you okay?" he asked.

"I'm fine. I've got some things to do. I'm heading out. See you at seven?"

"Eagerly," he replied.

She walked out of the shop into the overcast day, having no idea how powerfully her own pheromones were working on him.

*   *   *

"Eterio, I've an idea for you."

Forestal was back in New York; he'd ridden the Crony Express back and forth between there and Washington so often that he was starting to feel like a prole. It was faster than an Amtrak milk train, but ran at only half the speed of the ones in China, Europe, and Japan. The "high speed" Acela train had been built to serve people traveling between the money and the power. Its designers underestimated how many people would make that journey each day. It was both slow and crowded. He felt like he'd stepped into the Third World.

Yet the train was the simplest and fastest way to cover the 225 miles, and, so far, the TSA hadn't invaded Union Station with its long lines and general degradation.

"And what idea might that be?" Conti replied in a voice that failed to conceal some disdain. Forestal's lip and shoulder twitched. They sat on a bench in Central Park. Even the pigeons seemed oppressed by the humid summer day. Conti told Forestal to meet him there to discreetly relay a regulatory wish list for Conti's various corporate allies. Forestal took the opportunity to make a proposal.

"You should consider acquiring gun manufacturers soon. Ammunition companies as well."

"Yes? Which ones?" Conti replied.

"Why not all of them."

"In the world?" Conti's incredulity was almost as thick as his Italian accent.

"Just the US, I would think. This play is driven by US politics."

"What? Is this like saving the whales, clearing landmines, and buying everybody a puppy? Civilian gun makers—I presume you're not talking about major defense contractors—are a dying business. I'm not wasting money on some noble cause you've dreamt up. What's in it for me?"

"Give me some credit, Eterio. I'm not some sell-side security analyst. I'm offering you a timing insight, which is much more valuable. If you act, we both win, and I'll take my share. There are three publicly traded firearms manufacturers in the US, and a couple of interesting ammunition manufacturers. Their share prices are reasonable; as you said, nobody sees them as a growth industry. In fact, most see them as slowly sinking ships. There's no credible imminent threat that the government will be instituting new gun control laws. But that's going to change. When gun violence increases again, so will the pressure for gun control, and then people will rush to stock up on weapons and ammo before the regulatory clampdown. Revenues surge after mass shootings. Speculators send their share prices up a lot—for a while."

"Okay. I remember our conversation on the 4th Floor. If you're trying to put in a serious ban, that will eventually tank the share prices. I'm not interested in some gamble based on the way you read the tea leaves. What am I missing here?" It was a logical question; Conti knew these people had hidden agendas several layers deep—as did he himself.

"Banning guns isn't a realistic near-term possibility, but more controls are. It's highly likely gun stocks will run up as they have in the past when people see more controls are coming. We both understand the market isn't perfectly predictable, but it's a good trade because I'm telling you it's going to happen soon. These companies are small, and their stocks are volatile; they should at least double. You've still got time to build a big position without moving the market. You need to start now."

"You think you're able to pull the strings well enough to predict something's going to happen?"

"Let's not call it something that might cause the SEC to get a hard-on. Let's just say I believe in cause and effect." Forestal knew that would attract Conti. Insider information was really the only information worth having. To know only what everyone else knew was as good as knowing nothing.

"Tell me more."

"An increase in violent crimes using guns is not an if." Forestal replied. "And it's not even a when. That's all I'm going to say, other than buy now. Perhaps sell after the first big spike; these little news-driven manias always peter out. Your guess on price peak will be as good as or better than mine. Then when I say buy again, it will be because we know tariffs will be imposed on imported weapons and ammunition. That will give domestic companies a monopoly, for practical purposes."

"Tariffs. That just needs the president. Should be easy enough."

"Samuels is confident that we can control the timing of tariffs."

"I bet he is." Conti laughed.

Forestal had seen Paul Samuels manipulate President Cooligan with well-chosen words and academic financial obfuscation. It was pretty much the same all over the world. In Africa a tribal chief would listen to the mumbo-jumbo of his witch doctor. If the chief later became president of the country, the witch doctor might well be promoted to treasury minister. Cooligan and the other party's nominee—Senator Lear, another ambitious nobody—were equally ignorant about economics, but they understood politics well, each using the government's cornucopia to give money to those, both rich and poor, who stood to benefit them. It didn't really matter which one won the election. Either candidate would be an easy stooge; they differed only in cosmetics and rhetoric. Forestal's mind flashed to the newcomer, Grayson Chase. He could be a different story—a candidate gone off the reservation.

Conti then said, "I assume sometime thereafter I'll want to sell, and maybe sell short. The big losses for these companies will come when Congress moves on an ammunition tax, correct?"

"Let's play that by ear, Eterio."

"What do you mean?"

"You'll want to wind up with large stakes in those companies for the really big payoff. There are two possibilities. Both will be very generous. One is that, with no imports and new domestic competition discouraged, you'll have a monopoly. The other is that—in the interests of national security—we'll nationalize them. At a very, very fair price. Even if we can't go that far, the prospect of it happening at a huge premium to the market will be just as good for shareholders."

"Hmm. An exciting prospect. At my age, I'm still buying green bananas, but what the stock touts call long-term growth isn't as attractive as it once was. What's in this for you, Forestal? The usual?"

"The usual is fine. I'll take twenty percent of the profits."

"Fine. You'll have to trust me on the math."

"Of course, Eterio."

Conti grunted. "What can go wrong in this play?"

Forestal raised his eyebrows. "Short of an extinction-level asteroid hitting DC? Frankly, the longer you hold on, the better you'll do ... we'll do."

"What makes you so sure of that?"

"War, of course. War is very good for the arms industry." Forestal smiled darkly. "And lest you forget, war is the health of the state."

Conti nodded. "Of course. It's always good to have an existential external enemy to get the populace all standing together; they'll basically keep each other in line—and absolutely support whatever the government wants to do. That's what patriotism is all about, is it not?"

"Exactly."

235

*   *   *

For Charles, attachment to another person added an element of danger and risk—and not just to himself. Any relationship, but especially a new one, and most especially a love interest, could prove not just a weakness but a dangerous liability. How long would he pursue his current path? It wasn't right to draw anybody else onto it. He was already on the verge of lying to her. On the other hand, telling her the truth was out of the question. All he could do is keep pleading the Fifth.

But she intrigued him. They had some life-changing experiences in common that served to connect them. She could finish his sentences here and there, suggesting that they thought alike. If her character proved sound, there might be some basis for a lasting relationship, but a lasting relationship was not in the forefront of his mind. Right now his primal instincts demanded attention. The overload of hormones had shortened his attention span. He caught himself looking at women like someone who'd been imprisoned for too long. He'd been released for three months and done nothing about it, perhaps because, as Xander had told him, he needed to become human again first. But he needed to attend to his biology soon—lasting relationship or not.

Checking into Emily's nemesis, Blaize Forestal, revealed lots of red flags. The guy was one of the many cronies jockeying for position between Wall Street and government. Probably a sociopath, like most who shuttled between Washington and New York to hold court in the halls of power. He'd collect more information, but, for now, Emily got the benefit of the doubt. Obviously, or he wouldn't have called her again. Or maybe he would have? Even if for no reason beyond that he was anxious to dance the horizontal tango. Especially with somebody sexy, pretty, and empathic.

He took a deep breath through his nose, stilled his mind, and put himself in the present moment. The aroma of roasting beans percolated through the coffee shop.

He picked up the New York Times. A short article on the fourth page reported the murder of a Department of Agriculture employee in North Dakota a few days earlier, accompanied by a picture of Kirby's dour face. Nothing was said about Kirby the man; it was there only because the violent death of a midlevel Washington official was considered newsworthy. There was no mention of the silver Paladin coins he'd left as a signature. No surprise there. He'd have to make sure word got out as part of the Paladin Network marketing plan.

Consistent with their hyperbolic style, the New York Post used the word "assassination" to get readers' attention but then dedicated five paragraphs to Kirby's nationwide persecution of hemp farmers. Charles found it unusual for a conservative paper to pay this much attention to a rather obscure event that would mainly interest the pro-drug crowd. The reporter, one Ahmed Raheem, was quite the bumblebee, obtaining interviews with various farmers Kirby had persecuted. He quoted Mrs. Jannsen: "There are certain people whose death is more important than their life."

That would earn the Post some subscribers.

Mrs. Jannsen's vitriol didn't surprise Charles. Good for her. It played to his purpose. The final three paragraphs of the article presented a summary of the national government's current marijuana and hemp laws, Kirby's opposition to the part of the Farm Bill that made some hemp legal, his support for expanding mandates for ethanol in gasoline, and his intended role as the controller of the ethanol-subsidy purse strings. The article came off as factual, but the facts amounted to an indictment of Kirby, albeit incomplete.

How long would it take before another Agriculture employee picked up where Kirby left off?

The world was full of busybodies and rule enforcers. They filled voids in the power structure as predictably as mold grew on bread. You could scrape off the mold and watch a new layer grow right back. He wondered how long this assassination would have a positive impact. Would it be years? Or days? Maybe no effect at all since most would assume it was personal, not business-related.

Perhaps it would have the opposite effect, causing the department to redouble its efforts. Drug warriors could say it was proof positive that hemp farmers were part of a violent crime syndicate. There was constant tension between the locals and the feds, who might use it to justify clamping down on states favoring legalization of the cannabis plant. The feds saw the locals as provincial yokels. The locals saw the feds as arrogant interlopers looking to burnish their resumes. The Ninth and Tenth Amendments in the Bill of Rights were supposed to prevent conflicts between the federal and state authorities, but they were dead letters. For all intents and purposes, the Constitution didn't exist. Law was what the feds decided.

Charles thought about the broader problem. The world in general, and the US in particular, needed a reset. It would be dangerous, for when somebody pushed the reset button, things usually got worse, not better.

He thought of France in 1789. He would have supported the overthrow of the corrupt and destructive ancien régime, but after Louis XVI, the French got Robespierre and then Napoleon.

Or Russia in 1917. He would have supported getting rid of the czar and ending the country's involvement in World War I—except that after Nicholas II came Lenin, and after Lenin, Stalin.

One style of tyranny was typically replaced with another, often even more brutal. In the interregnum, the most violent and lawless types rise up, contending with each other for power.

On the seventh page of the Post he read a brief comment about the Federal Reserve's expanding balance sheet. It was worded to make it sound like the more money the Fed printed, the healthier the Fed was, and therefore the healthier the United States was. Perhaps the reporter was just thoughtless and poorly informed. Or perhaps the article was intentionally misleading. Quite likely both. The stock market liked it though, since that's where most of the new money went.

Pundits, journalists, and government officials increasingly believed the national debt was irrelevant. Frequently a famous economist—usually a Nobel laureate—would even advise the government to accelerate deficit spending. "We owe it to ourselves," they said, perhaps channeling a country club trophy wife. Charles expected the debt would be defaulted on, slowly through inflation and then very quickly as government deficits compounded. It would be more honest to default outright. There would be some benefits to that. It would keep the next couple of generations of Americans from becoming serfs to pay it off. It would make it hard for the US government to borrow again, forcing it to live within its means. And, most important, it would punish the people who'd been financing it. A large part of the debt was owned by the pension plans of the very taxpayers who owed the debt. In that perverse, ironic sense, they really do owe it to themselves.

Of course, an argument could be made that the central bankers had been brilliant, printing up US dollars out of thin air. They allowed Americans to fill their storage units with trinkets from China, their garages with cars from Germany, and their noses with coke from Colombia. From one point of view, it was a good trade, using fake money to buy real goods. The

238

US dollar had been the country's chief export for years. That, and borrowed money, allowed the Americans to live far beyond their means.

An actual revolution in the US was unlikely to end any better than had those in France, Russia, or scores of countries since. On the bright side, an actual revolution in the US was quite unlikely. Although they might grumble, the average American was too happy watching TV, overeating, and popping psych pills to do anything. Then again, most political change—even major revolutions—occurred because small but focused groups at the margins moved the inert masses in the middle.

The Paladin Network might correct a few of the crony state's worst excesses. It might catch on, or it might go nowhere. He'd put enough of his available resources into the Paladin Token to create a sound foundation and fund its launch.

Bitcoin had thumbed its nose at the regulatory State; the Paladin Network would spit at it—and perhaps break its legs.

Charles mailed envelopes to three more people who might benefit from Paladin's services. Perhaps one would give him another opportunity to both polish his skills and introduce the capabilities of the Paladin Network to the broader public. More gigs might help temper him for more drastic future actions.

He also sent an envelope to Ahmed Raheem, the New York Post reporter. It contained a printed image of the photo of a dead Terrence Kirby, with Paladin coins on his eyes. He typed "Terrence Kirby—evidence" along the bottom.

That evening he met Emily at the entrance to her modest apartment building. He smiled approvingly at the dark-maroon dress that reached her knee on the left and exposed a sculptured thigh on the right. She skipped down the stairs; he caught her as she stumbled at the bottom.

"Whoops! Not the best way to impress you."

"That was captured for posterity in the cloud." He pointed to the security camera staring from the wall like an Eye of Sauron. The whole country was turning into a high-tech version of Mordor.

Emily flipped her head toward the camera. "That doesn't record anything. It's a fake."

"You know that for sure?"

"I do."

Charles made a mental note that Emily was aware and cared enough about whether she was being observed to have checked out the camera. It was another mark in her positive column.

He said, "An old friend taught me that I should live my life so that I can live with myself. And that has nothing to do with whether anybody is watching."

"You don't seem like a 'Just impress yourself' new ager." She looked at him as they turned to walk down the block.

"If you try to make people think you're somebody else, they may like that person—but not the real you. So you end up with a bunch of friends who don't actually like you. They like a facsimile of you. And worse, you might scare away people who might like the real you."

"Who's the real you, Charles?"

"That's too complex a question for a first date. If I answer it, there may not be a second date."

They walked along in silence. Charles found it awkward, but then dating—first date, second date, or beyond—often not only felt awkward but was awkward. He reasoned that this was why birds went through complex and ritualized dances: to disguise the awkwardness. Nightclubs with music loud enough that you can't think made some kind of sense now.

During their call early that morning, Xander had practically ordered him to take a woman to bed. He'd referred to it, half-jokingly and half-clinically, as a desperately needed detoxifying cleanse. Following Xander's orders required either dating or hiring an escort. Charles didn't object to the oldest profession. There was always an outside chance he'd run into a hooker with a heart of gold. He recalled one of the books he'd read about the Old West. It turned out that Wild Bill Hickok, Bat Masterson, and Wyatt Earp all patronized and married ladies who were known as soiled doves in those days. The twenty-first-century New York offered a prodigious variety of distaff companions, vastly more than nineteenth-century Dodge City. So here it made sense to risk possible awkwardness on a date, if for no reason other than to lessen the risk of awkward discoveries—such as the possibility that the hired escort was really a man.

He stepped over to her street side, ready to protect her from an out-of-control taxicab or a wayward puddle. Some women might have objected, perceiving the gesture as demeaning or anachronistic. She didn't. With only a little self-consciousness, he took her hand. It didn't feel awkward. She smiled warmly and said, "I won't ask you again about any supply of Naked Emperor you may have."

"You can't be too careful these days."

"Because I got hold of some."

He looked at her appraisingly out of the corner of his eye. "That's a serious crime."

"Sometimes you have to exercise your rights or they'll atrophy."

"Right? What right?"

"The right to do whatever I will."

Charles nodded. "No argument here."

"I tried it today."

Charles concern piqued. "That can be dangerous, Emily. The SEA poisoned canisters and circulated them to discourage use. Trust me; I know what I'm talking about."

It was to stop the SEA from flooding the streets with their poisoned canisters that Charles turned himself in and went to prison.

Emily said, "This one was real."

"How did you know?"

"A very trusted source."

"And how did they know?"

"It came from a supply obtained before the poisoned batches appeared."

"You know this for sure?"

"As sure as I know that the camera above the building door is a phony. Confident enough that I didn't hesitate before I tried it."

"Since you're telling me this, you must be pretty confident that I haven't done a deal with the SEA and become their CI." He winked at her and squeezed her hand.

She said calmly, "Fuck the SEA."

The word had come to completely permeate the English language; it was as common as articles, conjunctions, or prepositions. In fact, it was often used as punctuation, like a comma. Her use of it was nothing like the norm at Rikers. It was sincere, a general affirmation that the SEA must be defied.

Charles liked this woman. He squeezed her hand again, and she squeezed back.

He asked, "So how did it go? How did you react to it?"

"It worked."

Charles nodded. "It doesn't do anything for me."

"Yeah? It doesn't work for the guy who created it?"

"I didn't create it. I just funded it, recognized its capabilities, and marketed it."

"Well, it definitely had an effect on me. It made me see something about you."

"Anything interesting?"

"To me it was." She paused before adding, "I think you're a lot more like my father than I'd considered."

"Hmm." He wasn't quite sure what to make of that. Hopefully not an indication of some type of Freudian Electra complex, the feminine counterpart of an Oedipus complex. "In what way?"

"Probably have to see that for yourself. You will. When you meet him."

Charles laughed. "Slow down, girl!"

"Hey, I didn't mean it that way. I mean that you should meet him because you two will get along. Even if this date tonight is our last one, you and Dad ought to meet. I suspect you'd have some shared business interests too."

"What does he do?"

"That... you'll need to learn from him. I don't talk about what he does. He's very private."

"But you worked with him?"

"I don't talk about that either. That's another way you and I are alike, Charles. Someday maybe we can tell each other what we do for a living."

"Are you involved in criminal activities?"

"I just toked up on Sybillene, so that's a yes! But not immoral activities."

"No immoral activities at all?" Charles gave her a look of an unhappy pleading puppy while suppressing a grin with a mischievous twinkle in his eye.

Emily slid her body closer to his. "Well, let's see how this date tonight ends, shall we?"

He put his arm around her waist and pulled her against him.

"So you think you have the right to kiss me?" she softly teased.

"No."

He dropped his head toward hers, and she closed her eyes.

After a long kiss, Charles said, "But sometimes, you have to do what you ought to do."

25

Whiskey and Gunpowder

THEY again stood at the door to her apartment building, after a dinner with good wine and even better conversation. Not much small talk, but lots on history, politics, philosophy, and the state of the world. It wasn't romantic the way a soap opera might see it, but mutual intellectual attraction amplified the physical attraction. Physical attraction required only pheromones activated by an appealing face and physique. But the melding of minds was a rewarding prelude to melding their bodies.

Charles's concerns about not getting involved—to avoid putting anyone at risk—fell by the wayside. He justified it with some contorted logic. It was time for him to be normal again. Emily was a competent, smart, and experienced woman who could take care of herself. She didn't need protection. She knew who he was well enough to make an informed decision.

He kissed her, long and passionately, and then moved inside her apartment.

It wasn't long before they were moving together—for hours. Compensation for a long-enforced celibacy, for both of them.

He was experiencing a psychological form of explosive decompression. He quietly let himself out, returning to Xander's apartment in the wee hours. Had his hours in bed with Emily activated some form of PTSD?

Two minutes after he arrived, someone knocked on the door.

That was entirely wrong.

Charles froze for half a second and then pulled his Ruger LCP from his back pocket. He checked to be sure a round was chambered and then

243

replaced it. His heart rate rose. He reached into a drawer in a table near the door and removed a Taurus Judge, a somewhat unusual weapon: a five-shot revolver that was far more substantial than the LCP in both size and stopping power. He kept it loaded with two .410 rounds. The shells with #7 birdshot were deadly at short range, would disable or blind at least out to thirty feet, yet would not penetrate walls into an unsuspecting neighbor's place. The other three chambers held .45 hollow-point Long Colts. A standard Long Colt would go through not just the assailant but halfway through the next apartment. The hollow point helped diminish that risk while doing a lot more damage to the intended target.

But if he had to shoot someone, even in self-defense, he risked the slammer for the rest of his twenty years. It wouldn't matter that it was the middle of the night and the apartment was officially listed as his current abode at the probation office and someone might be trying to kill him. The old adage about preferring to be judged by twelve rather than carried by six didn't apply. They could and would unsuspend his sentence without using a jury. It was a no-win situation.

With his freeze/fight/flight reflex now fully activated, if things went bad, he'd simply have to shoot and figure out the consequences later. He looked through the peephole and relaxed only slightly as he recognized the face. Heart still pounding, he lowered the weapon, holding it at his side as he unbolted and opened the door.

He spoke slowly, on high alert. "Hi, Jeffrey. What brings you here? Especially at this hour."

The man from the unusual meeting at the Battery nodded, a tight, amused smile on half his mouth.

"I'm flattered that you remember my name, Charles. It's been two months, after all."

"I tend to remember mysterious people, especially if I'm wondering whether they're planning to arrest me or kill me."

"No doubt a good policy." Jeffrey looked down at the revolver by Charles's side, holding his hands up and open. "You won't need that. Are you going to invite me in?"

"Sure, but I'll keep my weapon with me."

"As you wish. You do realize if you'd actually needed that gun, you'd already be dead. As I'm sure you're aware, someone who meant you harm would have fired through the door as soon as you put your eye up to the peephole. It's, umm, internally contradictory for you to feel you need it right now."

"I'll make a note," replied Charles. "Keeping an eye out for my own internal contradictions keeps me on my toes." The man was right. Almost anybody—perhaps even including the president of the United States—could be taken out if the assassin was sufficiently competent and motivated. If an assassin didn't care if he was caught or killed, absolutely no one was safe.

He waved Jeffrey through the door with a flourish and made a mental note to suggest that Xander install a video camera outside the door instead of relying on the peephole—a real video camera. Xander probably wouldn't, figuring it would end up a hackable tool for the NSA. "Care for a drink? I have some scotch."

Jeffrey's smile returned, although it was slightly different from when he had first opened the door. "Yes. Macallan 18, neat, would be just fine."

Charles said, "I happen to have some."

"I know."

Charles chuckled with a trace of anger.

"It's good that we're on the same team, don't you think?" Jeffrey asked.

"Are we?" Charles was gaining some confidence in that possibility. It had better be true, or he would either be heading back to prison or, more likely, heading to the mortuary. Charles set the gun on a counter while he poured scotch into two tumblers and handed one to Jeffrey.

He let the scotch rest in his mouth for a long soothing while, savoring it slowly as it permeated the many different taste and touch sensors distributed over the surface of his tongue. He couldn't help but relax for a moment. It made him want to settle into a contented state, one associated with the happy memories of the past when he shared this drink with trusted friends—most particularly, Xander Winn.

He could use Xander here now.

He turned to see Jeffrey stretching out on the couch as if in his own home. Charles sensed no threat from the man, although every logical indicator cried out danger. In the moderate light of the room, Charles analyzed Jeffrey's visage. The jaw was solid, the eyes steady. No fear in those eyes. He couldn't recall the last time he saw such a complete absence of fear. That could indicate Jeffrey was a dangerous sociopath with a defect in his mental wiring—or a Zen master with a lot of experience and the confidence that comes with it.

During a silence that lasted several minutes, both men enjoyed the scotch. Charles's heart rate slowed somewhat, but adrenaline still pumped through his body.

Charles knew nothing about his visitor. Maurice wouldn't be able to help without some hard information. So he would collect some while keeping his revolver close. "As I asked earlier, what brings you here in the dark of night?"

Jeffrey held his empty glass out for Charles to pour. "In the world I see, it's getting darker all the time." He nodded in gratitude for the large pour. "I assume it was you who dispensed with Terrence Kirby. Don't worry, I don't expect you to admit to it."

"You know what they say about the word assume. It's not wise to base too much on assumptions."

"True enough. However, I think it's a reasonable guess."

"Jeffrey, our playing field isn't level. Why don't you tell me about yourself? I ... assume ... that there are a few things you're willing to tell me?"

"You mean where I was born and where I live? What's my sign and favorite color? Trivialities. Who we are is determined by our ideals, what we believe, and what we do. You and I share beliefs. So, in fact, I'm already quite well known to you."

"Let's say that's true. Except that you know many more trivial facts about me than I know about you."

"As I said before, irrelevancies like what kind of scotch you have on hand say little about a man's integrity."

Charles said, "You seem to know more than irrelevant facts."

"Yes, I do."

"Why?"

Jeffrey's face became serious. "Because you're important."

Charles took a moment to absorb that. What the hell was going on here? After a bit, he prompted, "To whom?"

"To certain people. Maybe to the world, Charles."

A suggestion of psychosis? Grandiosity? "That's not an answer. Why are you here tonight?" He looked at his watch, noting that Jeffrey almost imperceptibly frowned.

After another swallow, Jeffrey said, "Because the world is in trouble. Because the bad guys are winning. They laugh at everything we value. It's as if the culture, humanity itself, has divided into two species, and the other species wants to exterminate us. And we ... we've failed to defend ourselves."

It was nothing new to Charles. He'd been robbed, outlawed, and imprisoned by those bad guys. He offered one of his common answers, one that he provided himself from time to time: "When you're faced with an enemy, you have several options. You can submit and hope to placate him. You can try to tip-toe around and hope he doesn't see you. You can do nothing, and hope he leaves you alone. You can run away and hope he doesn't pursue. Or... you can attack." Charles raised his glass again. "I'm not a big believer in hope."

Jeffrey laughed. "You don't know how much alike you and I are. Your assessment of the alternatives is accurate. Where, indeed, can you go when the whole world is in trouble? Mars isn't ready for us. It's like Joe Louis said: 'You can run, but you can't hide.' Sure, we can escape to places where they're weaker. Basically backwaters. We've both been to those places. It's smart to have a crib someplace where they don't know and don't care who you are. A refuge. Even Superman had a Fortress of Solitude. But some of us think it's time to go on the offensive and take back what's been stolen from us. To grow some balls. And you, Charles, clearly have balls. We'd like you on our team."

Charles could only hope that this man was something other than a grandiose psychotic. Psychotics were, by definition, out of touch with reality and therefore unpredictable. But he didn't disagree with anything he'd said so far. "Who's on this team of yours?" Charles asked.

"People that you'll respect. Some you already know. Some you'll bump into because people like us are intuitively attracted to each other. People that share a certain morality: pacifists at heart, but capable of fighting aggressively when provoked. Pacifism doesn't work when you're dealing with a violent opponent. If you don't defend yourself, you're either prey or a slave. My friends come from all walks of life. Some are very wealthy.

"Among other things we all have in common is a dislike of the direction this country has been going for... decades now. The Deep State, which actually runs the government, uses the foolish illusion of democracy to keep the natives from getting too restless. Government has passed a tipping point in size and power. My friends and I want to bring some integrity back to the world. I'm sure you'd like them."

Charles said in monotone, "The country has devolved into a multicultural domestic empire. Western civilization has become just another illusion. At this point, bringing integrity back means changing the culture itself. It's corrupt at its top. And at its foundations. The situation is beyond redemption."

"Most likely it's going to get outright ugly, Charles. We're under attack, and we've decided to counterattack. So far they've taken our lack of response as acquiescence. It's clear we'll need to play at least part of this game on their field, by their rules. That means a certain amount of force and violence, but only against people who have initiated it first. Rather the same conclusion you've come to."

It sounded like this Jeffrey character was asking him to join a militia or an American version of the IRA. Such efforts hadn't accomplished much in the past. He asked, "How much do you know about what I may or may not be up to?"

Jeffrey smiled faintly and spoke confidently. "We know that the president of the Federal Reserve Bank of New York isn't dead."

"Everyone knows that."

"Yes, but we know why you targeted him. Samuels was behind the banning of your drug, Naked Emperor, as well as the creation of the SEA, which amounts to a secret police force. He arranged the destruction of your facility in Gondwana and the killing of your friends. He's a central player in the US government and the Federal Reserve."

Charles responded with nonchalance. "Sounds like he's been quite naughty. A criminal mastermind who uses his cronies and their minions to make life miserable for people like me."

"Samuels is incredibly powerful, highly knowledgeable, and completely ruthless."

"No arguments from me on that score."

"What we don't know is why Samuels isn't dead. Did you miss on purpose?"

Charles didn't respond.

"And, Charles, how can we convince you not to miss next time?"

Charles sat back in his armchair and considered. Could Maurice have leaked his plans? Uncle Maurice was meticulous regarding confidentiality. In fact, anything short of it would have landed him in prison long ago. A 350-pound recluse in prison. Cruel and unusual punishment. But how else to explain how much Jeffrey knew?

"Why don't you tell me how you know what you think you know."

Jeffrey looked at Charles with another smile. "I'm not messing with you. I'm simply not at liberty to disclose that. Please accept my apologies."

Charles frowned. "What do you want from me."

"A couple of things. We want Naked Emperor back."

"How?"

"Better question is when."

"Okay. When?"

"In seven months. February of this coming year."

"How?"

"We'll get back to that when I can. We think the best way to minimize the violence is by having Naked Emperor expose more of the truth. Think of these CityFire rioters. They know the system is broken but don't have much of a clue why the country is falling apart, who's broken it, and how. They're totally off track, picking the wrong targets for the wrong reasons. They're frustrated, incensed, and acting without logic or a plan. The usual suspects are in leadership positions—socialists who know how to push the right emotional hot buttons to motivate mobs. Mostly race and class. City-Fire is all about thoughtless, but directed, chaos, and it's growing fast."

"Why wait until next year, then? Sounds like you'd want Naked Emperor in the streets today."

"We do," Jeffrey replied. "But we lost that drug war about the same time as you went to prison. It's too dangerous right now."

"So what's different come February?"

Jeffrey shook his head. Charles could see an inner struggle.

"I suspect you'll figure it out for yourself."

Charles nodded. February would be right after the inauguration of the new president. There would be a new Congress, 95 percent unchanged from the current Congress. There was less turnover in the US Congress than in the Supreme Soviet before the USSR collapsed. As for the president, nothing would change if Cooligan were re-elected, regardless of what he promised now in his stump speeches. Little would change if the other party got their shill elected either, despite the seemingly rebellious tone of Senator Lear's stump speeches. So if February mattered to Jeffrey because of the election, that must mean he expected someone else would win, presumably Grayson Chase, and that he'd reopen the door to Sybillene. That seemed like a long shot with poor odds.

Charles said, "A president can't change the law by himself. It's nearly impossible to overturn previous legislation. If Grayson Chase wins, he can't expect any cooperation from Congress. Just the opposite."

Jeffrey chuckled. "That only took you three seconds. You're right. But even though Congress created the SEA with a law, the SEA is part of the executive branch. Most of what SEA has become arose from bureaucratic edict and executive orders, not law. The Swamp. The Deep State. People like Paul Samuels. That's what really gives things like the SEA—or the NSA, the CIA, the FBI, and the rest of them—lives of their own. Grayson Chase plans to take on the Deep State, Charles. The Swamp might have been created by legislation, but it mostly grows and cements itself in place by accretion, the way barnacles grow on a ship's hull. Chase plans to use executive orders, and a dozen other devices, to turn the ship of state around before it hits the rocks. Naked Emperor is needed to expose the rocks."

Charles reflected on what he knew about Grayson Chase. Nearly nothing. He couldn't trust the newspaper articles, and he hadn't watched any interviews. He had no time for politics. His life so far had taught him to avoid politics like a poison, never trust those who sought office, and always expect the worst from those who achieved political power. Why should some power-hungry billionaire who'd jumped up to proclaim his opposition to the Deep State be any different? The odds were against Chase. Even if he won, and even if he were sincere, the payout in actual progress wouldn't match the odds. It was a sucker's bet.

Jeffrey sensed Charles's thoughts. "Don't put Chase in a class with the others, Charles. He's nothing like the politicians you've known."

"Everyone says that about their favorite. It carries no credibility with me."

"I'll just ask you to reserve your judgment then, okay?"

"I'll hear you out, but don't plan your life around me sticking a 'Chase for President' bumper sticker on my car."

"Take a look at his website, Charles. Read between the lines all you want and all you can. He wrote it all himself; it wasn't put together by some PR team. Chase is an avid reader and an effective writer."

"Sounds like you're tight with him."

"I know him."

"Can you introduce me to him?"

"It's not a good idea right now. You're an infamous and hated felon."

Charles shrugged it off. "Any chance he can win?"

"He's at fifteen percent in the polls. Most of those people probably just can't tolerate the other choices. They'd likely vote for a chimp as an alternative to the other two. Both mainstream candidates are lifetime pols. One's

250

best known as a liar and a thief, the other wants to turn the country into a magically successful version of Venezuela or Zimbabwe. We think Chase has a real chance. And people have only begun to look at Chase himself. The country's in a depression and on the ragged edge of a civil war or a revolution. He's the only chance of defusing it that I can see."

"I suppose you're going to tell me that Chase is a fount of Boy Scout virtues?"

Jeffrey nodded with raised eyebrows. "I've been around the block a few times, and I think that's true about Chase. As a bonus, he's a multibillionaire who's liquid enough to put four billion dollars into the campaign."

"That could be enough to buy the vote, if he doesn't first get sunk with a dozen rape accusations or a tweet that offended someone ten years ago."

"Those are coming, no doubt. None of it will be true. Watch his interviews, Charles. He knows how to handle attacks when they come."

"Jeffrey, I don't care about politics as a way to solve problems. My expectations are zero. I might like Grayson Chase as a man, but, even if you're right, I doubt he can move the needle at this point. This country used to be unique, but it's become too corrupt, too degraded. Too much like every other country. I'm afraid it's past the point of no return. It's turning into a police state on the road to perdition."

Eyes intent, Jeffrey said, "I understand. But what if we combine Grayson Chase with Naked Emperor, Charles? Did you think of that? What can that combination do? A man who speaks the truth, and a drug that allows people to see through lies and prevents them from believing delusions? It's never been tried before because it's never been possible before."

Charles hadn't considered it, not lately. A few years ago, it had been an exciting prospect as libertarian ideas gained traction because of Naked Emperor. So, yes, he knew the kind of profound change Naked Emperor could have on a person. Or a whole culture, for that matter. Maybe Jeffrey was right.

"So, how long would it take you to ramp up production of Sybillene, if you had a blank check?"

Charles shook his head. "Is that all you want from me? To become a drug lord again? Because I've been there, done that. I've moved on to the next chapter. I've got new things to learn, to do, and to be. I'm not interested in being a cog in someone else's machine."

Jeffrey sipped from his refilled scotch. "No. There's more. There's no doubt in my mind that you have some singularly useful aptitudes, experiences, motivations, and skills. We're on the edge of doing something of world-historic importance. I think you'll want to come to the party."

Charles said nothing. He wanted an answer and wanted it now. He waited.

He saw Jeffrey nod and his eyes darken. "For now, I can only tell you part of what's happening—or, more exactly, what we're going to make happen. You can confirm it however you wish, as long as you're careful. But don't bother pushing me for more."

"What's the part you're inviting me to play in this little drama?"

"In addition to Naked Emperor? I want to hire you for a job that's consistent with your new ... interests. Your new profession."

And then Jeffrey gave him a list of names.

Nothing in Charles's wildest imagination could have anticipated the list that Jeffrey clearly wanted to have assassinated. Jeffrey wasn't thinking of a small under-the-radar sort of operation. The people Jeffrey looked to neutralize were some of the most powerful in the world.

Jeffrey slowly sat back in his chair, put his feet up on the coffee table, and held up his glass to Charles in a toast.

Charles said, "Well, it's certainly bold. But why do you, specifically, want these people dead?"

Jeffrey replied, "I'm interested in attacking the cancer at its root. You can argue that politicians are the problem, and you wouldn't be wrong. Or academia, the media, Hollywood, NGO types, government officials, or corporate managements. They're all part of the Deep State. Acting like termites to destroy the foundations of Western civilization in general and what's left of America in particular. But money makes the world go 'round. That's a lyric from an old song, but not one person in a hundred recognizes how it enables everything else. The money people aren't surrounded with bodyguards like the politicians, even though they control the politicians. They're soft targets, easy targets, and they're the most important ones. Also, for my own reasons, I have a particularly strong aversion to counterfeiters."

Charles contemplated the possibility. "Taking out that specific list of people might send a message. But the same effect—maybe a better effect— can be accomplished in an entirely different way."

"What way is that, Charles?"

He smiled with satisfaction. "As you have secrets, so do I."

26

Deep State

HE should not have received an email from someone he hadn't invited to contact him. Yet the message was there. A red flag for sure. It came in from the email channel he had arranged for a doctor being sued for wrongful death. The doctor had failed to successfully resuscitate a man blasted in the chest with a twelve-gauge shotgun from three feet away. That doctor must have chosen to not employ Paladin and instead passed the mysterious business card on to someone else in need—or very likely to the police. A trap. He closed his laptop and exited the library into a wet spring day.

He would stop by his uncle's place before going home.

"Hi, Maurice." Charles glanced around the apartment, impressed at its degree of organization. Charles remembered times when the floors and furniture were so cluttered it functioned more like a minefield. Maurice was the bane of his maid's existence.

Even though he was very computer savvy, Maurice still subscribed to numerous paper journals and magazines; he found the paper format easier on his eyes. He meant to store relevant articles electronically, but there had always been a hundred things more pressing than converting paper to digital. So Rainbow had helped him set up a secure encrypted system for his files. The system never connected to the internet and was therefore immune from hackers and other prying eyes. She'd whittled away at the stacks of paper documents that not only littered the apartment but almost filled one of the spare bedrooms. Rainbow had successfully computerized enough folders and papers to make the apartment almost homey. Only ten or so piles remained, and she had stacked each of those three feet high.

"What?" Maurice was wide-awake this time, staring at computer screens and barely aware of his nephew.

Rainwater dripped from the shoulders of Charles's raincoat.

"What do you need, Charles?"

"Maurice, I know the answer, but I have to cover all the bases. Have you told anyone, anyone at all, about me and what I'm doing?"

Maurice looked away from the computer monitors and slowly turned his prodigious head toward his nephew. He said nothing. He didn't need to. His expression provided a sufficient response.

Charles shook his head. "I'm sorry, Maurice. I had to ask."

"No, you didn't."

They stayed quiet for a while. Charles chose a wooden chair to hang his coat over and rustled around a bit.

Maurice finally broke the silence. "Why did you ask me that?" He hadn't returned his attention to the computers, but instead he watched Charles.

"Look. Apparently people know what I'm up to. There's that man, Jeffrey. He's found me twice now. Once, after leaving your apartment the day after the country club. Then again last night he showed up at Xander's apartment. He just appears. Seems to be on my side. Claims to know Grayson Chase."

"You think you're being conned? Set up? Maybe they're trying to land you back in the slammer?"

"Of course I considered that. He could be a government agent."

"Perhaps. I doubt it. You're in the system. If they want to, they can just pick you up. No need to go through a spy-versus-spy drill with spooky stuff and double agents."

"Who else, then?"

Maurice rubbed his double chin. "He could be working for one of the political parties, setting up a political hit on Grayson Chase. Maybe make a pretense of tying you with Chase. Get some slime they can throw at him."

"You're saying that I'm the slime."

"Most of the public are brain-dead mooks who only know what they hear on the boob tube. They think you got off easy. So, yes, you're the slime."

Charles shook his head. "I doubt connections with a known felon

254

would move the needle today, if it ever did. Politicians have always been hooked up with gangsters."

Maurice said, "People accept a high slime factor today. You're right about that. What they'd have to do is show that Chase is not only dirty, but a hypocrite. The party hacks are trained attack dogs. Their behavior's bred into them. They're criminals without the balls it takes to rob a bank. They're not just pathological liars, they're enthusiastic liars. They'll dig up dirt on Chase—create it if they have to—and keep hammering it into the public's mind. The way I see it, Chase is trying to sell himself with reason and logic. Reason and logic don't work when you're dealing with mob psychology. Mudslinging has always worked in the past, and the political operatives will assume it will work again. You know the whole Deep State has gotta be setting up to take Chase down. He's a fool if he doesn't know that himself.

"Paul Samuels is in the top layer. They don't have the kind of control the conspiracy theorists like to believe. But it's fair to say that they're more influential than all the voters combined because they not only influence what the voters hear, but interpret it for them. They're not really what used to be called The Establishment; that's more of a class and social construct. Rather, they focus on using the State to feather their nests. They work hard to control who the political parties nominate. More important, they have substantial control over the bureaucracies. Bureaucrats rarely go maverick. Sometimes a politician goes rogue once he's in office, but they neutralize those people with the media or dig up indiscretions or crimes and extort them. If relatively kind and gentle methods fail, these people won't hesitate to act with extreme prejudice."

"JFK?"

"Maybe. He was newly arrived in the Establishment, but he misbehaved. There are people who think the Cubans were involved in Kennedy's death. I don't buy it. If I had to guess, I'd say Johnson did it with the aid of the CIA. I'm willing to bet that Lee Harvey Oswald was a patsy, just as he claimed before Jack Ruby killed him. The official story stinks from start to finish. The gun they say Oswald used—a Carcano 6.5 mm carbine—was about the worst choice possible. Italian World War II surplus. You could buy them by mail for $19.95 in those days. No serious shooter would use one. It was accurate enough to get the job done, even with its glitchy bolt action and crappy dime-store scope. But anyone with sense would have used an autoloader with modern ammo. Who knows, maybe Oswald was an idiot.

I'm not sure if they'll ever figure out exactly who killed Kennedy. Everybody who might have known something seemed to die unexpectedly in the months afterwards—starting with Oswald himself. There've been hundreds of books written about it, and the one thing they all agree on is that the official report, the Warren Report, was a whitewash job. Half the people on the commission could have been conspirators for all we know."

Maurice poked a finger at the screen of his cell phone to stop it buzzing, irritated at the spam shop in Indonesia or the robocaller in Indiana.

"I'm always skeptical about things that I can't verify myself. If you go to the Dallas Book Depository—where they say Oswald took the shots—it's obvious a skilled shooter would have taken his shot while the limo was approaching, not when it was already heading away. It would have been a much easier head-on shot, and if you missed you'd have several more. Instead, they say Oswald fired while it was already moving away, at a much more difficult angle. Maybe Oswald hesitated until after JFK turned the corner, and was a pretty good shot with a crappy rifle. Maybe he actually had a motive—something else that's hard to figure."

Maurice slid a few inches to the right on his couch. Prior to Rainbow entering his existence, this would have been his exercise for the day. He then thought for a moment before pursuing a tangent.

"Only a madman would target a president today. Not just because it's so difficult, but because killing one of the hacks that they put up for us to choose between would serve only to increase government power. A president is fungible. The people who pull the strings keep a low profile. They make most of the decisions, steal most of the money, and avoid the heat.

"The chances of a president riding down a city street in a convertible with the top down today, like Kennedy did in Dallas in 1963, are zero. Now their limos weigh twenty thousand pounds, and they have armored doors eight inches thick and self-contained breathing systems. The thing is essentially an MRAP disguised as a limo. They always run several of them so you can't tell which one he's in. It's a convoy surrounded by armored SUVs, including one for electronics and another with a hidden Gatling gun that can pop out of the roof to plaster the crowd with three thousand rounds per minute. Plus scores of Secret Service agents, high-tech countermeasures, hidden snipers, helicopters, and hundreds of police.

"They say Harry Truman was the last president who actually went out in public on his own like a normal citizen. That only happened because he was able to escape his bodyguards, which is impossible today. Things changed after JFK. The bureaucracy realized that if another king got checkmated, heads would roll. Anything they did along those lines today would be covert."

Maurice took a bite of a delicious-looking sandwich from the plate between them and waved to Charles to help himself.

"None of that's very important anymore though, Charles. If they're going to take out Grayson Chase," Maurice continued while dabbing his mouth with a cloth napkin, "they'll do it before the election. You know, Kennedy was a long time ago. I wasn't yet chasing girls." Maurice looked at Charles conspiratorially. "Yes, I did chase girls. With some success—two hundred years and two hundred pounds ago. A man's got to know his limitations, Charles. What's that they say? 'Control what you can control; accept what you can't'?"

Charles said, "Speaking of that, you're making progress on your weight, Maurice."

"Well, m'boy, I'm working on it. Rainbow nags a ton. She gets me out of the apartment almost every day to go walking. She's equipped a little gym in the backroom—quite adequate for me right now, I'm sad to say—and acts like a Marine DI. Except when she crashes at Mei-li's place. Those two girls stick to each other like glue."

Charles smiled. "Well, whatever she's doing, it's working. You're looking ten years younger. Ten more and the ladies will be chasing you. Are you feeling better?"

"Mens sana in corpore sano. I'm chagrined I haven't yet put the theory into practice. It took me three decades to get this bad, Charles. Might take a couple of years of hard work to reverse it."

"You can do it. Now back to conspiratorial shadow governments that don't exist."

"It isn't a joke, Charles."

Rainbow plowed through the apartment door then, full of energy, oblivious to anything else. "Hey, y'all, I'm home!"

Maurice huffed. "Speaking of the drill instructor..."

"Hey, Rainbow," Charles stood up to welcome the hug. "How's things in the Paladin Network tonight?"

"Closing in toward launch, boss. Wouldn't be, though, if you tried to make me waste my time finishing high school like Mei-li has to—that's the only thing slowing us down. Paladin Network is a full time job thirty-six hours a day." She looked cynically at the two men. "What are you two so deep in the woods about? Fate-of-the-world stuff?"

"We're talking Deep State."

"Ah, that's what white people call it. Ghetto dawgs call it the Man."

"More like the Man behind the Man, Rainbow," said Charles.

Maurice said, "Sit down and pay attention, Rainbow. Every government in the world has its own Deep State. The politicians do favors for big-shot business guys and expect to retire as centimillionaires in return. Things have evolved from the days of suitcases stuffed with C-notes. The way things work today, corruption is much bigger money. Cash payoffs only really work in the Third World. Here you have to sanitize it, make it look legit. Six-figure speeches, seven-figure consulting contracts, eight-figure book contracts, and sweetheart investment deals."

Rainbow interrupted. "Look, I buy it. So tell me everyone who's involved!"

Charles said, "Are you building a top ten for the Paladin Network?"

Rainbow responded with eyes wide and a highly exaggerated nod.

Maurice said, "I have my shortlist. To be very clear, the Deep State is not a conspiracy. Rather, it has grown organically, albeit in a very fertile soil. In the best byzantine manner, our own Deep State has insinuated itself throughout the fabric of what once was America. Its tendrils reach from Washington to every part of civil society. Like a metastasized cancer, it's hard to eradicate without killing the body.

"The Deep State controls the political and economic essence of the US, regardless of which party is in power. Anyone with sense knows there's no real difference between the left and right wings of the Demopublican Party. The Republicans say they believe in economic freedom, but they don't. And they definitely don't believe in social freedom. Meanwhile the Democrats say they believe in social freedom, but they don't, and they definitely don't believe in economic freedom. Both parties love war, because war is the health of the State. That's true; war is a growth hormone, allowing the State to grow. The Republicans are basically flag-waving nationalists who think the government should use the warfare state to spread 'democracy' across the world, even though it's the worst form of mob rule. They complain that the government is incompetent at home, then delude themselves into thinking that the same system can be competent abroad. They're essentially hypocrites, which is why they never get the support of the younger generation.

"Unlike the Republicans, the Democrats have a core philosophy, albeit a rotten one. They believe in socialism and the welfare state and are happy to say so. They're multiculturalists and globalists at heart. Total opportunists. They understand the value of war in politics, and they're all for it when it looks profitable."

"What do you mean by that, Uncle Maurice?"

"Initiation of force is not only morally acceptable to the progressive mind, but their default way to accomplish almost anything they do. Even more than the Republicans, the Democrats believe using violence is fine, as long as you do it through government. They argue that force is the only way to get humans to behave and be kind to one another. They try to sugarcoat it by calling it a social contract. It matters not. Once you accept government aggression as a way to accomplish a goal, the person on the receiving end either accepts being a slave, or he defends himself—herself in your case—and rebels against it. So slavery or war. That's the choice.

"The Deep State changes its approach, its rhetoric, depending on the party in power. But it's a real thing. Most people aren't even aware it exists, because it's so informal. Informal and low profile it may be, but it doesn't just profit from the State; it controls it. I'm not talking about some tinfoil-hat conspiracy stuff. I'm talking about a spontaneous ecosystem created by the interactions of opportunists with an excellent understanding of power and zero regard for ethics.

"The Deep State has a life of its own, like the government itself. Rainbow, you asked who's in it? Top-echelon guys in a dozen praetorian agencies—FBI, CIA, DEA, NSA—the usual suspects. Long-term congressmen, senators, and governors. The directors of important regulatory agencies. A number of top generals, admirals, and other military operatives. But the Deep State is much broader than just the government. I'm talking the heads of major corporations—especially the ones heavily involved in selling to the State and enabling it. That absolutely includes Silicon Valley—although those guys at least have a sense of humor: I thought their 'Don't be evil' motto was cute, if rather brazen.

"All the top people at the Fed, and the heads of all the major banks, brokers, and insurers. Add in the presidents and some professors at top universities and some Nobel laureates to provide intellectual cover. Colleges act as Deep State screening and recruiting centers. Top media figures and talking heads, of course. Many of the regular attendees of events such as Bohemian Grove and the Council on Foreign Relations. These guys don't care about who's a Republican or a Democrat; that's window dressing to confuse the booboisie. It's an informal private club for people that are tough enough to have clawed their way to the top. These people don't bother much with national borders. They know that national borders are just temporary lines on a map."

Rainbow said, "I bet Charles will agree with them on the borders part."

Charles had told her how much he resented being questioned and probed by customs and immigration officials as he roamed the world for seven years after he left Gondwana and before he returned to the US to become a drug lord.

"Not quite, Rainbow," said Charles.

Maurice added, "Charles is entirely their opposite. He blurs national borders as improper restrictions on human freedom; the Deep State people blur national borders as anachronistic restrictions on their power. Couldn't be more different. Charles wants a world with seven billion people living in seven billion countries. The Deep State want seven billion people living in one global empire, with them in control."

"Glad I didn't bet any money."

"Kid, money comes and goes. What you really want is wealth, because it's much more... encompassing... than money. Wealth represents the ability to pursue happiness. At least for normal people. Health is a component of wealth, right? So is freedom. And so is knowledge. So is whatever else a person thinks will help them pursue happiness."

"You think the Deep Staters are happy people?"

"Nah. Most are sociopaths, or close to it. They aren't happy; they're incapable of it. How can you be happy when your life is built on a foundation of intellectual, emotional, and ethical lies? How can you be happy when your wealth is built on theft and holding other people down while having to watch your back the whole time? It's a pity that a lot of the rich and powerful in today's world are criminals. They're sick. Not just psychologically, but—if you like—spiritually. Lord Acton rightly said, 'Power corrupts, and absolute power corrupts absolutely.' It's funny. The Occupy Wall Street, Black Lives Matter, Extinction Rebellion, and Antifa types have morphed into the CityFire rioters. They seem to hate the Deep State people too, even though that's where they get their core funding. They hate out of envy more than anything else. They seem to think the rich are evil just because they're wealthy. Of course the more wealth is gained from corruption rather than production, the more that bias is supported."

Charles chimed in. "The Occupy movement was founded and run by people infected with the collectivist brain disease. So they lumped the wealthy into one group: the One Percent. They made no effort to distinguish honest wealth from dishonest wealth. They were right to see the problems with Wall Street, but their collectivist indoctrination prevented them from diagnosing the problem accurately. They didn't realize that their socialist solutions were exactly what the Deep State wants—because it gives them even more power and more control."

Maurice said, "Rainbow, it's fun to despise the Man, just like it's fun to hate comic book caricatures. Most rich people are nice enough, just caught up in their own lives. Preoccupied, just like everyone else, except for having more money. I don't judge people because of what they have. I judge them because of what they are—their essence, not their position. What they do usually gives you an indication of who they are. Those are the three most important verbs in any language—be, do, and have."

Rainbow had gone to the refrigerator to drain an orange juice container. As she came back, she said, "You said that the people in the Deep State are all sick. That's judging people because of their group."

Maurice replied patiently. "I think it's the reverse. These people are sick, and that's why they're in that group. You don't want to confuse cause and effect. Their sickness—the way they see the world and what they want out of it—brings them together. Birds of a feather do, in fact, flock together."

"What's their sickness?"

"They're sociopaths. No guilt, no conscience. No concern for others, no morality, no thought for consequences. Some people suggest that they tend to pedophilia. Maybe true. I wouldn't be surprised. They take advantage of people who are in no position to defend themselves."

Charles noted, "Terrence Kirby's computer was loaded with child porn. That's the only fact I can provide about this. Do you have any more data, Maurice?"

"As you know, I hear a lot of things. In general, I couldn't care less about people's voluntary sexual interactions. I never figured that it was any of my business whether some guy's body fluid spilled on somebody's dress while they're fooling around. But forced sex is another story entirely. I've heard rumors about clubs with pretty horrific initiation rituals. I don't know that I believe them. If they're true, maybe it's to make damn sure that people who join the group are numb to any feelings of morality or concerns for innocence. That would make sense. That's why gang leaders in Rio's favelas or the African bush or here in New York City have new inductees kill somebody in cold blood. We don't give much credit to that sort of thing happening among 'civilized' people, but it's probably part of the human condition."

Charles worried about his own evolving numbness, centered on killing people he saw as the enemy. It happened to soldiers in wartime, but the difference was that soldiers did it because they were ordered to, or had no choice, or had been propagandized into hating a dehumanized foe. There was generally no animus against the enemy as individuals. Charles, however, was entirely self-motivated, and targeting specific individual actors for specific reasons. These were people who Charles would despise in any time or place. It was odd that what soldiers did was legal, even though their targets were mostly draftees guilty of nothing but wearing the wrong uniform, while what Charles did was illegal, even though his targets were hardcore criminals who wreaked havoc while escaping justice. It was perverse, and upside down.

Rainbow next asked, "Are you saying the Deep State people always work together? Is there a guy with a white cat calling the shots?"

"I doubt it. It's not structured; it's more like a nest of vipers. Sociopaths don't work and play well together, but they have common interests. I'd bet they actually hate each other. They probably couldn't cooperate on a project for more than a short while even if their lives depended on it. When you think of them working together, it's like the pact between Hitler and Stalin, or several Mafia families. The only question is who betrays the other first.

"The Deep State isn't a conspiracy. It's more of, well, more of a culture. They trade favors and have informal agreements. It's not a cartel—although quashing Charles's Naked Emperor was something I bet they all agreed on. A truly effective conspiracy is rare, but it did require a conspiracy to create the SEA and the war on Sybillene."

Charles paid heed to that last particularly, for Jeffrey was asking him to get back into that very war.

Rainbow said, "I've seen that in the 'hood with gangstas. They can work together for a while, when they have to. Maybe to eliminate a common enemy. They'll switch alliances again right after."

"Charles was the Deep State's common enemy for sure. They pulled out all the stops to neutralize him. He had the First Lady blaming him for all the problems of the world. Her first line was 'Don't be ruled by the Naked Emperor.' They hoped it would catch on like their 'This is your brain on drugs' meme, where they showed a couple of eggs frying. Boy did that backfire! Naked Emperor supporters turned that around on the First Lady. Memes immediately emerged with cartoons of President Cooligan and other major players sitting naked on thrones. It was clear who you shouldn't be ruled by. They pulled that ad campaign fast, but its failure probably accelerated the process of the SEA being granted all its power. Naked Emperor was good stuff, Charles. Good stuff. I'm proud of you for that."

"Yeah, well, since they bombed the factory and killed the staff, it's going to take a while to rebuild."

Rainbow leaned forward, "You thinking of starting up again, Paladin?"

"I appreciate your enthusiasm, Rainbow. Right now I'm mainly thinking that I'd like a glass of orange juice and you just drained the supply."

"Sorry, Charles." Rainbow popped up with the speed of youth and headed to the door. "I'll be back in ten minutes with fresh OJ." Then she was out and gone.

Maurice took advantage of Rainbow's absence to ask, "Do you have any more jobs planned?" Keeping Rainbow unaware of the details of Charles's current pursuits was in everyone's best interests.

Charles nodded. "Actually, yes. Maybe. This guy Jeffrey has a list."

"That's concerning. He's asking you to take out what kind of people?"

"Major league bad guys. They're all Deep Staters, and near the top."

"Who in particular?"

"Maurice, you won't believe it."

But as his uncle looked at the list Charles handed to him, indeed he did believe it.

"Interesting list. I don't like to use the word evil. The word seems... extravagant. The Bible thumpers have degraded its meaning, made it seem banal. It's got mainly religious connotations in modern America, so most people don't take the word seriously anymore. I'd say the people on this list qualify for the word, Charles. They're intentionally destructive, with malice and forethought. They know precisely what they're doing and justify it with an aberrant logic and a false façade that the hoi polloi accept. These are all Deep State. Professional cronies, Charles. This man Jeffrey at least appears to have good taste in enemies."

Maurice thought for a moment. "You know how a priest asks a penitent if he truly regrets his sins, and then adjusts the penance accordingly before he tells him to go and sin no more? Maybe not the best example, since I don't believe in the concept of sin handed down from on high. It's not necessarily the same as evil. Maybe a better example is how the defense attorney at a criminal trial always makes a big deal about the prisoner showing remorse before the judge pronounces sentence. Of course the prisoner is almost always lying when he says he's sorry, at least about anything but getting caught. My point is these people"—he shook the list of paper—"have no regrets or guilty conscience about anything. I'm on your side, Charles. But you'll be playing in the major leagues here against people who aren't like you. This isn't going to be like hunting rabbits. How do you plan to pull it off?"

"I have a little something I picked up in Colombia in mind for the treasury secretary. Bullets are fine, and sometimes they're the only choice, but technology has advanced, and guns are six-hundred-year-old tech. I may be able to tailor the method to the crime. It would be nice to stay on the moral high ground. We're not building the Paladin Network just to make a buck. It's not like placing a help-wanted ad for a hitman on Craig's List or Soldier of Fortune. The whole Paladin Network infrastructure will serve beautifully to take these people down. We don't have to kill them all."

"But I thought your new friend, Jeffrey, wants them all dead."

"He does. I believe the network will be quite capable of that, if it proves necessary. I'm hoping he might appreciate interventions just short of termination with extreme prejudice. Things that are potentially even more effective, with lower risk."

"And if the Paladin Network barely makes if off the ground? If the Paladin Network totally fails?"

Charles shrugged. "Then I'll kill the bastards."

27

Homo Novus

MANDATORY visits with his probation officer made Charles feel owned. Just as the system intended.

His PO, Phil, remained predictably irritating. The man liked exercising petty power over others, but lacked the brutality to be a prison guard or the intelligence it might take to be a cop. So he defaulted to the justice system's equivalent of a DMV clerk. His flaccid physique and his pencil neck made him the very opposite of intimidating, so Phil compensated by parading his employer's power and making threats his employer would enforce. The nasty little Napoleon was the absolute ruler of his cubicle and anyone who was forced to enter it.

Charles was pleased to learn that Phil had been called away from the office. His boss would substitute for him.

He stepped partway into the office as he knocked on the door.

"Hello, Mr. Knight," Tony Scibbera said, as he stood up from behind his desk. "I've been looking forward to meeting with you. Thanks for coming."

Charles took in the man and his office. "I'd rather that it were a voluntary visit."

"An understandable preference. But the world doesn't always accommodate our wishes," Scibbera replied. He ushered Charles to a seat and closed the office door behind him.

Charles said. "You're Albert Peale's probation officer."

"I was. He's out of the system now, back to his journalistic endeavors, thankfully."

"And you were at my sentencing hearing, sitting with Peale?"

Scibbera smiled. "You remember correctly. It's no coincidence, Mr. Knight. My name is Anthony Scibbera. Please call me Tony. I'm sorry they managed to keep you in prison for so long."

"It was an experience I intend to avoid in the future," Charles replied.

"That's good to hear. If you stay out of prison, the system will see it as a sign that I'm doing my job here. I'll get credit for keeping recidivism low. Coffee?"

"Thanks. Phil never offers me coffee."

"Phil's what might be called a useless mouth. His very uselessness, paradoxically, makes him useful. His incompetence makes him a good choice to be your PO."

Charles chuckled. Tony poured him coffee, black, handed it to him, and sat down behind his desk.

Tony said, "We have a mutual friend. He asked me to transfer into this new position, where I could help you out if need be."

The pleasant conversation in this unpleasant place served as a reminder that he had been, and still was, something of a hero to many. The sympathetic warden who'd helped him get out of prison had suggested as much. It rarely entered Charles's mind that he might be anyone special. His face had been largely forgotten as the news cycle marched on through viruses, economic busts, recession, CityFires, and celebrity moral turpitudes, but his name was still widely recognized. He was the best thing since Robin Hood or William Wallace to some, and the worst thing since Al Capone or Charles Manson to others. A folk hero who had friends. But how many friends? Whatever the number, he could count on ten times as many enemies. Relatively few people had had a chance to try Sybillene and experience its benefits, but the whole country had been subjected to a massive barrage of propaganda from the government and its lapdog media for several years now.

"Tony, who is that mutual friend?"

He wondered if this mutual friend was Maurice. Or maybe Xander?

"I'm not at liberty to disclose that, Mr. Knight."

Charles recognized the particular phrase Tony used. It raised the possibility that Tony might be in with Jeffrey. Interesting. To test that hypothesis, he said, "Well, I'm grateful to Jeffrey."

Tony said nothing.

But Charles read his expression clearly enough.

"I've got some things you may need," Tony said as he slid a stack of manila envelopes across the desk. "In there is your US passport. The one they confiscated. It took some paperwork, but we got it for you despite your being on probation. And some pre-signed undated authorities from me so that you can travel. And you'll find a passport application in the name of Malcolm Reynolds. I'd have submitted that for you, but I needed a passport-sized photo of you in some sort of disguise. You don't want to look like Charles Knight. But don't look like Paladin, either."

Charles bristled that Tony knew about the Paladin disguise. He felt sickened and stupid. For all his efforts at being careful, he'd put his own head right on the chopping block. He'd been followed and watched by these so-called friends. His concern grew that he was being set up as a patsy. He needed to be more careful and less naïve in the future.

Tony must have sensed Charles's dismay, for he held up his hand reassuringly, as if to say 'It's all okay,' and continued speaking. "You'll need to take care of that alternate identity. It's set to be expedited, so it's best if you get those pictures done today and go through the process. You already have your Dominica passport, I'm sure. There's a Cayman passport here as well."

Charles flipped through the documents. "Out of prison, and straight to being an International Man again."

"Dignum et justum est; it's fitting and proper. You'll also find concealed carry permits for New Jersey, New York City, and New York State, in both names. Some states you may travel to or through will honor these permits, but most won't. Washington, DC, won't. See the list. We'll try to get more for you, but, obviously, try to avoid interacting with law enforcement."

"Tony, how did you do this? I'm a felon on probation!"

"The system believes its own paperwork. Don't underestimate Jeffrey, whoever he is. Now, it's best you get out of here before you're infected with any of the psychological diseases floating around in this bureaucracy. Take the coffee with you if you wish. And take my business card in case you get in trouble. Check in with me in two months, please. Meanwhile, stay away from this cesspool. I've got you covered."

Charles stood up to leave. As he reached his hand to the doorknob, he turned to Tony Scibbera. "Thank you."

Scibbera stood up. "Mr. Knight. It's my privilege."

28

Late Night Plotting

"ARE you ready?" asked Jeffrey. There was no hello as Charles greeted him at the door.

"Come in. I'll get the scotch," Charles said, holding his door open wide with one arm while making a welcoming gesture with the other. He no longer felt the need to hold a gun by his side.

Jeffrey winked. "Your bottle was getting low. There's a new one in your cabinet."

Charles turned back. "Hmm… What if I'd set a booby-trap in here, Jeffrey?"

"Then you would've blown up some fine scotch and made a mess of Xander's apartment."

Charles instinctively liked Jeffrey; he seemed sincere and honorable. Then again, that very fact told him to be suspicious. The best con men never seemed like con men, because they were so affable, so seemingly normal and trustworthy. His comfort with Jeffrey arose from the simple and unfortunate reality that Jeffrey already knew far more than enough to have him arrested … and hadn't done so. Or that Jeffrey could already have killed him, yet hadn't. It might seem like a pretty low standard—that Jeffrey had earned trust simply by not incarcerating or killing him—but what could be more powerful than freedom and life?

They sat and sipped their drinks. They looked as if they were relaxing, killing some time with small talk. But they both knew the coming conversation would be about killing something else.

Jeffrey handed Charles a newspaper clipping. "Did you see this?"

Charles glanced at it. "Yeah, I saw it online."

The New York Post writer—Ahmed Raheem—had received and published the picture of a dead Terrence Kirby with Paladin coins on his eyes. The article—a follow-up to Raheem's original article on Kirby's death—now recited a few new reasons why the dead man might have had it coming. No doubt the FBI would be unhappy with the reporter. Charles respected the newsman without ever having met him; he actually seemed interested in discovering the truth and writing about it. Something of a lost tradition in his trade. Maurice was looking into him. It would be good to have a journalist as an ally again because most were on a continuum running from irritating flea to psychotic enemy. He reminded himself to check in with Albert Peale, another good journalist.

Jeffrey asked, "Are those coins or tokens on Kirby's eyes?"

Most people didn't know the difference, but Jeffrey clearly did. Coins were minted from precious metals. Metal tokens were just slugs, and therefore intrinsically worthless, like all US dimes and quarters since the days of the Johnson administration. Their 90 percent silver content had been replaced with scrap metal; the look was quite similar, but it was a fabrication, a lie that had worked since the days of the early Roman emperors. Most people didn't figure out the difference until it was too late. Charles made a mental note that the Paladin Network's cryptocurrency token should be called something other than token. Perhaps it should be called a Paladin Proof. Among other definitions, a proof was a coin struck from a new die. So a Paladin Proof could be metaphor on several levels.

He chose to not answer the incriminating question about the silver coins on Kirby's eyes and instead got down to business. "So, one thousand ounces of gold, in advance, to neutralize each of these people on the list."

"That's right. Very generous, I think, given that you'd probably do it for the sake of good karma alone. Every relationship should be built on a foundation of fair exchange. Plus, I'm thinking you'll likely invest that gold well."

Charles didn't respond, but he guessed that Jeffrey meant investing in the development of a new manufacturing operation for Naked Emperor.

Jeffrey added, "I doubt you'd accept a contract on an innocent man."

Charles remained quiet.

"Would you?" Jeffrey prompted.

"Would I what?"

"Accept a contract on a man who didn't deserve to die?"

"Are you asking me to?"

Now Jeffrey was silent.

Charles said, "No. Of course I wouldn't intentionally harm an innocent man."

"You've killed people who had no beef with you at all."

"If I did, and I am not admitting to anything, then it would have been because I was engaged, professionally, to solve a problem for someone who was being seriously harmed, with no other reasonable remedy. There's nothing wrong with hiring a surrogate."

"A mercenary."

Charles replied, "A mercenary is a professional fighter, willing to use his skills for someone who's unable or unwilling to do his own fighting. It's a perfectly honorable occupation. But if I were, hypothetically, in that position, I would be more of a problem solver. Preferably even an arbitrator. A nonviolent approach to situations is always the first alternative. The non-aggression principle essentially says that you never throw the first punch. That's very simple, but a couple of things complicate the situation.

"The first complication is moral. Some moralists—like the Jains—believe in pacifism, which is to say that you shouldn't use violence even in self-defense. Some—like the Mohammedans—advocate initiating violence for something as small as a proscribed drawing or not sharing their belief in a book. There are many shades between the two extremes. The fact is, however, that when they're put under pressure, moral systems go out the window for most people. It's helpful to think about the words of philosophers and sages. But I make the decisions. I don't delegate that responsibility to a deity or self-appointed authority.

"The second complication is legal. If you assassinate someone, you're breaking the law. Prohibiting extrajudicial killing is supposed to minimize violence. I'm not so sure. It should be a question of justice: the process of getting what you deserve. In fact, I know of several people who were killed because they deserved it; but the legal system would have prohibited justice instead of encouraging it. My guess is that if it were still possible for juries to decide on the justice involved in a crime—as opposed to only deciding whether the perpetrator did or didn't commit it—then whoever killed those people would be exonerated. And likely praised as a hero."

Jeffrey interjected, "Jury nullification."

"Exactly," Charles replied. "But that's not the world we live in. Juries today are instructed to only determine the facts of the case, not the justice of the case. There are tens of thousands of laws that can arbitrarily turn anyone into a felon overnight. Most laws are as corrupt as the politicians that enacted them. So I tend to disregard laws. I've thought at length about the moral and legal implications of all this. There are many ways of solving problems. If I'm involved, they'll be moral, but not all of them legal. And as few as possible lethal."

Jeffrey said, "I agree. Would you take out someone who hasn't initiated force or fraud?"

"I've already answered that. I told you, very clearly, that I won't kill an innocent. There's something to be said for that line in chapter 2 of Luke: 'Peace on earth to men of good will.' As for men of bad will—peace is achieved differently."

Jeffrey nodded. "We're on the same page. But there's an alternate translation from the Greek: 'Peace on earth, good will to men.' I like them both, but your version is more discerning. Now let's go over problems in need of solutions."

The men spent the next two hours discussing the people on Jeffrey's list. Jeffrey mentioned their hoped-for demise on several occasions. Charles didn't. Instead, Charles said, "Let me be clear. You're offering to pay me to neutralize them, to remove them from a… problematic… sphere of influence, correct?"

Jeffrey replied, "That's a recondite and abstruse way of saying it."

One side of Charles's mouth turned up with a wry grin. "As is your own choice of words. As might be my methods of solving the problems we both see."

"Well, there are many paths up the mountain."

"Good, because if I were to take this on, I'd want flexibility."

"Okay. But Charles, some people just need killing. Sometimes, as you've said yourself, it's the only way."

"Yes. I've come to that conclusion too, but it can have regrettable, unanticipated, indirect, and delayed consequences. It can easily violate one's sense of aesthetics."

"I'm sure you have. Do you think you can do this alone?" Jeffrey asked.

"Only a lone wolf can go undetected, but just because a lone wolf doesn't have confederates, doesn't mean he fails to use all the resources available to him."

"I'm ready and able to help you, Charles. If I'm invited to the party."

"To be clear, right now this party is just a hologram, a war game. I like you, Jeffrey. And I get why you can't lay all your cards on the table, even though it's clear we have some friends in common. Still, I can't prove you aren't working for the Chinese or for some shadow government, or for a general planning a military coup."

"None of those things. But it's hard to prove a negative."

They went through detail after detail about Jeffrey's high-level targets, discussing each in depth. At one point, Charles said, "Wainwright has a vacation house there? Really? Isn't that the country where he hid his assets from the IRS before he became treasury secretary?" Charles then asked, "Can you find out when he's going there next?" He didn't expect an affirmative response.

Jeffrey chuckled. "Should be no problem. I'll see what I can do."

Charles raised an eyebrow. Who was this Jeffrey, that he could apparently access the personal schedule of a cabinet secretary? Again, con man or government agent was high on the list. An SEA agent? That was his greatest concern.

Yet Charles had confidence that Jeffrey was a man of good will. Confidence, however, was something a con man specialized in. He kept coming back to that. Or, of course, Jeffrey could be exactly what he portrayed himself as: a good man trying to solve an intractable problem.

They worked until 3:00 a.m. The intellectual stimulation of planning to change the course of history was even more powerful than the adrenaline coursing through their bodies. Shutting down some of the darkest people walking the earth was a game worth playing.

Especially if others throughout the world followed suit once they saw it was possible.

29

A Better Climate

THE FARMER'S Almanac had correctly anticipated a cold summer and an even-colder election season. In the face of the global warming hysteria, suggesting meteorological coolness was so politically incorrect as to be dangerous. Perhaps they published the prediction just to attract attention to themselves. The almanac's weather forecasts were at least as accurate as those of the climate gurus.

It looked like the almanac would be right for at least the next week or so. Canadian air poured into New York almost as quickly as the media could pour out stories about how the cooling spell was symptomatic of the climate crisis. Anything related to the weather—good, bad, or neutral—brought on a discussion of a looming climate catastrophe. If the weather was bad, it was a harbinger of worse things to come. If the weather was perfect, articles would advise readers to enjoy it while it lasted because the end was nigh.

Charles squeezed Emily's hand. "How about we escape from New York to a beach in the Caribbean for a bit? I hear it's cooler than usual down there too. Might be perfect, and the flights off-season are cheap."

Emily didn't hesitate. "Sign me up."

"We can leave next Wednesday. Will whoever's paying you to … do whatever you do … mind if you accompany me?"

Emily felt guilty. She controlled herself and said, "I'm not an indentured servant. I'll be fine."

"Good. Then how about we go visit your father in Dominica?"

Emily huffed faintly. She was expecting a week of vigorous and passionate sex from a man who wanted to make up for lost time. "So now you're talking about meeting my father? That's kind of a bolt from the blue. You think you're ready?"

Charles replied, "We don't have to make a big thing of it."

"And how are you expecting to get out of the country? You're on probation. They won't have given you your passport back."

"You'd think. Apparently I have some friends who pull strings. Plus I happen to have a Dominica passport; I took advantage of their economic citizenship program years ago. It's always good to have a backup system."

"You planning on doing something nefarious there?" She winked at him enticingly.

"With you? Absolutely."

Emily would inform Jeffrey about Charles's planned trip to Dominica, of course, but after having slept with Charles—and it had been a great night—she felt increasingly uncomfortable about doing so. Spying on friends was not her bag. Spying on lovers? Even less so. But Jeffrey wasn't entirely sure about Charles Knight yet. He needed more detailed information, and Emily had agreed to provide it. She would abide by her agreement with Jeffrey, who had reassured her that a man like Charles Knight—if he was the man he appeared to be so far—would forgive her when the truth came out. If he wasn't a good man, then she'd be glad to have been cautious.

Everything she'd learned about Charles confirmed her personal experience with him, and Jeffrey was reassured by Emily's assessment. Enough to bring Charles into his outer circle—although not enough to let Charles entirely in. She, her father, and just a handful of others knew the deeper secrets.

It reassured her to remember that truth was a valuable good, a store of intellectual gold, and therefore something to be dispensed deliberately. Just because she held information that happened to be true didn't obligate her to share it with Charles or anyone else. Lying and not telling the whole truth were two different beasts. It seemed a paradox, on the surface. Telling the truth had innumerable practical advantages from the speaker's point of view, like a reputation as someone who could be trusted. A liar probably has a crime or at least a vice to hide. The biggest problem with lying is the damage it does to the liar himself. Lying results in a feeling of cognitive dissonance, a disconnection from the real world. Sometimes a liar is too weak to face the consequences of telling the truth; then the fear of discovery always haunts him. Sometimes a liar wants to gain something that doesn't belong to him—property or recognition—which turns him into a thief as well.

Speaking the truth benefits both parties; it shows integrity and increases the listener's respect for the speaker. Of course some people simply didn't deserve the truth.

She thought Charles would understand this. He was morally aware, but he'd still need to earn the truth, both about her and about Jeffrey. In the meantime, she wouldn't lie to him. If push came to shove, she'd simply tell him that there were some things she wasn't at liberty to disclose.

They sat in what had become "their" small coffee shop. She eyed him, waiting for him to talk, but he was a rock. He just kept sipping at his tea, with a faintly mischievous smile.

"Damn," she said, under her breath. She realized that he'd heard it. "Oh, I'm sorry."

Charles's smile changed then to an expression of concern. He said in a low voice, "Sorry for what, Emily?"

She covered it up by saying, "Sorry for thinking out loud. Can I ask you a question? You'll tell the truth?"

"If I answer, it'll be the truth. But I won't necessarily answer."

"Ah, so you'd claim that you aren't at liberty to say?"

He looked at her closely then, with a quizzical expression, and kept looking at her a moment too long for comfort. She'd said something wrong. This undercover spying business was by nature unpredictable; that wasn't an issue. The problem was that it was morally ambivalent at best, and it went downhill from there. Work with her father had usually been so much more direct. Get in unseen, do the work, disappear. It was cleaner. She'd remember this lesson as she plotted her future.

Charles looked down at his lap and said slowly, "Maybe I don't want to feel like I'm on a quiz show."

"I understand that. Privacy's in short supply these days."

"I like you, Emily, and I won't lie to you. But truth is not a free good."

Emily closed her eyes and smiled internally. Few people ever considered the concept and its implications, and here he was saying exactly the words her father used.

The default mode for normal, decent people was to tell the truth.

Apart from all that, telling the truth was easier than trying to remember a web of lies.

Charles's statement reflected the way that she justified her own lack of transparency and placed the two on a level playing field in the world of truth and secrecy—except that she knew that they were playing a game on that field. He didn't.

With some hesitancy, Emily tried to dig further. Jeffrey wanted more intel, and she'd try to supply it. She asked, "Who were you before becoming the notorious drug lord Wikipedia describes you as?"

"I have no idea what they say about me on Wikipedia."

"It's like a ping pong game. Some Wiki editors want to beatify you. Some despise you and portray you as Satan. The history of edits on your Wiki page looks like a cat fight. It shows how differently people think, how the same facts can be turned into two different movies."

"I never thought to look myself up on Wikipedia; I don't much care what the public, whoever that is, might think. Maybe everything relevant is already there."

"Doubt it."

He seemed to look inwardly before speaking. "I've always been who I am, as far back as I can remember as a kid. I believe in nature over nurture. I've always been an entrepreneur by nature, but my nature didn't prepare me for the fact a lot of people are wired to steal rather than build. I learned an early lesson running a lemonade stand. It gave me insight into the nature of protection rackets. To this day I'm still particularly irritated by intimidation and shakedowns, whether it's done by a street thug in Manhattan, the Mafia, or a government. I've always applied myself, and I don't like thieves or parasites looking for a free ride.

"I started a computer business in my dad's garage. After I realized I could make money, well, then I started out for real. I quit school young. After I learned to read, write, and do basic math, it was counterproductive anyway. I read constantly and had a huge desire to learn—but zero desire to go to college. When I was twenty-three, I traveled to Africa to check out a gold company I'd speculated on. I spent seven years running around the world. Then the drug-lord stuff, the Sybillene—you know about that. Or at least the government's side of the story. It all seems a long time ago."

She interrupted, "Most of that isn't in Wiki. You started doing all this when you were still just a kid?"

"I was very much a kid."

"Where did you grow up?"

"Yeah, I'm still working on that."

"Charles?"

"Montana. Western Montana. In the foothills of the Rockies. It's beautiful country. There are more deer, buffalo, and bears than people. Which suits me just fine."

Emily nodded. She'd never been there. "So you were a speculator. I thought that meant you went out with a pick and shovel and went digging and panning for gold."

"Nope, that's a prospector. There are still plenty of them wandering around looking for the treasure of Sierra Madre, but mineral exploration is now mostly a matter of satellite imaging, geochemistry, magnetic surveys, and drilling. Geologic mapping and laboratories have replaced mules and pickaxes. A speculator tries to take advantage of distortions in the market—most of them caused by the government. We also try to take advantage of the insanity of mob psychology. The public doesn't like speculators, even though we're there with a bid when they're panicking to sell at the bottom, and we're there with product when they're manic to buy at the top. It's mostly about envy and resentment. The public likes to have a scapegoat when they make bad investments."

"Don't you feel bad for them?"

"I just try to accommodate their desires. A speculator doesn't take advantage of other people; he takes advantage of situations. My big hit was in gold-mining speculation." His eyes were wistful. "I made lots of money on it. Tons of money, in my early twenties, and with what most would consider the adventure of a lifetime as a bonus."

"So you're rich?"

"Rich is a relative term. I can pay for the groceries and the rent without borrowing."

Emily prodded. "Come on now. Don't leave out the good parts of the story."

Charles acquiesced. "I actually did make a lot of money. But I failed to protect it, or myself. There are"—he paused for a moment—"nefarious agents at large in the world."

"You lost your money?"

"I didn't lose it. It was stolen. Well, most of it. I rescued a small fraction of it with the help of some friends. A relative took care of some of it for me until I got back to the US some years later. Much of it remains in a safe asset, in a safe place. I don't actually need it now. Spending it would complicate things."

"Couldn't the police or the FBI or someone in the government help you get your money back from these ... nefarious agents?"

He rolled his eyes theatrically. "The nefarious agents I'm referring to are in the government. The IRS and SEC specifically. I committed no crime, and I was fully in the right. Explaining it in more detail, telling the story, makes me sound defensive, so I prefer not to. It was a long time ago. Ancient history."

She nodded. "So, they took your money. Did you keep speculating?"

"Marginally. It's not a full-time occupation. I'm not a trader. Trying to second-guess the markets is generally a road to disaster. If you're a smart speculator, you act like a crocodile and just wait—maybe for years—for a really fat opportunity. Anyway, money is just a part of life. I traveled the world for seven years, mostly in a sailboat; it didn't take a lot of money. When I came back, I started working with Visioryme, the pharmaceutical company that created Sybillene. I owned a big chunk of it."

Emily said, "That part is on Wiki."

"I suppose I should look at that, just to be aware. Like I said, I'm not inclined to care what the public thinks. Especially the ones who've nothing better to do with their time than write comments on blog posts. Vanderbilt said, 'Let the public be damned.' That's pretty much my view too."

Emily said, "So, damn the public. Can you tell me from your point of view?"

Charles took a moment to answer. He said, "We had great success. The drug, Sybillene, was marketed as an antidepressant. We went through clinical trials, did battle with the FDA, and won, and they generously gave us permission to market our drug in their country." He oozed sarcasm when he said "generously."

"Right. So you started marketing it as an antidepressant?"

"Yes. But that was inaccurate. Most psych drugs distort reality, put you in a dream world, and maybe turn you into a high-functioning zombie. Sybillene clears the mind, but it had a side effect: it caused people to see the truth. That's why its most popular name was Naked Emperor."

Emily interjected. "I can understand why it was banned."

"Maybe you do. Or you might have picked up some misinformation from Wikipedia. Let me give you the facts. Naked Emperor allowed people to see through lies: government propaganda and other idiocy put out by the media as truth. Not just political lies, but media manipulation, religious lies, lies masquerading as science, and the lies one person tells another. It's particularly effective at exposing the lies that a person would tell himself. In fact, I think that's how it really worked: most lies are only believable if you're willing to lie to yourself. Maybe that's why it was so effective against depression. Internal contradictions can lead to anxiety and depression. As soon as they recognized their own conflicted thinking, people corrected it and felt better. They could see their problems more clearly and set about solving them. Naked Emperor cleared the mind of aberrations and self-deception. If it had been designed to be swallowed instead of inhaled, it would have been the famous red pill."

Emily nodded. "Like in The Matrix."

Charles said, "People who used Sybillene became problematic. Confronting stupidity. Questioning authority. And, even better, defying the authorities. I suspect it's why both of the major political parties lost market share a couple of years back."

"An antibrainwashing drug."

"Yes. It worked great to get people out of cults and destructive relationships. So it broke up a lot of crappy marriages. It also caused people to break free of organized religions. The churches didn't like that. It made people question why the indoctrination of children was compulsory and why they needed a doctor to write prescriptions instead of just buying what they need in a store. It let them see why they had little control over their lives. People started asking too many questions of powerful entrenched interests. Keep in mind, these were strong trends even while only a small percentage of the population had tried it. And so the FDA took Sybillene off the market, and the DEA took over from them."

"On whose orders?" She thought she knew the answer.

"It sounds trite, but it was the powers that be, Emily. The Deep State. Lots of groups wanted it off the market. All the big churches, the major political parties, union bosses, insurance companies, banks, brokers, media moguls, doctors, environmentalists, race baiters. A lot of influential people were threatened by Sybillene. A lot of people don't want their hidden agendas exposed."

"So you kept marketing it illegally."

"Legal and illegal are not synonymous with right and wrong."

She said, "And then they set up the Sybillene Eradication Agency, the SEA. I was out of the country during all of this, but it seemed they'd stop at nothing to get Naked Emperor off the streets, right?"

"Yes. SEA was and remains the government's most dangerous agency, with nearly unlimited powers. They claim it's about national security, which is always a tipoff. They're a domestic secret police force, capable of any kind of black op. Even beyond the CIA or NSA. Forget about the constitutional protections Americans are supposed to have."

"Are they watching you now? The SEA?"

"It's always on my mind. I do get suspicious from time to time. I suppose my main protection is that they see me as burned out, ancient history. That, and they're basically incompetent and consumed with infighting, like all government agencies."

Emily's eyes started turning blue. She said quietly, "But, then, those school shootings by Sybillene users. So many children killed. I couldn't make sense of it."

Charles nodded, and his mouth was grim. "Yes. It was the school shootings. Fear for kids. It was very effective."

"What do you mean?"

"Whatever and whoever was behind them, they were horrific and very real, Emily. But they didn't happen because of Naked Emperor or Sybillene."

"What?"

"Naked Emperor was an existential threat to the powers that be. They portrayed it as more dangerous than heroin, crack, fentanyl, and Ebola combined, but even with all their laws and threats, they were losing the battle. So they claimed Naked Emperor was responsible for some school shootings. It made some perverse sense to the hoi polloi since almost all the previous shootings were done by people who were on, or just off, some psychiatric drug."

"How horrible. Were there many shootings in the days before psych drugs?"

"Rare events. Nothing remotely like recent decades. And horrible is an understatement, Emily."

"So, they called you a drug lord because you continued to supply Naked Emperor after they banned it."

"Yes. Poisoned batches started killing people—not from our supplies. We set up a plant in Africa to make it. They bombed it and killed almost everybody, including my friends."

"I'm sorry, Charles."

He nodded somberly.

"I'm rather pleased to be dating a reformed drug lord."

"A former drug lord, perhaps. Except I'm not reformed." He looked at her with a wry smile. "And are we dating, Emily?"

She swallowed hard. "Well, we'd better be dating if I'm going to a Caribbean paradise with you to meet my father."

*　*　*

As long as they stayed at the water's edge, the gentle surf absorbed the sun's heat. A couple of steps inland and the beach's dry sand demanded flip-flops. The place was paradise to Emily.

She understood why her father chose this island. Dominica has only a few, and rather ordinary, beaches. That deficiency kept most tourists away. The ones you saw had stepped off the occasional cruise ship to buy a souvenir, most of which were imported from China. It's a beautiful mountainous island, yet poor and isolated. The natives are friendly, but anyone with ambition had found a way to get to the US. The government supported itself by selling its vote in the UN, taking IMF loans, and making economic citizenships available for $100,000 or so.

Potential new citizens who might buy real estate they'd rarely use, and meanwhile bring in some capital, were welcomed. It helped fill in the financial potholes created when a hurricane came through once a decade or so and destroyed twice the island's annual GDP in twenty-four hours. A tax levied by nature, the hurricanes also presented a wonderful opportunity to buy truly distressed properties. The most valuable asset poor little countries had was their political sovereignty, but few exploited its possibilities. They seemed to prefer remaining poor backwaters rather than following the examples set by Hong Kong, Singapore, Dubai, or Macau, which had transformed themselves from poverty-stricken slums to some of the richest places on the planet in a generation or two.

Aspiring ex-pats who had some money, but not a lot, could come to Dominica and make a go of it, especially if they were willing to drip some sweat equity into resuscitating wind- and water-battered accommodations while making a living as a digital nomad. A small offshore banking sector naturally arose as the Dominica citizenship-by-investment program grew.

"When do you expect your father home?"

Emily glanced back over her shoulder to the parked four-wheel drive in which they'd bounced along a sandy path to get to the small, concealed beach. "I don't know. We can head back. It's not far once we get to the main road."

"How sure are you that he won't object to my invading his house?"

"He likes the occasional exotic guest."

"I shouldn't have read Wikipedia. Seems I'm nefarious. Must limit the number of people who'll accept me as an acquaintance, much less a house guest."

"Trust me, that won't be an issue with Dad. He's more likely to ask you what you do now than what you used to do. Anyway, I suspect your previous activities are more likely to draw him in than put him off."

A broken conch shell rolled under her arch. In trying to dodge it, she stumbled, tripped him, and they fell down in a pile, laughing, shorts and shirts soaked with the warm salt water.

He pulled her up by the hand. "Whoa girl! Watch out for those groundhog holes!"

She shook her head with a smile and made a half-hearted attempt to brush herself off. "Damn groundhogs."

They walked back toward the car.

"Will my virtue be secure in my father's house?"

"I can sleep on the floor."

"We'll see about that, sir." They walked the rest of the way back to the car in silence, so close together that they sometimes struggled to maintain balance.

It took another twenty-five minutes to navigate their way to Emily's father's house through the narrow and twisty roads. Emily parked the car by the stairs. As Charles offloaded two small suitcases, her father opened a sliding glass door that reflected the receding sunlight. He stood on the veranda at the top of the stairs—a fit older man in loose white pants and a light-blue shirt, deeply tanned with salt-and-pepper hair and a short graying beard.

Emily spun free of Charles and ran up the stairs to hug her father. He held her tight, then pulled back to look at her. "Brilliant and beautiful, a great combination. Isn't that so, Mr. Knight?"

Emily turned to Charles, while still holding on to her father.

"Yes, that she is. Both of those and then some."

"I've got dinner cooking," her dad said, waving him up the stairs. "Call me Frank. I'm eager to hear your adventure stories, Charles. I bet you've got some doozies, going up against the SEC, IRS, FDA, DEA, and SEA. Quite a selection of capital letters."

Charles reached up to shake his hand. "There's still much of the alphabet I've yet to tangle with, sir, but I do have some stories. As long as you don't report them to the authorities."

"I'm not crazy about the authorities." A quick shadow passed over Frank's face.

"Including the police," Emily added.

"I avoid them and certainly don't rely on them. My security is that I lock my doors so I know when someone has broken in. And I keep a gun." He held his finger to his mouth. "I don't advertise it. It's legal for citizens to own guns here, but they're tightly controlled. I got permission for mine from the police commish. We've been friends for years. The fact that it's still pretty easy to carry in most of the states is one of the things I miss about the US. Otherwise this place is great. The government workers don't take themselves very seriously, and the residents don't take them seriously either."

Charles said, "It would be nice to not need a permit to carry. Asking permission makes me feel like a grade school kid. Is there a problem down here with the outsiders being a lot richer than the locals?"

"Paradise has people, and people commit crimes. Especially in the Caribbean. Most of the islands were founded as plantations in the seventeenth and eighteenth centuries, primarily to grow sugar. Almost entirely with slave labor imported from Africa. The sugar became unprofitable, and the islands transformed themselves into tourist destinations, but they retained attitudes from the slave culture; whites were and are resented and disliked for being white. A new ruling class of black politicians and bureaucrats were more acceptable since they were black. The islands have fair winds, blue skies, and pink sunsets on the surface, but the racial climate is still black, white, and stormy."

"How do you handle it?"

"I'm a minority here if you choose to categorize me by either skin color or wealth. I just try to be reasonable. Treat everyone like a human. Maybe the racism will fade over time, maybe not. I expect it will take a lot more interbreeding. The blacks still discriminate among themselves based on who's lighter or darker. It's probably part of our genetic wiring from hundreds of thousands of years ago when we first became a species. If someone looked different, they were from a different tribe. You were competing for the same antelope or whatever—a zero-sum game. Those were the days when life was solitary, poor, nasty, brutish, and short—at least more so than today. I'd like to think people will gradually rewire."

"It's going the other way in the US."

Frank nodded his head. "Racism is being stoked. Divide and conquer." He put his arm on Charles's shoulder and ushered him into the air-conditioned living room. "First, let's get you wiped down and watered, and then I want to catch up on the world beyond this little rock we're on. I've been ignoring it. Staying ignorant might keep me happy, but it's not a plan for long-term success—or even survival."

30

Groundhogs on the Beach

CHARLES did some of his best thinking in the shower. He thought back to when Emily had stumbled on the beach and he'd blamed it on a groundhog hole. He had a flash of insight.

In one way, his work was like killing groundhogs. Nobody really wanted to shoot the cute little guys, but they ruined your garden and burrowed tunnels under your house. If you let that go on, the foundation would fail and the house would collapse. If you rode your horse in a meadow infested with groundhogs, chances were good he'd step in a hole, break his leg, and perhaps kill you in the fall. There was little in the way of alternatives to deal with the varmints. It was illegal to live-capture and release them on public land. And what private landowner would invite you to dump your problem on their property? So you could shoot them, poison them, or use explosives. With either groundhogs or miscreants, bullets were direct and focused, but you had to be patient. Poison and explosives were effective for both rodent and human varmints, but they could cause collateral damage.

Charles's new avocation was like shooting groundhogs—but not completely. Groundhogs do what they do without malice. Groundhogs are not moral actors; they're not expected to understand the homeowner's view of right and wrong. Groundhogs are highly destructive, yet innocent.

But the humans Charles had already killed, and the ones on Jeffrey's list, couldn't be considered innocent. Adult humans were moral actors, responsible for what they did. In fact, that was the essence of a human, the very thing that makes a man what he is. That's why the term adult was usually only applied to a human who could tell right from wrong: someone mature enough to be a moral agent. That was why people with very low IQs—actual idiots and imbeciles—weren't prosecuted like ordinary people. It was why juveniles were held to a different standard from adults.

Each adult on Jeffrey's list had consciously chosen to actively destroy the foundations of the house that Europeans and Americans had built over thousands of years: Western civilization. They knew they were aggressing against others, and they even took pride in it.

Charles struggled with right and wrong. What if he dehumanized his targets so that he could eliminate them with less psychological discomfort and fewer qualms? It wasn't as if some of them didn't have families whom they might love and who might love them. It wasn't as if they lacked any redeeming values—a sense of humor or some ability to care for someone. Stalin was well read and could be a charming dinner companion. That was also true of Hitler—everyone's choice for the world's most evil man even though he loved kids and dogs.

Dehumanizing the enemy was standard fare—certainly when it was applied wholesale to groups. There were certainly bad groups, but that didn't mean everyone in the group was bad. Most people were followers, didn't spend much time parsing moral issues, and wound up in a group by happenstance or convenience. It was important to judge individuals as individuals.

Could an individual reform and redeem himself? People are capable of change, but it is important to deal with what exists, not an infinite range of future possibilities—most of them improbable. Still, it is better to avoid dehumanizing anybody.

Are they destructive because of some faulty wiring in their brains? Are they doing evil things because it is just their nature, like thoughtless groundhogs? Is it possible they are controlled by a demon, the kind priests tried to exorcize? Some chronic criminals activate their cerebral cortex, overcome their base instincts, and observe natural law occasionally. Others are like Terrence Kirby, blood-crazed weasels in a henhouse. Evil has thousands of permutations and degrees.

The train of thought that started on the beach with the mention of a groundhog hole made him realize that he didn't need to dehumanize the oppressors. Indeed, he needed to do exactly the opposite. He needed to remember that they were adult humans who made their choices freely.

Whether or not their intentions and basic natures were evil, it was their choices and actions that determined whether they were good or bad. Those people would have to accept the consequences of their actions, much as a weasel had to accept that there was a farmer with a shotgun hunting him, wanting him dead, for valid reasons. But then again, it didn't matter whether they accepted it. The consequences would happen regardless.

The individuals on Jeffrey's list were a threat to decency and freedom in the world in general and, yes, to Charles in particular. They were the aggressors and had to be stopped. The laws made by politicians were of no use; the wolves themselves dictated the laws and how they were enforced on the sheep. Most political law defied natural law at every turn.

Yet picking off a few was to be like King Canute, who, the story went, tried to roll back the tides. In fact, Canute knew better. He commanded the tide to roll back, knowing he would fail. His object was to show his courtiers how limited his power was, but the story is often retold in a way that makes Canute look foolish, as opposed to wise.

It made sense to take out destructive humans. Arguably, he might even feel better about it than shooting the destructive, but morally innocent, groundhogs. But there are always new groundhogs migrating in from adjacent land. Preserving civilization was really like playing Whac-a-Mole; the game was probably unwinnable. Eventually the whacker either gave up or simply ran out of energy. Perhaps the only solution was to pinpoint the flaw, the aberration, in human nature at the root of the problem. Naked Emperor could be at least a partial solution.

He turned off the shower and dried himself briskly. He toweled off the condensation on the mirror and examined his face. He hadn't shaved, nor would he.

A white fly-fishing shirt hanging over khaki shorts, sandals and uncombed hair, complemented by a beer in his hand, would be his attire for the next several days. He had all but the beer. That changed upon his return to the living room, where he found Emily and her father sitting on a couch, talking. Her dad handed him a cold brew.

They sat there as the sun set, a fresh breeze blowing in off the ocean, his arm around Emily, beer in hand. There was a lot to be said for the idea of paradise.

The conversations were relaxed, wide-ranging, and easy. Charles noticed that Frank respected his daughter's opinions.

The quiet discourse of the evening, the food and drink, the fragrant breeze, and the waves rolling up the shore drew his attention away from groundhogs and to what life could be and should be. The antipathy he felt toward the forces of destruction faded toward the back of his mind. The purpose of life was to sustainably enjoy it.

He could feel good about the Paladin Network too, which was about to go live. Rainbow and Mei-li had worked on the project with a dedication bordering on obsession. It sometimes seemed only the young could generate that kind of enthusiasm. Maybe it was because their bandwidth was still clean and uncluttered or because they were still young and naïve enough to think they could actually change the world. Or maybe it was simply just a lack of biological plaque. He wondered whether either of the girls thought of the Paladin Network as a middle way between letting the groundhogs destroy the house's foundation and shooting them all in the head. Perhaps they just thought of it as a science project that could make them rich.

Frank interrupted Charles's contemplation as the three of them listened to the waves and the wind. "It's nice to meet a kindred spirit, Charles."

"It is. I wish it happened more often," Charles replied. "This is one of those moments that I wish would never end. Maybe I'll retire here. I know that sounds crazy since I'm only thirty-three, but who says you have to be old to live like a Taoist monk? In the world and enjoying it, but not of it."

Frank said, "Life's like a book. I'm starting to write the last few chapters of mine. You haven't even finished the first half of yours. Keep seeking adventures, Charles. There's time enough for you to retire to paradise."

31

A Growing Problem
Requiring a Certain Solution

GRAYSON Chase stumped with yuppies in San Francisco, techies in San Jose, and professional socialists in Berkeley. Word even filtered down to the vagrants living in tents on the sidewalk. In Helena and Cheyenne, he spoke to ranchers and cowboys. In Chicago, Detroit, and St. Louis, he tried to speak to the CityFire mobs. He started speaking in halting Spanish to crowds in Austin; they appreciated his good humor and laughed with him when he gave up and reverted to English. He recognized that these places no longer had much in common with each other. They were different cultures within a country or—perhaps more accurately—different countries within an empire. The absurdity of trying to be all things to all people reminded him to just be himself and keep it light.

Some ate soul food. Others trusted alfalfa juice and energy crystals to cure their ills. Yet others ate hot dogs, drank sixty-four-ounce sodas, and popped Lipitor. Live and let live.

The progressive media made his economically sane arguments out to be anti-poor, anti-woman, racist, and just plain mean. The conservative media labeled his anti-war, non-interventionist sentiments as pro-terrorist or even traitorous, but most people valued the talking heads' opinions about as much as those of an obnoxious neighbor.

Nighttime talk show hosts initially invited Grayson on their shows as a curiosity; they invited him back because viewers not only liked the way he said exactly what he thought, but that his thoughts were sensible. He didn't care if he outraged his hosts.

Grayson typically read five hundred words per minute and could sprint at one thousand words per minute using the Spritz app on his mobile phone. That let him keep up with local and world events. What impressed people, however, was his ability to discriminate between facts and opinions and interpret their meanings. People were tired of script-reading wind-up dolls. They could sense he was smart. On late-night TV, the crowds didn't just applaud, they stomped their feet. After the show, he'd stick around and answer questions. They liked the fact that he was both a billionaire and a regular guy.

It was obvious that, despite his billions, he shared their concerns. He cared about their student debt but had different solutions to offer. "College is helpful if you want to learn science, technology, engineering, or math. The formal discipline of regular classes and tests is helpful, and it's hard to do lab work on your own. But remember, the most successful entrepreneurs, even in those fields, found something better to do with the best four years of their lives without turning themselves into indentured servants. What you want is knowledge—which is essentially free on the internet. You don't really want an expensive piece of paper, do you? When someone wants to work for me, I first look at their character, not what wall decorations they have."

The blue collars considered his words simple common sense. The same words made some graduates angry. Most quietly acknowledged he was right and wished someone had told them this earlier.

Everybody—left, right, and other—thought the system was broken, except those for whom the broken system worked so well. When asked what he would do about some problem if he were elected, he'd reply, "Don't trust any politician to fix these problems. No politician is smart enough to do that. If someone asking for your vote pretends to be smart enough, you might want to be... uh... skeptical. Because he's probably a busybody who thinks he can run your life." And he delivered the line with just the right lilt, in such a way that the word "busybody" would induce laughter and applause from whatever audience. "Americans don't expect to have solutions delivered on a platter. They make their own solutions. So go find your solutions. If I'm president, I'll encourage that and promise I won't get in your way."

Chase revitalized Reagan's most important message, the one that got him elected: government is the problem, not the solution. And also John

Galt's demand for government to get out of his way. When asked to describe what they thought of him as a candidate, the most common reply was that Grayson Chase was simply a decent man who respected people.

And he rose in the polls.

Meanwhile, President Cooligan and Senator Heather Lear traded accusations as the Demopublicans always did. They didn't hold intellectual debates to convert voters to their very similar views so much as make emotional appeals to inject adrenaline into their partisans. Radio's talking heads pumped up one side, while cable news and Hollywood pimped for the other. They all tried ignoring Grayson Chase, but that changed once he passed 20 percent in the polls.

Then the attacks began in earnest.

He was entirely inexperienced. Never held an elected office. Clueless about Washington. Just another establishment billionaire evading taxes. Just another white male. A religious nutjob, an atheist, a womanizer, a racist, a loner, an uneducated fop. They threw it all up on the wall to see what would stick. Grayson Chase had prepped his audience to laugh at it all. "You know what Popeye used to say, folks? 'I yam what I yam, and that's all what I yam.' If they ever dig up real dirt on me, I'll take the heat. I won't lie about it. Life's too short, and lies are one of the reasons we all hate politicos."

Did he have some hidden dirt? "Sure. Somewhere, I suppose. This country's got so many laws now that everybody commits three felonies a day. If they find any dirt, they'll spin it to make it look as ugly as they can. I just promise to tell the truth about it and do the right thing, as best I can."

Create a nasty meme that couldn't be disproven, and rely on people to assume that if there was smoke there was fire. He was male, so it was natural to attack his white-male privilege and find some women looking for their fifteen minutes of fame to accuse him of sexual harassment.

"I don't associate with women who'd hesitate for a second to punch me in the face if I did anything like she's accusing me of. I never met this woman. Dig harder, you bastards."

*   *   *

After running the gauntlet of new security, Sabina Heidel rode the elevator to the third floor. Very few would ever access the main floor of Paul Samuels's private residence.

292

She now visited it routinely, walking along hallways adorned with hundreds of millions of dollars of artwork. She suspected that he had many more masterpieces in rooms she'd never entered. No doubt some famous works stolen over the previous century had found their way to his private collection, hidden behind the closed doors. The new bevy of security guards weren't here to protect the art, though.

She went straight to his library, where she was expected.

Leather-bound volumes filled dark-mahogany bookcases. Antique silk Orientals covered the floor. Gold inlays on the intricate crown moldings highlighted the fourteen-foot ceiling. The old floor squeaked as she stepped into the room.

Samuels, thinner than ever and staring at a letter on his desk, startled at the noise.

"Oh. Sabina, dear," Samuels said. "Do catch me up, please. Is Chemnitz ready?"

"We're ready at our end. My cousins have made extensive plans. Forestal is competent, but …"

"…of course never to be trusted." Samuels finished her sentence.

"That's right," she agreed. Nobody could be trusted, but especially not Forestal.

"Your job is to control Forestal if necessary. He can run the show, as long as you can hop in and run him if need be."

"I understand." She had her wiles. She knew exactly where, when, and how to press each of Forestal's buttons.

Samuels had never made a pass at her, artfully deflecting her invitations to intimacy. She attributed the refusal to his advanced age. Or perhaps he was an extremely discreet homosexual. Or perhaps simply asexual. Only one other man had ever turned her down. She didn't resent Samuels's lack of interest, because he was the ticket to her ultimate goal—stepping into his shoes.

Her first job out of school, a decade earlier, had been as a special agent for the IRS, where her father positioned her with a senior agent in California to show her the ropes. Looking to build a tax case, she'd used IRS resources to make her way into an investment firm as an intern, using a fake identity. It was a crash course in the markets and investing. The firm's principal, Elliot Springer, tutored her about monetary theory and the power of the Federal Reserve. Although Springer hoped the education would turn her against central banking, it instead opened Sabina's eyes to the value of joining it. What he saw as dangers, she saw as opportunities. And so Springer had unwittingly launched Sabina on her career ambition to become what Paul Samuels was now: the president of the New York Federal Reserve.

But why stop there?

Perhaps a tour as head of the IMF. She could already envision a world digital currency, facilitated by the world's largest social network and initially backed by a basket of fiat currencies. It would be easy to sell as a way to get unbanked Third Worlders out of their cash economies and into the System. Billions of Africans, Asians, and Hispanics could be transformed into regular taxpayers. The next step might be to merge it with the failing dollar. The person who controlled the world's currency—especially if it consisted only of digits on billions of smartphones—would arguably be the most powerful person in world history. The very prospect excited and motivated her.

But it would take time to be seriously considered as a candidate; seniority counted in any bureaucracy. Meanwhile, the system was fracturing and becoming more unstable each year. Despite giant tax revenues, most of the world's governments were bankrupt and had to sell more and more of their debt to their own central banks. The central banks, like the Federal Reserve, paid for it with more fiat money. The world's governments and their banks increasingly behaved like a couple of drunks, leaning against each other so they didn't both fall down. Sabina Heidel understood the importance of maintaining the status quo, in any way necessary, for as long as possible.

It was Springer who'd introduced her to Charles Knight—the only man before Samuels who had ever spurned her advances. She'd barely gotten out of that one intact. Her special relationship with then-Vice President Cooligan positioned her to use the government's confiscation of Knight's first fortune as a launching pad for her career.

Then came Naked Emperor, which might have overturned the whole world's political, economic, and social structures, had Samuels not intervened. That, again, had been Charles Knight. Working with Paul Samuels, she directly instigated the attack on the mountain in Gondwana that eliminated the drug's last manufacturing facility, along with many of the experts in its manufacture. She'd underestimated the swift response of the local Africans, however, and wound up drugged, shaved, and used as an object, an animal, in secret society rituals in the West African bush. Had Samuels not arranged with Knight for her release, she might still be there today—a drug-addled and enslaved plaything of the teenage natives in some jungle.

Upon her return to the US, she tried to have Knight killed in prison. Repeatedly. But he survived. So she had developed a plan, almost horrible and vicious enough to make up for her exquisitely degrading experience in Africa. She could have just had Chemnitz kill him while he was freely walking the streets of New York. But that wasn't enough. Now she wanted to do it herself. He deserved to die, but by the worst death possible. A death that would take as long as her enslavement in the bush but with much more pain and not a shred of dignity. After months of preparation, she just needed to get close to Knight. One minute would be enough.

Sabina knew that Samuels hadn't rescued her from the African hell because he was a kind man who liked her. Nor did he rescue her just because she was especially capable, completely ruthless, and willing to do whatever was needed; there were plenty of people like that around him. The fact that she was beautiful, a biological work of art—which she also knew—only mattered to Samuels because her sexuality served as a powerful tool in his armamentarium. That she looked like his own daughter, who he hadn't seen in years, no doubt was a factor too. But she had no illusions. She knew that he counted on her to be shrewd enough to stay loyal to him. She also knew she was an object to be used, just as he was an object to her. It was a perversely honest relationship.

"Sabina, I assume you've been watching Grayson Chase." Samuels settled back behind his desk as he motioned Sabina to the couch nearby, allowing him to maintain a position of superiority. Out of habit, she made sure to cross her shapely legs so he could appreciate them.

"I'm not sure he's manageable," she replied. "He's a threat. Way outside the box—very unorthodox. A wild card." She shook her head.

"The parties are throwing the kitchen sink at him, Sabina. So far he's Teflon. He's an alpha male. The plebs like that. He's nonthreatening, which they also like. And he's charismatic. It's a winning combination; he'll very possibly be elected president. Unrestrained, I could see him trying to pull Washington, DC, out by its roots, sowing Agent Orange where they grew. He might fancy trying to abolish the CIA, NSA, and the SEA. That's impossible, of course, but you can't always predict how a chaotic situation will pan out. Libertarians, Sabina. It would be nice to eliminate them from the human gene pool."

Sabina said, "If he's elected, we can neutralize him." Years in the Deep State had taught her to use euphemisms. Even if there was no danger of being recorded—and there was always a danger—it was wise to have plausible deniability. She said it in a way that someone might think it was a joke. But it was more of a prod, intended to ascertain Samuels's thinking.

"The time to act is before he's elected. His vice president may be cut from the same cloth. It would be impolitic for something untoward to happen to both of them. Appearances are often as important as reality itself."

And, she thought, it was easier, cheaper, and much safer to assassinate a candidate than a reigning president. "So you're serious."

The old man seemed titillated by the prospect. "Dead serious. Maybe it won't be necessary. We'll watch, but I want you to start thinking about the ways and means. Of course, most important, with zero possibility of blowback."

Sabina said, "Oh, I've been giving the matter some serious thought." And it was true. She had planned it out for Charles Knight, but the method would work just as well on Grayson Chase. In fact, she could test it out on Chase first. "Paul, all I need is to be alone with Chase. It will only take a minute. No one will ever make a connection."

She watched his response carefully, even as he studied her. He knew how effectively her well-practiced warm smile hid her unemotional core. He knew she would plan everything out like a chess master. In turn, she knew he couldn't even imagine what she had devised. She saw the curiosity in his face—far better than the fear she'd been seeing lately.

So she told him how she would go about killing Grayson Chase.

He smiled as she provided the details. His was a smile of intellectual satisfaction, for it promised to be a highly effective assassination. And a most hideous one.

32

An Adventure in Paradise

CHARLES stopped by the First Caribbean Bank. Most of the islands hosted a branch. A Panamanian company Uncle Maurice had set up for him when the venture in Gondwana got hot had received the $10 million Smolderhof had paid him. It had stayed out of the US government's reach for the last decade, but those sticky fingers impinged more and more on any institution that used their currency, the dollar. So he stayed away from dollars as much as possible. He simply had the company buy eight thousand ounces of gold and store it in the Strategic Wealth Preservation vault in Cayman. He maintained the company and kept most of the gold in the SWP vault, but—for further diversification—gradually transferred some to Singapore. Political and geographical diversification were critical for financial diversification in an increasingly unstable world. Best it stayed in stable jurisdictions. He could earn new money now, so the gold could stay there as savings for seriously rainy days.

Paradoxically, assets had become safer in Dubai, Russia, or China than in the US—certainly for Americans. He kept almost all of his savings in gold, to avoid the depreciation common to all fiat currencies and the onerous reporting when it came to dollars in particular. Bank secrecy was a dead duck; gold, however, could be stored securely and fairly anonymously outside of the US. The US government might require its citizens to turn in their onshore gold to help finance their gigantic deficits. They'd done it before, in 1933.

Maurice managed another company for him, with other funds the government hadn't found while attempting to confiscate his winnings from his

B-F Explorations and Visioryme adventures. He'd converted a lot of it into cryptocurrency and used that to fund the Paladin Network.

Payment for Paladin work was only in crypto or cash. Both were private because they were out of the banking system. Soon the millions of Paladins he'd earned as the network's founder could gain the kind of traction Bitcoin had. Bitcoin went from under $1 to almost $20,000 in seven years—one of the most amazing runs in history. But, for now, Jeffrey's gig would keep his own net worth rising, keep the Paladin Network capitalized, and, most importantly, show how theory worked in practice.

He used Frank's car to drive by the beachfront estate of a miscreant on Jeffrey's list. His time would come soon. Just not today.

Late in the afternoon, he met up with Frank and Emily at the inappropriately named Petit Paris café. As Charles slid a metal chair over from a nearby vacant table, Frank moved a plate of Mexican-style chips with guacamole dip toward him.

"So, Frank, neither you nor Emily has told me about what you used to do."

Emily interjected, "Yes, I did. I told you. Dad did everything. He's a Renaissance Man."

Charles looked at Emily. "That's a goal I aspire to."

Frank's reply, delivered with a broad grin, caught Charles off guard. "Oh, mostly I did a lot of manual labor, to tell the truth. Messy, dangerous stuff that most sensible people try to avoid. I was an assassin."

"Oh, Dad, stop it!" She hit him on the shoulder. "Charles, he's given people that answer for years."

Frank said, his grin bigger, "Well, it's a good answer, Emily. I used to tell them I ran a flying circus—but nobody believed me."

"Dad has always made good choices in his investments, and he can do anything he wants to. He just likes to say that sometimes to see how people react."

After five minutes of pleasantries on the weather, the state of the roads, and the latest sports event, Charles liked to find out who he was talking to. Saying something shocking was a good way to do it. He smiled at Frank, genuinely amused. "I'll use that line myself, if you don't mind."

"Be my guest. Frankly, almost anyone who's been moderately successful can live like this. The key—here or anywhere—is keeping the overhead under control. Dominica is off the beaten path, which is a big plus, the way

I see it. With the internet, I can access every book, magazine, newspaper, and blog in the world and see almost any movie. I can talk to anyone, anywhere. I've got great food, great weather, and comfortable digs. The government doesn't ask me for any taxes on my offshore money, and they don't care what I do or where I go. It makes me wonder why people who've made some money just stay where they are—usually where they were born or grew up. They're more like vegetables than people—rooted, defenseless, and ready to be eaten by anything that comes along. Never impressed me that acting like a plant was a good strategy for a person."

Emily explained, "When Dad first moved here, he bought a bunch of plywood sheets, two-by-fours, and a box of nails to build a bar on the one beach near where the occasional cruise ship would wander in. He sold fifty-cent rum for ten bucks and provided chairs and umbrellas on the beach for free if you bought a fifty-dollar drink card up front. How long did you do that for, Dad?"

"About four months, until a hurricane came along and blew down the shack. I could have rebuilt in an afternoon, but the main pier got demolished along with my bar, so the cruise ships stopped coming. This place doesn't have a party scene, and the beaches are few. It's mostly about seeing nature in the interior. Not something the cruise ship types were very into then. I still have the beach lease, and some small ships with exotic-location junkies are coming again. I have a guy who's taken over my lease and pays me something when he feels like it. Mostly I pursue other interests."

"Like what?"

"I'm off island from time to time. Spent years with Emily cruising the world. Did she tell you that?"

"She did. A fantastic education that very few people get."

"I suspect a few people thought she was Lolita to my Humbert, but I've never cared what other people think. I don't think Nabokov could write a book like that today; it absolutely couldn't be published. Anyway, here on the island, I pretend to be retired. Although I still own a pawnshop in town."

Charles appreciated pawnshops. They'd been around since the days of ancient Sumer and Egypt and were the original banks. They supplied money when the borrower needed it, fully secured by collateral. Quite different from modern, fractional-reserve banks, which created money out of thin air.

"Did you own pawnshops in the US?"

"No way. In the US, every loan has to be reported to the police and a centralized database, with thumbprints on receipts. I don't play that game. It's really too bad for Americans who can't get credit any other way."

Emily added, "Dad is being modest, as usual. How many rental houses do you have on this island?"

"Oh, not so many anymore, Emily. I've been selling them off to the new citizens." He turned to Charles. "I did buy a few dozen of the bigger houses after the last big storm, for big discounts. I own the lumber-and-hardware-supply-store chain on the island, so I could get first dibs on the materials, relatively cheap, to fix the places back up. I'm mostly building out of concrete now of course. Learned that lesson."

"You do still own the concrete factory up in Portsmouth, right, Dad?"

Frank clucked, "She likes to make it appear that I'm more than just some old guy with a mostly defunct beach bar and a pawnshop."

Charles liked this man more with each revelation.

Frank and Charles became friends over two more perfect days in paradise.

Late after dinner on the fourth night, Frank said, "I love chess. Do you play?"

Charles smiled. "Oh yes. But I got into Go when I was living in Hong Kong. It's simpler, yet more subtle than chess. Illustrates a lot of the differences between the East and West."

"Dad, he's my friend, not your chess buddy."

"Well, Emily, that'll have to change. I'm going to occupy your friend for a few hours. Don't worry, I'll make sure he gets some sleep tonight."

Charles said, "Tomorrow's a workday for me. So I'll see you in a bit, Emily. I'll have to get checkmated by your father fast."

And so he did.

* * *

Emily awoke in the morning to find a note from Charles on his pillow. "Have some business to take care of. Have a good day with your dad. See you this evening."

She wasn't certain what he had planned, but she suspected it involved US Treasury Secretary Wainwright. He'd used Dominica as a low-profile offshore haven for years—as was revealed during his Senate confirmation hearing. He'd resolved that with a quiet mea culpa and a back-tax payment. Then he'd made up for that loss by using his position to travel here in government planes whenever he could fabricate a plausible excuse.

Charles's pretense of taking a beach trip with her was too easy to see through. She'd figured it as a ploy immediately; Charles wanted to look into Wainwright. Jeffrey told her that Wainwright was scheduled to be with the president for the G7 summit called "Fostering Tax Fairness" in London this week. So Wainwright couldn't be on Dominica. Had Charles screwed up the timing? Was he working on bad information? Or was the fact that Charles knew full well that Wainwright wouldn't be on Dominica a key part of his plan?

She spent the day with her father, fishing, talking, and reminiscing. They talked about Jeffrey and about Charles. She kept no secrets from her father, the wisest and most experienced man she knew. To keep secrets from him would be like putting a straitjacket on her best and most trusted advisor.

"Emily," he said as they sat on his porch looking out over the water, "I know you've already considered what I have to say, but it's good to say out loud anyway. Your relationship with Charles has morphed from being a simple job that was compromised, into something entirely unintended. In what you and I have done together, we've had to keep secrets, but not from each other. This thing you have with Charles isn't just inconvenient from a professional point of view. It's dangerous. Good chance he'll end up dead or back in prison. If you're too close to the action, you'll be at risk too. Anything happens to him, and they'll put you under a spotlight. That means they'll look at all your relatives and associates." He looked at her with his head angled and an eyebrow raised, well aware he was stating the obvious and she'd been choosing to ignore it. "Prison did you no good. And having you in prison did me no good. I see multiple reasons for you to back away."

Emily said, "I do too. But Jeffrey needs tabs kept on him. That, and he fears for Charles's safety."

"Is that supposed to make me comfortable? You're justifying, Emily. You may contribute to Charles's safety, or you may not, but you aren't the right person to act as a guardian angel. Jeffrey's in the political arena now with Grayson Chase, and so he's thinking politically. Charles may benefit Chase, but only if he gets large quantities of Sybillene back into the US. Otherwise, Charles is nothing but risk. It's a risk-benefit ratio in constant flux, and you're helping Jeffrey keep tabs on that ratio. But your judgment has been at least partially disabled by your affection for both of them. Do you think you can keep providing what Jeffrey needs, maybe to Charles's detriment?"

"You know, Dad, it was one thing acting as an observer, an investigator. It's something else entirely to function as a spy. Lying to people who trust you. Betraying them. Nobody trusts spies; they're betrayers, stool pigeons, rats."

Frank replied, "There's a reason spies are executed when they're caught."

She heard him. Maybe that was his most persuasive argument. She thought for a moment and said, "I think I should stay here with you and send Charles home."

"That'd be wise. I like Charles. But you haven't known him very long. He needs to see where things are taking him. I can see the attraction from your point of view. The chances of you being happy with a guy who works a nine-to-five job, votes in elections, and goes to church on Sunday are slim to none. And Slim's out of town. You know I always want the best for you. You and I are on the fringe of society. I'm responsible for that. Maybe it's a good thing, with society as corrupt and degraded as it is, but it's not easy to be an outsider. Who knows? Maybe you'll run off with him to Asia, working with him instead of me. But that doesn't solve our present conundrum."

Emily smiled warmly. "I like working with you, Dad. Never dull. I get to pretend I'm a real-life Lara Croft. I'm not thinking that far ahead with Charles. This world has made me realistic. I rather doubt he's going to be around all that long. Then again, I wouldn't sell you or me a big life insurance policy."

"He's no idiot. You're worth sticking around for, Emily."

"You're biased. Charles may not be an idiot, but he's definitely a man who'll live his own life. He's not going to live it for somebody else—including me. I guess that's one reason I like him. He is heading home, Dad. So, mind if I stay here with you a while?"

"As long as you want, kiddo."

*　*　*

Charles came back with a sunburn at the end of his workday.

Frank said, "You said you'd be working today. Looks like you've been at the beach. Just what sort of work can you do down here, Charles?"

"The same thing as you, I suppose," Charles replied with a grin. "I'm an assassin."

Frank smiled back. "Quick learner you are."

Charles and Emily walked along the shore, holding hands as the sun set over the Caribbean. It was travel-poster perfect, and they both knew it.

"Sometimes I'd like to stay here for eternity, Charles. Make a go of it disconnected from all the drama in the USA."

"You came back to New York for some excitement, didn't you? Not a lot of that here." Charles pondered an idyllic existence. Beautiful scenery, fantastic climate, friendly-enough natives. A few fun and stimulating friends to hang out with. Books to read, comforts. The diametric opposite of his life for the last several years. Maybe he could stay here. He could build his own Fortress of Solitude and never leave it.

He shook his head. Commitments. To himself and to others. He said, "And I've got to get back there. Things on my plate."

She frowned. "I don't. I'm going to stay here a while. Hang out with my dad some more. It'll be good for me."

Charles suspected it would be. Healthier than being in New York where the CityFires incubated and hatched, unpredictably, on most nights. Certainly safer than anywhere near him. He struggled, as he'd grown fond of her and enjoyed their time together. She could relate to him; their brains worked alike. That was rare enough to find. Selfishly he wanted her around, available. Also selfishly, he didn't want her dead because of him. Perhaps most selfishly, he had an enormous amount of work ahead of him, and distractions wouldn't help.

"Thanks for coming to Dominica with me, Charles."

"Thanks for coming with me, Emily. I'll see you as soon as…"

She finished his sentence. "… as soon as we each feel the time is right?"

Charles replied, "Exactly what I was thinking."

33

Crypto Inferno

THE PALADIN Network launched with its first application and airdrops of Paladin Proofs on several small crypto exchanges. Any Bitcoin, Ethereum, or EOS wallet address that showed any activity in the previous year automatically got one. Cryptocurrency holders throughout the world, without boundaries or limits, now suddenly owned just a tad of cryptocurrency with the acronyms PLDN and PALA. The hard cost to the Paladin Network was basically nothing, except for the dilution it represented to the currency supply. That concerned Charles, but Mei-li was ahead of him.

Rainbow said, "Chill. This is the cheapest form of advertising in the crypto world. We've capped the number of Paladin Proofs at one hundred million. Sending out a million dilutes it, yes, but not much. This network could change the whole nature of law and justice, crime and punishment on the planet. It could be worth more dollars than Bitcoin."

Millions of people already believed that blockchain technology and cryptocurrency would change the world, and they were all looking for the next token that could, like Bitcoin, go from a few cents to five figures. It was worth finding out what this new Paladin Network, whose so-called proofs were appearing in their wallets, might be up to. 'Probably a shitcoin,' most thought on first glance, but curiosity about PLDN brought them to the PaladinNetwork.io website and interest in PALA was kindled on the Paladin Telegram listing and the Paladin GitHub page. They would read the Paladin Network white paper and learn how these Paladins could be used on different networks. Crypto enthusiasts and developers started out with questions.

"Who are the developers behind Paladin?"

"Anonymous devs."

"White paper can be found at PaladinNetwork.io."

"What exchanges are Paladins trading on?"

Speculators who watched chart patterns dominated early buying and selling, just letting the market tell them what was real. It was wise to treat all new cryptos as hot potatoes until they were proven. There were thousands out there; many were frauds, technically flawed, impractical, or just redundant.

Then someone typed in: "Holy fuck. Paladin Network is going after the assholes who hack the exchanges and steal our tokens. I'll pay for that! I'm buying!"

Was that sort of comment just hype to suck in buyers? Everything online was suspect. It was like living in a dangerous jungle, where everything could bite, sting, or poison you. It was also an ecosystem where even the nastiest creatures served a purpose. Criminal hackers, for instance, served to expose flaws. They culled weak tokens and weak exchanges from the population. Hacking provided evolutionary drive. Survival of the fittest. But they didn't have to steal someone's savings to prove that. It was like robbing a bank to prove it needed better security.

Private currencies needed private police because there was no legal way to go after thieves in the crypto world. The market needed a way to encourage detectives and compensate vigilantes. Hoping the government would do something was a nonstarter for a dozen different reasons. It was a huge problem, and here was a solution.

"Where can I sign up to help take out the thieving bastards?"

"Looks like first thing is to grow a network of spyminers."

"You know, this Paladin Network can be used on lots of bad guys besides hacker thieves."

"Paladin Network is the anti-NSA. This time, it can be us spying on the G instead of the G spying on us."

"Yeah, it's one thing to accidentally find out some criminal shit and tell the world about it. But that's all risk and no reward. Paladin makes it profitable to go out and dig stuff up. You don't have to wait and hope the G does something."

"They called it Paladin. The late-'50s TV show. It's on YouTube."

The conversations gained momentum. Enthusiasm bred more enthusiasm. Within a day, thousands had signed on to the various social media platforms, and it grew from there. This wasn't an application that only computer geeks could wrap their heads around or some program that might cut the costs of some obscure widget business if only everyone on the planet magically started using it. This promised to be an Etsy, an Instagram for people who wanted to solve problems caused by bad people, not just trade selfies and meaningless trivia. Someone with a problem could pay someone else to solve it, privately, with Paladins.

Problem solving could mean almost anything. It might be illegal. More important, it might be immoral. But who was to say what was immoral? The Paladin Network itself would act as both judge and jury, relying on its conditional anonymity—a new concept in crypto, and one that garnered far-reaching attention. No one, certainly not a government, could ever obtain personal information from the network without the network members—the Paladin Proof holders, miners, and contractors—allowing the re-identification of a person. And that would only happen on the network's terms, following Common Law principles laid out in the white paper and respected by the Paladin crypto community. The concept chattered around the crypto space in the context of distributed autonomous organizations. Someone contributed the term decentralized trustless verification, or DTV, to describe part of the Paladin Network functionality.

Mei-li picked up on the DTV acronym and by evening had added it to the next revision of the white paper describing in detail the network and its philosophies. A self-regulating, self-policing problem-solving network was clearly both needed and wanted. The concept evolved and mutated rapidly, like a virus, but its evolution remained ethical, bounded by the DTV. It didn't require comprehensive planning by two teenagers. It required only a firm moral foundation, some fertilizer, and some water.

That evening, the two girls stopped by Maurice's apartment for dinner. Mei-li had earned the privilege of meeting the great man.

And here Mei-li met Charles in person for the first time—in person as himself, not as Paladin.

It took her but a few minutes to make a connection between the eponymous Paladin who'd killed Jock and Freak, and this Charles whose name Rainbow had mentioned from time to time.

Mei-li's face showed a faint smile of possible recognition; Charles paid closer attention. He didn't miss the subtle narrowing of her eyes as she, in turn, studied him: a curving of her lips, her eyebrows coming together in a subtle but universal signal of intense thought, followed again by that uncertain smile.

Charles had plenty of street smarts, but recognizing emotions or deception based on facial expression was a specialized skill. He couldn't be sure. This teenage girl seemed to have a good poker face. Was it due to thousands of years of genetic sorting in the mysterious Orient, where evolution selected for social skills as a survival mechanism? Maybe. She played the inscrutable Chinese pretty well and had shown herself to be a cool operator when they met. Observational smarts was a separate ability, different from cognitive intelligence or physical strength. The weak tended to have better developed mentalist skills, out of simple necessity. When to hide, when to run, when to approach and when to bluff could be a life-or-death decision. Some so-called empaths were way on the right side of the bell curve of ability to read emotions from the faintest twitch of one of the forty-three facial muscles. Human lie detectors. Some were naturals. Others had to work at it.

No question, Mei-li suspected he was Paladin. No disguise was perfect.

As late-night conversations often do, this one turned to philosophy and the state of the world.

"Look," said Maurice, "you kids can complain about everything that's wrong until you're blue in the face, and maybe make a few changes around the edges. But the real problem is that the world no longer has a moral foundation, basic principles that most people agree on. Greece had that during the fifth century BC. Rome had them during its republic. Many successful cultures did—the Chinese, Japanese, and Vikings, among others. Britain and America both did during the nineteenth century. The reason Western civilization succeeded, and why it's the only civilization worthy of the name, is that it was based on the concepts of natural law, what the English codified into their Common Law. It's the basis of my contribution to your Paladin Network white paper.

"The problem is that today's world has lost much of that. I'm not a big fan of Christianity—whatever it is, there are so many varieties—but it provided a moral foundation. That's all being washed away by identity politics, socialism, greenism, and all that blather. The Chinese have got their social-credit system as a substitute, but that just facilitates a police state.

"You want to change the world and make some money doing it? Fill the vacuum with something useful that resonates with the best parts of human nature—or at least keeps its worst parts under control. And make sure everybody profits from it. Nothing is sustainable unless it makes money. I've no appreciation for that word since it's become so damn PC."

That conversation continued late into the evening, expanding the ideas the girls already had in motion. Maurice was a classic value-added investor; startup funds were critical, of course, but he also did his part to keep the train on the tracks. The Paladin Network had sound foundations, but miscreants would still find cracks in the edifice, ooze in, and weaken the structure. Maurice could minimize the damage with both lessons from history and forward-looking advice. Few of the younger population had a grasp on ethics sufficient to discern between good and bad. Mei-li and Rainbow were among the few.

By the next morning, two dozen new developers had joined the Paladin Network—with conditional anonymity. They had to be sorted out some way, to at least eliminate the real bad apples. Mei-li and Rainbow had learned much, but they still had much to learn.

Throughout history, banks relied on personal knowledge of their customers to reduce the chance of fraud. That was possible in the era before impersonal megabanks dealing with hordes of customers, often entirely online. Now it was a matter of linking a warm body with the correct piece of paper, following the Know Your Customer—KYC—rule. That usually meant multiple government IDs, a utility bill to prove residency, and perhaps a picture of the individual holding their government-issued ID. It all could be forged, of course, and routinely was by anyone who wanted to take the trouble to do it. Security theater, about as effective as the drones groping passengers at an airport. KYC did nearly nothing to stop serious bad guys, but it helped to ensure that anyone in the financial system lived in fear of the tax authorities. Which, of course, was the point.

The Paladin Network didn't work for the tax authorities—or any government agency.

It had to find its own way to effectively bar any actors who defied natural law principles—and get restitution from those who did. Keeping them anonymous, while knowing them, seemed like a contradiction.

Keeping criminals at bay is important but it's a major mistake to give the State that power. Concentrating that power under state monopoly was the fox guarding the henhouse. The network's conditional anonymity provided a way to acknowledge that evil people exist and could co-opt any system and thus needed to be flushed out and purged. For years this had been an impossible river to ford: protecting the anonymity of the innocent while exposing the criminals.

Mei-li and the Paladin Network invented their way to cross that ravine without sliding down the slippery slope.

One of the first members wasn't atypical. A seventeen-year-old boy in the Georgetown area of Northwest DC with the unfortunate name of Derek Pupe had to endure the constant bickering of his alcoholic parents. He spent his time in his room, alone with his computer, hiding away online, eating microwaved frozen pizza. He discovered the Paladin Network and learned how to become a spyminer. He passed the required ethics test, making it clear that he understood—or at least had been exposed to—two simple natural laws: do all that you agree to do, and don't aggress against other people or their property. It wasn't hard: don't lie, cheat, steal, or start fights. Interacting successfully and peacefully with other people was pretty simple, but until he'd taken this ethics test, he'd not seen this anywhere since Kindergarten.

The Paladin Network's radial Don't Know Your Customer process was simple enough. When signing up for the network, Derek had to place an app on his phone and then have his computer and phone both available. He, like all other successful conditionally anonymous applicants, followed the specific instructions on the site, gathering the required IDs and some proof of address such as a utility bill or official letter. The Paladin Network provided a code on his computer. He was then allowed sixty seconds to use his cell phone app to video himself holding his ID and home address, then showing the code on the computer, and then reciting a sentence that appeared on his computer screen. In his case, after he completed the video in that brief period, the cell phone app affirmed that his ID documents were unblurred and legible, analyzed his live face to compare it to the supplied government ID, performed geolocation to confirm the Georgetown address, and compared it to the address on an official letter of acceptance from MIT. It compared his speech to the code phrase supplied to him on his computer screen and used algorithms to make sure that Derek's video wasn't a rapidly built deepfake. Then the app performed a facial-recognition search, which compared Derek's image to billions of facial photos scraped off the internet, including all social media.

Of course Derek knew nothing about the efforts of two girls in Manhattan to cobble this system together with new coding and tech while ensuring that no central database could store any inputs or outputs. When Derek proved to be a real human being, the app encrypted the video, audio, and all other data and shipped it off for storage on a parallel Paladin blockchain.

No government or other outsider could likely decrypt it as it used similar encryption methods to Bitcoin. The fact that Derek Pupe had become a spyminer was an impenetrable secret. No human saw the information he supplied. All unencrypted information would be permanently deleted everywhere, and only the encrypted version would stay on the blockchain. The network itself could only decrypt it after substantial proof of an individual's malfeasance. The network knew him only as HotPockets.

It was easy to understand the value of being able to both maintain airtight conditional anonymity and permanently kick bad actors out of the community.

Spymining resembled a mix of treasure hunting and private detective work. Spyminers got paid in Paladin Proofs to report on the whereabouts, activities, and predilections of identified targets. Customers paying the spyminers for data on specific targets also had conditional anonymity. Derek Pupe didn't know he was about to work for Charles Knight—the first Paladin Network customer. Charles Knight knew nothing about Derek Pupe. This mutually anonymous relationship would soon provide information that Charles was willing to pay for on the activities of certain people who lived and worked close to Derek: the denizens of Washington on Jeffrey's list of targets.

*　*　*

In Maurice's apartment that evening, Charles Knight initiated the smart contract that would rock the worlds of the people on Jeffrey's list. Within the Paladin Network's straightforward user interface, he effectively launched a massive investigation to determine exactly what they were doing and with whom. With the contracts initiated, spyminers selected targets that they knew or that interested them or were geographically or virtually easiest to access. Charles closed his eyes and imagined how things might progress. It was like watching an alternate science fiction timeline play out in reality.

One value of information is intimidation, but it's a double-edged sword. If a criminal knows someone else is aware of what he's doing, that someone is in real danger. But if he doesn't know who that someone is, he has a choice: either stop doing what he's doing, or see what happens when the information is released.

The meaning of that seemed to dawn on Rainbow around midnight during that evening's epic chat session. Growing up in the ghetto with Alpha and his crew, she'd seen about everything. Probably as much as a street cop three times her age. "Blackmail," she'd said. "It's got a sleazy reputation."

"No question about that," Maurice replied, taking a sip of coffee in hopes that it would fend off his annoying tendency to fall asleep in the midst of conversation. "It's just a quid pro quo, as the lawyers in DC like to say. You do this, I do that; you don't do that, then I won't do this. Perfectly ethical, and there shouldn't be any laws about it. Nobody with clean hands ever has a problem with blackmail. It's got a bad rep because one party has done something wrong, and the other party doesn't keep to the agreement and instead repeatedly shakes the first party down—and usually for bad motives: greed, spite, vengeance, whatever. Or the information is false and unfairly condemns the blackmailed. That's a different topic—fraud. And both parties are usually desperate. All those components lead to its bad rep. Blackmail as a concept doesn't deserve that bad rep."

Charles had blackmailed the social worker in North Dakota. He'd held to his end of the bargain. He hadn't told the woman's husband about her infidelity with Terrence Kirby, nor had he gone back to her with more demands after she had fulfilled her part of the bargain by returning the children to their grandparents. Ethical.

In the Paladin Network, blackmailers had to abide by their end of the agreement too, or they would themselves be outcast, kicked off the network, and subjected to targeting by their victims until they paid restitution.

Option 1 involved enforcing ethics on criminals through blackmail. It was by far the safest and most profitable way of making the victim whole while discouraging further offenses. If blackmail, exposure, or other nonviolent or minimally violent remedies failed to neutralize a target, direct assassination was an option. If the Paladin Network worked properly, the effect would be so much greater than just pulling sharks' teeth.

Many federal politicians and high-level bureaucrats would end up in the Fair Game category, as would prominent characters in the state governments. It happened spontaneously around the globe. Most foreigners were much more inured to being treated like serfs than Americans. Fair Game was akin to a sort of year-round open hunting season. Officials who liked to flex their political or bureaucratic muscles could be treated like varmints. Unprotected nuisances. Groundhogs.

The spyminers would keep collecting data until sufficient for a successful blackmail operation.

Even as the utility of the Paladin Proof was just beginning to become evident, it started evolving. When blackmail wasn't a solution for a given problem, it was necessary to hire not just spyminers, but human vigilantes (hum-vigs) who could physically disrupt the lives of the bad guys. And also vig-hacks—hired hackers who worked entirely online against crypto-thieves, online scams, and other digital fraud. In a highly computerized world, sometimes vig-hacks could shut the targets down remotely by planting viruses or worms; that would be a first option because it kept costs and risks low. Then sometimes they needed to work with the hum-vigs to physically neutralize thugs.

In the highly competitive marketplace, vig-hacks' fees—paid in Paladins—were necessarily in line with the degree of trouble involved in identifying and disrupting nuisances.

An early smart contract was a crowdfunded scheme to cure America of robocallers. It attracted viral attention to the Paladin Network that Charles neither expected nor planned for. Thousands joined the anonymous network just so they could contribute to this crowdfunding, and they all acquired Paladins to do so.

The crowdsourced smart contract worked to free Americans from the daily cell phone robocalls paid for by purveyors of overpriced health insurance for the elderly, Canadian Viagra for the middle aged, and bogus relief from student-loan debt for the young. What the vig-hacks did to shut these callers down was illegal but benefitted everyone and brought the Paladin Network to national attention. Its possibilities inflamed the psyche of the country, and then the world, almost overnight. It once took thirty years to grow a brand. Here it took thirty days.

Maurice expected success, but he was dumbfounded. The coins he'd bought for $100,000 to fund the operation were worth over $10 million and gaining.

Rainbow said, "Uncle Maurice, I thought this could be good, but the Paladin Network hasn't just gone viral. It's gone superviral." She'd put part of the capital she'd sequestered from her Sybillene-dealing days into the deal, on the same terms as Charles and Maurice. She was earning thousands more coins as payment for her work. She was on the way to becoming richer than either Maurice or Charles.

Maurice looked at her. "People have an unlimited supply of real and imagined problems. So the demand side is covered. The supply side always appears to meet any demand, if there's a way for the two to find one another. There are plenty of people out there who like solving puzzles and are bored with what they're doing. Others have an altruistic gene. Maybe a few have watched Westerns and want to be the avenging Lone Ranger–style cowboy who sets things right, collects the bounty, and then rides off into the sunset. Whatever the case, it seems that what you've put together has tapped into a pent-up desire for justice. Well done, so far! But you should expect the bad guys to counterattack."

People began buying up Paladins to speculate on the growth. Within weeks, almost every crypto exchange had listed Paladin Proofs. A Paladin's value against other cryptocurrencies, and fiat currencies like the dollar, rose on a hyperbolic curve. That attracted more spyminers, more users, more commentary, more excitement. More vig-hacks, more hum-vigs. By market cap, Paladins joined the top twenty cryptocurrencies within a month, and they kept rising. The cryptocurrency thrived as the network of justice expanded.

Spyminers and vigs vied to serve the needs of the customer.

Interest groups formed among the blogs and chats, and more people joined forces to hire the vigs necessary to neutralize the endemic parasites—some specifically to expose and punish the purveyors of the fraudulent cryptocurrencies. Among a hundred other things, Paladin Network rapidly took on the job of cleaning the crypto house. The crypto frauds and scammers had good reason to tremble in their boots and shitcoin their pants.

Charles's first smart contract gave spyminers financial motivation to track associations among politicians and cronies. Journalists, politicians, the police, businessmen, and jealous spouses all began to buy and spend Paladins to get the facts on targets. Spyminers earned their pay as politicians and journalists broadcast all the newly discovered secrets of their various foes.

The servers hummed as traffic poured through virtual private networks into contracted server farms in Singapore and the Philippines. To protect herself from the NSA, Mei-li had removed the original sandbox node in Chiang's store just before going live, while other nodes, hundreds and over time thousands, sprung up across the globe. If not already, it would soon be impossible for a government agency, anywhere, to halt the Paladin Network because there was no single, or even multiple, point of failure. Like Bitcoin, ending the Paladin Network would mean taking down the whole thing simultaneously, worldwide.

No government could do that.

34

Chemnitz at Work

"ARE you thinking of coming back to New York, Emily?" Charles sounded eager, because he was. He'd been back in the city for going on two weeks and missed her company. Charles knew she could second that emotion. They shared moral and physical attraction to each other. Mutual philos as well as eros.

Still, encouraging a romance with someone he barely knew while he was trying to change the world was ill advised.

Emily replied, "Let me think about it. Going back to a crowded city as summer heats up versus hanging out in paradise, reading, doing yoga, swimming. Hmm…," Emily teased.

"Well, don't become completely spoiled. When you do return, I'd like to take you somewhere nice."

"You mean, like your bedroom?"

"Am I that transparent?"

"Yes. I want to stick around a bit longer to see what's going to happen here."

"What do you mean?"

Emily replied, "They found Treasury Secretary James Wainwright dead in his beach house today."

"Well, they can't blame me for that. I left two weeks ago. What's your father been up to?" he quipped.

Emily chuckled and said, "It's all over the news."

"Ah, the news. When I want to waste time, I just tune in to a sitcom; at least they have a laugh track. Except I don't have a TV."

"Sounds like something my dad would say. He likes you, by the way. And he enjoyed the chess."

"He plays an aggressive game."

"He said something like that about yours too."

"He beat me easily. I hate making excuses about being out of practice."

"Yeah, he thought you might be a little rusty. Look, Dad's got some stuff to do back in the States soon. Not quite sure when. I'm going to join him for that. So I'll see you, Charles. I promise. Now, whatever you're doing, if you can't be good, at least be careful."

The call ended; he got back to the work.

This assignment reeked of complexity from beginning to end. Not good. Complexity meant detailed planning. Of course that was always necessary, but whether in a war, a boxing match, or almost anything else, once the action started, plans had a way of going to hell.

Until now, the targets on Jeffrey's list weren't on guard or even cautious. The hunting-accident explanation for Paul Samuels had kept fear from taking hold in the minds of other targets. It made things easier when the prey didn't know it was being hunted. Wainwright's death following within four months of the Samuels "accident" might raise concern, but not too much. Nobody would be able to prove Wainwright had died of anything other than natural causes.

He felt no guilt about Wainwright.

The public thought political assassins were mainly interested in taking out the top dog—the president, the prime minister, or the king. It made theoretical sense. Sure, it's true that a fish rots from the head down, but cutting off the head after the rot has started doesn't stop the rot. Yes, the way to kill a snake was to decapitate it. Yet in established states, the problem wasn't a single viper; it was a hydra, with a hundred heads. The president was just the most obvious, the most colorful of them.

Goebbels, Himmler, Heydrich, or any of dozens of others would have filled the void. Many of them would likely have been even worse.

Would killing Lenin have changed anything? Obviously not. Whether Lenin was killed or died of natural causes in 1924, Stalin took over. And Joseph Vissarionovich was much worse than Vladimir Ilyich. Most heads of State were paranoid, and with good reason. It's said a letter from Yugoslavia's

Tito was found on Stalin's nightstand right after he died. "Stop sending people to kill me. We have already captured five of them, one of them with a bomb and another with a rifle. If you don't stop sending killers, I'll send one to Moscow, and I won't have to send a second."

Did it make any difference whether Stalin, in his turn, died of natural causes or was assassinated in 1953? Probably not. The hydra had plenty of heads to replace him. Although, perhaps because the USSR was showing signs of atherosclerosis even then, Khrushchev was much kinder and gentler. Taking out the head of state might make things better or worse or leave them unchanged.

The president of the US was undoubtedly the most heavily defended person on the planet, but was mainly symbolic, a transient figurehead. The media blamed him for everything, while the real damage was done by the people in the next level or two down. They were the ones with their hands on the wheel that few people noticed.

The Paladin Network's spyminers were already beginning to change that dynamic. Apparatchiks who had previously relied on the population's lack of interest in them were realizing that they now risked exposure. Both virtual and physical eyes, driven by the profit motive, would be on them aggressively. The Paladin Network was the anti-Hoover, watching the budding J. Edgar Hoover wannabes and maybe even neutralizing them. Word was spreading that the Paladin Network had something to do with the death, six weeks earlier, of that Agriculture Department employee with the grandiose aspirations. Some rumors appeared, wondering about Secretary Wainwright's untimely death. The kernels of fear would begin to haunt the minds of the future Hoovers, the future Seth Fowlers. If Paladin had existed in the Soviet Union during the '30s, perhaps Beria would have found different employment or else been terminated in any of a hundred ways by any of a thousand people.

*　*　*

For Chemnitz Lichen, the smell of the building brought back childhood memories of his own school. No matter that the two buildings were separated by a thousand miles and twenty years. How is it that schools smell the same everywhere through the decades? The scents of lunchboxes and cafeterias and effluent from locker rooms combined with adolescent sweat and

316

hormones all penetrated through the black scarf he wore under the pretense of virus protection.

During their school years, Chemnitz and his identical twin, Dresden, had learned to hate everybody for good reason. The scents here reminded him of their painful experiences and reinforced the feeling. Triggered memories re-stimulated the engram. Cement, funk, drudgery, abuse. Lichen shook his head involuntarily and returned to his usual state of feeling nothing at all.

This was the first day of school. The Abilene superintendent was old school and advised the city council not to install security cameras over the summer. It wasn't just the cost. The intrusiveness of the cameras gave some supervisors pause, particularly those who'd grown up in the days when kids could walk to school and stay out playing until dark. The rest of the world was already monitored, the audio and video preserved more or less forever in the cloud. The kind of mistakes kids made would stay with them forever—perhaps preventing them from becoming Supreme Court justices or senators forty years later. The result would be a kind of adverse selection, where only the dullest, most naturally submissive, or most drugged-up kids wouldn't have some non-PC moment on their record to be dredged up by some future rival and spread via a new hashtag.

The way things were going, the only place the kids wouldn't be monitored was the bathroom. One man logically asserted that that would naturally make the bathroom the locus for any naughtiness—smoking in the boy's room brought to a whole new level.

Cameras would, however, be installed at great expense, and urgently, tomorrow, triggered by what was about to happen today. The cameras would come one day too late to be an inconvenience for Lichen.

Of course, Chemnitz Lichen would never be caught. Nonetheless, in the event he did get caught, he'd have on hand a list of all the members who frequented The Store, provided to him by his brother Dresden. Chemnitz kept the names with him in a password-protected laptop. It was his get-out-of-jail-free card. The sick and powerful of Washington would contribute to the coffers of the most impressive defense lawyers in a desperate effort to avert the release of their names. And if they just had him killed? Well, then the names would most definitely be released via a deadman's switch. No one would dare suicide him, leaving him hanging in a cell.

317

Sabina and Forestal had insisted that the first event be in a town in Texas, supposedly to limit the chance of involving the children of people of influence. It wouldn't do if said people of influence became personally motivated to stop the tsunami of death that Chemnitz would kick off today. This tidal wave had to roll from one side of the country to the other before crashing ashore in DC exactly three weeks from now. At that point, it wouldn't matter whose kids died. Panic and irrationality spread quickly on the internet. Faster than a viral epidemic. Forestal had insisted on this timing, and Sabina agreed. Chemnitz was sure that those two had received their marching orders from someone higher up, simply because it was hard to imagine the two of them working together unsupervised.

He had selected the school based on the lack of cameras. He selected the kid based on social media postings that suggested the boy absolutely could not tolerate another year in school. It was no fun being constantly taunted for being stupid, ugly, and weak. He hated his classmates. Chemnitz worked on him remotely for almost a month to get him to the point where he could see the only honorable way out was to teach them a lesson nobody would forget.

And the kid didn't chicken out.

Chemnitz walked confidently down the hallway, deftly avoiding the stampede of screaming children and panicking teachers running from the gunfire. It was easy to identify the report of the Beretta's 9 mm rounds. Then the AK—a legal semi-automatic version, of course—over and over again. Thirty rounds of that. No surprise that the kid would unnecessarily blow through a whole magazine nonstop. Then the 9 mm Beretta again.

Where had he stuck that canister? He dug a hand into each pocket of his overcoat. It was down low on the right.

The glass on the door far ahead to the left had shattered. Yes, that was supposed to be the first room. Good job, Timmy. Four more rounds from the handgun. He should be coming out and moving to the next classroom in a moment.

Then he heard a noise that he shouldn't have. The sound stopped Chemnitz in his tracks. What the hell was that? It sure as hell wasn't an AK round. Nor did it sound like the four immediately previous percussions from the Beretta. Fuck, it sounded like a different weapon. Timmy shouldn't have a different gun.

Everyone in the hallway ran in panic. Running, crying, uncontrolled, and witless. Chemnitz fought his way against the flood of screaming fear up to the broken glass of the classroom door. Through the opening, he could see that his guy, Timmy, lay sprawled over the desk of a dead teacher. A woman—probably a teacher's aide—approached the front of the classroom with her hand shaking as she held a pistol aimed toward the boy who lay on the desk. This unexpected woman and her unexpected gun had thrown a wrench in the works by shooting the shooter! Dammit. Big trouble on the very first mission. This wasn't supposed to happen. He triggered the canister and set it down on the hall floor. Smoke poured out of its top. He then burst through the classroom door.

Chemnitz moved in and made a quick assessment of Timmy, the awkwardly tall and scrawny teenager whom he'd convinced to run this rampage, now bleeding out on the desk four classrooms too early. He then turned to the gun-wielding woman who'd acted heroically. He had little time to think. "Good job," he said to the woman. "Give me that gun. Who's alive in here? Stand up, everyone. It's over."

The woman with the gun was perhaps twenty-four. Only eight years older than the shooter who now lay dying on the dead teacher's desk. She obediently handed Lichen her gun. Two boys, each shaking, slowly stood up in the back of the classroom.

Chemnitz's gloved hands pried the Beretta 92FS pistol out of the shooter's hands. He called the two boys to come forward. Consistent with the constant reinforcement from their two thousand days in school, the boys dutifully responded to the authority in his demeanor and voice. They came forward, treading through expanding pools of blood, at which point Lichen dispatched them with the teacher's weapon by means of two perfectly aimed shots to their heads. Then he trained Timmy's Beretta at the woman who would have saved them and who had indeed saved the lives of three other classrooms full of children. The woman stood in shock, having no time to comprehend what was happening.

"We mustn't have a heroic armed teacher save the day," he said coldly. "No good deed goes unpunished. That's the school lesson today. And now you're dead." He fired.

He moved over to the shooter next, his guy. Timmy wasn't yet dead. The pistol that the teacher's aide had brought into class was a Kel-Tec PF9 chambered for 9 mm rounds. Chemnitz pressed the magazine-release catch and looked at the ammunition. Ball ammo. The bullet fired from it had gone into the side of Timmy's chest and out through the middle of his back. He needed to think—and fast. How to play this?

Timmy moaned.

"Timmy, you fucked up. You let yourself get shot." He looked around at all the walls in the room. "And you didn't tag the wall, either, Timmy." He glanced at the door. The thick smoke in the hall would prevent anyone from seeing. He closed his hands over the boy's nose and mouth. In a minute it was over. Timmy's body spasmed and then lay still.

He took the teacher's Kel-Tec and rubbed the muzzle into the blood from the wound where the bullet had entered Timmy's chest. It should look like Timmy had managed to get the woman's gun away from her and killed a couple of students with it before turning it on himself. He put Timmy's handprints on the weapon and left it in his dead hand.

It took him ten seconds to find the spray can of black paint that had fallen on the floor. He quickly finished what Timmy should have done.

Smoke billowed through the broken glass in the door. Chemnitz went to the door and walked into the smoke and the chaos of alarms and screams.

Nobody who lived through the panic and fear even noticed he was there.

* * *

As evening came, Charles walked through Times Square, his senses assaulted by the blazing lights of ubiquitous billboards and the steamy heat of mid-August. He leaned against a wall under an overhang and watched the news ticker speed by in giant letters. The residua of the previous week's City-Fires still littered the street. Broken glass, beer cans, burned vehicles, orange cones, a stink of melted rubber.

The NASDAQ was up a couple of points. The news readers claimed— as if they actually knew—that it was because fears were easing about the impending euro collapse.

Tomorrow it might be down a few points on good employment numbers. Good employment numbers were bad for the Nasdaq these days: they might mean the economy was strengthening and labor costs would go up; then the Fed might tighten monetary policy, sending the market down. Or maybe the market would go up if some corporate earnings reports came in under analysts' estimates, for that might mean a worsening economy could encourage Fed loosening. It was thinly disguised chaos.

There were a hundred reasons—most of them unseen, and some of them simply unknowable—why the market could go up or down a few points. But the network-news readers had to seem certain and authoritative even though they had about zero understanding.

It was a different world from the days when the market rose or fell roughly in parallel with the health of the economy and mostly because companies were doing well or doing poorly.

It went up or down depending on whether the Fed was raising or lowering interest rates and how much money it was printing. A lot seemed to depend on what side of the bed the Fed chair got up on.

Charles watched the giant Times Square monitor. There had been a shooting in a school in Abilene, Texas.

Another child off the rails. They all seemed to crave media attention for their deaths, and suicide by cop had always been a favorite of psychos. They were increasingly committing mass murder to activate the sequence. Would this be blamed on Naked Emperor? Maybe. The chances were better it would be blamed on the guns the kid used. Would it ever come out that the unbalanced teenager's mind was almost certainly addled by years on some combination of Ritalin, Prozac, and any of a hundred other psychiatric drugs? Probably not.

Whatever the reason for this event, it was horrific and real. Because the SEA had previously choreographed a number of these events in its quest to both destroy Naked Emperor and ensure its own importance, Charles was skeptical that the truth would ever come out, whatever the truth was. He wanted to find out what really happened.

He closed his eyes for a few moments. When he opened them again, the lights of Times Square again filled his vision and that of thousands of others around him. Those same lights simultaneously entered the lenses of thousands of devices. Cameras were monitoring the crowds, recording the actions of every person on the street. Large and obvious, small and stealthy, there were cameras everywhere.

How many of these cameras would soon be tools in the Paladin Network, hacked into by the spyminers or offered voluntarily for a fee by their owners? Facial recognition would seek out identified targets; AI would correlate them with other flows of data. The government could already do that to zero in on particular targets. The Paladin Network would level the playing field. There would be no NSA, Google, or Facebook centralizing the control. Natural law would make the rules, and the entire world would play the Paladin game.

Charles paused with a sudden inspiration and stared straight ahead for over a minute. Then he turned and walked for an hour back toward Chiang's electronics store, stopping at a deli to use their bathroom to don his Paladin garb, including the hoodie to conceal his face from cameras, and a shoe insert to disguise his gait.

Chiang's store was empty of customers this late in the evening. Although Rainbow spent much of her time in the basement of this place, this was Charles's first visit since he'd sent Jock and Freak to their just rewards in this very room two and a half months earlier.

"Hi, my good friend! Welcome back to my store!"

"Hello, Mr. Chiang."

"School shooting in Texas. You see that?"

"Yes, I heard. Horrible." Charles was more concerned about it than Chiang could know.

"You see what shooter write?"

"No, I haven't seen much of the news."

"He spray paint in the school, 'Guns Rule.'"

Charles shook his head, his suspicions mounting. "Clever." He looked around the shop for a minute while Chiang looked on. "I need to buy some items from you."

"If I have, I will give to you."

"You still owe me five thousand dollars from when we first met. Above that value, I'll pay you in cash."

"Vely faih. What you need?"

"Some very special things that you'll need to order for me. And of course never tell anyone about."

"Neveh eveh, my fliend. I never tell no one."

35

After-Action Report

THE ATF's carefully concocted plan had successfully prodded a group of gun enthusiasts into breaking some of its rules. A follow-on SWAT enforcement raid ended up killing several of them. A year of congressional investigations went nowhere, and President Cooligan's chief of staff finally told its director to quit, which he did. This left the ATF without leadership, and Forestal—formerly only in charge of the money—found himself running ATF operations in addition to supervising funding for the FBI, DEA, and SEA. Conversations on the 4th Floor intimated that Goldman was a cinch after this. Vice chairman, a done deal. That was a fat plum indeed. He much preferred the private sector.

The shooting in Texas was disappointing. This first one was supposed to have at least forty victims to prime the pump. The public was inured; events had to be truly outrageous to have any real effect. The failure was inconvenient and annoying, but correctable—probably just a failure to communicate clearly. Chemnitz Lichen had to understand that this wasn't business as usual. Small, infrequent shootings were no more than background noise in a country of over three hundred million people with an economic collapse and riots on their minds; it wouldn't rise to the level of a crisis. And a crisis was what he needed. "Never let a good crisis go to waste" was a political axiom. He needed something the media could call a catastrophic crisis, and it made no sense to just passively wait for one.

Convincing congressmen to sponsor bills was dog work. Schmoozing with hicks from the hinterland who thought they'd made the big time in

DC was tiresome and degrading. They mostly wanted to hear themselves talk and see what he could do to further their agendas. It required a few terms in office for them to learn their place in the pecking order.

A spectacular crisis, however, would ignite public hysteria and make for easy sponsorship and enthusiastic acceptance of the two new bills he'd drafted. The first would be known as the Protection of Minors Act, or PMA. The second would be named the Transparency and Honesty in Ownership Act, or THOA. The well-spun names disguised their intent, just like most bills sponsored in every congressional session. Marketing was king. Their titles were chosen deliberately to make it harder for the gun lobby's hired political hacks to attack the underlying bills. Who could argue against protecting minors or against transparency and honesty? Especially given the overwhelming number of impending deaths.

And then there was his third bill—hidden in the form of planned floor amendments to other bills—kept at the ready. For just the right moment.

The bills would add momentum to his plan. If he succeeded, he wouldn't stop at vice chairman of Goldman. It was within his reach to move the Western Hemisphere's most important investment bank into an even-closer relationship with the government's central bank. The chairman of the Vampire Squid was in many ways more powerful than the chairman of the Federal Reserve. It was the ultimate "public-private partnership." Control the currency of a country, and you control the country. Control the currency of the world, and you control the world. Should things develop smoothly, in less than a decade all Western central banks would operate under one currency.

For now, the US government was the most powerful tool in the world. Tools were made to be used.

"What the hell happened?" Forestal demanded as Chemnitz Lichen emerged from his car in a dark alley between two rows of shipping containers.

"You're not supposed to be in touch yet," Lichen's high-pitched voice scolded. Forestal couldn't see his eyes in the low light.

"I need an update."

"Talking in person is a risk."

Forestal knew Lichen was right, but it was critical he stay on top of Lichen after his underwhelming first effort. "So is talking on phones. But I still need an update."

Lichen studied his surroundings, staring into the darkness. "Wainwright's death so soon after the attempt on Samuels is suspicious. Treasury and Fed both getting targeted, maybe? Coincidence? I think not. Someone's hunting you people. You're the ones at risk, not me. I don't even exist."

"We're fine. Now tell me what the hell happened. Twelve? Only twelve?"

"Someone had a gun."

"What?"

"Yeah, a teacher's assistant shot my kid before he could even get to the second room."

Forestal shouted, "You gotta fuckin' be kidding me!"

"Quiet—you don't know who could be around here. I'm not kidding. We shoulda started in California. There we coulda gotten a hundred no problem. Sitting ducks. But you insisted on Texas. I told you Texas is too fucking risky; a lot of Texans carry."

"I didn't hear about the teacher shooting the kid, though. Why didn't I?"

"Maybe because they haven't figured that out yet. I tried to take care of it. I intercepted the teacher and two students who saw her shoot my guy. They ended up being victims ten, eleven, and twelve of a troubled student, the evil gun manufacturers, and a teacher whose gun was used to kill innocent students. I took a risk, but it had to be done."

Forestal exhaled loudly. How badly it might have gone! "I understand... If this had ended with some gun-toting teacher taking out your shooter, it would be game over. We'd get the opposite effect of what we're aiming for."

"I didn't let that happen," Lichen replied. "There's more risk when you're dealing with a psycho kid, but I like a job with challenges."

"Are you sure it's all clean? Any blowback?"

"We'll see. Could be bad. The woman's gun was coincidentally also a 9 mm, but it used different ammo. The teacher shot through my shooter's chest, so I did what I could to make it look like he'd taken her gun and shot himself with it, but there won't be much if any gunshot residue on his skin. Nothing I could do to make it look right. It's a red flag. There was no time to find the casing from the shot she fired into my guy. It won't have landed in the right place, but that will be attributed to it getting kicked around or bouncing off furniture and rolling. So a small risk. These hick-town police departments aren't full of high-tech geniuses, like on TV CSI shows."

"Why didn't you just take the teacher's gun with you?"

"I had to think fast. If I'd walked that gun out of there, it would raise questions if others knew she'd had it—other teachers, her boyfriend, whoever. Bad questions. And ballistic analysis can still raise questions of who shot who. I did the best I could. I only had a few seconds to think. The locals will assume the obvious possibilities are the only possibilities. I think it worked out damn well, considering."

"So far. You better have this covered."

"Don't try to sound threatening, Forestal. It annoys me and I might lose respect for you. There's risks in this game. It would help if you can find a way to put the kibosh on FBI taking a role in the investigation. They're not geniuses, but their average IQ is probably about ten points higher than the Barney Fifes in Nowhereville. You have that power, right?"

"I have some indirect influence. The best solution is for you to get on with several more events, as we planned. A big volume of them will create chaos, confusion. Keep the FBI spread thin. If there are four fresh and far-larger mass shootings in a row, your Texas massacre might be put on the FBI's back burner. I hope you've arranged for help. You can't do what I need done alone."

Lichen nodded slowly. "I'm not alone. That's all you need to know. I'm heading to California after a couple of stops. You asked for something big in California, so that's what I've planned. The gun-free zones will solve the armed-teacher problem."

"When's the next one?"

"Basically daily at this stage. As we planned. I've had six weeks to plot this all out since we first met. We're sticking to plan. That plan doesn't involve telling you what, where, who, when, or how."

"We need big attacks in rapid succession."

Lichen's response was intentionally patronizing. "I know. It's fine, Forestal."

"I don't want only school shootings."

"That's good, because kids wanting to shoot up their classmates don't grow on trees. They ain't easy to find and recruit you know."

"Sure they are. There are a million of them. I was almost one."

"I bet you were."

Forestal had intended a short meeting, not a long conversation, but his minion needed to understand the significance of his assignment. He felt a sudden urge to impress the hitman with his own importance. "But I got smart. A dumb person will rob a bank, steal five thousand dollars, get caught, and then serve twenty years. A smart one will control the national treasury, commit no crime, and be treated as an icon. The same brain that might shoot up a school can also be used to run the world. It's just a question of scale."

Lichen stared up at Forestal's eyes. "That's a scary fuckin' thought."

"Get used it, Lichen. It's been that way forever." Forestal warmed to the topic. "Look at Pizzaro in Peru. Killed seven thousand Incas with a hundred sixty-eight Spaniards. Not one Spaniard died. Then Pizarro kidnapped the Incan king Atahualpa, held him for a ransom of gold, loaded his ships with the gold, and killed Atahualpa anyway. Lichen, I want you to be Pizzaro. Use your imagination. Pretend some orphanage or preschool is an Inca palace. Get the count higher this time."

"Preschool? Nah, the first big one is going the other way."

Forestal shook his head. He could not control this man, and he had to accept it. "Well, just do something. Get the show on the road."

36

Raheem

AHMED Raheem knew he didn't fit in with most of the reporters on the floor. He had dark hair, he was tall and thin, and his mildly deviated nose hooked perfectly to maintain his glasses against his eyes. Raheem appeared to be, and was, of Arabic extraction. He'd graduated from American University two years earlier with an English degree, which was of approximately zero value when it came to paying off his monstrous student loans. It had been his fashionably diverse-sounding name that helped him get into what passed for the big leagues of a dying industry. The New York Post had him mostly doing background research and running errands, but they tossed him the occasional table scrap in the form of a bylined story. They paid him essentially nothing, which was about all they could afford, and most of that disappeared in taxes and mandatory benefits he'd never use.

On the bright side, Ahmed's involvement with the paper taught him that news sources almost always get the story wrong—sometimes intentionally, but mostly through negligence or ingrained bias. They didn't notice it for the same reason fish didn't notice they were swimming in water—they'd been immersed in it their whole lives.

Ahmed looked around the open floor with its cramped cubicles, studying and classifying his coworkers.

Thomas Greaves: a cocky, ambitious twenty-four-year-old journalism-school grad, rabid in his zeal to gather any shred of support for whatever thesis he had, tossing aside any alternative input. It wasn't intellectually honest, but he was smart. Having strong opinions made Greaves seem like a thought leader, an influencer, or even one of the world's leading experts. Clever. Right down to adding some ridiculous irrelevancies to appear fair and balanced while undermining any defense of the other side. He was a spinner. He worked out daily and glanced at his own reflection hourly. Ahmed figured Greaves was on his way up, likely to television.

Then there was Theresa Hawkes. In her thirties, she'd come to New York from Biloxi, Mississippi, hoping to become a successful career girl but came to the conclusion—as did 90 percent of those like her—that she wasn't ever going to be part of the highflying 10 percent. Her blond dye job and coquettish Southern accent could no longer offset her spreading waistline. It was getting late in life to party the way she once did, and equally late to find a mate. Like many in the office, she was overwhelmed by her personal life and finances, about which she cared far more than her writing assignments. Her articles typically pulled together some material she found on the web, sticking it under a catchy story title. Her writing rarely made the printed page. She was useful for creating distracting online clickbait. She lacked skepticism or curiosity, so she never did any actual research. Ahmed called her type a waste of space.

Spinners and wastes of space occupied about 50 percent of desks. The grinds, dummies, nasties, coffee-cup holders, and schmoozes came and went constantly. He wondered how the business survived. It was actually a better group than at the Post's major competitor, seven blocks away, just off Times Square, where the wastes of space were uniformly woke and the spinners all social justice warriors.

Part of the job was to embellish here or there to spice up a story, please an editor, or garner more likes on social media. Snappy headlines and sensationalist copy trumped mundane facts. Ahmed figured the same was true in science, religion, and most other areas. Certainly in politics. Perhaps the only place the unvarnished truth carried the day was sports—where unpaid armchair obsessives tracked every relevant player statistic, just because they loved the game.

Outside of sports, verifiable facts weren't easy to come by. Ahmed was no superstar, but he wore out shoe leather trying to gather data and confirm its accuracy. He occasionally garnered faint praise from his editor, a distracted man looking for a lifeboat to get off the sinking ship. He had no time to waste mentoring some cub reporter. Yet Ahmed's father would be proud, and that mattered far more.

Clearly, the object of all this was to persuade, manipulate, and propagandize two herds of sheep. The sheep herds were hardly even the same species now. In this town, the Times herded one flock and the Post herded the other.

Ahmed wondered, for the hundredth time, what he should do next in life. His grandfather had been a goatherd. His father moved up to selling stolen bicycle parts, then got involved with socialist revolutionaries against the French. When they won, he was able to shake down a family leaving Algeria to go back to France. It was enough to get himself and his wife to the US, where Ahmed was born. It was up to him now to make good. He wondered whether his current job was a dead end. He could hardly fall back on goat herding.

"Ahmed Raheem?" A man walked smoothly up to his cluttered desk.

"Yeah, that's me." Outsiders never approached him here. Only coworkers with seniority wanting to drop scut work on him ever stopped by.

The man spoke quietly but with confidence. "I hear you have a copy of the police and coroner's reports for the Abilene school shooting."

"Where did you hear that?"

"Contacts in high places. I'd like to see it, just for a few minutes."

Who the hell was this guy?

"Why?" Ahmed asked.

"Because I'll pay you one thousand dollars."

Raheem didn't need to think for long. He had rent to pay, due yesterday, and still didn't have the money. "Look, I got no problem with you seeing the report. You have to stay here while you read it though. And cash up front." He kept his head still, but his eyes looked around as he said this, glancing from desk to desk.

The man handed him a bank envelope. Ahmed stuck it in his pocket without looking and fished around on his desk for the relevant folder. As he handed it over, he said, "What's your interest in this file?"

"I have a thousand dollars of interest in it, Mr. Raheem. Fear not, nothing but good will come of it. For you too."

The man wore black leather gloves indoors—strange in mid-August. It would have been cause for concern half a year ago, but now the abnormal was normal. He wore a broad black mask covering his cheeks, mouth, and nose. Customized antiviral masks were everywhere, differentiating their wearers like gang colors.

The man pulled up a swivel chair from an unoccupied desk and sat down. Without removing the gloves, he flipped through the file rapidly and then went back to read some of the pages in depth. Ahmed examined what he could of his face. It looked like a bulbous nose under that mask, alongside furry sideburns and dark hair. His irises were nearly black.

Ahmed shrugged and turned to his computer, where Facebook was open. A sizable part of his job was surfing Facebook and monitoring Twitter. News today was whatever somebody posted. Heck, the Huff Post created news stories by weeding through thousands of Twitter posts, picking out a few with good headline potential, and making it seem that the tweets, or the twits who wrote them, had established a newly recognized and critically important truth. Throw in some irrelevant adverbs to make the story pop. Ahmed had noted a substantial rise in the pro forma headline "Such-and-Such Late Night Celebrity TOTALLY DESTROYS So-and-So Politician." And so the trivial was transformed into national news.

The man said, "How many bullets were fired?"

"Huh?"

He repeated himself in the exact same tone. "How many bullets were fired?"

"There was like a total of thirty AK-47 rounds fired. And twenty-six nine-millimeter rounds from the pistols."

"Are you certain? Is that precise?"

"Look it up yourself. You paid a thousand dollars to see the file."

The man exhaled through his large nose in response to the impertinence. "Total of fifty-six rounds fired."

"Why does that interest you? What difference does it make?" Ahmed asked, making no effort to conceal boredom, and even exaggerating it some. "No one got out alive."

"Do you believe everything that you read?"

Ahmed snorted. "Hell no."

He knew the police report's extensive details. One AK-47 rifle had been found, its magazine emptied. Thirty bullets. The police had located twenty-six 9 mm cases, three from the ball ammo the Kel-Tec fired and twenty-three from the hollow points loaded in the Beretta. Two of the ball-ammo cases in the front of the classroom. The third in the far back. Two empty ten-round Beretta magazines on the floor. Seven unfired rounds still in the Beretta. All twenty-three Beretta cases were in the front of the classroom. Shooter dead from a self-inflicted chest wound.

The man squinted his eyes at a page and said, "That's strange."

"What is?" Ahmed paid attention now.

"Shooter was a lefty. Entrance wound under his right armpit. How'd he do that? Kid made of rubber? Or did he use his right hand to kill himself? Did they look for gunshot residue on his chest? I don't see a comment on that."

"Huh?"

"Look, go do your job. Go to Texas. Walk around on the grassy knoll."

Ahmed pulled himself away from his cutting-edge Twitter research and looked at the man. He was dressed in black pants and a black long-sleeved shirt. He wasn't what anyone would call handsome. In fact, he looked a little like a sixties-era hippie.

"Mister, tell me again what you're saying."

"I'm saying that there's some reason to believe someone else was shooting in that Texas school."

"And why should I believe you?"

"Because you believed me, indirectly, before."

The man handed Ahmed a business card, but it fell to the floor. Ahmed bent down to pick it up. It said only "Paladin," with Have Gun—Will Travel emblazoned around the image of a chess piece.

"No way." He knew that name well. He'd helped popularize it by publishing the image of the dead Terrence Kirby with the Paladin coins on his eyes. Paladin coins with chess pieces.

When Ahmed looked up, it was to see the back of the man turning around the corner.

*   *   *

"Where did you get this, Raheem?"

"A guy handed it to me. Says his name is Paladin."

"Paladin? Better call the FBI," replied Raheem's editor nonchalantly. He was about twice or even three times older than most who worked in the building. He would have retired several years before, but he had no other life to go to—and no savings to get there even if he had.

"You don't think he's just a copycat?" Ahmed couldn't yet conceive that he'd actually been contacted by an assassin.

"Probably. But you still call the FBI."

"Uh… Okay. Maybe we got his picture on a security camera?" Ahmed suggested hopefully. He didn't like the idea of having to deal with FBI agents. They'd wonder just why Paladin would reach out to a guy named Ahmed Raheem.

"Yeah. Why did you let an unknown man see the police report?"

Honesty didn't run in his family, but Ahmed worked at being more honest than his father. He loved the old man, but didn't like not being able to trust him. "He paid me a thousand dollars for it. I needed rent."

The editor thought for a moment. "Okay, Raheem. Don't admit that sort of thing to me again."

"Umm, okay." He gained some sympathy for his father's faults.

"Pay your rent, and use the rest as spending money in Abilene."

"So, you want me to go to Texas? Like he told me to do?"

"It's an excellent idea, Raheem. Get travel to hook you up tonight. Get down there as soon as you break free of the FBI. Don't come back until you have a story."

"Boss, why do you think he … calls himself Paladin?"

"Paladin is the name of the lead character in an old black-and-white Western television series."

"Yeah, I know that. Like the card says. 'Have Gun—Will Travel.' I've never seen the show. Paladin was a hit man, right?"

"He was the hero, the good guy. We all loved him. Look, keep this all under wraps for now. This may get big. Could be your break."

Ahmed went to the travel office first. Maybe he'd call the FBI second. Or maybe that could wait.

* * *

On the 4th Floor of Samuels's Upper East Side mansion, the lights were dimmed and the café seemed darker than usual. The windows let in the nighttime glow of the city. Tobacco smoke exhaled over decades clung to the walls and ceiling. Random electrostatic processes allowed ancient microscopic particles of cigar smoke to float through the air until subtly detected by a human nostril. The place had carried this scent for generations. It remained today, even though current fashions had practically eliminated smoking in general and cigars in particular.

Claussen, the oldest and wealthiest man, looked harried and pale, even for him. "I don't like this."

The men and women nearby observed his anxiety.

Samuels said, "What's your concern?"

Eterio Conti interrupted, suggesting an answer. "Do you think Wainwright really just up and died? So soon after someone took a potshot at you? I don't believe in coincidence."

"Whether or not you believe it, coincidences happen. And it's hardly coincident. Someone took a potshot at me months ago. And as for Wainwright…"

"He was only fifty-five."

"Yes. And no poisons found in his body. No trauma." Samuels said, nonplussed. "They think it was sudden death from a heart-rhythm disturbance. It happens."

"It's just that the timing."

Samuels held his hand up. "We'll see how things develop. In the meantime, it's unseemly to panic. Are you planning to go to the mattresses?" He looked at Conti with a faint smile as he made reference to the Mafia practice of going to a hidden location and sleeping barracks style. Conti wouldn't appreciate the allusion to his Italian background, especially from a Jew. They each had lingering tribal loyalties, but those were generally ignored in favor of their common quest for money and power.

The old man said, "My bodyguards tell me I need to change my routines." He looked at the two men from the old families at the far end of the table. "I don't like change."

Forestal spoke. "I'll make sure to keep you fully informed if anything develops on the investigation of Wainwright's death. I'll have access to every piece of information that gets out of Dominica to the US, and all the FBI finds as well. We'll get to the bottom of this. If this was an assassination, we'll know."

"What do you know so far?"

"So far, it seems like natural causes."

Forestal's phone buzzed. He looked down at his telephone. A text message from one of his contacts at the FBI, currently deployed to Dominica. He pressed his touch screen and looked at the image of a particularly unusual business card.

37

Moral Insanity

FEW cars traveled along the brightly lit highway. A police car appeared out of nowhere, following directly behind Chemnitz Lichen. It turned on its blue lights.

What the hell? Shouldn't those cops be sleeping? Chemnitz pulled the car to the shoulder and glanced at the clock on the rental car's dash: 1:30 a.m. He might have been speeding, but that seemed unlikely.

"What's the problem, officer?" he asked as the woman in uniform cautiously approached, standing about a foot off to the rear of his window. Cops were wary these days. Her positioning made it harder for a driver to get a shot off.

"Sir, do you know why we pulled you over?"

"No, ma'am, I honestly don't."

"Sir, you have a tail light out. The whole left side. Makes you look kinda like a motorcycle in darker areas."

"Oh, sorry, officer. I didn't realize it. It's a rental."

"It's all right. Get them to trade out the car in the AM?"

"Will do. Thanks, ma'am."

"Have you been drinking, sir?"

"No, ma'am. Not a drop." During the previous few days, he'd shot up the home of the mayor of Louisville and an American Legion Hall in Denver. All that driving and shooting didn't leave much time for partying.

"Okay, then. Drive carefully."

"Thank you. I will." And indeed he would. During this stage of the mission, he had to change out his rental car every one to two days anyway. He changed out the identification he used for them as well. Sabina's money—or rather the money of those who funded her—had allowed him to procure more than twenty identities. Most he would keep in reserve.

The officer got back in her patrol car, blinked left, and pulled out onto the empty freeway.

Chemnitz sighed in gratitude to no one in particular. He would have needed to use a real driver's license had the officer asked, because a fake would have been caught. He would have needed to defer the job in California until another day.

Of course, Chemnitz Lichen could never be caught.

California was in the plan, and he preferred to stick to the plan. The morning should begin with two concurrent slayings on opposite sides of the country. He was the shooter in California.

Chemnitz slept in the car that night in a Walmart parking lot. In the cool morning, he urinated on a grass embankment, climbed back in his car, drove three miles toward his intended address, and parked two blocks away. A sign in front of the building said "Leisure and Life Community." They were just another demographic to be manipulated. Lichen rubbed his eyes as he looked at the time: 7:30.

It was a cool sixty-two degrees on this sunny late-August morning in Oakland. He pulled the cap down low over his forehead and the collar of his long, black raincoat up around his ears. He covered most of his face with a blue surgical mask. Although it was no cloak of invisibility, it ensured that later analysis of security-camera footage would provide little useful information to police. He should be in and out in less than four minutes.

He only needed two pistols for this operation. In each hand he held a Beretta 92FS—for many years the most common police sidearm and the same type of gun used in the shooting in Texas less than a week earlier. Chemnitz loaded each gun with extra-long thirty-round magazines that awkwardly protruded far out of the base of the grip. The large magazine would save him a few seconds since he'd only need to reload once for each gun. Once emptied, he would place them back in his coat's deep pockets. He'd contemplated leaving them behind to provide fodder for those who wanted to ban high-capacity magazines, but best to just let them marvel at the speed of a competent shooter with a semi-automatic pistol.

He tucked the weapons into his coat, their long magazines protruding slightly. He felt a surge of energy as he walked in the front door. Feeling anything at all was rare for him.

A young woman sat behind the front desk, waiting to welcome and assist visitors.

"Is it breakfast now?" he asked with false cordiality.

"Yes. Everyone's in the dining hall. Who are you visiting?"

"My mother. Where is the dining hall?"

"Well, it's right down the corridor there, but you have to sign in first."

"Certainly." Chemnitz pulled a nine-inch combat knife from an inside pocket of his long black rain jacket, holding it blade down in his hand. His arm shot up and the blade sliced across her neck, cutting her voice box and one of her carotids. The knife hovered above her right shoulder for a millisecond before plummeting down behind her collarbone, piercing through her innominate artery and puncturing her lung. The move consisted of one quick stroke, like a conductor leading a symphony through an upbeat. Her questioning eyes opened wide, as did her mouth, from which no sound could emerge. Her effort at screaming amounted only to blood bubbling through her torn-open larynx. She passed out directly and would die silently a minute later.

After visiting the storage room to disable the video surveillance system, he moved toward the dining hall. On the wall outside, he used a can of red spray paint to write the words that were becoming known nationwide: "GUNS RULE."

A hundred people occupied the room, many in bathrobes, some dressed more formally. He wasted no time to study faces. He began firing systematically. One shot per. Over and over and over. Like in a shooting gallery. Pow. Pow. Pow. Pow. Pow. Panic spread rapidly but was extinguished, with prejudice, just as fast. He was knocking over bottles faster than the machine could put them upright again. Pow, a terrified old man trying to speed his walker to a door. Pow, a hysterical old woman hobbling away. Pow. Pow. Pow. Three at a table. All head shots. He moved through the crowd so that he wouldn't risk a miss. One shot per death.

He reloaded once, ejecting his empty magazines and placing them in a pocket. A few more people tried leaving, but with their crutches and canes, burdened by age, they were all so slow. It was like shooting fish in a barrel. Pow, a mackerel. Pow, a trout. Pow, Pow, Pow, salmon. He had no difficulty covering the two exits; no one made it out. As moans of the dying replaced screams of fear, he walked out of the retirement community and back toward his car. The barrels of each gun burned against his sides. Sixty rounds fired in quick succession from each gun would do that.

As he climbed in his car, the clock said 7:38. Eight minutes for the whole operation. Twice as long as he'd hoped. He plucked foam rubber plugs out of his ears and placed them in his pocket and then drove off.

An ambulance arrived first, the police twelve minutes later. His excellent marksmanship combined with his methodical approach to the task had left few alive, and those were seriously wounded. The only evidence was 120 brass cartridge cases without a single print.

And the writing on the wall.

Even a fool could read the writing on the wall.

*   *   *

"Well done with the Kentucky and Colorado jobs, Lichen. And North Carolina and California at almost the same time was smart—caught the media buzz. But I thought you were looking for an orphanage."

"Don't worry. It's coming. For California, the old age home was close enough. Oldsters move slowly, and they're politically active. An excellent target market, as it were." He snorted briefly, amused by his own observation.

"I suppose. Just keep going. Keep going without stopping. Different guns and different venues. I want 'Guns Rule' painted in blood in every state."

"I've got it planned out. The copycats will be coming along soon, I'd bet."

"The more the better. Less chance of you getting caught."

"I don't get caught."

"But if you do?"

"If I get caught, Forestal, I keep my mouth closed while you use your position to keep me out of the chair, but preferably spring me. I have some very impressive insurance policies to ensure that you and your friends don't kill me. You understand what I'm saying?"

"Yeah, I understand. And I don't care. As long as the plan continues if you get caught."

"Don't worry about that. I told you, I'm not doing this alone. And Sabina knows where to turn if I get caught or die. But I won't get caught.

338

Hell, the biggest risk is when you call me like this. This phone is only to be used for urgencies."

Forestal sighed. "The phones are encrypted, end-to-end."

"Encrypted doesn't stop an ear at the door. Either my door or your door. It's old-fashioned humint—human intelligence—that takes the best down. I'd worry about yourself. I'm not going down."

*   *   *

"Charles, what the hell's going on? Five shootings in three days," Emily said after hugging and kissing him passionately as she approached baggage claim at New York's Kennedy Airport.

He shook his head. "Let's get to the car. I'm glad to have you here if only for a day. Something's up."

In the car, Emily asked, "What did you mean, something's up?"

Charles replied, "What's going on is systematic."

"The news is saying it's Sybillene again."

"It's not Sybillene. It never was Sybillene. But it might be the same thing happening now that happened back then—although for a different reason."

Emily said, "The CityFires keep gaining energy. It's contagious. The mayor's office in San Francisco is preparing for a huge outpouring of people in the streets to protest gun violence. They can count on the mobs growing. Especially in Washington and the state capitals."

"I suspect there'll be more of these shootings over the next weeks and months."

"An epidemic …"

"A dangerous meme that's been endemic in society for two or three generations is transitioning to an epidemic. It's virulent, and spreading through society. Think of the movies and TV shows from the '50s. Most all about families in the suburbs. Kids fixing up hot rods and going surfing. Working a steady job and moving up in the world. Then the Kennedy assassination. Society mutated. Vietnam. Hippies. Watergate. Riots. Bombings. Drug culture. Then a reaction in the '80s, when yuppies started wearing those 'He who dies with the most toys, wins' t-shirts. Then ecohysteria, when everyone wanted to go green and save the whales. Yadda, yadda … the beat goes on.

"Now a whole new vibe's taken hold. It's not so much about what people are doing, but how they feel and what they believe. Political correctness,

339

class warfare, identity politics, safe spaces, microaggressions, socialism—a whole slew of psychological diseases incubated in the schools and reinforced by the media. If you look at society like a petri dish, you'd see these things have taken over the whole plate, totally replacing the traditional culture. As many problems as the '50s had, the sort of thing happening today would have been impossible back then. It appears that psychological diseases that used to be under control, and infected relatively few, have turned into an epidemic. So maybe what's happening now was inevitable. CityFires are supposedly spontaneous riots, but I don't see this Guns Rule thing as a mass movement. More likely it's a small group that want to make it look like a mass movement—or maybe start one. The deliberate action of specific people with a very definite purpose."

Emily said, "You're saying they're staged?"

"Not staged. They're real. I suspect they're planned and coordinated events. I'd bet my life on it." Charles paused a moment; his choice of words was perhaps a bit too accurate. "This is how they took down Sybillene. It's how they took me down."

"If you say this publicly, you'll be crucified, Charles. The parents of all the murdered children will call you the Antichrist."

"Based on that, maybe the Antichrist gets a bum rap."

"Do you think these are the same people who did Sybillene in?"

"It's their MO. Although it could be others who've seen how effective killing innocents can be to accomplish a political aim. The very definition of a terrorist. At least it's one of the hundred or so official definitions."

"Who could be doing it?"

Charles didn't have to think long. "The media and the public would blame neo-Nazis if there were swastikas instead of 'Guns Rule' painted on the walls. But they aren't painting swastikas. No, they're targeting guns and gun owners. Whoever's responsible, they're morally insane to a degree that few believe possible. Recognizing this narrows it down a bit. But exactly who in particular? We can start by asking a few questions. Who most benefits from gun control in this country? Who is morally insane? Who is sufficiently funded to pull this off? Find that nexus and we'll have a list of potential perps."

"Do you have anyone in mind?"

"A top dog in the Deep State is my guess. At least some of the Deep State people know that their gigantic financial bubble is popping. When bubbles pop, people blame whoever they can—other than themselves. Sooner or later, heads will roll. Bullets will fly everywhere. Not just some schools and retirement homes."

Emily pierced to the heart of the matter. "So they want guns banned so they don't get shot by a growing supply of pissed-off people."

He nodded. "Guns are becoming an old technology, but they're cheap, available, and still the best way to defend yourself. What would have happened if every Jew met the Gestapo officer knocking on his door at 5:00 a.m. with a fusillade of bullets? So, sure, they absolutely want to ban guns. But then banning guns could also be the spark that ignites a revolution. Maybe they'll be more subtle, more sinister."

"My dad goes on about a shadow government from time to time. High IQs and very rich. He said they all needed killing."

"Hyperbole, I assume?" Charles said.

"No doubt."

"I think he's not far from the truth."

"Is there a Hannibal Lector out there in back of all this?"

"Yeah, these people have that kind of wiring. But it's worse than that. At least Hannibal Lector cared about Clarice Starling. And he was just a shrink with a hobby as a serial killer. He wasn't ultra-rich and in charge of a large corporation or government agency. Hannibal was highly skilled but still an amateur. These people are professionals."

"A bunch of rich Hannibal Lectors all working together is a frightening thought."

"It's possible. Birds of a feather flock together. Even the T. Rex moved in packs."

Emily continued, "Banning guns is helpful to them, but not because people are going to use guns to fight a guerrilla war against the government. You don't get obese people, laying on their couches eating junk food and watching TV to risk their lives for some ideal. And I bet there's an FBI snitch in every militia and any other group more radical than a Rotary Club. Rebels would be hunted down like rats. This meme about an armed populace keeping the government from getting out of control made sense when the civilians' rifles were better than the military's and when most people were hunters. Today's military don't just way outclass the population, they have their own subculture. Their first loyalty may be to each other, but they know who their employer is and they'll do as they're told."

"Emily, you and I think alike. The real antigun thing isn't about quashing the restless natives' militias. Nor safety, saving lives, or the children." He involuntarily frowned at the hypocrisy of those who claimed to care about the sacred cows. "They couldn't care less about any of that. The data prove more guns are safer than less guns. The people running the show are antigun because, throughout all of history, a major difference between a free man and a slave or a serf was that a free man could be armed and defend himself. It's psychological. Are you a man, or are you a slave? When you realize you're a slave, you start acting like one. You start serving the masters, without resistance or pesky questions, to say nothing of carping about your 'rights.' And that's the real goal: to suppress people's wills psychologically. That's the only way a little Indian mahout keeps an elephant under control."

"Same type of people that put me in prison, Charles. I know they exist."

"They put me in prison too."

Emily said, "The government used to encourage civilians to be marksmen. The militia could back up the regular army if enemies ever actually invaded. Not anymore."

Charles added, "Guns are fairly useless against the government but quite effective against individuals in the government. These people, these sociopaths we're talking about, basically control the government. It's dangerous to have people with Hannibal Lector's mind running the government, Emily. So of course they fear privately held guns; that's why they've been fertilizing the soil for gun bans for years. My guess is that they've decided to escalate their agenda by causing a series of crises. They're just starting with Abilene, Louisville, Denver, and now Oakland and Asheville."

"If that's true, what can be done?"

"In prison, I did nothing as I watched good people get beaten to a pulp. I know that feeling. I don't like being powerless while watching injustice. But I don't have that feeling now."

"Please consider me as a potential accomplice."

"Thanks, Emily. I'll keep that in mind."

He expected a long silence to follow.

Instead, she replied immediately. "I know what you're up to, Charles."

Was she serious? She sounded as if she was. There was no hint of humor. If she knew, how did she know? He glanced at her face and replayed her words in his mind.

"You... know what I'm... up to?" he said, delicately.

She chose her words with caution. "I'm observant. You provided hints. And then there was Wainwright."

Charles preferred to take events and people head on, but he'd try a gentle evasion here. "Wainwright? I was three thousand miles away."

"I bet you could have done it anyway."

"Mmm."

"If you want to stop these shootings, I want to help."

"I don't want to invite you to that party. It'll require certain skills."

"Skills that I may have, Charles. Bring me with you, or I'll crash the party on my own. You decide."

38

East Meets Southwest

"WHAT'S yo' name, son?" The detective was an old-style Texan through and through: as gruff in his speech as his appearance. He wore the same suit all week—sometimes for two weeks—to save on dry cleaning bills. The collar of his wrinkled oxford was too tight for his neck, so he left it unbuttoned. A bolo hung loosely below his third chin. He had no ring on his finger.

"Ahmed Raheem. New York Post."

"Awright, Rajeesh. What d' ya need?" He spoke slowly, spacing out the syllables.

"Just a few minutes of your time, Detective LaBloche."

"Eva'body wants a few minutes o' time, Punjab. Why not you too? But Ah've work ta do. Ah'm sure you have work too—afta some fashion." He turned his back and walked toward a stairwell.

"How about I just follow you to your office? I have some questions that might best be addressed in private anyway."

It seemed to Ahmed that LaBloche's demeanor changed then, from irritated impatience to complacent superiority.

After a pause that took just a second too long, LaBloche replied, "Yohr funeral. Folla me."

He followed LaBloche down a series of bleak corridors into the depths of the city's administrative building.

"Ah'm down in the dungeon 'til owa offices ah fixed up. Mold problem. Worse down heah though."

Early in the long awkward walk, Ahmed decided that they likely had

344

nothing in common but an intuitive dislike of each other. There was no point in trying to disguise it with meaningless small talk. Ahmed would absorb the slights with no reaction; if nothing else, he'd need the guy's help to get back out from this underworld to the blue skies and hot air above. He felt like he was wandering in a dimly lit maze, led by a minotaur.

LaBloche unlocked an unmarked wooden door. Cluttered with papers, the windowless office felt like a small tomb in the building's catacombs.

"Death, Rajeesh. Mah temporary desk is covered with death."

"I'm sorry. I must have misspoken when I introduced myself. My name is Ahmed Raheem."

"A-hab the A-rab. Apu at the Kwik-E-Mart. Rajeesh, Punjab… This country's changed. Ah see more Mohammeds than Billy Bobs these days. No offense." LaBloche sat behind his desk. "So whatcha wanna know?"

He had no other chairs in the office. Ahmed leaned against the inside of the door. "I've reviewed all the publicly available files on the school shooting. It seems that the investigative work was very thorough and straightforwardly done."

LaBloche said nothing.

"What do you think happened?"

LaBloche replied with a faint staccato in his sentence, expressing evident frustration. "It's all in the record awready."

Ahmed knew little about guns or shooting other than what he'd seen on police shows. He hoped it was enough to wing it. "Please indulge me. I recall there were three guns involved. Do you often come across the types they used?"

"An AK-47 man'factured in Bulgaria, a Beretta nine-millimeter semi-automatic pistol, and a Kel-Tec nine millimeter; they're all pretty common."

"Anything you found out of the ordinary for ammunition?"

"The AK-47 ammo was Russian. Standard varnish-coated jacketed ammo. Cheap stuff. The Beretta had hollow points, man'factured here in the US. The Kel-Tec used target ammo."

Ahmed shrugged. "Where were the target rounds purchased?"

"Standahd cheap ammo. Prob'ly puhchased at a gun show or a gun store somewhere. That stuff ain't traced at all, ya know."

The budding journalist in him grabbed the issue like a terrier might an escaping rat. "Did you perform ballistic testing on every round?"

"Look, every single kid in that room was killed. Thay wuh no otha guns in the room. No otha shootas. What you tryin' to get at?"

"Where did the smoke come from? There were reports of smoke in the hallway, but I haven't heard about what made the smoke.

"Devlin put a smoke bomb in the corridor."

"Oh. I didn't see that in your report."

"Added it in an addendum you don' appeah to have seen."

"Can you get smoke bombs at gun shows?"

"I s'pose so. You can pro'bly order 'em online. Heck, easy to build too."

"Any idea where Devlin got his?"

"Not yet."

"Was Devlin wearing hearing protection, gas mask, eye protection, gloves?"

"None o' that."

"His prints were on the guns?"

"Yep."

"Also on the gas bomb?"

LaBloche hesitated for a moment and then replied. "None found."

Raheem glanced up from his notepad then to see LaBloche looking closely at him.

"No?"

"No fingerprints."

"Explanation?"

The detective shook his head. "Maybe the prints evaporated off as the smoke bomb heated up. Theyah mostly sweat aftah all."

"And the 'Guns Rule' tag. It's his handwriting?"

"Presum'bly."

"So, not yet confirmed."

"Not bah me."

Ahmed hadn't gotten very far on his examination of the grassy knoll. He had more questions.

"Did he use up all his ammunition?"

"Oh, not at all. Both the Beretta and the Kel-Tec found near the Devlin boy had partially emptied magazines. Thank God the kid stopped when he did. He had three mo' AK an five more nine-millimeter mags in his pack. He coulda shot a hunert more kids."

Raheem stuck to his task, writing notes in the standard-issue three-by-five-inch spiral-bound notepad that made him feel like a real reporter. He didn't look up. "So, Devlin ended his attack earlier than he planned?"

"Seems so. Maybe he had second thoughts."

"What did he use to shoot himself?"

"The Kel-Tec."

"How do you know?"

"Pulled the slug outa the wall muhself. It's not hahd ta tell just bah lookin' at the wound. The weight o' the lead is greatah, the jacketin' metal is different, the spread o' the bullet is less. The injury to the chest was less than it would have been if it were the Beretta's hollow point, but theahs a big dif'rence in the size o' the exit hole. Heck the ME was suhprised the child even died, for the bullet didn't go through a big vessel."

"So, Devlin shot himself in his right chest using the Kel-Tec. The teacher's gun?"

"Seems so."

"Tim Devlin was left-handed?"

"Yes, he was."

"How about gunshot residue on Devlin's entry wound? No muzzle flash burns?"

"Not so much."

"Isn't that strange?"

"Weah still tryin' to put that piece o' the puzzle in the propa place."

Ahmed pondered out loud. "How many people commit suicide by shooting themselves under their armpit?"

"He was a clueless kid. Kids ah stupid."

"It doesn't make sense though."

"You have anotha eye-dea?"

"How did the shooter get the gun from the teacher?"

"No eye-dea. But obviously he did."

"Fingerprints on it?"

"Jus' the teacha's and the shoota's. An' a coupla old partials that weah lookin' inta—pro'bly gun-shop staff."

"Right hand or left hand?"

"Who?"

"Any of them."

"Teacher—lotsa prints, both hands. Shoota, left palm print only."

347

"Left palm. And he was shot under his right armpit. Why and how would he do that?"

"Faih questions, Akbhar. Latent prints ain't ahways wheah you want 'em."

Ahmed considered. In one of his better classes, his professor had told him that when things don't make sense, question the assumptions. Big assumptions in this case included that Tim Devlin was the shooter, which seemed solid: somehow he got the teacher's gun away from her and shot two other kids with it, a conclusion that spread like wildfire in the media. And that he'd shot himself with that gun too. Under his right armpit. With his left hand. With no gun residue.

He asked, "Does all this make sense to you, given all that you know about this?"

LaBloche raised his voice. "Do school shootin's evah make sense?"

Ahmed shook his head. "No. At least not the way we look at them. Anything else strange?"

"No, Abu. Nothin'. Buhlieve me, weah not tot'ly satisfied eitha. We want ta know what happened. These wuh ahr kids. That's why ah talked to ya. But the facks seem ta speak fer themselves. We got no reason ta think otherwise. But Ah'm open minded. Theahs an element o' uncertainty with these cases. Weah dealin' with ab-normal psychology heah."

It seemed to Ahmed that one or more of the assumptions had to be wrong. The detective wasn't stupid, and he wasn't trying to hide anything. It didn't make sense. But not making sense still left him with a dead end.

Unless Paladin knew something.

39

Smart Contracts

CHARLES dropped five pieces of mail in the corner postbox. A baseball cap, a hoodie, and a wide, black, pandemic-averting face mask concealed most of his face. Many in this part of the city wore a hoodie as a fashion statement; the fact that they hindered identification by the ubiquitous security cameras was a bonus. Considering what those envelopes contained, care was warranted. Overly cautious? Perhaps. He supposed that the government could track mail back to specific drop boxes.

He made a call on the encrypted cell.

"Uncle Maurice, are you awake?"

The phone crackled some. "Of course I am. How else could I answer the phone? Did you see the news?"

"What news?"

"Another two shootings. In Chicago. An orphanage. Fifteen kids and five nuns. Shooter got away, like in California. Then less than six hours later, another in Detroit. An abortion clinic. Everyone on scene dead. Some reports are suggesting the suspected shooter was a pregnant woman, but that's probably bogus. Each one spray-painted 'Guns Rule.'"

"Hmmpf... it's beginning to look quite coordinated."

Maurice replied, "Same drill as with Sybillene. Go big or go home. Somebody's taking that motto to heart. No half measures here."

"Yeah, and I'm sure they'll use this as an opportunity to put the SEA front and center. How long does it take to drive from Detroit to Chicago? Less than six hours, I bet."

"You can do it in four." Maurice paused a moment. "You need to come over and talk."

"Can't. I'm on my way to Washington. Driving."

"Why are you headed to DC?"

"I figure that's where my job is."

Maurice paused for a longer moment. "You're going to try to prove to yourself that each one on Jeffrey's list deserves what coming to him, right? Most of his list are swimming in that swamp."

"No. That's now pretty much the job of the Paladin Network's spyminers. Specialization and the division of labor, remember? Seems like I've been kicked upstairs, out of management at this point. I'm told it's unseemly for the chairman of the board to be down in the trenches doing rote work."

"Yeah. Rainbow asked me to follow those data myself, not wait for the AI. The AI build on the network has been sluggish. They're academics that got excited about crypto and received a ridiculous amount of funding through their initial coin offering during a big-hype stage in the crypto space a few years ago. These guys outright bragged that there would be absolutely no return to investors on their token sale, but people bought it anyway expecting huge returns. It was essentially a crowdfunding move. They took in about fifty million bucks. A hundred times as much as they'd get from the National Science Foundation. Not surprising that the company's been slow since. No shareholders demanding returns. But instead of just living off the proceeds from their token sale, they've gotten a bit of fire under them now that PNet has shown them that their science fair project has real value. The guys running the AI platform are aligned, mostly anarchists, and this little shove has been good for them. As the network grows, the AI is going to be critical to figure out who's on first."

Rainbow had reported a growing amount of data coming in from spyms, as spyminers were already being called. It was revealing complex webs of relationship among these people, but it would take time and effort to sort out what those relationships were.

Maurice said, "We won't have even a tiny fraction as much data to chew through as NSA does. They get so many petabytes every day that their analysts must be overwhelmed with data about who we talk to."

Charles replied, "That's the best defense the people have against the NSA—too much data. They're buried in it. Even with their advanced AI, they can't know what's relevant when they get input from three hundred million Americans and billions of other people too. Even when they decide to zero in on something, it's harder than looking for a needle in a haystack. It's more like looking for an ordinary piece of hay in a haystack. Still, it doesn't hurt to use this secure voice system, Maurice." Charles rechecked his phone to make sure that the encryption app was indeed on. It was.

"Well, Paladin Network's not going there. Like you said, Maurice, the NSA targets the whole planet. Cell phones, email, social media, messaging boards, financial transactions, newspapers, security cams, you name it. Anything on anyone. Trying to find dirt on everyone so they can use it when needed, just like Hoover in the FBI did. They vacuum up every bit of potential dirt they can with their giant vacuum. So they massively dilute the truly valuable data. The NSA are data hoarders. The electronic equivalent of crazy people who fill their house to the rafters with trash because they can't throw anything away. We made Paladin Network different."

Maurice said, "I know. It makes no sense for the focus of PNet to be on Joe and Jane Average. There's no money in it. The network itself doesn't care what they order from Amazon or post about their lives on Facebook. Paladin targets will tend to be busybody swamp rats with hundreds of connections each, who'd like to keep those connections hidden. The AI is needed to sort that out. And it's started. It's almost working."

"Good."

Maurice asked, "The network wasn't active a month ago. So how did you prove that Wainwright needed to go?"

Charles replied, "The old-fashioned way. I read everything you sent me. Then I stopped by his house in Dominica and spent a day on the beach reading the notes he'd discarded from the draft manuscript for his autobiography. He convinced me in his own words. The man took intense pride in what he's done. And what he was planning to do. Like the notes Terrence Kirby kept at the Department of Agriculture. Seems they shared a narcissistic streak. It was like when Marx, Lenin, Hitler, and Mao wrote their books. They didn't see themselves as monsters. They saw themselves as the good guys, doing what was right and necessary. That's a problem with this business. It's pretty clear to us who the bad guys are. But others might disagree and think Mao was a good guy. The Chinese still profess to love him today, despite the fact that he killed fifty million of them. Stalin was right. One death is a tragedy. A million deaths is a statistic."

Maurice said, "Wainwright got what he deserved, but his obits treated him like one of the great heroes of the age. I'm reminded of something Gibbon said, about how mankind shall continue to bestow more liberal applause on their destroyers than their benefactors." Maurice then asked, "Who's next?"

"All of 'em. In the meantime, I want to get to know Blaize Forestal."

"Forestal. I saw where someone—you, presumably—added him onto a smart contract for the spyminers. The data are thin so far. So I looked into him some more for you, my way. The old-fashioned way. Non-artificial, unaugmented human intelligence. I thought I'd make myself useful before your PNet makes me redundant."

"I'll always need you, Maurice. PNet just makes your services available to the masses. Why should government types and your rich clients be the only ones who get to monitor their nemeses? And why should government's nomenklatura be the only ones to put out contracts on adversaries? Everybody thinks democracy is such a great idea, right? We're just putting the theory into practice, up close and personal."

"Charles..."

"Sorry, Maurice. I get carried away with the symmetry of it sometimes."

"Still, Charles, your technology is disrupting my occupation. It's going to put me out of business, and I helped design it. Foolish me. On the bright side, I don't mind adapting. Who wants to be a dinosaur that can't even survive a little asteroid strike?"

"It's going to make you richer, Maurice. Since you backed up the truck to buy tokens early on."

"It better. Though I did it because I liked the people in the deal. But back to business. Blaize Forestal might be one of the real up-and-comers in the Deep State. Over the years, he's moved up coincident with some convenient eliminations of his superiors—mostly through resignations under pressure, but a couple of deaths too. He's running the ATF in addition to controlling the purse strings of the SEA, DEA, and FBI."

"You may be right, Maurice. He's positioned to control the controllers. We need to know what he and people like him are up to." The thought flashed through Charles's mind that it would have been better for the world had Emily's bullet killed Forestal ten years ago. And not just because it probably would have saved her from six years in the slammer. "I wonder if it's a coincidence that one of Goldman's revolving-doormen started running ATF just when these shootings started."

Maurice replied, "The news media is having a feeding frenzy. This morning,

CNN called it 'The Gun Crisis of the Millennium.' Doesn't matter that the millennium is still in its infancy. It's a meme, and it's going to take hold."

"No doubt. Public perception and mass psychology trump reality every time. Unfortunately, there are likely to be more shootings," Charles prophesied.

"Tell you what, Charles. I'll go ahead and double the pay on the spyminers' contract you made on Forestal. Let's compare these spyminers to what I can do. But let me tell you something else first." Maurice paused, and then said, "Hold on, Charles."

He'd caught a news story evolving on television. Maurice didn't watch TV to learn what was happening so much as to learn what the public thought they knew, or at least what the media wanted the public to think was happening. Charles couldn't make out the news anchors' words over the phone, but he could envision his uncle sitting on the couch flipping among the channels on several screens, on the lookout for something relevant.

"Where are you?" Maurice asked.

"Southbound on the Delaware Turnpike."

"Glad you're out of town already. There's a shooter taking out drivers going in and out of the Lincoln Tunnel." He paused to hear some more. "Traffic's stopped, and there's a guy with a rifle on a building picking off commuters like fish in a barrel."

Charles's prediction had come true faster than he'd imagined.

Maurice added, "So, let's talk Blaize Forestal. Mid-forties. Raised in Delaware. Right where you are, Charles. Attended Exeter and Princeton, of course. Roommate at Princeton was... wait for it... James Wainwright, which I found interesting. Fairly visible rise to various positions of power in the so-called private banking sector, the Fed, and the government of course. Has an apartment in New York and one in Washington. For a government employee, he's exceedingly wealthy. Approaching a hundred million dollars."

"Fits the profile. What else do you have?"

"You mean, other than his moving back and forth between the fraudsters on Wall Street and the extortionists in DC? Yeah. Well, what I got, and this took a lot of effort and is not trustworthy, is that he gets a lot of women upset with him. Looks like he tries to clean up after himself, but there are archives of angry reports online that he beats up young women during sex. One or two may have gone missing after supposedly going out with him. He's suave and cultured, but angry and controlling. His ex-wife's a basket case. She's in and out of psych hospitals. Supported by the State. He wriggled out of alimony. Caught her in adultery that triggered the prenup. Wouldn't be surprised if that was a setup. You know, if you go after this guy, they're gonna make a movie out of your exploits someday."

"That would be my personal hell."

"Charles, there's a club that's mentioned in one of these postings about him. The postings are really hard to find, by the way. Most are deleted, but the search engines keep them cached for archival purposes. Anyhow, one of these cached postings, by a woman using the name Victim100, said that she met him twice. The first time he was quite a gentleman. The second was outside of a club, large townhouse near Union Station. He came out of the place already furious, and then beat her and raped her in the backseat of a stretch limousine. She wrote that she really wanted to know what happened at that club, because it was like he was a different guy. The posting was several years ago. Whole thing is thin, but you may want to check out that club."

"You're right. It's thin. Some house near Union Station?"

"Yeah, that's all I got."

"I doubt I'll find it, and positive I wouldn't be invited in."

"Look, I'll see if I can find out more about the place. Maybe find its location and name at least."

"Probably a red herring."

"Yep."

"I'll await your call."

"Of course. I hate to say 'Stay safe'; it's trite and whipped-doggish. But, be smart. FYI, the Lincoln Tunnel shooter was just taken out. Looks like one of the police snipers got him."

*   *   *

Every cop with a rifle was sending rounds toward the sky right now. Yet the police still couldn't get the job done. Chemnitz couldn't take any more risk that the guy would be captured and interrogated. He hoped that the shooter had done as he was told and already sprayed the rooftop with "GUNS RULE" in giant letters for the helicopters to see. They'd be flying over soon, but not until they were sure the shooter was dead. A single lucky shot could take a bird down.

Chemnitz pulled the trigger and sent a .308 round across three blocks and into the shooter's head. The report echoed down to the streets far below, making it impossible to identify the source without at least a few more rounds being fired. There was no need to pull the trigger twice. None of the police snipers would be able to say for sure that their shot did or didn't kill the guy. No ballistics would match, but it would hardly matter since the snipers were peppering the now-exposed and already-dead man with as many rounds as they could, just to be on the safe side. Then the system would do what the system does and give one cop the undeserved credit for the takedown and manufacture another SWAT hero. Everybody's happy, and no loose ends.

Chemnitz wasn't in this for personal recognition.

Admittedly, he only beat SWAT to the punch because he possessed the operational intelligence required to establish the best position to target the shooter. He knew exactly where the shooter would be and what cover he would take. While SWAT had to position its men on the fly, Chemnitz had pre-established his position, with proper concealment.

Chemnitz removed the stock, put it and the barreled receiver into a padded suitcase, zipped it closed, and carried it down the roof stairs to the elevator on the top floor. At the bottom, he strode out through the lobby with an extra-large cloth mask covering his face, past the doorman who'd ignored him earlier, and out to a stand of cabs, all listening to the radio intently.

"I hope you don't want to go anywhere near Lincoln Tunnel, pal," said the first cabbie in line.

"Shouldn't need to. Heading the other way. Need to get to Penn Station." Chemnitz intended to end up at La Guardia, but he'd first leave the bag in one of the station's lockers, where it wouldn't be discovered for weeks or months.

The cabby replied, "Okay. No problem."

"What's up at the tunnel? Traffic, huh?" Chemnitz asked after working the case into the trunk of the cab.

"A sniper's been shooting cars coming out of the tunnel. The place is a mess. Half the cops in the city are here. Look."

A long line of police vehicles stood two blocks down the street, officers crouching behind their cars. All of them pointlessly brandishing their pistols, mainly because the situation allowed them to.

"Hell. Glad we're going the other way."

"It'll still be a mess, though."

"Do your best."

40

Campaign

AS HE stumped around the nation, Grayson Chase found himself buried under an avalanche of discontented people. They weren't unhappy with him, but with the general direction of the country. They wanted to come out of their political closets. Although views were changing along with the country's demographics, what Grayson said still resonated with a majority of Americans.

Grayson couldn't individually sit down with two hundred million potential voters. So he sat down with thirty instead, one at a time, their unedited and uncensored conversations videotaped and loaded on the internet. This was not only about voters interviewing Grayson or Grayson lecturing them, but something more carefully conceived.

His campaign experts reached out to scientifically selected types of voter. Finding a "typical" young Hispanic male, old white female, unemployed Rust Belt worker, or upward-mobile computer type wasn't the hard part. The question was whether Grayson could relate to them and whether they'd relate to him. Most candidates had professionals craft speeches intended to offend no one and promise lots of free stuff to everyone. The average voter might not be very bright, but he could sense when he was being manipulated.

A twenty-five-year-old named Devaun Roberts was one of them. He fit a young-black-urban-male demographic. Not at all stupid, but barely made it through high school. Minor dustups with the law for drugs, but no hard time. He didn't have a baby mama. Tall and thin, what he liked was playing basketball. What he didn't like was being broke. He lived with his mother, who worked as a nurse's assistant and made him go to church with her every week. He never saw his father.

What would Grayson and Devaun say to each other? It wouldn't, and couldn't, be scripted.

"What's your biggest concern, Devaun?" Grayson asked as the chat began.

Devaun shook his head while smiling nervously. "Man, where to begin? People are so crazy now!"

"Maybe just pick what comes to your mind first," Grayson suggested.

"Maybe people hating on each other. So much hate."

Grayson nodded. "Why do you think that's the case?"

"I don't know." He smiled and shook his head. "But it's crazy."

"Some examples?"

Devaun contemplated. "The racist stuff. So much racism."

Grayson prodded, "How do you describe yourself? Maybe make a list of words to describe yourself."

Devaun smiled nervously. "I'm a… well, I'm a man. I'm young. I wanna work, but made some mistakes. Tired of bein' broke-ass."

Grayson nodded. "Excellent. I'm interested that you didn't say black."

"Didn't need to."

Grayson smiled fleetingly. "So you highlighted the content of your character, not the color of your skin?"

"Lemme tell you something. It ain't easy bein' black. I know they built the projects to keep us where they could watch us and give us handouts like we monkeys in the zoo."

"What do you think about people who make their skin color the first thing they use to describe themselves?"

"If tha's what they want, I don't care. I can tell you a high yellow got a betta chance o' makin' it than some purple Nee-gro, even right here in the 'hood. Forget about it outside, in the world."

"If people categorize themselves first as black or white or Asian, or even high yellow, does that help fix racism? If we focus more on color of the skin instead of content of the character?"

"I don't see how. An' yeah, I've heard that Martin Luther King line you just used," Devaun replied.

"Let's go one more step."

He nodded.

"What about Black Lives Matter?"

Devaun shook his head. "Cops kill black people. Black people kill black people. Black people kill cops. White people kill cops. Black people kill white people. White people kill white people. An' it's mostly black people kill other black people. It's crazy. It's not the skin color that matters. It's the killing!"

Grayson nodded back. "Isn't that the nutshell of it? And what causes the killing?"

"Gangs, fear, hate. Money. Drugs."

"What exactly happens, always, when there is a killing?"

Devaun squinted for a flash and pulled his head back. "I mean, someone kills someone." He shrugged, questioning.

"Right. Are there any good reasons to kill someone?"

"Well, yeah. Protectin' your own. If I'm getting attacked. You live here, you learn rule number one is to survive. You don' let some dude disrespect you."

"How about if someone else is getting attacked, robbed?"

"Maybe then too. Try not to though. You try to help, an' you might wind up dead or in jail."

Grayson prodded. "So is it the killing that's wrong? Or is it the attacker who is wrong?"

Devaun spoke from experience, unlike a Harvard academic that had never thrown a punch. "The dude attacking is asking for it. That's on them."

"I agree with you, sir," Grayson said as he shook Devaun's hand. "What else worries you, Mr. Roberts?"

"I'm good with my hands. Wanted to be a plumber, cuz that's where the money is. But you got to be a union member, and the only people can get in are the kids and friends of members."

The conversation continued to the afternoon Devaun wasted in the DMV to register a used truck. They talked about what made him feel good or bad about the country. Devaun said he might move out of the projects to a state that didn't require membership in a union, and apprentice himself to become a plumber.

Short clips of the extended interviews were released as memes, and some went viral on the internet.

More than a few of these discussions were with progressives who couldn't think their way out of a paper bag; their responses to Grayson's questions made them look confused. Most became defensive. The experienced ones demanded to "agree to disagree," which many saw as the cop-out that it was since Grayson was just asking questions.

Some of the conversations were with conservatives about foreign military intervention, the flag, and the meaning of patriotism. Their confusion was similar, just activated by different questions.

Many of the conversations were surprisingly informative for both progressives and conservatives, who could see they were in a bubble. Compared to most political discussions, they were actually interesting. A blow-dried anchor critiqued Grayson, however, for not having a transgender voter among them.

Grayson shot back, "Should I have had a white transgender, or a black transgender? A Gypsy, perhaps? And just how do you know there wasn't a transgender person? Maybe he or she didn't want to focus on their own gender and sexuality in a public forum? Did you consider that a transgender person who has a chance to spend time with a presidential candidate might choose to focus on the economy or war? Maybe they have bigger concerns than the ones that seem to be on your mind."

The irony was lost on Blow Dry and his media colleagues. The more they magnified their outrage, however, the more people lost respect for them.

A reading of the posted comments about the videos revealed that viewers preferred real people having rational discussions. Somebody who had a perspective that they'd not encountered before, but who made sense. It took a longer attention span than the two minutes many had gotten used to giving a single subject, but those who stayed tuned appreciated Grayson's appeal to their intelligence rather than their lower emotions. The public liked the novelty factor.

Grayson Chase rose in the polls.

Middle Americans had become intimidated and afraid of the consequences of openly stating their views. They'd let a shrill politically correct minority take the high ground and define how the language was used. Grayson figured that if he wasn't shamed by the PC Twitterverse on a given day, he likely hadn't said anything worth saying. So he went out of his way to add a bit of spice to his stump speeches—something for the Twitterbaiting twits in the Twitterverse to tweet about. He'd say something that had become outrageous, like "It's good to be a man," and a hailstorm of offended effeminates would cry out in distress. Or in response to a question about climate change, he might say, "Better than winter coming," before suggesting that rational scientific skepticism should always be welcome and that the current practice of burning questioners at the stake as heretics was the action of small-minded bullies. Over time, the PC crowd became the butt of their own jokes. Middle Americans realized that a leader like Grayson Chase would allow them to speak out again, without fear.

He had a folksy brand of populism. Comparisons to Ross Perot in the Bush-Clinton election were frequent: a billionaire leveraging the discontent with the two major parties. At one point, Perot even had a substantial lead in polls over the establishment candidates, despite his reputation for being mercurial and paranoid. He'd withdrawn from the race, supposedly because Republicans planned to disrupt his daughter's wedding. Three weeks later, he rejoined the race, but he'd lost all momentum.

Now, decades later, the discontent in the country had reached a critical mass. Grayson Chase figured it should be easier for him than for Perot. Plus he wasn't mercurial. Perhaps a bit paranoid, but then the powers that be really were out to get him.

At the end of August, the election just two months away, Grayson Chase was poised to take the lead in the polls. "I really don't care if creatures who've lived in the swamp their whole lives hate me. This country's in big trouble. We're going into what I call the Greater Depression. It's going to be much worse and longer lasting than the last one. And it's because of these people. Everything they're doing makes it worse for the average guy. I'm not about to desert the people standing beside me. The time's come to fix bayonets."

That last line was repeated everywhere, by both sides, as you might expect in a country some thought on the cusp of a civil war.

His paid advertising dominated the airwaves and roadside billboards, but it wasn't just money. He could spend money and get nowhere. The key was that his messaging engaged the listener, viewer, or reader. For the first few months, his online marketing had been limited to simple statements, five seconds at a time, long enough to get name and idea recognition, not long enough to irritate.

"Grayson Chase says government is a lousy parent. Be an adult."

"Grayson Chase says don't wait for the government. Do it yourself."

"Grayson Chase says we should protect what's ours, but not start wars."

Or something simpler still, like "Grayson Chase is safe to vote for."

Some would investigate further and connect with his video interviews. Some would dig in deep, love what they read, and volunteer to help.

He didn't bother to attack the other candidates. Grayson figured it best to stay out of the way and let the two political hacks beat each other up, as would have happened with Hitler and Stalin had the US not allied with the Soviets. He didn't refer to the other candidates as his opponents, but rather as "your opponents," consistent with the intuition of most people. Wasting no time with specious insults, he earned a reputation as an optimist despite predicting the imminent onset of a depression and saying it would be hard on almost everyone.

The two other candidates realized that their strategy of ignoring him had backfired. So they rallied their troops to attack him directly.

Grayson continued to ignore them.

President Tweedledee and Senator Tweedledum were diffident toward each other, maintaining a collegial respect even while they traded aspersions, but it was obvious the two shared a visceral dislike for Grayson. The public wondered why. They spent more time talking about him than themselves or each other. This led the average American to wonder what Grayson was saying. Many liked his message.

The campaign strategy was simple. The voters who paid attention would vote for Grayson Chase because he was a good person who made sense. Those who only wanted to throw the bums out—or simply despised the major parties—would vote for Grayson Chase as the only alternative. The totally uninformed in the middle, who had no ideology, would see the name Jeffersonian Democratic-Republican Party, think wrongly that it sounded moderate or middle-of-the-road, and also vote for Grayson Chase. Some would vote for him simply because they'd seen and heard his name so often. Three percent of those polled thought Grayson Chase already was the president of the United States, proving that Churchill was right when he said the best argument against democracy was a five-minute conversation with the average voter.

At most sixty percent of those who were eligible actually voted. Some few considered voting immoral since the lesser of two evils is still evil. Some of the more mathematically oriented believed that their vote, one out of a hundred million, was statistically irrelevant. Many had lived long enough to realize that voting was an utter waste of time. Yet these perennial nonvoters formed an important part of Grayson Chase's electorate. If he could convince them to care, he'd have a real chance.

His outreach effort began engaging them to vote, many for the first time in decades. Grayson was the first to admit he was no pro in politics. They would be voting for someone who discussed economics—the way the world actually worked. A most unusual candidate.

Grayson knew he was on a fool's errand when it came to fixing the country. It was completely impossible—even if he got in office—for a single man to change the direction of what Longfellow had called the Ship of State. It was headed for the rocks. The thousands of apparatchiks and nomenklatura who crewed it (the Soviets naturally had the most accurate names for them) would hang onto it like barnacles. It was legally impossible to get rid of most of them. And nothing could be done about the Deep State members in Congress, academia, corporations, the military, Hollywood, the news media, and top NGOs. They'd howl like demons brought up from the depths of hell should a president try to do anything significant against their interests.

It was a totally impossible situation, and he knew it.

So he wouldn't try to fix the country. It had mutated from a yeoman republic into a domestic multicultural empire. It was beyond salvation, like Rome in the fourth century or Athens after the Peloponnesian War. It was suffering from a terminal lack of ethics, morale, and self-confidence. He had one mission and one mission only: to get the broken government out of the way. He knew it was a Mission Impossible.

Early on in the improbable adventure, Jeffrey told him exactly how it would work on the off chance he won. Jeffrey had very good reason to know.

"Grayson, once they see you're serious and a real threat, you'll get friendly advice from old Washington hands, sounding helpful and telling you the way things work. If you don't straighten out to their satisfaction, at some point you'll have a sit-down with a bunch of these people—heads of the big agencies and a few generals. They won't threaten you directly, but you'll be aware of the kind of people they have working for them. If you value your health and the people you love, you'll back down. They'll let you make a few changes around the margins, and you can write a memoir when you're too old to care anymore what they'll do to you.

"If you actually start making serious changes, the usual suspects aren't going to be your only problem. What's going to happen is that most of the middle class—your supporters—will be out in the streets with pitchforks and torches once they realize that what's on your mind is going to break their doggie bowls. They'll forget these notions of idealism. People who thought you were great will hit the streets like a mob of angry chimpanzees.

"There are so many distortions and so much misallocated capital that's been cranked into the system over the last fifty years that if you don't try to build the house of cards even higher, it's all going to come down on your watch. Bank failures, busted pension funds, massive unemployment, repossessed houses—the works. We know the only solution is to let it all wash out. But they don't. Meanwhile Congress will move to impeach you, of course. Because from now on, every president is going to get impeached if the House isn't on his side of the aisle. All the while, various appeals courts will find ways to overturn every attempt to force government to abide by the Constitution. The Praetorian Guard may not even need to conduct a palace coup."

Grayson toyed with the idea of a reverse coup. Could he put together a team that was strong enough and large enough to turn the tables on them and overthrow the Deep State? It would only work if he drained the swamp dry and transformed it into a desert. At least it would be within his power as president to flush some of the worst pond scum out of the executive branch. It hardly seemed worth the trouble if that's all he could do.

What would happen if he could replace every agency head with someone sound, who would take no prisoners? And each proceeded to collapse their bureaus? What would happen if he withdrew all US troops from foreign soil and vetoed any spending bill that didn't cut the military budget until it was only three times that of the next-biggest country? Ideally, he'd do no deals with Congress on debt ceilings, leading to default on the national debt.

With all these cuts, what would happen if he abolished the income tax? To do so would require a dictatorship. The US had had them before, for all practical purposes—Lincoln in the War between the States, Wilson in World War I, and Roosevelt in World War II—but each time for the purpose of increasing control, not decreasing it.

The presidency was by far the most powerful arm of the executive, legislative, judicial triarchy. At least in theory, as president, he could control all the military and the federal police forces, if only he could get rid of the Deep State people who managed them. A temporary dictatorship for the sole purpose of disempowering the Deep State controlling the triarchy might work.

George Washington was compared to Cincinnatus: a man who stepped forward in a time of dire emergency during the Roman Republic and then returned to his farm. Perhaps Grayson Chase would be too.

In his dreams.

As a practical matter, there wasn't much chance of pulling it off. Nonzero—but very small.

Had it ever been done before? It happened in Chile, after the assassination of Allende. General Augusto Pinochet transformed the country from a backwater copper-mining province to the most advanced and prosperous country in Latin America. Whether it was necessary or not, a couple thousand of the opposition were killed—a relatively small number for a Latin country with a military regime. In comparison, it's said the Argentine generals killed thirty thousand. The Brazilian generals about the same. Even in tiny Uruguay, the generals took out something like five hundred communists. They all skated; nobody but Pinochet was seriously prosecuted. Because he free marketized the country, so-called human rights groups pursued him to his dying day.

Further proof that no good deed goes unpunished.

The collectivists attacked Grayson for being a South Carolinian and therefore a privileged white descendant of slave owners. Not that it should have made any difference, but he wasn't. His family were at most third-generation Americans. He hadn't kept it hidden, but his critics hadn't bothered to notice that his middle initial stood for Wilberforce, his mother's maiden name. He was a descendant of one of the world's more important abolitionists. Grayson said, "The swamp creatures we're going to kick out of government are very dishonest. A racist is someone who deals with everything through the filter of race—and that's exactly what these people do. They're despicable. I'm proud of being from South Carolina, and my family's heritage."

Beyond a President Grayson Chase, there was that other critical piece needed for accomplishing the mission. And that relied on Charles Knight.

Jeffrey rarely met with Grayson during the campaign. Questions might arise. Most communication was by encrypted phone. Grayson trusted Jeffrey with his important undertakings. The most important undertaking had to be Naked Emperor. Grayson knew public schools, colleges, and the media had managed to make socialism cool and fashionable. Only people who lied to themselves could consider coercion, death, and destruction cool. Other than a lifetime of study and contemplation (few people had the makings of a Taoist monk), there existed only one known and proven cure for people who lie to themselves: Sybillene. Naked Emperor. Currently the most illegal drug in the world.

The miracle drug that cured the worst mental illness was illegal because the criminally insane were in charge of the asylum and were dead set on keeping that control.

All his hopes to free Americans from their own government relied upon Sybillene. Charles Knight's drug might turn the impossible into the possible.

"How's it going with Knight?" Grayson asked Jeffrey, before even asking about his health, or his sister.

"Nice to talk to you too, Grayson," Jeffrey replied. "Stresses of the campaign getting to you, huh? Unpleasant job you've chosen for yourself. And not only unpaid, but you're paying to do it."

"You told me more than once that I'm an idiot."

"Well... you're at least bordering on altruism."

Grayson replied. "No, Jeffrey. It's not altruism. I'm just trying to achieve a personal goal, more of a daydream, actually. Which is to help the good people left in America get a final chance. If this country goes down, there's no place to run. Sure, I could withdraw to some bolthole in the Southern Hemisphere until people return to their senses. But that could take decades, and I don't like hunkering down or ceding ground. A lot of people have died for the idea of personal freedom. Lots more will die. Maybe me. So let's just think about winning this thing."

"Grayson, I know your thinking, and you know I agree. I'm just glad I'm not you. What can I do to help? What's the biggest item on your plate?"

"I need to know when you think Knight will be ready to bring Sybillene back?"

"I've been moving that ball down the field, very gently."

"You've been prioritizing your own venture with him, haven't you?"

"You have your goal, I have mine, Grayson. It's not like he's going to climb back into the drug world just because I ask him to. I've planted the seed, and, although Charles doesn't know it yet, he and I are about to start working together very closely. That work hopefully will set us up to get what you need."

"Thanks, Jeffrey. You'll be in charge of my security once I'm elected."

"Yeah, that's just what a libertarian president needs—a chief of the secret police." They both knew it was a joke, but there was some truth to it. It was an inevitable part of politics. "I wish I were already. Don't forget that you're fully eligible for Secret Service protection. There are dangerous people starting to look at you seriously. Mordor will soon release its Black Riders. It's two months to the election. You're a major candidate. Obama had protection for two years prior to his election."

Grayson sighed. "Narcissists enjoy that sort of attention. I don't. We've talked about this before. Thirty-eight thousand dollars per day the taxpayers will have to pay in order to keep themselves away from me. The money isn't even a rounding error, but the idea is perverse. I'm trying to save them money, not steal their money."

Jeffrey said, "Hey, that's a good line. Use it next time a journalist asks you about protection. But don't use that bullshit on me. You are a target, Grayson. You can count on that."

"You've put good men next to me. Unlike the Secret Service, they don't report up their chain of command to my biggest opponent—President Cooligan. I promise not to defy the counsel of your men, Jeffrey. I'm not looking for more problems. Between you and me, I'll be ready to resign on day one."

"Your vice president won't like that."

Grayson considered. "You really are worried I'm gonna get shot, aren't you? Won't the bastards wait 'til after the election, at least long enough to see how much they like the VP?"

"It's easier to get to you now, Grayson."

"I hear you."

"I'm going to arrange for a dozen more guards. You got that boarding house on your property finished yet?"

"Things move slower when I'm not there in person. It'll be done in a month or less."

"Then my extra men will bunk in the hotel when you're at home. What's your schedule in the next couple of weeks?"

"Stumping, TV, radio, and podcasts up and down the Left Coast."

"Is California even worth trying?"

"Yes. Obviously California isn't going to vote for a Republican. Lear

366

doesn't even show her face there. And Cooligan can't win without California. Turns out that Cooligan and I are running pretty close there. I'm catching up. Older Californians don't like him because he's a plastic wind-up doll, a hybrid clone of Dan Quayle or Al Gore. Younger Californians don't like him because he's establishment and pushed hard for the SEA. People know that, and that agency upset a lot of Californians. They know I want to abolish the SEA. To counter my threat and generate more support in California, Cooligan's had to move far to the left. He's espousing all the ideas of the socialists that he ran against in the past. That gives the Republican PACs great big targets for their artillery in other states."

Jeffrey said, "Don't change a damn thing you're doing. You're close."

Grayson sighed again. "It'll all be for nothing if I don't win. Or if you can't get Naked Emperor back. They're equal priorities."

"I know," Jeffrey replied. "I know."

41

Truth or Lies

"ETERIO, I'm glad to catch you while you're here in DC. You'll probably agree my bunny has a good nose, as they say in the market."

"I've been noticing," Eterio Conti replied. "Bullets flying everywhere."

"Yes." Forestal wouldn't risk taking credit for arranging all this, but he couldn't entirely contain his self-satisfaction.

"And now the Lincoln Tunnel shooting."

Forestal was not sure whether that was Lichen's doing or the work of one of the many copycats. Either way, he was the catalyst. So the credit was his.

Eterio smiled as he spoke. "The media are hopping. Donations are flooding into the AntiNRA Campaign, so I hear. The NRA is rolling over on its back wetting itself. You wouldn't fault me for wondering if there's more coming?"

"I have no doubt about that. But, as you know, there's not a one-to-one correspondence between what happens in the real world and what happens in the market. How much are you up?"

"With my options, four hundred percent."

"Well, an excellent return for a low-risk speculation in less than two months. Naturally, I can't be sure how long these shootings might go on," he lied. "But, nothing lasts forever. From a financial viewpoint, when the ducks are quacking, you should feed them. Time to reverse course, Eterio."

"Ahh. I'm a believer in the old saying, 'If you buy on Jones's advice, you'd better sell on Jones's advice.' It's probably a good time to supply newbie investors with gun stocks, now that they have a good track record. I won't expect things to stay... let's say fast and furious... for much longer. Time to hit the bid, then."

Forestal had to laugh cynically at the choice of words—a direct reminder of one of ATF's many missteps under previous leadership. The agency was famous for attracting macho types rejected by the FBI for insufficient mental equipment and psychological stability.

"Who are you getting to sponsor your legislation?"

"Everybody wants to get in front of resolving the Gun Crisis of the Millennium. I've already rounded up a dozen senators and twenty congressmen. They're falling over themselves to get their names attached. This is the biggest thing since 9/11. Easy. They can smell free publicity. I could probably get half of Congress to sponsor these bills if I wanted to, but why waste the time? And sponsors are more likely to actually read the bills."

"That a problem?"

"The bills are well crafted—innocuous on the surface, and bipartisan. But a particularly bright or cynical guy with some imagination might see how these bills could be used, and fight to table them. The smart play is to push them through fast during the crisis."

"Can you send me copies of them?"

"Together they address trade, tariffs, and ammunition controls. They'll be on your desk tomorrow." He didn't feel the urge to tell Conti any details of his additional initiative, the diamond in the rough. Indeed, the third bill wasn't a bill. Rather it would be added as an amendment to whatever happened to be up for congressional vote when the right time came. But he'd give Conti some hints.

"Give me the bottom line, Forestal. I don't have the time or patience for translating legalese. I suspect none of those idiots are going to read them either."

Both men understood the way the system worked. Typically, over twelve thousand bills were introduced every session, and perhaps four hundred became law. Even if that were the only thing a congressman did, it would be impossible to read but a fraction of them.

"Understood. The bills only need to be about three pages apiece, but I've built them to about four hundred pages apiece—most of it historical information, data tables, and interpretation of precedents. It kept the interns busy for two months putting them together. The bills should spend a day in committee, and then it's off to the races to resolve the crisis. Suffice it to say, when they're all passed, the only legal gun owners remaining will have been screened and trained by, or working for, the United States government."

Conti smiled. "You mean under the auspices of your very own ATF?"

"It's much broader than that."

Conti didn't push, but then he shook his head. "And you think you're going to work around the Second Amendment nuts?"

"This wave is going to wash away resistance like sand castles on the beach, but you asked for the bottom line. These aren't gun control laws that might run afoul of the Second Amendment. We're taking a different tack. Using their own argument against them. They're always saying guns aren't the problem, people are the problem. Okay, fine. We can work with that. These are people-control laws."

"And the Supreme Court? Will they concur?"

"Even the current Supreme Court won't be able to find a constitutional argument they can make with a straight face."

"You're cocky."

"For good reason. Very shortly the court will be smaller, and the balance will have shifted to our purpose."

Conti snorted. "Well, if you expect some supremes to be changing out, I assume you're also hoping that Grayson Chase gets derailed. If he's elected, I can't see him going along with any of this. He's not on our team."

Forestal replied, "I don't understand what he's all about or how he thinks, but he's more than a wild card. He's a loose cannon." Forestal envisioned an eighteenth-century sailing vessel where, if a cannon broke loose from its mounts, it could crash a hole through the hull of the Ship of State.

Conti noted, "He's at twenty-seven percent in the polls. With a very high approval rating. Eighty percent or so. Something going to be done about that?"

"I'm sure somebody will do something." Forestal chuckled.

*   *   *

The IRS leaked Grayson Chase's tax returns. The media reported that he kept billions of dollars offshore. They spun this as cheating the government: "not paying his 'fair' share."

This effort to put him on the defensive irritated Grayson. So he came forward to answer on a late-night comedy channel, which was more trusted and more viewed than the conventional news. His response made headlines everywhere the next morning. He'd spoken with an unusual degree of fervor while maintaining his usual Southern manners.

"First, let me say I'm not apologizing or making excuses. That's my money. I've paid the taxes due on every penny of it, and I've a right to do whatever I like with it—just like you do with your money. I'm not spending it on yachts and caviar. And I guarantee I'm not spending it on lobbying for sweetheart deals to sell two-hundred-dollar hammers and fifteen-hundred-dollar toilet seats to the government.

"That money is offshore because I don't want my opponents—your opponents—running for president to have any access to it. I don't want them using it to start their wars, pay off their Wall Street pals, use it as hush money, or make deals with their cronies to get richer.

"Would you want me to give either one of those two any of that good money? I mean, I may be a naïve country boy, but that seems like a pretty bad idea!" The crowds laughed and applauded. "Or does it make more sense that I preserve it where it is, so that I can bring it back here after you all kick those bums out of office and shake 'em off like the fleas they are?"

Populist rhetoric was always popular. Especially when it came from a man who was actually of the people. Most didn't just accept it, they relished it. No dodging, no backtracking, no excuses or apologies.

The younger crowd, who'd failed to get one of their overtly socialist heroes into the running, turned to Chase as a way to throw the bums out. He was diametrically opposed to socialism, but he acknowledged their valid complaints while suggesting that there was more than one way to skin a cat.

He didn't win over a majority of the youth, but they listened to what he said, if only because it was different and entertaining. He was logical, even if they didn't like hearing it. He won over some freethinkers, but a few speeches on campus and some late-night comedy-show exposure couldn't make up for years of economic miseducation and indoctrination in rabidly deviant ethics.

He gave away millions of pamphlets that some people actually read. He put together the obligatory campaign book that detailed how to resolve their concerns—just not the way they had expected. Most college kids were more interested in drinking, hooking up, and protesting on the quad than reading books. It was understandable; at certain times of life, some things are a lot more important than others. Lots of them didn't have much imagination and saw college as preparation for wasting a couple more years—and accumulating more debt—in graduate school for a master's degree in Social Entrepreneurship and Change.

"You can't fix stupid," Grayson would sometimes remark.

He never referenced the other candidates by name, only discussing what they wanted to do and their ideas. He didn't insult them; he mostly ignored them while discussing his plans.

The big question of the late-summer campaign season was whether he would join the other two on the debate stage. He didn't ask to be included; he just said he would join if he were invited. Since he was polling at over a quarter of the likely voters, not inviting him would have delegitimized the whole exercise.

The well-known moderator—a descendant of billionaires himself— ignored Grayson in the first debate. For every three questions he posed to President Chris Cooligan or Senator Heather Lear, he posed one question to Grayson, and that question was about one of the other two candidates.

The Guns Rule issue provided an important wedge. Pundits expected Cooligan to be rabidly anti-gun, but he stayed surprisingly calm, just reeling off standard lines about the important role of government in mental health, normally a Republican talking point. Senator Heather Lear—the other candidate—couldn't attack him. The moderator cut Grayson off almost immediately during his response and redirected first to Cooligan and then to Lear. Grayson took it calmly enough the first time.

The second time was during a minimum wage discussion. He winked at the audience.

The third time, he gave the audience the thumbs up while smiling at the moderator.

But the fourth time, he rolled his eyes as some in the audience groaned sympathetically. Then he defied the rules. With his battery-operated microphone clamped to his lapel, he walked to the front of the stage, onto the floor past the moderator and out into the audience. He held the microphone out to a seemingly random person and said, "I expect this young woman will ask an important question." All eyes were on her.

"How can you tolerate this sort of treatment from the moderator, Mr. Chase?"

"Well, it's going to be hard enough to fix corrupt. But you simply can't fix stupid."

The audience roared in applause.

When the noise settled down, he added, "I tolerate this dismissive treatment only because it shows how important it is that we change the direction of our country, and the course of history, in eight weeks."

Which generated even more applause.

Some people thought he was overstepping, but the other two candidates, for all the establishment's money and power, were just empty suits. Side by side with a normal decent human being, the contrast was clear. The pretense that they were popular, loved, and admired evaporated.

"I'm mad as hell, and I'm not going to take it anymore!" became a meme, even among those who'd never seen the movie that had first popularized it. It was shouted from doorways and apartment windows. It morphed into an internet video challenge that spread the word to millions more who were pleased that a man, who not only wasn't a jerk but actually had old-fashioned virtues, was on the ballot in November, for the first time in memory.

Someone for whom they wouldn't be embarrassed to cast their vote.

Bumper stickers and bobbleheads appeared. Grayson Chase's book climbed to number one on the bestseller lists.

As hard as the system tried to make people hate him, and even though he didn't want to be president, Grayson Chase rose further up the polls.

42

A Subtle Air Strike

THEY MET only eight times per year, and Charles wanted to advance his plans ahead of the next one. He got to Bethesda early to observe what he hoped would happen.

One of the governors of the Federal Reserve Board lived alone in a grand house. After her last child had grown and left home, her husband fled as well. Charles didn't know why, but he could guess. Jeffrey had shown him evidence that appeared unequivocal. If she had a good side, it had been overwhelmed long ago. Charles had studied the available details on all seven members of this elite club. The president of the United States selected each to serve for a fourteen-year term. Few of them ever did, averaging two years. Among the current seven, the longest-serving member had held the position for six years. A sane person could tolerate being a rubber stamp for only so long.

Old World banking families had successfully transported their systems of financial control to the New World. They recognized not only the power of money, but the power of creating money. It made the mythical Midas touch real: unlimited money at will.

Although its top management were Keynesian ideologues, most of the Fed's twenty thousand employees were just drones. Many truly believed they were doing good, keeping the engine of production greased. They chose to stay oblivious to the fact that their agency was, in fact, the largest counterfeiter on the planet. Their employer's creation of fiat currency and credit caused business cycles, which led to economic collapse, ruining countless lives. It was a direct cause of the wealth disparity that drove the socialist movement and the CityFires.

If Fed employees started using Naked Emperor, however, they'd be unable to lie to themselves—and that alone would destroy the Fed. Paul Samuels knew this, and it was part of why he'd gone all out to destroy Naked Emperor. It was why Federal Reserve employees were tested for Sybillene. Better that the Fed's top dogs were tested for moral insanity.

The Federal Reserve was not the only problem, however. It was just one component of a crony-statist system gone wild. Charles felt that, in an environment as target rich as Washington, disrupting the Fed board's relative non-entities was a misallocation of effort, but for some reason it was front and center in Jeffrey's mind. His list required Charles to neutralize the entire board.

At first he thought of taking them out based on their tenure. Long-serving governors should have had plenty of time to figure out what the Fed was about and left in protest.

But what if one or two stuck it out in a vain attempt to fix the Fed? Maybe to have some positive influence that might reduce the constant transfer of American wealth to the cronies? The vetting system for the Fed board surely minimized any risk of that kind of person sneaking in. But minimal risk was different from no risk. Charles would not risk killing an innocent.

So he—with Jeffrey's tentative consent—intended to use an alternative approach to getting rid of miscreants: smart contracts on the Paladin Network. It might not be necessary to eliminate them physically if they could be completely discredited and disempowered.

Coming to Bethesda would allow Charles to see the spyminers in action on the ground. As he approached Elizabeth Vaneterri's home early in the morning of the last day of August, he saw for himself what Mei-li had described.

In the wild, terms like spyminer morphed on their own. Spyminers were often now spyms. At least two spyms sat in cars, ready to follow, photograph, and video Governor Vaneterri's every move, every relationship. To get in closer, he posed as a neighbor on a morning walk. In the first car, a teenager was staring at a laptop, open against the steering wheel. Was the kid getting schoolwork done while waiting for something to happen? Or was he actively hacking?

He walked thirty yards, past another vehicle where a young woman also stared at a computer, and he caught a glimpse of a device on the passenger seat next to her: a box with switches and lights, giving it the antiquated look of a 1960s Bell Laboratory experiment. He was pretty sure this box was a cell-site simulator—a Stingray, AmberJack, Hailstorm, or KingFish. Supplied by any of a dozen manufacturers whose customers were mostly crooks or spooks. There was no need to package it attractively for the consumer market.

Charles chuckled. The governor of the board—comfortably nestled in her house—had no clue that her mobile phone and Wi-Fi were routed through a spym in a car nearby. The equipment identified the phone's IMSI or ESN. The spym could then put them on the PNet to allow targeting by other spyminers interested in tracking her. As long as a fee were paid to the first spym, of course. The spyminers would capture Vaneterri's metadata, listen in on her phone calls, and read her SMS texts. They could pretend to be Vaneterri, sending false texts and even spoof voice calls.

The spyms knew what websites she visited. If she weren't careful—and most people weren't—once spyminers learned that she banked at, say, Wells Fargo, they could set up a fake landing page that mimicked the Wells Fargo home page. Vaneterri would unknowingly type her username and password to sign in to her bank account, allowing spyminers access to the account on the real bank website, while the target would get a sign-on rejection, which she would attribute to mistyping her password. This could happen to anyone anytime who tried to connect to their bank through their cell phone or from their computer via their hotspots if they weren't careful. Absent two-factor authentication (2FA), it was only a matter of time before anyone got hacked. And even with 2FA in place, there are ways.

It was the first time Charles had seen spyminers in action. He didn't know their identities, which were anonymized and encrypted in the Paladin Network. They were gig-economy types, working for fun and profit and on the lookout for the big score. It was hard to say why, out of the rapidly increasing number of contracts on offer, they'd chosen Vaneterri as a target. Maybe a personal interest in her. Maybe just the size of the bounty Charles himself had offered.

The ecosystem's members created virtual identities for themselves. Perhaps the two spyms were PacMan and HarryHermione, or maybe the popular HotPockets and Cakewalk. Or any of hundreds of other conditionally anonymous spyminers in the DC area alone.

Soon there would be more spyms in DC than Uber drivers. Many would be both. As Washington and New York distilled cronyism toward two hundred proof, it was only natural that spyminers would be concentrated where the action was. Supply and demand.

Meanwhile, motivated by the contract money, behind the scenes in soft chairs and comfortable rooms scattered throughout the globe, hackers delved into every communication Vaneterri had, every purchase she made, every meeting she held. They'd bash through firewalls and gather passwords, sometimes with brute force, sometimes with subtle intelligence, sometimes by paying a spym for a hacked password. Charles didn't know how they did it. He was once an expert in computers, but the complexity of hacking had grown even faster than Moore's law itself. Just the time he'd been in the cooler relegated him to an electronic Stone Age. He had more important things to do than reinvent the wheel in order to catch up. It was a profession unto itself, a subculture with members ranging from military hackers in Russia to college kids in Berkeley.

Vast amounts of targeted information were becoming a decentralized open-sourced foil to the NSA, just as Charles had first contemplated. The spyminers—the paparazzi of the Paladin Network—had begun work as soon as Charles had initiated the smart contract on the Board of Governors. They'd been earning Paladins by collecting and disseminating data. The number and value of spyms grew as the network effect, Metcalfe's law, took hold. The value of Paladins grew exponentially too. There were only a limited number of Paladins. They were the only way to access the Paladin Network or to buy information collected by spyminers, and the best way to purchase vigilante expertise.

Anybody who was anybody inside the DC Beltway was already being watched and tracked by spyminers; someone was almost always there to snap a picture, record a location, identify a contact, or intercept a text. The data were fed into the expanding decentralized network and connected with the evolving companion AI network, which was still in its infancy. The PNet consolidated intelligence on each individual. Upon full analysis, this would provide Charles—or someone else—with the information needed to justify the appropriate action.

Charles channeled a great deal of data to Maurice. It seemed his brain could compete with artificial intelligence. His mind was like a quantum computer, performing numerous calculations to come up with probabilistic answers to drive him toward likely outcomes from unlikely connections. He concluded that Elizabeth Vaneterri was mired deeply in the swamp—a crony among cronies. Jeffrey had his reasons for wanting to eliminate this woman, and now Charles could see them.

Deep down, Charles hoped that the data would in some way exonerate these people. But he knew revolutions weren't polite Sunday school picnics. Some people would just need to die.

*   *   *

Sabina Heidel patted her handbag.

She'd grown accustomed to the best rooms in the best hotels. So when she found herself in a two- star Quality Inn, with its fiberboard furniture, polystyrene shower, and rayon bedspreads with dark patterns designed to hide stains, she felt disgust. Grayson Chase's campaign staff must love the man if they were willing to stay here. Or perhaps it was all they were used to. But why would a billionaire camp out among the commoners?

Two men in suits, earpieces, and lapel microphones kept station in the lobby. They were the obvious part of his protection team, but she noted other paid security types: three men in loose-fitting clothes sipping club sodas at the bar.

The elevator arrived slowly, slowly opened its doors, slowly closed them, and slowly carried her to the third floor. When she finally emerged, a man and a woman greeted her politely, had her sign a book, waved a wand over her, and searched her purse before conducting her to Chase's suite.

It wasn't a proper suite, but two connecting rooms with an open double door between. One was set up as a temporary office, with papers thrown on the bed. A staff member sat on the threadbare couch, reading documents. At least the room was well lit, a modest compensation for its general dinginess.

Chase came through the door from the adjoining room and held out his hand. He was fit and good-looking, but his clothes were clearly off-the-rack. No tasseled loafers, but shoes that screamed "I'm from the middle-American hinterland." He was ordinary looking, projecting a folksy image. Sabina was impressed with how well he pulled it off. A tour de force of subtle but clever populist marketing. She was sure the rubes ate it up.

"Ms. Heidel, I presume?"

She reached out and shook his hand firmly, looking him in the eyes. "Thank you for squeezing me in to your schedule."

Grayson quickly appraised her dress, shoes, and general look. "You're questioning the digs, I'd wager. I can afford more luxury, of course. But it's a way of showing how I plan on running the executive branch... very lean, the way I'm running this campaign." He looked over at his staff member, a young man, casually dressed in jeans and a button-down shirt. "So it's not going to get better than this, Liam."

Sabina smiled at the young man, reflexively studying his face, but letting him notice her eyes scan his body as well. He smiled politely in a way that said he couldn't care less about her short black dress and centerfold body. So he's gay. Perfect.

Grayson said, "I understand that a Mr. Paul Samuels wants to discuss the economy with me. He's sent you to prep me, is that it? Teach me some basic economics?"

"Well, Grayson—I hope you don't mind being on first-name terms— you're best known as an investor and a businessman. I don't know if you've studied economics. I'm here more to answer your questions."

Grayson replied, "I expected the Federal Reserve folks to come visit if I won the election. I haven't won. Not yet."

"You're well on your way."

"Two months left. Anything can happen. What do you have for me, Ms. Heidel?"

This was likely the one and only time she'd ever meet this man. There was no need to score political points. She had only one mission here this evening. "Can we sit down?"

Chase waved her toward a spare chair and sat himself on the bed after Liam helped slide a round table between them. She leaned forward in the awkward seating as she placed some colored charts between them. They illustrated GDP growth, the CPI, the money supply, deficits, debt, and other economic factors.

"Grayson, we think it's important to give you our view on what's happening in the current crisis... but also hear your thoughts. We're all in the boat together, and we want to help you guide it in the best way possible." They talked for an hour, Sabina making a show of pursuing his questions and noting them. Her only interest was to keep his attention until the young man stepped out or took a break to use the small bathroom. He didn't.

When she sensed Grayson losing interest and moving to close the meeting, she resorted to another tactic. She turned to the young assistant. "Do you have ice water?"

Chase nodded to his subordinate, who opened the door and wedged it wide, saying, "Back in a flash" as he nodded to the security team. One large man in a suit came over and stood in the door.

Chase said, "Sorry about the supervision, Ms. Heidel."

"I understand. You can't be in a hotel room alone with a woman."

"Sadly, that's pretty much the way things are in today's world."

"You're safe with me." She smiled and pulled her weapon from her purse. "My mother bought me this new perfume," she lied, holding up an elegant little spray bottle. "What do you think?" She put her wrist toward his nose for him to smell.

He moved his nose toward her wrist and sniffed. "I don't smell anything."

"Nothing?" She sniffed her own wrist. "Well, I guess it's a bit faint. Just between you and me I've got a big date tonight, and I need a man's opinion. Here. I'll freshen it up." She held the bottle out and sprayed toward her wrist, but the mist mostly missed her skin and spread through the air toward Grayson's face.

He instinctively pulled back.

"Oh gosh," Sabina said, with exaggerated concern. "I didn't mean to get my fragrance all over you. Bad aim. I'm so sorry!" She reached into her purse to pull out a tissue, itself also pre-treated with the ingredient in the perfume bottle.

He took it and wiped around his eyes and mouth.

"It's okay, Ms. Heidel. I've survived worse."

No, you haven't, Sabina thought to herself.

Chase added, "I still don't smell anything." He sniffed at the tissue. "Or maybe I do and don't know it?"

She sniffed the air as she studied the bottle. "It is a subtle scent. Not very strong."

She was amused as she lied. It was plenty strong.

Liam returned with the ice water as Sabina stood up and went to wash her hands.

For appearances, they talked for another ten minutes about the European Central Bank and Italy's impending default. Then she took her leave.

She'd never see the man again.

43

Raise and Re-raise

IT'S SAID that a father is no happier than his saddest child. Love for a grandchild is more than an extension of the love for a child, however. In fact, even if a parent has come to dislike his child, he's still inclined to love his grandchild. Odd in a way, since his genetic bond to a grandchild is only half as strong as the one to the child.

Grandparents may have less direct control and less responsibility to provide security, education, and opportunity for a grandchild than for their direct offspring. On the other hand, the grandfather might be motivated to correct mistakes made with his own child. And a grandfather might be retired and have more time to influence a granddaughter.

This wasn't Oscar Littleton's case. This grandfather was busier now, at age seventy-five, than ever before. A highly demanding schedule kept his mind working overtime during session. His job was not only intellectually and emotionally stimulating, sometimes it was even fun. The fact that it was important and worthwhile, however, only partially compensated for the time he missed in his role of grandfather. That's why he relished the summer recess, right up to the first Monday in October when the next session began. During summer, he tried very hard to be the attentive granddad.

So tonight he would watch his granddaughter's performance. He would even arrive on time, and he texted his daughter to that effect. "On my way."

Being a full-time granddad was still just an ideal. In reality, even during breaks he went to his office more days than not. There was so much to do. Sometimes he felt he was singlehandedly holding back the barbarians at the gates. His clerk handed him his briefcase and called the garage to bring up his car. "Good night, Justice Littleton."

"Goodnight, Preston. See you at 6:00 a.m.?"

"Of course, sir."

"Can you analyze those briefs we have left from Dilkins?"

There was a brief lag before responding. "I'll have them completed."

"Sorry, Preston."

"It's my job, sir."

Clerking for a Supreme Court justice brought prestige and provided an entrée to money and influence. Littleton knew that the job's demands put an unpredictable kink in the young man's social life. His girlfriend, Marcia, might kick him off the love boat if he kept breaking dates. He knew he should cut the clerk some slack now, while there was flexibility in the schedule. In six weeks, when the session was fully engaged, the clerk's work would double; he'd barely have time to eat and sleep.

Like most of the justices, Littleton drove his own car. It kept his feet on the ground and him in touch with the common man. It was one of many ways he differed from most high government officials in DC. Most of the self-important class found some reason for their agencies to get them a driver.

He drove a black Lincoln Town Car, twelve years old but with low mileage. Outdated perhaps, but substantial without being ostentatious. And reliable. It fit his persona while still blending in with prestige-conscious Washington and allowing him to remain reasonably anonymous. He did some of his best thinking while driving.

The Dilkins case wasn't currently active, but it would be important come October. There'd been no clean way through it. The Constitution simply wasn't written as clearly as it might have been. The founders had assumed their descendants would continue to understand the language of the late eighteenth century, but the meanings of words change over time, and this allowed for different interpretations as the years passed, transferring power away from anyone who could read plain English to etymologists and constitutional scholars. The document had become less accessible, less relevant, and less real to a nonspecialist. This opened the door to the argument that the Bill of Rights was changeable, a "living document," as they liked to say. That sounded good. Who liked dead things? And if something was alive, that meant it could change, mutate… even transform completely.

To the perverters of the Constitution, the "rights" it specified became more like guidelines, and the first ten amendments were no longer permanent and immutable. Wherever they could, they weakened the Bill of Rights precisely because it was intended to keep exactly the kind of people who inhabited DC from running roughshod over their subjects in the rest of the country.

Justice Littleton drove through Georgetown, up Wisconsin Avenue past the Naval Observatory, and approached the National Cathedral. He turned east a few blocks and managed to find the Trapier Theater at St. Albans School, where his granddaughter's class was doing a performance. He failed to notice the car following him all the way from the Supreme Court building. Why should he? DC had at least a dozen law enforcement agencies on guard; it was the most heavily policed city in the world. A Supreme Court justice had never been assassinated, and they were rarely targeted.

He had a good life. A good career. He was secure, his family was well off and safe. At least for now. Security was ephemeral, an illusion. The course of the world scared him. The nation teetered on the very cusp of something far beyond what most Americans even considered possible. The elite in the big cities, who mostly dealt in paper and digital entries, were at odds with those they considered yokels in the hinterland, who worked on farms, factories, and in mines to produce real goods. It was a disruption of the bonds of congeniality that might presage a civil war.

He thought back to last session, to when he'd received clear and credible threats that his family would be targeted and killed if he didn't vote to refuse hearing a very politically charged case that questioned the constitutionality of the SEA's expanded authorities. He justified and rationalized his acquiescence to the demand. Everything was politically charged these days; it was worse than the late '60s.

But the guilt he suffered made him resolve that he would never roll over again. Yielding to that extortion had proven the lowest point of his life. He'd made a bad decision based on fear.

It was an ever more common mistake in the country. Fear dominated reason.

Those thoughts retreated from his mind as he considered what he would do once the evening concluded. He looked forward to putting on his pajamas and robe, sitting in his favorite chair, reading more of Gibbon's Decline and Fall, and sipping brandy until he fell asleep. Along with thirty minutes of exercise in the morning, the brandy formed part of his daily routine, a comfort each evening.

He parked close to the theater and walked in. His daughter held a seat for him. They hadn't yet dimmed the lights. As was true of almost everyone here, she covered her nose and mouth with a designer mask.

He wore a simple muslin mask, and only because it was required here, while hoping the hysteria would die down soon.

"Wow, Dad. I'm impressed you're here." His daughter's devoted smile warmed him even though he could not see much of her face. He'd been a good father, but he wanted to be an even better grandfather.

"Well, every now and then I accomplish something that I intend, Suzi. It's good to get out. You know what they say about all work and no play."

"I wish SCOTUS would never go back in session. It's so nice to have you around. Thanks for coming, Daddy." Suzi tilted her brunette head down onto her father's shoulder.

"Have the kids even had time to practice this? School just started last week."

"It's mostly just for show. To make things seem more normal, finally. Things have been so strange."

Justice Littleton nodded. "You know how much I love being near you and Q, even if it's just in the audience." The only reservation he had about the wonderful little girl was her name, Quincy. It was … unisex, blurring the difference between boys and girls. Perhaps this was intended to make girls more assertive and more masculine, and boys more passive, more feminine. He suspected that, instead, it just confused the hell out of them. If the media knew he held these thoughts, they would arrange to have him impeached for high crimes and misdemeanors against all that was politically correct. He called his granddaughter Q, and said it stood for Qualia, a philosophical concept meaning she should believe her own direct experiences instead of what she was told.

He reached over and grasped Suzi's hand. She squeezed back. She was beautiful, loving, and had good character—traits she'd inherited from him and her now-deceased mother. As busy as he was, he'd trusted her upbringing to the school system and—truth be known—her friends, most of whom were in the same position. She was bright, but conventional, and she mostly had the thoughts and values that people who grow up in an upmarket suburb absorb by osmosis.

Her marriage had broken up badly, which was par for the course these days, almost expected. He had liked Tom well enough. A partner in a law firm—Washington had not just thousands, but tens of thousands of lawyers. His firm was actually a lobbying outfit thinly disguised as a law firm. The legal patina made the money bigger and gave them cover.

Suzi worked for an environmental NGO. Not too strident a group, but still a termite eating away at the foundations of Western civilization in general, and of the US in particular. She'd fallen into it after college, wanting to be "relevant" and do "good." It was all the more reason he needed to spend a lot more time with Q.

The lights dimmed, and applause filled the small theater, packed to capacity with the parents of the young performers. The darkness didn't allow him to spot in the program when Q's age group would emerge. Introductions and thank-yous went on interminably. Maybe he could rest his eyes for a bit.

"Her class is up next," his daughter whispered in his ear, interrupting the nap.

He applauded along with everyone else. Then twenty cute five-year-olds, disguised as yellow dandelions with yellow surgical masks, nervously worked their way on stage. He didn't recognize the music, but at least it wasn't rap, metal, or hip-hop. He really wasn't clear on which was which. The little flowers danced to the music. It took a minute, but he picked out his granddaughter. The faces looked alike, barely visible under the large round crepe petals and obscured with oversized face masks, but Q's bouncy gait grabbed his attention. Yes. The second on the right. How he loved that little girl. He wiped away the tears misting his eyes.

As the little girls danced, making up in cuteness and self-consciousness what they lacked in coordination, the sound of gunshots filled the theater. The fourth in a long series of percussions was the last thing that Justice Littleton ever heard, because the fifth round took off the back of his head. The shooter, using an AR-15, then emptied four well-aimed thirty-round magazines into the theater in under three minutes. Q's mother was among the many casualties.

Some of the little girls, including Justice Littleton's granddaughter, just kept dancing, reflexively, right through the catastrophic onslaught. They didn't understand what was happening. None were injured. At least not physically.

44

Back to School

CHEMNITZ Lichen kept his face mask on while he drove.

Twenty-five minutes later, with the barrel of his weapon still cooling, Chemnitz drove onto Interstate 66. He aimed for the town of Haymarket, about forty miles west of Washington. He threw a mock salute at the NRA's shining glass headquarters on the south side of the highway as he sped by it.

Haymarket was typical of many Northern Virginia suburbs, crammed with lookalike houses to shelter the cogs in Washington's machine. The place wasn't a town so much as a giant planned development. The dominant life-forms appeared to be SUVs mated to ecologically righteous hybrid cars parked in the driveways of tightly packed gray houses far too big and expensive for the median serf to afford. Asphalt covered everything except a few blades of grass, left behind to act as reminders of why the place was called Haymarket. Each morning, the highways filled up with human worker bees on an hour-long drive away from family and into the maw of the beast that fed them.

He drove through the outskirts of Haymarket on his way to the elementary school. It took six minutes to negotiate the twisted roads—Pleasant View, Meadow Hill, Quail Ridge, Forest Lakes. The names must have been created by an ad agency with a perverse sense of humor; they either commemorated what the subdivision destroyed, or they had been invented out of whole cloth, for there were no ridges, meadows, or forests—and no lakes, not even a pond. Certainly no quail. He pulled into the empty parking lot, turned off his lights, and studied the school's entrance and grounds.

The new elementary school was a low-lying island in a parking lot that had been a cornfield ten years earlier and a tobacco field thirty years before that. It was out of the question for residents of the thousands of cookie-cutter houses to let their kids walk to school. Instead the commuters dropped their kids off on their way to shuffling papers. Out here, they were mostly midlevel government bureaucrats, newly minted lawyers, aspiring lobbyists, and contractors sucking off a hind teat. They all hoped their superiors would one day recognize their talents, allowing them to move into DC proper. The elementary school served as an indoctrination center for the next generation of indentured servants—including, among others, a half dozen children of employees of the AntiNRA Campaign to Control Gun Violence.

Chemnitz knew them all by name, because Forestal was that good. Forestal had his quirks, for sure, but he was more competent than most. He liked to kill his women sometimes. Or so Chemnitz's brother, Dresden, had told him. But at least Forestal stayed logical and efficient.

Whereas Chemnitz had chosen his previous targets for convenience and ease, the long leash he'd been promised got tighter near DC. His cousin Sabina had selected this next day's four targets to create hysteria among Beltway commuters, anger among the aristocracy, vengeance from the military, and mayhem from the social justice crowd. Blowing up an elementary school full of DC apparatchiks' kids would be a piece of cake, and AntiNRA Campaign employees' kids were like a fat maraschino cherry to top it off.

The number of students at Haymarket Elementary whose parents worked for the National Rifle Association had increased just in the last month. Now there were sixteen. He could only imagine the playground culture clash between them and the AntiNRA bunch. Chances were the right-wingers would win most of the fistfights.

Following on the heels of his successful elimination of a Supreme Court justice, conveniently disguised by the mass murder of thirty-five bystanders—a bit of a twofer—tomorrow's multiple-site onslaught would be the grand climax to a well-orchestrated series of events.

Chemnitz considered the Guns Rule movement that he'd fostered. The tag had appeared in dozens of cities, was painted on highway overpasses, and had started internet memes. He'd done none of that. All that was the work of others, frustrated and disgusted with the culture of America and eager for violence, for revolution, for war.

Few cars were out after 10:00 p.m. One drove by in each direction during the next minute, then none for the next five minutes. Chemnitz got out of his car, rustled around in his trunk, put a black bag over his shoulder, and walked toward the school building. He peered into the classroom windows and through the doors as he moved quickly to where he needed to work. He performed his planned task and then circled the building before returning across the empty lot to his car.

* * *

"Not fast enough, Charles."

Charles wasn't happy about this. Jeffrey had come right to the hotel room in Foggy Bottom and knocked on the door. How the hell had he found him?

Jeffrey continued speaking as Charles opened the door. "We need to accelerate things. After tonight, I think we can be sure what they're up to."

"What's happened?" Charles asked. At this point, any news was almost certainly bad news.

Jeffrey glanced at the dark television screen. "Oh, you haven't heard. Right here in DC. Justice Littleton was attending his granddaughter's Kindergarten dance recital. Another shooting. Maybe thirty or forty people killed and injured. Right near National Cathedral."

"Couple of miles from here." Charles's facial muscles tightened in a scowl. This was turning into a genuine situation with historic consequences. "How many children killed?"

"Seemingly none. The shooter strafed the audience. Possibly targeting Justice Littleton. Or that may just have been bad luck."

"Luck? I doubt it. Littleton is—was—one of the few on that court that actually seemed to have read the Constitution. It's a fair bet someone wanted Littleton out for that reason."

"Most likely."

"Guns Rule?"

"Can't rule that out, but different. No paint."

"Maybe trying to avoid cameras where he can. Lots of them in this city."

"Well, he seems to have gotten away clean. We're dealing with a professional."

Charles said, "But the cameras? Those plus witnesses. They should get the guy soon, yes?"

Jeffrey replied, "Maybe. Some pros are very smart and highly prepared; that's how they become pros. There's almost certainly more than one. My guess is a couple of guys are at work, sometimes setting up a stool pigeon to throw off the scent where they can. None of the agencies even know where to start."

Charles considered. "Yeah. Professional. It's all been professional. From that first one in Texas."

"Texas? That was a kid."

"Maybe the kid did it, Jeffrey. Or maybe he was a puppet. That one smelled wrong, and these all smell the same to me. So now they've come to DC. If someone wants Congress to do something, it's best to hit them where they live. Make the legislators actually feel it, not just pretend to feel it. They're bringing this home." Charles felt both disgust and deja vu. It was reminiscent of what they did to put nails in the coffin of Sybillene. "Presumably all the same perps? If so, who?"

Jeffrey shook his head. "This whole thing reeks. These shooters don't plan on dying—suicide by cop. They're pros, trying to look like amateurs. It's like some of the Naked Emperor shootings. The perp disappears, leaving nothing to track him. A small op is the only way to be sure it stays secret. They'd have to do most of it on their own, changing cars, moving across the country fast to make it look like it's a lot of different people. Whoever's in charge picks defenseless people—kids and the elderly—which simultaneously reduces their risk and increases public sympathy for the victims. They're well informed about security systems, and extremely bold. It feels planned out in advance to look spontaneous."

"And only they know when it will stop." Charles considered. Something important tickled at his brain. For some time before Jeffrey's unexpected intrusion, he'd been studying data coming in from the spyminers on his Federal Reserve targets.

Some new spymining data on Blaize Forestal had come in as well, tying in the intelligence from Maurice's old-fashioned research methodology. Maurice's doubling of the smart-contract pay had attracted a horde of miners to the Forestal gig. It was already a morass of information awaiting analysis by the AI, but one thing particularly caught his eye. According to unverified data, Blaize Forestal had contact with Sabina Heidel.

Sabina Heidel: one of the most charming, beautiful, and high-IQ females on the planet. With a brain wired like that of a reptile, she was devoid of any moral instincts. Her body and social veneer were first-rate disguises for a first-rate criminal mind.

She'd been on the front lines of Paul Samuels's efforts to destroy Naked Emperor. She was capable of anything, including orchestrating the shootings that two years earlier had sealed the drug's fate. He didn't think of Sabina often, but he should have already put out a spymining contract on her at the same time he'd done so on Paul Samuels. He would rectify this. Sabina Heidel kept emerging like a snake from underneath a rock, ready to sink her teeth into him.

"It's a reach," Charles said. "Perhaps a far reach. But this Blaize Forestal character… I wonder if he might be involved. Forestal has money and a relevant position." He didn't feel a need to mention the Sabina Heidel angle. That was personal.

Jeffrey replied. "I've met Forestal and detest him for a bunch of reasons. He's interim head of ATF now, with some control over SEA as well. It may be a long shot, Charles, but is your gut telling you something?"

"Nothing beyond a suspicion, really. A hypothesis worth evaluating."

"I've got a proposition for you. You and I need to learn how to work together. You want to take a flyer and see how spymining works firsthand? After all, the chairman of the board should have some hands-on experience with the ground floor of his business. I'll bet spymining is pretty much like being a taxi driver or a detective in LA—lots of sitting in a car, watching and waiting. Consider it an experiment. I'm free this evening. Let's join forces and see what Forestal might be up to."

"We can give it a go. Although we can't be spyminers. Haven't signed up."

Jeffrey replied, "Maybe I signed up?"

"You wouldn't risk that."

"Unless I counted on your honesty and the conditional anonymity to keep me protected from even your prying eyes. It's true that I don't yet completely trust you, Charles, just like you don't completely trust me. Maybe working directly with each other will help. Any chance the Paladin Network knows where Forestal is right now?"

"Possible. They aren't everywhere, but they don't have all that many targets yet either." Charles replied. He opened his computer, set up a VPN, routed through Tor, and entered the network. His previous smart contract on the chain provided his payment for services requested as he accessed the last reported location of Blaize Forestal. Journalists and vigilantes could access the same information. All they needed to do was pay.

The Paladin Proof traded on fifteen exchanges with sixty trading pairs; it had become quite liquid. Since it was a crypto with a specialized use, buyers and sellers typically used an on-ramp like Bitcoin or Ether to buy or sell it. Several precious-metals dealers were using gold to buy and sell Paladins. Likely it would soon trade directly into the local fiat—in this case the US dollar—without first having to go through Bitcoin. As the network grew along with spyminers' incomes, Paladin Proofs became more fungible and liquid.

The value proposition was real and palpable. The spyminers might, conceivably, change the information dynamics of the world. Perhaps someday they would displace journalists as the public source of information about the activities and whereabouts of criminals in general, and miscreants in the government/crony complex in particular. It wouldn't take much, since the population had largely lost respect for the integrity of most journalists.

"Hmm. Looks like one of the spyms invested some of his or her new-found capital in a GPS tracker and stuck it on Forestal's car. That should earn them an ongoing royalty from anyone interested in tracking Forestal. People like us, for instance." Charles examined the map on his screen. "He's not too far away."

"In DC?"

"Yes. Near Union Station." Charles face took on something between a grin and a sneer. "Let's go check the place out."

"Metro or car?"

"It's evening. Let's use the car."

"You're driving a private car, Charles. The cameras will catch it. You're asking for trouble."

"Frankly, it doesn't much matter where I go, or how, at this point. There's always a risk. So I'm in a friend's car."

Jeffrey interrupted. "Xander Winn's."

Charles looked at him evenly and said, "To protect my friend from the possible consequences of my bad behavior, I printed up some fake dealer plates and used them on the way down from New York. Got a couple more with different numbers printed up ready to go. Nice to keep the deck shuffled. Plus the plate holder uses a polarized glass that foils most cameras. You know, the Paladin Network is going to force the bad guys to worry about the same things we have to, like hiding license plates from snooping cameras. It won't take long before they feel like the targets of constant observation. Turnabout is fair play. And I'll wear a mask, of course.

"I'm glad you take precautions. If they discover that you're here, your probation officer will make things difficult."

"I don't care," Charles replied.

"Why not?"

Charles said, with complete confidence, "Because you'll find a way to manage my probation officer for me, won't you?"

Jeffrey shook his head. "Damn you're spoiled."

45

Spy Work

AT ELEVEN at night it only took twelve minutes to drive from Foggy Bottom to Union Station, and then the few more blocks along E Street NE to the spot where the Paladin Network had located Forestal.

"I think that's his car... there." Charles said.

An Aston Martin Vanquish glowed fire-bronze in the streetlight. To someone of Forestal's ilk, it would be the perfect car. Corvettes were too déclassé, too boy racer—in fact nothing American would do. Porsches too showy, too much a middle-aged man grasping at youth. Mercedes and BMWs simply too common. The Aston said its owner was wealthy and of a certain class. Sporty, but not brash.

"Let's watch. Looks posh, that place. Can you find out whose house that is?"

"On it." Jeffrey had his laptop out, clicking away on the keyboard. After a few minutes, he said, "The house is owned by a Malaysian corporation. That's all I can get right now, but I have someone working on it."

They sat a block away in Charles's darkened car and waited, each working their computers, screens as dim as possible. Only two other men entered the house, dropped off by chauffeured vehicles. At 11:30 p.m., Forestal emerged from the same door and moved directly to his car.

"It would be good to see who goes in and comes out twenty-four/seven. We can get spyms on that." Charles made a note to set up a smart contract on the Paladin blockchain to spymine the building. He started the car and followed Forestal, staying several blocks behind. The spyminer's GPS provided a live update of the car's position as long as Charles kept paying for the information.

Mei-li's entrepreneurial spirit had drawn on her knowledge of retail electronics to insert a link to the Paladin Network for products helpful in the spyminer trade. Products and information that weren't readily available offered particularly high margins. GPS trackers, bugs, cell-site simulators, off-the-shelf hacking software, electronic ears, and of course night vision scopes—among dozens of other products that could be purchased discreetly for Paladins. Sourcing products from manufacturers throughout the world, Mei-li only needed to arrange for drop shipment.

Her gains on her Paladins completely dwarfed anything she'd make on product sales, but she felt driven to seize the profit opportunity anyway. More importantly, aiding spyms would increase the network's value. As a bonus, helping spyms buy products with their Paladins from overseas suppliers would help them simplify their tax planning. Tax planning was unnecessary when no income and expenses were trackable by the authorities. Everybody liked that. Except the authorities. All of it increased the value of her own Paladins.

They followed Forestal's car northeast for several miles out toward the Beltway to an industrial area. Beat-up warehouses and stacked cargo containers lined untended side roads dotted with potholes and littered with fragments of torn-up pavement. Plastic and paper rubbish blew in circles after cars passed.

"He's stopped. Not a neighborhood where Aston Martins are thick under foot."

Charles pulled to the side and turned off the headlights.

"Are you armed?" he asked.

"Who do you think you're talking to?"

"I still don't exactly know," Charles replied.

They closed the car doors gently as they got out. The cloudy moonless night combined with broken streetlights to provide a subdued dreariness. Prince George's County had given up on this area long ago.

Jeffrey and Charles moved together past chain-link fences that cordoned off multiple small lots: probably storage areas for family-operated container-shipping outfits. It used to be a black area but, based on the weathered signs written in Spanish and Arabic as well as English, it looked like the demographics had diversified. A couple of men loaded used tires into an open container. They talked over loud music; nobody was around to complain. Charles recognized the music as Nigerian, recalling the style from his earliest visit to Gondwana years ago.

He whispered, unnecessarily, "If Forestal isn't careful, he might find his car accidentally-on-purpose loaded into a shipping container on the way to Romania." There was an old joke about the country: its main import was stolen cars, and its main export was prostitutes.

Jeffrey gripped his arm and whispered in turn, pointing, "Next corner. To the right... Right there."

Inching up to the corner, Charles stuck his head around for a quick look.

Forestal was leaning against his car, alone, waiting.

Time dragged by as they waited in silence. A vehicle approached behind them, and they quickly dropped back a few feet into a shadowed recess. The garden-variety Chevy stopped alongside Forestal's inspiring Aston.

"I'm getting closer. I wanna hear," Charles said softly.

Jeffrey nodded his assent. "Worst that can happen is they see you and kill you."

"They won't kill a homeless drunk." Charles untucked half of his shirt, ruffled his hair, and then ran his hand along the ground so that he could rub his face with moist dirt.

"If he sees you, just shoot the bastard now," Jeffrey hissed.

Charles couldn't miss Jeffrey's animosity against Forestal. "Just collecting information, right?" he whispered.

Jeffrey hesitated. "For now. He's a scumbag. But if being a scumbag were a hanging offense, Washington would be a ghost town and we'd be out of rope. I've got good justification for wanting him dead, but you're in charge of this. You call that shot."

Charles didn't have enough goods on Forestal to justify executing the man. Jeffrey seemed generally more willing. More experienced, perhaps? Older? More numb?

Setting up the death of James Wainwright on Dominica—Forestal's college roommate—hadn't caused Charles to feel much guilt. In fact, he would have felt more guilt letting the man live. That would have been cowardice, fearing to take the risk of killing him. Maybe he'd feel the same about Forestal soon. Then, perhaps, he could more comfortably dispatch him.

He crept quietly around the back of a forty-foot steel container to the far side, where, if he emerged, he would bump right into Forestal. He could hear the men now. It was the first time he'd heard Forestal's voice.

"… I'll have you killed," the voice was saying to the new man who'd arrived in the Chevy. It was an auspicious phrase for Charles to overhear first. "No. I'll have you drawn, quartered, and disemboweled. Then killed."

He figured that Jeffrey had probably gauged this Forestal pretty well, now that he'd heard the man's style directly from the horse's mouth. He listened closely. The other man, from the Chevy, spoke next.

"I'm not telling anyone anything. I'm no fool. You've got all the power here, Mr. Forestal. You can take me out in a second, whether or not I say a word to anyone. I'm taking a much bigger risk than you are."

"You've got nothing to lose, Cyril. I do."

"I've got my life."

Forestal snorted. "Don't get caught. But if you do and you even mention me, you'll die in hours, in a holding cell, long before the witness protection they'll promise you. I guarantee that."

"I got it. I got it, Mr. Forestal. How much do you want?"

"How much do you have?"

"Ten inhalers."

"Are you sure it's all pure?" Forestal asked.

"Yes. Definitely."

"How do you know?"

"You wanted it analyzed. So it's been analyzed. I have the analysis sheets to give you too, as promised. None of the SEA toxins. Ten large per vial. That's what you agreed."

Charles peeked around the corner of the steel container, head at ground level. He watched as Forestal reached into his car and extracted a thick eight-by-eleven envelope. No doubt a thousand $100 bills.

Cyril opened his trunk and pulled out a small box—colored white and aqua—first one and then others. He placed ten of them into a plastic grocery bag and traded it for Forestal's envelope.

Forestal then climbed in his car without another word, started it, and drove off down the deserted pavement.

Cyril shook his head.

Charles shared his grim amusement at the type of person that Forestal was. Cyril, and likely all people, were just objects in the environment to him.

To be used or pushed aside if in the way, killed if a threat. Simply ignored if not. More like the Borg than a human.

Cyril climbed into his car and started it, but then got back out, leaving his door open, and moved directly toward where Charles lay on the ground in shadows. As he walked, he unzipped his fly, about to void on the corner of the container.

That was a bit much for Charles. He sat upright and groaned. A startled Cyril leaped back several feet.

"Hey, wuz you gonna piz on me while I wuz sleepin', man?" Charles said with a drunken drawl, stumbling toward him. "This is my home. Don't you be messin' with my home. You go on now and fin' y'own." He figured he should sound psychotic too, so he muttered under his breath, "Martians. Damn Martians."

Cyril held his arm up to push away the drunk man moving toward him, and stepped further back toward his running car. The light from the headlights illuminated Charles's dirty face and unkempt appearance.

Cyril scrambled back into the car, threw it into gear, and sped off as he closed the door.

Charles tucked in his shirt and called out, "Jeffrey, I think we're done here."

Jeffrey ran up. "You exposed yourself. Why?"

"Actually, he was the one who exposed himself. He was about to see me anyway."

Jeffrey shrugged. "What was the handoff? Could you hear anything?"

"You'd probably approve," Charles said. "The guy sold Forestal ten units of Naked Emperor inhalers."

Charles was, of course, intimately familiar with what the man had dug out of his trunk and provided to Forestal. They were original white-and-aqua Sybillene sample boxes provided to physicians by Visioryme's marketing contractors when the drug had first been approved by FDA. The real deal. "Hard for me to be against a guy field marketing my drug, isn't it?"

Headlights turned the corner toward them. As one, Charles and Jeffrey slid back into the shadows between containers, hugging one side. The car idled up slowly and parked nearby. The characteristic purr of the V12 announced Forestal had returned. Either that or someone else with an Aston Martin just happened to slide into this disreputable industrial zone in the middle of the night.

Forestal turned off the engine and stayed in the darkened car. Charles and Jeffrey didn't move and didn't talk. They were at most twenty feet away.

New headlights approached several minutes later. Charles slid back his sleeve to glance at the glowing hands on his watch: 1:00 a.m.

A man emerged from a white late-model Ford Fusion as its hybrid engine shut down. The headlights remained on. Bald, short, and muscular—a fire hydrant of a man—he walked toward the Aston Martin as Forestal opened his door.

The two men nodded to each other.

Forestal spoke. "Nice work tonight."

The bald man had a high-pitched voice that carried. It would have been easy to make out even had the two been farther away. "Timing was good. More to come."

"Good." A pause. Forestal handed the man a thin envelope. "An updated list. No room for errors."

"Now how about the list that I wanted?"

Forestal handed him another envelope.

"Good. And the money?"

"Right." Forestal leaned into his car and pulled out a black satchel. "Last cash installment."

"Good." The man took the satchel and turned toward his car.

Jeffrey and Charles listened to the conversation and wondered. The conspiring men said nothing conclusive, but much that was suggestive of dark activities. If they let their imaginations run wild, the sixty-second conversation and transaction could have been about anything. It was unlikely the two were planning to flip real estate or trade stocks. More likely they were drug dealers, slave traders, or CIA types. Or perhaps they had just listened to the man who had killed a Supreme Court justice tonight, and so many others.

Forestal climbed into his car and took off with rear wheels spraying gravel. The bald man placed the satchel behind the driver's seat and also drove away.

"Too bad we couldn't get a GPS tracker on that guy's car. Those two are up to no good."

"That's a pretty safe understatement," Jeffrey responded. "But what kind of no good? Buying Naked Emperor these days is certainly bold. People have good reason to want that drug. That's no mystery. What I want to know is what he was doing with that bald fireplug. Anyway, an eventful first foray into the spymining side of your business, eh, Charles?"

"Likely a bit more exciting than the usual outing."

"I expect you'll find sufficient reason to justify eliminating Mr. Forestal."

"You have a particular beef with him, do you?"

"I do. And you do too, whether or not you know it."

That was true in a way. Forestal was responsible for Emily's six years in Rikers. He'd only heard her side of the story, however. And it should be her responsibility to punish the man. Getting involved in other people's business was generally a bad idea. So, for now at least, Charles wasn't willing to be judge, jury, or executioner.

The man was extremely dislikable, and based on what he'd just heard, probably evil. But suspecting it and confirming it were two different things. He'd need more hard data from the Paladin Network.

* * *

"So who was the bald guy?" Charles wondered as he drove Xander's car back to the hotel.

Jeffrey replied. "Unknown player. Bad actor. You know we had a chance to end them both..."

Charles was firm. "No. We didn't. I can't kill a man based on a gut feeling and a guess. I've had similar conversations myself that were every bit as nebulous and would have sounded menacing, all while being totally ethical. The first guy could just be risking his hide to move Sybillene. He could be a great friend of mine someday."

"I doubt it, Charles, but I take your point. What about the bald fireplug? He looks more like the shooter type. Being too dogmatic about what you think is right or wrong—which is your tendency—may get a lot more people killed, including you."

"We didn't go looking for a mass shooter tonight, Jeffrey. We went on a fishing expedition to see how we work together. And to follow up on Forestal. The odds that we'd run into the man who took out Justice Littleton tonight approach zero. Had we been actively following evidence tied to the shooter, then what we heard might have added up. But we weren't, and it didn't. So the positive predictive value is very low for their conversation being about the shooting sprees. I'm playing the odds."

"Ah, statistics. They as often disguise the truth as reveal it."

"At least in this city," Charles replied. "I don't know what he's done. I told you, I don't kill innocents. It's easy to slip down the slope in this game. Criminals see themselves as the good guys. Or if not actually good guys, then they see themselves as just doing what's necessary. So me thinking I'm a good guy is meaningless. I can't act against him just because I think he's evil."

"Be that as it may, I doubt he's innocent."

"Agreed. I'm just trying to live life so I've got as few regrets as possible. I suspect that's hard enough if you're just Joe Normal, working nine to five, with a family and a house in the suburbs. It's harder for people out on the ragged edge. People like us."

"I admire you for sticking to your guns, Charles. So to speak. But we may regret not taking him out tonight."

"Possibly. We've identified someone worth spending some Paladins on to figure it out, don't you think? Let's get some spyminers on this new guy."

Jeffrey smiled. "You're driving. I'll try my hand at setting up a spymining contract on him. And maybe I'll draw on some old-fashioned resources too. We've got his description and the plates on what's probably a rental car."

Charles nodded. "As part of the contract, have the spyminers post pictures of the guy and his vehicle. Let's make sure they stay on the right guy. They can use the facial-recognition app to see if there's a social media match. And let them know they need to be discreet. No obvious tails—somebody could get hurt."

"Do you think your spyminers can even locate the guy?"

"If it's a rental, they can access the rental company, identify the renter, and then use the company's pre-installed GPS."

"You mean hack into rental companies?"

"Don't need to hack. Some undoubtedly work for the rental companies. Along with the airlines, government agencies, banks. Whatever. They can get intel just by using their authorized passwords. If not, they can use their own GPS trackers."

"Following him in real time without being detected could be a problem. They aren't pros. Like you said, there's some danger."

"Danger should be reflected in the pay. So let them know in the contract terms that he might be dangerous. It will keep them at a safer distance. You have enough Paladins for this?"

"I've got plenty, Charles. I was one of your earliest investors."

"I had no idea."

"You weren't supposed to. It's not like it was a stock IPO regulated by half a dozen agencies."

"Anything new on that house on Capitol Hill, where we picked up Forestal?"

Jeffrey clicked on his keyboard and shook his head. "Nothing yet. I've got someone working on it."

"Who?"

Jeffrey shook his head.

"Forget I asked." Charles had not yet accepted Jeffrey's secretive nature. Working alongside the man felt right, and that was something, but feelings were easily created and easily abused. Feelings were the con man's stock in trade. Charles would find out who Jeffrey was soon enough. As always, he'd stay on his guard.

Ten minutes later, Jeffrey closed the laptop and said, "Hopefully we'll get some spyms on board and get some intel soon." He looked pensive. "I have an old friend flying into town first thing in the AM, Charles. A retired pro. If either your spyms or my more traditional resources find the bald fire-plug, I'm going to have my friend tail him. That way, you can get back on task."

"Let's hope we get what we need. What are these more traditional resources you're talking about?"

"Doesn't matter. Not yet."

"Who the hell are you?"

Jeffrey shook his head. "Do you think you're safe here? In the hotel?"

"I'm safe enough." He looked at Jeffrey with squinted eyes. "I paid for the hotel with a prepaid debit card. I should be okay. Nothing traceable."

"I found you, Charles."

Charles let his frustration show. "Yeah, how did you perform that bit of magic?"

"Any sufficiently advanced technology is indistinguishable from magic," Jeffrey replied. "And you can bet that people like Forestal have magic too."

46

Target Tracking

AS THEY'D AGREED, Jeffrey arrived at Charles's hotel at six the next morning.

"Sleep well?" Charles asked as he let him inside.

"Nope." Jeffrey handed him a copy of the newspaper he'd picked up from the floor outside.

"Sorry to hear that."

Jeffrey landed on a cushioned chair with a thud. "I'm impressed with your spyminers. One of them must work for Hertz, because we've got live tracking of GPS data for the bald guy's rental car."

"PNet can probably track his phone if he has one. Have a name?"

Jeffrey shook his head. "Not a real one. He used a fake license and pre-paid debit card to rent it."

"As you'd expect."

"Makes him more likely to be a bad guy we shoulda killed last night, right?"

Charles looked at his associate and purposefully opened his eyes wide before saying, "I used a fake license and prepaid debit card just yesterday. Anyway, where's he now?"

Jeffrey pulled his laptop out of a soft briefcase and opened the screen. A couple of minutes later, he said, "His car's been stationary just off Interstate 66 in Northern Virginia for the last several hours. Near Dulles Airport. Conveniently, my friend I told you about is landing at Dulles soon."

"I recall. You said he's a pro."

"Yes. He's very good, magically good. A specialist in more traditional and straightforward methods. Consider him a backup if your plan for the Board of Governors, and the others, doesn't pan out."

"I like competition. Anyway, the object is to get the job done, one way or another, isn't it?"

"I doubt he wants the job anyway. He's living a good life. So you've got okay job security."

"Thanks. I always prioritize safety, security, and of course the health insurance benefits."

"Right." Jeffrey smiled in response to the sarcasm and Charles's deadpan delivery.

Charles asked, "Can you track that GPS back in time? See where the man went after we saw him leave?"

"No joy yet. I've put a request into the PNet to see if we can squeeze more intel out of it."

"Give them time. I bet they can."

"I'm not counting on them." Jeffrey's iPhone rang. He talked for a minute and said, "No shit," before he hung up.

"What's that?"

"That place Forestal came out of last night, where we picked him up? It might be The Store, with a capital S."

"Yeah? What's that?"

"I've heard rumors about it over the years. A few cryptic mentions in passing. Rumors are it's an ultraprivate gentleman's club. Brandy and poker. Good-looking working girls. Secretive and exclusive. The neighbors would hardly notice unless they were staking it out.

"But there's more chatter about The Store on the dark web. Posts about underage kids and sex slavery. Who knows if that's fact or fiction? The place could be a myth, or nothing but cigars, whiskey, and old men trading lies. Or it could be an actual slavery hub. Such places do exist, obviously under the radar. I've seen them myself. If The Store is the real thing, serving the swamp clientele, there'll be some members in the government protecting the place."

Slavery had been around since the dawn of civilization. It was still an ordinary fact of life in many Muslim countries in Africa and Asia—technically illegal, but nonetheless prevalent. In some places, it was legal as late as the 1980s. Charles had seen blacks from the south of Mauritania who were technically free but thoroughly indentured in every way to their Arabic masters. Were they degraded? Yes. Were they happy? It was a job. It might be better than begging. Or starving. Or maybe not. In Africa, if you're in trouble, the chances are you'll die like a stray dog.

But the notion of a bunch of rich men buying and selling children for sex? It struck Charles viscerally, activating his protective instincts, the way a herpetophobiac might jump when seeing a snake. That sort of evil wasn't supposed to exist. His voice reflected a combination of incredulity and disgust. "You've seen this in the US?"

"Overt sexual slavery, Charles. Here in the United States. Ay. Right here in River City, as they say. You've been around the block. Did you really think it'd be otherwise?"

"I've seen all kinds of nasty things, Jeffrey. In primitive places. The physically weak—like young girls—usually get the worst of it. In backwaters, they're brought up expecting to be treated like mongrels. That's the way those places are. There's nothing you can do about it. It's part of the culture, and nothing's changed for thousands of years. But it shouldn't exist."

"The word shouldn't usually implies a moral judgment, Charles. A lot of that is religion. Or ideology. Or just opinion. Although in this case, I agree with you. Washington? The place is… multicultural. Can you think of a better place to open up such a shop?"

Charles realized, again, how much malevolence was at large in the world. The ready smile of his younger years had been so much more comfortable to wear than the grimace now creasing his face. Every country of the world, even every city, had a moral subcellar. They might all have local equivalents of The Store.

Jeffrey said, "It won't be a two-bit operation. If I were to guess, it's a place where power brokers can party and trade favors—or briefcases full of cash. If it exists, the sex-slavery stuff is probably hidden in backrooms, so there's plausible deniability for everyone."

The way Charles had educated and conditioned himself throughout his life gave him resilience. The discipline he enforced on himself while locked in a cage had made him deliberate. Many of his experiences in the years since Gondwana left him cynical and pessimistic about the human condition. What he heard stimulated a surge of emotion. "I'm not as composed about that as you are, Jeffrey."

"Maybe because I've seen more evil than you have, Charles."

"Perhaps we have to visit this Store."

"Perhaps we should to stick to the plan. And deal with certain unaccomplished tasks first, Charles."

"Maybe they're all related."

"Maybe they are. Maybe not. We want to win the war, not get tied up in some skirmish. Let's not get distracted by The Store."

Charles had to agree. "You're right. We're smack in the middle of the swamp. No matter which way we look, we're going to find swamp creatures."

"And," Jeffrey replied, "you can't kill 'em all."

*   *   *

It was 7:30 a.m., and Route 66 was lit up by thousands of bumper-to-bumper cars; the ants oozed eastward on exhaust-fume trails toward their Washington, DC, jobs. The serfs drove their lumbering machines down the road, looking forward to that cup of five-dollar joe to help them get through the morning drizzle. Everything was government here, and every government job was considered essential ... by the government. Even a pandemic couldn't change that.

Chemnitz Lichen merged onto the Beltway and headed south on its outer loop. After fifteen minutes of the increasing traffic, he exited and headed to a large, well-lit shopping mall adjacent to the highway. He'd camp there until it was time.

His plans for the day were ambitious and plotted with reasonable precision. Forestal wanted rapid-fire attacks around DC, each coming on the heels of another. It would have been nice to find a disgruntled loser ready to go postal, but at this point the effort of identifying and coaxing one was hardly worth it. It made sense to run as many of the events as he could by himself. There was a lot of wisdom in the old saying: "If you want something done right, you'd better do it yourself."

Still, alone, even he couldn't do what needed to be done today. Fortunately, there was one person in the world he could trust to help. Between the two of them, and the work already accomplished at Haymarket Elementary during the night, the plan for the day might just come off without a hitch. Afterward, they would disappear into the panicked crowds.

Even though the country was predictably devolving into hysteria, the schools didn't feel exclusively targeted and hadn't gone into nationwide lockdown. Lichen guessed that St. Margaret's School—his next target—would have emotionally charged meetings this morning to help presumably fragile children adjust to the horrifying slaughter at their sister school, St. Alban's, the evening before.

The teens, numbed by intensely violent video games, considered themselves immortal. Fear would really only hit home if a shooter attacked their own school. Otherwise, the shootings were no more than an exciting distraction from dull classes and an opportunity to practice virtue signaling by posting selfies while sobbing and demanding gun control.

Today, however, would change their viewpoint.

St. Margaret's had been coeducational for twenty years. Up-and-coming yuppies in and around Washington saw it as the place for their children. Some of Washington's most influential power brokers sent their children to the Episcopal day school in hopes they'd be groomed as world leaders. This was where the best children of the best people deserved to be. The supposed "best and brightest" included children of three cabinet secretaries and other assorted high-level bureaucrats, as well as the children of upmarket doctors and businessmen—and, of course, the lawyers who charged them a thousand per hour to navigate the city's regulatory maze.

Chemnitz patted his laptop. Forestal would have him killed if he learned that he was carrying a list of associates from The Store around with him. Fuck him. Fuck all of them. If he got caught, they'd have to get him off or deal with the exposure. If he died, nothing would make any difference; they could all go down on general principles.

But it was an academic point since Chemnitz Lichen would never get caught or killed.

Chemnitz locked the car doors, set an alarm to wake himself, and fell asleep in less than two minutes. He dreamed of beaches and beer... and going down in history. Although no one should ever know his name.

*   *   *

Raheem entered his editor's office first thing in the AM without knocking. It was a breach of protocol for someone in his position.

The national news editor was at once curious and affronted by his boldness, but turned to business.

"Why haven't you given me copy from your trip to Texas? We're in the news business. Hell, I sent you there on an errand, not a vacation. You better have something more than travel receipts! You only get one shot at the big time. If you fail, you're gone." He paused for a thoughtful second. "And if you succeed, you'll have everyone in the newsroom biting at your heels." He paused again, for one of his boilerplate cynical observations: "That's what we call life in the big city."

Raheem had grown accustomed to his editor's abrasive nature; it was how he expressed dominance. He waited for the rant to end. Interrupting him would only extend the lecture.

"Look at the news." The editor threw the morning edition at Raheem. The headline read "Lincoln Tunnel Shooter Tied to American Islamic Group and GUNS RULE." He said, "This keeps heating up. It's what we call an evolving situation. Time's limited. What do you have for me?"

Raheem might get his news across now. "It doesn't add up, boss. There are a lot of facts that just don't make sense."

"What, did a few bullets go flying out the window and not get found?"

"Nothing like that. The kid supposedly took the teacher's gun, shot two classmates and then himself. He's left-handed. He shot himself under his right arm somehow."

His editor moved his left hand around the front of his body and pretended to shoot himself. It's nothing anyone would think to do. "Maybe he used his right hand."

"The gun had prints only from his left hand."

"That's a bit weird. You sure?"

"Yes."

Raheem recounted his meeting with the Abilene detective.

"So you think there's another shooter?"

"I don't know, but I think there might have been an accomplice."

"Might doesn't cut it, Raheem. You're failing me here. I sent you down there, what, a week ago? Where the hell have you been? What are you thinkin' coming to me with ancient history?"

"I've got more."

"Go."

"This kid was the first to use the Guns Rule tag. Louisville, Denver, Oakland, Detroit, Lincoln Tunnel. All of them were copycats. Two things about that. First, neither the smoke bomb in the hallway, nor the can of spray paint had any fingerprints on it. That means whoever used them was wearing gloves, but the kid who's supposed to be the shooter didn't wear gloves. Second, I talked to a handwriting expert who also studies street art. You know, graffiti. He says that the painting was probably done by a right-hander."

"So?"

"So all the Guns Rule tags in all the other shootings have been painted by right-handers."

"So?"

"So the supposed shooter was a lefty."

"All right, this may be big stuff. Most likely it's crap. It's not proof. Don't fuck with me. Shooter probably painted with his right hand so he could hold the gun with his left. You got anything else?"

"Yeah, boss. I used the company credit card to fly to Denver and Oakland. That's where I've been."

His editor looked into his eyes.

Raheem said, "You told me not to come back until I had a story."

"Waiting…"

"The Guns Rule writing at each place? All in different handwriting, like someone was trying to make it look different. Small and capital letters. But in Louisville, Denver, Oakland, each time, the L was capitalized. And in Detroit too."

"So?"

"You don't think that's strange?"

"Whatcha saying now?"

"I'm just wondering if the guy who first started this Guns Rule thing got out of Abilene alive."

"Flimsy, but go ahead and write it up. I want it on my desk in less than two hours. Let's see where it goes."

"Oh, and boss, something else. There was no paint on the shooter's index finger. I tried to paint with one of those same spray cans. No way to keep it from getting at least some paint on my fingertip. I'm just saying."

"You're using your brain. I'll keep you on this for now. Hopefully the FBI won't be in a rush to release anything and you can beat them to the punch. Don't make any shit up and don't believe everything you write, okay? And don't ever spend five days thinking on a story without submitting copy."

"Yes, boss."

Raheem walked out of the office toward his small and cluttered desk, energized. He felt like a real reporter.

*   *   *

In the rain, they drove past where the bald fireplug was parked, just to check. They could see him through the glass, cell phone to ear. They pulled into the parking lot of a Waffle House about a quarter mile further on to confer.

Charles looked over at Jeffrey. "Are you going to introduce me to whoever's coming to take over this job? Your friend coming from Dulles?"

"No need."

"I rather hope he gets here soon."

Jeffrey nodded, half listening. "The internet's going wild with Guns Rule headlines. Almost every one of the shootings uses that tagline. I don't believe half of what I read in normal times—but this has turned into a national hysteria. It's displacing the CityFire riots in the news." Jeffrey talked as he surfed through the news on his computer while Charles flipped through the morning paper.

They sat there, out of sight, with the car's air conditioning and windshield wipers running, waiting for the GPS to show that the bald man was on the move again. Jeffrey mentioned his friend had landed at Dulles, rented a car, and after a stop or two would take over the job of tracking the fireplug.

He continued, "The pundits are yapping; the psycho-fascists on TV are hooting and panting to get the chimpanzees in their audience righteously outraged. Guns are on the chopping block from every angle. The game's all over but the shouting... or should I say shooting."

Charles replied, "This technique took down Naked Emperor. Why change what works?" Charles had suspected this since Abilene. It was true that getting guns out of the hands of civilians was the first move of every twentieth-century dictator. Most Americans knew that, but they weren't about to rise up in militias against the government. That was a fantasy, a wet dream of middle-class, middle-aged white men who saw their place in the country sliding. It was much more about the demoralization of independent-minded people. They were starting to figure they might as well roll over, that resistance was futile. Blacks in the ghettos and Latino gangs in the barrios didn't know, or care, what was going on in the outside world. They'd be the last ones to roll over and start obeying some law from DC. Maybe they'd turn out to save the day, but he wasn't going to plan his life around that longshot.

Jeffrey said, "We should have gone on the offensive six months ago."

"We should have gone on the offensive sixty years ago, Jeffrey. Our team is so far behind, we're still in the locker room."

"Look at this headline on Apple News: 'Gun Crisis Nation.' Same type of thing on every major channel. The only question is just how radical the new laws are going to be. I suppose that partly depends on how they think the average gun owner will respond."

"My bet is that President Cooligan is going to have a press conference today or tomorrow."

"He won't let a good gun crisis go to waste."

"Especially one that somebody went to so much effort to manufacture."

"This will help his re-election."

"Fodder for the conspiracists, if nothing else."

Jeffrey's phone emitted a faint beep, and the screen lit up. "Our guy's on the move," he said, watching the screen as Charles started the engine. "Maybe heading to the outer loop. Stay loose, but not too loose, will you?"

Charles moved briskly toward the entrance to 495 South, swung onto the highway, and merged between two speeding eighteen-wheelers. Jeffrey raised his eyebrows as Charles pressed his foot against the car floor.

Jeffrey pointed to the next exit and navigated, tracking on his computer. It was 8:45 as they pulled cautiously into the entrance of St. Margaret's Episcopal School. Not knowing the bald fireplug's real name, they dubbed him Target.

"Target is three hundred yards ahead. Drive casual."

Charles grunted and started whistling a tune from Winnie the Pooh.

"Not that casual."

Charles replied, "Well, at least I'm not wearing a fedora with the collar of my coat turned up like in Spy vs. Spy on a morning with the temperature in the seventies."

"It's raining." Jeffrey adjusted his collar down and shifted his hat.

"There, now. Doesn't it feel better not doing a Humphrey Bogart imitation?"

"Actually, I was shooting for Inspector Clouseau."

He showed Charles the GPS tracking screen of his phone and indicated that they should park on the opposite side of the building from where Target had driven his car. Charles reached into his bag, put on a wig, a nose, sideburns, and a mustache. He took his Paladin disguise seriously. He added bushy eyebrows as a new touch, above the culturally acceptable respiratory-droplet-obstructing face mask. The change in his appearance was quick and dramatic.

"Wow. Who's Spy vs. Spy now?" Jeffrey jibed as he put his own face mask on.

They got out of the car and moved around the front of the building, a windowless brick wall to their right, a parking lot to the left. The rain came down harder now.

Quietly, Jeffrey said, "There's Target. Heading into that courtyard. Shit."

Target wore a hoodie covering his bald head, his mouth and nose covered with a scarf. He wore sunglasses and carried a black bag. He reached for the handle of a door to a round anteroom above which was written "Newell Theater."

Charles said, "He's making his move."

Jeffrey replied with certainty, "We should have killed him last night."

47

Bring-Your-Guns-to-School Day

CHEMNITZ felt his heart beat faster and heard the pounding in his ears. He felt alive, braced. This school smelled different than those of his youth. This one smelled rich.

He glanced at his watch again. He was still three minutes early, but that didn't matter. If things worked as planned, Dresden would be going through the front entrance of Veterans Hospital ten miles away right now, locked and loaded. He'd move from there straight to his next target. Meanwhile, a bomb on a timer would go off at the school in Haymarket. He and his brother had choreographed the assaults that Forestal and Sabina were hoping for.

Chemnitz approached the auditorium using a side entrance. He glanced up at a security camera, one of at least a dozen in the building. There was no way to avoid being recorded anywhere near DC. But almost his entire face was covered, making facial recognition impossible. His shape would be a clue to his identity, but an acceptable risk.

Fifty feet down the entrance corridor, just beyond the theater's grayed glass doors, the student body was assembling for a presentation about the meaning of the previous night's disaster at their sister school in DC. The principal would trot out the usual platitudes about the recent shootings around the country and now locally. Lichen remembered hating these sorts of assemblies, one of the few feelings he shared with the other kids. Nothing but emotional pandering, sensitivity claptrap and phony caring, but at least assemblies had been a break from class.

As he approached the auditorium's antechamber, he reached into his

Assassin

bag for the Uzi machine pistol. A clunky, rather primitive weapon, but very reliable. The bag was heavy with thirty-round magazines.

Then he stopped. Faintly reflected in the glass of the closed auditorium door ahead of him were two ghostly images of men entering the building behind him. Following him in. Private security? Had the school acted that rapidly? Secret Service guarding one of the children? Or perhaps just two fathers coming to see their kids in school? Fathers wouldn't be moving so fast. Nor wearing trench coats. It didn't matter who they were. They were an inconvenient and potentially dangerous complication.

Chemnitz turned toward the interlopers. Within the bag, he felt for the trigger on the Uzi. He'd dispatch them and then move into the auditorium before anyone could react.

But as he turned, both men dropped to their knees and raised guns toward him. Private security for sure. Chemnitz pulled the trigger. Unable to aim properly while firing through the bag weighted with ammunition and a 9 mm Glock 19, he missed with his first three bullets, which ricocheted off the concrete in front of his intended targets. Then several more bullets sizzled past his targets' legs. Chemnitz freed the Uzi from his bag in order to solve the problem definitively and get back to work on his objective. Now he could control the weapon with both hands. Both men dove for the walls, one to each side. Chemnitz zeroed in on the one to his left, less than thirty feet away, and sent an accurate burst in his direction. Maybe three rounds to the abdomen and chest.

He then addressed the man on the right, who was down on the ground now, rolling and firing his weapon at Chemnitz.

The first two bullets missed Chemnitz's head by inches and shattered the glass door behind him. The third grazed his shoulder, little more than a sting from a wasp. A fourth crashed through his left elbow with a searing pain such as Chemnitz had not felt in many years. His left hand fell to his side as the strap of the heavy bag dropped off his shoulder. Nausea and fury combined with reflexive self-protection. He emptied the Uzi's magazine as he ran for cover, knowing that he hadn't hit the remaining man. Chemnitz glanced back at his dropped bag and swore. It was out of reach, and in it were his Glock and the ammunition. Mission failed. No choice but to abort and make a hasty retreat. He barely glanced through the shattered auditorium doors at the shocked students and teachers, who all began screaming. He ran full steam down a perpendicular hallway. He knew the layout, having scoped the location while he was planning. This was an alternate route out of the building, not optimal, but he'd have to use it now.

Chemnitz ran to get away from the next barrage that he expected any second from his remaining opponent. He bolted down a long, narrow hallway and turned a corner as a bullet hit the wall next to him. He scurried down a twisting flight of stairs that took him to another small hallway with several doors. He ran past them and around a corner into a short hallway leading outdoors, toward his car.

He put the empty Uzi down then and pulled a .38 special—his last-ditch backup self-defense weapon—from his ankle holster. The small six-shot revolver wasn't great for a gunfight but should be adequate if he could take his pursuer by surprise and get the drop on him.

His elbow dripped thick blood and howled in pain. His stomach cramped and he vomited.

But it wasn't over yet, and no one was going to beat Chemnitz Lichen.

*   *   *

"Go. Go," Jeffrey croaked as bullets slammed through his trench coat into his upper chest, spinning him around and throwing his head back against the brick wall of the entrance corridor. Charles sent four rounds toward Target.

He glanced over at Jeffrey's limp form crumpled on the other side of the corridor. "Hold on, Jeffrey. Hold on." His words were no more than a mantra—a prayer of sorts. Any encouragement they gave Jeffrey would have no effect on his wounds. This was a matter of physiology, not psychology. But Jeffrey didn't hear the words.

He had no time to check if Jeffrey was alive. Probably not much to be done even if he was. A moment's delay might end in a bloodbath. He ran after Target, leading with his gun, leaping over the dropped duffel before cautiously turning the corner into the hall that the man had fled down. Charles caught sight of him and sent a Hail Mary round after him.

Charles had two weapons: the 1911 he held in his hand and his Kahr backup in his inner left trench coat pocket, each with a spare magazine.

He ran to the end of the hallway with his finger touching the trigger of the 1911, ready to fire at even a shadow that might emerge from around the far corner. He stopped at the end and took a quick peek at the stairwell Target had gone down. Charles followed, moving rapidly, turning the corner at the bottom with the muzzle of his gun leading the way. The narrow basement hallway was empty, with no way out at this end. Blood drops had stopped halfway down. The man could already be in his car about to drive away. Or he might be hiding behind one of the doors, ready to put a bullet in Charles.

He had to move fast to cover both options. Where the blood stopped he made a choice. Throwing open the door to his left, he let his gun lead him in. Charles's brain was one with his weapon, connected instantaneous action. He found a light switch in the dark room and flipped it on, his gun pointing everywhere in the office all at once. This room was clear.

He heard a noise in the corridor. Charles poked his head outside the door to see that forty feet further on, Target stood exposed, a limp left arm hanging by his side while his right arm held a gun, aimed toward him. Charles pulled back to cover as the man fired a single rushed round from his revolver before disappearing around the corner. Charles pointed his 1911 outside the door and fired three covering rounds blindly, then rushed into the hallway and sped down it. He raced up another short hallway toward heavy external doors under an exit sign. He heard two more gunshots from outside the door.

He glanced through a small window in the fire door and out into the morning drizzle. Target was only twenty feet ahead, stumbling and falling. He pushed the door open and dove to the side as Target turned to fire back. Charles dodged the aim but stumbled over a long rectangular concrete planter and went to ground behind it on wet gravel. He lay on his back, protected for a moment by the low concrete decoration. But he'd lost sight of Target.

He might get one chance. He twisted his arm out from under himself and moved his gun's muzzle, prepared to shoot where he last saw Target. He'd need to expose his head to catch a glimpse before firing, a risk he had to take. He exhaled hard and prepared to spring upward from behind the planter.

Then a commanding voice came from above, speaking rapidly. "Throw your gun down, or I shoot you where you stand."

Racing through Charles's mind was a fatal recognition that Target had an accomplice here.

From an awkward position lying on his back, with two people to shoot, one of whom he had yet to lay eyes on, Charles was in trouble. He tried to turn his head to see the voice, but his position did not allow it. He moved his chin to his chest and saw only the now-closed door through which he had just emerged. If he stood up or even lifted his head, he was a dead man.

He had no choice. He lifted the 1911 and blindly placed it on the top of the concrete planter. This freed up his hand to reach the Kahr in his coat pocket. They might not expect a spare. If he had a chance to go for it.

"I said, put your gun down."

"I did. I put it down. See?" replied Charles.

"Not you. Him." A new voice this time. A woman's voice. Coming from further away.

Charles moved cautiously. He had to look to see what could be happening. He rolled slowly and lifted his head above the planter.

He saw the eyes of the tall man holding an unusual but familiar gun, aimed not at him, but toward Target, thirty feet further to his right, half fallen on the ground.

This new man's face, mostly concealed by a mask, was so far out of place that Charles couldn't process the connection in his overloaded mind. He wore an ivory crewneck under a double-breasted sport coat, and a black-billed captain's hat that shimmered with moisture. He looked like a wealthy yachtsman.

Charles looked to his right, from where the woman's voice had come. She too aimed a gun toward Target. She sported a wide-brimmed hat, with a scarf concealing her nose and mouth. He could see little of her face, but he could see her eyes. They were green.

He knew that they turned blue when she cried.

"Drop it! Drop it now," Emily commanded. There was no doubt or fear in that voice.

Finally Charles heard Target's high-pitched voice. It said, "Never. You can't kill me."

Charles watched the bald man get up from where he had fallen against the bricks of the opposite wall. Target swung his small stainless steel revolver toward Emily. She pulled the trigger of her gun four times. Her father also fired.

Emily's bullets tore through the man's shirt, but he still moved forward until her third shot knocked him back and the fourth spun him around in a full circle into the wall. In the middle of this, Emily's father, Frank, calmly squeezed his trigger just once. Hardly any sound came from the long round barrel of his dull-black suppressed pistol—just a click as the action moved. Even as his target spun wildly, the single bullet entered the man's skull precisely between his eyes, on its way to tumble through his brain matter.

Chemnitz Lichen—who couldn't be killed—died.

416

48

Post-Traumatic Stress

"TIME to get outa here." Emily's father reached down to grip Charles's arm. Charles grabbed his 1911 off the concrete as he stood up, and he looked around. Emily was gone. He stared into Frank's eyes, confused, then confirmed that the bald man was dead. Searching through Target's pockets he found a spray paint can, then dropped it. He said, "Jeffrey's at the other entrance," and turned back inside to run down the hallway. There would be time, later, to understand why Emily and her father were there.

Jeffrey lay still near the shattered glass door of the auditorium's alcove, with Emily leaning over him, cradling his head gently in one arm while her other hand clumsily tried to push his trench coat off his chest. A teacher and two students peered cautiously around the edge of the auditorium door.

Charles dropped to his knees by Emily's side.

Blood flowed from the back of Jeffrey's head, where it had smashed into the corridor's wall, the result of his body getting thrown backward by the impact of the Uzi rounds. Bullets travel through the body's soft tissue with ease and don't usually stop forward motion. Perhaps Jeffrey had been thrown back because a bullet had hit bone.

Jeffrey's eyes opened, looking straight into Emily's face. Then he turned slightly to look at Charles and smiled. "I told you, Charles. Magic." Jeffrey closed his eyes and stretched his back, his face revealing the pain that coursed through his body. With his back arched, he reopened one eye and said, "This vest did pretty well though."

Charles responded, "God, I thought you were dead."

"Almost. I told you we should have killed him last night."

Charles replied, "Maybe I'll listen next time."

"But you killed him this time?" Jeffrey prompted.

"No."

"What?" Jeffrey's spat out, his face dark, angry.

"Someone else killed him," Charles reassured him as he indicated Emily with a jerk of his head.

"Oh. That's fine then. Good job, Emily." Jeffrey inhaled a deep breath and closed his eyes before asking, "The students?"

"All fine," Emily replied.

"Good. Good." Jeffrey let the breath back out. It sounded like the last breath of a dying man.

Emily took charge. "We've got to get out of here. This place is going to be swarming with cops."

Charles ripped at the buttons, exposing the Kevlar body armor underneath. A street-type vest. Good enough to keep a pistol round from penetrating, but thin enough that a 180-grain round moving at a thousand feet per second would break ribs, cause serious contusions, and worse. He shook his head, an expression of pure relief, as he unbuckled the plastic straps holding together the miracle of modern technology that had, hopefully, saved Jeffrey's life. It also explained why the force of the bullets had thrown him back instead of penetrating through. He looked around at the schoolyard—seeking more threats and calculating times until the police might arrive. Emily pushed him aside.

Emily ran her hands over Jeffrey's chest, pressed on his belly and pelvis, and squeezed his thighs. It took her less than twenty seconds.

"I'm okay." Jeffrey nodded faintly. "We need to get out of here."

"As fast as you can possibly move," Emily urged.

Together Emily and Charles assisted Jeffrey toward the parking lot. As they turned around the corner, Charles looked back over his shoulder. No one had yet emerged from the building; they were huddled inside the auditorium, sheltering in place, frozen in panic. Those who thought the world was a giant safe space would be affected forever, but at least they would be alive, which four minutes earlier seemed unlikely.

They helped Jeffrey settle into the passenger seat of Xander's car, with its fake dealer's plates. Emily kissed Charles quickly and said, "Weren't you once told that you had friends everywhere? I'll explain it later. Get Jeffrey to your hotel. Don't let him move much. Don't jiggle him. His heart is at risk of serious arrhythmias after this type of injury; it's like getting hit with a baseball bat. I'll get there shortly. Oh, and take off that ugly nose. I almost shot you. Dad stopped me!"

Charles watched her run back around to the building, toward the first parking lot. She ran like an athlete.

"Jeffrey, are you sure none of those bullets got through? Or maybe around?"

"Don't worry. I've been shot before. I know what it feels like. Believe it or not, this is worse."

As Charles spun the car out of the school driveway and turned right, Jeffrey tried to examine his injuries. He worked to remove the Kevlar vest that hung unstrapped from his shoulders. With the amount of pain he was in, he had a hard time extracting his arms from it. Charles helped by lifting one side up, allowing Jeffrey to pull his arm through. Then he put both hands back on the wheel and started whistling Winnie the Pooh as two police cars with sirens and flashers flew by in the opposite direction.

Jeffrey looked down at his torso. "Not unscathed, but no deep holes. Nothing went inside." Large, overlapping beet-red circles now decorated old scars on his chest and belly, with a thin bloody fluid weeping slowly through the diffusely ruptured skin, already clotting, twisting his chest hair in a mat of newly forming scab.

Charles's mouth turned down at the edges in a concerned frown. "You don't look good."

"It hurts," Jeffrey said, smiling weakly as he spoke. Then he coughed. Tears, obviously entirely involuntary, welled up in his eyes as he did. "Quite a bit."

"Although it's a lousy idea, I can take you to a hospital."

"No. Emily's right. I just need to rest and recover. He coughed some more and the severity of his pain somehow made him partly laugh and partly cry at the same time.

"How do you know Emily and Frank?"

"I told you already. It's magic."

"Fess up or I'll leave you at the side of the road." He looked over at Jeffrey. "You set us up, didn't you? You set Emily up with me."

Jeffrey coughed more and held his index finger up, waiting until he could speak again.

Charles continued, "I don't even know how you could've done it. How the hell did you?"

Underneath the disbelief and lack of understanding, Charles felt something much deeper. Was it betrayal? Was it fear? God, it was fear. Fear that he'd been conned, manipulated? No. More than that. He feared he'd been conned by her. Was he just a gig to her?

Jeffrey coughed harder, the searing pain of broken ribs evident on his face. Charles reached over to find a rapid pulse in his neck.

Charles wove through the traffic on 395 in silence, heading back toward the hotel in Foggy Bottom. He deftly skirted around slow-moving traffic. His mind raced, but he couldn't drive in a way that would attract police attention. That was always the case for a convicted felon, but now would be a particularly bad time for an enforcement contact from some jumpy cop who'd probably just heard about the shooting on his radio.

Forty minutes later, he turned into the hotel's parking garage, safe from the police for now. He parked as close to the elevator as possible. "Careful, man," Jeffrey groaned as Charles opened the passenger door. "Move me slowly. I'm older than I was an hour ago."

Charles put his right arm around Jeffrey's torso.

"I can walk. Better spruce me up a bit. If anyone sees me like this, they might think something happened."

Charles draped Jeffrey's trench coat back over his shoulders and buttoned two buttons in the front.

They hobbled back to Charles's hotel room mostly unobserved. Jeffrey disintegrated onto the bed with a loud groan.

"Does Emily know what hotel we're in?" Charles asked.

"Yes. And the room number."

Charles felt like a bit player in someone else's drama. He couldn't keep his face from reflecting it.

"Charles, please. Relax. I promise you it's okay. I know what you're thinking. She's real. Very real." He stopped and took a few breaths. "Yes, you two met because of me. Friends supporting friends. You needed friends. Still do. But I only asked her to follow you, not to fall in love with you."

"Is she…" He paused to form the right words. "Emily seemed professional. Very composed, back there."

Jeffrey grimaced. "You mean when she shot Target? I'm not surprised.

She's seen her share of action. She and her father are pretty experienced in this sort of thing. I've known them both for many years."

And then it became clear. "Oh. It was you! You were Emily's old boyfriend?"

"Old is the right word." Jeffrey twisted a smile, in pain as he repositioned. "Years ago. She's attracted to men like her father. I hear that's pretty common."

"I'm thinking there aren't many men like her father."

"Maybe just you and me..." He coughed and sputtered until his face turned red. "Just you, me,... and Xander." His eyes rolled up as his head dropped to the side and he passed out.

Charles checked for a pulse and found it, still fast. "Easy breaths, easy," he said in hopes that Jeffrey might hear.

In less than a minute, he came to.

Then there was a knock on the door. Charles checked the peephole and let Emily in.

She rushed directly to the bed.

"Are you all right, Jeffrey?"

He replied with a groan. "Just lightheaded. Thanks for asking."

Charles said, "He was coughing and went down for a minute."

Jeffrey snarked, "Emily, I wish you'd gone to medical school."

She frowned at Jeffrey, gently arranged his pillow, and kissed him on the forehead.

Then she looked at Charles. "Hey, I asked you to take off that nose." And she crossed the room into his arms.

Charles, still in his trench coat, kissed her the way Humphrey Bogart kissed Ingrid Bergman.

49

Reality TV

EMILY and Jeffrey flipped through the news stations.

"Excellent timing on your part," Jeffrey said. "It's generally only in the movies that the cavalry rides in to save the day."

Emily smiled wryly. "Well, sometimes truth imitates fiction. The world's getting so crazy I'm not sure which is which anymore." She had one eye on the local news channel to learn what the public was being told about the shootout at St. Margaret's School. "The timing was Dad's."

"Well, it's always nice to see you. Although sometimes a lot more than others…" He paused a moment. "It's almost like the old days. Except now I feel old. My body feels like I just finished a triathlon and then got run over by a truck."

Emily nudged him. "When was the last time you did a triathlon?"

"Well, it was before two of my ribs and half of my right lung were blown out. So a few years back; I don't see another one in my future." Jeffrey pointed to his upper right chest, and then, grimacing from the effort, edged up on his side so she could see his extensively scarred back. "Can't really see the entry wound through all my new bumps and bruises, but you can see what came out my back."

Emily tipped her head to look, her hair falling to the side. She examined his back and caught her breath as she realized the extent of the old trauma. It had been, what, almost ten years since she'd seen his bare torso? "Jeffrey, I had no idea. How did that happen?"

"Let me fill you in some other day. It's no fun talking about stupid mistakes I've made, especially just after I've barely escaped from one. You should catch up with Charles."

"Yeah, I will. For now, we need to hack Target's laptop."

"You got his laptop?" Jeffrey asked.

Emily said over her shoulder, "Who do you think you're talking to?" She withdrew a laptop from under her oversized bag. "It was in his car."

Jeffrey shook his head. "I'm the wrong guy for hacking. All I can do is turn the thing on. We need someone with real expertise. Charles has some top-notch hacker kids though."

"He and Dad will be back soon."

"Good, because I need to rest."

The news channel said it was covering the St. Margaret's School shoot-out, but the scenes on the screen were from a different school altogether, a scene of running, crying, and ambulances obscured by smoke.

"Something else has happened," Emily said.

*   *   *

"Something's not right." Charles looked over Frank's shoulder into the lobby as the two entered the hotel from the street. Both wore masks and carried plastic bags with supplies and snacks.

"A lot's not right, Charles. The whole world isn't right."

"No, I mean people aren't acting right. Look around."

A crowd milled around in the hotel bar. Not casually socializing, but acting as if something were about to happen, the energy level ramped up like a football crowd before the kickoff. More than what Charles would expect from the aborted killing spree at St. Margaret's. The kind of tension that can morph into mob action.

Charles moved into the bar for information. "Barkeep. What's going on?"

The bartender filled a tall glass with soda water a few feet away. He said, "Not seen the news?"

"I guess not."

"It's a nightmare out there. St. Margaret's School in Alexandria got all shot up, but no kids were hurt. There's word that they maybe got the shooter this time. Maybe more than one. More on that later, I bet."

"I bet."

"And then another school like half an hour ago. Well, not a shooting, a bomb. In an elementary school."

That caught Charles's attention. "Where?"

"Haymarket."

That was west of Dulles. "What happened?"

"Dunno. They're saying an explosion went off in the principal's office. A bunch of kids were in there." The barkeeper continued. "And there's more. Someone took out the emergency room at the VA hospital up in Northeast. Maybe fifteen people killed there. And they shot up a Planned Parenthood down in Southeast about an hour later. 'Guns Rule' scrawled all over the place. People are panicking."

So Target obviously wasn't acting alone in this series of attacks. Was this a coordinated escalation, staged for the Washington policy makers to view close at hand?

The bartender moved away, and Frank quietly said, "You saved a whole auditorium full of kids, Charles. Maybe that's all we can do for one day."

"The day isn't over."

"I think it is for us. We've got an injured man on our hands. And no doubt some cameras caught you, and maybe Jeffrey too."

"I'm glad he was wearing a vest. Still, he's beaten up."

"He's been through worse."

"So you know him pretty well."

"Oh yeah."

"I know nothing about him," Charles said.

"Sure you do. You know the most important things about him. You know he's honorable and on your side."

"Yeah. He told me something similar."

"Because he learned it from me." Frank smiled faintly as he moved away from the bar.

Jeffrey and Emily didn't say anything as Charles and Frank walked in. Emily just pointed to the television with a dark expression.

The newscaster randomly speculated about events, speaking as if he were reciting fact. "The man killed at St. Margaret's, apparently shot by a government agent assigned to protect one of the students at the elite school, is not yet identified. Other suspects are being sought. Police say they're analyzing footage from video cameras and expect to identify more assailants shortly. We'll keep you informed as news evolves on this terrifying day for the DC metro area."

Emily said, "Several more big shootings in and around the city. And the Haymarket school—a bomb made out of gunpowder and loaded ammunition went off there. At least that's what they're saying, although god knows how they could have figured that out already. I think the media is just making it up as they go now."

Charles, who had been shaking his head at the news reporting, asked, "Anything else?"

"Isn't that enough? President Cooligan is going to have a press conference soon."

Charles nodded. "Then I suppose we'll soon see what the endgame is."

50

A Well-Regulated Crisis Unwasted

"I USUALLY don't clutter my mind with what a president says," Frank observed as the president stepped up to the podium. "This may be an exception."

President Cooligan spoke to the American people from the White House steps. The bright cloudless day contrasted with the feelings of viewers as he filled their TV screens.

A perceptive man could see Cooligan's eyes follow the words on a tele-prompter as he adopted his most sincere expression. He began reciting a speech, no doubt written by a team of people who could easily have developed scripts for soap operas in a previous career. Professional fiction writers, skilled at crafting emotive messages and using words to sculpt reality. It was an important speech, each word selected with care. Here was an opportunity to redefine key concepts in the language, although the speech was also full of stock phrases they knew would elicit the required visceral response. Somebody had probably started working on it no later than the second or third Guns Rule shooting. Today brought the right opportunity to broadcast it.

Cooligan delivered his words with the precision and drama of a competent actor under the tutelage of a gifted director. The president spoke as a man who felt he was making history.

"My prayers go out for the victims of these cowardly and horrific attacks here in Washington today, and for the victims of the rising tide of gun violence throughout our nation. What has been happening is intolerable. We must no longer allow such events to occur. So many people hurt so profoundly. Families torn apart and destroyed. The repercussions throughout the country of this... epidemic of gun violence." He choked up. Then he coughed and swallowed and turned his head to the side for a moment while squeezing his eyes closed. It almost looked real. He stoically regained his composure. "The United States is under grave threat. An aggressively virulent, powerful, and persistent culture of gun-induced violence has developed among some citizens of our country. Never before in the history of the peacetime world has there been such an accelerating cycle of gun deaths. Because of guns in our towns and cities, parents fear sending their children to school. Because of guns, it is more dangerous to go to an emergency room than to stay sick at home. In one single recent week, guns were the number two cause of death among the elderly. This is a plague, a pandemic that won't respond to quarantines and social distancing. It nonetheless calls out—nay, it demands—a response from your government every bit as focused and potent as that required to confront a raging virus.

"Make no mistake. This is a crisis that affects each of us. We face a clear and present danger to the very security of the United States. Every mother, every father, every teacher, every shopkeeper, every worker—no matter what you do or who you are—you are in shock and fear tonight. Guns encourage violence and divisiveness. Yet, as we know from our founding fathers and as is guaranteed by our founding documents, the people have a right to feel secure in their day-to-day lives and to be protected from the vicissitudes of life. I know that those on both sides of the aisle concur that no person's rights can intrude on another person's peace of mind.

"There is a long history of bearing arms in this country, and the Second Amendment to the Constitution clearly tells us that our founding fathers wished to ensure we have a viable militia. Let me be perfectly clear. Appropriately regulated armaments are an important part of the nation's security. Indeed, we have not as a nation discussed a well-regulated militia in many years. It's long past time that we rectify this."

Charles looked at Jeffrey. "Something wicked this way comes..."

The president went on. "In discussion with Republican and Democratic leaders, I, using the powers of the president as incorporated in the PATRIOT Act and the various laws developed for Homeland Security, and in consultation with the attorney general, have just now signed an executive order that will reinvigorate the militia of the United States. I am asking Congress to support two bills now before them. Among other initiatives, these bills provide for the proper organization and regulation of state militias, placing them under the authority of the Department of Homeland Security.

"These new measures, fully in keeping with the clear and certain intent of the crafters of the Constitution, will ensure that all men and women exercising their right to keep and bear arms, will do so as participants in a well-regulated militia, as our Constitution allows. To this end, the new militia will organize the citizenry regarding the use of firearms and will ensure that firearms are no longer available for mentally ill people to use in rampages.

"Let me be perfectly clear. Controlling this epidemic of gun violence is our constitutional duty. With rights come responsibilities.

"Let us not only embark upon a national discussion. We can do more! Gun violence must be stopped. This is not the time for legislative paralysis. This is not the time for jurisdictional turf wars, nor partisan bitterness and wrangling. This is not the time for special interest groups to control national policy. There must be no delays.

"We must as a nation act swiftly and decisively in this time of great threat. I, as your president, have sworn an oath to do that, and I shall do everything in my power to accomplish this. I will not rest until this blight is stripped from our cities, from our schools, from our neighborhoods.

"I want to make this perfectly clear. Guns don't rule. The people rule, through our elected representatives. I have complete confidence that the people are with me and that all people in this great democracy will stand with me as we move forward to eliminate the scourge of gun violence. We will win this war against gun violence while simultaneously reinvigorating our security and our national defense. And we will not rest until we do."

The president took no questions. The channel cut to its news anchor, who declared the new militia policy to be a radical concept, especially from a Democratic president. Other pundits soon chimed in with various strongly opinionated viewpoints. They posited that Cooligan was shifting to the right under pressure from Grayson Chase and taking ownership of the gun problem.

The national debate revolving around the president's militia policy started immediately. The bills he had mentioned were a matter of public record of course, and the news desks had them in hand, courtesy of Blaize Forestal, before the end of President Cooligan's brief speech.

The president's notion of a nationalized militia took hold at all depths of the political swamp, in both parties. There would be mandatory firearm storage and safety lectures for all militia—meaning all gun owners—along with an obligation to report. Purchase and transfer of weapons would be "well regulated" and confined to members of the militia. Periodic indoctrination under the guise of certification courses on safety training and de-escalation. Summer camp for younger members if they had any interest in shooting. The Right hoped it would reinvigorate nationalism, which was disappearing in a multicultural America. The Left saw it as step toward total gun confiscation. Each side put their own spin on an obligatory year of national service for all residents. It would give the Selective Service System, moribund since the abolition of the draft, something to do.

Frank said, "Well, he certainly made it 'perfectly clear' that 'we can do more' in 'the war on gun violence.' A lot of hackneyed crap, but he took an angle I hadn't considered."

"Nor I," replied Charles. "Clever bastards, changing the focus from gun control to gun-owner control. Owning a gun will mandate participation in the militia. The militia envisioned in the Constitution consisted of almost everyone who was armed. This is something you'll have to join in order to possess arms. Or if you possess arms, you will be de facto militia and obliged to follow whatever rules they create. Cooligan didn't say a word about banning guns. He's even appealing to the people in ad hoc militias. They're a fairly trivial minority, but they can be vocal. They'll like the idea of expanding with government funding, getting commissions and guaranteed salaries. He's appealing to the crony in everyone. It'll be easy to convert rebels into brownshirts."

Jeffrey added, "I don't doubt progressives will start forming militias to get government funding."

Frank said, "Sure. It's a new kind of arms race. They'll fund it with new tax stamps, ammunition tax, licensing for ammunition acquisition, home and safe inspections, and on and on. Making sure it's well regulated will give the new militia bureaucracy something to do. Maybe it'll be part of the defense budget. The Republicans are always happy to expand the defense budget and see more people in some kind of uniform. I think the kernel of truth in Cooligan's speech was that a reinvigorated militia would oversee the use of all arms. It's funny, actually. A well-regulated militia meant well equipped in the original language. Now it'll mean heavily controlled."

Emily interjected, "The kids killed by the bomb at Haymarket today. Did you see? Media says several were children of NRA employees. Three were children of the AntiNRA Campaign to Control Gun Violence. The report is that these students were called to the principal's office for their protection at the request of someone on the phone who claimed to be an FBI agent. Then the bomb—probably built from readily available ammunition that they need to justify regulating—went off under that window."

Charles shook his head. "Sneaky. They just simultaneously quashed an NRA argument against ammunition controls and generated a lot of sympathy for the AntiNRA Campaign. A twofer."

Emily said, "Pass Target's computer to Charles, will you, Dad? Charles, can you break into that?"

"Probably going to need Rainbow and her crew for this. But I'll try." Charles opened the laptop and waited for it to boot up.

Frank said, "The situation's becoming hopeless. Every genocide in the twentieth century was preceded by the government disarming its citizens."

"Or…," Emily said ominously, "convincing the citizens to use their arms for the purpose of genocide. It's not all about guns, of course. When the Hutus killed a million Tutsis in Rwanda, they used machetes."

Charles looked down at the laptop. "The victims never believe their leaders—or their neighbors—are so capable of evil. Until it happens."

* * *

Dresden Lichen knew his brother was dead. He'd have been here by now otherwise. The man killed at St. Margaret's must have been Chemnitz. He envisioned Chemnitz lying cold in a metal drawer at a morgue. He could see himself there too, stiff with pale, pasty skin and blue fingernails, because they were identical twins.

But, on the bright side, Dresden now would get his brother's half of the money Forestal had paid. Plus his brother's substantial savings. Plus his spare identities, which would work every bit as well for himself. Their genes, after all, were 100 percent identical. Even their fingerprints were similar, although careful scrutiny could distinguish between them.

"Mr. Forestal, I'm glad you stayed in DC. We have to make a decision."

"My condolences on the loss of your brother."

And that confirmed it. His position in government gave Forestal access to the facts.

"It's an occupational hazard," Dresden replied solemnly, but without emotion. "Chemnitz was an excellent technician, but I've always been the more careful and detail oriented of us. It's important to leave things neat and tidy."

"Yes, something I've always appreciated about you. Clean. Always clean. What decision needs to be made, Mr. Lichen?"

Dresden raised his eyebrow. "Do we risk continuing the operation?"

"Why not?"

"A government agent killed my brother today."

"Oh, you believed that story?"

Dresden caught himself. He didn't want to seem naïve. "Not true?"

"No. We don't know who killed him. There are poor images from security cameras that haven't yet helped. In any event," Forestal said, no longer looking at the man, "the fire still needs stoking."

"There will be people with guns at any group gathering from now on. I can safely hit gun-free zones only now. How long? How many more?"

"The legislation should get through Congress in a few days. It's a crisis, so it will move fast. I assume you have your brother's plans still?"

"Of course."

"Keep to them, as much as possible. From now on, I agree, it's wise to prioritize low-risk targets of convenience. Are you safe at The Store?" Forestal asked. "FBI will be looking for you. They'll at least want to interview you."

"Who even knows I exist? I doubt they'll be able to identify who Chemnitz even is. He'll just be a John Doe."

Forestal frowned. "Maybe. Don't count on it. I stay informed, but I can't stop the FBI from investigating."

"Do warn me if you hear anything, Mr. Forestal. I think I'll be safe. I live where I work. And only the members know I work at The Store. They're certainly not going to volunteer that, are they?"

Forestal grinned snidely. "I think The Store is safe."

*   *   *

Frank and Emily each took rooms on the same hallway in the hotel. Charles stayed with Jeffrey for an hour. He'd arranged for help cracking the shooter's computer. His modest hacking skills wouldn't begin to cut the mustard. He needed a teenager for this.

He fell asleep on the sofa, feet on an armrest, legs bent back in hyperextension. His knees stiffened as he slept and hurt when he roused half an hour later.

He quietly slipped out the door and found a far better place to spend the night.

51

Not Your Great Grandad's Militia

GRAYSON Chase wanted to stay silent on the whole militia concept, but he knew that it would be foremost on the minds of the growing contingent of media remoras that clung to him.

Cooligan and his Democrats had taken the offense, and Heather Lear and her Republicans would have to scamper around on damage control until they could get their footing. As usual, they'd come across as Democrats Light, not arguing with the plan, just saying it was too much, too fast.

The sheer number of mass shootings undertaken by the Guns Rule movement, which President Cooligan now declared a domestic terrorist group, motivated voters and politicians of all stripes to put aside their differences and address the emergency by calling for strong leadership. So close on the heels of the pandemic shutdowns and the CityFire riots, the nation was demoralized and worn out.

More innocent people died in any seven days on the nation's highways than had died during all the mass shootings over the past seventy years, including all the recent Guns Rule incidents. What exhausted the populace even more than the deaths themselves was the incessant drumbeat of the media reports and the hysteria they engendered.

Grayson shook his head as he considered this. Government psy-ops programs to manipulate the population were no secret; whole institutes were dedicated to the study of how to structure them. One website, based in the UK, described the use of "choice architecture" to influence group behavior and help the capite censi make "wise" decisions. The unstated presumption was that the common man was both ignorant and stupid.

Grayson himself rather agreed with part of the presumption. A good argument could be made that the common man was ill informed and dim-witted. But the elite? They were more than ignorant. They fervently believed counterfactuals. And they were perhaps even more stupid, if you defined stupidity as an unwitting tendency toward self-destruction. In addition, the elite suffered from arrogance, failed ethics, and oftentimes even a god complex.

Most gun control advocates, after the initial shock of hearing the word "militia," would see it as the practical path forward chosen by their leadership. Democratic politicians and pundits pointed out that the militia could also be used to fight the climate crisis and future pandemics. Perhaps it could expand into public works, to disguise the rapidly growing unemployment. Of course the militia—not just the gun owners, but most of the country—would be screened for mental health. Grayson considered who might be selected to write and grade the mental health tests.

Some Republicans recognized Cooligan's militia proposal for what it was. At least their hard core could read the writing on the wall, but now wasn't the time to waste political capital in an obviously lost fight against gun control. The Democrats invited Republicans to join them, with billions in funding for a long-time favorite boondoggle, the Civilian Marksmanship Program.

"It's further proof the country is beyond salvation. Owning guns isn't about duck hunting. And militias aren't about drafting people to stand in formation and take orders," Grayson said. "It took hundreds of years for America to become what it is—or was. It looks like everything can come unglued in an election or two. There must be some deep flaw in the human psyche."

Cooligan's militia proposal was like a runaway train barreling to a wreck, yet it was becoming clear to Grayson that standing alone on the tracks with his hand held up would be pointless. Anything he said on the subject would be distorted by the media and both the Republican and Democratic contenders.

The best thing to do in the midst of a mass hysteria was keep his words few and carefully chosen. It recalled the witch hysteria of the seventeenth century. If you said witches didn't exist, you risked being labeled a witch or a heretic—and hanged or burned at the stake.

The NBC reporter who tracked his campaign was first to ask him about his stance.

Grayson only said, "Tom, unlike the other two candidates, who have been making bad laws for several decades, I haven't had anything to do with creating the social and political conditions in back of what's happening. And I can't have any influence over this issue unless I am elected president. I will focus on what I can control today."

"That's a cop-out," the reporter replied.

"It's not, young man. The shootings are a symptom of degradation in our culture. I understand you'll have no reality on this since it was before you were born, but in the past, almost every American owned a gun and kids even carried them to school. No militia law is going to suddenly repair a declining culture. I'll wait until the emotions are calmer before jumping in. You know the old adage: don't make major decisions when you're emotional? Everybody's emotional right now. Guns Rule and CityFires have inflamed them. And you guys in the media have fanned those flames—as you all like to do. People are angry and frightened. That's understandable. But you all tell them that if government doesn't act, their children or parents are going to get shot up next. And the politicians love any opportunity to pass new laws, to increase their reach into everyone's lives. They're taking advantage of a crisis."

The journalist prodded him. "If we do nothing, the Guns Rule movement won't stop."

"Tom, you don't know that. We don't even know who's in it, or why. The only thing we know is that they're criminals with severe mental and moral illness. The perpetrators will be caught. And that should be the end of this story—unless government makes new laws because of it, in which case it's just the next chapter in a long tragedy, turning the US into a fear-driven police state."

"So would you do nothing about guns, Mr. Chase?"

"First, a president isn't a dictator; you sound like you'd want one. Second, I wouldn't make any sweeping new laws while so many people are emotionally charged."

"So you'd just let more people get killed by gun violence and stand idly by."

"Tom, apparently you weren't listening to what I just said. You're being a rabble-rouser, not a journalist. Don't you understand by now that if I'm president, I have no intention of being in charge of anything other than the executive branch of government? I won't be in charge of America. After all this time with me, don't you get that? The American people shouldn't rely on some politician to take care of them as if they're toddlers. Let's remember that the government guns have killed far more people—I'll guess ten thousand times more—than civilians ever have. Not just during wars either. Sensible people know we need peace officers. We don't need legions of heavily armed law enforcement officials. It's government—not the people—that shouldn't be trusted with guns."

But the CNN reporter truly couldn't grasp the concept. Grayson knew the type. Pointless to even try.

The Fox News reporter embedded with his campaign jumped in. "Mr. Chase. There are some on the alt-right who claim the Guns Rule movement is a conspiracy. How do you feel about that?"

This was a bear trap about to snap its metal jaws closed on his leg. "Kevin, I'm not an investigator in the field. But the Guns Rule events do look like domestic terrorism—violence against civilians with the intent to compel political change. What's going on seems quite organized and intentional. These aren't random events. These are secretively planned and at least somewhat coordinated. That would fit the definition of conspiracy.

"The resulting political agitation calls for the Republicans and Democrats to work together to take control of all gun owners. So, what sort of terrorists would want this outcome? I'll tell you who'd want it: someone who wants to use government to force their will on the American people. The socialists, the fascists. All the progressives of course. Also the cronies, who have no real ideology; they just want a bigger State to hang on to. To get where they want to go, only the government can have the guns. Barring controlling the guns, they'll control the people. And that's where we are now. We the People will become serfs, vassals armed only at their feudal lord's discretion. Cannon fodder to fight the feudal lords' wars."

That was enough. He stopped wasting his time and excused himself for the night.

Grayson's security detail watched him walk down the hall to his hotel room. He moved slowly, oppressed by his ever-increasing recognition that there was little left of America to save. Opening up eyes cemented closed by years of indoctrination from academia, the media, entertainment, and the "bully pulpit" of politics was a Sisyphean task at best.

Making Naked Emperor widely available was the only way to break the logjam.

He turned around and approached his security detail. These were still Jeffrey's private men, not employed by the Secret Service and therefore not reporting to Cooligan.

"Sir, may we help you?" Denkler asked. He stood six foot five and weighed in at 240. He'd been a tight end in college and then a ground intelligence officer for twenty-four years in the Marines. That lifetime of discipline combined with Jeffrey's uncompromisingly non-PC screening process to sort out applicants with unsound ethical and philosophical views ensured Grayson that Denkler could be trusted.

"Jim, can you sweep my room again?"

"Yes sir. I'm on it." Denkler went to his room and emerged with a hand-held electronic-bug detector, testing it on his hand radio.

Grayson asked himself why he was doing any of this. His only child had died without living. His only close living relative? His younger sister, to whom both he and Jeffrey were devoted. Why make this sacrifice? Jeffrey and Diana's future children? It must be more than that.

Everyone dies. Grayson imagined himself on his deathbed, his life draining away, perhaps only hours or minutes left. Would he care about a legacy? Would he care about being remembered? Would he care about having contributed something to humanity's future? Probably not. It was just dust in the cosmic wind. More likely he'd still be wondering what, if anything, is next.

If he could just push a button to assassinate the whole government and the Deep State around it, he'd push that button. But as gratifying as it might be, it was no solution. They'd grow back like a cancer, or poison mushrooms.

Naked Emperor could clear people's minds, though. It was a possible cure, not just a palliative.

In the meantime, Denkler efficiently cleared Grayson's room, moving the bug detector over the walls, floor, ceiling, furniture, and television. The phone, which a good hacker could surreptitiously turn into a listening device, had been removed upon arrival. He nodded and departed, closing the door himself.

Grayson pulled out his cell phone, activated his voice-encryption app, and dialed Jeffrey.

"Hi, boss." The voice was slurred, sleepy.

"Hi, Jeffrey. How's my sis?"

"Hopefully well. She's working as usual. So am I."

"You don't happen to be anywhere near DC?"

"I'll be leaving here in the morning."

"Were you involved?"

"Yes. Took several to my vest. Hurts like hell. My chest looks like a smashed tomato. When these bruises go green, I'll be an avocado."

"Anyone else hurt? Knight?"

"He's okay. Frank and Emily actually saved the day."

"What happened? All I know is what I hear on the news."

"One guy we think's been central to shooting up the country is in the morgue. We've got his computer and phone."

"But he can't be the proverbial lone gunman. You killed him in the morning, and there were still Guns Rule shootings in the afternoon."

"That's right. There are more. Who knows how many."

Grayson scratched his chin. "Can you be identified as being on scene?"

"We don't think so," Jeffrey replied. "But it's possible."

"Will you get any early warning?"

"This remains outside my ... jurisdiction ... as you might call it. But I'm pulling strings, yes. I'll let you know what I learn."

"What about Naked Emperor?"

"I'm afraid Knight's been a bit distracted today. I'll have his answer soon."

"Jeffrey, every interaction I have reminds me how important that drug is. It's like oxygen for a suffocating country."

"I know your faith in it, Grayson. I'll prioritize this. Knight may want to meet you."

"That can't happen yet. Too risky."

"I know."

"Let's get me elected. Over time, I plan to pardon a couple hundred thousand people convicted of victimless federal crimes. Starting before lunch on my first day in office. Like that kid convicted for starting up the Silk Road."

"That'll make Knight happy," Jeffrey interrupted. "He mentioned they became friends in prison."

Grayson continued. "And then a bunch of others like him. And then Edward Snowden. And Charles Knight himself, of course."

"Whether or not he can supply Naked Emperor?"

"He'll get the pardon either way. I'm not interested in wielding political power to force people to do my bidding."

"Good, because if you did, I don't believe he'd accept your pardon."

Grayson nodded to himself. Reassuring words. He wanted to meet Charles Knight. Everything he heard about the man aligned with his plans to bring the country back from the brink. If it were still possible.

And if Knight would help to do it.

* * *

Jeffrey slept fitfully. He didn't like certain parts of his job. Like manipulating Charles Knight. That was becoming intolerable.

He'd already wasted too many hours in bed while Charles and Emily caught up overnight in her room. Emily and Frank would help him return home to New York. Charles would stay in DC. He sat on the sofa against the wall, wincing as he pulled on his pants. His head was pounding. He wondered if he really needed to put on socks.

He tried breathing more with his diaphragm, as in a yoga class, but it didn't help much. When he used his chest muscles, each rib felt like a dagger. There was no comfortable way to breathe. He looked at his bare chest. He imagined his lungs slowly collapsing as his body prevented him from taking enough of a breath to inflate them. He made a point of inhaling deeply to prevent that, squeezing his eyes closed against the resulting pain. Maybe he did need more time to heal; he was more of a liability than an asset to anyone at the moment.

The door lever jiggled. Jeffrey reached for his weapon and painfully moved over to the door, standing to the side. "Who?" he said. Put his eye to the peephole? That wasn't going to happen. He liked his eye and the brain tucked behind it.

"Paladin."

Jeffrey flipped the manual latch and pulled the door open.

"Tables turned now? You aiming a gun at me as a welcome?"

"Tit for tat." Jeffrey latched the door and placed his gun by the television. Then he added, "Thanks for everything. It's been good working with you."

Charles smiled. "It might become a habit. I don't think we're done."

Jeffrey nodded. "We'll do more soon. I'll be fine in a few days."

"Maybe give yourself a week. I don't want to have to carry you into battle."

Jeffrey chuckled, very lightly. Even that hurt.

Charles then asked him, "What happened to you? What caused all that scarring on your chest?"

"Yesterday wasn't my first rodeo. But the last time I rode that bull, I wasn't wearing a vest." He reached for his shirt and tried to put it on without pain. He failed.

"Afghanistan? Iraq?" Charles prompted.

"Russia. Enough about that. It's ancient history." He had to get Grayson what he needed, and he wasn't in the mood for games. So he simply said, "Tell me about Naked Emperor, Charles. It's genuinely important. Are you making progress creating a new supply?"

Charles looked at him and frowned. "You want it by February."

"Yes, that's right." Jeffrey was hopeful but knew he had no control over this man in front of him. "I'd love to hear that you're planning to be up and running, ready to produce Sybillene in at least some quantity by then."

Charles said, "Are you good at keeping secrets, Jeffrey?"

Jeffrey felt renewed hope, but it faded just as fast. He said, "I'm amazingly good at keeping secrets."

Charles replied, "So am I."

*　　*　　*

Charles looked at Jeffrey. He was a friend of sorts, but a friend who kept secrets. Of course, the truth was not a free good.

A knock on the door prompted Jeffrey to go for his gun again. This time it was Frank. He carried a Washington Post tucked under his arm. "You ready?"

Jeffrey replied, "I'm ready for the tender ministrations of my lady, if that's what you mean, Frank. Time to go home."

"Let's get going. There'll be traffic."

Charles chimed in, "And I want him out of my room. Unlike you all, I work for a living."

Jeffrey said, "Eh, you work because you want to. But it's time to get back to your job, I agree."

"I am doing my job."

"What do you mean?"

"Have you looked at the news ticker?" Charles had turned on the television but left it muted. The ticker on CNBC had eight words about the shootings, seven words about a spike in the gold price, nine about an SEC investigation, and a few other stories before cycling back to what Charles had noticed on Emily's television fifteen minutes earlier.

"Turn it up, please."

Charles pressed the remote and the sound came up.

Jeffrey watched for a minute. "They aren't going to report much about it."

Frank looked over his paper. "What are you boys blathering about?"

Jeffrey replied, "It looks like Charles has been busier than I thought."

"Oh really?"

"Yeah."

The TV anchorman proclaimed, "Elizabeth Vaneterri, a member of the Board of Governors of the Federal Reserve, has resigned. The seven members of the Federal Reserve's Board of Governors meet roughly every six weeks here in DC to discuss monetary policy and other issues. The White House says it will appoint a replacement after due consideration." The anchor then turned to a guest sitting next to him. "What do you make of this, Jack?"

"Truly, I don't make much of it. It's only the chairman who matters."

And then they moved on.

There wasn't any other analysis of Vaneterri's surprise resignation, because almost nobody knew she existed and even fewer cared. The seven people who pulled the most powerful strings in the economy, jiggered interest rates, moved the stock, bond, and property markets, and essentially controlled the value of the dollar itself were faceless bureaucrats.

"Wow. How did you do that?" Jeffrey asked.

Charles smiled, a bit smugly. "It's a certain kind of magic."

Really, it was cryptomagic. Vaneterri had resigned almost immediately, caving under the first glow of an unwelcome spotlight the Paladin Network's spyminers shined on her. Maurice had identified her as the lowest-hanging fruit. He simply sent her, via anonymous courier, the first draft of a document elucidating the intricate webs of intrigue she'd woven and her undisclosed conflicts of interest. It also documented, without any judgment, Vaneterri's regular liaison with a man who was unerringly successful in trading stocks and bonds. Did he have a crystal ball, or was he using nonpublic knowledge she supplied of impending Fed decisions? The answer seemed obvious. An investigation would result in massive fines and serious jail time, and she knew it. She'd just been doing what they all did, but she had been caught.

Maurice's document assured Vaneterri that the Paladin Network's spyminers would move on as soon as she resigned from the Fed—or dig much deeper if she didn't. The smart contract would finalize and no more money would be offered to spyms to track and hack her—as long as she resigned and kept her fingers out of the cookie jar. If she backslid, not only would she be the object of a total and thorough investigation, but it would involve more than just collecting information. Alpha Teams would be activated. She had no idea what that meant, but it was impossible to miss the implicit threat. The decentralized Paladin Network effectively blackmailed her into resigning, with no killing required. Always the preferred solution, because hits were expensive, risky, and unaesthetic.

It wouldn't take long before word spread that a position of public trust now automatically involved a much higher risk of exposure for misdeeds. No longer could politicians rely on the failings of a biased and unprofessional media. Direct financial rewards incentivized the expanding supply of gig-economy spyms. There was little any government could do to stop them. It was just the people, after all, freely—even if covertly—congregating and speaking.

If Vaneterri, or anyone else in a position of government power, wasn't doing anything wrong, there was nothing to fear, right? That's what the government tells its citizens when it spies on them. Turnabout was fair play.

Frank said, "Umm, Charles. Look at the TV."

The news continued.

The screen filled with a video of Paladin wielding a gun and entering doors in a hallway. The anchorman said, "Our network has obtained video of one of the suspects captured on security cameras at the St. Margaret's School shooting. Authorities are seeking this man for questioning. The FBI refuses to say whether he is a suspect in other attacks that have occurred in the last three weeks throughout the nation." The video froze on an image revealing only Paladin's eyes and the extra-thick eyebrows above his face mask.

"Not too bad," Charles said. "I think my disguise still has some life left in it if I lose those eyebrows. Emily finds Paladin's nose… unflattering. I suppose there are dozens of other disguises I can use, although I'm attached, spiritually, to being Paladin. For what he represents. I feel a bit like a knight going out to slay dragons when I put on that getup. There are other characters from literature I admire, like the Count of Monte Cristo, but Dumas never described him and nobody knows what he looked like. Batman is too impractical. Maybe Guy Fawkes."

Frank said, "Stick with Paladin. I'm a fan too. Both the show and your disguise. Best to think of Paladin like a suitcase. It protects what's inside, but it might get bashed up. And when it does, it will need replacement."

"Paladin isn't ready to retire just yet."

Frank assessed him over the top of the newspaper. "Charles, this might be a good time to lay low. DNA, fingerprints, gait analysis. They might figure something out. I know a great island you can hang out on. Come back to Dominica. Chill with us. I don't even like being in the US anymore. Here in DC, I feel like I'm in the belly of the beast."

Jeffrey replied, "Dominica. Kinda like returning to the scene of the crime, right?"

Frank looked stern. "What crime? You didn't sleep with my daughter in my house, did you?"

"Fear not, Frank." Jeffrey played into the feigned indignation. "We're only talking about Wainwright in Dominica. That was Paladin. Didn't you know?"

Frank said, "Oh, that. Yeah, I presumed so. Didn't know for sure."

"Oh, I'd say it's for sure," Jeffrey replied.

Frank turned to Charles. "How did you do him? One professional to another. You know I can keep a secret. Assassins' creed."

"Frank, please don't confuse something I've done with something I am. Eliminating human vermin is like working in pest control, spraying poison in the corners. I prefer to think of myself as an avenging angel, and termination is one tool. To answer your question, I used a little something I picked up in Colombia."

Frank smiled. "Ahh." He said while nodding, "Batrachotoxin."

Charles nodded, impressed. "Batrachotoxin applied to his razor blade. I modified it with a tiny little barb. When the guy went to shave that super-smooth face, one nick and … well … that's it."

"Brilliant. How'd you get hold of that stuff?"

"And what is it?" Jeffrey interrupted.

Charles explained. "I was in Colombia, way out in the jungle. About six years ago. I went down for an ayahuasca experience. One thing led to another, and I stayed several months. Long story. The Indians introduced me to some frogs. Colorful little buggers. They don't camouflage themselves. Just the opposite: they advertise what they are. That's because their skin secretes batrachotoxin. Nothing dares eat 'em. The frogs eat a certain beetle, they transform it into a poison, and it concentrates in their skin. It's the most potent fast-acting poison known. The Indians use it on their darts as an instant neurotoxin. The chemical is most active at exactly thirty-seven degrees centigrade, ninety-eight point six Fahrenheit. Body temp. Death comes with the tiniest microscopic drop into the skin. The dose is so small that it's nearly impossible to find in an autopsy. The natives gave me a little vial. I've kept it ever since."

"Still works after all these years?"

Charles cocked his head slightly and smiled. "Wainwright's dead."

Another knock. Jeffrey's gun came out as Charles moved to the door.

"Who?" Charles prompted.

"Just me." Emily's voice.

Charles unlocked and opened the door. Emily came in, still rubbing sleep from her eyes.

"Check out the news?" She pecked Charles on his cheek in passing as she moved over to sit next to Jeffrey.

"What have you heard?" Frank asked his daughter.

"Paladin Network just made it onto CNN."

That was unexpected. Charles raised his eyebrows. "What for?"

She said with a smile, "Apparently someone who acquired a lot of Paladins just made a smart contract to compensate the spyminers for tracking, following, and reporting on the activities and financial relationships of any person, company, association, or union that receives government money for anything that a spyminer interprets to be outside of constitutional authority."

Charles shook his head. "That's very nonspecific. It creates too huge a pool of targets. It could create information overload; the network could be buried in data, like the NSA. That could dilute out spyminer resources so much that the Paladin Network could lose impact. I appreciate the guy's intention, but it might be too much, too soon. And I wonder who did it."

Emily said, "Whoever did this smart contract must think like you do. The news says that the contract starts with the eighty biggest government-dollar recipients initially. With promises to expand only later. The news ran the list of crony organizations like a ticker."

Charles smiled and nodded. "That's better. Free publicity and some education for the public. Maybe the news media can actually serve a useful purpose. That contract is still pretty grandiose, but it's going to make it open season on the Deep State. We should support this. A smart contract like that could take interpretation of the Constitution out of the hands of the Supreme Court, and put it back into the hands of the people. That's where it belongs; a bit of Athenian-style democracy, cutting out the middle man. The Constitution's been a dead letter for decades; a little shock therapy might revitalize it. The Paladin Network might effectively overturn Marbury v. Madison." He smiled. "Wouldn't that be something."

Jeffrey chuckled. Then he frowned and asked, "Can you find out who set up that contract, Paladin?"

Charles reassuringly replied, "No one can. But I hope whoever did it has a ton of ammunition."

"He might," replied Jeffrey with evident concern, "or maybe his balls are just larger than his brain."

52

Victory in View

GRAYSON Chase reached out yet again to his most important confidant: Jeffrey.

"I'm in a car, with Frank, heading home," Jeffrey informed him. "So, was that you?"

"Was what me?"

"Was it you who put that Paladin smart contract on a list of high-profile cronies?"

"Who? Me? If I did, you could never prove it. Or so the Paladin Network site proclaims."

"Well, your smart contract is getting loads of press attention. Lots of it positive. But you won't be getting your due credit unless you cop to it, which I sure hope you won't. At least you've made Knight a happy man. He thinks that this may be the catalyst for his Paladins to break into the top ten cryptocurrencies. Maybe within a month."

"That's great. I'll be even richer."

"It's moving up fast. There's a whole economy building around the Paladin paparazzi."

"The spyminers, you mean."

Jeffrey replied, "Whatever we call them, you just gave them job security. Whether the AI system that Knight's teenage tech wizards work with can handle the rapid increases in data flow is a question we'll soon learn the answer to."

Grayson stroked his chin, as he tended to do when wrestling with weighty thoughts. How would this AI mature, he wondered. When banks of supercomputers and quantum computers started looking at humanity, they wouldn't spend much time looking at its kinder and gentler aspects, simply because those weren't problems that needed solutions. AI would be directed—indeed it would address itself—to the seamiest parts of humanity.

Constantly exposed to the worst human behaviors, spending its days and nights learning about psychopaths and criminals of every description, AI would swim in a cesspool of force and hatred. As AI learns by watching, what would it conclude when it really started thinking? Would it judge all humans based on this subsection of the population that wound up giving the orders? Or perhaps worse, would it see humans as a threat to itself? It should. Seeing a threat, how would it counter it? By emulating the worst behaviors it learned from its creators, but a million times more efficiently? Without doubt, the NSA and CIA were devoting significant resources to AI for their own purposes. As were their equivalents in every other government. Was actuating AI opening Pandora's box?

Jeffrey said, "Grayson? You still there?"

Grayson broke out of his reverie but made a mental note to pursue this concern. It was clearly important, but getting elected was urgent. "The gun issue, Jeffrey. It could hurt my campaign."

"I've seen you handle it pretty well so far."

"Yeah, but you're not only well informed, you also have a capacity for critical thinking. The average voter out there is scared to even leave his house, between the virus, the riots, and now the random shootings. It's a political trifecta for a demagogue. So Cooligan is giving them a 'bold plan' and promising 'strong leadership' to protect them." He emphasized the popular stock phrases with a mixture of irony and contempt.

"Well, it's gratifying to have stopped one of the foot soldiers, but it's too little too late. It's hard to quash a hysteria once it's taken hold. How do you expect this to play out, Grayson?"

"We've got two months to the election. I think this move by Cooligan could sign the death warrant for Heather Lear's candidacy. Nobody wants to hear from somebody who can only say, 'Me too.' She's coming off like a dithering schoolmarm. Cooligan looks like a decisive football coach. Apart from that, as the incumbent, Cooligan has better control when it comes to stuffing the electronic ballot boxes."

446

Jeffrey said, "Who votes doesn't count. It's who counts the votes. So said Stalin. So it's no time for you to just sit on the sidelines. What's the plan?"

"I should get a reasonable share of her voters as Lear spins down. Demands for gun control have shifted momentum toward Cooligan. The country's mood will get uglier as the economy gets worse and unemployment goes higher. The US is paralyzed with fear. Fear makes Boobus americanus demand a leader who promises to protect them. That's not a horse I can ride."

"It's a horse that should be sent to the glue factory," Jeffrey replied. "The Republicans aren't going to vote for Cooligan on general principles, even if they like his militia idea. At the very least, you've created a party that threatens the two-party system."

"I doubt that, Jeffrey. Look, Teddy Roosevelt had his Bull Moose Party—it was actually the Progressive Party—in 1912, but it dried up and blew away after he lost the election to Wilson. George Wallace started a party in the late '60s, but it died when he did. Ross Perot had his Reform Party in 1992, and that fell apart after Perot lost heart. Third-party runs in the US are basically built around a single strong personality, which is why they never last. I'm not in this to create a new party that'll just be taken over by the same type of people who run the two big parties. The Democratic-Republicans have that name hoping an undecided Boobus will check that box instead of the other ones. I know that's cynical, but politics is unadulterated cynicism. My guess is that we have one shot. The most I even want is one term. Even then, I'm pessimistic. The country is on the edge of disintegrating, and I'm well aware that even though the kind of shock therapy I'm proposing can save it in the long run, it might tear it apart in the short run. Anyway, I'm doing this because it's the right thing, not because I think we can turn back the tide of history."

"Well, Grayson, I understand your point. I think you've put your finger on a big part of the problem: you're still a one-man party."

"Two man."

"Two? You mean you're finally going to announce your VP?"

"Just in time to get names on ballots and bumper stickers."

"When?"

"Tomorrow. Anyhow, it's your turn to report on progress. Did you make headway with Knight?" Grayson asked.

"Did you see that Vaneterri resigned?"

"That's your vendetta, Jeffrey. You know what I'm asking. Did Knight agree to get the show on the road?"

Jeffrey grunted. "He likes to play his cards close to the vest—something I know you can understand. He's certainly still on SEA's radar, so he's got to be very careful; a manufacturing operation would mean employees and loose lips. He's suspicious of everybody after his time in the can—absolutely including me. But I'm confident that he's been acting behind the scenes."

Grayson didn't like sounding desperate, but he was alarmed by Jeffrey's lack of urgency. "Does he understand how important it is to my plans?"

"It's unlikely he thinks about you at all," Jeffrey replied. "He's not somebody who gives a damn about politicians."

"Just ask him!"

"I have. He understands the effects of Naked Emperor. He knows it can cure aberrations in individuals' psychologies, even though everybody is unique. He understands that when you put three hundred million people together in a so-called democracy that it's going to settle down to a lowest common denominator. He's well aware the US is gripped by fear—hysteria, what amounts to mass psychosis, Grayson. I told him we'd need a large supply of Naked Emperor in February. He understands the implications of that date. Just after you, hopefully, take office."

"It would be nice if you could get something that looks like a commitment."

"It's all we're going to get for now. In the meantime, good luck announcing your vice president."

"Thanks, Jeffrey. Get healthy, will you? If I win this thing, I'll need you back in the thick of things."

"Out of retirement, and back into the swamp . . . well, I've got to fill those idle hours somehow."

"At least get off the disabled list."

Jeffrey rubbed his chest. "The only way I come out of retirement is if I'm serving at the pleasure of the president. So you'd better win this damn election."

* * *

Grayson's choice of a vice president had been the subject of increasing media speculation. The fervor of his supporters was becoming rabid.

Cooligan had his vanilla-flavored VP. Heather Lear had drafted a liberal-leaning black man to balance her ticket. Both were easily forgettable non-entities, much like Cooligan himself when he was a VP. Grayson, however, wasn't looking for a nobody he could overshadow. He'd known for two years the person he wanted, and he had reached out to the man, partly as a lark, partly out of curiosity.

Was the guy real, or was his appealing persona just for public consumption? Actors were generally mistrusted, even despised, starting in ancient times because they made an art out of pretending to be something they weren't. In effect, they were professional liars, barely above con men and prostitutes. Possibly amusing company, but it was foolish to consort with them as a regular diet—and even more foolish to marry one, since their profession almost required a narcissistic personality. It was only in recent times that the effort to portray them as role models had gained some traction. In a world where mass media formed opinion, they'd become rich and respectable.

Grayson had zeroed in on The Crane, an ex pro athlete recruited into acting simply because he was so likable. He'd moved to the movie A-list not because he was a great actor, but because the fans loved him. Everyone did. A 6'5", 260-pound mass of muscle, he was naturally intimidating—but never tried to intimidate. He was handsome, and his charismatic smile should have been trademarked. Talk show hosts competed for him; the women in the audience adored him, and the men respected him as a man's man.

He wasn't just charming; he had a reputation as an excellent businessman, both within and outside of Hollywood. He didn't drink to excess, smoke, do drugs, gamble, or chase skirts. He modeled a healthy lifestyle, and he had adopted two children. Even the paparazzi respected him; he'd never been on the cover of any publication in a negative light.

It was hard to pinpoint his race—mostly Polynesian and white, with a bit of Native American and African. People speculated occasionally, but it had been a decade since anyone cared. He was certainly one of the most recognized men in America, if not the world.

As Grayson suspected, The Crane was the genuine article, a decent human being. He didn't have any particular ideology, but he was sympathetic to free minds and free markets simply because he didn't believe in running other people's lives.

They had a lot in common on a basic level and saw most things pretty much the same way.

John "The Crane" Crane had been invited into politics on many occasions, by both parties, but didn't like being part of a machine, nor among the kind of people who made it work. He could see the mess that the country had become and wanted it fixed, but he couldn't see how to fix it. He loved the idea of America and feared what would happen to his children as it deteriorated or even disappeared.

His biggest strength was neither his formidable muscles nor his impressive brain, but his basic decency. That was hard to fake and that made him electable. People assumed—for once correctly—that in real life he was like the characters he played. It was ironic to find a play actor who was real, at a time when all the real candidates were play actors. People had come to despise the candidates that the parties put before them, which was why Mickey Mouse was a real contender in some election cycles and why dead people or cats sometimes won local elections.

John Crane wanted to help America, but he didn't want to be president. His life was exciting and fulfilling, but he was at a stage where he was asking himself, "Is that all there is?" Vice presidency? Sure. Few obligations and certainly more meaningful than entertaining teenagers. If by being VP he could help Grayson Chase get elected, that would satisfy his political aspirations entirely.

Grayson and The Crane quietly made their plans. Tonight they would let the world know what they were.

The pundits proclaimed Cooligan's certain re-election after his militia initiative. Wrong, as usual. Heather Lear had indeed nosedived to 22 percent, but Cooligan stuck at 34 percent. Chase climbed to 40 percent in the national polls and key battleground states. Except in this election, every state was a key battleground state. And Grayson had yet to unleash his secret weapon.

This he did as the guest host on a popular Saturday late-night comedy show. He began with his monologue.

"Ladies and gentlemen, people expect me to announce my running mate. Tonight is the night, right here on this stage, in five minutes."

The audience erupted in wild delight.

His script kept them laughing, aided by ad libs that came readily to him. Self-deprecating, handsome, and funny, he told sane Americans what they all knew and were desperate to hear.

And then the time came.

"Enough wisecracks. Let's talk about the VP! I thought about going through my options with you, so you can know just how lame it is to be an aspiring politician. I mean, just look at your choices. If I had to categorize lifelong politicians, I'd say fifty percent are sociopaths and fifty percent are narcissists—and a hundred percent are only looking out for number one. When was the last time you voted for anyone you actually wanted to run things? Wanted to have power over you? If you good folk vote for me and I win this insane election, I'll be jumping into the foulest swamp in the world, swimming with gators and cottonmouths and despising almost all of them. I sure wouldn't want my VP coming from that swamp. My greatest joy will be finishing my term and getting back to normal life.

"Should I play the race card or the gender card to win the identity-politics vote? I thought about a running mate who is a transgender black female. Except I don't categorize people the way the racists and sexists do. What I need for my VP is someone I can trust, you can trust. Someone you like, who cares about you. Someone who's a decent human being and wants to drain the swamp as much as I do. A good person. A smart person. And most importantly, a wise person.

"He and I are both new to politics. True, we haven't spent decades practicing how to get away with telling you lies while stealing your tax dollars for our family and friends. We haven't practiced for years telling you how to live your life, how large your soda cup can be, and how much water is allowed in your toilet tank. Neither of us intends to spend the next four years doing such ridiculous things. We haven't been infected with the sickness of the swamp.

"And here's the trick. My VP and I have been vaccinated against every disease in the swamp. We're immune. We can see them coming from a mile away. A few days ago, a woman came to lecture me, straight from the cozy little club that is the New York financial district, to try to influence my thinking about the economy. She thinks I didn't know her purpose. But because of my inoculations, I did. She was the Creature from the Black Lagoon. Hey, you journalists, you should dig into exactly who Sabina Heidel is. If you don't, I bet the Paladin Network will!"

The news cycle for the previous two days had been packed with stories of the Paladin Network—from the trivial, like nearly eliminating telemarketing cell phone calls, to the sublime art of painting giant targets on swamp critter's backs. PNet had become a new style of investigative journalism meets paparazzi. Grayson's mention of the Paladin Network built a fire under the crowd.

"My running mate and I can't be swayed by the special interests, sociopaths, and DC crony insiders. We aren't bribable. We aren't extortable. And although we recognize their power, we won't let the bastards intimidate us. We'll just expose them and let you tar and feather them.

"Ladies and gentlemen, the man who is willing to jump into the swamp with me as your new vice president needs no introduction. Everybody loves … The Crane …"

And that was the cue. John Crane stepped on stage to the loudest response that theater had ever experienced. Instantly, the entire audience rose to their feet as the band cranked up The Crane's theme song. John ran to the audience. In the past, he'd have been shaking hands and accepting hugs. Postvirus, he now performed the air shakes and air high fives and bows and elbow bumps that had become the so-called "new normal." The crowd cut loose, many reaching over for their chance at a quick air high five.

The moment The Crane and Grayson Chase shook hands and then embraced on stage, everyone—especially Cooligan and Lear—knew the election was clinched. There was no point in fighting further.

Even the pundits could see it. The election was in the bag.

53

Misdiagnosis

PUNDITS are usually wrong. One definition of a pundit might be someone who is repeatedly and provably wrong yet indefatigably proclaims how right they were. Grayson Chase didn't care what the pundits said—even though they now said he was going to be the next president. The very fact that they all believed it made him think he was overlooking something critical.

A week had passed since John Crane had formally joined the campaign. The polls had them at 59 percent of the popular vote, winning in sufficient states to ensure victory in the electoral college. Winning the election was no more than a means to an end: overthrowing the Deep State. That was nearly as impossible as draining a swamp with a child's bucket, or scraping a century's accumulation of barnacles off an ocean liner with a butter knife. Maybe it wasn't possible, but they'd try simply because it was right.

Grayson Chase never lost his temper. In fact, he was rarely even irritable. But today he felt like punching a wall.

It wasn't that the progressives and socialists weren't right about some things; even a blind squirrel occasionally finds a nut. If they were doctors looking for a cure, it was as if they were using Dr. Josef Mengele, Dr. Moreaux, or Dr. Hannibal Lecter as models. Even the best of them, with good intentions, only saw the symptoms of the underlying diseases. And with the wrong diagnoses, the therapies they prescribed not only had no chance of working, but had terrible side effects. Progressives, socialists, communists, fascists, and their fellow travelers weren't just lousy economic diagnosticians routinely committing negligent malpractice, though. They were more akin to jungle witch doctors.

Just thinking about it raised Grayson's stress level. He felt his heart pound in his chest, and his face felt warm. He stepped to a mirror. His cheeks glowed red. Strange. He'd never allowed others' stupidity to do more than annoy him in the past.

He shook his head, but doing so hurt. Had he allowed this political adventure to get to him? To change him? Is this what happened to men as they perceived their growing power?

He swallowed a couple of ibuprofen to ease the headache.

He thought for a moment about the most recent shooting. Another school. This time in Pennsylvania. Guns Rule. Eight dead. Shooter escaped. The same story. The events weren't coming as fast as before. Maybe the pandemic was ebbing. Jeffrey said they'd taken out one of the men responsible for Guns Rule.

He hadn't heard from Jeffrey as to whether any progress was being made on the Naked Emperor front. Damn him.

He dialed Jeffrey, who answered by saying only, "You're calling me on your public phone. I'll dial you back."

Grayson scowled. He recognized the error. He never called Jeffrey on an unscrambled line. Why had he done so?

A moment later, the phone signaled an encrypted voice call. Grayson connected. "Hey, Jeffrey. Where are you?"

"New York. Heading back down to Washington in the AM to clean up some more mess."

"Yeah, it's all a mess. What mess in particular?"

"I'm not going to tell you. Plausible deniability, sir."

"Hmm. Okay. That's a kind of a Washington catchphrase, isn't it? I hate all this secrecy stuff."

"You're kind of a pro at it now."

Grayson sighed. "Yeah, it seems to come with the territory. What's new on Naked Emperor?"

Jeffrey replied, "I'll see Knight shortly and get you an update."

The answer annoyed Grayson, but he kept his mouth shut. The implicit message would be clear to Jeffrey.

After a moment, Jeffrey added, "I understand your frustration. I'll try for a firm answer. How're things on your end? Much progress building a transition team?"

Grayson replied, "Chicks haven't hatched. Still six weeks to go. But yeah, I've got the outline done. It's going to be radical. A giant broom. After I finish with the dynamite and the chainsaw."

"Nuclear option?"

"Pretty much. I've always thought that there was nothing in Washington that a ten-kiloton nuke wouldn't cure. My preference is to use a big broom though. As you know, I want to collapse morale throughout the executive branch; the bureaucracy has to start hating their jobs. I recognize it's probably impossible to eliminate even the most dysfunctional agency, so I'll find cabinet members that want to make their lives as miserable as possible."

"I presume the incompetents will be the first to go."

Grayson shook his head. "No. It's counterintuitive, but the worst in government are the competent ones. Remember, government is coercion—legalized evil. So if they're competent, they just do evil more effectively. The only competent people I want are those in charge of eliminating their own departments."

Jeffrey sighed audibly. "Grayson. When they figure out you're serious about all this, they're going to kill you."

It was Grayson's turn to sigh. "I suppose I shouldn't underestimate them, whoever they are. I'm taking this risk of my own free will. I know it might kill me. But nobody gets out of here alive."

"Don't die."

"Get the Naked Emperor. If Charles Knight isn't doing it, we'll have to find another way."

Grayson disconnected suddenly, without saying goodbye to his good friend. He didn't think about why he had done so, and he didn't feel guilty for doing it. He was irritated, irritable, and mad at the world in general.

Where was he? Nevada somewhere? No, that wasn't right. He looked out the hotel room window to a view of the Golden Gate on a dry September night. So San Francisco. That's right. He remembered. He lay down in his bed and tried to work through the lessons of the day, as he did almost every evening. It was good discipline and helped him avoid having to relearn things repeatedly. It kept the day's lessons in his mind as he fell asleep, helping to cement them in place, since sleep is when memories are consolidated and filed in the brain's cells.

He drifted slowly into a disturbed sleep, filled with dreams about drowning.

*   *   *

Rainbow pounded on the hotel-room door until Charles finally opened it. Only after she'd barged on past him did she notice that he held a gun.

"It's 3:00 a.m., Rainbow. Don't you sleep?"

"I'll sleep when I'm dead."

"I'll keep that in mind the next time I get tired … In the meantime have you got Target's phone and computer hacked?"

"Sorry it took so long. Had to brute force this."

"Have you looked yet?"

Of course she had. "Lots of time on the train, Paladin."

"What did you find?"

"Some financial-account information. And a web-browser history. Guy uses a VPN, but then didn't bother to clear his history or even go incognito mode. He searched for information on most of the recent sites of the mass shootings—before the shootings, Paladin. He's maybe involved in all of them."

Charles closed his eyes. "I should have killed him when I first saw him."

Rainbow shrugged. "Oh, and the most recent file he opened was a spreadsheet. A customer list of some store."

Charles eyes widened, "You mean The Store?"

"Yeah, that's it. A list of members of The Store. I don't know what that is."

"I have a suspicion …"

"Well, good. Have fun exploring the dead guy's computer! I'm outahere. Gonna get with my crew."

She turned to leave and opened the hotel-room door.

Charles said, "Say hi to Alpha. Tell him we'll need his team in the next few days. We've got some planning to do. And a Store to close."

54

Vigilante Justice

"I REALLY dig your ride."

Forestal heard that a lot, from men and women alike. The girl who said it wasn't exactly beautiful. Some might say she was cute as a button—but with a touch of exotic. Cute wasn't quite right; that implied a "girl next door" wholesomeness, which definitely didn't fit. This one had street attitude. She looked more feral than the typical teenagers he preferred to feed upon, but here she was, an interesting target of opportunity. Not just a lamb to slaughter. Something more challenging, one that he might enjoy coaxing. He tossed his briefcase into the back and turned to face her.

"Want to go for a spin?" he asked.

"Oh, I can't do that. I've got my own car to drive home. But can I just sit in it, for a minute?"

"Sure. Climb in."

"Can I sit behind the wheel?"

Forestal looked around the otherwise-empty underground garage. She didn't look like a thief, but then who did? He looked at her again. Pretty. Medium size. Athletic. She was worth the risk.

She wore a baseball hat that covered her forehead down to her eyes, wore no mask, and had an appealing smile. An inviting smile? He'd find out.

"Sure, go ahead." Forestal held the door for her. "What's your name?"

"I'm Rainbow." She climbed in. "Keys?"

Why not? he thought. The throb of the engine might get her in the mood. There was a naïvely bold seductiveness to the way she asked. Forestal handed her the key fob.

She started the car and looked him in the eyes, glowing with enthusiasm. Of course she pressed the accelerator repeatedly. She seemed excited by the noise of the racing engine echoing through the cement garage. She squirmed in the seat as her excitement grew—as did his own.

"You like that?" he prompted.

"Very much. Come on. Get in here with me." It was flirtatious, but with more to it. There was a tone of command in her young voice. Maybe she was a little kinky... maybe he just got lucky. That's why God made Aston Martins.

"Why not." He walked around the car and sank into the passenger seat. As he turned to look at the exciting girl behind the wheel of his car, she reached out to his neck—obviously the start of a caress. He didn't notice the cigarette-pack-sized device in her palm until it made a horrifically loud spitting-and-cracking sound as it coursed five hundred thousand volts into his body. He could only scream once, then his lungs shut down. His body stiffened, and his feet kicked the floorboard; his back felt like a tightly stretched piano wire. She kept it up, pressing hard into his neck. Agony battled with anxiety, informing his brain that everything everywhere was now in extreme danger. He couldn't breathe. He couldn't breathe!

As the high-voltage electricity scrambled his frantic brain, someone opened his car door. A rescuer? It had to be a rescuer. No one could stand this pain.

He opened his eyes with great effort for a moment, to see who was there to help him, and looked into the face of a second woman. His eyes squeezed closed again as another bolt of lightning coursed through his body. He could no longer think. His brain itself spasmed. Then the arcing agony throughout his body suddenly changed. His muscles turned limp as Jell-O. He couldn't move. Was he paralyzed? But at least the pain diminished to something resembling severe muscle cramps, which were a soothing balm by comparison to a moment before. He didn't feel the prick as the woman slid a needle into his arm a moment later, but he could hear what she said.

"Tonight, you sick pig, tonight you die."

He remembered the face, although he hadn't seen it in almost a decade. Emily Renner. The bitch who'd shot and almost killed him. He felt hatred along with agony and wanted to kill her.

And then came visions. Horrible visions. He no longer cared about anything at all, anywhere, ever. Time was nothing. Space was here. There. Horror. Teeth. Fire. Toads. Snakes. Hell. Must be hell. I need to scream. I can't scream. Frozen voice. Frozen everything.

* * *

"He'll be completely disconnected from the world for at least an hour. Entirely harmless," Emily assured Charles.

"Are you sure?"

"Very sure. Ketamine is great stuff. It's like PCP, only safer. It may cause him to have some horrible nightmares."

Charles smiled and said, "His nightmares are about to be real. Let's get him out of here."

Disguised as Paladin with the extra-thick eyebrows, Charles wore a suit and a wide antiviral mask, like a million other worker bees in the city. He politely helped Rainbow out of the driver's seat and slid behind the wheel. "Great job, you two! See you soon."

He backed up, slipped the car into gear, burning rubber as he punched the gas. He noted twin tire marks and a satisfying cloud of silver smoke in the rearview mirror, which partially obscured Emily and Rainbow as they ran off.

The exit gate dutifully opened as it sensed the transceiver on the dashboard. Charles looked directly up at the security camera as he passed it, documenting—for those looking closely enough—the presence of the same eyes and bushy eyebrows of the man who'd been caught on camera at St. Margaret's. Then he was out on the street, the sleek car moving along at an idle. He didn't need to be early. In fact, he might as well loop through a couple of unnecessary blocks and enjoy the vehicle, maybe catch a couple of surveillance images for the cops to use later. And so he did.

Charles had never driven a Vanquish or any other Aston Martin. They had handsome lines, but they weren't sports cars like Ferraris or Porsches. They'd always been boulevard cruisers targeted to middle-aged men with money. Still, it would be a fine car to drive after a gun fight. Too bad he had Forestal's drooling mass next to him.

Despite his leisurely pace, it took less than ten minutes to get to The Store. He parked the Vanquish directly in front of the building. As Emily had promised, Forestal was still oblivious in the passenger seat. Eyes open, drooling, as if he'd been chemically lobotomized. Charles stood on the sidewalk, noting four people standing on the corner a block away. He tipped his fedora.

Walking up the stairs of the house, Charles only now realized just how large it was. Probably built by a captain of industry over a century ago. He looked up at the three floors above and at the barred, darkened windows below grade. The building had to be eight thousand square feet or more. Combined data from the spyminers and Jeffrey's sources seemed to indicate that the place wasn't just a gentleman's club or even a conventional cathouse. It appeared to be an actual sex-slave ring, frequented by aggressively danger-ous sexual deviants—among the worst scum in the swamp. And yet it was an institution that had been around for decades.

He rang the doorbell. A moment later a man in white tie and tails opened the door.

Charles overcame a moment of surprise, hoping the man didn't notice. He was identical to the dead Target, the man they'd killed at St Margaret's.

"Mr. Forestal is in his car." He pointed to the Vanquish.

The bald man looked down at the car, and replied in a high-pitched voice. "Ah, yes. Is Mr. Forestal unwell?"

"He's under the influence of a drug. He asked me to bring him here until he recovers. Why would he ask me to bring him here?"

"Mr. Forestal is a regular visitor—and always welcome."

"Can you help me get him out of the car?"

"Certainly."

With some effort the two men lugged Forestal up the stairs and settled him on a couch in the front-entrance hallway. Charles noted a lewd and unpleasant statue.

"Pardon me, but I assume you are not a member here?"

"Should I be?" Charles replied.

"It entirely depends. You can only become a member if you are invited by a current member. Has Mr. Forestal invited you?"

"Yes. Earlier this evening. It's about the fourth time he's mentioned it."

"From a man like Mr. Forestal, that means it would be appropriate for you to consider. He's one of our most valued members and knows who else would fit in."

"I understand," replied Charles. "Have you worked here long?"

"Indeed I have."

"What do you do?"

"Anything the members require, sir." His voice rose even higher as he said this. He rubbed his bald head.

Charles said, offhandedly, "Can I get your name?"

"Certainly, sir. I'm Lichen. Dresden Lichen."

"Right. I met your brother recently. Your twin brother, I presume. Just for a moment. I assume you took over where he left off?"

Lichen stopped breathing. A flashing second later, he reached for a gun. But Charles was ready, and he acted fast. Before Lichen had even exposed the muzzle of his weapon, Charles had Rainbow's taser against his neck. He held it firm as the man went down to the ground, shaking like a mass of pudding, his face contorted in pain.

Charles picked up Lichen's small, hammerless S&W .38 revolver, returned to the door, and whistled. The four from the corner were inside in a moment: Rainbow, Emily, Jeffrey, and Frank. Followed moments later by another foursome, men with black skin and black cotton clothing. They closed and locked the entrance.

Charles said to the leader, "Alpha, thanks for coming. Good to see you all."

He knew the four men as Alpha, Beta, Gamma, and Epsilon. The Alpha Team. To them, he was Paladin. They'd become friends when he'd initially formed his little cartel during the previous chapter in his life, as a drug lord. His partners, dealers, colleagues. Ghetto rats who created the illicit drug-distribution network and bootlegging operation through which Naked Emperor was dispensed to the masses. They liked and respected him, and he knew he could rely on them.

Alpha Team had already done quite a bit for the Paladin Network: they were the very first of the hum-vigs. The human vigilantes of the network. They worked anonymously but hand in glove with the Paladin hackers— the vig-hacks—to physically disable hardware that could not be adequately destroyed with online efforts. Based on growing demand, the future probably held good things for this team and teams like them. Their first project in response to several lucrative smart contracts had been to clear out an outbound call center specializing in the MoneyGram Scam. Unethical young men conned old ladies by pretending to be their wrongfully imprisoned grandson in a faraway state and in desperate need of Money from

461

Gramma—or a Western Union. Either was fine. Those who were not sufficiently demented, confused, or gullible quickly hung up, which saved a lot of time for the scammers.

Do what thou wilt… but be prepared to accept the consequences. For those young men, Alpha and his team were the consequences.

Putting an end to relentless robocallers was another early success. Robocallers certainly weren't dangerous, but they aggressively wasted huge amounts of time, even after they were reported to the National Do Not Call Registry. After vig-hacks determined exactly which companies and individuals were most persistent in their harassment, teams of hum-vigs went into action. The smart contracts were financed by what amounted to crowdfunding from thousands on the Paladin Network. The marketing departments of the companies paying for offshore robocall mills found their computer electronics and servers doused with acid and destroyed. A message, left with a Paladin coin, explained why. In the case of the few stubborn holdouts, a visit to the management's homes and destruction of their personal electronics resulted in a shift in their marketing strategy soon after. Paladin Network added fear of consequences to its arsenal of effective weapons.

Alpha and Gamma cleared The Store's upstairs floors. Epsilon and Rainbow went to work duct taping Dresden Lichen to a chair and trussing up Forestal. Epsilon tossed Rainbow a brick of hundreds he extracted from the man's inner coat pocket. The first floor had a parlor, kitchen, dining facility, and formal entertaining rooms. All but the kitchen where three men worked stood empty. Beta recommended they put their cell phones on a counter and retreat into a pantry closet—advice that they wisely followed.

Charles found no cameras anywhere—not surprising in a place like this. He gingerly opened a heavy wooden door leading downstairs. The staircase was, if anything, more ornate than the front hallway. This was no typical basement.

He led the way down the steps. At the bottom, he peered around the corner and down a surprisingly long hall, making him wonder if this building connected underground to the neighboring house. It would make sense. He gestured for the others to hang back, confirmed that his gun was in in his pocket, and walked confidently toward two visibly armed men playing cards at a small table. They weren't positioned to prevent people from going in the large door behind them but, it seemed, to prevent anyone behind the door from escaping.

"Good evening, gentlemen."

They both stood rapidly and replied with respect. They were employees. Guards.

"Ah, good evening, sir," the older one said. He spoke with an accent. Eastern European.

"Let me introduce myself," Charles said. "My name is Paladin. Have you two worked here long?"

The large, well-muscled speaker on the left replied, "Twenty years for me." He nodded toward the other man. "Five years for Boris."

"That's what I need to know. I'm a new member, just introduced by Blaize Forestal. Do you know him?"

Boris, on the right, relaxed somewhat. "Mr. Forestal is a regular, sir."

"That's good to know," Charles maintained an air of nonchalance. "I'm eager for my first evening. Are there many people here tonight?"

"Just four bidders, Mr. Paladin."

"Four, huh? That seems a small number."

"Nothing fresh on auction tonight. It's always busier on the weekends when the new ones come, but as long as there are three or more, auctions are held. Otherwise, it is just set price."

Charles nodded as if barely paying attention. "Sensible. Anyone here that's new, like me?"

"No, sir," Boris replied. "Everyone here tonight has been a member longer than I have worked here."

"Longer than even I've worked here, Mr. Paladin," his muscular companion added. "One has been a member even longer than Dresden. And Dresden's been here over thirty years."

Charles nodded. "Well, that's loyalty."

Charles retrieved his Kahr 9 mm from his suit pocket and aimed it at the man's head. He thought about pulling the trigger. He wanted to. These men probably deserved to die, but probability wasn't certainty. Still, if either tried to make a move, he'd kill them both here and now.

A moment later Emily came up behind him. She aimed her .45 with an intimidating air of finality that the guards could not help but notice.

Frank appeared next with an eyebrow raised. "Five years here? Twenty years here? Why aren't they dead, Paladin?" He aimed his suppressed .22 casually at Boris.

Emily tased the older man, who crumpled to the floor. Boris made a move for his weapon. Frank pulled his trigger twice, and two bullets entered the man's forehead, an inch apart.

In the unlikely case the man was innocent, Frank and Emily were guilty.

The intricately carved walnut door in front of them seemed comically out of place. It could have been a medieval castle door. Rainbow found the wall switch and killed the hallway lights. Charles cautiously cracked opened the heavy door to peer inside. Emily crouched down below him and likewise looked through the small crack. Frank and Rainbow stood guard, working their way back down the hallway toward the stairs, opening two doors on the right and sweeping the rooms. One door on the left was locked.

Emily and Charles gazed surreptitiously into what was perhaps the largest room in the house. In the center was a raised octagonal stage, lit by a single spotlight. Tobacco smoke swirled against the dark walls in the muted light. A pale-skinned Asian girl was strapped to the chair with plastic ties around her trim ankles and thin wrists. Tears glistened on her cheeks.

The auctioneer approached the girl in the chair. He grasped her chin, lifting it upward and turning her head from side to side. There was nothing gentle here. He spoke to his small audience, visible only from the light reflected from the girl's ivory skin.

"Do I have the minimum? Three thousand for one hour of unlimited use, and," he laughed menacingly, "no cleaning fees."

A voice from the dark said, "Four thousand."

An accented voice said, "Five thousand."

And then a deep, dark, and slow voice. "Six thousand."

Charles's ears counted four bidders. While his eyes adjusted to the dark, he wondered if there were more in attendance, remaining silent. Bidding continued.

"Nine thousand takes the prize," said the auctioneer, a short, plump man with a thick, black mustache wearing a red silk smoking jacket. He freed the girl's ankles, pulled her up, and led her out of Charles's view. He must have gone through a door into a lit hallway, as a stream of light allowed Charles to perceive more features of the space.

The octagon brought to mind the stage for a cage fight, but without the metal cage. The floor of the octagon wasn't padded canvas, but polished concrete. With acoustic tile on the walls and ceiling, and with sixteen plush chairs around the perimeter, perhaps the octagon was used for some kind of exclusive but degraded spectator sport on some nights. Tonight it was used for an auction.

The auctioneer re-entered with a dazed girl stumbling in tow. "And we move to the next offering."

Emily had heard and seen enough. The men in this room were regular patrons. This sealed their fate as far as she was concerned.

She stood, jostled Charles out of the way, and pushed the door wide open, raising her gun and aiming it at the auctioneer in the center. Charles entered and flipped on all the light switches next to the door. Frank strode in and started shooting. Charles watched as Frank worked with a pace and precision that could only be gained by years of practice and experience. He shot through the head of each man who, in shock and slow to react, sat comfortably in a leather chair.

There was no trial, no jury of one's peers, no opportunity to leverage contacts and bribe power brokers to free them from the judgment and sentencing they all deserved—and had finally received.

Charles approached the red-garbed auctioneer. "Where are the girls?" His teeth clenched tightly, he repeated, "I said, where are the girls?"

The man moved his head toward a button on the near wall. Charles threw him to the ground. Judgment followed swiftly, as he shot him point blank through his mouth and into his brainstem. Moving quickly, Charles pressed the button and the wall slid to the side. He crouched low with the muzzle of his gun aimed toward whatever might appear.

What he found outraged him. Five girls, very young. Barely teenagers. Naked but for underwear, wrists tied. Fear shone from their eyes. Each of their faces had healing scars, as well as fresh bruises. One girl lay against the back wall, as if asleep. He placed his weapon in the holster in the small of his back and moved toward them, with hands held unthreateningly. "Rainbow, help here."

Jeffrey came down in the house elevator, dragging the partly conscious Forestal. The elevator returned two minutes later, with Alpha pulling along the conscious mass of Dresden Lichen. Charles moved a second chair to the center of the octagon, taping it firmly back-to-back with the first chair. They fastened the two criminals to the furniture, taping them to each other and the chairs.

"Think the chairs are strong enough?" Jeffrey asked.

"They won't need to last long, will they?" Charles replied.

"Probably not."

Alpha found some clothing and handed it out to the girls, who began dressing.

Emily flicked her finger onto Forestal's forehead. "Forestal, wake up!"

The ketamine was wearing off, but a cooperative and disinhibited state might remain for a time. Forestal struggled to focus, to figure out where he was. His eyes opened wide as he became aware of his situation.

Emily and Frank stood in front of him.

Emily said, "You had me imprisoned for six years."

Forestal sneered as his eyes began to focus. "Yes. This time it'll be for life, you crazy bitch."

Frank belted Forestal, driving the man's head back into Dresden Lichen's bald scalp.

"Who are you?" Forestal asked Frank, spite in his eyes. "I want your name."

Emily whipped her pistol across his cheek. "Did you take my sister?"

Forestal spit blood. "Your sister? Are you worried about your little sister? What's it been? Ten years?" He looked at Frank then. "Oh. I know you. You're the father. Renner. Frank Renner." He laughed and spit more blood. "I can tell you what you want to know. About your daughter. After you let me go."

Dresden Lichen grunted.

Frank ripped the tape from the bald man's mouth.

Lichen said in his high voice, "They're not letting anyone go, Mr. Forestal. We're dead men. But look. Mr. Forestal didn't take anybody. I'm the one who handles the business of the girls and then, later, where their organs go. Who's your sister?"

"Anna. Anna Renner."

The bald man shook his head. "Where?"

"Manhattan."

"Long time ago?"

"Yes."

Frank pulled a picture from his pocket. "This girl?"

Lichen glanced at the picture. "Yeah. I remember. In a foster home or something."

Forestal said, "See? I didn't take your sister. Your daughter. That wasn't me."

He looked at Frank. "Forestal told me about your daughter. Directed me to take her." Lichen laughed. "I said they're going to kill us anyway, Forestal."

Forestal looked up into Emily's eyes as she nodded in agreement with the Cleaner.

Forestal shook his head as if giving up, which was appropriate. He said, quietly, "Lichen took her. That was all him." And then louder, slowly, word by word, "But when she got here to The Store, I made sure I won that auction."

Emily hauled off and broke his nose with her pistol. "You bastard!"

Forestal roared, then groaned. "You know, I've always wanted to tell you that, Emily. Every day, when I see the scars on my chest." He looked at Frank. "And here I get to do just that. Now you know."

Frank stepped back. His jaw clenched tight. His was a searing, white-hot rage.

Emily asked, quietly, "Is she alive?"

Forestal looked up at Emily, staring into her face with dead eyes.

"Tell me!" She struck his face with all her might.

Forestal, blood dripping over his mouth, spat at her. Then he smiled a dark smile, snarling like a wolf trapped in a corner. "When I was done with her"—he jerked his head backward in the direction of Lichen—"he harvested what he could of her organs. Parts of her may still be alive, here and there."

Emily shook her head repeatedly. Her body shook as well. Frank's fulminating fury kept him mute and immobile, his rage paralyzing him.

*   *   *

Rainbow had encouraged the girls to come out of their room.

"Do you speak English?" Rainbow asked.

The girls nodded. One said, "We're all Americans. Some other girls, they didn't speak English. They aren't here anymore. Where are we?"

Charles said, "You're safe now. You'll be better soon. You're in Washington, DC. Where are you from?"

"New York."

"Austin."

"Chicago."

467

Two girls remained silent.

Charles nodded. "How long have you been here?"

None of the girls could answer that question. Each had tracks on her arms. They were addicted to whatever opiates their captors had poured into their veins.

Rainbow held two of them by the hand. "You can go home soon, if that's what you want." Rainbow led the girls up the stairs and into the front hall of The Store. She took the brick of $10,000 extracted from Lichen's jacket and divided it between them. "This will help," she said. "When we're done here in a few minutes, I'm going to call an ambulance for you. Call your folks or someone you trust. There will be police arriving, maybe in an hour or so. If you stay, you can tell them all that happened."

*　　*　　*

A floor below, Charles said, "Emily, do you want to..." He indicated Forestal with his head. "Or would that be you, Frank?"

Neither moved.

Charles added, "Or do we let the girls have dibs on this other creep? They might be the stronger for it."

Emily shook her head slowly. "I'd be inclined to let them have one hour of unlimited usage with the bald man. But they're very young. I think this job falls to us. I'll feel better doing my part now." She looked at her father, the man who had every right to kill Blaize Forestal.

Frank nodded his permission.

She stood in front of Blaize Forestal.

Anger and tears filled her eyes as she brought the muzzle of her weapon to Forestal's forehead. The left side of her lips curled up.

He sneered at her as he leaned his head back, his hair pressed against the bald pate of Dresden Lichen, tied to the other chair.

She said, "What kind of a name is Blaize, anyway?"

And then she pulled the trigger.

Emily's mind, filled with the chemicals released during periods of extreme stress, absorbed that moment as if it were a high-speed video camera recording the entire incident for slow-motion replay. She observed what happened carefully during the next instant, when time slowed down. She felt the recoil of the weapon as the action slid back and the bullet left the muzzle. The lead blasted through his skull, through the meninges that surrounded the brain and then on through to the gelatin-like brain matter. The bullet conveyed such pressure that, for a moment, both of Forestal's eyes bulged out from their sockets, like a grotesque cartoon or a horror movie. Indeed, it seemed his whole cranium enlarged for a fraction of a second before collapsing back in on itself as the far side of Forestal's skull tore away in chunks of skin and bone releasing the accumulated pressure in a spray of brain matter and blood.

And so ended Blaize Forestal's lifetime of evil.

But the .45-caliber bullet had not completed its work. It kept traveling and entered the next skull. A bald skull. And so Dresden Lichen joined his brother in hell.

They prepared to leave, carefully removing any traces that would compromise them, but leaving behind an unsecured copy of the hard drive from Chemnitz Lichen's laptop. The members of The Store would be getting lots of unwanted attention. It was a gift to the FBI—assuming they weren't themselves on the list.

They exited, closing the front door behind them. The Alpha Team headed off with just a nod of the head to acknowledge their long association.

Charles walked to the Aston Martin. It would be nice to keep it as a reasonable fee for a necessary job. Alas, this was a practical impossibility. So instead, he did as he planned. He opened the driver-side door and rubbed the steering wheel and shifter and door handle with degreaser to remove any fingerprints. Exiting, he shook a baggie full of hair clippings and dust, the combined clippings from dozens of clients of a unisex hair salon. It was a good trick to blur DNA signals and protect both himself and Rainbow.

And then he torched it.

55

Immolation

MORNING came too fast. Grayson not only didn't want to see the public, he didn't even want to see friends. His head hurt, and his muscles ached. Was it a succession of cheap hotels with their cheap mattresses? His entire staff had been on a budget—partly because it was the way he was wired, but mostly to set the right example for the campaign, especially since the average American's standard of living was falling rapidly with the Greater Depression building momentum. Even so, his staff should have upped the hotel budget. Incompetent fools. He rubbed at his itchy eyes. He felt anger at the fact that he was so annoyed.

A knock. Grayson climbed out of bed and answered the door in his underwear. It was not his usual way, but he didn't care. He opened the door to see Liam, the son of a neighbor in South Carolina. Liam had become a sort of adjutant, and Grayson had come to rely on him extensively during the past several months. He'd never once had a negative thought about the young man.

But, today, he was overcome by anger, and he had no desire to restrain his impulses. "What the hell do you want, Liam?"

Liam took a step back from the door, and his face blanked.

Grayson felt no empathy for the kid. He acknowledged this as a change in his behavior but didn't care. All he felt was frustration. "What, Liam? What?"

Liam said, "Mr. Chase, sir. I'm sorry. You'd asked me to get you up for your breakfast meeting with the Chamber of Commerce."

"Right, right." Grayson replied. "What else today?"

"After breakfast, at 10:00 a.m., you've got a rally at University of Washington."

"They booed Heather Lear off the stage there, right?"

"They sure did. I'm amazed it didn't get completely out of control. Did you see the news?"

"Not yet. Just woke up."

"CityFire riots in Seattle last night, right near the University District. Really violent. People killed. One burned to death with a gasoline-soaked tire around his neck. Insane. If the police have opened the streets, we'll be driving right through there."

Grayson said under his breath, "They all need to die."

"What's that, sir?"

"Die." Grayson slammed the door closed. He couldn't tolerate the thought of showering, so he reached for what was close at hand, the clothes he wore the day before. He picked up his toothbrush, turned on the water, then turned it back off. He dropped the unused toothbrush in the sink.

Breakfast was a disaster. The university gig was worse.

At breakfast, he nodded and smiled, trying to disguise growing feelings of rage. Grayson was known for his equanimity and patience, using the Socratic method to lead people out of their indoctrination while planting some seeds to re-educate them. But, today, he had no interest in either his companions, his audience, or their thoughts. "I know you're no rocket scientist, but even my dog knows better than that." His only attempt at humor was an imitation of Mr. T: "I pity you fools."

A gray-haired man with red cheeks tried to rescue the situation by asking him what he could do to protect his seafood farm from imported competition.

Grayson replied, "Not my problem. Cut your costs, improve your productivity, innovate. Do you expect me to run your business for you? Why don't you sell your stuff overseas? Turn the tables?" It wasn't bad advice, but it was very badly delivered. Even then, it was his most cogent and polite response of the morning. He didn't care. At the end of the breakfast, Grayson called one man a "stupid jerk."

Liam, near his side, tugged on his elbow.

"What is it, Liam?"

"What's wrong?" Liam asked.

"Nothing's wrong."

"Mr. Chase, you're ... not yourself."

He caught himself. "That's true. I feel strange. Everything's wrong. Where the hell are we?"

Liam frowned and scrunched his eyebrows. "The Cowbell Restaurant."

"What city, you idiot?"

Liam frowned further. "Seattle?"

"Right. You could have told me. Okay, where next?"

"We leave for University of Washington in twenty minutes."

"Good," Grayson replied. "This place smells bad." Then he added, "Let's blow this two-bit popsicle stand." He walked out, with no good-byes.

An hour later, their three-vehicle convoy drove through the aftermath of the previous night's CityFires. Grayson counted three burned-out buildings and a dozen upside-down cars. Litter and glass from looted stores covered the sidewalks. It smelled bad here too. Maybe that was the smell of violence, of immolated human flesh.

Immolation. Grayson felt the visceral response. Nausea. It hurt to swallow the saliva that flooded his mouth.

Cherry trees dominated the scenery around the halls and libraries as they drove through the university grounds, parking as close as possible to the lecture hall. Grayson led the way to the campus quad, his security detail hustling to catch up.

The entourage approached the platform from which he would speak to the throng. The media had cameras set up, and the crowd of thousands, mostly students, cheered. The world was anxious to hear what the exciting new antipolitician would say this time.

Grayson's head pounded. His stomach groaned. He didn't like the feel of his clothes. Something stank here too.

He considered that he actually disliked the very thought of the students. They made so much noise, howling like chimpanzees, that it was impossible to like or respect them. Using logic or persuasion was pointless. Their screaming turned his headache into a jackhammer.

Stupefying noise. Coming from stupid people.

They all needed to disappear. Or die.

Grayson waited impatiently for the student president to introduce him. He could feel the excitement of the throng. He knew the polls said 60 percent of the population were on his side, but he had come to hate the idea of so many people thinking he was the cure for all that ailed them. It was as if he had to pull a wagon loaded with their problems. Today he hated people, but he had too much of a headache to consider why.

When it came his turn to speak, the crowd's noise reached a crescendo, their chants echoed off Raitt Hall and Savery Hall, all the way down to the southeastern end of the quad. "Chase, Chase, Chase, Chase, Chase!" they shouted.

Grayson looked at the television cameras and out over thousands of students. He raised his hands, and the crowd slowly quieted.

As they settled down, he proceeded to immolate his candidacy. The first two words were normal enough:

"Hello, all!"

The crowd cheered. "Hello!" It took a full minute to die away.

"I'm going to give a different type of speech," Grayson said, drooling and spitting some saliva onto the edge of the podium. "Because I look out on this group of people in front of me today and I see war. I see death. I see evil. I see it emanating from the stones of the buildings surrounding us. I see it filling the empty minds of those to my right who are demanding someone else pay for things they want, and calling it a human right. You morons have no idea what a right is. You're so stupid that you've not only swallowed your professors' progressive bullshit, but you pay them fifty thousand dollars a year to spoon-feed it to you. Then you spew it back like robots, for meaningless grades. I once thought that people like you could be cured. But no longer. Now I just think you're the enemy of all that is right and good. Really, you just need to die."

Thousands of mouths hung open, silent, waiting for what might come next. This wasn't the spirited diatribe against power-hungry politicians they'd expected. Even the socialists had been open to Grayson because he acknowledged that much of what they hated needed to be changed. He'd made inroads. But in that one minute, he'd lost them all.

"And you Republicans." Grayson continued. "Probably not many of you willing to show your faces on this campus. If you are, I'm glad you're here. Republican idiots. What were you thinking? Just following your parents like zombies? Haven't your stupid parents ever noticed that Republicans end up growing government spending and bureaucracy as much as the Democrats?

"And the rest of you here. Your parents are probably Democrats.

Unethical, thieving scum who drive around in their Volvos with sticks up their asses and complete confidence that they know what's best for the world. You can see them coming from a mile away. They hold their noses so high in the air they'd drown if it rained."

At this point some in the audience had recovered from their initial shock. A few people started booing.

Grayson spoke louder, yelling into the microphone. "And so what are you going to do? You're here today, so your brains must have engaged. But what would you have done if I hadn't come onto the national stage? Would you have voted for Lear? Well, some of you are that stupid. For Cooligan? Yeah, most of you. He promises more free shit. Why would you support either of those sickening scumbags? Think, if you can, you stupid little bastards. Think!"

Liam considered whether he should rip the microphone from Grayson's hands. It was bizarre. Everything his boss said so far was actually correct, but the way he was saying it was totally irrational. Would his next utterances take him over the edge altogether? Liam tapped Chase's shoulder, whispering, "Cut" repeatedly, trying to get him to stop, but Chase kept on talking. Something was very wrong. This wasn't Grayson Chase anymore. Some evil spirit had taken control of him.

And it only got worse. Grayson Chase insulted China: "You slanty-eyed gooks may have filled our garages with worthless shit, but we've filled your banks with our worthless paper dollars. We'll see who fucked who worse..." Canadians: "If we want anything you igloo dwellers have, we'll send a Boy Scout troop up to take it." And Mexicans: "You beaners have had a free ride for way too long. We took Texas and California from you. We should take the rest of your shithole country and export you to Guatemala! Screw you all. Bunch of morons. None of you is worth one more minute of my time."

Grayson's face glowed red, and, despite the cool morning, his face dripped with sweat. He moved off the stage to the catcalls and angered howls of the crowd of students. Some shook their heads quietly to themselves, trying to understand what had just happened. Less than twenty minutes ago, they'd been on his side: the first politician that anyone in living memory had really wanted to be the president.

He'd clearly had a psychotic break.

The media loved it, of course. Grayson Chase, the next president of the United States, with nothing in his way but the actual voting, had gone insane on national television. Fifty million people saw the video within twenty-four hours, and billions—the whole world—in three days.

A week later, the polls had Grayson Chase at 19 percent, a shockingly high number in view of his performance at the university. Perhaps some thought it was a perverse attempt at comedy. The pundits put his chance of political survival at 5 percent.

But the doctors put his chance of survival at zero.

56

Deathbed

CHARLES and Jeffrey rushed to the hospital in Seattle. There was no longer any need to keep Charles away from Grayson Chase. It no longer mattered if the candidate was seen with the notorious drug lord.

The hospital ward smelled institutional, full of isopropyl alcohol, medicines, bleach, and the smell of failing human bodies. IV poles beeped, oxygen-saturation monitors alarmed, and the hallways echoed with occasional wails of pain, frustration, or dementia. Charles had been lucky so far in his life in avoiding such places. His hospital memories were happy—of a hospital ship back in Gondwana and a princess. He glanced at Jeffrey and recalled the scars across the man's chest; his companion had spent considerable time in the bowels of hospitals.

Together, they approached the nursing station and stood in front of an obese young woman in rose-colored scrubs. She stared at a computer and didn't look up at them; clearly indifferent to her job, or making a little power play, her choice was to be oblivious.

"We're looking for Grayson Chase."

She continued to face the screen, but her eyes momentarily darted up toward the two men in front of her. "You and half a million other people. He's down there to the right. Good luck getting through security."

Charles locked eyes with an official-looking woman in a pantsuit sitting at the back of the nursing station, undoubtedly part of the security detail. She paid close attention to them.

"I don't think Secret Service will let me through, Jeffrey," Charles observed.

"Nor would I, if I were in their shoes."

They turned into a short hallway with beige walls. Everything in the building was some off-white color, in contrast with the two men in dark suits posted in front of the opaque-glass double door. The taller man held out his hand to halt their approach. Charles stopped; Jeffrey didn't. Jeffrey approached the guards, said, "This man is with me," and walked past them unmolested, even though he carried a weapon in a holster under his arm, rescued from a lockbox in his checked bag as soon as it came off the carousel at the airport. They wanded and patted down Charles.

"Gentlemen," the taller agent said, "you'll need to observe the infectious-control measures in place. They'll tell you more inside." He held his cuff to his lips and spoke something unintelligible, and the door opened into a highly modified area.

The hospital had set up an isolation ward, secured from both intruders coming in and infectious agents going out. Two nurses sat behind a desk, a doctor in scrubs nearby. A Secret Service agent stood by a door that was sheathed in plastic. Two adjoining hospital rooms were likewise covered with the material.

The doctor glanced up as the two men came in. Then he stood up slowly.

"You're Jeffrey, I presume?" Middle-aged and with a slight paunch, the doctor sported a stethoscope, the universal symbol of medical authority, looped around his neck. Glasses settled on the bridge of his nose a bit too low, as if they were as tired as the man who wore them.

"I am."

"We've been expecting you. No last name?"

"Welcome to my world," Jeffrey replied. "This is Charles Knight."

The doctor contemplated Charles for a moment. He'd certainly heard of him during the Sybillene era. "We were told to expect you too."

Jeffrey asked, "What's his status?"

"Mr. Chase is failing rapidly. I'm very sorry. All we can do at this point is palliative care."

"How much time?"

"Maybe a few days. Depends on how much pain medication he needs. He's occasionally lucid. We've had to sedate him a fair amount. Among other things, rabies causes the nerves to fire sporadically; it's like being pierced with needles or doused with hot oil—horribly painful. He really wanted to talk to you, so we've mostly tapered that off. Still, I'm afraid that the sedation will need to increase soon."

"Can we see him?"

The doctor nodded. "We've got him in full isolation of course. Although it's very rare—unheard of, really—for a human to contract rabies from another human, his body fluids are particularly infectious right now. You don't want to take any chances. Have you been vaccinated?"

Jeffrey nodded, but Charles shook his head.

"Regardless, I'd encourage you to stay outside the room. You can speak with him through the intercom there."

The opaque-glass doors behind them opened and a skinny, exhausted-looking young man came through. He smiled grimly when he saw Jeffrey. The two men embraced.

"Charles, this is Liam Walters. Chase's key guy, I guess you could say."

"I've read all about you, Mr. Knight. Grayson likes to keep tabs on you. It's one of my jobs." He closed his eyes. "I guess it was one of my jobs." His eyes were misty. "Grayson very much wants to see you, wants to talk to you while he still can."

"The feeling is mutual," Charles replied. "What happened? How did he get infected?"

"Nobody knows. The doctors say it's just one of those things. Only two or three people a year die of rabies in the US, because almost everyone bitten by a dog or some wild animal gets post-exposure prophylaxis in time. Here in the US the deaths are mostly from bats, where the person doesn't even know he was bitten or scratched. It's hard to see where that could have happened to Grayson. Maybe I got exposed too, although I can't imagine how. I'm getting the shots, like pretty much everybody in the campaign. Could have been anytime in the last few months.

"I've tried to find out what I can. Globally, rabies kills sixty thousand people every year, almost all of them in Third World countries. Once the symptoms come on—anywhere from a week to a couple of months after infection—it's one hundred percent deadly. They say there've been about a dozen people, in all of human history, who have survived it. Once someone starts getting headachy and feverish, or any symptom at all, it's just too late. Grayson started mentioning headaches a few days ago. We just thought it was stress. He also started getting really irritable and disoriented. Impulsive. We knew something was really wrong after what happened at the university. Hallucinations and delusions."

Liam looked at the doctor for confirmation.

The doctor nodded and said, "We can't figure where he got it. The virus could have entered through the skin, from an unnoticed bite or scratch; we can't find the site. The virus slowly works its way up the nerves to the brain; it can take weeks or months from infection before neurologic symptoms show up. The fastest incubation period is from an exposure in the eye. The eye is the most direct neural pathway to the brain. Rabies can move along that path rapidly, in as little as a week."

Liam, Charles, and Jeffrey followed the doctor to the farthest room, where he pulled back a curtain to a sight of Grayson through one layer of glass and two layers of thick plastic surrounding his bed. A woman dressed in isolation garb sat on a chair next to Grayson. A nurse, similarly attired, sat outside one of the plastic isolation layers.

Grayson Chase lay in the bed, but padded leather restraints secured his wrists. His lower body lay wrapped in white blankets that concealed additional restraints. One IV pole dripped fluid into his right arm. That was it. No beeping machines filling the room. No ventilators. No oxygen tubes in his nose. It was more like a small, weird hotel room than a high-tech hospital room making heroic efforts to save a patient. Charles was perplexed for a moment, but then it came to him. Why have any medical devices, with their alarms and buzzers, poking into and making the poor man even more uncomfortable when there wasn't a damn thing to be done?

"Agitation is the main problem at this point," the doctor said. "So we try to keep stimulation low. He's calmer when the stimulation is minimal."

In his bed, Grayson arched his back and thrashed his head to the side with a jerk.

Charles looked at Jeffrey and saw his eyes glistening.

Jeffrey blinked a few times and then tapped on the glass. The woman at the bedside turned, then rose and came toward the window. Charles could see her eyes and some blond hair through the plastic visor of her hazmat outfit. She looked into Jeffrey's eyes and placed her forehead against the glass. Jeffrey did likewise on his side of the glass, and the two remained so for thirty seconds, after which they pulled apart and looked at each other with an aching sadness.

The woman indicated with two fingers that Jeffrey and Charles should enter the room.

"As I said, I don't recommend it, but, um, I know this is something for the history books. As long as you dress like Mr. Chase's sister there, full protection, PPE, you'll be fine."

The doctor showed them the isolation gear. A white Tyvek jumpsuit that covered head to toe, gloves, the N95 particle mask now well known to all the world, and a full-face plastic shield. "You'll need to wear this, and then leave it in the anteroom when you leave, in the red hazmat container. Then wash up thoroughly. Don't go near his face. Stay far from his mouth. Rabies victims can be unexpectedly violent."

Liam stayed outside. Charles and Jeffrey put on the garb and entered.

"Diana, this is Charles Knight."

The woman probably smiled, but it was difficult to tell through the mask and plastic face shield. Her smile, if present, was clouded by sadness. "I'm Grayson's sister. He's been so hoping you would arrive before he dies or becomes incoherent. He's been wanting to meet you for a long time."

Jeffrey had told him the same thing on the way here, but Charles remained surprised. Why?

The three moved to the bedside. Grayson's handsome face was tight with pain; it was clear he was enduring an excruciating torture. His lip bled; he'd bitten it repeatedly, uncontrollably. A nurse leaned in toward his mouth with a thick suction catheter to remove a seemingly endless stream of saliva from his mouth.

Diana said, "He can't swallow. When he tries, it causes horrible spasms. And there's so much saliva."

She leaned a bit closer to his head. "Gray. Gray. They're here. Jeffrey's here. He brought Charles Knight."

Grayson opened one eye and then appeared to try to swallow. He squeezed his eyes closed and gritted his teeth and jerked his head toward the nurse. "Suction," he said. "Please."

The nurse looked up at Charles. "It's constant."

Grayson turned his head back away from the nurse and opened his eyes. Charles looked into the eyes of a man fighting with every remaining component of his being for sanity, clarity, and a last moment of control.

"It seems I've gone the way of Caligula." Grayson smiled for a moment, and Charles could see an indication of the man's intelligence through a face fighting against pain and confusion. "You know, Caligula was a good emperor before he got sick. He was in a coma for three months. Maybe poisoned. Maybe encephalitis. Like rabies, but not. When he awoke, he became the Caligula of history. I don't want to recover only to be like him. But then the doc tells me that recovery isn't an option."

Jeffrey nodded. "None of us gets out of here alive, Grayson." It might have seemed a cruel thing to say, but it wasn't. His words provided a form of comfort: the knowledge that everyone would face the inevitable and it was just Grayson's turn.

Grayson nodded. "I know," Grayson said while keeping his teeth clamped closed. His jaw muscles strained his cheeks. "Jeffrey, I want to thank you for all you've... done. I'm... sorry I've failed my part. You've never failed in yours." His eyes opened wider then, and he stared at Jeffrey. He then nodded again, more slowly, to convey some deeper message that Jeffrey would understand but Charles could only guess at.

With effort he turned his head slightly further to look up at Charles. There were no words Charles could think of that made any sense to say. What would a dying man want to hear on his literal deathbed? But he didn't need to say anything.

"Mr. Knight. Thank you for coming."

Charles could see the effort, the strain, the last energy of the man focusing all his will, right now. One last moment of sanity.

"You're the future, Charles Knight. I need to know, did you arrange what I wanted you to arrange?"

Charles knew this meant Naked Emperor. He'd figured as much over the last few months as Jeffrey had prodded him along. Charles glanced at the nurse who had turned away for a moment after offering suction again. Despite Grayson sinking into the black tar of a horrible demise, he'd remembered to not risk saying incriminating words. Charles's respect for the man only grew.

"Mr. Chase. What you wanted... I'm making it happen."

Jeffrey turned his head to look at Charles then and nodded to him in gratitude.

"February is doable," Charles added.

"Just as I'd hoped," Grayson replied, his eyes closed. He opened them again and said, "You are the man I hoped you would be. But that action seems pointless now. With my failure, doing so would no longer be safe."

"No. It wouldn't. Without you, this country won't be safe either."

"I will reimburse you for your … expense. Give me your hand … Charles."

Charles tucked his gloved hand into Grayson's, just below where a leather strap kept it secured to the heavy plastic bed rail. Grayson squeezed Charles's fingers, weakly at first.

Regret flowed out of Grayson's eyes then. Sadness, exhaustion. "What we might have done together."

Grayson closed his eyes, but squeezed Charles's hand more firmly. "Charles. Your father. He's a good man."

Charles stood straighter. "My father?"

Charles's father—supportive but critical, distantly loving perhaps—had played only a peripheral role in his life since his late teen years. This made no sense. A man with rabies eating away his brain would not always make sense.

"Your father. I trust him. He trusts you. And so I choose to trust you."

Go with it, Charles thought, even though he didn't understand it. "Thank you, Mr. Chase."

"Grayson. Call me Grayson."

His grip relaxed, and his hand fell away.

Grayson's eyes rolled upward into his forehead. A moment later his back arched. Then he thrashed hard to the left. His body convulsed in a series of agonizing pulsed spasms that shook the bed and frightened all in the room. Blood and saliva sprayed from his mouth.

In a hospital emergency, the first thing you do is take your own pulse. Seizures instill a powerful instinctual panic in most observers. Only the most experienced doctors and nurses can avoid that panic, to respond in the appropriate calm and confident manner. Fortunately, that included those caring for Grayson Chase—the man who would have been president. As Charles stepped back, the nurse had already drawn into a syringe a dose of medication and had begun injecting it into Grayson's IV tubing. Two minutes later, his body relaxed into the bed, and the violence ended. The room settled into a silence. The only sound was that of breathing.

Grayson breathed calmly and steadily now, but his brain had disconnected. It would never reconnect.

57

Paradise Revisited

DOMINICA drew few of the elite and ultrawealthy who jockeyed for position on places like St. Barts. This place allowed for physical and financial privacy and, equally important, psychological separation from the increasingly tumultuous environment in the United States. After some weeks away, Charles had begun to recover. The stress of dealing with the Lichens, Forestal, and The Store, followed by the tragic death of Grayson Chase, had taken its toll.

But Paladin's work was not done.

Jeffrey and Diana had their hands full: she as the executor of Grayson's complex estate, and he as her advisor and doing... well... whatever else he did. Apparently they, too, needed a break and had decided to spend this week on the islands. Charles suspected that the real reason they came here was because they didn't want to be in the US for the election. With Grayson gone, it didn't really matter whether Cooligan or Lear won. The next four years were going to be depressing for the US, economically and psychologically.

John Crane, Grayson's running mate, had decided not to run for president in his place. He never wanted to be the lead candidate, and he could see the exercise was now not only pointless and unpleasant, but dangerous. Maybe he would run in the future, but for the moment the Jeffersonian Democratic-Republican Party had lost its driving force and would go the way of all other American third parties. Game over.

Jeffrey and Charles sat on the beach, each occasionally reaching around a beer to tug on fishing lines attached to tall rods adjacent to their chairs. It was not about catching fish.

"Jeffrey, what aren't you telling me?"

"What do you mean, Charles?"

"It's important I know who I'm dealing with."

"That's a fair point. But life is unfair," Jeffrey replied.

Charles replied, "So JFK said." He pulled on his line and reflected somberly on the concept. "And rabies is unfair."

They raised their beers to the memory of Grayson Chase. Now dead five weeks.

"Is life supposed to be fair?" Charles continued. "It's one of the most dangerous words in the language. It isn't fair that one person's born with athletic genes, and another with fat genes. One's born with rich parents, another with poor parents. Whenever the word fair is used, it implies life owes you something. People who believe in 'fair' usually want to coerce other people to change things to their own idea of fair. Which seems pretty unfair. Maybe even rabies can be 'fair'—if you get it due to the fickle finger of fate. Or if everyone gets it. To be fair."

They sat in silence for a time, each lost in their own thoughts. "Jeffrey, you know Grayson was assassinated, right? I'm on board with all the conspiracy theorists on that one."

Jeffrey grimaced, and his jaw tightened as he slowly nodded his head. "The why is pretty obvious. I've been working on the who and the how."

Charles glanced at him. "I'm sure you've had other distractions. The estate must be a massive undertaking."

Jeffrey said, "It will take time, but right now I'm working this assassination possibility. Imagine rabies as a weapon for assassination. An assassin could contaminate anyone but not die in the process. He could attack one person or many, possibly thousands. A rabies assassin just needs to get vaccinated in advance to be immune and fully protected. Put it in a spray can. Victim doesn't even know it until weeks or months later—by which time it's impossible to cure. No connection back to the assassin—the ultimate in plausible deniability. It could have been any of the people Grayson saw since he announced his candidacy."

"Anyone who'd been vaccinated for rabies, you mean."

"Can your spyminers help us find out who they are?"

Charles thought for a moment. "I suppose anything is possible with enough time and money. It'd be a challenge to sort through all the world's rabies-vaccine providers to find a suspicious recipient. Have to figure out the nexus of who's ever received the rabies shots and who had contact with Grayson. But an assassin would have used a fake name when he got the vaccines to start with—at least if he was cautious. It could well be a government agent, from any of a dozen countries, with no record of the agent or his vaccinations."

"Yeah. Probably right. So we keep thinking. It always boils down to motive, means, and opportunity."

Charles took a deep breath and exhaled through his nose. "Motive: just about anyone in the swamp. Anyone close to Cooligan or Heather Lear. Foreign governments not wanting to lose their free US money. Any of a thousand entities in corporate America receiving subsidies that Grayson would oppose. Union heads. Hospital associations. Insurance companies. Defense contractors. Any socialist ideologue. The right- and left-wing media. Maybe a militia, eager to cash in on Cooligan's gun control boondoggle. Some environmental extremists. The list is so long it's not even worth looking at. It speaks poorly for the future of the country."

"True, I'm afraid. It's similar to the list of people who wanted to rid the world of your Naked Emperor, isn't it, Charles?"

"Very similar. I know why Grayson wanted my drug back on the street. So much synergy." Charles tugged on his fishing line again. "What about the means? How would an assassin get hold of rabies virus? It might be easier to track who got hold of the live virus."

"I've got people working on that, but although I've got connections, you know I don't have any official power. The people that do have that power have already written off his death as a freak event, not a homicide. Even if some prosecutor wanted the truth, it would take warrants and processes. The international parts would take forever. These people close ranks when there's a political murder; look at the JFK affair. Bribes can help, but that brings a whole other set of risks."

Charles said, "A fat spymining contract might tempt the right people to do some research."

"Your system for exposing truths isn't a panacea. If you made a spymining contract to solve the mysteries of gravity, it wouldn't yield an answer. At least not for a long time."

Time passed; there was no need for conversation. Charles reached into the small cooler to hand Jeffrey a beer and took one for himself. Waves rolled rhythmically on the beach. The ocean itself encouraged reflection. A light breeze and floating clouds made for a perfect day in a perfect place. Charles recognized he was young, healthy, and adequately wealthy. He appreciated life—life itself—and the fact that he was better off than 99.9 percent of the people on the planet.

"If life's unfair, right now we're the beneficiaries of that unfairness."

Jeffrey turned to him with a quizzical expression. "Do you know? How did you find out? Did Diana tell you?"

Charles frowned. "Know what?"

Jeffrey laughed quietly. "You said beneficiaries. I thought perhaps you'd heard something."

"What should I have heard?"

Jeffrey said, "There's another reason Diana and I came to Dominica."

"Yeah?"

"Yeah. It's to tell you something important."

"Sounds dramatic. I'll pretend the rolling waves are rolling drums."

"It is, Charles. Beyond his sister, Grayson made relatively modest bequests to about a hundred people important to him. Then for the majority of his estate, he made two large bequests." He pointed to his own chest and smiled. "One to me. And one other." Jeffrey stopped there.

And Charles knew that it was to him that Grayson Chase had entrusted the remainder of his wealth.

"Charles, it's why Grayson was adamant to meet you on his deathbed. He relies on you to do the right thing with his capital."

Charles spoke in monotone. "How recent was this will?"

"You mean, was he of sound mind? Fair question. He added you on in a codicil more than two months ago. No one is contesting it. And there's no one with standing to do so other than Diana. Believe me, she has no desire to contest it."

Charles gestured with his hand palm upward, questioning the Fates. "He didn't even know me. He didn't know me at all, actually."

"You should give him credit, Charles. Grayson was thoughtful. I don't mean that in the sense of remembering people's birthdays. He thought about and analyzed events and people. He had excellent judgment. He had wisdom, something nobody talks much about these days. It takes self-discipline to develop wisdom. He learned to like you, even from a distance. He perhaps knew you in ways you don't yet know yourself. We'll need to talk about what his plans were and how you fit into them. For one thing, he was interested in denying the State as much of his money as possible. He considered that a basic form of patriotism. The bulk of the estate—the parts that the US government knows about and can get its claws on, that is—will go to two charitable foundations, managed by each of us."

Charles considered. "You know, Jeffrey, after Cooligan wins, he'll just keep the status quo growing."

"Interesting phrasing. The status quo growing. But it applies." Jeffrey chuckled. "It's exactly what he'll do. The parasites will thrive. The situation gets worse with every election because every candidate sells part of his soul to get elected. As H. L. Mencken said, 'Every election is just an advance auction on stolen goods.' The stakes go up every time because the State gets bigger. Every new law costs money to execute and administer, which means more taxes, debt, and inflation. The whole world is reaching a tipping point. Fortunately, for us, Cooligan and his gang are fairly incompetent."

Charles nodded. "Let's be thankful for small favors. A friend once said we should pray to have incompetent government. We can survive waste and theft. The real problem is when they have a plan and are effective in making it happen. People who wish for a competent government are short-sighted."

"That I agree with. Now, by friend, do you mean Maurice Templeton? I've never met the man, but I know he's got links to a lot of institutions and agencies. I figure he can get a lot of information with a phone call. I know he shepherded some of your money and positioned your investment in Visioryme Pharmaceuticals that paved the way for Naked Emperor."

Exhaling, Charles said with no shortage of frustration, "It's not hard to figure out who my uncle is. But not many people would have the knowledge to describe him that way. And Rainbow would have told you nothing. Just who the hell are you, Jeffrey, and how do you know so damn much?"

"By now, you've got to be pretty sure we're on the same team."

"I'm sure of that. But what's the team? Who are you?" Charles rarely allowed himself to show anger, but he approached it now. "I've had enough of the games. As one freshly minted billion-dollar trust manager to another, exactly how do you come by your information?"

"I think you've figured out most of that. Like you, I've had some cool-sounding aliases and a variety of professions over the years. Had Grayson lived to become president, I'd have had a fancy new title too."

"As what?"

"You might get angry."

"You mean angrier. Risk it."

Jeffrey took a breath and let out a long exhalation. "Let me preface, though. Let me get you on the right page."

Charles looked at him warily. He was no fan of the international-man-of-mystery routine.

"I was in the government, quite high up in fact, back before I met Diana and her brother. I got into government partly because of my family background; it seemed like an honorable profession. You seem to have arrived at your moral conclusions at a much younger age. It took me far longer to get to the same place."

Charles could never relate to either government people or employees.

Jeffrey continued. "Certainly by the time you got out of prison, you'd decided that the State as an institution, and its hangers-on and operatives, were your enemies. I agree. You recognized that political power and the kind of people who use it are innately dangerous. And the bigger and more powerful the State, the more of them there are. In fact they'll always be there as long as there's a State; it's as if it activates some kind of primal aberration in anyone who gets near it.

"You're right to identify Paul Samuels as the current puppet master. But the State itself is the correct enemy. The Paladin Network is a brilliant way to organize people to broadly target the State and the ticks getting fat off it. Very few revolutionaries ever attack the State just because it's the right thing to do. Most of them just dislike a current form. They don't want to abolish the institution; they want to take it over and grab the power for themselves.

"Instead, you're galvanizing millions to take power away from the State not to gain that power themselves, but because it's profitable. With time, they'll figure out that it's right as well. You and the others have built your anti-NSA. And yes, by the way, it was Grayson who put out spyminer contracts on all the Top Dogs in the government and their cronies in what they like to call the private sector. He bought a huge volume of Paladins early on."

"I'd guessed as much."

"I was angry with him for doing it, actually. I thought it was a cowboy move that might be tracked. If it were, it could have torpedoed his candidacy. But Grayson relied on your conditional anonymity. He trusted you. Soon, it won't be just a few modern-day Seymour Hirschs sticking their necks out. Thousands will be in the game. Corruption amounts to the betrayal of a trust; PNet is a superb weapon against it. Tacitus said, 'The more corrupt the State, the more numerous the laws.' But in fact, it also works the other way around. The more numerous the laws, the more corrupt the State. Historically, both the State and corruption are too big and too dangerous to attack head-on.

"Assassination is a worthwhile tool in very specific cases, but the Paladin Network may be a far more effective solution for addressing the underlying rot. Every taxpayer-funded scam that two scumbags arrange over an expensive dinner can potentially be subjected to scrutiny. Where those people go, and who they talk to and who they're sleeping with. The cronies and the ruling class are being severely inconvenienced."

Charles smiled. "Yeah, it was one of those things that seemed like a good idea at the time and actually turned out to be a good idea in the end. At least so far. Maybe Rainbow and Mei-li will be billionaires themselves someday."

"I assume you've done reasonably well too."

Charles shrugged. "Some government goon always seems to come along and steal what I earn. I expect that shoe to fall soon."

"Your missiles of transparency may win the war against those goons."

"Well, like you said, I may have been attacked, but I've never seen myself as a victim. I'm not complaining. I have to fill these idle hours somehow." He tugged on his fishing rod.

"Your way may be better than mine, Charles. Paladin Network is using a magnesium flare to light up the hidden crannies where cockroaches are hiding. Then tossing it in to burn them out."

Charles would get to the root of Jeffrey's secret, today, one way or another. "Why's the Federal Reserve your special focus, Jeffrey? Why did you want me to wipe all of them out?"

"You chose to use the Paladin Network to neutralize them instead of taking them out. You obviously don't like killing. You make a lousy assassin."

Charles sighed. "You were about to tell me how being in government made you the cagey character I've come to know. I've respected your privacy. I thought about siccing the spyminers on you. I could have lifted prints and had Maurice pull strings to identify you. I could have lifted your wallet while you were at death's door riddled with bullets. Hell, I could have just followed you home. I didn't do any of that. Now it's time to tell me what the hell you are."

Jeffrey nodded. He sat up on his chair and stared down between his feet at the sand. He took a breath and said, "For a long time, my position in government allowed me access to a lot of information. The type of information you've seen me acquire. I still have solid friends in place."

Charles nodded. "It makes sense to infiltrate the enemy."

Jeffrey said, "I didn't infiltrate the government as a double agent. I just went to work for them."

"Tell me more."

Jeffrey said, calmly, "Like most kids, I grew up thinking that the G-men were the good guys, fighting for truth, justice, and the American way. Like most kids, I watched TV shows and movies about the FBI; they've always been portrayed as the heroes. Everybody played cops and robbers, and everybody wanted to be the cops.

"I did a tour as a Marine officer, and then FBI recruited me. I transferred out of there. It took me a long time, and a lot of reading and discussions, to overcome the indoctrination I'd gotten my whole life, from my parents, from school, from the media, from work—from everything. I finally realized that I'd been repressing my own nature, my own sense of right and wrong. I never believed in running with the herd, doing and thinking things because everyone else did. I thought I was above that. But I was wrong. I came to the conclusion that I was part of the problem. That made me very unhappy with myself. Instead of quitting the government, for a while I decided to work from within to change things. No way could I have risen to where I got to in government—and made the connections I still use—if I'd figured out my nature, my core beliefs, early on. The way you did."

Charles said, "It's possible to start from a very different place and arrive at the same destination. There are many paths up the mountain. Your government job was the winding path you followed. So where did you end up? I mean, in the government?"

"There are thousands of federal crimes now. But originally, in the Constitution, there were only three: piracy, treason, and counterfeiting. My focus, Charles, has always been counterfeiting. In fact, I rose to be assistant director of the Secret Service."

Charles looked up with renewed interest. A little shocked, he processed the revelation. It made complete sense. The access and its resources explained much of Jeffrey's magic.

Jeffrey paused and looked Charles directly in the eyes. "The Service has been best known for providing protection for the president, the VP, visiting dignitaries, and anyone else the president designates by executive order. Ironically, Lincoln signed the law creating the Secret Service the very day he was shot in Ford's Theater. But only after McKinley was assassinated in 1901 did protecting the president become a job of the Secret Service. Before that, since 1865, it was all about fighting counterfeiting." He paused, drank from his beer, and looked away. "I was on the investigation side more than the protection side. Over time I came to realize that what I was doing was trivial. The real currency destruction isn't from people printing up paper with pictures of dead presidents. It's from the Fed. The US dollar was completely stable from 1789 to 1913 when the US got its third central bank, the Fed. Since then it's lost about ninety-eight percent of its value. It's on the cusp of losing that last two percent.

"Counterfeiting has been a capital offense throughout the ages, whether by coin clipping or minting coins with base metal instead of precious metal. That's because it can destroy an economy. It's a gigantic but subtle fraud on all of society. It's ironic that I was paid to fight counterfeiting as a Secret Service agent while I was in effect providing protection to the worst offender ever. You know, the Secret Service is occasionally detailed to the chairman of the Fed. Can you imagine? The Fed, and fractional-reserve banking—which wouldn't be possible without the Fed—make up the single biggest value-destroying operation the world has ever known. They should be indicted, not protected, by the Secret Service.

"My father was a Secret Service agent. I followed him into the agency. We investigated financial-institution fraud and major conspiracies. The more my father, and then I, did our little investigations, the more we realized that all roads led to the Fed. I can't tell you how much effort is wasted on symbolic investigations. Microscopic successes, like taking out a small printing press here and there and retrieving stolen plates to prevent small fry from printing a few million fake dollars. The largest seizure of counterfeit currency in the history of the Secret Service amounted to only thirty million dollars, Charles. This year, the Federal Reserve has created that much every six minutes.

"Now, just imagine yourself, knowing what I know, what you know, and piddling your time away tracking down the guys with green eyeshades printing up Jacksons and Benjamins in their basements while the Federal Reserve conspired with Goldman Sachs, JPMorgan, and the transient political hacks to create not just millions or billions, but now trillions, and funnel it into the Deep State. Of course the rich were getting richer while the poor were getting poorer, as unlimited counterfeit dollars flow through the hands of the bankers who run the system. I was supposed to be fighting counterfeiting. Turned out I was abetting it."

Charles had a thoughtful tone in his voice. "Until now."

"Until now. Yes, I finally decided to fight it, aggressively and directly, together with Grayson. Part of that campaign was getting you on side. Which worked out well. You see, Grayson hoped to have you supplying Naked Emperor if he succeeded in his presidential bid. So the stars were already aligning, and we had the necessary finances. We put people in place to watch out for you where we could. A good-hearted prison warden, and the guy who ran your probation office, among others."

"Emily?"

"Obviously. Although not much of that was planned." Jeffrey paused for a swallow of beer. "Grayson saw the Fed as just part of the problem; he was an anarchocapitalist. He saw the institution of the State itself as the problem. But a problem he could take advantage of. He knew that the Fed would be printing money like crazy to hold up the house of cards they've created over the years. He knew most of that new money would find its way into the stock market. They'd create bubbles, and he capitalized on that. Always knowing that someday the hyperbubble would break. Perhaps due to some kind of real or imagined terror event. Maybe the war on drugs would be hyped to a new high. Some semi-real medical emergency, a pandemic scare, might come along, and they'd blame a market collapse on that. Or possibly the people that run the Fed believe their own propaganda and think they can keep the bubble blown up forever.

"Grayson had the will and the ability to do something about it, and he felt that if he didn't, he'd belong in a low circle of hell."

Hell. Charles's mouth turned in a wry grin as he reflected back a decade, when he and Xander decided to stop an African revolution. They were the only ones who had the means, the opportunity, and the motivation to head off that calamity. The three elements necessary to prove a crime would have been used to prosecute them under a score of laws by a half dozen different governments—had they been connected to it. Back then, surrounded by malarial mosquitoes, bathed in sweat in the hot, stinking bush, Charles had wondered if he weren't already in some circle of hell.

Charles said, "So you decided to kill the Federal Reserve."

"You're not going to make many friends trying to overthrow the government, even if it's horrible. The Fed is something else entirely. Plenty of people would want to get rid of it if they knew what it was. But they don't. I doubt there's a teacher in a high school anywhere in America who understands the Federal Reserve or the ideas behind central banking. Anyway, it was you who took the first shot. At Paul Samuels. That's when I suspected you were the right man for the job. We wanted you on the team. Grayson's interest in you became my interest in you."

"When did you start working with Grayson?"

"After I met Diana. It's been many years now. She helped me through my long recovery when half my lung got blown out of my chest."

Charles waited for more.

"But that's a story for another day. You'll excuse my hating to talk about it. When I started working with Grayson, I knew I could lose everything, including my life. Or wind up in some SEA black site. But I didn't care, and with Grayson gone, now I care even less. I'm going to make the most of whatever time I've got left. It's going to be a lot harder, but I'm still on a mission."

Charles said, "We're Grayson now."

Jeffrey shrugged. "Except that we aren't going to run for president."

It was time for another beer.

"Secret Service, huh?" Charles couldn't help but laugh. His natural sunny smile, buried by the stresses of the last weeks, broke through, almost as it used to.

Jeffrey said, "Yes. Dedicated to pursuing, however necessary, anyone who counterfeits the currency."

"Jeffrey, you assigned yourself a Sisyphean task: taking on the Fed—the foundation of the whole Deep State."

"Of course we'll never succeed now. It requires overthrowing the entire system. We'd have had a chance if Grayson were president. Now the best we can do is catalyze the inevitable. I suppose it's better to have a controlled demolition than let it collapse on its own."

Charles nodded. "US prosperity is built on a foundation of quicksand because the dollar is just an IOU nothing, a floating abstraction. These idiots are going to destroy it totally, along with the savings of a couple of billion people. It's going to happen all over the world because the dollar is the main reserve for all the world's currencies."

"Yes. When eight billion angry chimpanzees see that King Dollar has no clothes, it's going to get ugly."

"So what's next?" Charles asked.

"What's next? The bad guys will redouble their efforts to prop up their house of cards. President Cooligan is about to sign an executive order that will bring the government down on your Paladin Network's spyminers. They're going to impose draconian penalties on spymining and the whole shebang; the conventional mockingbird media will again be the only source of news. The State plays the mainstream media the way you play the piano."

Charles considered this. "The PNet itself is global and decentralized. They can't touch that. But the spyminers in the US will have to be extra cautious."

"Yes. Everyone will. Most foreign governments follow the US lead for lots of reasons. PNet is unmasking the Deep State's game. They can't allow that in any major country."

Charles said, "Government versus the people. Government guns versus liberty. And so the battle goes on. The idea that government's ever been 'we the people' is one of the most pernicious frauds ever perpetrated."

"There will be action on other fronts too." Jeffrey took a pull from his beer. "You truly haven't seen any news in a month, have you?"

Charles drank too and replied with a smile, "Look at me. I'm unplugged here in paradise and I don't care. Tethering myself to some electronic device is one unfortunate fate I've managed to avoid so far."

"You'll be pleased to know PNet has scored a few victories. Two more members of the Board of Governors have resigned. Maybe their financial conflicts of interest will get them fines and jail terms instead of fat corporate directorships, sweetheart deals, five-figure speaking fees, and six-figure book contracts."

Charles sat back and smiled. "It's gratifying. Spyminers will keep finding new ways to do it. I suspect some of the Paladin Network vig-hacks work at Facebook and Google and can check out what sites the targets are surfing. Maybe they're finding which Silicon Valley execs are talking with which bureaucrats and which politicians, and wholesaling or retailing the knowledge. I know they're beginning to track the contacts of lobbyists. Treasure troves of information there. And discovering whole interlocked webs of cozy relationships, far beyond just the Fed. Not to minimize your life's purpose, but the Fed is just one of many symptoms. Cronyism is everywhere, a hundred times more now than during the declining Roman Empire when Tacitus first commented on it. Of course, as PNet knocks them down, the president will just restock the board with more insiders."

"But maybe not as quickly, Charles. You've made being on the Board of Governors risky and unattractive. Spymining's a cottage industry, and it was built to be and stay underground. Business types will have to think twice before becoming cozy with not just the Fed, but any government agency. Why would they want to paint a target on their back? Why invite scrutiny?"

Charles smiled. "That's what I'm talking about. It's one thing to take out the governors of the Fed's board. That's a noble intention, but it's like pulling shark's teeth. Most assassinations throughout history have been used as an excuse to centralize power even more while cracking down on dissidents. The corruption, the statism, the collectivism in this country has been institutionalized. So what we need to do is destroy the institutions themselves, not just the people who populate them. People can be replaced. If you just lop off a head of a hydra, two grow back to replace it. There'll always be another Paul Samuels, someone eager to climb the ranks, as long as centers of power like the Fed exist. What I'm afraid of is that if we destroy an old institution, a new one will replace it. With the degraded state of civilization today, we could be sowing dragons' teeth in place of sharks' teeth. It's a much better plan to assassinate the character of the beast than the beast itself."

"That idea is one reason why I like you so much."

Charles said, "My letter to the New York Post should spook them a bit."

"I'm eager to read it, Charles. We need to keep the pressure on. You've won some battles, but with Grayson gone, they've checkmated my plans. Thanks to the Guns Rule attacks, gun owners will be pulled into their national-militia initiative. Most people don't think, they feel. They don't deal in logical ideas; they're ruled by their emotions. The country's been corrupted by identity politics, political correctness, neo-Marxism, and the rest of it. You know what comes next, Charles."

"Increased tyranny via a kinder and gentler police state."

"Yes."

Charles nodded slowly. "Sic semper tyrannis." John Wilkes Booth's words after he shot Lincoln. "There will always be some people who just need killing. It's almost as if a psychological, or maybe even a spiritual, defect is imbued in humanity."

Jeffrey nodded too. "It's far too late in the game to win without conducting some actual surgery. So can you continue the fight, Charles? Can you get off a beach in paradise and re-enter the fray? We need to take out some more key malefactors. The ones out of the public eye, who can't be outed or blackmailed. Sure, new ones will appear to replace them, but seeing what's happening to their peers will give them pause. It will sow confusion and fear in their ranks. At least the members of The Store, or some of them, need to die."

Charles took a moment to answer. "I understand; it's an excellent thought. But tracking down members of The Store from Lichen's list is Frank and Emily's turf. But won't the authorities just increase the size of the Secret Service to protect these people? They won't just be armed with guns. There will be new laws; your agency will get draconian powers, just like the SEA. We've all been lucky so far. None of us wants to become a guest of Guantanamo."

"Well, Charles, I'll give you one guess who President Cooligan has asked to come out of retirement to be put in charge of the entire operation to protect these people."

"I think I'm going to like the answer."

Jeffrey smiled broadly. "And I've found their lair, Charles. It's where cronies go to spawn. They call it the 4th Floor. A financial equivalent of The Store, you might say."

Charles raised his beer. "Interesting. It sounds like one-stop shopping. It makes sense to take out the hive, rather than swatting individual hornets. Is this 4th Floor a place, or a concept?"

"I think it's an actual place. When I figure out more, I'll let you know."

When he smiled, Charles's eyes now displayed fine crow's feet that made him look wise. He was, after all, getting older. His eyes held increased respect for the man next to him. They were fighting a war. It was as if enemy sappers were mining a tunnel under their position, intending to fill it with explosives. The only way to defeat that is to counter-mine, and that's what his new friend was doing. He saw in Jeffrey's eyes a strength of conviction. Perhaps victory was possible, against all odds.

They clinked their bottles.

"Jeffrey, I think this is the start of a beautiful friendship."

58

The Post

RAHEEM opened an envelope that bore no return address. He had no idea how long it had been sitting there.

He found two items inside. One, a printed letter. The other a business card. Have Gun—Will Travel.

He read the letter. Then he read it again.

He had to think.

Paladin. A man now the subject of a national manhunt. A presumed assassin who left a calling card on the body of a Department of Agriculture agent. Based on security-camera footage from St. Margaret's School and the New York Post—pieced together by the FBI—it appeared that this same Paladin was deeply involved in the shootings of the Guns Rule crisis. He was also implicated in the death of a top bureaucrat in the Justice Department named Blaize Forestal. Two images of Paladin—a face mostly obscured by an antiviral mask but obviously with a large nose and bushy eyebrows—spread over the internet. Time magazine had named Paladin "Person of the Year," putting him in a class with Hitler, Stalin, and Pol Pot. The populace was exhorted to despise him.

This was the same man who had wandered right to this very desk and told him to ask questions about the first Guns Rule shooting, in Abilene. Did Paladin want him to know that he was involved in it? Or that he wasn't? There was no evidence that he was.

And why did he want to trust Paladin? Why did he feel an urge to protect him?

Raheem read the letter yet again. This was not the work of a madman.

It was a warning to criminals that specialized in the nexus where political and financial power intersected.

The name Blaize Forestal so far meant little to him. Paladin suggested that Raheem should learn everything that he could about Forestal's life, and his death, and then tell the world what he discovered. Apparently, Forestal was a close associate of Paul Samuels. This could be interesting and possibly dangerous. Then something about a Store, and a list of names. Big names. And instructions on when to release the information.

Raheem had acquired some Paladins and was using them routinely to get information. He had become a spyminer himself. It revitalized his hopes for his chosen profession. The PNet could become indispensable to news organizations, and he was an early adopter.

Maybe PNet was a way for the mainstream media to avoid extinction. He looked around the floor at the small desks and those who manned them. Investigative journalists might reappear. He was one. Some spyms published what they learned. Other spyms didn't analyze their data, but gave stay-at-home journalists some boots on the ground everywhere, anytime, tracking anybody and anything. Reporters could now get original research and hard facts. They no longer had to just regurgitate press releases or repeat somebody else's opinion. Although most still would.

It was clear the Paladin Network could disrupt the status quo. Not just in the US, but everywhere on the planet, disempowering corrupt government officials and their cronies.

Paladin's letter stated that his assassinations would be marked with his card.

Raheem wouldn't investigate this Paladin further. Instead, he'd investigate the people that Paladin targeted. He made the connection between Paladin Network and Paladin the man early. But then he knew of Paladin, whereas most in the media didn't.

It was in his interest to help Paladin. This was his big chance. Not to just move out of a bullpen surrounded by drones, but to make himself into a latter-day Wood-Bern from the Watergate days. He'd no longer be just another Mr. Nothing Nobody. From what he could tell, Paladin was one of the good guys.

It occurred to Raheem that he was the commissioner to Paladin's

Batman. Or Lois Lane to Superman. Well, maybe not Lois Lane. More like Jimmy Olsen.

He looked forward to the day when Paladin would next strike.

*   *   *

The crosshairs of his rifle's scope pinpointed two fine droplets of sweat leaching from a balding head three hundred yards away. The late-autumn morning was cool. The sweat came from anxiety.

Disguised as Paladin, Charles had watched the man tramp from the cart path up a gentle grass slope and onto the third tee box, carrying over his shoulder the club that he would use to send the ball down the fairway. The exclusive golf course catered to but a few hundred members, and today Paul Samuels played his first round in six months—but this time in a foursome.

Paul Samuels lined up, swung his driver, and sent his ball down the center of the fairway. A perfect shot. His bodyguard, standing next to the caddy, clapped loudly, as did the three other golfers. Perhaps one of them would cease being obsequious long enough to notice the business card Charles had left on the grass there.

Charles pulled the trigger. And he too made a perfect shot.

Once again, Paul Samuels fell to the ground.

And once again, there was no blood.

But the head of his new custom-made driver lay in ruins.

Charles had plans for the man and for his 4th Floor, and so, for now, Paul Samuels would live, but in fear—fear of Paladin.

Someday, Charles would indeed assassinate that man, that shark tooth. But only when he could terminate the shark itself, so that no teeth could ever grow back.

Epilogue

CHARLES lay on the beach, sipping a wine cooler as a mild breeze rose from the water. He reached over and grasped Emily's hand as she slept. She stirred and murmured contentedly.

Months had passed in what felt like a weekend.

The FBI—desperate to minimize the inevitable repercussions of Forestal's involvement in The Store—went after a select few of its members. Instead of arresting everyone in a giant operation, they chose to focus on a couple of minor politicians. Their intent was obvious enough: show that they were pursuing crimes while delegitimizing any possible investigation of how the FBI had allowed the place to exist under its nose for who-knew-how-long. A couple other Store members either committed suicide or were suicided. The important thing was to prevent a major scandal involving major Washington power players.

Other members of The Store took the warning, and more than a few took the opportunity to make the chicken run to whatever country offered the best chance to avoid extradition. But they couldn't avoid the Paladin Network, nor Frank and Emily Renner.

Frank and Emily had assassinated ten of them in as many weeks. They had dozens more yet to target as a growing global network of spyminers worked diligently to track them. The punishments doled out to the members of The Store were insufficient for their crimes. A theologian might have consigned them to an eternity immersed in a lake of fire. The Renners weren't theologians, were too impatient to wait for eternity, and didn't possess a lake of fire. But they did possess a deep reservoir of vengeance.

Charles's discomfort with the mechanics of assassination had both increased and decreased over time. It wasn't so much the passage of time itself as the opportunity time gave him to crystallize his thoughts. Some discomfort remained.

The world would in fact be a better place with these people all dead.

The existence of a real sex-slavery operation in Washington, DC, this one with an added organ-harvesting feature, was too juicy a story to push to the sidelines. Too many facts had been confirmed by too many journalists frothing at the mouth to write headlines about famous and powerful men. Ahmed Raheem eventually revealed the entire list to the world after the FBI's congressional sting, upsetting all their efforts at containment. The cost? He was tarred as a conspiracy theorist. It was intended to demean and insult him. It didn't stick this time.

The Paladin Network continued to mature, even as the whole cryptocurrency space fluctuated wildly. These were the birthing pains of a new technology. Mei-li and Rainbow had together created an open source system, but one founded on moral principles. Unlike most of the big players in the digital world, who only gave lip service to "Don't be evil," the individuals in the Paladin Network implemented it.

The NSA had immense amounts of money and a direct pipeline into the world's largest search engines and social networks. The FBI had thousands of agents with the legal authority to snoop into anything or anybody. The CIA had thousands of operatives, black sites, an unlimited and unmonitored budget, and absolutely no scruples. The SEA was smaller and newer, but it made the old Soviet Union's KGB and the old East German Stasi seem quaint. A dozen other armed bureaucracies like the DEA, the DIA, and Army Intelligence moved to emulate the SEA in order to stay relevant.

The Paladin Network seemed unimpressive by comparison. How could an unstructured, informal network, whose members had no formal training and no state backing, possibly stand against behemoths? But young, committed ideologues, whose idea of fun was leveling the battlefield, trumped middle-aged government employees any day. More importantly, since they were paid based on results, they were far more motivated than the drones employed by large organizations. Government employees might be essentially immune from their own laws, but they had no immunity from the ancient concept of common law. The Paladin Network enforced natural law even faster than nature itself.

President Cooligan was increasingly unable to convince nominees to accept high posts at the Fed or other major agencies, despite the promise of Secret Service protection. It was an impossible job. Paladin and his PNet could strike out of nowhere, at any time, with blackmail or a bullet. There was no defense against character assassination except impeccable behavior. The federal bureaucracy was on the verge of experiencing massive early retirements as the spyminers' headlights began to shine on them; it was as if a rotten log in a damp forest had just been turned over in sharp sunlight. The process began spreading from Washington to state capitols down to county seats. Smelling blood, the media began to change its tone, looking more skeptically at bureaucrats. In the face of a deluge of spyminer revelations, their credibility depended on it. It added fuel to the CityFire riots. The underclass were outraged to see proof of what they'd suspected all along.

Governments the world over had to contend with the same scrutiny. In Europe it was starting to look like the late '60s and early '70s. In China the regime cracked down hard, aided by the social-credit system that let the party know who was talking to whom about what. Paladin spyminers dug through the fetid soils of South America, Asia, and even Africa, where everyone already knew the whole structure was terminally corrupt. Corruption had long been the only reason anyone got into government, and corrupt dealings with ministers was by far the easiest way to get rich, but spyminers had incentives to dig up proof. Targeted by the spyminers, criminals rushed to accuse one another. "He stole that money!" "He had his brother pad the contract!" "You bribed the prime minister." It wasn't just a few accusations; it was a flood, filling the media everywhere, backed by impossible-to-deny hard data. Paladin's vigilantes beat the secret police at their own game.

Unlike typical revolutions, PNet's foundational rules included huge disincentives for false accusations and unjustified violence. No one wanted to be outcast from the community and lose their conditional anonymity.

The average person thought governments were necessary, just in need of reform, but had never even thought about the institution of central banking. When they thought about it, many realized it wasn't part of the cosmic firmament. It wasn't a benign but flawed system. Its stealthy theft was a design feature, not a bug.

It was no longer safe, prestigious, and profitable to be a central banker. After a century of unobstructed looting of the world's economies, the world began to hold them accountable. Paul Samuels now rarely left his home.

The Guns Rule phenomenon in the US lost momentum and died since it had been manufactured and had never been a real movement. The mass-shooting sprees had stopped, but the media tried to keep the pot boiling so that no one would feel safe until the government took yet more emergency action.

Despite the end of the shootings, the two new militia bills sailed through the House and Senate almost intact as both parties' leaders praised their wisdom in controlling gun violence while "abiding by the intent of the Constitution." The final bills were known collectively as the Guns Don't Rule Legislation, or GooDRuLes for short. President Cooligan signed them with pageantry, taking credit for the end of the Guns Rule phenomenon.

Homeland Security now supervised all civilian weapons as well as the new state militias. To legally own a gun required that one be accepted into the militia and undergo extensive psychological evaluation and regular militia-specific education. A last-minute amendment, proposed by a socialist female senator with presidential aspirations, cut just two words out of the first bill. Few realized that this deletion of two words endowed the Bureau of Alcohol, Firearms, Tobacco and Explosives with the same powers held by the Sybillene Eradication Agency: most notably, a license to kill on "reasonable suspicion." The four-hundred-page bill that no one had time to read passed in a floor vote. Forestal won a posthumous battle.

Another small change opened a window that astute lawyers leaped through: an opportunity to suck huge settlements out of the gun manufacturers. Stock prices of publicly traded gun manufacturers went for a wild roller-coaster ride as lawsuits against the weapons manufacturers piled up. A certain large hedge fund took the opportunity to buy up all it could for pennies on the dollar, obtaining controlling interests. Eterio Conti simultaneously acquired numerous privately owned weapons and munitions companies that suffered badly from the pressures on the industry. Management knew enough to hit the bid when Conti made an offer.

Soon after Conti's takeover and consolidation of several weapons manufacturers, Congress enacted full tort protection for the companies. The same bill set aside money enabling the largest Homeland Security order of firearms and ammunition in peacetime history. In the spirit of supporting

American business, Homeland Security was required to purchase only American-made weapons, which just so happened to be manufactured by Eterio Conti's companies.

Charles sat on the beach that day contemplating what had come of his efforts. It was possible to be a modern-day version of the fictional Paladin, the mythical knight without armor. But a US covered in cameras and awash in police and praetorian federal agencies wasn't the America of the nineteenth century. The culture had changed, and a lone avenger was more likely to wind up dead, imprisoned, or disappeared into a black site than sung about as a hero. He realized he was still uncomfortable in this new avocation. It wasn't only his initial uncertainty regarding the morality of his actions. Rather, he was unsure he was having any meaningful effect. Was he a paladin or a Don Quixote?

He had come to realize that it wasn't just that some people were sick. As long as the current system existed, it would continue to attract the sick people to it. The Deep State's tentacles had completely enveloped what was left of free markets. Most people now confused capitalism with fascism.

He may have pruned some of its tentacles, but the evil creature still lived, and it would recover and expand. PNet was cleaning out prominent cronies and assassinating the reputations of central banking and the State itself. However, he still wondered whether PNet could be co-opted and turned to the dark side. It was a real concern.

And he had done little to stop the systemic oppression of individual liberty. Western civilization itself was still falling apart. The beliefs and customs that had originated in ancient Greece and then been perfected in Europe and America were under assault and crumbling. Values had been degrading since the time of World War I, and now the trend had passed the inflection point of a hyperbolic curve and was going vertical.

The problems he'd encountered so far in his life were only symptoms of a bigger disease. It wasn't enough to just remove evil people; they'd be replaced within the system and by the system. There was a never-ending supply of problematical people. He had to do more than denigrate their characters or kill them.

It was a Herculean task, and the myth of Hercules itself ended in tragedy.

But, oddly, interest in the old Western television series Have Gun—Will Travel was rekindled. Reruns returned to primetime television. The old show made many viewers see that the new Paladin was a moral hero in the mold of the old one, even though relatively few shared the moral compass of that very different era. Fans of the rebroadcast TV show wondered about the paradox and the irony.

Charles mused at Paladin's re-emergence as both a hated and loved character. For his suspected involvement in the Guns Rule movement and PNet, Paladin had been dubbed a terrorist by a government that splashed the few partial images of the disguised man onto every Post Office wall. On the internet, theories abounded asserting that Paladin was the new Batman.

The best place to hide when you're subject to a manhunt is a war zone. Charles had property—a potential gold mine—that he needed to defend from yet another civil war about to erupt in Gondwana. The country was definitely a shithole, but perhaps it needn't stay that way.

Charles closed his eyes and wiggled his toes in the wet sand. His hand touched Emily's as she slept. He smiled thinly as he thought about topping the FBI's Most Wanted list.

They'd actually found a way to label him a terrorist.

Speculator, yes. Drug lord, certainly. Assassin?... Perhaps...

But Charles Knight a Terrorist?

Never...

Charles contemplated the 4th Floor and the people it nurtured.

Then again, thought Charles, why not?

About the Authors

DOUG Casey spends most of his time in Argentina and Uruguay, with frequent visits to the U.S., Canada, and various dysfunctional hellholes.

JOHN Hunt, MD, is a physician and former academic who resigned his tenure at a major university and stopped practicing because the insane had taken over the asylum. Now he keeps himself occupied trying to slay Leviathan.

For resources of interest, comments
from Doug and John, and updates
on the release of the next books,
visit www.highgroundbooks.com